**Typewriter Pub**, an imprint of Blvnp Incorporated
A Nevada Corporation
1887 Whitney Mesa DR #2002
Henderson, NV 89014
www.typewriterpub.com/info@typewriterpub.com

ISBN: 978-1-64434-145-2

**DISCLAIMER**
This book is a work of fiction. The characters, incidents, and dialogue are drawn from the author's imagination and are not to be construed as real. While references might be made to actual historical events or existing locations, the names, characters, places, and incidents are either products of the author's imagination or are used fictitiously, and any resemblance to actual persons living or dead, business establishments, events or locales is entirely coincidental.

# THE KING OF ALL VAMPIRE KINGS

*The Awakening Series*
## BOOK ONE

## SONDREEN J.

type
writer
pub

*To my four blessings, this is for you and your father.*
*I know that he's smiling down on all five of us. This is also for my soul mate,*
*thank you for shining light into my soul when I was in a dark place.*
*Thank you for giving me the second girl that I always wanted,*
*and most of all thank you for trusting me with carrying our son.*
*I know he's also smiling down on us. Together for ever.*

*In 2081, an unexpected war plagued the world, changing the lives of humans forever. "The Awakening," as what the media called it, was the act of the vampire species coming into awareness of the human world. Armies from all continents were defeated, world leaders were publicly executed, and the human species was on the brink of extinction.*

*After the Awakening, any human that survived could only pray for death. They were stripped of their rights, and seven vampire kings claimed each continent as their own.*

## The Seven Kings of the World

**North America** is ruled by **King Cyrus**, a ruthless king. He is known for his wicked ways and knowledge of various methods of torture.

**South America** is ruled by **King Luscious**, a savage king that despises the human race. He is known for his barbaric, reckless nature. No human stands a chance in his kingdom. For him, they are nothing but mere cattle or lamb to feast on.

**Europe** is ruled by **King Marcellus**, a malicious king that enjoys the sound of humans screaming. He is known for his mischievous ways and hosting a series of sick games. He promises humans that if they are somehow able to defeat the odds and win, they will be set free from bondage—well, free after they take their last breath. No human has ever survived the games.

**Africa** is ruled by **King Seneca**, a violent but quick-witted king. He is known for breaking humans physically and mentally. He starts with mental torture, disturbing every inch of their minds by turning their worst fears into reality. He is always successful in driving them to the verge of insanity until they beg him to end their lives.

**Asia** is ruled by **King Rufus**, a short-tempered king. He demonstrates little to no patience with humans. His bark is as big as his bite. Humans barely inhabit his kingdom because only a few are able to survive.

**Australia** is ruled by **King Cornelius**, a dominant and sadistic king. He is known for forcing humans into submission in the most sexually painful ways they could ever imagine. Only masochists thrive in his kingdom—the land of the breeders, the official birthplace of all humans born after the Awakening.

**Antarctica** is ruled by **King Xander**, a cold-hearted king. He is known for his unsympathetic and unloving nature. He is the executor of humans, only existing for one purpose, and that is to drain them of every ounce of their blood. His kingdom is the final resting place of millions of souls.

$$*\qquad *\qquad *$$

I'm a human who prays every day and night for my eighteenth birthday to at last come. It's the day when I can finally escape this hellhole I live in, where death is better than having to wake up another day. I'd rather be sent to Antarctica and drained of my blood than be trapped in this godforsaken world. My plan is simple: go to school, do everything possible to piss the leeches off, and be marked as a "feeder." It is that simple. Well, at least I thought so, but that funny word *fate* had other plans.

Unfortunately for me, fate decides to say, "F*ck you," and on my eighteenth birthday, I'm marked as a *chosen*. You see, all the kings who rule over Earth are cruel and calculating, tyrants in their own right. They answer to one vampire who is known to be the most-barbaric of them all.

# CHAPTER ONE
## The Awakening

CLAIRE

I'm a legal property of another creature. Unfortunately, that's all I will ever be. I'm nothing but a slave, and they do whatever the hell they want to me. However, it really doesn't bother me at this point because all humans are eventually forced into slavery anyway.

On May 3, 2081, the shadows cast by the moon fully blocked the brightness of the sun, bringing about what we humans now know "the Beginning of the Awakening."

*Awakening* of what? You might ask, so let me tell you about it.

During the Awakening, major cities were the first to fall, followed by everything else in between. Our military stood no chance; our soldiers were slaughtered, gutted like pigs, then eliminated. Vampires killed for sport, and no human was safe.

On the second day of the war, a national broadcast filmed our world leaders as they were being tortured and drained of their blood, one by one. It was the vampires's way of announcing the Awakening.

Ha, that's funny. Who did they think they were fooling? Those bloodsuckers are never asleep if you ask me. They've been in the shadows, patiently waiting for the right time to strike. The video was simply a hoax formed to scare the sh*t out of the human race and to force us into submission. And it worked, obviously. I must admit they are pretty clever—well, as clever as you're going to get when you're a bloodthirsty monster.

I've watched that video every single miserable day since I turned five. I've watched those humans being beheaded after having been tortured for hours. Most children at that age would believe a live recording like that was a nightmare. Sadly enough that was not the case for me. Their deaths were actually a fairy-tale ending.

When I watched the video for the very first time, I had a realization that death has to be better than living in constant suffering, because when you die, you are finally free. You no longer have to feel the pain of being tortured. You're just dead—lost and gone forever.

The public massacre of our human world leaders was just the beginning. Trust me, it only got worse. Each continent was claimed by a vampire king, and all those declarations and rules of human society were long forgotten.

Antarctica, my personal favorite and now known as the Kingdom of Bleeders, was the first to fall. Any human that had been graced with the honor to visit that kingdom would never see the light of day again.

Australia was the second continent that met its end. It is the new birthplace of every human born after the Awakening. Ironically enough, most human girls, except me, pray to go there. Don't ask me why; they just do.

When vampires took over the world, they wanted to crush the ties of human family bonds once and for all. They wanted to make sure that we humans would never experience the feeling of being loved, including a mother's love of course. However, there was only one thing that stood in their way: blood. A vampire needs human blood to survive, at least that much was true. So they had no other choice but to allow humans to procreate, so vampires had to develop a way for humans to reproduce without understanding the power of love. Those sadistic pieces of sh*t came up with a perfect system, and for some strange reason, human girls—well, at least the ones that I have met—still believe to this day that it's their best chance for survival. The Kingdom of Breeders was designed for one purpose and one purpose only, and that is for breeding.

Yup, you heard me right. It's the land of reproduction. A human male and human female are assigned to have sexual intercourse until the latter falls pregnant. When the baby is born, vampires rip it out of the mother's arm and exchange them with another breeder family. Once the child turns five, they are sent to North America. There they grow up in one of the boarding schools built for humans. It's my current place of residence by the way.

This is no normal school with a normal curriculum. That would be too kind. In Vampire 101, we are taught to become perfect slaves—vampire kings most certainly have a sense of humor. While other human girls that live here put their best foot forward to be the perfect slave, I make it my life's purpose to get under the vampires's skin, doing everything in my inner power to be marked as a bleeder.

Now, remember my words *inner power,* because on the outside is where reality takes place. I'm powerless, but this crazy human girl purposefully wants to become a bleeder. I would rather die than spend the rest of time in this world pleasing the likes of them. Spending eighteen years of my life living under their rule is already bad enough. Death should be better than this.

I must be out of my mind, but I'm not. In fact, I'm the only human that is not on the brink of insanity. The other girls are doomed and brainwashed, every single one of them. Perhaps it's the effect of the generational curse the vampires inflicted upon us. It guarantees that we will never be able to understand how it feels to be loved or even provide love. For the last one hundred years of living and surviving under their rule might be all our species has known. However, one thing is certain: I will never allow them to break me.

*　　*　　*

The loud sound of the alarm ringing wakes me up from my deep slumber. For the first time in history, I'm actually excited to hear that dreadful buzzing sound. Today is my eighteenth birthday! Whoop-dee-doo! Finally, it's the last day I will have to endure this godforsaken place.

I release a small sigh while stretching my arms out. I then roll out of bed and quickly rush to the bathroom, hopeful to be the first one to enter today. It's so hard to try to take a shower in a tight and confined space, especially when several other girls are continuously fighting over washing their butts.

I nearly dance with excitement when I open the door and see no one inside. Thank God. I don't think I could survive another episode of battling over the hot water. The girls around here will find any reason to pick a fight. Honestly, I can't blame them. Picking on people weaker than you typically makes others feel invincible. We have learned that from the best Vampire 101 Aid.

My birthday is actually starting off on a good note. After taking a shower, I'm the first student to enter the cafeteria. A vampire staff member watches me carefully as I grab a piece of toast and fill my cup with orange juice.

I slowly attempt to make my exit when Mr. Rouge unexpectedly asks, "Aren't you going to grab something else to improve your blood flow, Claire?"

*No. If I was, don't you think I would have filled my plate with the garlic eggs your kind so graciously provides us with?*

One good thing I can at least say about the vampire teachers is they love to give us healthy meals that are sure to boost our blood circulation, for their own benefit of course.

4

I clear my throat and reply, "Of course, Mr. Rouge. I just want to be the first student at the ceremony. Today is my eighteenth birthday, so it's kind of a big day for me."

His eyes flash with excitement. I catch his beloved Mrs. Rogue's eyes also glint with excitement. She turns to face me, muttering under her breath, "Allow her to go, darling. By the end of the day, she will be marked as a bleeder anyway."

I don't respond. There's absolutely no reason to. It's funny they believe I'm afraid to be marked as a bleeder. They have no idea it's exactly what I'm banking on. Dying means I will no longer have to put up with seeing their ugly faces, any of them. Problem solved.

Students start to fill the cafeteria.

*Oh boy, I really hope I can make it to class before they arrive. It looks like my luck has quickly run out. Time to go.*

Before I can make my sweet escape, Victoria—my archnemesis—and her posse walk into the cafeteria.

"Aww, you're wearing red today. How fitting! At least you've already accepted your new role openheartedly," she teases once her dark eyes center on me.

Of course, her posse back her up with snickering and fits of giggles.

I breathe in sharply and exhale through my parted lips.

*Ignore them, Claire. They only have one last day to bother you.*

I roll my eyes and decide to listen to my inner voice. I walk right past them. Screw them, they're not worth it. Those red-headed sluts only hate me because unlike them, and the rest of the student body, the vampires haven't succeeded in brainwashing me.

*Just breathe in and out. Breathe in and out.*

The bell rings, and my vision snaps back to reality. Students start swarming the hallway, rushing to class. I wipe off some sweat that rolls down my forehead. I always sweat when I'm surrounded by a lot of people; humans or vampires—it makes no difference.

After smoothing out the wrinkles that formed in my dress, I head to class before anyone else arrives.

5

Our instructor saunters toward the center of the room once all the students finally get settled, her heels clicking with every step she takes. "I know most of you have been informed that you simply will have to walk to the stage and bow. However, that is not the case this year. The ceremony has changed," Ms. Fox announces.

Gasps echo throughout the classroom. A couple of whispers ensue, but of course, no one questions her as it has been implanted in us not to, except me I guess. I'm the only one who courageously asks, "Why the sudden change?"

Vampires never change anything, ever.

The entire classroom falls quiet, and every single pair of eyes flickers to me.

Ms. Fox walks to my desk, a wicked smile tugging at the corner of her mouth. "Instead of auctioning you all off together, we have decided it's best that you enter a room one by one," she answers.

I am under the impression that she is done when she continues, "Our vampire kings will be present this year to decide your fate."

*Wait, what? They are barbaric. They might drain us on sight.*

Abruptly she backhands me in the face, sending me straight to the floor. I'm pretty sure a bruise is formed on my left cheek. I should have expected that. They hate it when we question them.

Two strong vampires come into the classroom.

"Take her," Ms. Fox instantly demands. "She's up first."

*Freak! I've really screwed myself over this time. I should have kept my mouth shut.*

The two vampires drag me out of the room, and for the first time ever, I feel scared—terrified of the unknown. I just hope and pray they make my death quick.

# CHAPTER TWO
## The Chosen

The bulky vampire guards throw me into an unfamiliar room so hard that my butt stings from the impact.

*Assh\*les,* I think. I stand to my feet and take a moment to survey my surroundings. *This must be the room vampires use to prepare us humans for the most-important day of our lives.*

There really isn't anything special about it apart from a stand in the center that's full of unfamiliar items and a huge mirror attached to it. A small red chair is directly in front of the stand. A tub full of water is on my left, and on my right is a rack of many different styles of red pieces of underwear and bras in every size.

*I guess all the rumors are true. They really auction us off in nothing but a bra and panties. They wouldn't have it any other way. Vampires are nothing but some sick sadistic sh—*

"Claire, is it?" a high-pitched voice interrupts my train of thought.

"That depends on who's asking," I sarcastically reply, flipping my rose-blond hair in the direction of the female voice.

To my surprise, it isn't a vampire but a very pretty human wearing a red lace bra and matching panties. She has long chocolate-brown hair. Her skin is flawless, not a single scar in sight. I have never seen a human so put together. I mean minus the fact that she is in nothing but her undergarments, she actually is . . .

How should I say this? She's . . . Well, I don't have a word to describe her, but I've never seen a human like her.

She wrinkles her nose in disgust. "Aren't you a feisty one? I guess that's why your instructor sent you to be slaughtered first. Hmmm. Too bad for you," she says. "Please take a seat and don't give me any trouble. I would hate for the guards to whip you before you're presented. When was the last time you washed your hair? You look horrible!" she adds.

*Who the hell does she think she is? This wench is acting like she's one of them. I'm ready to give her a piece of my mind.*

I stop in my tracks when one of the bulky vampires steps back into the room.

"Is everything okay, Jasmine?" he asks her.

She doesn't respond.

Who I now know as Jasmine is staring at me with an eyebrow raised, her penetrating green eyes dancing with mischief.

I follow her command and take a seat in the only chair in the room, crossing my arms in the process. I guess she decides to ignore my childish antics because she remains silent as she runs a comb through my long, tangled hair. The guard disappears from sight shortly after. I flinch every time the comb touches the top part of my hair. I hate that damn thing.

"Take your clothes off now!" she demands, slamming the comb down. "This isn't going to work."

*She's got to be kidding me.*

"No, I'm not taking off sh*t!" I respond.

She said I'm going to be slaughtered, but at least I can go with a little dignity.

Jasmine taps her heel impatiently. It wouldn't take a rocket scientist to figure out she is used to other humans following her every command. That's when I realize exactly what type of human she is. She's one of the chosens, which explains why she's so high-maintenance.

8

A chosen is a human a high-ranking vampire personally picks to perform certain tasks. They receive more privileges than most, but they are still slaves, just maybe a little more polished than the average ones. At the end of the day, chosen slaves are still nothing but mere humans.

Jasmine's patience is wearing thin. That much is obvious, but I don't give a flying crap. It was already bad enough that my instructor nearly knocked my face off moments ago. I will not allow another human to intimidate me.

"I'm going to give you one more chance to take your clothes off. If you still have them on your body in seven seconds, you will regret it," she murmurs with that annoying high-pitched voice of hers.

She should know that regret is my middle name and death wish is my last, sarcastically speaking of course; that's exactly why I do what most typical humans don't. I flick my middle finger in her direction to further infuriate Little Miss Uppity.

"Guaaards!" she yells a little too loudly for my liking.

*Drama queen. She will definitely fit right in with Victoria and her posse. As if that could scare me. Screw them all.*

I laugh out loud just to ruffle her feathers more, then an unfamiliar vampire in a gray dress suit walks into the room. He looks at me, then his lips curl into a wicked grin.

"What's the problem, slave?" he asks her.

I don't like the evil glint in his bright-green eyes as they travel up and down my body. Just thinking about what this sadistic assh*le is capable of doing makes me shiver.

Jasmine bows submissively. "The king doesn't want any of the girls touched before they are presented, but this human is itching for it."

I continue to laugh. This girl really thinks she is one of them. She's f*cking delusional to believe she's anything more than me.

9

"Don't worry. I'll teach the little wench a lesson. Give me a couple of moments alone with her," he responds nonchalantly.

My laughter turns into a sneaky snicker. I'm always doing things to piss the vampires off, but even I am not this careless. I don't know what has gotten into me.

As the vampire takes a step closer, my snickers decrease. I know he isn't going to hurt me. Like Little Miss Uppity confirmed, kings ordered that we remain untouched. No vampire ever disobeys any of the kings.

"I can hear your heartbeat, you know?" He stands in front of me.

*Go screw yourself. Like for real, who gives a sh\*t?*

I stare into his now glowing eyes with defiance as their red color darkens with every second that passes. "Just get it over with!" I shout.

The next thing I know, my back already hits the stone-cold wall. I hold back a scream, refusing to give him the satisfaction of causing me pain. I prepare myself for his strike. I take a deep breath, in hopes of relieving some pain.

His touch never comes, well at least not in the way that I expected it to. Instead, his cold hand grips my left breast, and shivers travel down my spine.

He leans in closer toward my ear. "You know the best part about humans coming out of these facilities?"

I don't respond. I will not give this creep the satisfaction of hearing how scared sh\*tless I actually feel.

"Answer me!" he roars.

The volume of his voice does nothing. I will not speak, I will not break, and I will never allow any of these monstrous creatures to control my mind. They can control my body; they can control my life, but not my mind. Just because I grew up as a slave, that doesn't mean I'll break into a thousand tiny pieces. I haven't, and I'm not going to start now, especially on the day I will at last gain my freedom. Today is my day. Screw them all.

My silence must piss him off further.

He turns my body around so I face the wall and then he roughly bends me over. I know what is coming next. I have experienced this over and over with Mr. Rouge and the other male vampire instructors in this school.

He unbuckles his pants, and my heart rate starts to increase. I close my eyes, like I always do when they take what they want from my body. There is no need to fight him. I will lose. Resisting would only hurt ten times more. If I struggle, my body will suffer more than it has to. I have learned that. If you stay in place and allow them to have their way, they finish faster.

He picks me up by the back of my neck and abruptly dunks my head into the tub full of water. I struggle to breathe, and my eyes sting. I kick my feet out behind me, attempting to fight this unexpected attack.

Eventually, my body goes limp. He pulls my head back up, and I gasp for air right before he plunges it back into the water. It hits the bottom of the tub, blurring my vision. The clear water is now turning bright red.

Just when I think about my wish finally coming true, he lifts me up for air once again. This time, I don't want to breathe. I'm ready to let go.

"Oh no, you don't, slave. Death is too good for you."

I feel his hard manhood as he presses it against my back. The voice inside my head is pleading with me to fight him, but I can't. No, I won't fight him. It would just excite him more. I'm not going to be the one to provide him with that sort of thrill.

My jeans scrape roughly against my legs as he yanks them down and rips my undergarments to shreds. He then thrusts his disgusting manhood into my walls with such brutal force, causing me to release a blood-curdling scream. Tears flow heavily from my green eyes, down my face, and into my mouth as quiet pleas for him to stop escape my lips.

I have been raped numerous times by different vampire instructors, but the pain he is inflicting on my body is indescribable. Hearing his sick, joyful moans only makes me cry even harder. Blood pours from the right side of my head as he slams himself mercilessly in and out of me. I feel my consciousness slipping, my pupils dilating.

He wraps my hair around his hand and forces my head back into the water, never once stopping the cruel attack on my body. He increases his thrusts and the water rushes to the back of my throat. Another scream is forced from my lips, and I start to choke, but he only pulls me out much quicker this time while still pounding in and out of me in the process.

When he finishes degrading my body, he yanks me upright by the hair and throws me onto the floor. The door opens instantly, and Jasmine walks in with a smile. She hands him a towel, and they whisper back and forth.

"She's going to make the perfect breeder, trust me. I'll recommend her new status to the kings once she's presented to them."

"There's no need to put any makeup on her, or even do her hair. Present her with nothing on but red," he responds, as he finishes wiping himself off. He throws the soiled towel at my face, then walks out of the room. Now the only thing I hear is the sound of Jasmine's heels.

Seconds later, she throws a cherry-red bra and underwear in my direction. "I'm giving you five minutes to clean yourself up. There is no need for you to put in too much effort. You will experience the same fate once you reach the land of the breeders. I know it sounds tough, but look at the bright side. At least you will have a purpose to live for."

She's crazier than I thought. I guess living so close to those monsters would do that to any human. Most other humans must hate her, but I don't. In fact, I pity her. Jasmine is not one of us. She sold her soul to the devil a long time ago. Anything that made

12

her human was ripped away from her. She already lost her humanity.

When the annoying clicks of her heels disappear, I gather enough strength to drag myself toward the stand. I pull myself up and search for anything that could be of use. A sharp-pointed item that I believe is a razor blade is what I manage to grab. The only challenge is to hide it.

I search the room in a panic, and my eyes land on a red silk robe. I put it on and wrap a piece of tissue around the blade before sticking the small weapon into my underwear. The door swings open, and the two bulky vampires that dragged me into this room appear.

# CHAPTER THREE
## Kings: Part I

Jasmine is waiting on the other side of the door. I look into her eyes for any sign of remorse but was unable to locate a single ounce. She completely lost her humanity. Even Victoria wouldn't approve of what the vampires do to us. However, Jasmine is just as monstrous as the vampires. In fact, she's a disgusting excuse for a human being. If I could have my way, I would slit her throat with the razor blade.

My attacker's voice rings in and out my head: *"Death would be too good for you."*

He is right. Death is too good for me, and I plan on having that luxury sooner than he can possibly imagine.

I follow behind them in some sort of frenzy even though I have been through it before. It's just one of those things I will never get used to.

As we walk further down the hallway, one of the bulky vampires announces, "The kings are ready for her."

My heart starts to race, pounding louder with every step I take. No matter how brave and prepared I am to die, just thinking about entering the room with all seven of the kings in it is enough to scare the bravest of humans sh*tless.

We enter into another room I've seen for the first time. I inhale deeply as Jasmine guides me in the center of a stage. I take a look at my surroundings in surprise. Never in all my years of living here have I ever seen a room so well-crafted. It has several red velvet chairs set in groups, and at its far side is a stand full of different bottles containing many various liquids. Gold lighting with shiny objects hangs from the ceiling. The entire room is also filled with what I believe are called *paintings* from the time of the humans.

As the lighting dims, the vampire kings come into view. They have human girls with them—each of these female humans wears nothing but a collar around their neck connected to a leash. They are sitting on their knees beside the vampires, appearing calm and relaxed as they converse with each other.

*I was expecting the seven vampire kings. Who is the eighth vampire without a pet?*

They shift their attention to me, and their expressions transition from that of curiosity and then into something I can't describe. The first thing I notice is they all are extremely handsome and have the most-stunning eye colors. Vampires are known to be beautiful, deadly creatures. I guess their kings are a testament to that.

*Sh\*t. I hope they get this over with quickly.*

Jasmine drops to her knees instantly. Call me crazy, but I can't stop rolling my eyes at her actions. She really is the perfect little slave. No wonder she's a chosen.

"King Cyrus, King Luscious, King Marcellus, King Seneca, King Rufus, King Cornelius, King Xander, and King of All Kings Nicklaus, I present to you . . . Claire, the first human of interest," Jasmine hesitantly announces.

My eyes open widely.

*Did she just say "King Nicklaus," as in the King of All Vampire Kings Nicklaus?*

I was under the impression I was only going to be auctioned off to the seven kings. The king of all vampire kings never presents himself to humans, and from what I was told, that is a good thing. No human has ever lived to tell the tale of meeting the king of all kings. It's just unheard of, and this is worse than I expected. It only means one thing: I will be marked as a breeder.

I'll kill myself before that ever happens. I know very well that King Nicklaus is known for making humans suffer. It's common knowledge that his various torture methods are far worse than all the ideas of the other kings put together. Rumor has it that King Cyrus of North America reaches out to him for new methods of torture. Like seriously, who actually reaches out for such? They are all crazy. No, screw that. They are psychopaths.

I start shaking uncontrollably, and my heart is beating so fast that I can feel it nearly falling out of my chest. Being the first human to be in the presence of the world's most-dangerous predators is so nerve-wracking.

*Why does God have to be so cruel? Why can't I just die peacefully?*

"Sires, shall we . . . begin?" Jasmine's high-pitched voice murmurs hesitantly.

I swear the sound of it annoys me to the very end.

King Cyrus stands up. He is a handsome vampire with fair skin and tousled, thick dark-mahogany hair. Out of the eight vampires who sit before me, he is the first I am able to identify.

News flash! I have lived in North America for as long as I can remember.

His deep, baritone voice rings loud and clear when he declares, "We were expecting a human that is more obedient. This slave has no manners. My good friend doesn't have time to break it."

*Good! They will be presented with thousands of girls with manners. He's absolutely right; I'm not one of them. This might go better than I actually thought, so maybe I should speed up the process.*

Jasmine slowly rises to her feet. "This slave was nominated by the academy, and I don't know why. The instructors were very adamant about presenting her first," she states.

"Did we ask for your opinion, slave?" questions a gruff voice.

16

Seconds later, a vampire with angular features and silver-cerulean eyes that pierce straight into my soul stands directly in front of me. I know we were taught to never stare directly into their eyes, but I can't help it. This king's eyes are not only stunning in color but also hypnotizing in beauty—electrifying in all aspects—and the fact that he is extremely handsome doesn't help. His thick lashes and heart-shaped lips would drive any girl crazy.

Jasmine falls to the floor, shaking uncontrollably while I just continue to stare like the crazy human I am.

*He is so beautiful.*

"Do you like what you see?" he asks, winking.

"Of course not!" I roll my eyes.

*Wait a minute, I'm speaking to one of the kings.*

I smack my hand over my mouth.

*Oh, sh\*t. I didn't just speak out loud to one of the kings.*

Yup, I'm officially going to meet the worst death. Welp, in my defense, he did ask me a question.

To my surprise, his lips curve into a soft smile. He turns to face the other kings. "What do you guys think? I believe she will make a lovely pet."

"Lady Gwen will suck her dry." A vampire with sun-kissed and dark features chuckles, his milk-chocolate eyes shining with amusement.

"If he doesn't drain her first," adds another vampire while running his hand through his golden hair.

I turn, and they all watch me in amusement. I shiver when the vampire beside me strokes my hair.

"You're very brave for a human. It's not wise to turn your back to me," he says.

Once again, I roll my eyes. Screw him, and screw them. This conversation they are having in front of me is not going the way they want it to. They are actually talking about keeping me and not killing me, and I can't have that. Nope, it's not going to happen.

17

I turn around and spit in his face. "I'm not scared of any of you. Go to hell!"

Several growls roar around the room, and my brain stops functioning for a second.

*What the hell did I do?*

He stares at me in shock, obviously unable to process the fact that a human girl had the balls to spit in his face. I wish this were King Xander so I'd earn myself a ticket straight to the bleeder tank.

*F*ck, I should've paid more attention to the Vampire 101 history class instructor. I'm unable to identify him. In fact, I recognize only King Cyrus.*

"You should have," his husky voice states as he wipes off his face.

My face nearly falls to the floor.

*I should have what? No there's no way he could possibly know what I was just thinking. I'm losing my mind, that's all.*

He flashes an award-winning smile, and my heart skips a beat. "You see, little human, I would very much enjoy ripping your heart out and feasting on your liver, but there's only one thing stopping me," he states, his voice turning dangerously low as he yanks my bra off my body.

Adrenaline runs cold through my veins. I immediately start to pound his chest with my fist, only to feel like I'm hitting a brick wall. Intense pain travels throughout my body after landing my first punch.

He pulls me into him with force and cups my breast firmly. The vampire kings purr in approval, except one of them. I don't know which one, but I'm pretty sure he just growled.

He places his hand over my nipple and squeezes it gently. His cold and calculated laugh sends fear traveling inside my core.

I feel violated, my tears streaming down my face.

*No, not this again, not on the same day. No, no, no . . .*

The vampire freezes before pushing me to the ground. "This human would rather die than live the rest of her life as a slave," he says.

"I'd love to break her!" one of them shouts.

"And so would my dick," another vampire king chimes in.

*This isn't happening. I won't allow them to break or stick their dick anywhere near me.*

I notice icy silver eyes flashing crimson red.

"I'll rip your dick off before you have the chance!" I scream.

The kings burst out laughing in unison. It's the scariest sound that has ever hit my ears. I swear I can feel the walls around me trembling.

The vampire beside me forcefully pulls me by the hair. "You will be my slave, and you do whater and however I please. I will feed on you, mentally torture you, and explore that tasty little body of yours when I see fit," he tells me, his eyes the color of blood.

Again, another growl is heard from the crowd, but I ignore the anger surfacing deep inside me. This is the day I'm supposed to die, not announced as one of the chosen slaves of these lunatics. I'll be damned to allow them to deny it to me. If I have to take drastic measures to ensure that I die, then that's exactly what I shall do. There are thousands of other girls who will kill to be in my place. F*ck, I wish they were here to do me the honor.

Jasmine is apparently no use. She's still on the ground, bowing with such grace like the perfect little slave she was raised to be.

The vampire king throws me onto the ground, and a soft whine escapes my lips from the unexpected impact. "Strip!" he barks.

*Wait, what? I'm already without a bra, and he expects me to willingly take off my underwear? If he hasn't discovered by now that I don't value my life, then screw him. I'm not removing anything from my body.*

19

Certainly, he's going to take my head off. His eyes are now bulging and bleeding red. "I, King Nicklaus, the king of all vampire kings, demand you to strip!" He tries again.

Panic settles within me. Not only am I clearly defying the most-feared creature in the world . . . Oh well, if that's what it takes to die, so be it.

In the next instant, he yanks Jasmine by the hair, and she screams. "Strip, or she dies! Her blood will remain in your conscience."

*He's crazy if he believes I give a f\*ck about her dying. She's the reason I was just recently taken advantage of for crying out loud.*

He immediately sink his fangs into her delicate neck, and Jasmine's high-pitched scream echoes throughout the room.

*Oh sh\*t! He's not bluffing. But that's not fair. He didn't even give me a second to choose.*

The life in her smoky green eyes starts to flicker in and out as she silently pleads with me to help her.

*Sh\*t, sh\*t, sh\*t!*

"Stooop! I'll do it," I announce in defeat. I can never allow a human to die because of me, not even one like Jasmine.

# CHAPTER FOUR
## Kings: Part II

King Nicklaus releases Jasmine and tosses her back to the floor. Her blood still lingers on his face, trailing down the side of his mouth that is now curled into a smile. He gestures for me to follow through on my promise. I exhale deeply and pull my underwear down in a hurry, grabbing the tissue with the razor blade in the process.

Following orders from the kind that imprisons my race is the hardest task to complete. I'm not a student that follows the rules. In fact, I have been whipped many times because of my stubborn nature. Luckily, the sadistic kings passed a rule that if a human is whipped before the age of eighteen, they must be healed. If they hadn't passed that rule, I'm pretty sure I would have severe scars all over my body, just like the breeder woman who raised me.

King Nicklaus nods in approval, his eyes roving over my naked body. "What do you guys think?" he asks, addressing his audience

I cringe. He can't be serious. They are not going to talk about how I look naked. This is absurd.

The vampire with sun-kissed skin flexes his broad shoulders as he yanks his pet's leash harshly. "I'm not impressed," he comments. "Don't you already have a blond toy to play with at home?" His unfamiliar accent deepens and his milk-chocolate eyes turn into rich dark chocolate. "Kill the b*tch!" he demands.

21

*Yes, kill me please, and get it over with.*

"Gwen is not a toy. She is your future queen, Lucious," King Nicklaus murmurs, tension rolling through his frame. "You must learn to respect her."

*So, this is King Luscious of South America? What a joke! Compared to the rest of the kings, he looks like a wimp.*

King Nicklaus's eyes rake over my body in pure amusement. His facial expression says it all. He is listening in to my thoughts. Leave it to a vampire king to invade my privacy.

*Get out of my head, jerk face,* I think, causing him to release a small warning growl.

"Turn around," he barks in my direction.

A huge part of me wants to disobey him until Jasmine's lifeless body pops into my head. I follow his command and yelp in surprise when I'm met by another king standing right in front of me, his icy gray eyes paralyzing me. Caught off guard, I take a single step back. He is just as handsome as King Nicklaus. After searching his expression as if I were his match, I can't help but feel lost in his stare.

He trails a single finger down the side of my neck. "I say you keep her. Any human that has the balls to spit in your face earns my approval." His voice is just as cold and smooth. Snowflakes cover his well-kept facial hair that goes perfectly with his dark hair.

"Who are you?" I ask without thinking.

Instead of getting upset like the other vampire kings, he seems to be just as enchanted as I am. "My name is King Xander, but you may call me Xander, brave one," he says.

I stare at him in shock. His public display of affection is very unusual and unheard of in my world.

*Could it be that for once the rumors aren't true? Is the King of Antarctica actually kindhearted instead of coldhearted? That makes no sense.*

A dark chuckle interrupts our moment.

22

"The cold-hearted king is touched by a mere human. I vote for allowing her to participate in the games this year. Xander can sponsor her."

I know who he is just by the words that have come out of his mouth.

*King Marcellus proves my previous thought wrong. Rumors are usually formed through some truth, so there is no way King Xander or King Marcellus can ever be more than what they are known to be.*

Hurt flashes through King Xander's eyes, but it quickly disappears.

*Wait, can he also read my thoughts? And why on earth would he show any sympathy about how I feel?*

I look into King Nicklaus's eyes, and they reflect jealousy.

*Okay, now I know I'm officially going crazy. If they were listening in to my inner monologue, they've both simply ignored it.*

Xander storms off the stage and yanks his pet along with him in the process. "I will not take part in this nonsense. I'm going to view the other humans in the next annual auction. The king has already claimed her as his chosen. This is a waste of my time." He slams the door, leaving us all in silence.

*Fate is so cruel. They could have presented any other human. They would love to be the chosen of any of these kings. None of this makes any sense.*

So far, I have identified four of the kings, including the king of all vampire kings. Now that leaves three.

"So, it's settled then. You have selected your chosen girl. I'll take my leave as well." The blond-haired vampire moves toward the exit, dragging his pet human behind him.

On the way out, she makes the mistake of tripping over a seat. Without a second thought, he buries his fangs right into her. A high-pitched scream slips from my mouth as her lifeless body is thrown in front of me. I know instantly who the king is: King Rufus, the short-tempered king. As I said before, all rumors are formed through some sort of truth.

The vampires don't even bat their eyes.

23

I drop to my feet and whisper, "Your fight is over." I close my eyes, tears streaming down my face.

"Jasmine, go fetch the guards to dispose of the body of that thing!" an unrecognizable voice directs her.

I look through my glassy vision, and icy blue eyes meet my stare. It's another vampire king.

Jasmine stands up and follows his direction without defiance.

Something inside me twitches, fury overriding my pain as she walks past me. I lunge at her with the razor blade, slicing her delicate skin, and she falls to the ground in a panic. "You stupid b*tch, I saved you!" I hiss, striking her square in the face.

How could she follow their orders without a fight, especially after they proved how quickly they would dispose of her?

I'm just about to land another strike when unexpectedly I am knocked to the floor.

"How dare you prevent her from following my orders?"

"F*ck off, you perverted leech!" I spit, fury running hot through my body again.

King Nicklaus chuckles. "Ignore her, Cornelius. She will soon be broken."

"F*ck you too!"

"This human needs to be taught some manners. F*ck her being your chosen. I say you give her to me, Nicklaus. Every vampire in my kingdom will love to break her stubborn nature." King Cornelius's voice lowers dangerously at the end of his sentence.

"And how do you plan to teach her, Cornelius, besides f*cking her to death?" King Nicklaus responds coldly.

I hurry to my feet and jump onto his back. Unlike King Nicklaus, King Cornelius does not have much patience. He grabs my hair and throws me off with ease. The sound of my rib cage cracking echoes throughout the room as I hit the floor.

"I'll show you how to handle this type of human!" he yells. He clamps his hand around my neck, his eyes bloodshot.

I cry out in pain and claw at his arm, attempting to free myself, but it has no effect. I'm no match for his power. He undoes his pants with his free hand, and panic rushes through me.

*No, I won't allow him to have his way.*

"Enough!" King Nicklaus commands.

But King Cornelius continues.

"I said enough!" King Nicklaus roars, then he yanks the other king to his feet.

I fly off the stage in the process due to the force, and somehow land in one of the kings's arms.

"I got you, little human," King Cyrus consoles me, as he runs his hand through my hair.

I quickly bounce out of him. "You're all crazy," I hiss. I attempt to make my sweet escape, only to slam right into King Xander's chest.

"I knew you would come after me." He winks with a smile, leaving me breathless.

*How do they manage to move so quickly, and why would I chase after him? Oh yeah, I forgot the kings are known for their sense of humor,* I think, answering my own question.

Behind us, King Nicklaus is beating the other king to a bloody pulp. Each strike is like a crack of lightning reverberating off the walls.

"Take her, Xander. Monster has taken over," he roars from off the stage.

The red robe is placed over my body while I'm in so much pain. We are outside in a crowd of excited vampires in the next instant, and I can hear loud chatter all around me.

King Xander bites down on his wrist. "Drink," he says, as his blood flows like a river.

*He's crazy. I'd rather be a bag of bones.*

25

A loud scream fills the air, and my eyes shift to a large similar stage like the one back in the room. It displays thousands of naked humans standing straight in a row. I immediately recognize Victoria, who is crying her heart out as a vampire inspects her harshly. It is a horrible sight to see.

Most humans would pray for the day to see their archnemesis's reign crush, but I'm not one of them. Seeing her so broken is killing me. The evil vampire who just recently took advantage of my body plunges his finger inside her private area.

I cringe, unintentionally burying my face in Xander's chest. He freezes, and I can feel rage course through his veins. I take a step back. I'm certain he's going to show his true nature and live up to the cold-hearted brute he's known to be. However, he takes me by surprise.

"You touched her without consent," he states, his voice filled with hatred.

Shock waves swarm around my core, and I swing my head in the direction of the stage. The vampire who attacked me stands there with his glowing green eyes opened wide in fear. Xander is shaking with fury, his gray eyes now midnight black. The vampires around us grow silent as they witness the scene with great interest.

"Your Highness, I'm only doing my job."

"Punishing a human girl for disrespecting another slave is not your job," Xander responds.

*Disrespecting a human girl . . . ? This is unheard of . . . but why the hell does he care?*

My mouth gapes open. For the second time today, this vampire king has displayed kindness in public for a human. He's displaying kindness toward me.

King Xander turns around and searches the stage. His facial expression brightens when he finds what he is looking for. Out of the corner of my eye, I notice the king who murdered his pet staring intensely my way. He knows what this is about. Judging by his body language, he clearly is not happy about it.

26

A loud whip cracks through the air, forcing my attention back to the stage.

"Strip, peasant, and lower to your knees," King Xander orders.

The vampire follows without a fight, his green eyes probing the crowd and blazing with hatred as they land upon me.

My mind refuses to believe that this is actually happening. A king of vampires is actually defending me. This is so unreal.

The whip slashes across the vampire's back, and the other vampires roar in approval. Their barbaric nature causes me to shiver. They cheer and chant for one of their kings that is publicly humiliating their own kind. The whip snaps across his skin again and again. Blood rains down from his back, splattering across the floor off the stage. King Xander's eyes are on me the entire time. He only stops his attack when a very angry growl is released.

"What the f*ck are you doing?" King Nicklaus spits, his voice booming with authority.

# CHAPTER FIVE
## Sweet Escape

One thing is clear: King Nicklaus doesn't approve of Xander's actions. I mean King Xander's actions. I have no right to call him by his first name.

Once the crowd of vampires recognizes his voice, they all go down on their knees in submission. The other vampire kings are now present. It is obvious King Nicklaus and Xander—who are having a staredown battle—want to rip each other's throat out.

F*ck, I called him by his first name again. What has gotten into me?

Xander drops the whip to the floor and spits, "Exactly what you should be doing. This piece of sh*t raped a—"

"There is no law that forbids raping a human," King Nicklaus abruptly cuts him off as his eyes flicker to me.

"It is a crime to rape a human who has not been auctioned off and classified," Xander snaps back.

King Nicklaus raises a hand forward, and Xander falls silent. He walks through the crowd, his gaze smooth and graceful. He is the king of all vampire kings after all. As much as it kills me to admit it, there is no denying he oozes supreme authority. The humans on the stage are frozen in fear as his eyes scan the crowd.

I look down, not wanting to cause any more attention to myself than I already have.

"Come, slave," he commands, his voice powerful.

28

Without looking, I know he is referring to me. Knowing it is best to not disobey him in front of an audience, I follow his order with ease.

*Don't get me wrong. I do have a backbone, but even the bravest of slaves know when to fall in line.*

*"Oh really? Coming from the stupid human girl that spat in my face."* His voice pops inside my head, literally.

Before I can react, he continues, *"Stay calm, human."*

And just like that, my body goes limp.

What the hell? That has never happened to me before.

Xander places his stormy gaze upon me, his irritation reflecting clearly in his eyes.

"My loyal subjects, I apologize for my brother's unacceptable behavior. You have all been called here to choose your new slaves. The untouched slaves will be classified and released into the kingdom that could utilize them the most. Choose wisely, as this event only comes once a year," King Nicklaus announces.

The vampires cheer and then continue to shop for humans, completely ignoring the fact that one of their kings has taken a stand for a human.

*Wait, did King Nicklaus just call him his brother? They are brothers? No f\*cking way. I have not been the best student in Vampire 101, but I'm one hundred percent positive that not one of the history books indicate that any of the vampire kings are related.*

Xander breaks my train of thought when he releases me from his hold and knocks the scary vampire out with one punch. "This red-haired human is mine," he declares and snaps his fingers.

Seconds later, some vampire guards come and grab Victoria. She screams, her entire body trembling. I know she's aware of who he is rumored to be, but she has no idea she is super lucky. Well, as long as he decides not to classify her as a bleeder, she will actually be better than me—lucky tramp.

King Nicklaus startles me with his low, animalistic growl grumbling throughout his chest. He wraps his arms around me and then waves in the guard's direction. "Take my chosen to the vehicle as well. We shall depart shortly."

*No, this isn't happening. He is seriously taking me with him?*

I start to panic, going crazy in his arms.

*This is not happening! This is not happening! This is not happening!*

He restrains me with ease, and my attempts of freeing myself from his hold fail miserably.

Xander's eyes meet my own, and I silently plead with him to save me from this fate—I seem to secretly trust this king for some strange reason. His stormy eyes turn black. He doesn't intervene. Instead, he turns his back to me and storms off the stage.

All hope is lost, and my fear heightens to a new peak. King Nicklaus roughly throws me into a huge, scary vampire's arms.

I start punching him in the chest, ready to fight him with my last breath. "Let me f*ck go, you piece of sh*t!"

The crowd abruptly settles down and focuses on us. This is a rare sight for them. Humans in this day and time don't fight back, especially those that are being auctioned off.

The vampire guard's eyes flash red and land on King Nicklaus and then suddenly his lips curve into a wicked grin. "You stupid human b*tch, now I have to teach you a lesson about obedience," he spits before intercepting my next punch and twisting my wrists painfully.

A snapping noise is released into the air, and I softly whimper as pain shoots through me. However, I continue to attack, refusing to back down without a fight until a sharp, cold object pierces my skin. I scream as my body instantly goes numb. My eyelids feel heavy before everything around me turns black.

\*  \*  \*

My skin tingles like wildfire. I open my eyes slowly, then massage the left side of my neck to ease the sharp pain. Gosh, it stings like crazy. The right side of my head is pounding. My neck is sore and cramped. My bones ache, my vision blurry.

*What the hell did happen?*

I'm surrounded by darkness, but there is no way to miss the amber-eyed woman staring directly at me. She has a chain around her neck.

I try to pull myself up, but my body has another idea.

"If you try to stand quickly, you will hurt yourself," the woman speaks.

I groan as I attempt to roll to my side and pull myself up once again. I feel super dizzy, drowsy even. Somehow, I manage to pull myself halfway up, right before I crash back down.

The woman continues to watch me.

"Where am I?" I ask, my eyes adjusting to the darkness.

She is way too pretty to be a normal slave, but the tight collar around her neck says otherwise. I have never seen a silver collar like that before. The woman has long jet-black hair that blends perfectly with her milk-chocolate skin, even in its matted state. Whichever vampire has taken possession of her must be pure evil. The poor thing's bones reveal to me that she has missed many meals. Despite her malnutrition, her rare beauty still shows.

She licks her dry lips. "You shall figure that out soon enough," she answers, the tone of her voice irritating me.

*How great! Of course, they would pair me with another heartless human! Hopefully, once I make it to Antarctica, I'll meet some who are a little more in tune with their humanity. Wait, Antarctica . . .*

A vampire with icy silver eyes suddenly pops into my head, then it all comes back to me: the vampire raping me, the king of Antarctica displaying his fondness of humans, then him . . . King Nicklaus, staking his claims over me. I'm his. He made me his, his chosen.

31

I scan my surroundings in a new light. We are in some sort of cage that smells like piss and vomit. The stench of death hangs in the air. No wonder this woman beside me is in such a sh*tty mood, but she is the least of my worries. I have been marked as the chosen of the king of all vampire kings.

My eyes open widely, and somehow I find the strength to stand. I need to get out of here fast. With my newfound energy, I bang on the cell. Hopefully, I'll annoy the wrong vampire, and they will drain me and release me from this horrible fate once and for all. Out of the corner of my eye, I see my cellmate watch me with great interest.

"You've figured it out sooner than I thought. It's no use trying to run away. Trust me, I tried, and I'm a lot stronger than you." She tugs on her collar like it's some sort of proof.

Once again, the tone of her voice bothers me to no end.

"What are you trying to indicate by saying you're much stronger than me? You don't know anything about me. The last time I checked you were human just like me, so stop acting like you're better than me right now, you stupid little twit."

Her hearty laughter fills the air. She moves her head from side to side, cracking her neck in the process. I've realized something is strangely different about this woman. Her eyes flash bright yellow, and I swear on my life, her skin has just changed to fur! All my attention is confined to her immediately, sensing my new threat. My entire body is frozen in place.

"Now what were you saying . . . human?" she says, her voice dangerously low.

"Let me out! Let me out now!" I release an ear-piercing scream.

A menacing-looking vampire appears, kicking the front bars of the cage. "What's going on in here?" he yells with a rugged voice.

I attempt to find the words to explain what I just witnessed, but no matter how hard I try, my tongue refuses to form

32

a single syllable. Deciding it may be best to just show him, I turn around. To my surprise, the beast woman appears to be lying on the floor, sound asleep.

My eyes widen. *She was just . . . but I saw . . .*

I turn back around to face the very impatient vampire. His eyes flash red. He does not seem so happy about me interrupting whatever the hell I interrupt with. Oh well, it serves him right. He should have never placed me in a cage with this beast woman.

I return his hateful stare with a penetrating gaze of my own, and he steps inside with a smirk.

"Haven't you been advised not to stare us in the eye, little girl?"

*Little girl! Oh please.*

I mimic his actions with my own. "F*ck you."

Apparently, I've stated the wrong choice of words. Quickly, he grips my hair and yanks me out of the cage. I kick and scream as he drags me out—I wouldn't be myself if I didn't. He is so focused on me that he doesn't even notice the beast woman crawling out of the cage behind me. I release another scream when her sharp canines bite down on his neck. He drops me instantly, and I struggle to gain control. I force myself back to my feet. I don't know where I'm going, but I'm getting as far, far, far away from whatever the f*ck she is. Vampires don't put that much fear in my heart, but that animal scares me sh*tless.

I run down a dark narrow hallway, not once looking back. My heart is racing a million miles per second.

Physical education was the only subject I excelled in during my time in that human-housing school. Unlike the others, I knew the importance of maintaining my strength despite what the vampires taught us to believe. Having a little strength is necessary for our survival. Welp, I was okay in that category, but like Ms. Fox would say, "There is always room for improvement."

I peek over my shoulder to find no one coming after me, then suddenly my body slams straight into a rock-solid surface.

# CHAPTER SIX
## From the Dream House to the Dungeons

"Leave it to the human that so boldly spat in my face to find a way out of her cell."

His husky voice sends chills down my spine. He picks me up off the ground and throws me over his shoulder. My buttocks still sting from the impact of the fall.

"Let me down this very instant, you, you, blood-sucking leech!" I scream, pounding on his stone-hard back.

King Nicklaus drops me on the floor with a thud—just like that.

*Assh\*le. I hate him with a burning intense passion. I hate all of them.*

"Suit yourself, sweetheart. From the looks of it, I guess you are already aware of your werewolf cellmate that has escaped."

I gulp as the memory of the woman beast's transformation into a werewolf, like a real live werewolf, flashes across my memory with a vengeance. I was under the impression that their kind had gone extinct a long time ago.

Werewolves are cruel, menacing creatures. (No wonder my body naturally sensed her presence as a threat.) Just like vampires, they believe they are a superior race. Legend has it that the vampires and werewolves had been at war long before the Awakening. We humans didn't come into play until after the Awakening. The history books made it seem like vampires demolished the werewolf kind before they presented themselves to the human race.

Just thinking about the beast woman's scary yellow orbs makes me jump onto Nicklaus. Surprisingly, his big magnificent body accepts me with open arms. I bury my face into his shoulder, hovering away in fear.

How silly of me to run away from one monster only to depend on getting saved by another monster!

His body visibly goes stiff, and I'm quite sure he is about to throw me flat on my ass for the second time until his minty breath fans over my skin, his lips trailing dangerously close to the crook of my neck. My heart thunders to a new beat inside my chest, crashing. The top of his body is completely bare, and I can feel his muscles visibly flex.

*Oh my, they feel glorious.*

I so foolishly pull my face away from his neck as he lowers his lips closer to mine. His head abruptly snaps up, and once again, he drops me flat on my ass right before a furry creature slams straight into him, enough to bring me back to my senses. I jump to my feet just in time to see him and the creature spiral into battle.

"The little wolf found her way out of the cage after all," he taunts, moving too quickly for my human eyes.

The beast woman shifts her attention to me. My entire body freezes as I realize what's happening. Before her massive wolf paw can take a step in my direction, she is knocked onto her side. Muffled sounds escape her lips when King Nicklaus effortlessly breaks her neck in a second.

"I knew that silver collar had no effect on that b*tch. She was really under the impression she could fool me," he says with a smirk. His eyes trail me. "Leave it to my chosen to be the one to get the dog to speak. I knew I could depend on you."

His words register in my head.

*He used me. He put me in that cage on purpose to test a theory. I could have been killed by that dangerous creature, not that it would matter in the end but still . . . It's the point that he used me to his advantage.*

Anger blazes up inside me. "Leave it to your kind to utilize humans as if we are at your disposal," I snarl.

"You are at my disposal, little firecracker. You're mine, and I can do whatever I please with you, remember?" He makes his way toward me.

*I hate him. I hate him. I hate him.*

"Oh really?" He raises an eyebrow. "You didn't seem to hate me when you jumped into my arms," he teases with that annoying smirk of his.

I ball my fingers into a tight fist, ready to swing if he tries anything stupid.

*I don't care if he's the king of the leeches. I'd rather die than allow him to have his way with me.*

"That's funny, coming from a human that was scared out of her mind of a scrawny she–wolf," he taunts further before bursting into a fit of laughter.

"Stay the hell out of my head, you f*cking leech!" I roar.

The sound of his laughter pisses me off more. This cocky dickhead annoys me to no end. Why is he laughing anyway? Isn't he supposed to be some creepy blood-sucking tyrant? This is exhausting. First I get picked by the likes of him, then the king of Antarctica nearly beat one of his subjects to death for disgracing me, and now, I'm in a dark, creepy dungeon with a dead werewolf lying in front of me. Meanwhile, the king of vampire kings is acting like a childish human.

I slump onto the ground with my back against the stone wall. I'm so lost in thought that I don't even notice the king of the leeches has stopped laughing. I slowly raise my eyes, only to be met by his blazing red orbs. My heart rate increases sevenfold.

*What did I do? He was just enjoying himself, making fun of me. It's not like I said anything in my head that I haven't said out loud.*

36

I bang the back of my head against the wall in an attempt to make my sweet escape. His penetrating gaze causes fear to surface in raging waves. Surprisingly, he scoops me into his arms and walks out of the dungeon without another word.

"Are you just going to leave the beast woman there?" I raise an eyebrow.

He bursts out into another fit of laughter. "I've already sent some guards to take her back to her cell."

*Wait a minute, the beast woman is alive? That's impossible. He snapped her neck. I saw it with my own eyes. It made a crunch sound—snap, just like that.*

"It takes a lot more than snapping their neck to kill a werewolf, especially one as strong as her. The only way is to shoot them in the heart with a silver bullet," he answers my question. He has once again invaded my privacy.

"What do you mean by saying 'one as strong as her'?"

"You are a very brave human, fragile but brave," he says, changing the topic of the conversation.

*Maybe it's best not to learn more about the beast woman. I don't even want to see her again.*

He breaks into another fit of laughter. He seriously has a laughing problem.

"The king of vampires just gave you a compliment, and all you can think about is the she-wolf, or should I call her the beast woman?" He chuckles while holding me tighter against his chest.

I hate to admit that my body loves the feeling of his bare chest swallowing me whole.

I take a moment to look at my new surroundings as we emerge through a massive set of double doors into the fanciest place I have ever seen in my life. Portraits of every single vampire king hang on red walls. Some are pictures of them all together or with others. If I didn't know any better, I would believe they are what we humans never get to experience to have—a family.

A huge gold light with rows and rows of diamonds hangs in the center of the room, directly over a gold table with fancy diamond decor. I believe the instructors indicated that the light is called a chandelier. I never thought I would actually see one in my life.

In a flash, King Nicklaus heads up a massive red marble staircase. The place, beautifully grand, reminds me of pictures from *Fairyland* books I used to sneak and read back at the human academy. We humans could only dream about being in a spectacular place like this.

We enter a few more doors, passing several kitchens, three libraries, two pools, and numerous other rooms that I'm unable to identify.

*How on heaven's earth am I supposed to navigate myself through this house? There is no way.*

Finally, we arrive in front of another massive door, but unlike the others, this one is gold. We enter and King Nicklaus locks the door behind us, then we walk into a huge bedroom that may be bigger than the entire human academy. He sits me down on a very comfortable red rug that's in front of a cozy fireplace. In the center of the room is an enormous bed neatly made with black and red bed linens.

I look through a glass door on my left and see a balcony that provides a perfect view of a large body of crystal clear water. "Where are we?" I ask, mouth agape.

He makes his way over to the bed and settles in. His eyes sparkle with mischief. "We're in my room in one of my homes. As my chosen, it is your duty to stay close to me. I'll give you this one-time courtesy of choosing where you would like to sleep. You have two options: on the floor or on the couch. Take your pick."

I snort, not because I have to choose between the couch and the floor, but because in all honesty, they're both way better than any bed I have ever been forced to sleep in, and because he deliberately stated, "I'll give you this one-time courtesy . . ." like I'm a freaking dog.

"How about I take the balcony? That way I can be positive that you can't touch me when the sun rises, unless you want to become a burning corpse that is," I joke.

He rolls his eyes. "Very well. I'm a man of my word. There is an extra blanket and pillow in the closet. The sun will be up soon, so I suggest you get ready for bed. I have a meeting with a good friend of mine tomorrow night, and you're attending. Good night."

He mumbles something about the sun not having an effect on him or something of the sort and then he rolls over, indicating that the conversation is ended.

I walk toward what I suppose is a closet, but it actually reminds me of another room. If it weren't for the racks and racks of clothes, I would believe it is. I notice that one side of it is filled with women's clothes. Now, why would the king of vampires have a closet stocked with women's items?

The material of each piece of clothing is very beautiful. Wondering how it would feel like against my skin, I run my hands along a lovely emerald-green dress—curiosity kills the cat. The fine material feels as good as it looks.

*"I'm pleased to see you show some interest in your new items."* His deep voice startles me, and I jump and fall flat on my ass—typical me.

*Hold up! Did he just say they're my new items?*

I check the size of the dress, and it's actually my size! In fact, every single piece of clothing is my size.

My mind goes crazy as I move item after item to the side. My eyes nearly pop out of my head.

*"Are all these really for me?*

He responds with a chuckle.

*"Sleep now."* His voice appears in my head, then my sight surrenders to darkness.

# CHAPTER SEVEN
## Pervert

The warm sensation that beams onto my skin feels heavenly. A strange and salty smell fills the air as the sound of crashing waves invades my consciousness. I open my eyes and am greeted with a half sun that's hanging low in the sky, confirming that the night shall begin shortly. I pull myself up and further search my surroundings. I'm on a bed that has been placed in the middle of the balcony.

*Hey, this wasn't here last night. Nonetheless, I'm very grateful. That was the best sleep I have ever experienced in my eighteen years of living.*

I look down at myself. The beautiful emerald dress clings to my skin snugly at the top and flows loosely down my legs, my skin glistening in the sunlight.

*Wait a minute, I don't remember putting this dress on, and I damn sure didn't take a bath.*

The honey, milk, and oats fragrance of soap that booms out of my pores says otherwise.

*That only means that the blood-sucking leech changed my clothes! Pervert! He must have washed my body in my sleep. Speaking of which, I don't remember falling asleep or leaving the closet to come out here.*

A white bird lands on the bed. It has a long brown beak, its beady black eyes staring at me as it moves its bald head side to side. I have never seen this type of bird before. Honestly, I have never really seen a bird in person at all. Deciding to feel its texture, I stretch out my arm slowly, but it squawks at me and flies away. My hands grip the comforter.

*If only I knew how to escape this place, I'd open the door and fry his ass to a crisp.*

With that thought, I roll out of bed and scan my surroundings for a second time, attempting to locate some sort of landmark that would identify where his kingdom is located. I may not have been very keen on learning any other subjects in that god-awful school, but geography always fascinated me. I paid close attention to the different climates of each continent and very close detail to certain landmarks in order to tell them apart. The vampire instructors only filled our minds with a little knowledge of important subjects, focusing on teaching us how to be perfect slaves instead of how to be smart beings. Thank God I wasn't that dumb to fall into their trap.

A moment passes, and I'm still unable to identify any landmark. More birds like the one that sat before me continue to fly in circles, closer toward the water.

*Bird, water, and sand . . . They don't help much. Birds, water, and sand . . . Birds! That's it. Right there, birds! If I can manage to sneak into their library, I'm sure I can find a book about birds. Even I know that certain types of birds only live in certain places of the world. Bingo!*

I move around in a victory dance, then I lie back on the bed and vividly memorize each detail of the birds flying over me. The sun starts to fall, disappearing and bringing forth the night.

I guess I shall head inside and get ready for this meeting with whatever blood-sucking friends of King Nicklaus. I wonder what he's doing. I'm pretty sure he was aware of the exact moment I woke up. The vampire instructors always seemed to be able to identify when we were awake or asleep. If they could, I know he is no different.

I take one last look at the large body of water. Not one picture in any book I have ever read actually captures the true beauty of this. I slide the glass door open and step inside his room.

The blood-sucking pervert is still fast asleep. It's so strange he actually looks like a harmless human—well, a supermodel, badass, sexy kitten human—while he's asleep.

*Sexy kitten . . . Really, Claire? Pull yourself together.*

Okay, more like a sexy tiger that will rip a human into shreds while they're asleep.

I blow some air out of my mouth and make my way toward the bathroom. My eyes nearly pop out of my head again. Like seriously, is every room in this house so freaking fancy? I can't decide if I want to take a shower in the wide walk-in shower with several golden shower heads that seem to hang in every direction, or sink inside that huge golden tub I have to climb up a few stairs to get into. The tub itself appears to be big enough to house the entire body of water outside.

*Decisions, decisions, decisions!*

I squeak in excitement. Of course, I'm taking a shower. I untie my dress, allowing it to fall to the floor. I turn the shower on, and water flows out of each shower head in different speeds.

*Heaven, heaven, heaven.*

Chanting the words inside my head, I hop right in. The water hits my back from all different angles, filling me with pure happiness. I place my head under the shower and enjoy the feeling as the water trails down my body. I grab the purple soap that smells exactly as I expected—just like honey, milk, and oats.

*I know that pervert washed my body last night. That is so creepy, someone washing you in your sleep.*

I guess it's expected. Vampires have no respect for human privacy. If they like it, they take it. And based on King Nicklaus's reaction when Xander decided to punish one of my attackers, he's no different.

King Xander's stormy gray eyes suddenly flash through my head somehow, piercing straight into my soul. One thing's for certain, King Xander does know how to leave a good impression on a lady, especially one like me—I'm only a human.

I continue my shower in a peaceful-like state. Once I finally have enough, I turn the shower off, then grab a towel and dry myself off fairly quickly. I realize I didn't bring any clothing into the bathroom with me, so I look for the dress I was wearing before my shower but unable to locate it.

*I must be going crazy. I know that dress was right there.*

Steam hangs heavy throughout the bathroom, and fog covers the mirrors and other bathroom surfaces. I heave a long sigh.

*Perfect! Now I have to walk out of here in nothing but a towel. That pervert must have snuck in here and taken my dress with him. Pervert, pervert, blood-sucking pervert. I hate him with a passion. Gosh!*

Anger soars through me as I walk out of the bathroom. The devil himself is sitting on his bed with my dress in his hand.

"Forgot something, firecracker?" he teases, barely holding back his laughter. His broad shoulders flex as he twirls my dress in his hand. And that's not it, he is wearing absolutely nothing! That's right. He's as bare as the day he was born or created, or whatever happens when a vampire awakens.

My eyes open so wide, wider than I could ever imagine, and zero in directly on his manhood.

*Oh my, he's gigantically big! There's no way that's real.*

"Wow!" I place one hand over my eyes and the other over my mouth. "Cover please."

His laughter fills the air, booming against the walls. "Oh come on, baby. You know you like it. Come get some," he teases me further.

I run into the closet, banging my head into the wall in the process.

Ouch, that hurt like a b*tch. I can't blame it on my own clumsiness. No, this time it isn't my fault. Not too many people can see with their eyes covered. I can't believe I just blatantly eyeballed his cock like that, out in the open and with no shame. I couldn't look away even though I wanted to. He is so huge, so gigantically

43

huge, even bigger than a horse's dick. And I'm here to tell you horses have really big, thick, and long junks.

I rake through the closet for some clothes and find a black lace bra and pantie set.

After some struggle of placing the undergarments on my body, I grab some skinny jeans and a comfortable olive-green V-neck shirt. Once covered, I start to panic again. My back hits the door, and I slide down in embarrassment. Water drips from my damp hair, providing the perfect sound effect. I can't believe I've just smacked my head.

*Pull it together, Claire. You are not one of those brainwashed humans you grew up with. He's evil, very, very evil, and your enemy. Pull it together, Claire,* I mentally tell myself over and over and over again.

He's not even acting like himself. That is not the vampire king that inspected me at the auction. All of this playful nature and kind little gestures must be some sort of act. Maybe he's trying to make me fall in love with him, my abductor. Yeah, I have read that many vampires did that to humans before the Awakening.

The more I think about the change in his behavior, the more my head spins. Maybe I should have behaved in school so my plans could have actually had a chance of playing out. If I'd behaved, I would have been invisible. The instructors wouldn't have had it out with me. And just maybe Xander would have been the one to choose me at the auction and take me straight to the bleeder kingdom.

"Little firecracker, come out. Come out wherever you are," he calls in a teasing voice, once again irritating me to no end.

Oh boy! The king of all vampire kings acts more like a human teenager. How on heaven's earth did he manage to lead his race to victory against nations of different humans?

I rise to my feet and drag myself back into the room. He is still on the bed, no longer naked but still looking handsomely good. I hate that he is so attractive. God, I wish I could knock that sexy little smirk right off his good-looking face. He truly is so f*cking appealing.

*Pull it together, Claire. Pull it together, Claire.* The little voice inside my head starts to chant once more.

"Yes, pull it together, Claire." He chuckles again, then he stands up.

"Stay out of my head, you stupid, blood-sucking vampire leech!" I snap.

*Stupid vampire powers. Gosh, he is so annoying. Damn it! Can a human girl have a little privacy around these blood-sucking monsters?*

*"You mean perverted, blood-sucking, monstrous leeches?"* His voice pops into my head without a word actually escaping from his mouth.

I give him the stink eye. Yeah, I can be as childish as him.

*I hate your kind. I hate your kind. Burn in hell. I hate your kind.*

His hands go up in the air as he takes a step forward. "I get it, you hate my kind. News flash, baby! My kind hates yours too, so we're even."

I'm just about to form a jazzy comeback when he opens his big mouth again. "Your shirt enhances the color of your eyes. I have always loved that brilliant green color. They're fascinating," he says, pulling me closer toward his God-given body.

My body freezes, then I melt. I'm a puddle—a very, very large puddle.

"Claire." His minty breath blows softly as he calls my name in a hypnotizing way.

*My name . . . He actually said my name, not chosen or slave but my name.*

"Yes?" I manage to answer.

"You will follow my every command the entire time at this dinner because I own you."

45

# CHAPTER EIGHT
## Compulsion

A vibrating sensation tugs at the back of my mind, and the power to act or think on my own slips away. "I will follow your every command the entire time at this dinner. You own me." My lips move of their own accord.

*No, the hell I will not! He doesn't own any part of me. That's not even my voice. I sound like a robot or some type of zombie.*

"Good girl. Now keep your head down and follow me," he speaks to me like I'm his pet.

He pisses me off even more when he pets me on the head. However, just like the perfect pet, my legs move on their own. I walk behind him with my head down.

*"You blood-sucking leech,"* I say, well at least try to say, but no words leave my lips, not even a single syllable.

"I'm a powerful, blood-sucking leech," he corrects me, his eyes in my direction.

I glare daggers at him in my head. *This blood-sucking leech is listening in on everything I'm saying.*

"Of course I'm listening to you, baby. It wouldn't be any fun if I didn't. Now behave yourself before I make you stand on one leg, hop like a bunny, and bark like a dog."

*You wouldn't dare,* I think to myself.

He turns and pets me again, his mouth curving upwards into that devilish smirk of his. "Try me."

"F*ck, I hate you."

He doesn't respond to my comment. He heads down the stairs and through several double doors. I really wish I could see the details of this beautiful place, but his stupid commandment doesn't allow me that privilege. I just walk behind him with my head held down the entire time.

We enter a dark room, but I don't know what type of room it is because I can't see sh*t but the shine of the marble floors. I can hear voices as we approach.

"All hail King Nicklaus, who has finally found the time to grace us with his presence," a deep familiar voice says to him. "And you bring your chosen. Nice to see you manage to break her so easily."

*I'll show you broken, you piece of sh*t, blood-sucking leech. Whoever you are,* I say to myself.

King Nicklaus's deep chuckle presents itself inside my head, and I can't help but release a giggle of my own—inside my head of course.

"It's always a pleasure for a king to spend time with his peasants, even one like you, Cornelius."

My bravery falters as soon as King Nicklaus speaks his name. My last encounter with that monstrous king scared the sh*t out of me.

My heartbeat increases, and my palms become sweaty.

*"You have nothing to fear, little firecracker. No harm shall come to you."* King Nicklaus's words appear in my head again, but this time they are very welcomed.

I heave a sigh. I'm starting to feel thankful he did whatever he did for me because I honestly don't believe I could control myself around that vampire. Maybe I should thank him. On second thought, that would be too nice. He doesn't deserve my kindness.

"You may sit, human," King Nicklaus commands, and I follow, somehow finding a seat without needing to look for one.

"You're seriously not going to allow the dog to eat with us?" King Cornelius asks, stirring a wide range of curse words in my head.

*I don't care if I'm scared of him or not. I'll smack his gorgeous face. How dare he call me a dog?*

"Even dogs share food with their owner, Cornelius."

I recognize King Cyrus's voice as he comes to my defense. Well, at least I think he's defending me on his own way.

*If King Cyrus and King Cornelius are present, does that mean I will be dining with all the kings tonight? Hopefully, Xander is here.*

"Enough with this foolishness. Why are you two here? Both of you should be governing your kingdoms like everyone else, not discussing dinner arrangements," King Nicklaus speaks to them and answers my question at the same time.

*Welp, I guess it's just the four of us.*

The smell of mouth-watering spices lingers in the air, hitting me hard and strong. My belly growls in response. Whatever it is, it smells *a-maz-ing*.

I hear the clink of some items being placed in front of me.

*"You may eat,"* King Nicklaus announces inside my head, and my body follows his command.

I finally have the chance to view my surroundings. I'm seated in front of a long table with at least a hundred red chairs up and down its sides and a variety of different foods covering its center. It is directly in the middle of a very huge dining room. The kings sit at the left far end of the table, already enjoying their meals. In front of me is a plate of what should I call dog food? That's exactly what it is—human chow food. Of course, they feed me scraps while they eat grandly.

*I'm dining with the kings who place my race in chains. F*cking assho*les.*

Someone on the opposite side of me sneezes, gaining my attention. On my right is a very thin human girl, barely dressed. She is holding trays of food in her hand. She is young, my age or

48

younger, and has a pie-shaped face, rich mahogany-colored hair, and mesmerizing hazel eyes. She heads over to the opposite side of the room, her six-inch heels clicking against the floor. To my surprise, she doesn't fall or trip and somehow manages to place the plates in front of the kings even though her eyes are averted and hands are shaking.

My heart goes out to her, especially when King Cornelius abruptly pulls her by her left arm. He forces her to sit on his lap before plunging his fangs into the right side of her neck. The human girl releases a soft whimper, attempting to free herself as he hungrily fills his belly with her blood.

*Let her go, you blood-sucking leech!*

My eyes land on the other kings. They do nothing, not affected in the slightest. They can't be serious.

I try with all my might to say something, anything, or just a single curse word, but nothing comes out of my mouth.

*"Please save her. He's killing her,"* I plead with King Nicklaus inside my head.

He doesn't respond.

*"This is ridiculous. You're barbaric!"*

"Cornelius, that's enough. Dinner is served," King Nicklaus finally interrupts him, but the tears that have formed in my eyes during his ungodly performance are already sliding down my face.

King Cornelius releases the poor girl. She scrambles to her feet and bolts out of the room. He picks up his fork and dives into his meal, her blood still traveling down the side of his mouth. He doesn't even have enough decency to wipe it.

The contents of my stomach flip. I lose my appetite after witnessing that horrific scene. I stare at my plate of food. I really don't understand why I feel so disappointed about King Nicklaus not stopping King Cornelius quickly.

*It would be against his nature to give a sh\*t about anything other than himself. I bet Xander would have saved her.*

49

"Enough!" King Nicklaus slams his fist onto the table so hard that it cracks. His eyes glow red as they land on me, the other kings's eyes searching around the room in bewilderment.

"What the hell is wrong with you?" King Cyrus asks, confusion clear on his face. He watches him staring daggers at me and then a look of understanding washes down his features.

King Cornelius hasn't seemed to put two and two together at the moment. He honestly looks bored or more like stuck on stupid.

King Nicklaus suddenly laughs and then stuffs his mouth with food as if he didn't just have an outburst.

*Bipolar much!*

He chuckles again. He finishes chewing his food, then starts the conversation. "You two never explained why the hell you are in my kingdom."

King Cyrus rolls his eyes, and if I didn't know better, I would say a ghost of a smile tugs his lips.

King Cornelius's clueless ass answers, "Cyrus is here because of his dog problem, and I just tagged along for the fun of it.

That sparks my interest. *What does he mean by "dog problem"?*

King Nicklaus pushes his plate and relaxes back into his chair. "Don't tell me you can't handle a single pack of mutts? Cyrus, I expect more from you."

*Why do they have to refer to other species as animals? It's really annoying.*

King Cyrus's expression becomes more serious. His golden eyes flash red. "If it were just a pack of mutts, I would have put them down by now. The challenge is that the mutts have teamed up with the pack of wolves."

King Nicklaus grabs a glass full of red liquid I didn't notice before, then he takes a sip. "What do you mean? They are wolves . . ."

*Wolves? Are they referring to werewolves?*

50

Once again I'm thankful that King Nicklaus prevented me from speaking out loud. I'm pretty sure I would have been drained dry by now.

King Cyrus shakes his head from side to side. "They have teamed up with lycans, Nicklaus."

My neck snaps in his direction. I don't know how I manage to do it, but I do.

*Did he just say lycans, like eat you alive? Lycans teaming up with beastie break-your-bones werewolves . . . No wonder he came running. I would have run too.*

King Nicklaus spits the liquid. A low rumble leaves his chest. "Now does that make things interesting?" He wipes the liquid from the sides of his mouth. "I guess it's time to put the b*tch to use."

"Speaking of which, how was your little experiment?" King Cornelius queries, and I feel his penetrating gaze make its way to me. "Did the b*tch take the bait?" The sound of his voice sends adrenaline flushing through my veins. He sounds creepy, and I have a feeling he is referring to the beast woman.

"As expected, my chosen exposed her," King Nicklaus answers, a sheepish expression creeping across his face. "She even managed to stay alive."

My body goes visibly stiff.

*Here he goes again talking about me like I'm nothing but an item that he can dispose of whenever he pleases.*

King Cornelius's eyes are still on me, and I feel little under his gaze. "Interesting," he comments.

King Nicklaus clears his throat, placing the attention back on himself. "Not really. So, Cyrus, I guess you came here to ask my permission to wage war relating to the abomination of a species?"

"You know me better than that my friend. I come to ask you to help me erase the abomination of a species off the face of the earth once and for all."

King Nicklaus stares into space for a long moment.

51

"Of course I'll partake in the war," he finally speaks. "However, I have something to attend to before coming to your kingdom and—"

"I have no problem lending a helping hand," King Cornelius cuts in.

"There is no need, Cornelius. You may return to your kingdom. If I'm in need of your assistance, I will send word," King Nicklaus responds. He takes another gulp of his drink. "Besides, Xander will be notified to assist since he's the one who started this uprising in the first place."

# CHAPTER NINE
## Spaghetti

As soon as Xander's name leaves his mouth, my heart rate accelerates and butterflies swirl in my stomach, making me feel all mushy inside. The three kings all turn to face me. One stares at me in amusement, another with great interest, and the other—King Nicklaus—is sending daggers my way, sort of like scorching hot daggers that have been placed into the fire, just like silver daggers with neon orange and neon red blending together at the sharpest point of the knife, straight-out-of-the-fire type of daggers. The intensity of his stare is that serious. He's way past the point of being pissed. I don't have the slightest clue why. I've lost track of the whole conversation once he mentioned Xander's name.

"We shall finish this conversation," King Nicklaus growls through clenched teeth.

The other kings vanish in the blink of an eye without saying a word, just like that. They're gone while I'm still sitting in my chair, looking dumbfounded and left all by myself with this very angry-looking vampire king. Like seriously, what did I miss?

He continues to stare intensely at me for a long-drawn-out moment before finally breaking the silence. "Come to me, Claire," he commands, his voice sparking something inside me. "Now, Claire!" he barks, holding the edge of the table so hard it cracks.

I must be going insane because I rise instantly, and my feet move in his direction. But this time, my mind actually agrees with my body's reaction. There's something about how he calls my name. It stirs a strange reaction deep within me, burning flames that match the color of his glowing red eyes.

I take a seat on his lap without being told to, shocking the hell out of myself. He doesn't move me; he doesn't even look surprised, not in the slightest. He continues to stare at me with blazing red eyes that seem to burn brighter by the second, red flames dancing away. I am caught in some kind of a trance. My heart rate increases, my heart beating so fast that I feel like it might jump out of my chest and form little legs before taking off. The butterflies that once were flying inside me turn into buzzing bees, stinging the surface of my gut.

King Nicklaus continues to stare at me and then his lips curl into a deadly smirk. "This is the only reason your heart rate should speed up, firecracker." He trails his finger down the side of my face, never once breaking eye contact. "You belong to me, Claire." His voice sounds compelling, but this time it doesn't feel like he's reminding me of my place. His words are spoken with more emotion, in a possessive but passionate way.

Passionate way—yup, I'm losing my mind. Whatever he does to me would explain exactly why I'm reacting like this. It's not me. This is him, controlling me again. That's the only reason why I feel so comfortable sitting on his lap, or why I so foolishly believe he's claiming me in another way, a passionate way to be exact.

His smirk deepens. "At this moment you're free from my control, Claire." His finger makes its way to my chin. He lifts my face up high, holding it in place and making sure we're sharing eye contact. "And I mean what I say in every single way that's running through that pretty little head of yours."

Shivers run down my spine. I part my lips to speak, but he cuts me off before a word can come out.

*"Forget everything you saw or heard tonight. Eat your dinner until I suggest otherwise . . . Oh . . . and stop drooling over my brother."* His words echo loudly inside my head.

My mind drifts off in a misty haze. I blink rapidly, feeling like I've just had one hell of a dream. Silver-cerulean eyes are gazing directly at me, while I'm sitting on the lap of the king of all vampire kings!

My eyes grow wide, and I leap into the air and stumble back. "Um, what's going on?" I turn around. I take in a table filled with mouthwatering food.

He chuckles, bringing my attention back to him. "You must have hit your head harder than I thought."

"Hit my head?" I sit in a chair. Usually, I don't eat anything given to me by a vampire, but for some strange reason, the spaghetti is calling out to me—practically screaming my name—so I place a huge amount onto a plate and dive in.

*Yummy. This is delicious. Really, really good.*

I nearly moan from the taste.

King Nicklaus clears his throat. "How's the food?"

I twirl some of the tasty noodles with my fork. "It's actually pretty good," I answer with a slurp. "My head is killing me. What did you do? Hit me with a sock full of rocks?"

He laughs. "You tripped, remember?" He points his finger at a crack on the table. "Hit your head and landed right onto my lap, like the clumsy little human you are."

"And like my knight in shining armor, you caught me." I stick my tongue out at him, demonstrating his immature vampire behavior. I'd rather be a clumsy human than a blood-sucking leech." I slurp the last of my spaghetti and then add some more on my plate. I'm not even hungry, but I still feel as though I didn't eat enough. "I bet it killed you to have to share your seat, with you being a privileged vampire king and all."

He wiggles his eyebrows. "On the contrary, I never told you to move, sweetheart. I actually enjoyed the feeling of you moving around, sitting fairly close to my own balls."

My whole face heats up. *F\*cking pervert!*

"Speaking of balls, I know you have eaten enough," he says.

I place my fork down, suddenly no longer having enough room to finish my food. He's wearing a slightly amused and slightly conceited expression.

"You sure know how to stop a girl from finishing her food, pervert," I sass him, stretching the last word out.

He leans closer, hovering over a few chairs that separate us. "You have no idea how true your statement is, angel face," he confesses, curving his lips into a full-fledged, seductive smirk and flashing his pearly white teeth.

My breath catches in my throat as he leans much closer, his broad shoulders brushing against my left arm. Having close contact with his muscular frame is enough to make any girl faint.

I bite my bottom lip. *Why does he have to be so goddamn handsome, so goddamn good-looking?*

He stands up straight and presses himself against the side of my body. If my face was on fire before, it is burned to a crisp at this point. Because of his height, this new position places his waist directly in front of my face.

*His spaghetti balls are practically served on a platter, meaty and plump enough to eat.*

Realizing my eyes are set in stone, staring at the hanging jewels, I jump out of my seat.

*Oh God, his balls were in my face and I thought about them being good enough to eat!* I mentally smack myself.

"Still hungry?" he asks, wiggling his eyebrows again and adding more to my embarrassment.

*I totally forgot that he can read my mind.*

I cover my face with my hands in a failed attempt to hide the red blush on my cheeks.

"It's okay, Claire. There is no need to be shy. You can't help yourself, with me being a blood-sucking leech and all," he teases, forcing my blush to spread all over my face.

I don't know what to say. This situation is already awkward enough.

The sound of clicking heels comes to my rescue, saving the day.

A young girl with a round face comes into view. She curtsies and then kneels down. "Your Highness, I apologize for interrupting you. King Cyrus is requesting another audience," her soft voice announces.

She looks very familiar, but for the life of me, I cannot place my finger on where or when we met. It's very strange that I believe we have met before. I have lived in the school my entire life. I know for a fact she didn't attend the academy with me.

She is wearing six-inch heels and a tight-fitted black dress that complements every inch of her curves. Her dark-mahogany hair is pulled into a high bun, revealing her slender neck.

My eyes zero in on two tiny puncture holes followed by a trail of blood. "Who fed on you?" I choke, jumping toward her to further evaluate her neck.

She flinches, cowering away in fear but doesn't respond. The poor thing is terrified out of her mind, petrified even.

"Claire," King Nicklaus calls out in a warning tone.

*Claire my ass.*

"Who did this to her?" I turn to face him, not giving two sh*ts about his status or the strength he possesses to overpower me. This is some sick sh*t, how dare he?

"Don't forget your place," he hisses, revealing his fangs.

*My place . . . my place . . .*

That does it. I swing my hand out, jabbing him right in his face. It feels like punching a wall. A snapping sound soon follows, alerting me that I may have cracked my wrist. Disregarding the pain, I continue my attack.

"You blood-sucking leech! You blood-sucking leech!" I land punch after punch, my temper flaring rapidly by the second as I scream. The ground trembles beneath me, the air whooshing. My back abruptly hits a wall, and I close my eyes through the process. Regardless, I continue to fight, swinging, kicking, and biting. I have to admit the taste of his skin is satisfying to my taste buds.

He grips my hips gently but firmly enough to keep me in place.

"Get your filthy hands off me, leech. You f*cking monster!" I continue my assault, attempting to ignore his warm, intoxicating vanilla scent—gosh, he smells so good.

"Calm down, little firecracker."

His smooth and compelling voice settles my anger immediately. I then realize that his entire body is coating my own. My mouth seems to dry up. My heart races, running its own personal marathon inside my chest.

"Look at me, Claire."

My eyes pop open.

"The only human that will ever feel the pleasure of my fangs piercing their flesh"—he pauses for a second—"is you."

Booming laughter and hand clapping sound off from behind us.

"Nice show. Like seriously, you guys really put on a great performance," a voice full of amusement states.

King Nicklaus's muscles twitch. "Didn't I tell you we would finish our conversation later?" He turns to face King Cyrus, who is sitting in a chair and smiling brighter than the early morning sun. "Get out!" King Nicklaus presses his tall frame against me, intentionally hiding me from King Cyrus's wandering eyes.

"Aww come on, man. Don't be such a grouch."

I can't see his face, but the tone of his voice confirms he's holding back laughter.

"I just wanted to—"

"Get out!"

"Okay, okay, okay." King Cyrus stands. He holds his hands in the air, no longer being able to contain his laughter. "I'll go but before I take my leave, I thought you would like to know that—"

King Nicklaus taps his foot. I can tell his patience is wearing thin. "I don't give a—"

"Honey dumpling, I'm home," calls out a high-pitched voice.

King Nicklaus's neck snaps in the direction of the door.

# CHAPTER TEN
## No Choice

A beautiful vampire woman in a tight, stylish black silk lace dress walks in, a naked human chained to a leash crawling behind her. Her dress is short in the front—revealing her long and slender legs—and trails to the floor in the back, glorifying her curvy frame with every step she takes. Her beach-blond hair is pinned into a tight, high bun. Not a single hair is out of place. Her hips sway as she walks. Her light-blue eyes shine brightly, focusing on him.

I have no doubt in my mind what or who she is to him. One look says it all. She is his beloved.

Her cheeks catch on fire. She throws the leash on the floor and crosses the room in inhuman speed to embrace him. His body stiffens slightly before he wraps his arms around her. She wastes no time capturing his lips with her own. He responds to her kiss instantly, nibbling on her bottom lip with his fangs. She sticks her tongue down the back of his throat, deep enough that I'm sure if he weren't a vampire, he would have choked. They suck each other's face, completely disregarding the fact that I'm currently locked in place behind him.

I wrinkle my nose in disgust as their intimate moment stirs some unknown emotions inside me. My chest burns, and without thinking, I pound on his stone-hard back. I then start wiggling myself from side to side, attempting to break free. "Get off me, you blood-sucking leech!" I scream, throwing a tantrum like a seven-year-old child. I don't know what's gotten into me. I don't even know why I'm so mad, but the burning sensation within me clouds my better judgment.

I feel his body go dangerously still while her eyes flash bright red, acknowledging my presence for the very first time since she stepped into the room. I soon realize my error. Disrespecting King Nicklaus or their kind is a crime punishable by death—a crime I've already committed once when I spat in his face—and the fact that his beloved is now a witness to it is going to put me in deep sh*t.

Seconds after her eyes land on me, she leaps over him with her fangs bared, ready to end my life. Surprisingly, he shoves his beloved, gently enough not to cause her harm but hard enough to send her stumbling back.

His muscles flex as he crouches slightly in front of me, his shoulders cramping of tension. His back still presses against my frame, holding me in place. His beloved smashes the table, and light snickering can be heard from the other end of it. I can see King Cyrus barely able to hold in his laughter while both human girls watch the scene with wide eyes. I can't blame them. It's not like you see vampires protecting humans on a daily basis.

"What the hell, Nicklaus!" she screams out in utter shock.

King Nicklaus doesn't even flinch. "You will not touch my property without my permission," he growls low, his tone more than a warning.

I freeze in place.

"That filthy thing disrespected you," she says, voice raised and eyes glowing brighter with every word. "She disrespected our kind. She's . . . a human!" she screams, her face bright red. She studies his expression, eyes quickly searching his face.

I can tell she's trying to understand what just happened. We all are.

King Cyrus is rolling over with laughter, damn near losing his mind.

King Niklaus's features soften as he struggles to contain his anger. "And she will pay for it," he speaks through clenched teeth.

My temperature rises to a new height once I see the soft expression on his usually inexpressive face. He cares for her, and that bothers me on a whole nother level, sending a storm of emotions to flood through my veins.

Now that his guard is down, I manage to break loose of his hold. I dive toward the table and grab a plate. I know I'm overreacting, but he means nothing to me. I'm human, and he's a vampire. With all that being said, that doesn't stop me from throwing the plate in his direction, hitting him square in the face.

King Cyrus's laughter stops completely. The door swings open, revealing another extremely beautiful vampire woman with hair as dark as night. She's wearing a skintight black leather suit that seems to be painted on her slender, milky frame. Unlike his beloved, this vampire's bloodshot, narrowed eyes go straight to me.

King Nicklaus blocks me from view before I can drink in any more of her features. I have overstepped the boundaries. I know that. Speaking against him is bad enough, but a human attacking a vampire—no matter how small the attack is—is one that cannot go unpunished.

He stands in front of me, appearing so much taller. I want to cower away in fear, but I somehow manage to find the courage to stare at him head-on, unshaken. I purposely ignore another rule that should result in my death, not caring that both of the vampire women's eyes flash brighter.

"Cyrus, bring me the girl!"

His words catch me off guard.

King Cyrus stands to his full height. "Which one, Your Highness?" he asks, his eyes fixed on me. The amusement he once showed has disappeared completely, and I notice he has addressed him with his formal title.

"The one she tried to protect."

My heart drops instantly as King Cyrus pulls the human girl by her mahogany hair, slinging her across the floor without hesitation.

"No, please. Don't do this, Your Highness," pleads the girl.

My attention shoots to him as I open my mouth to defend her.

*"Silence, be still, and pay attention,"* says his voice in my head.

I feel his commandment sink into my bones, preventing my body from fulfilling my mind's true desires.

King Nicklaus holds the girl by the back of her neck; her sobs and screams penetrate the air. Tears flow heavily from my eyes as I try to break free, utter a word, and do anything to stop this punishment that I've caused. But no matter how hard I try, I can't move and speak. I'm just frozen in place, forced to watch this monstrous act.

King Nicklaus tightens his grip.

"What does this human have to do with that human disrespecting you, Nicklaus?" asks the newcomer, as she makes her way toward him.

"To train an animal, you must first break their spirit, Mother." He grips the girl harder. "As you can see, this human doesn't fear losing her life. However, ripping away another life because of her actions will do the trick." His voice becomes dangerously low. "Her death is in my hands," he hisses in my direction, cutting me deep.

My tears match the human girl's own, spiraling out of control.

Who I now know to be his mother nods in approval.

King Nicklaus places the girl in front of me. She looks me in the eye, still screaming and lashing out as her fight for survival kicks in. I try so hard to look away, but my eyes are locked on her, unable to break his command. My heart pounds loudly, beating against my chest.

*"Please, don't do this. Take me instead,"* I beg him inside my head.

His angry expression turns to stone, void of any emotions.

"I-I . . . did . . . do . . ." The girl hiccups in between her words, sobbing and trembling with every breath she takes.

Déjà vu swirls inside my head. I am reminded of the events that took place the first time we met. This is not the first time the true nature of one of the kings is demonstrated in front of me, but this is different.

"No, you didn't." His eyes found their way to me as he points in my direction. "She did."

More words that don't come out of his mouth float in my head. *"You gave me no choice."*

King Nicklaus sinks his fangs into the side of her neck, and ear-splitting screams fill the air.

Pity floods King Cyrus's expression whereas King Nicklaus's beloved smiles from ear to ear. Her pet shoots a quick glance at me, watching my reaction and sending guilt to swallow me whole—blaming me as she should.

*This is my fault. I've caused this, and for what?*

I can't explain the feelings flowing through me while he drains every ounce of her blood, his bite becoming harder. Her screams eventually go silent, and the life in her eyes slowly fades away. He removes his fangs and tears her head off her neck, catching her limp form before it hits the floor.

That very moment reminds me of what he's capable of and who he is—the ruler of the others and the most-heartless, barbaric vampire of all time. How could I forget so quickly? His boyish behavior when we were alone was all a front. He is still a vampire, and I'm just a human. I will not make the same mistake twice.

His words swirl in my head: *"To train an animal, you must first break their spirit."*

Everything starts to make sense. It was all an act.

With utter fear, I stare at the girl's headless body. I can only pray she can forgive me for causing such a savage death.

"Take her to the dungeons, Cyrus," King Nicklaus orders. His muscles tense. He pauses, and a look of hurt flashes in his features, or so I think. "Place her in the cell across from her original one."

King Cyrus freezes in place. "Are you cer—"

"Take her now!" King Nicklaus storms out of the door. His beloved snatches her pet's collar, dragging her while following behind him.

His mother watches me for a long-drawn-out moment. "Do as my son ordered!" she hisses in King Cyrus's direction.

"As you wish, Queen Mother," he responds.

The sound of her high heels clicking out of the door as he follows behind him gradually fades away.

My chest heaves up and down. I fall to my knees the moment I'm no longer under his control. My breathing is heavy as I hug my body. Guilt, regret, and unbearable pain all swirl together, forming a tight circle in the center of my chest.

*I killed her. I did this.*

The human's body is still lying in the center of the room. Her head is in front of me, his lifeless eyes staring at me.

Tears flow heavily down my face as I sob, my body shaking.

King Cyrus's golden orbs meet my own. He lowers down to my level, forcing my attention away from her. He releases a soft sigh. "Please, calm down. You left him no choice."

# CHAPTER ELEVEN
## Dogs and Leeches

Water drips on my forehead, bringing me slowly into awareness. Shivers travel down my spine when the cold, damp air escapes my lungs. I lift my head slightly and listen to the hissing and howling coming from all different directions. My back cramps and my legs are sore from sleeping on the hard cot. The water still continues to drip down, further provoking my body's discomfort. The smell of urine, feces, and vomit hits me hard and strong, causing me to gag. I make my way toward the toilet as memories of before I lost consciousness flash like a movie inside my head: King Nicklaus, his beloved, and the human who lost her life because of me.

*I killed her.*

Hot tears are the only warmth I feel as they flow like a chaotic river down my cheeks. Vomit erupts the moment my body hits the floor in front of the toilet. I empty out my stomach, moving my golden hair out of my face just in time. My entire body trembles and shakes while my tears continue to flow, staining my red cheeks.

I fight to gain control of my pounding heart. Once I finally find the strength to calm down, goosebumps trace along my skin and the coolness of the air seeps into my veins. I manage to crawl my way back onto the cot. I press my body against the stone wall and place my head in between my knees, balling my body into a protective shell. The howls seem to become more distant as I lose myself, drowning in my own personal pit of guilt.

I don't know how long I stay in that position—a minute, an hour, or perhaps all through the night—but I'm sure I never move as guilt continues to swallow me whole. I have never been that scared of falling asleep in the dark. In fact, I have always welcomed it. I have prayed for the day that my life ends for good while I'm encased in a deep sleep and tucked away safely in darkness. However, tonight or today, is different. I can't sleep. Every time my eyes close, that poor, sweet girl's head detached from her body continuously pops into my head every single time.

Tugging of chains and a low growl from the jail cell across from my own break my train of thought.

"You didn't last long," a soft feminine voice says from the far back of the cell.

The darkness surrounding us makes it hard for me to see the figure's movements. I sniff and wipe away my tears, deciding to ignore the voice, until the figure decides to make its way to the front of the cell. The small light hanging in the center provides me with a perfect view, and I gasp as soon as she is in plain sight. It's the beast woman, or at least what's left of her. She is much thinner than the first time I saw her, literally nothing but bones. Her long jet-black hair is still matted but now with blood. Her chocolate skin has purple and black bruises as well as numerous marks of fangs, but the right side of her face completely captures my attention. There is a strange, unique silver scar slashed across it, starting right above the corner of her eye and ending about mid-cheek. Despite all the damage her body has endured, she's still deadly beautiful, and somehow the scar only adds beauty to her face.

I pull my eyes away. She leans closer, holding the bars of the cell to support her fragile body. A chilling chuckle leaves her lips, then she tilts her head to the side.

"Why are you back here, human?" she asks.

"Why are you here, werewolf?" Sarcasm drips from my tongue.

I don't like the way she utilized the name of my species while asking me a question. The last time I checked, we were both behind bars, enslaved by the quote, unquote "superior race." What gives her the right to look down on me?

"Someone's brave now that they are safely behind the door of another cage." Her lips curve into a little smirk as she holds the bars a little tighter. "Typical human," she adds. Her eyes flash bright yellow while she balances herself on the bars of her cell, her fingers replaced with claws. "Let's see how brave you are once I make my way out of this cell." She taps her claws against the bars, in hope of giving some spooky effect.

I roll my eyes and bang my head against the wall. "I'm not afraid to die." My voice seems to be caught in my throat, and moisture starts to build on the brim of my eyes. "So there is no need to be brave or scared of you. Do us both a favor by escaping to end me, until then shut the f*ck up and piss off, dog!"

She growls menacingly, sounding just like what I called her—a dog, a very large dog at that. I completely tune her out. My heart rate doesn't increase as I keep ignoring her even when she starts to claw at the bars.

Eventually, she gives up. I hear the clanking of her chains, followed by a moment of silence before her face hits the bars. She sniffs the air a few times, relaxing her shoulders. "You're really not afraid, are you?"

Her question catches me off guard. She is just as bipolar as the leeches.

I ignore her for another moment before I finally give in. "Why should I be? I'd rather die than continue to live the remainder of my life as the vampire leech's slave."

Just thinking about King Nicklaus sends glass shards straight into my heart. I quickly shake the perfection of his handsomely crafted face out of my head.

She presses her ear through the bars of the cell. A light giggle escapes her lips. "Leech!" She continues to giggle. "Dog . . ." She is now hunched over with her hand across her stomach while she laughs so hard, tears threatening to escape from her eyes. Her chains shake and rattle with her movement. "You really know how to get underneath another species's skin, don't you?"

"Yup," I answer popping the *p*. "Apparently, that's what I do." I stretch the bottom of my V-neck shirt out, pulling it over my legs. At least I have clothes on that gives me some sort of warmth.

The beast woman is completely naked. I glance at her, her glowing yellow eyes meeting mine. She looks me up and down, analyzing me carefully. Her eyes linger on my attire. I know her next question before she even asks it.

"Where did you get your clothing, human?" She tilts her head from side to side. She laughs again and then she leans her head closer to the bars of the cell and sniffs the air. "You smell like their king."

She's so strange and certainly bipolar.

"Their king can burn in hell for all I care." My words feel like acid as they slip from my tongue. I rest my head against the wall, and memories of what transpired with the king and me swarm around my mind. "He provided me with the clothes, by the way," I answer her question, feeling like I am obliged to. I know she may be a beast woman who doesn't have all her marbles, obviously. But even with all that in mind, something about her seems welcoming, as if I could tell her anything and everything. Maybe I have been stuck in this cage way longer than I thought.

*Having a fondness for a werewolf, really, Claire?*

I guess that happens when you're never good at making friends or even being able to hold a conversation.

"And why would the king of leeches do that?" she asks an open-ended question, looking lost in her thought.

69

"I'm his chosen," I answer. There is no need for me to pick her brain. "Or at least I was," I finish, sounding more disappointed than I intend to.

She tugs the chains and scratches the skin covered by the collar around her neck. "That must suck. No wonder you were crying."

The bitterness of her voice bothers me, not to mention she sounds extremely harsh.

I make my way off the cot to sit in front of my cell, ignoring my aggravation. "Why are you here?"

Curiosity starts to get the better of me. Hopefully, I don't push any buttons that will stop our conversation or prevent me from receiving insight from another species about the vampire race.

"I was under the impression that your kind was extinct." A light bulb flickers in my head. "You're not the last of your kind, are you?"

She slides to the floor, relaxing her head on the bars so we can be at eye level. "My kind is far from extinct."

"But the history books say—"

"The history books you read in those academies"—she stops—"are bullsh*t." Her eyes flash yellow before they close altogether. "The outside world is nothing like you were raised to believe it to be like, human."

When I part my lips to speak, she stops me by releasing a small growl.

"There's something about you, human," she says. She watches me closely as if searching for a reaction. "I don't know what it is." Her facial expression becomes tight as her eyes trail into space. "But my intuition never lies, and my wolf has never steered me wrong." She inhales and exhales a deep breath, seeming to be battling with her own thoughts.

"What do you mean by 'the history books are bullsh*t'?" I ask. I can only focus on those words.

"Just exactly what it sounds like—bullsh*t." She smirks. "Nothing is ever what it appears to be, human."

Of course, she wouldn't forget to mention my species.

"So you're not a werewolf?" My sarcastic tongue can't help itself.

"No, human." She sniffs the air. "I'm a she-wolf. A werewolf is a male wolf. Most werewolves are a lot stronger than she-wolves. Of course, they are males." Her eyes seem to drift into space once more. "A typical she-wolf wouldn't be able to last more than a couple of years with what you call leeches."

"How long have you lasted?" I ask, my eyes unintentionally traveling down her bruised body.

She catches me studying her. She tilts her head from side to side, then sniffs the air again—her behavior is so strange. "Since 2041," she says nonchalantly.

I gasp. That's way more than a couple of years. That's over a hundred years. There's no way she could look like a teenager and not somebody's ancient grandma. It's just not possible unless werewolves, or she-wolves, age just as slow as vampires. On top of that, if what she claims is true, then it means she had been here long before the Awakening even started.

"How can you claim the history books are bullsh*t if you haven't been on the outside world in over a century?" I call her out with her bluff.

"I have my ways."

She's not making any sense.

"So how have you survived so long"—I lean closer toward the bars on my cell—"with you being a typical she-wolf and all?" I believe this time I can catch her in a lie.

"Who said I'm a typical she-wolf?" Her lips form into another smirk. "Human," she adds.

I roll my eyes in defeat as her smirk turns into an annoying grin.

"What's your name, human?" She sniffs the air again, but this time her eyes glow.

"Would you stop calling me human . . . if I told you—"

"Maybe." She shrugs.

I make my way back toward the cot, over this conversation. She stands up, her chains tugging at the wall with her movement. I turn to face her one last time before getting settled into the hard cot.

"I'm Claire. What's your name were— I mean she-wolf?"

A ghost of a smile crawls on her face. Her eyes glow yellow, reminding me of a night light. "Mecca," she responds.

# CHAPTER TWELVE
## Blankly

I don't know how long I've been down here—a couple of days, maybe two weeks or so? I'm not certain, but I know it's been a while, and Mecca and I have grown pretty close. Well, as close as we could be, I guess. She still talks to me like I'm less than her, with me being a human and all. And let's not forget about her prize-winning growl she releases whenever I call her *dog*. Other than that, she's actually a very interesting person.

Listening to her stories about the different werewolf tribes and learning about their saviors, the lycans, became the highlight of my day. I even found myself fantasizing about becoming a mate of one of the famous alphas, or a "destined" of any of the powerful lycans—which would never happen of course. Nevertheless, it's still pretty exciting and absolutely romantic to daydream about it.

The love stories that Mecca told me were super intense, terrifying even, yet they still managed to warm my heart. She explained to me that each vampire, werewolf, witch, gypsy, hunter, and lycan were all split into two and are meant to find their other half regardless of place, time, or circumstance and they will instantly become one.

It's really unfair that the other species are born with another half. Only a few humans have reported having that special companion of one of the other species. It's extremely rare.

She also informed me that the Awakening happened because the vampires had become bitter toward a human destined to be with a lycan, specifically because she happened to catch the eye of one of the vampire kings. Apparently, she broke his heart, and because of it, he started a rebellion to enslave her entire race.

Could you believe that? My entire race has been enslaved because of hatred and bitterness toward one human who did nothing but find her other half. I guess that could be expected. Vampires are selfish and cold-hearted creatures.

Mecca's voice is the first thing I hear when I wake up. My stomach growls because the food I had was not enough as I have been sharing my rations with her.

"Little human, the leech king came to visit you again while you were sleeping." She giggles. "He even brought you a blanket. How cute!"

I sit up, just in time to see her sniff the air.

"Now, how strange is that?"

Her question seems to be directed more to herself than to me.

A mischievous glint beams around those amber irises that flicker the fascinating color of neon yellow. Mecca has healed a lot because of me sharing my food portions with her even though she doesn't take much—a little bread and water here and there.

I stretch my arms out. "That is pretty strange," I confess, rolling off the cot.

I haven't seen King Nicklaus during my entire stay in the dungeon, but Mecca has watched him from the shadows, coming to visit me every night. This is not the first time he has left me something. He already left me extra water or a change of clothes. I don't know why he does it, but he does.

I try not to dwell on his strange actions too much because every time I think about him, a piercing ache surfaces in the center of my heart.

A few moments of silence go by, then Mecca starts to fiddle with her collar. "I have come to my own conclusions of his strange actions," she informs with a low growl.

"Is that so?" I draw my brows together. As soon as I stand up, my body begins to shake—it's colder than usual. I grab one of the sweaters that King Nicklaus has provided for me, then an idea pops into my head. "Do you think you can do that creepy she-wolf thing and stretch your arms out of the cell?" I ask Mecca.

She moves closer to the front of her cell.

"Creepy she-wolf thing!" I say.

She leans against the bars of her cell, her hands now replaced with sharp claws and furry paws.

*Creepy, just like I said.*

After I quickly pull the sweater over my head, I grab the wool blanket that the leech king has left. I move toward the front of my cell, pushing my hand between the bars. "Here, take this," I offer, searching the dark hallway that separates our cells. You need it more than I do. At least I have clothes on." I watch her tilt her head from side to side.

"I hope I'm wrong about my conclusions." She grabs the blanket. "It would really be unfortunate."

I tilt my head to the side. Her statement has already caught me off guard, but her tone does more.

"What are you talk—"

We hear footsteps approaching, stopping me from finishing my question.

Mecca sniffs the air and turns to face me. "We should meet again, human," she states, as her eyes glow darker than I have witnessed. She fully transforms into a she-wolf, then she growls viciously in the direction of the newcomer.

I shift my eyes to the guest as well, only to be met by two glowing red orbs. I take a few steps back. Red eyes are always a bad sign in my experience.

Mecca continues to growl.

75

I instantly recognize the vampire as I reach my cot. "King Xander?" My mouth hangs open as I am slightly in a moment of shock.

He doesn't respond, his red irises scanning over me briefly before they land on Mecca, who is in her full-fledged wolf form. Abruptly, he slams against the bars of her cell. She pounces on them, her yellow orbs dancing with hatred.

I watch their exchange in silence even though I'm fully aware of what she is. It's not like every day you get to see a woman turn into a gigantic brown wolf. Mecca never demonstrates fondness for vampires, and who can honestly blame her for it? However, this is different. The glint of detestation in her eyes says it all.

"Claire," Xander hisses, unlocking my cell without taking his attention off Mecca, "let's go now." He's in my cell in the blink of an eye.

The next thing I know I'm already in front of the familiar door that leads us out of the dungeon. He moved so fast that I didn't even realize when he took me out of my cell until the door came into view. I didn't have a chance to say goodbye to Mecca, but at least I was able to give her a blanket.

I fight the urge to ask him why he hates Mecca so much, reminding myself of my place and that others are left to suffer due to my actions.

Painted portraits of the vampire kings hanging on the walls meet us.

*Mecca told me a story about the lycan's destined human. I wonder which king started it.*

"You have grown fondness for that she-wolf, haven't you?" Xander asks.

*I forgot he can read my mind. I have to be very careful around him.*

I wrap my arms around myself. "Mecca is interesting. She's . . ."

He steps in front of me, and I instantly run into him. His hard, muscular body makes me feel as if I ran straight into a brick wall, knocking me off balance. Thankfully, he catches me just in time.

"She is a she-wolf"—he pauses, as I struggle to balance myself from the unexpected impact—"and a very dangerous and bitter one at that."

*Apparently, you all are.*

Lucky for me he wasn't reading my mind. I'm sure he wouldn't appreciate my sarcastic remark.

Once he realizes I'm not going to respond to him, well at least not out loud anyway, he turns around. He knows I'll follow behind him without being told. The warmth of the mansion bubbles against my skin, and sweat starts to drip from my back. The sweater is perfect for the dungeon but not so good for this new environment.

Unlike my first impression of the place, this second encounter is not so glamorous. The stories that Mecca shared with me provided me with vast knowledge of what the vampire kind truly is. Every item in their possession, including this palace, has a horrific story.

Xander glances over his shoulder, at me. "You're a lot less talkative than I remember."

*We only met once, when your brother and king decided to take me as his chosen without my consent, of course!*

"Staying in a dungeon would do that to a person," I reply with my head down, thinking about my previous remark. "My apologies. I didn't mean to disrespect our king."

"Our king." He stops in his tracks in front of one of the many red doors. "Since when did you form respect for *our* . . . king?" He stretches out his question. His now stormy gray eyes study me as he waits patiently for my answer.

I breathe out deeply, calculating the right way to respond.

"You don't have to pretend to be something you're not in front of me, Claire . . ." his voice trails off, as he holds the door open for me to step in. "I don't know what that mutt has implanted in your head about me, but I'm sure whatever she said was a single version of the truth."

*The single version of what truth? What makes him believe she just patronized him? What am I missing?*

We enter what seems to be a bedroom with rich décor. It isn't as massive and expensive as the one in King Nicklaus's penthouse, but it is still impressive. It is very spacious but not a single drop of sunlight could burst through the covered windows. There's a massive black sofa set in the living room, matching the loveseat set in the center. All the furniture is black, sleek, and stylish, but it does nothing for the gloomy vibe of this room. In the center is a grand staircase that must lead to other bedrooms.

"Claire, did you hear anything I said?" Xander closes the door behind us.

I nod, waiting for further instructions. I'm under the impression that he's escorting me back to King Nicklaus, with me being his chosen and all.

"Where are we?" I ask, allowing my thoughts to slip out.

He reaches for my arm and drags me toward the couch. I flinch at the unexpected touch.

"You're in the room I reside in whenever I stay in Nicklaus's kingdom. Is that alright with you?"

*Does it matter?*

"Well in fact it actually does," he answers my unspoken question.

*Stupid mind reader.*

He smiles and takes a seat. "You don't like me invading your thoughts, do you?"

I continue to stand and watch him warily.

"You have my permission to be blunt, Claire. And please take a seat."

78

Without thinking, I obey and remain silent for a moment.

"No, I don't," I finally answer. "But it really doesn't matter now, does it?"

My eyes drop to my lap. I study my fidgeting hands while I try my best not to disrespect him. He notices my feelings toward Mecca, and if he's anything like his brother, he will not hesitate to hurt her. I will not be able to live with that, not again.

"Claire, look at me."

The tone of his voice startles me. I slowly bring my eyes up, following his command.

His body tenses visibly as he answers my question, "Yes, it actually does matter to me."

# CHAPTER THIRTEEN
## A Game of Chess

I am about to respond, but he raises his hand to stop me. His stormy gray eyes watch me intensely as he leans over the sleek coffee table that separates our couches.

"When we first met at the auction, I thought I made the affection I feel for you quite clear. The courage you demonstrated in the presence of the world's most-dangerous predators amazed me, not to mention your intoxicating and extremely rare beauty." He pauses and my heart rate seems to increase by the second. His eyes darken, then he continues, "If that wasn't enough to catch my eye, you also have a heart of gold. You allowed yourself to be humiliated, all to save the life of a human who didn't show an ounce of remorse when you were raped.

"Humans in this day and time don't possess such qualities. My kind made sure of that, but somehow, you managed to slip through the cracks, Claire."

I open my mouth to respond, and this time he doesn't stop me. However, I am at a loss for words. I don't know what to say. No one has ever said anything so nice to me. I'm only human, and he's a vampire, a king at that. He should hate my kind.

*I don't . . .*

"Claire, I want to respect your wishes and not invade your privacy by not reading your mind, but you must converse with me if we are ever going to have an understanding."

His smooth voice breaks my train of thought.

*An understanding?*

"I'm sorry, King Xander b—"

"I told you, call me Xander."

King Xander, I mean Xander, has been kind and affectionate since day one. Still, it's strange hearing him say nice things to me and compliment me with my character. I don't know what to do with this information. It's not like every day humans receive compliments, especially from vampires. This is foreign.

"I just don't understand," I confess. 7

He leans further over the table and takes my hands. His eyes darken as he speaks, "I know you were taught that you exist only for the benefit of my kind. I know you don't understand what it feels like to be adored and cherished . . . and I take full responsibility for that. I will right my wrongs, if that's the last thing I can do. And I want that to start with you, Claire."

If I was speechless before, now I'm mute. I've totally lost the ability to speak, breathe, or even think properly. 7

*This is unreal. I must be dreaming. That's it. That's exactly what this is. It's just some sick and twisted dream.*

I let go of his hands and do the only thing I can think of. I pinch myself, literally digging my nails into my skin. The dream-like king tilts his head to the side and bursts out laughing. That's right. He laughs his ass off, nearly stumbling over the coffee table in the process.

"You're not dreaming, Claire. This is reality. I'm real," he says in between laughs.

*He can't be. There's no way a vampire, especially a king, would ever in a million years say what he stated to a human, let alone me.*

He moves in a flash, and now he's sitting right beside me. His beautiful silvery irises melt ice inside my soul. "Claire, you have no idea how I wish this were a dream. Before I ever laid eyes on you, I had been content with the way things in the past played out.

I buried my decency deep within me and allowed my society to turn me cold."

His eyes hold so much pain, and I feel like I'm staring right into his soul.

"Your fearless nature awakened something inside me that had been long buried," he confesses, never once breaking eye contact. You are my savior, Claire. All our savior."

*All our savior.*

Okay. This conversation has done nothing but confuse me from the start. Although I can feel the honesty of his words, I still don't understand them, nor do I get why he's even saying this.

"Xander, I'm human. How could you possibly say I'm a savior? I have never been able to save myself. I'm nothing but the property of King Nicklaus. Nothing you are saying makes any sense."

*He's really starting to seem crazy. He must be doing everything to belittle me. Calling me a savior or saying sweet things about me is just not right. Is this some kind of trick?*

He leans back, providing me with much-needed space. I breathe in, allowing the oxygen to flow inside my body, and it feels like my first breath of air in ages.

"You are right about one thing," he admits, raising an eyebrow. "You are Nicklaus's property, and you belong to him in every way. My loyalty has always been with my brother, the king. Despite what you believe, he is truly a remarkable ruler. You may not see that due to the unfortunate circumstances of your upbringing, but in time, you shall agree."

He turns to face me, still allowing a short distance to remain between us. "I vow to protect you and show a more . . . How should I say this? a more . . . a more . . . human side of my species. Claire, you have no idea how important you are to me, how important you are to my species. As long as you continue to stay true to yourself, there is no doubt in my mind that you will change everything."

He stands from the couch and starts to walk his way up the steps. "I apologize, Claire. I know this may be hard for you to understand." He chuckles softly. "If it weren't for the bond Nicklaus and I shared, I wouldn't understand it either. Let's just pretend we never had this conversation and allow fate to work its magic."

*Forget? No, I'm not taking that. I shall get him to explain himself and this ridiculous speech.*

I quote his words, "If it's the last thing I can do," I will get answers.

"You don't honestly expect me to just forget this conversation. How could I just forget a conversation like that?" I ask him.

He not only said things that vampires have never said about my species, he even had the nerve to attempt to fill my head with lies. The reality of this situation is starting to sink in. King Xander is trying to get me killed. Yup, he really believes I'm that foolish.

Something inside me ticks.

"Do you believe I'm some sort of fool?" I cross my arms, anger rising with each second. "You keep speaking in riddles, and it's starting to piss me off."

*He wants me to be blunt, right? Cool, I'll show him blunt!*

"Your kind hates my kind with a burning passion. Your noble king drained a girl to teach me a lesson." I stand up, tears forming in my eyes. "There is no way you, or any of you, will be able to demonstrate humanity, especially one who shares the same bloodline with the leech king."

There I said it. How's that for remaining true to myself?

Xander is in front of me as soon as I've finished my sentence. His icy breath fans my neck. I'm pretty sure I have signed my death warrant, but he asked for it.

"There she goes. That's the girl I met a couple of weeks back, little brave one." He smiles wryly, acting as if my statement

83

amuses him. "Keep that same energy at all cost, and I promise to protect you against any species that will try to silence you, including my brother. I can guarantee Nicklaus will never harm you, at least not physically anyway." He lifts my chin so we are at eye level. "Have you ever played chess?"

"What does that have to do with anything?"

"It has everything to do with it, Claire. What's a king without a queen? When you play a game of chess, the goal is to put the opponent's king under direct attack, in which escape is impossible," he answers with a smile. "The players are so focused on the king. They truly underestimate the power of the queen. My brother is extremely powerful. His only flaw is not accepting the true queen, and I take full responsibility for playing a part in that."

Here he goes with his riddles again. Okay, I finally give in. This conversation or as what he calls "understanding" is just not understandable. I saw King Nicklaus accept his leech queen with my own eyes, and what in the hell does that have to do with me?

I smack my forehead in defeat. "I disagree, but sometimes it's best to just agree to disagree," I state, speaking freely once again. My head is starting to pound.

I can admit Xander is not like any vampire I have ever encountered. He is sweet, charming, and nothing like his brother. I honestly do not know how he received the reputation as a cold-hearted king.

"I don't understand why you keep advocating for your brother, or why you even feel the need to do so."

"He's my brother, and as I stated, players always underestimate the true power of a queen, but you shall not be one of them. No matter what happens, I want you to remember a king is nothing without his queen, Claire," he says, speaking in riddles for what seems like the thousandth time since our conversation began.

"Why do you keep speaking in riddles?"

"It's the only way I can explain things to you, for now anyway."

My stomach growls at his response. Xander raises an eyebrow, and I take a mental note that he does that often, most likely absentmindedly.

"Where are my manners? You haven't had a proper meal in a while, have you?"

A soft knock on the door prevents me from responding. Something in his eyes flashes as he grants access.

"Come in."

Seconds later, the red door swings open, revealing a recognizable, fiery red-haired woman.

"Victoria?" I ask the question more to myself than to her.

She doesn't respond. She curtsies, her head held low. She is patiently waiting for Xander to acknowledge and give her further instructions.

I bite my bottom lip as I turn to face Xander. This is a really bad idea for Victoria to be in King Nicklaus's kingdom. Now don't get me wrong. We were never friends. In fact, I should hate this slut because she participated in making my life at school a living hell. I should want her to suffer for every single time she made me cry. If Xander meant anything he said, I'm sure he would end her without question if I truly desired for that outcome, but I'm not that person. No matter what she did, it wasn't her fault but the vampires's because they encourage humans to belittle other humans. She was just trying to survive.

*I honestly don't know why I'm surprised that she's here. I knew Xander took Victoria under his protection. As much as bringing her here may have good intentions on his part, it will only end in her death, and I can't allow that to happen.*

Xander watches me with a calculated gaze. I'm pretty certain he's reading my thoughts, invading my privacy again. I glare back at him, and his stormy gray orbs sparkle with delight.

*My instincts were correct. He's listening in.*

85

"Forgive me, brave one. I just couldn't help myself. And please remember it's all a game of chess," he responds out loud to my inner monologue, his words confusing me once again. He turns his attention to Victoria. "Rise, slave," he commands, and I notice the shift in his demeanor.

# CHAPTER FOURTEEN
## Red-Headed She-devil

Victoria instantly stands up, her shoulders high as she stares straight ahead. She never once makes eye contact with Xander, and she somehow controls her human urge to blink.

I take a moment to look at her, really look at her. She appears the same. I mean it's only been a couple of weeks, but Xander has treated her well. She looks way more polished than a mere slave. She's wearing a tight long black dress with a long slit on each side, exposing her slender legs and flawless porcelain skin—scar-free of course. The dress was made for her although it reveals too much cleavage for my liking. Victoria is a very attractive girl with a face like an angel. However, looks can truly be deceiving. She is the devil's child, if not the devil herself.

Memories of how cruel she could really be flash through my head.

\*     \*     \*

I close my eyes and imagine a world where I don't have to listen to the leech teacher asking the class to repeat after her.

"As a slave, I should do . . . As a slave, I shouldn't do . . ."

*If I have to listen to this slave lecture bullsh\*t more, my head may explode. I really don't understand why they have to drill into our heads how they always have thrall over humans. They won, and we lost. Big f\*cking deal. Why* *can't they just let us be? I imagine a time my race is out of chains, free from dictatorship. Free. Free. Free.*

Yes, I'm in my own little world, dreaming and tuning Ms. Fox out completely until she directly asks, "Claire, are you too good to repeat after me?"

*Uhh!*

I open my eyes and take a quick glance toward the other Claire's direction. To add fuel to the fire, of course, the entire class turns their attention to me. They're all waiting for my legendary, sarcastic remark. They all know I don't give a flying f*ck. I may even be the only one in this classroom with some balls. No, I'm taking that back. I may be the only human in this entire school with some balls. What's the point of sucking up to these leeches? They want to drain us dry anyway, so f*ck it!

I clear my throat. "Of course I am, Ms. Fox, but you already know that."

And here come the fireworks and the chorus of giggles, filling the room.

Ms. Fox's eyes are now red.

I roll my eyes. I can't help myself. Seriously, how many times do I have to provoke her to just end me? God, I can't wait until the day I turn eighteen so that I can finally escape this bullsh*t once and for all.

My lips turn upward with my legendary smirk. Ms. Fox is in front of me in a heartbeat—vampires and their f*cking speed. Before I know it, I feel her hand collide with my face. The effect of her smack echoes throughout the room. All the giggles completely subside, except Victoria's. She obviously enjoys Ms. Fox's retaliation.

My hands ball into fists, ready to give her a taste of her own medicine, but Ms. Fox beats me to the punch. She sinks her fangs into the side of my neck. Her teeth pierce my veins so deeply that I can't hold back the high-pitched scream from escaping my lips. It's the first time ever that a human has ever been publicly fed on in this school. All people in the room stare at the scene with wide eyes and horror-filled faces, except Victoria, who is watching with a smirk. Her laughter trumps my screams. She enjoys the show; she enjoys my suffering.

*     *     *

I continue to analyze Victoria, assessing every detail of this polished she-devil. She remains standing with her head held high and her shoulders straightened. This girl perfected the craft of playing the part—from top to bottom—effortlessly. Xander has her full attention, but she hasn't acknowledged me once since she came in the room.

*I hate how she still somehow makes me feel invisible even after our selection and placement into the vampire world. It's as if we never met, as though we were complete strangers or something. I wish for her sake at least.*

My reaction doesn't go unnoticed.

"This is Claire, as you already know," says Xander, appearing taller.

*Jerk's face is still listening in on my thoughts. I see.*

"She is the chosen of King Nicklaus," he continues, sounding amused. "Even though she's still human and is nothing, her status is considered higher and more valued compared to yours. I expect both of you to get along and guide each other in your new role as the kings's chosens."

*Get along? That's never going to happen, and did he just say she's his chosen?*

My eyes snap in Xander's direction. My stomach turns as his sentence sinks in. Xander made her his chosen. Of course, he did. He was under the impression that we were friends, thanks to my reaction at the auction. To make matters worse, he placed me on a pedestal. I don't like it one bit.

I already received backlash from the other slaves, with me being King Nicklaus's chosen. And now, I have to worry about the

89

sneaky, red-headed she-devil? There's no doubt in my mind she will try her hardest to plague my character. Victoria doesn't like coming second to anyone, especially to another slave.

"Do you understand what I'm indicating?" Xander's voice seems to darken.

"Yes, sir," was Victoria's short reply.

"Good. Why don't you assist Claire with preparing for dinner, after showing her around the slave quarters? Claire hasn't had a chance to see the slave quarters, and she needs to pack. We have a long journey ahead of us. I expect both of you to be full and well-rested," he goes on, not waiting for a response.

"Xander, my items are in King Nicklaus's room," I call out right before he reaches the door.

He turns to face me and raises an eyebrow. *"Every good chess player was once a beginner. Please don't forget to add 'sir' when addressing me in front of other players."* His voice echoes in my head.

*"Huh?"*

*"Say 'sir' out loud, Claire, and apologize."*

*"Oh."*

I stare at him wide-eyed, then give him my best bow. "My apologies for speaking out of line, sir."

He nods in approval, and a ghost of a smile tugs at his lips.

*"Practice makes perfect."* His words once again float inside my head.

"Your items have been delivered to a private room in the slave quarters, slave," he addresses me out loud. He grabs a suit jacket off the coat rack I didn't notice was there. He strolls out of the room and slams the door behind him.

I can't help but roll my eyes. *Jerk's face.*

*"I heard that, brave one."*

*"Stay out of my head, jerk face."*

He chuckles.

I swear it feels like we are actually having a conversation.

*"I tried, but you made it so hard. Don't forget to play the game, and play nice."*

*"That's easy for you to say . . . I'm the one left with a she-devil."*

He chuckles again and then he's gone, leaving me alone with Victoria, who is currently eyeing me from head to toe. Her stare is full of hatred, her voice sarcastic as she states, "You're still a troublemaker, I see."

I ignore her passive-aggressive behavior. Remaining silent is sometimes the most-effective approach.

"How could you possibly get kicked out of the king's room so quickly? He must have gotten tired of the boring f*ck."

*You know what? Screw this.*

I walk past her and can't help but bump her shoulder in the process. "Unfortunately, King Nicklaus didn't have the pleasure like King Xander, who obviously didn't enjoy his time with you. I mean, that has to be the only reason he made it a point to state that my status is . . . How should I say this? Considered higher and more valued compared to yours," I sass her, reciting Xander's words just to get under her flawless skin.

Victoria's eyes instantly widen.

Haha! I would usually ignore her, but she asked for it.

Before I can open the door, she catches up with me and takes a hold of my shoulder. "Listen here. I don't care what King Xander says. You will always be beneath me, and deep down inside, you know that."

Someone's mad about their fall from grace. If I were her, I'd be mad too.

*This is going to be fun,* I think to myself, snatching her hand off my shoulder.

"Oh really? That's not what you stated to King Xander moments ago, when he reminded you of your position. As what I remember, you simply agreed with a 'yes, sir' and a bow of your head, completely ready to open your mouth and cater to his every need, just like the red-headed slut that you are."

Her eyes narrow instantly as she catches my insult. She's about to snap back with one of her famous comebacks when someone clears his throat from behind us.

We turn in unison, only to be met by King Cyrus. A puzzled look covers his features. Victoria lowers herself into another curtsy, her neck bent to the side in complete submission. He ignores her presence completely and focuses on me, studying every inch of my curves. I honestly don't know how I feel about that.

"Have you forgotten that you're in the presence of your superior?"

"Sorry, sir." I curtsy, trying my best to mimic Victoria's action. It might not be as graceful as hers, but I've managed to do it.

King Cyrus seems to approve of my attempts because I could feel his attention shift from me to her.

"Why are you here, slave, or should I say red-headed slut?" he asks, and I try my best not to laugh.

Victoria is not going to show her irritation in front of him. Obviously, she is too good of a slave for that, but she's pissed. I can practically feel her wrath, tucked away under the fake smile she gives.

"King Xander directed me to escort Claire to her chambers, sir," she speaks with a soft voice, once again putting on a great show.

I stop myself from rolling my eyes. This girl is good, maybe too good.

"You're dismissed. I shall escort Claire," King Cyrus replies with a smile.

My heart rate increases.

*I'm like a magnet to these kings. One leaves and here comes another. God, please save me.*

Victoria casts me one more glance and then she turns around and walks away, her heels literally clicking with her every step. King Cyrus heads in the same direction Victoria goes, and I don't have a choice but to follow as he walks at a slow pace down a hallway I haven't seen before. I really want to check out my new surroundings instead of fidgeting with my hands and keeping my head down, but I have to play the part.

Our walk to the slave quarters is actually peaceful and quiet until King Cyrus stops in his tracks. I can feel his eyes on me again, looking me up and down.

"I wonder if you taste as good as you smell, Claire," he speaks.

# CHAPTER FIFTEEN
## Judgment

The color from my face drains away. Before I can react, King Cyrus slings me around by my shirt and smashes me into the wall. He is holding me in place like I'm nothing more than a mere rag doll sandwiched in between the wall and his body. The impact of his swift movement is nowhere near scary as the animalistic look in his eyes, like he's ready to devour his prey—to drain every ounce of my blood.

All hope is gone. Screw playing a stupid game of chess. I'd rather play hide and seek, running and hiding away from my new captor.

His thick dark-mahogany hair is smothering my face, and I can feel his eyes bore holes into my skull. It's so nerve-wracking that I think I might faint.

"Is that fear I smell? What happened to the brave and foolish human we analyzed at this year's auction?" he asks, his voice sounding extremely dangerous.

*Brave? F\*ck no. Foolish? Hell yes.*

"Sir, please."

"You're begging now, Claire?" His voice holds a sound of amusement. His laughter follows after his words. "I thought you would put up a better fight." His dark laughter does nothing to ease my fear. "Pity. I guess I was wrong about you being different. Every human caves in to the law of the land eventually, how could you not? After all, you're nothing but a weak and submissive human."

The tone of his voice and his words change my stricken fear into a melting pot of rage. I don't like his statement one bit. This filthy leech doesn't have the right to speak to me like that, king or not. I don't even allow King Nicklaus to get away with speaking to me as though I were nothing unless he forces me to, with his creepy leech control. Either way, I will not stand for it. I'd rather die first.

With my newfound courage, I respond with a mouth full of venom, "If you're going to end me, just do it, you blood-sucking leeeech!" I stretch out the last word just to piss him off, then I purposefully stare straight into his eyes, doing exactly what I do best—getting under his kind's pale skin.

Vampires hate it when humans stare into their eyes, especially while talking to them. It is the same as asking them to kill us, as if declaring we are their equal, and that's one thing their kind refuses to accept. They have too big of a blood-lust ego.

His hazelnut orbs change into lava. "Are you challenging me, slave?"

The darkness of his voice sets me back on edge, but I refuse to back down. I continue to stare him in the eye head-on, challenging him further.

A second later, the anger in his features disappears completely, nonexistent. He abruptly releases me and turns on his heel, continuing to walk in the direction we were originally heading in. He's acting as if nothing ever happened.

Shock drenches my soul as King Cyrus walks away like I didn't disrespect everything his kind stands for. I take that moment to breathe. I lower my head and allow my racing heart to calm down—wrong move!

Suddenly, his strong hand grips my golden hair. He yanks a handful of it and throws me across the hall. I scream, but it is short-lived as he catches me by the neck and crushes my windpipes.

"Rule number one, never take your eyes off your enemy," he states, his voice dangerous and his stare dark.

I attempt to free myself, but it's no use. Every move I make, he squeezes my neck tighter, cutting off my air supply completely. My eyelids start to feel heavy and dots cloud my vision. I no longer have the will to fight my destined fate. I don't even know why I all of a sudden care. This is what I've wanted, and I'm finally going to be free—unchained and unclaimed.

"Aww, don't tell me the foolish human is losing her will to fight? Little Claire, are you really that easy to break?" He slightly loosens his grip.

Oxygen invades my lungs like a crashing wave, but the newfound air only lasts for a second.

Another wave of air envelops my whole body, and King Cyrus is suddenly thrown off me.

I gasp and cough up my own personal storm, desperately seeking the air that gets in my lungs with full force. I notice a figure standing in front of me, blocking my entire body from receiving another attack.

"You must have a death wish," states the voice that haunts my dreams every night, and I forget my fight for air.

I look up to see King Nicklaus's muscular frame directly in front of me. I don't have to see his face to know that his eyes are an inferno and his fangs are flashing dangerously—completely lethal.

"Calm down, Nicklaus. I was only having a little fun," King Cyrus responds, his voice once again filled with amusement. "It's not my fault. Your chosen was walking the halls freely."

"Get the f*ck out of my sight!" King Nicklaus growls, his muscles flexing with every word that leaves his mouth. "Now!"

I hear a whoosh of air and King Cyrus's dark chuckle. "Don't blame me. Blame your b*tch," he mocks.

And then I hear nothing, confirming that he's long gone. The only sound now is my heart that's pounding a million beats per second.

The momentary silence is quickly replaced with King Nicklaus's haunting growl. "Get up!" he orders, anger still very present in his voice.

My heart continues to race and my throat stings, but I somehow manage to scramble to my feet.

"Who let you free?"

His question sends a chilling fear to my bones. I can't speak. I can't think. I'm stunned, literally mute. It's not helping that his well-defined body is blocking me, intentionally preventing me from any chances of escape.

He is wearing a black button-down silk shirt that looks soft enough to touch. I suddenly feel the urge to run my fingers down his godlike frame. My heart rate starts to increase for a whole other reason as the air that's just been my savior quickly shifts into my doom. I'm completely breathless.

A ghost of a smirk appears on his beautiful face. I might be imagining it's actually there.

My cheeks are now strawberry red.

*What the hell has gotten into me? I need to get away from him, as far as my human legs can take me.*

"Oh now you want to escape?" he huffs. "After you managed to find yourself in another near-death experience, now you're thinking about escaping?"

*"Managed." Is he indicating that this is my fault? Yes, I wanted to be almost choked to death. Well, if you think about it, he may be right. I mean I don't care about dying, but blaming me for his sick and sadistic friend nearly crushing me is a little ridiculous.*

The hot desire I just felt is flushed away by anger. I open my mouth to finally tell him about himself, but he disappears as quickly as he arrived. The only reminder he's been really here is his husky voice floating inside my head. *"Go to the slave quarters with your head held down the entire time before I decide to grant your wish."*

M y body moves of its own accord, my feet directing me to the slave quarters even though I've never been there. I try to touch

97

my aching throat, but my stupid hands refuse to follow my own command.

I hate this! I hate them. It's extremely frustrating that I can't control my body movement. What's even more frustrating is that my legs are following the leech's order—that stupid sex god of a leech. Gosh, that man is so hot. He's unearthly. Really, no man has ever appealed to my taste.

But that's the point. King Nicklaus is no man. Even though he has the power to make any woman stop in their tracks, he's still an immortal, a monster who took an innocent girl's life just to prove a point. He's barbaric, and I'm a monster for feeling even the slightest bit of attraction for him. I have to remain strong no matter how mesmerizing he is. He is a leech, a blood-draining leech who participated in enslaving another species. I must remember that at all times.

I wouldn't be surprised to learn that he led the attack that resulted in the enslavement of my species to begin with. I wonder if he's the jealous monster that Mecca warned me about. Of course, he is. How else did he become the king of all vampire kings? It's not like they aren't all deadly creatures. King Cyrus was just seconds away from crushing my windpipe just because he wanted to, and King Nicklaus blamed me for his friend's outrageous actions, just like he blamed that poor human girl for falling for another species.

Everything starts to make sense now. I'm attracted to a monster, and the reality of the situation makes me sick to my stomach. I feel my body go down a flight of stairs before jerking to the left and entering a new hallway. As soon as I hear voices, I gain control of my body again. I search the new environment in complete awe, and for the first time since my arrival in King Nicklaus's palace, I'm surrounded by my own kind. It feels as if I stepped into a whole new world. I also see vampire soldiers in golden armor walking amongst the humans, paying them little to no attention. The only way I'm able to tell they're not human is their muscular frames and pale skin tone. They are way too pale to be considered living beings.

This wing of the palace is almost as magnificent as the other side, *almost*. And just like the other side of the palace, it has red walls filled with portraits of the vampire kings. These portraits, however, are not similar to the ones I have seen, of them smiling and enjoying their time together. As a matter of fact, there are no group portraits—paintings of them together. They are all separate, staring right back at you, guarded.

Several gold lights with rows and rows of diamonds hang from the ceiling, following me with every step I take. The first chandelier I saw was fascinating, bringing light to such a dark place, but these are hanging still in time. They provide the perfect effect for my fast-approaching appearance to the humans of this place. Speaking of which, human men are dressed in white button-down shirts and black pants whereas human women are in tight-fitted black dresses and six-inch heels, just like that slave girl whose life was taken because of me.

The idle chitchat is quickly replaced with silence once everyone notices my presence and starts judging me with curious eyes. The silence stops me in my tracks. It doesn't take long to determine how they view me. They blame me for the girl's death as expected, and they should.

Out of a sea of unfamiliar faces, I recognize three. First is Victoria. She looks like the goddess she-devil that she is while sending daggers my way. Another is Jasmine, the slave who was the cause of my sexual abuse. She's wearing a golden gown that also reveals too much cleavage for my liking. Just like Victoria, she's flawless. I look into her hazel eyes, searching for any sign of remorse. Of course, I see none.

Then there's the human girl that King Nicklaus's beloved dragged that day, naked except for a chain. She stands in the middle of them all, now fully dressed. Her crimson gown hugs her tiny frame. Just like her friends, she is extremely beautiful. The only difference between her and them is the softness in her big brown eyes as she watches me carefully just like she did when that poor girl lost her life, tears threatening to escape from her eyes.

They all stand out like a sore thumb, beautiful like so many and well-dressed and beauty queen-groomed like no other. No one around me makes a move, and all I hear are indistinct whispers.

With as much courage as I can muster, I continue to walk through the hallways until I hear someone to my left say, "That's the one that got Helen killed."

I snap my head in their direction, only to be met with another whisper of accusation and then another.

Finally unable to take their judgment, my own kind's judgment, I run down the hallway and enter the first room that comes into view.

# CHAPTER SIXTEEN
## Beauty Bias

The moment I slam the door, my tears flow freely down my face without an ounce of shame.

I hate this, every part of this. I should be long gone, deceased, and free of judgment or blame. I did everything in my power to make sure of it—breaking every rule, thinking that my disobedience was enough for them to sentence me to certain death. How foolish of me to believe that a human could have a little power over their own future?

I sink onto the floor and pull my sweater over the top of my knees—the sweater he provided, the one the killer brought to the dungeon for me, and of course I accepted it without any complaint. I don't understand how or why I became his chosen. Just thinking about the vampire king that forced this life onto me makes my heart ache with another round of pain. I'm so selfish, and I feel totally disgusted with myself.

I quickly pull the sweater over my head with no hesitation, foolishly believing that removing the king's gift will provide me with some sort of dignity. But it doesn't. I'm a monster. I may even be more monstrous than him as I accepted his stuff without a second thought, although it kept me warm in that horrid dungeon he put me in.

I even felt attracted to him before and after he killed that poor human girl. I betrayed my species, and they have every right to judge me. I would do the same exact thing if I were in their shoes, forming my own biased opinion of another girl who was picked to be his chosen. So how can I judge them?

Suddenly Mecca comes to mind. I can't help but wonder how she is doing. I have only been free an hour or so, but one hour in the dungeon can feel like a lifetime.

*Mecca has to be the most-bizarre creature I have ever encountered, but I care about her. I have to find a way to see her again. Maybe Xander will help me despite their differences. I forgot to ask him why they hate each other so much.*

The door opens, pushing my thoughts away.

"What are you doing in here?" queries a soft voice.

Quickly wiping my tears, I bring myself to look at the person. I'm thrown off guard when my eyes are met by the soft brown eyes of the pet of King Nicklaus's beloved. At least I think she's still her pet.

Most pets are typically chained and dragged around, but this girl is now polished and groomed like a chosen. Her posture is straight, her head held high. She's trained in the art of beauty just like her friends, the she-devil b*tches. The only question that remains is, How did she manage to learn how to play the role so soon? I couldn't have possibly been incarcerated that long, could I?

I stand up, refusing to look weaker than I already feel. I can see her now running back to Jasmine and Victoria, laughing about my moment of weakness. This is a dangerous world. Even if you're dealing with a human, you must show no fear. There's time and place for everything, and this is not the time to break down.

"I was just leaving. No need to be a b*tch about it," I snap.

Being standoffish is better than being approachable. It's better this way, and it's not like she doesn't already have her mind made up about me anyway.

I brush past her, not bothering to waste any more of my time staring into her judgmental eyes.

"You know, being a chosen is way easier when you have at least one friend."

Her words stop me right in my tracks.

"Friend?"

How could one word sound so foreign as it rolled off my tongue?

"Yes," she answers with a shrug. "Friend. I have climbed the ladder from pet to a chosen. Believe me when I say, if I can do that, anything is possible."

She walks over to the two beds now I realize placed in the center of the room. I scan the room briefly. Its walls are painted yellow, with golden trim. The beds are draped in golden comforter sets and fluffy golden teal pillows sewn into some sort of flower design.

"If you mix rose petals, fresh water, and a bergamot leaf or two with a heavy yellow, fine-grained bark of sandalwood, what do you have?" she asks.

"What?"

"Don't think, just answer," she tells me, staring mischievously with those big brown eyes of hers.

I replay her words inside my head, but they make absolutely no sense.

"Aww! Come on. I said no thinking."

If her question didn't catch me off guard, the playfulness of her voice most certainly did.

"Um . . . I don't know," I respond. "To be honest, I don't know what those things are, except a rose of course."

"I do, and trust me when I say it smells amazing," she says with a smile tugging at her tiny lips. "It even sounds like a really good aroma, don't you think?"

"Perhaps." I am unable to stop the smile that forms on my lips.

She walks over and stands directly in front of me. She holds out her hand. "I'm Jadis."

103

"Claire." I repeat her gesture, feeling awkward when she shakes my hand.

It's not like I haven't seen it before—someone so small shaking another person's hand. The problem is I've never experienced it. No one has ever done that to me. I'm the troublemaker. No one wants to be my friend.

"So, Claire, what do you say about my proposal?" she asks without letting my hand go.

This girl is strange but a friendly stranger, friendlier than any human I have ever met.

She tilts her head to the side like she's waiting for something.

*Oh, that's why. Right, she asked me about a proposal.*

"I'm sorry, but what proposal are you referring to?" I suddenly feel extremely stupid.

I don't even know what a proposal is. I mean I've read about a proposal happening to characters in books, but I've never experienced someone asking me about a proposal to be able to identify what she's actually referring to. I feel even more stupid than I did after admitting the truth about not understanding her question.

"To be friends, silly," she replies, surprising me again.

"Um okay."

She pulls me into a hug, and I don't know if I should run away or hug her back. This girl is definitely not what I thought she was.

I pull myself out of her arms, suddenly feeling tense. I judged her just like all the others did to me. Just because she was standing next to the she-devils, I expected her to treat me the same way as one of them did.

I suddenly experience déjà vu while Jadis continues to stare at me. I remember the look in her eyes when King Nicklaus ended that girl's life. She was analyzing me, judging me. Now it all makes sense. This must be some twisted joke that she and the other

104

chosen girls came up with. That's the only thing that can explain why she suddenly wants to befriend me.

"Is this some sick joke?" My voice comes out a bit hostile, but who can blame me? This girl asked for it. "Did you really believe I would fall into your trap so easily? Do you think I'm that foolish?" I take a step back, waiting for her to own up to it and laugh in my face.

But she doesn't. She doesn't even seem to be taken aback by my mood change. She sits on the bed and stares into space, refusing to make eye contact and confirming my speculations.

Maybe I misjudged her. Victoria and Jasmine must be the puppet masters. She probably just wants to fit in.

I watch as she licks her lips.

"I have been a vampire's pet since the age of ten," she speaks, gaining my attention.

That's impossible. Such title is not given until after the age of eighteen. I am about to object, but the ghostly glare in her eyes stops me. She's telling the truth. We can tell a lie with our words, but our eyes reveal it all.

I sit on the opposite side of the bed and wait for her to continue.

"My mother was no ordinary breeder. When she found out she was pregnant, she escaped the Kingdom of Canberra, Australia, and settled in Melbourne, along with another group of human women that escaped King Cornelius's rule. We lived in our little settlement for ten years, and we were never once been detected by vampires or anyone else." She buries her head in her hands.

I can tell she is lost in her own memories. My heart cries out for her. I'm ashamed. Once again I judged a book by its cover. She doesn't deserve that.

"When we were finally detected and brought for justice, the vampires raped and drained our mothers in front of us. There were a total of six children in our little village. I'm the only one whose heart still beats."

"Why didn't they kill you?" I ask, unable to stop myself.

She shrugs. "King Cornelius ordered the guards to spare me. He gave me to King Nicklaus as a gift, asking him to spare my life to be his personal trophy. He then gave me to Lady Gwen, who decided to make me her pet."

Without thinking, I rush over to Jadis and wrap my arms around her. There's no need for her to continue. I know the rest of her fate. I saw it.

Jadis's tears flow freely, and I allow her to release her pain. As humans, we don't get to experience family ties. We don't feel the pain of losing a mother because we never have that mother-and-child bond. However, Jadis did and she lost more than any human I have ever met in my life. She truly loved and lost someone.

Her mouth parts slightly, and I want to stop her and tell her she no longer has to explain herself to me. Who am I to judge her in the first place?

"Claire, I had lost myself playing doggy to my captors. I had tasted freedom and stopped fighting for my own the moment my mother was killed, until you came along."

I release my hold on her. I don't know how to respond. I don't even know how to process what she just said. "I don't understand," I tell her honestly.

"I don't either," she admits before standing up and wiping her tears.But I do know this. The night when I saw you stand up to the vampires, you reminded me that our lives are worth fighting for; that's why I want to befriend you, Claire. You reminded me that dying is better than living in chains; that's why I walked into King Cornelius's chambers and demanded he should free me and make me his chosen."

"You did what?" I gasp.

King Cornelius is a sadistic king. He would have f*cked her and slit her throat if she really walked into his chambers and demanded anything from him.

"Were you trying to get yourself killed?"

Her face brightens as a smile graces her lips. I like the way she looks when she smiles. She deserves to smile. She has been through enough.

Her eyes wander into space again, and I can't help but notice that her big brown eyes hold a golden tint around their irises. Her copper hair blends perfectly against her face. She is truly beautiful, but she is a maniac. This is not a laughing matter. Why is she blushing?

Jadis's face catches on fire. "I'm his beloved," she blurts out, taking me by surprise.

Yup, she's a maniac.

# CHAPTER SEVENTEEN
## Stockholm Syndrome

"I mean, well, I think I'm his beloved," she says while staring into space for the millionth time.

I stand quietly, watching her. Once again, this girl has me lost for words. I'm not surprised she believes she is his beloved. It's just I really feel bad about her upbringing. I was hoping she was smart enough not to flock with the rest of the birds. Vampires are charming, elegant, and very attractive creatures. A lot of humans like to think they can escape this hell by capturing one of their hearts. Some have even formed a one-sided bond with these monsters, believing that one day a vampire will return it; that is why I'm not surprised that Jadis thinks she can be a vampire's beloved. I'm just disappointed. I refuse to be one of those humans. It's absolutely ridiculous. Vampires have chained our entire race into submission. Because of them, we are nothing but like mere cattle running to the slaughterhouse with no will to fight.

"I know what you're thinking, Claire," she confesses, looking a little troubled. "King Cornelius is a monster. I know that. I have seen it with my own eyes. He kills with no remorse. He slaughters others without batting those long, thick, merciless eyelashes of his."

I'm going to pretend she didn't just compliment that leech and call him a monster in the same sentence.

She looks at me curiously. "He is a sadistic king, and I'm the silly human girl that finds myself lost and chained to his hold," she tells me.

There's sadness in her soft brown eyes as they wander into space again. I look closer and notice a heart-rending distress gleaming in their depths.

"I had never been so afraid in my life until the day my mom was murdered. The vampires, King Cornelius's soldiers, pulled me and the other children by the hair and tied us to a horse, allowing our bodies to be dragged until we entered his kingdom.

"By the time we did, the others were already dead. I was the only one who made it. They brought me directly to King Cornelius. I remember feeling like that was my time, like I was about to be drained and would be an example of . . ." She takes a moment to collect herself.

"Until . . . until . . . I saw him for the very first time. When they threw me onto his throne floor, he stopped in his tracks and assessed me from head to toe. And just when I thought that was it, I was a goner for sure," she explains, reliving that horrific day. Her lips tremble. "He ended every last one of their lives, but he saved me."

"Just because he saved you, that doesn't mean you are his beloved," I tell her, sounding a little harsh.

I get it. Demons killed her mother, and the devil slaughtered them because of it. She idolizes him, thinking he is her knight in shining armor. However, believing he is her beloved is more than a little far-fetched.

Mecca's story about a vampire and his human beloved comes to mind. I don't know why King Cornelius did what he did. It is very strange, but Jadis is not his beloved. No human could be a vampire's true beloved. That's what Mecca believes. She is a she-wolf and has way more experiences with those creatures than Jadis and me. She has also lived a lot longer.

Jadis ignores my statement and enters the closet. She exits with a beautiful long scarlet-red gown in her hands. "Here, try this. We don't have time to fetch your belongings. We are late for dinner."

"Dinner?"

*Dinner. Oh yes, dinner with our owners.*

My heart starts to pound all of a sudden. The last dinner I attended didn't end so well—a girl was murdered. I don't want to go to dinner anymore. I can't eat with those things, not again. There has to be a way I can get out of this.

"Don't worry, it will be okay," Jadis suddenly says.

"You don't know that!" I practically yell.

Wait, she doesn't deserve it. She is only trying to help.

*I'm sorry. I'm just . . . I'm just . . .*

"Scared? It's okay," she reads my mind, without actually reading my mind, because that would make her like King Nicklaus—the leech I'm being forced to have dinner with.

Jadis is still looking at me. I guess she's giving me a chance to calm down.

"The sooner we go, the quicker we can leave," she speaks again.

I let out a much-needed sigh. "I'm not going to stop you from trying to hump King Cornelius," I joke, attempting to lighten the mood.

"Oh, now why would I do that?" she answers too quickly, kind of excited even. She smirks and doesn't bother hiding that mischievous glint in her eyes.

"Yeah, why would you?" I ask her back. I try my best to hide my irritation.

She arches an eyebrow and crosses her arms over her chest. Well, there goes trying to hide my irritation. She catches me, as expected. I have never been good at concealing anything, trust me.

I know I might be overreacting as we have only been friends for like seven seconds. We just properly introduced ourselves a moment ago. Regardless, I truly want what's best for her, and this attachment she has for that leech is not good. It's very, very, very bad. It's not healthy in the slightest.

Jadis wanted to be my friend, and she got it—a very protective, loving, and loyal friend who refuses to allow anything to happen to her. Mark my words, Stockholm syndrome cannot have her. Sorry.

*Oh great. Now I sound like I'm obsessed with her. I wonder if there's a word for first-time-friend protection obsession.*

"Earth to Claire, earth to Claire." Jadis waves her hand in front of my face.

*Hey, when did she get there?*

I blink rapidly.

"Look, Claire, we really need to go."

"Okay, let me just go to the ladies's room," I tell her.

She taps her foot impatiently, her heels clicking. "You're stalling."

"I am not."

"You are!"

"I am not! Okay, maybe I am," I confess, giving in.

\* \* \*

Thirty minutes later, we are finally making our way toward the dinner hall. Thankfully, the kings have decided to have dinner later tonight so we aren't late after all. In fact, we are early, even arriving before Victoria and Jasmine, who both give Jadis the stink eye when they finally walk in.

I can't help but roll my eyes. I'm over them.

The long dress that Jadis loaned me fits like a glove. It's elegant and revealing. The scarlet color is daring and inviting, just as the vampires like it. I guess it is safe to say that this dress will please King Nicklaus. I don't really care, but I'm sure it will.

I close my eyes. I can't do this.

111

Jadis grabs my hand right before I have the chance to make a run for it. She's a lifesaver.

"Relax. You look extremely good, girl. Thanks to me." She winks. "This will be over, quicker than you think."

I highly doubt that, but she's right that I do look great—thanks to her doing my hair in an updo bun and putting a little makeup on my face, just enough to enhance my features. She really is a doll.

Servants are everywhere, running around like chickens with their heads cut off. This time the dining area has a lot of candles placed around. The marble floors shine away, and the flames from the candles provide a little more light. However, it's still a dark room.

I can't help but think about the slave girl lying in her own blood, her lifeless wide eyes boring into my soul. It's like her soul is here right now, haunting me. I'm about to freak out when Jadis saves me again.

"We shall be just fine," she reminds me, her tone soothing.

That's exactly what I need—a friend.

"Bow, Claire," she tells me in a low, hurried voice before I can even thank her.

I didn't get a chance to follow her lead. Well, at least not on my own because seconds later, his voice commands inside my head, *"Bow, Claire."*

My body obeys. That velvety tone does it every time.

King Nicklaus is the first to enter. He's the king after all. Out of the corner of my eye I can see his unbuttoned shirt, providing me and every other servant a full display of his rock-hard and beautifully-sculpted chest.

*He looks really, really strong and hot . . . smoking hot but dangerous. I hate it.*

I roll my eyes at my own thought.

*Of course, he looks dangerous. He is dangerous and hot, and so are all the kings. Vampire kings are inviting and exciting monsters. I must remember that.*

I must have been lost in thought for a while because I didn't notice anyone else coming in. Damn him. His muscles distracted me.

"You may come, slaves," he directs us. His voice sends a tidal wave of fire crashing to my core.

Damn that silky tone of his voice. If that isn't enough, those eyes are. And just like a fool in love, I am stuck. I can't move.

*"Come sit beside me, Claire, and don't stare no matter what,"* he instructs inside my head again.

That's when I notice he isn't the only king in the room. They are all here, including Xander, whose stormy gray eyes speak a thousand unsaid words. He is amused. My reaction does not go unnoticed.

Why the hell am I reacting like this in the first place? I'm acting like the other humans, like a silly little girl. I don't get it. It's as if I didn't see him earlier today. What has gotten into me?

My eyes flicker in Jadis's direction. She is walking toward King Cornelius with a confident, seductive swish of her hips. Victoria crosses her legs as she takes her place near Xander. Jasmine is strutting toward King Cyrus, whose eyes are glued on me. He growls deep in his throat, and I quickly lower my gaze.

*Oh sh\*t! Don't stare at them. Don't stare at them. Don't stare at them.*

Easier said than done, especially when all the kings are staring at me like a bunch of hawks. If it weren't for their cool, calm, and collected postures, I would make a run for it. Like for real, it's nerve-wracking.

*Why are they watching me anyway? Do I have something on my face?*

I notice the other kings don't have a chosen, but they all have naked pets chained on a leash. Creeps.

"Now that my chosen has decided to take her seat," King Nicklaus announces, placing his penetrating gaze on me, "we can feast and discuss the matter at hand."

*Oh, so that's why they are watching me. I'm the last one to take a seat. Well, that's not my fault. He needs to blame himself and that damn chest of his.*

I try to keep up with his words, but his eyes are hypnotizing me again. No matter how hard I try to listen to him, I'm super distracted. Gosh, I'm such a hypocrite.

"Brother, thank you for inviting us."

Xander gains my attention. He looks just as good as his yummy brother. Now that I think about it and see them sitting beside each other, I can't help but compare them. King Nicklaus is handsome in a prince-of-darkness type of way, with his irresistible features: compelling and controlling yet intoxicating and inviting. On the other hand, Xander, a dark warrior, is gorgeous, muscular, alert, intimidating, and unattainable. They are both beautiful, deadly creatures—brothers.

I briefly look at Xander. He's questioning why his brother brought him here. Every once in a while I feel his eyes bore into me, and I can't focus on listening in. My nerves are shot, and it's King Nicklaus's fault. His well-crafted, well-built six-pack has my undivided attention.

Out of the corner of my eye, I see King Cyrus watching me again.

*What's his problem? He's such a creep.*

Xander and King Nicklaus are now arguing.

"The council will not approve of going to war, Brother," Xander states.

"F*ck the council!" King Nicklaus responds.

*Wait, what war? What did I miss?*

I'm finally paying attention. Unlike the other chosens, I decide to watch their argument openly with my eyes moving from the King of Darkness to the Dark Warrior King, foolishly

114

forgetting one small rule that I'm not supposed to break. Immediately, they stop talking.

*Oh sh\*t. Oh sh\*t. Oh sh\*t. I was directed not to stare.*

"What are you looking at, toy?" asks a dark, chilling voice.

*F\*ck. I can only hope the toy he's referring to is any other toy and not me.*

My eyes travel in his direction. Now why would I do that?

# CHAPTER EIGHTEEN
## Royal Traditions

No sooner than my eyes land on him—by accident—King Cyrus smiles from ear to ear, fangs showing and eyes gleaming.

*Jeepers creepers! What is this vampire's problem?*

"I see, someone still doesn't have manners," he hisses (an ugly, chilling, bone-chattering hiss).

*He is so creepy. I just don't understand why he keeps intentionally f\*cking with me. First the incident in the hall, now this. What does he want from me?*

*Your blood,* says my own little voice inside my head.

That's exactly what he wants, to end me. The funny thing is that all he has to do is ask. I won't fight against it. Seriously, he will be doing me a favor, a big one.

King Nicklaus slams down his fist, getting everyone's attention. "Cyrus, we have much bigger issues to discuss! My toy can wait." He pauses for a second and places his gaze on me, and I drop my head instantly. "It shall be dealt with," he adds.

"It," I state.

Cyrus's smile widens, and the rest of the kings's attention is now on me.

Xander shakes his head—in a no motion—but it's too late. It has already started.

"It." I make a face at King Nicklaus.

I can't believe he just called me an it, not a chosen, not a pet, not a slave. I mean none of those words is much better, but an "it"?

"I am a person with a name, not a f*cking 'it,' you weak piece of sh—"

"Quiet, slave." King Nicklaus's voice silences me. *"You have drawn enough attention to yourself tonight. Now is not the time, trust me. Keep your mouth shut, mind blank, and head down. Please, Claire,"* he says inside my mind.

I'm absolutely stunned.

*He said "please." He said "please." No. He said, "Please, Claire." He used my name.*

*"I said, 'your mind blank,' Claire,"* comes his voice again. *"I can't block your thoughts for much longer. I need you to bow your head and apologize."*

*"What?"*

*"Please, Claire."*

*"Alright. Sorry."*

*"Say it out loud, Claire."*

That's when I notice that the others are still staring at me with blazing red eyes, ready to sink their fangs into my neck. Xander is also watching me, but unlike the others, his eyes are stormy and dark, almost black. I don't get it, but right now is not the time. I have other things to focus on, like the fact that King Nicklaus is actually speaking to me with manners.

"I apologize, sire. Please forgive me," I say, even going as far as standing just to bow.

"You may rise, slave," he tells me. He stands up, showing off those perfectly hardened abs.

I try to concentrate on the task at hand but without success. My focus is on his body. The sight of him is making my mouth dry and my knees weak. How can I stand? It's taking everything in me not to drop to my knees.

117

King Nicklaus's lips curve into a smirk. "Stand, slave, and take a seat."

My body complies of its own accord, compelled.

He walks to the center of the room without sparing me another glance. There's no denying the power and dominance that beam around him.

"Now that we've solved that issue, let's focus on the true problem." His eyes roam over each and every king's face. "As my brother said, the council will not want to declare war. However, the dogs need to be put back on a leash. Any suggestions?"

King Luscious is the first to respond. I remember when I first laid eyes on him. I assumed he was the least scary out of all the kings. I even went as far as calling him a wimp. Now, I'm not too sure. There's something dangerous and lethal lingering in his eyes as he speaks, "Dogs aren't a threat in my territory, so I don't see the point of going against the council's orders."

"But hunters are," King Nicklaus points out, shrugging his shoulders. "Imagine how big of a threat the werewolves would become in your territory if they learned that over ten groups of hunters inhabit your lands. They would team up, and with your land being King Cyrus's neighboring kingdom and a great distance from the circling kingdoms, I'd say it's likely they will do just that."

*Circling kingdoms? What does he mean? There's so much I don't understand about these vampires and the other species.*

I make a mental note to do some research. I was never that student who actually paid attention to our Vampire 101 class. Honestly, I didn't believe it was important enough to listen to. I was wrong.

My eyes move in King Luscious's direction. I don't know what a hunter is, but I do know one thing based on the look on his face. Hunters and werewolves working together equals double-trouble. If he notices that I'm watching him, he doesn't say a word. Instead, he rubs his dark chin hair for a long-drawn-out moment. He seems to be lost in his own thoughts, pondering.

118

"Good point," he admits. "That would be a serious problem. I honestly haven't thought about that." His eyes flash red as they center on King Nicklaus, and a look of determination settles on his face. "I have worked hard for my territory. My people and I are content. We are well-fed, and no one has the balls to defy me."

*Duh! I may not have focused much on Vampire 101, but I did in vampire sociology. Each lesson always revealed that they are reckless and barbaric creatures, especially King Luscious. No one with a brain would dare to defy him, and of course he's well-fed because he buys slaves just to slaughter them.*

King Nicklaus raises an eyebrow as his eyes flicker in my direction. I keep forgetting that he can read other people's thoughts, and based on his reaction, he doesn't approve of mine. I should be more careful.

*"You should focus on keeping your mind blank."* His voice appears in my head.

*Now that's easier said than done,* I think to myself, knowing very well he's still listening in.

Xander chuckles out loud, and I can't help but wonder if he's also reading my thoughts.

"That would all change if those dogs and savages decide to tangle," King Luscious interrupts our private conversation. He gives King Nicklaus the side-eye. "That's exactly why I can't partake in this war. I refuse to leave my territory unprotected and without a ruler," he adds.

"And so do I," King Marcellus chimes in, running his fingers through his inky-black hair.

I take a moment to soak him in. King Marcellus is a living piece of art, literally. He has art painted and carved all over his pale skin. His vivid green eyes scream masterpiece. He's handsome, that's for sure, but dangerous. He even has a ring piercing in his nose—scary.

"Europe has too much land and unmarked territory as is. It would be foolish and extremely stupid to leave it unprotected and

119

defenseless to participate in a war. I can't do that, especially when the wolves haven't attacked anyone's kingdom besides your favorite's." He looks at King Nicklaus, then says his next words with caution, "This is not about our species. This is about your undying loyalty to your best friend."

*His best friend? Who is his best friend?*

My question is answered seconds later when King Cyrus releases a gruesome growl, his eyes bloodshot red.

Now it makes me think about the time when I was at school. I'd heard rumors numerous times, about King Cyrus and King Nicklaus sharing torture ideas. I don't know why I didn't put two and two together. Honestly, it makes sense. I just don't understand why King Nicklaus stopped his best friend from draining the life out of me earlier today.

King Cyrus moved from his seat and is now standing directly in front of King Marcellus. His movements were too quick for my human eyes to catch.

"I don't need anyone to protect my territory, just like I don't need any help with ending your life."

King Marcellus seems to be unfazed. "I will enjoy seeing you try," he responds nonchalantly, rubbing his pet's head.

As if on cue, eight half-naked servants walk in, all of them smiling and holding trays of food in their hands, just in time to save the day.

"Cyrus!" King Nicklaus sighs deeply. "Please take a seat and eat. Killing each other is not the solution to our problems. If anything, it would only create more problems. Both of you are behaving like two little children, arguing over your favorite toys. Calm yourselves."

For some more while, King Cyrus glares at King Marcellus before he finally takes a seat. Without being asked, Jasmine sits on his lap and then bends her head to one side to provide him with easy access to the veins in her neck. She is giving him complete dominance. He growls in approval and plunges his fangs deep into

120

her skin. She moans loudly, and her eyes roll to the back of her head—she enjoys it.

My stomach turns. That's sick; she is sick. I wrinkle my nose in disgust. She's such a submissive little slave, ready to do anything just to please a leech. F*cking wh*re.

Surprisingly, I'm not the only one who's annoyed by their public feeding, or maybe he's just annoyed with Cyrus in general.

"That's right. Follow your master's orders," taunts King Marcellus.

King Cyrus quickly removes his fangs. "You're dead!" he yells. He jumps back up from his seat, knocking Jasmine to the floor in the process, then storms back over to King Marcellus's end of the table.

"I said calm yourselves!" King Nicklaus snaps, throwing a chair at them.

The chair breaks into a million pieces as it slams onto the floor. The authority in his voice cannot be ignored, his tone deadly. His eyes are flashing red as he walks toward them. He leaves no room for arguments. He leaves no room for complaints. King Nicklaus meant what he said.

I can't take my eyes off him. I can't help myself, chills traveling down my back. The power in his voice sparks something within me—a fire in the center of my core. It is like a burning flame of tender poison, slowly moving through my system. And I welcome all of it, unlike the other chosens. They are hovering in fear, scared for their lives. I have never felt this alive in my life. All my attention settles on him. He has it all. The other kings are stoic.

"Take a seat now, Cyrus!" King Nicklaus orders, making his way back to his own seat. "I don't want to hear another word from either of you unless it's about solving our problem as a whole. We are all in this together."

King Cyrus picks Jasmine up off the ground, then sits back down. King Marcellus lowers his head, his eyes on the table. They both look pissed, their jaws clenched. I can tell they want to say something, but they choose not to.

Make no mistake. All these kings can be scary as f*ck. They can scare a person straight with just one look. With all that being said, no matter how scary they all may seem, King Nicklaus is unquestionably the scariest of all. As I said, he is the king and his word is final.

The servants continue to stand around the table with the trays of food in their hands, their eyes averted.

King Nicklaus clears his throat. "Now that we all have calmed down, you may serve."

They obey and serve each king one by one.

The kings nod in approval and start joking with one another. Even King Marcellus and King Cyrus are now talking to each other like they weren't just at each other's neck. Their behavior confuses me.

Now it makes me realize that my vampire sociology instructor never mentioned what type of relationship the kings have.

*"I'm waiting for you, Claire,"* comes King Nicklaus's voice inside my head again. He damn near causes me to jump out of my seat. I was not expecting his sudden arrival.

*"Waiting for what? I don't understand."* I look up and see everyone's attention is on him, including the chosens. So, I duplicate their actions.

King Nicklaus raises his hand. "This food is a gift to my brothers. We should dine as one, think as one, and become one as we discuss the task at hand."

The moment they repeat after him, something clicks. This is the Feast of the Brothers. It is a royal tradition that vampires are rumored to have. It is said this is a tradition that each vampire king had passed down from generation to generation way before the humans even knew about their existence. I don't know much about vampire history, but I do know this feast is considered to be their most-valued tradition.

I focus on King Nicklaus, watching his every move with great interest. He picks up his fork with his left hand and bites into the meat first. The others follow suit, indicating that they will always follow his lead. It's a sign of respect.

*Wait, he's left-handed?*

Vampire kings are trained to utilize both their left and right hands to perform tasks. A king does everything with his left hand until he finds the person who is meant to sit on his left side, only then will he perform a task with his right. I don't know much, but I'm absolutely certain about that—which only means he's hasn't claimed his beloved.

*Lady Gwen is not his beloved?*

# CHAPTER NINETEEN
## War Plans

*She is not his beloved!*

I don't know why discovering that information sends a million and one butterflies spreading through my entire body. I shouldn't be that excited. It really shouldn't matter to me. Just because he hasn't claimed her as his beloved at the moment, it doesn't necessarily mean he won't eventually. Maybe he's just taking it slow. He's the king, and he can make his own rules, right? I have to admit it's strangely satisfying to learn that he hasn't, though.

The kings enjoy their feast with no interruptions. The chosens and I aren't allowed to eat with them. We just have to sit and watch them stuff their mouths with all this amazing food. I bet they wouldn't feed us at all if it weren't for the fact that they need us to be healthy. If slaves are healthy and well-fed, it means a good blood supply. And let's face it, vampires need to drink our blood, like how humans need to drink water. They can eat human food, but in order to survive, they need blood, healthy blood. That's why it doesn't surprise me when the servants place salmon, avocado, and a glass of green tea in front of me.

Honestly, I'm sick of this dish. Now don't get me wrong. The food is not bad. Actually, it's amazing. The zesty orange sauce is rich to the taste, and it's one of my favorite dishes. That's probably why I crush my meal in five point two seconds.

"I mean no disrespect," King Marcellus starts the conversation back up after wiping his mouth with a handkerchief, "but you know I have a point. Europe holds a lot of lands that I can't afford to leave it unguarded."

"Save the sh*t, Marcellus," says King Rufus, slamming a knife onto the table. "Asia has more territory than any other kingdom. We have marked and unmarked lands. With that being said, I'm still willing to go to war."

"And so am I," says another king with crystal-blue eyes. His face is covered with an ungroomed long golden beard. His hair, just as long and untamed as his beard, trails down his back.

I realize this is the first time he has spoken. He is the only king I haven't identified, so I eliminate all the other kings's names I've heard from my mind and find the answer. He is King Seneca of Africa, the violent and quick-witted king.

King Seneca picks up King Rufus's knife and plays with it. "Africa is the second-largest territory," he speaks through clenched teeth, his voice low. "I will partake in the war. My governors can handle the lands without me. Those dogs will die. An attack on one king is an attack on all. We shall destroy each and every one of them."

"Attack?" King Marcellus laughs out loud, bending over and tugging on his pet's chain in the process. "A pack of mutts freeing one group of transported humans is not an attack. We shouldn't leave the circling kingdoms unguarded for too long. They can have those humans!"

He pulls his pet roughly by the hair, causing her to release a small whimper. Her neck is bent to the side, and even my human ears can hear her heartbeat.

"We have their entire species. Why should we declare war?" His intense green eyes blaze with menace. "We are at the top of the food chain," he says. He plunges his fangs into her neck, and unlike Jasmine, his pet releases a high-pitched scream.

125

I flinch and shut my eyes. I can't watch this savage act. I try my hardest to tune out the pain in her voice as she begs and pleads for him to stop. She screams for what seems like hours and doesn't stop until her heartbeat does; he has killed her.

I can hear the guards dragging her lifeless body away. I open my eyes, only to be met by King Nicklaus's stormy cerulean orbs. He is watching me attentively, cautiously. He clearly expects me to overreact, offering myself up instead. If only it's that simple.

Once Marcellus gets himself back together, he hisses in King Seneca's direction, "Plus, you are only agreeing because you and Cyrus are good friends."

King Seneca says nothing. He simply continues with his meal.

King Nicklaus keeps on watching me for a long-drawn-out moment.

"You're right, Marcellus," he finally speaks. He takes a sip of his drink.

My stomach lurches, and food starts to resurface as I look at the thick red liquid that occupies his cup.

"We can't leave the circling kingdoms unguarded. Most of our people reside in those lands, and they must be protected at all cost."

"We have people in Antarctica and Australia," Xander adds. "And unlike the other kingdoms, they are the least protected."

"Those creatures will not survive Antarctica's climate," King Marcellus speaks again. "News flash! No one lives there, so why would they attack the land of the dead? Everyone knows once a human is taken to your territory, they're dead."

I must admit, he has a point.

"Your territory is the least likely to be attacked, that's why it's your territory, remember? We wouldn't want you to relapse and avenge your long, lost lo—"

"I suggest, you mind your tongue before you lose it!" Xander growls. His eyes flash red and his body visibly shakes, providing evidence that his threat is real.

All eyes, including my own, are now on him. I can't help but wonder why he's so pissed while the other kings do not seem to be surprised by his outburst, and this piques my interest even more.

King Nicklaus stands. "Everyone has a point, and I respect every single one of your opinions." He turns to face King Cornelius. "We have yet to hear yours about the war."

King Cornelius doesn't immediately respond. He faces Jadis, and my heart starts racing.

*I can only hope he is not going to use her like King Marcellus used his pet to prove a point. I won't be able to just sit here and watch it like a good little slave. I will really kill him.*

"I agree with King Marcellus," he answers, twirling his finger around a string of Jadis's hair. "Going to war because the dogs freed a few pets is just not worth the trouble." He stares at her, and the others at him.

I take that opportunity to grab a knife on the far end of the table.

*I meant what I said—he will die.*

"Very well," speaks King Nicklaus, nodding. He shifts his focus onto me. He must have been listening in.

I gulp. My heart rate increases threefold. Surprisingly, he doesn't call me out. Instead, he continues with their conversation.

"As I said before, I respect your opinion, and I have taken everything that was stated into consideration." He walks to the center of the room. "With that being said, I have made my decision."

The other kings stand in unison.

"I declare war on the dogs and any other creatures that decide to come to their aid. As King Marcellus pointed out, we can't afford to leave the circling kingdoms unguarded."

*What are the circling kingdoms? I'm still lost.*

King Marcellus smiles, but it's short-lived.

"That's why I've decided that Seneca, Rufus, Cornelius, and Luscious will stay in their territories."

"What? That's bullsh*t!" King Marcellus objects, grinding his teeth. "They can stay at home and guard their kingdoms, but I must get invloved in the war?"

King Nicklaus walks toward the upset king, who is having a b*tch fit. The others watch with smirks. "Are you defying orders?"

King Marcellus glares at the others while they are now holding back laughter. "Of course not. I just don't see the point."

"The point is," King Nicklaus growls, "as you stated several times tonight, the neighboring kingdoms have too much precious territory that we cannot afford to leave unguarded. Asia and Africa have more lands to guard than Europe does, which means that your governors can withhold a threat. And because of Europe being a part of the neighboring kingdoms, Rufus or Seneca can come to its aid if need be." He turns to face King Luscious. "Just like I expect you to come to our aid in the war if things don't go as planned. With you being the closest to Cyrus's territory, I expect that it shouldn't be a problem."

"Not at all." King Luscious takes a bow. "My governors shall be notified just in case I have to take action."

King Nicklaus's facial expression turns dry. "Xander, I suggest you notify your governors about our plans."

Xander bows, then exits the room without another word. Victoria
soon follows after him.

"Now that we have discussed war plans, you all may return to your kingdoms to make proper preparations. Be very discreet. If the council found out about our plans before we take off to war, it would do nothing but cause me a headache. I shall meet Xander and Marcellus in North America before the new moon. You are all dismissed."

128

Just like robots, the kings bow and take their leave. Jadis hesitates to follow after King Cornelius. I can tell she wants to say something but might be terrified of the consequences. I, on the other hand, am not. I run in her direction, refusing to allow my first and perhaps only friend to leave without a proper goodbye. This may be the last time we see each other.

"Thank you," I tell her, giving her a hug, "for wanting to befriend me." I tighten my hug around her tiny little frame. Out of the corner of my eye, I notice King Nicklaus and King Cornelius watching our interaction. Thankfully, neither of them intervenes.

"Hopefully we shall meet again," I add.

She smiles a truly genuine smile. "We shall. Stay safe and stop allowing things you can't control to get to you. I don't have to tell you to stay strong because you're the toughest human I know." She pulls away and walks out of the door.

I stare after her for a little while, praying for her safety. I hope we shall truly meet again. And if not, I'll be okay as long as she is safe and breathing.

King Nicklaus clears his throat, and I turn to face him. We are now the only ones in the room.

"You must return to my chambers. We have a couple of nights before we take our trip. I suggest you pack lightly."

"Wait, trip?" I raise an eyebrow.

"Yes. As my chosen, you are required to accompany me. I have to be at my strongest, so I need my food directly from the source."

*Food from the source? I can only hope he means I would be hunting rabbits or deer for him. I can't allow him to feed on me. I can't, and I won't.*

"You will," he declares, sending shivers down my spine.

I'm pretty sure my face is blue like a blueberry.

"I can bite you now so you can get used to it. I promise it will not hurt. All you shall feel is an intense pleasure."

Now my face is colorless. The color has damn sure drained away.

129

I have been bitten many times, and I know it hurts like hell. I don't know why Jasmine moaned when that savage ripped into her skin. I guess some humans are like that—they like pain—but I'm not one of them. He will have to catch me first. I won't go down without a fight.

He takes a step closer, and I take a step back.

"*Claire, don't,*" warns King Nicklaus. He's in my head again. He knows I'm about to make a run for it.

Oh well, I do, rushing toward the door.

It doesn't take him long to catch me, not even a second. He grabs me by the shoulder with force and holds me in place. His crimson eyes and pointy, monstrous fangs are on full display.

I panic.

"Be still, Claire. I promise it won't hurt," he coaxes, then my body goes still right before he sinks his fangs into my skin.

# CHAPTER TWENTY
## The Bite

His fangs tear into my flesh, piercing my skin. I feel like a hot blade has been lodged into my neck, followed by a rush of scorching fire burning in my skin and making my blood boil. It stings really bad. I release a scream so loud that my lungs tingle along with the sound as King Nicklaus sucks greedily and takes what feels like gallons of my blood in one sip. I can feel my heart hammering inside my chest, exploding. My body has blasted away into tiny little pieces. I'm nothing but a puddle of blood. My skin has evaporated.

His promise of pleasure was nothing but a lie. This is a kind of pain I've never felt, like I am burned alive. His fangs are a sharp blade digging deeper and deeper into my flesh. He yanks my hair as he bites down harder. If there is really a never-ending fire in hell, this is it. I'm screaming as though I were a sinner being punished, in an unavoidable torment for the rest of eternity. I try to find the strength to push him away, to fight him with every ounce of my being, but I can't. I'm not strong enough.

My hands feel heavy as I grip the knife. If only I had the strength to plunge it into his neck and make him feel the same pain he is forcing onto me. I wish with all my might that this monster would disappear and go back into the hole he crawled out of. I would dig a grave for this savage. If I were strong enough, his karma would be real. The problem is I'm nothing but a weak human. Unlike him, I don't have any supernatural strength. He has won. This dangerous predator has hunted his prey, and now he is feasting on it. He is no longer starving. No. He is taking his fill, and my blood is his greatest meal.

The more I fight, the harder he bites down. And it continues to sting, burning my flesh as he sucks, pulling and taking whatever he can get from me. My blood is his.

Just when I feel losing consciousness is when I decide to let go, and the knife falls to the ground. A wave of cool water washes the fire away. My screams of pain turn into a piercing cry of pleasure. My body relaxes, and his bite becomes softer. The fire is extinguished, my pain melting away.

King Nicklaus releases a husky moan of his own as he slowly massages my hair with his hand in a circular motion. It sends little sparks of electricity across my body, clouding my mind and better judgment.

I lean my head to the side, providing him better access to my neck. My body is acting of its own accord, and this time, he doesn't have to compel me to do what he wants. I feel like I'm in a haze, wanting to give him as much blood as he wants to take. I want this just as much as he does, and he can have it all. He can take my life away. He can have all my blood.

My head is spinning, and my eyelids begin to feel heavy. He releases his fangs, and I can't help but cry out, suddenly desperately wanting more. Just when it starts to feel amazing, he takes away the mountain of joy.

"Please, don't stop." My voice is no more than a whisper, and my throat feels like sandpaper, dry and hoarse.

"That's right, firecracker," he responds, his voice husky and deep.

I shiver.

"Relax and beg for the bite." He leans in closer. He takes his other hand and digs his claws deep into my back.

I can't find my voice, but I beg and plead with him inside my head. I feel his Adam's apple roll as he takes a deep swallow. His muscles flex while my legs feel like jello. The suspense is killing me. I need him to finish what he started.

The most-intense pain I have ever felt quickly turns into a rush of hot pleasure. I want more. My eyes are shut tight, but even without looking I can tell his eyes are glowing like lava, sending fire to my skin with just a glance. King Nicklaus blesses me with his soft lips, trailing kisses around his bite mark. His magical hands cup my face before traveling to my breasts. I start to explode for a whole other reason when he fiddles with my dress. He pinches my now swollen nipples, bringing my pleasure to a new height. My dress blocking his touch feels like torture. I want him. I need his fangs, right now. My body is begging for him to bite me again. If I have to take the pain to get that type of pleasure, be it. I need his bite more than I need air. He can have me, all of me.

How quickly the tables have turned? I don't want to run away anymore. I want to smash into him. I have turned into an addict finally allowed to have a fix, craving his fangs. I pull his head into my shoulder and lean my head all the way over to the side to give him easy access to my veins.

"You have to beg, firecracker. Beg for me," King Nicklaus says. His fangs nibble on my bite marks, gently and patiently. He won't bite down until I ask for it. He wants me to scream for it. His wish is my command.

"Pleeease!" I scream. "Please bite me."

He bites down, and this time, I welcome the burning fire and crashing tidal wave of cool, pleasurable pain. A soft purring sound leaves my chest as he sinks his fangs deeper. Liquid drips down my legs, down to the floor. He grips my legs and lift them off the ground, then pins my back to the wall. I can feel his member in between his legs. My God, it's gigantic. His huge Johnny pokes through the tight confinement of his dress pants. I can feel it reaching for my opening, desperately wanting a taste, just like his master that has been feasting on and taking the cool liquid that flows inside my veins.

This bite is nothing like the first. This bite is answering the call of my soul. I can feel him. We are one at this moment, and it feels so, so, so good. Oh my, this is the most-phenomenal feeling in the world. It's like a high caused by a very strong drug.

His member is rock-hard as he dry-humps me through his pants. My fingers dig deep into his equally hard chest, and my entire body is drenched in so much pleasure. I have never enjoyed sex or the emotions that come along with it until now. Vampires only take and never give, but this? This is different. King Nicklaus is giving me an experience I never want to end.

"Take all of me, Nicklaus."

He bites a little deeper, and everything around me disappears—everything but him. All I can see is the vampire king, and for the first time in my life, I'm glad to be his servant. Pleasure fills every inch of my skin, creating magic as blood continuously flows out of my veins. I can feel my body going limp. He is taking too much blood, but I welcome the darkness. My life is fair game. He can have it.

Right before the lights go out, King Nicklaus growls and his grip on my legs deepens. My knees buckle, and I start to wobble as I hear a voice, followed by a hard pull of my flesh and a stinging pain. Then, it all goes dark.

\*      \*      \*

A pounding pain awakens me from my deep sleep and brings me back into consciousness. I can feel a cool rush inside my veins. Seconds later, a warm cloth is placed on top of my forehead, providing aid to the ache in my brain. I try to open my eyes, but I can't. They're glued shut. My eyelids feel like chains. Panic starts to set in when I notice I can no longer feel my legs, feet, and hands.

The only sign telling me I'm still alive is the throbbing pain on the left side of my neck.

*What the hell has happened to me? Is this what heaven feels like, a state of living without actually being able to live? This cannot be it.*

I'm just about to allow myself to drift back into a deep slumber when I hear a voice.

"What the hell were you thinking? You almost killed her."

The man sounds familiar, but the hatred in his voice makes him unrecognizable at the same time.

"I lost control," says another voice.

*Wait, I know that voice. I would be able to identify that deep, husky, chilling voice in a sea of voices. It's unforgettable.*

Memories penetrate my brain. Our last moments bolt to the forefront of my head like a strike of lightning, replaying the fire that burned me alive and the cool wave that flushed that fire out. Suddenly, the memories of him asking me to beg for what I wanted before he gave it to me all flicker through my mind like a movie. The memory of his bite hits me the hardest. I begged for it, and I loved it. That's so f*cking embarrassing.

"How does a vampire at your age and with your skills lose control?" questions the other voice. "You have more control than all of us, that's why you're our king, Nicklaus!"

I can hear something is being smashed.

"I know what she is to you, and I refuse to allow you to make her suffer because you're not man enough to accept her," the same voice continues.

"Shut up!"

*If I could, I would run and hide from his terrifying tone. Thank God, I can't move.*

"F*ck you! It's not my fault you can't handle the truth. That's your problem! But when Claire is involved, I will not remain silent."

*Claire . . . who, me? Is he referring to me?*

King Nicklaus answers my question.

"She is my chosen!" he snarls. "I can do whatever I want with her body. I could drain every ounce of her sweet blood and plunge my dick into her core if I wanted to!"

*No, he cannot.*

A deep, ear-splitting growl fills the air, and commotion shuffles around me. My heart thuds, and although I can't see, I know what hell is breaking loose around me. A loud, threatening roar booms through the air. I swear the surface underneath me shakes.

"Xander! Nicklaus! What the hell is going on?" another voice hisses. It's a woman's voice, filled with venom and hatred.

When I realize Xander and King Nicklaus are the ones fighting, a rush of adrenaline invades my system, forcing my eyes to pop open, only to be met by their mother's glowing red orbs.

# CHAPTER TWENTY-ONE
## Royal Family

"What the hell is a human doing in your bed, let alone this defiant little pet?" King Nicklaus's mother sneers. "Have you completely lost your mind?" Her eyes grow redder with every second that passes. She is obviously one of those vampires whose hatred for humans runs deep.

"Relax. She is only recovering, Mother," Xander reasons with her. "Nicklaus lost control during their feeding session, taking more blood than he should have. She was bleeding out on the dining room floor. We wouldn't want to damage the marble, now would we?"

His choice of words—soaked in sarcasm—mocks her. I don't know what type of relationship these two have, but based on his attitude, one thing comes to mind: Xander is not the mama's boy type. Hopefully, I don't end up in the middle of some wicked son-and-mother dispute. Xander and King Nicklaus already got their panties in a bunch because of me. Besides, I don't like to be placed in the center of a family fight.

*They should value one another. None of them has a clue about what it feels like without a family. I really shouldn't care as they are the reason why I don't have one of my own, but that would be inhuman.*

"Watch your tone, boy," his mother warns. Her glowing orbs now zero in on Xander, whose eyes also glow bright red.

I can't help but notice how similar they are, appearance-wise anyway. The kings and their mother all share pitch-black hair and angular noses. I don't know the true shade of Lady Akasha's eye color since she's always walking around like Queen Evil whenever I'm in her presence. I wouldn't be surprised if she was born with red eyes. She's the Queen of the Walking Dead, with a black heart. It's not ironic for her true eye color to be red. The Queen of Evil with Crimson Eyes—yup, that fits her.

I wonder if Xander and King Nicklaus inherited their eyes from their dad. Their eyes are icy. However, Xander's irises are gray, kind of like the sky before it snows. King Nicklaus have more like silver-cerulean orbs that cause my heart to feel like it's in the center of an ice storm. Those eyes of his always give me chills.

"Mother, calm down. It's not that serious," King Nicklaus pipes up. His stormy orbs are at their normal shade, sending icicles to freeze my heart.

Lady Akasha looks at him in a different way than she looks at Xander. I can see that warm motherly affection, sort of. I mean, I think I can. Honestly, I don't know how a mom should look at her child, but I suppose it should be similar to how she's looking at him. I can also see the love beaming out of King Nicklaus's eyes.

From what I've observed, he usually seems intimidating and cold when he's with others. He tends to appear guarded around the other vampire kings and slaves, but right now he doesn't. His cool and calm demeanor at the moment has me on edge. I don't know what to expect, but it's different—a good different. It's weird and kind of foreign watching a mother and a son interact.

My mouth feels dry as I continue to witness their interaction. You would think I'm invisible. No one seems to be paying attention to me as I can't help myself staring directly at them.

"That's funny coming from you, especially when the only reason I'm here is that you and your brother were just fighting and shaking the entire castle. I suggest you take your own advice and then maybe I shall follow suit," she states.

King Nicklaus's calm demeanor shifts before our eyes in less than a second. Here comes the devil-may-care king. He doesn't like her tone, mother or not. From what I have deduced, this king doesn't tolerate disrespect from anybody, mother included. I don't know how to feel about that. Now, don't get me wrong. I don't like this woman. She seems to be more treacherous than King Nicklaus and would drain me in a second without a doubt, but she is his mother. That should count for something, right?

King Nicklaus grinds his teeth. "About that, Xander and I had a minor disagreement." His eyes flit to me before they land elsewhere quicker than I could blink. "Our issue is now resolved. He understands his place, so now, both of you can take your leave."

"My place?"

"Keep quiet, Xander!" Lady Akasha snaps. She turns to face King Nicklaus. "May I ask what the fight was about?" She crosses her arms gracefully, waiting for an answer.

The look she gives tells it all. She will not leave this room until her sons explain themselves, and neither of them will. Maybe I'm wrong. King Nicklaus may have more respect for his mother than I thought because if any other vampire intentionally defied his orders, there would be hell to pay.

"Mother, did I not make myself clear? I dismiss you both."

"I'm not one of your flunky kings or your slave wh*res," she spits, pointing in my direction.

It takes everything in me not to give her a piece of my mind.

*I can't believe she just called me a slave wh\*re. What the hell is up with these leeches calling me everything under the sun but my name?*

"You shall show me the respect I deserve, Nicklaus. I am still your mother!"

"And you have it all. Now please, can the both of you get the hell out of my room?" he yells.

I feel the urge to laugh. If it weren't for the dryness of my throat, I'm sure I wouldn't be able to hold it in.

King Nicklaus looks more like an annoyed human than a scary vampire king at the moment. This is fairly entertaining. So, is this how it is to have a family? I wonder if all families are like this. I used to dream about having a mother who would annoy me to the very end. I used to wonder from whom I inherited my hair color—from my mom or my dad? Maybe we all share similar features, but I guess that's just something I'll never know.

"Bye, Mother." King Nicklaus turns to face Xander. "That goes for you as well. Mother is losing her temper, and we don't want anyone else to suffer because of it, now do we?" He gives Xander the side-eye.

Xander's thin lips curl, and his eyes flash neon red.

I expect King Nicklaus's words to have a hidden meaning. It's obvious he is referring to me. I know Xander doesn't like his tone or his choice of words for that matter, and I expect Xander to jump into a quarrel. However, astonishingly enough, he doesn't respond. He doesn't even disagree. He only grinds his teeth—just like his brother did seconds ago—then starts to take his leave. Right before he steps out of the door, he turns to face me.

*"Continue to remain quiet, brave one. Our mother is just as bad as she looks."* His words appear inside my head as the door closes behind him.

Usually, I would be startled, but this time I kind of expected it. Well, I'm kind of becoming used to it. Xander has had no problem showing how he feels about me. I assume he is only leaving this room for my benefit. Unlike his brother, he cares about my safety, strangely enough; or at least I would like to think that he cares.

Out of the corner of my eye, I can see their mother watching me. She must have noticed that Xander's eyes lingered before he headed out of the door. If she could kill me with a look, I'm almost one hundred percent positive that I'd be dead.

She opens her mouth and moves her tongue over her fangs. Yup, she certainly wants to drain me. I feel extremely uncomfortable, and the dryness of my throat makes it ten times worse. I roll over, trying my best not to look at her. She shoots me an angry glare, and I want to sink underneath the covers. She is giving me a jeepers-creepers type of vibe. Seriously, her stare promises death. Oh great, that's just what I need.

I'll soon to have a swarm of vampire enemies. The list is soon to fill up, starting with King Cyrus, who decided to attack me for no reason. Now Lady Akasha's glare speaks a similar threat. I might as well paint "Hate me, vampires," in bold bright-red letters on my forehead. Speaking of which, my head is pounding. F*ck, it hurts.

"Very well. I'll leave you to play with your slave wh*re for now."

Yup, she has just officially assigned herself to my list. She hates me. Oh well, join the hate-her vamp club.

"Thank you, Mother." King Nicklaus kisses her left cheek.

She cups his face in return, and I catch a glimpse of her true eye color. It is similar to both of her sons's: stormy, cerulean-silver—almost white—chilling orbs. King Nicklaus and Xander inherited their beautiful eyes from her.

She left, and now it's just me and King Nicklaus. At first, I was relieved as I watched her walk out of the door, but now I'm not quite sure. The last time King Nicklaus and I were all alone, it didn't go so well for me.

*No, this is not good. This is a really, really bad idea. Hopefully, Xander will save me.*

"Don't count on that," King Nicklaus speaks, startling me. He makes his way to the bed.

*When the hell is he going to stay out of my head?*

This time he doesn't respond, well at least not with words. He just flashes that devilish smirk.

141

"Here, drink this," he offers. He holds my head up slightly and puts a cup of cool water to my lips.

I down the liquid without a second thought. This is exactly what I need.

"I apologize, Claire. You should have received water the very moment you awoke."

Once the cup is empty, he hands me another. "You have already received something to stop the pain in your head," he states, massaging my temple.

My heart rate starts to pick up.

"Your headache should end soon." He snatches his hand off my temple as if I'd burned him.

"Why are you acting strange, Nicklaus?" I ask, not bothering to put "King" in front of his name. I expect his eyes to flash red and his blood to boil.

Shockingly, he does the opposite. He laughs. "Little feisty thing, your balls grow bolder by the moment. It's nice to see that you're back to your usual self. I truly do apologize for hurting you, Claire."

His words stun me. For a second, he almost has me. I don't know what to say.

"I was listening in on your thoughts when my mother was here," he confesses, climbing onto the bed.

My body visibly goes still. We're lying right beside each other. I can feel his hard chest brush against me, making my mind go blank. He wraps his arms around me, and everything goes haywire. Sparks of electric fire hit me hard, setting my body alight. What is he doing? Better yet, what is my body doing?

I attempt to provide some space between us, but the ache in my body prevents me from moving.

"Claire, calm down. I won't bite you again or dishonor you. I'm going to command that you go to sleep. When you wake up, we should discuss arrangements for finding your parents."

"What? Find my pare—"

"Sleep, Claire," he whispers, then it all goes dark.

# CHAPTER TWENTY-TWO
## WTH

The moon beams through the balcony door when I open my eyes. The beauty of late night is shining into the room. My neck feels stiff, and the throbbing, searing pain is way too hard to ignore. I feel like I'm in a dream state, yet oddly content and at peace.

Strong arms lock me into place. I turn my body over, only to be met by unapologetic, glowing silver-cerulean eyes. King Nicklaus is awake. He is staring into my irises while I feel like I'm looking into the depths of the coldest sea—a dark, roaring, raging sea. I'm lost, adrift even, but I don't want an SOS. His eyes are perfect. The moonlight glowing on his skin makes him look even more desirable. However, in the back of my mind, it feels like something isn't right. I shouldn't be so drawn to him.

He doesn't say a word. He pulls me even closer to his muscular frame. He looks at me, assessing my reaction—obviously waiting for me to oppose or put up a fight. I'm not objecting, even if I should. If I'm going to be completely honest, I have to ask myself, Who would? Rejecting his embrace is like declining the offer to walk through the gates of heaven. No one is that stupid.

I can smell his aromatic cologne and his unique scent. He smells so rich, and it reminds me of cedarwood burning in the fresh, crisp air. It's addicting.

My head is on top of his chest. I know this looks bad since this vampire is my captor, but this feels right. Something is different about us. I can't place my finger on it, but it is. I don't know what happened or when it happened, but I no longer have the desire to stab him with a dagger. I just want to stay in his arms forever and ever, plus another forever. I just want to live in peace alongside him. It may sound silly, but I do, even if we never actually have peace. A girl can't help but imagine a life with him.

*Who am I fooling? There will never be peace between a vampire and a human. I know this.*

A little voice inside me screams at me to snap out of it, but that still doesn't stop me from wrapping my arms around him and snuggling closer. Just for tonight, we can pretend to be something special. If that makes me a nutcase, so be it. I'm going to enjoy my night with him as I lie in his arms.

King Nicklaus—scratch that—my Nicklaus, runs his fingers through my hair. My nerves are shot, especially when another one of his fingers slowly trails down my skin, gently brushing the throbbing pain on the right side of my neck. I shiver. That one single gesture makes my knees feel weak, and I'm not even standing. Can someone please explain to me how this is even possible?

I look into his eyes that are now glowing like lanterns, lighting the room.

"Now that you're awake, I'm going to grab you some food from the kitchen," he tells me, after another moment of lingering silence passes between us.

"I'm not hungry," I quickly respond, stopping him from rolling out of bed. "Please, don't go. I just want to live in this moment. Stay."

I know that I sound desperate, and probably a little hypocritical. Okay, I sound really, really hypocritical. I hate humans that bask in the glory of vampires's affection. I always have something bad to say about them, just as I did to Jadis. Now, look at me, I'm begging for him to stay, just like I begged for his bite. How desperate does that sound?

"You lost a lot of blood, Claire. You need something to eat. Eating food will help you regain your strength." He rolls out of bed and ignores my frustrated sigh and complaints. "Besides, once my venom is out of your system and your high goes down, you will hate me for taking advantage of you."

I make a face. "I'm not high. Now, please come back to bed and take advantage of me, Nicklaus." I poke my lip out—the same way I'd seen other slaves do back at school when they tried to get their fix from a vampire bite. Now I understand their childish behavior. My vision is crystal clear. King Nicklaus is like a drug, and I really want a fix. Suddenly, the desperation of those girls now all makes perfect sense.

"You know, begging is only appealing to me when my fangs and your blood are involved, otherwise, it makes you look like a puppy barking for a bone," he says with a taunting grin. "I can take advantage of you, Claire. I can have my way with you right now, and you won't even put up a fight, but that's no fun. I like it when you fight." His eyes flash demonic red.

The lust he holds for me is swirling inside his red orbs. He shakes his head, as if trying to shake a picture out of it. He is struggling. The monster in him wants to lie with me. The monster in him wants to taste me again. The monster in him wants me just as I want him. I can use that to my advantage.

"Nicklaus, please come back to bed with me. Please, sire," I plead again, the voice not my own.

Maybe he's right. I may be way too high, on cloud nine, and my mind is breezing through the trees. Oh well, I don't give a f*ck. It feels good.

His eyes are back to their normal shade. I can tell he is struggling to contain his laughter. He enjoys this—good!—so, that makes two of us. He pulls me gently out of the bed, and I'm finally back in his warm embrace. I sigh dreamily. Back to heaven I go.

"I won't take advantage of you, nor will I feed on you again." He gently tips my chin up with his index finger. "At least, not until I can remain in control."

"But—"

"I said no, Claire, and that's final. You need your rest. Besides, this is not how I want to claim you." He runs his hands through his hair.

I can't tell he is frustrated with me, or himself. Honestly, I don't really care. I'm just happy to be in his arms. This is exactly where I belong.

"Furthermore"—his voice catches my attention, and his glowing eyes make my heart skip a beat—"when I claim you, and trust me when I say I shall claim you in every way, every single inch of you, I want you to be mine, Claire.

"I want you to be yourself, my firecracker . . . the spirited, defiant, human-sympathizing, vampire-hating girl that you are," he says, not breaking eye contact. "So I won't take advantage of you, but I will make a confession."

His lips curve into an unapologetic smirk. "I will tell you a little secret and then make you forget everything I've said until the time comes for you to learn the truth." He continues to stare into my eyes as I stare into his, waiting for him to continue. "I confess that I will claim you, my little firecracker because every inch of you belongs to me. You are mine."

I feel the air shift around us, and his intense eyes lock me in place.

"I'm your chosen. Hey, that's no secret. We both are aware of that," I tease him, smiling from ear to ear.

He doesn't smile. Nope. There's not an ounce of playfulness I can detect anywhere on his face. He looks rather fierce and hungry, determined even. I can't explain it, but those glowing eyes are holding me captive. My heart starts to hammer, beating like a jungle drum inside my chest.

Nicklaus leans closer into me, only stopping when our faces are a few inches apart. Oh God, help me. He's more perfect than I thought. This close, I can see every detail of his breathtaking features and smooth, flawless skin. The moon shining down on him is not making it better. If anything, the glow makes him look more like a god than a vampire. He's right. I'm high of his venom. That's the only logical explanation why I feel all warm and bubbly inside. I must be higher than a kite.

The air zaps straight through us. His chest moves up and down while he stares at me like I'm his prized possession. I can't move or stop looking into his eyes even if I want to. I can only hear the sound of us breathing hard and heavy. We continue to get lost in each other's stare. The world ceases to exist, and there's nothing around us at this moment. The beautiful glowing moon seems to have evaporated, the bed has dissolved, and the walls have melted. All I can see is Nicklaus. It's just the two of us, sitting on nothing. K-I-S-S-I-N-G.

First comes love, then comes marriage and then comes the baby in the baby carriage. I'm really freaking high. Oh my gosh.

"Claire, you . . ."

The emotion in his voice brings my high down a little. He sighs deeply before finally deciding to get everything off his chest. He huffs, puffs, then blows the houses down. Just kidding. I'm higher than a kite.

"Claire, you are my beloved. I will have you in every way. You belong to me," he states, making my kite explode.

# CHAPTER TWENTY-THREE
## Traits of a Queen

NICKLAUS

I've commanded Claire to fall asleep and forget everything we discussed. I watch her sleep for a moment, admiring her beauty. I love how her plump red lips part slightly as she releases quiet snores. I'm in love with her silky, soft golden waves that have grown a great deal longer over the last couple of weeks. I love her full, luscious lashes that highlight her smoky green eyes. I'm in love with how peaceful she looks when she is asleep. Just watching her sleep makes me feel at peace. I'm in love with her. I'm infatuated with this human girl.

Claire's stunning features and intoxicating scent have somehow managed to make my still heart beat. She has no idea how much control she has over me, and I plan to keep it that way.

I continue to watch her sleeping. She looks paler than usual, but that can be expected since she lost so much blood. I still can't believe I went out of control. Not once had it happened until she came. I have lived for a very long time—six hundred and nineteen years to be exact—and no one's blood has ever put me in a vampire frenzy, except hers. The very first day I laid eyes on her, I knew right then she was special. I had never entertained the auctions, but when I got my hands on her file and read over it, I couldn't get those smoky eyes out of my head. I had no idea she was my beloved until we officially met in person.

The school requested that I mark her as a bleeder. I couldn't allow that, so I did the first thing that came to mind: I claimed her as my chosen. It felt like I was doing the right thing, the only thing to keep her safe; or maybe that was just what I wanted to believe. The truth is that I'm too selfish to let her go. I could have granted her freedom and allowed her to live a life without chains. I could have had her delivered to the hunters, and they would protect her and teach her their ways. She would be happy. Most of all, she'd be safe. The only issue was I couldn't. The urge to claim her as my chosen was very strong. Now, I'm putting her life in jeopardy. My family would have never allowed me to claim her. They would kill her! Everything is my fault, and I would be the cause of her death.

I run my fingers along her soft skin and place a gentle kiss on her forehead. Her beauty bewitches me. I kiss her forehead softly once again and give her one last glance. I leave the room and my sleeping beloved before the sun starts to rise, only to ensure that a servant will bring her breakfast. She hasn't eaten in a while, and I can no longer give her my blood without someone becoming too suspicious of why I'm aiding her. No one but Xander is trustworthy enough to know who she is to me. Cyrus can't even be trusted with my secret even though he's my best friend.

My head is spinning. All I can think about is keeping Claire out of harm's way. I must speak to Xander at once. I consider him my most-trusted adviser despite our occasional disagreements and different upbringings. He must know what to do. He always does. Besides, he has an experience with this type of situation. He shall help ease my roaming thoughts.

Xander and I are so close that our mother hates the bond we share. She has tried everything in her power to break it. I figured her hatred for him stems from the fact that he's a constant reminder of her past—a life she lived long ago when she was Antoinette, a French courtesan. She used to be one of the most-desirable courtesans of her time, but she fell from grace tremendously when she got pregnant with a duke's bastard son.

I also assume that played a part in her hatred for humans. I don't know what she had gone through, but I know it turned her heart cold. Things only became better for her when she met my father, King Apollyon. He is one of the oldest and most-respected vampires of our kind. He is her true beloved. He accepted her completely despite the fact that she was human and already had a child before they met.

My father's bloodline is vampire royalty. The other vampire kings also come from noble families of our vampire monarchy. My family had been the ruler of our kind long before the Awakening was even thought of.

In my father's eyes, I was nothing but a spoiled, privileged brat. He didn't think I was ready for the throne. Nothing I did was ever good enough for him. In fact, I waited for a very long time before I got to take the seat on the throne.

My sister Daniela is a born ruler according to our father. If she had been born a boy, I'm pretty sure he would have handed her the throne on a silver platter. She is his favorite while he resents me just like my mother resents Xander, that's why Xander and I understand each other so well.

My father abdicated the throne when I successfully won the Awakening War. Now, nothing or no one can stop me from ruling how I see fit. The Awakening has placed our kind higher than we have ever been. My family is no longer just a ruler over our kind but over other species as well. I finally did something right in my father's eyes—I claimed the world.

He has never been more proud, but that will all end if I claim Claire as my beloved. Before the Awakening, we could claim our true beloveds regardless of their species. However, times have changed, and so have our laws. We cannot turn humans no matter who they are. In order to stay on top, we vampires have to breed with our own kind. We cannot have a turned ruler because it would shift the balance of power. We should view humans as nothing but food to us.

Claire has proven many times she will protect a human with her life. She will not understand our laws. Only a trueborn vampire can understand their importance. My queen must rule with an iron fist, and our trueborn women are groomed to play that role. Each and every one of them comes from respected vampire families. They are strong, beautiful, and vicious. They will ensure that our enemies are crushed and our slaves stay in their place.

My people deserve a strong queen, and my father has chosen Lady Gwen. He truly believes she's the best candidate. After our first courting, I accepted the arrangements without question. Lady Gwen presented herself as the strongest candidate. I even believed she was born to rule by my side. She is strong, beautiful, and deadly. She also cares about the well-being of our people. She is the queen that my subjects need, but Claire is what my heart needs. I can choose to claim Lady Gwen for my people's benefit or claim my beloved for my own benefit. I'm torn.

My people will never accept Claire, and if I keep her around, I'm not sure how much longer I can control my emotions. My kind will see her as a threat. They won't like the fact that their king is claiming a human. Even my own family would want her head on a spike. They will try anything in their power to eliminate her, but I can't allow that. I will protect her from my entire race if I have to, even if it means risking my life.

After sending a servant to deliver Claire's breakfast, I make my way to Xander's wing.

I have been standing at his door for a while now, debating with myself whether I should go in or get back to Claire.

"How much longer are you going to stand out there?" Xander asks, opening the door.

I accept his unspoken invitation.

"I'm busy. You have five seconds to tell me what you want, Little Brother," he says, using the nickname he only uses in private. He crosses his arms.

Good! He's not that mad.

"Four seconds."

"I need to talk about Claire." I run my hand over my hair, then I shift my gaze to meet his own.

Xander's face softens. His arms are still crossed, and I can tell he is still irritated. At least he's not counting anymore.

"What did you mean when you said you know who Claire is to me? Everyone knows she is my chosen."

"Nicklaus, you can't make a fool out of me. Claire is your beloved. I know, and you know that. Soon everyone will know if you don't keep your emotions in check."

He's right; he always is. He wouldn't be my big brother if he wasn't.

"How am I supposed to do that? Claire isn't just any human. She makes it almost impossible to stay in control. She's defiant, challenging, stubborn, beautiful, and she's—"

"Fit to rule as a queen."

"What?"

Now Xander has lost his marbles. I didn't expect him to sound so shallow. He knows very well that a human can never rule as a queen. He knows our laws were made for a reason.

"You know that's impossible. Our people will never accept it. How can—"

"Our people can go to hell! Their ego and sense of dominance over Claire's race are the only reasons they will refuse her. We have sacrificed enough to live out your father's dreams, and I have lost enough. You have two choices. You can let her go, and I will protect her and allow her to live freely in my kingdom, or you can claim her and not make the same mistakes that I have."

"It's not that simple. You know that better than anyone. She is human. Our people will do everything in their power to

153

remove her from the crown. They will slaughter humans just to hurt her. I can't allow her to be hurt because of me."

"They won't touch her. I won't let anyone hurt Claire. She is your beloved, your other half. She was born for you. She was born to rule." He walks over to a chessboard.

"I was born to hold the crown and lead by example."

"What's a king without his queen, Little Brother?" He throws the queen chess piece in my direction. "Your crown will never be secure without your true queen holding your left hand."

"I have a queen."

"Gwen is not meant to be your queen!" he yells, throwing the pawn chess piece. He storms out of the door, going to check on my beloved, I'm sure.

For a long while, I continue to stare at the chess pieces. I'm not too fond of the game. It's more of Xander's thing, but I do know that the queen is the most-powerful piece. She can change everything; Claire can change everything.

# CHAPTER TWENTY-FOUR
## The Truth Will Set You Free

CLAIRE

"Wakey, wakey, wakey . . ."

Xander's deep voice breaks into my consciousness like a character straight out of a horror movie, disturbing my very comfortable slumber.

*Go away.*

"Wake up, brave one. It's time for your first lesson."

*Go away! Go away! I never liked school.*

"Claire, wake up."

*So, he's not going to go away?*

"No, I'm not. We have less than three days before the new moon, which means you have less than seventy-two hours to make your first move."

*I don't want to move. Nope. I want to stay right here, wrapped in these silk sheets, sleeping on this fluffy silk pillow on this comfortable big bed. Yes, this is the life—sleeping my life away in this bombass bed. I like it.*

Xander must have finally learned how to stay out of my head because he doesn't respond.

*Thank you. Thank you. Thank you. I knew my smart mouth would eventually pay off. Thank you, Miss Smarty-pants, for gluing the blood monster's mouth shut. I would have made a kick-ass big sister, chasing my sibling's bad dreams away.*

155

I'm very close to catching some more *zzz*s and extremely close to snoring when I hear plates clattering and the most-delightful smell invades my senses.

*F\*ck! The blood monster comes with reinforcements. He is breaking down my defense. He knows I can't win against this smell—this mouthwatering aroma of maple syrup, butter, and pancakes! Oh geez, it would even wake me up from my deathbed.*

I open my eyes and see Xander standing in the center of the room. He is holding a platter filled with stacks of pancakes topped with powdered sugar and dripping with maple syrup. My stomach roars, and I quickly jump out of bed.

Xander grins like a Cheshire cat, showing off his pearly white fangs. "The school is required to document every single time a student misbehaves," he states proudly. He moves the plate filled with fluffy heaven from left to right, my eyes following it. "With that being said, it wasn't that hard to find out about your little arrangement with the school cooks."

*Oh my gosh! I can't believe they actually documented how many times I bribed the cooks. So what? Who wouldn't blackmail a person to make pancakes?*

That's a little too much, don't you think? No one should know that I would do anything, I mean anything in my power, to have those delicious flour cakes with sugary contents on top. They are just that good.

I lick my lips. "Okay, you win. I will complete whatever lesson you want me to study. Just give me those goddamn pancakes."

Xander smirks triumphantly. I'm starting to hate that deadly, beautiful, evil, goddamn smirk of his. He passes me the tray and nods after I grab it. I could only hope it is a gesture indicating that I can now eat. With or without it, I will dive in anyway.

The moment the tray is in my hand, I waste no time doing exactly what I said: diving right in, devouring the fluffy and heavenly pancakes that taste as good as they smell.

Xander is watching me with a smug look on his face, looking like a kid gifted with a shiny new toy. He has found my weakness. He clears his throat (for the effect, I'm sure). "Now that I brought you breakfast in bed, we can start with your first lesson of the day."

"I meant what I said. I didn't do that well in school. Vampire curriculum was never my thing, but you already know that with you having my file and all, don't you?" I ask, making air quotes with my fingers just to add my own effect.

Ha, two can play that game!

"You're right." Xander pulls a folder from behind his back.

*Where did that come from? I know the pancakes were a perfect distraction, but I still should have noticed the folder, especially with my picture attached to it.*

"You earned a *D* in vampire studies, which means there's room for improvement for you to learn more about our history, society, and culture. That also tells me that you passed some lessons." He pauses, raising his eyebrow. "If I had to take a guess . . . I'm banking on you having passed the vampire sociology lesson. Right?" He pauses again, lost in his own thoughts, pondering.

"You received an *F* in slave hospitality, an *F* in marketing, an *F* in linguistics, an *F* in agriculture and forestry, an *F* in merchandise, and a *D* in chemistry, physics, earth science, and biology. Your mathematics courses are decent, and so are your dining skills"—he shrugs his shoulders—"after watching you eat."

I feel like I'm in the headmaster's office again for the thousandth time in my life as I continue to devour the delicious pancakes, sucking my fingers and tuning out as much as possible. This is exactly why I hated school so much. We are expected to be excellent and meet certain standards, without room for faults. We are expected to pass stupid tests on what another species expects us to know when really, we should be taught how to turn a negative into a positive and work on our flaws. Life is not about being excellent. It is about making mistakes and living and learning how

157

not to make the same mistake twice. If Xander wants to teach me anything, he should be showing me how to flip my negatives into positives, not point out what he thinks I failed in, based on lessons that someone else believes I should know.

Xander stops talking, just to further study my file. I hate that file. I hate that another person—or vampire—has a piece of paper to tell others their observations of me. No one knows me but me. F*ck that piece of paper.

Xander clears his throat again. "As I stated before, the schools my kind built are meant to break and classify you." He throws the file in the air, then shifts his attention to me. "I don't want to break you, Claire. I don't want you to be the perfect little pet or a grade-A student who sees the world how I expect you to see it," he states, finally gaining my attention.

He makes his way to me, and I stare at him blankly. He returns my stare with his beautiful, stormy gray eyes. Usually, his eyes are icy gray, like the snow. Now I don't understand why they suddenly take the shade of a tornado. I'm only used to vampire eyes turning red. I have no idea what it means when they darken. Maybe I should have paid attention in school, just maybe.

"I don't want to classify you and place you where I believe you belong. No, I don't want that at all."

"So, what do you want?" I place my plate on the nightstand.

I don't have time for his riddles. It's time for answers. Does Xander want to play teacher? Okay, he can play teacher as long as he wants, but I will ask questions.

"You know what they say, 'No question is a dumb question'," I quote Ms. Fox.

"The real question is, What do you want?" he asks, using reverse psychology.

Not knowing how to reply, I remain quiet and just continue to look at him blankly. He takes a seat beside me, and the entire bed sinks due to his big frame. We stare at each other quietly

158

for a long-drawn-out moment, and I find myself getting lost in his dark stare.

*Xander is a handsome vampire. He makes me nervous sometimes, but I can't compare how nervous I feel around his brother. Thinking of that makes me wonder where King Nicklaus is. The last time I saw him was when they were arguing. I miss him a little. Okay, I miss him a lot, but no one needs to know that.*

"Aww, that's sweet," murmurs Xander, poking out his lips to make a smooching sound.

My cheeks grow hot and red. Goodness gracious, vampires with their damn mind-reading powers!

I look away, but he continues to stare at me. My cheeks are flaming red from this sudden change of topic. Someone, please save me.

"Don't be shy, Claire. It's okay to like him."

"I don't know what you're talking about." I shrug, staring out of the window. My cheeks probably look like tomatoes right now.

"Right. Let's just tackle one task at a time. I need to know what you want, Claire." His smile widens as he changes the subject. "Be honest. I want you to think like you're talking to another human."

*Right. That's easier said than done. Xander might be the nicest, sweetest, and most-easygoing vamp I know, but he is still a vamp. He is still a big, fast, powerful, sexy, and malicious vampire.*

"Hey, you'd had me until you called me malicious," he teases, obviously reading my mind again.

I turn to face him. "Stay out of my head, Xander."

"I won't have to be in your head if you just tell me what you want." He flashes his pearly white fangs.

Well, he has a point, but I won't admit that to him. He is already cocky enough, and that smile? My God, that freaking smile of his!

"Well, right now"—I smile back—"I want to wipe that perfect, sparkly white smile off your perfect vamp face."

He wanted honesty, so how's that for honesty?

Xander laughs a melodious laugh, and I can't help but join in. He is such a cool vampire. We laugh for a long time, only stopping to catch our breaths and then going right back to laughing again—a laughing party. I have never experienced anything like this.

"Xander, you are such a joy," I admit in between fits of giggles.

He freezes and then pats my lap, finally settling down. He is smiling, but it's not that genuine smile that I received only moments ago. The air in the room shifts completely, going stiff.

*Wait, did I say something wrong? Freak, I'm not good at having a good time. Is it really a crime to say someone is a joy? Is that some kind of vampire no-go area? I don't think it is. Freak. Good job, Claire. You really know how to ruin the mood.*

He stands up and turns to face the window. "You never answered my question, Claire. What do you want?"

"I want to die."

He snaps his neck in my direction. His eyes quickly shift to a blazing red as I gaze into them.

I hold up my hand to stop him from interrupting and take a deep breath. "I want to be free," I say. "I want to live a life without chains. I want to live without fear and worry that today will be my last. I yearn to see my people out of slavery. I yearn to see human children grow up with their parents and siblings. I want to see humans going to school to be taught about our history. I yearn to see humans simply being humans, not pets, not chosens, not slaves, not breeders, not bleeders, or whatever label your bloody kind sticks on us.

"I want to be free. I want my people to be free and far away from the ones who call themselves masters. The only way I will achieve that type of freedom is by death. We all will be free by death."

Anger seeps through my pores, and I know I have the right to feel that way. Vampires are the reason for it—Xander, Nicklaus, and every one of those vampire kings who conquered the world.

Just thinking about what I want and knowing that I will never have them makes me angry. Being human makes me angry. Hell! Just being Claire, a name they gave me, even makes me angry.

Xander doesn't say anything right away. His eyes are still burning red, ablaze with the anger of his own. I know my words about his kind hurt him. However, in my defense, he asked for the truth.

Seconds turn into minutes and then it starts to feel like hours of silence. His eyes begin to shift from red to a dark, stormy gray. He has never appeared to be so scary. Since day one, he has always been the opposite of what I expected him to be. He has proven everyone wrong. Now, I'm not so sure.

I hold my head high, keeping my eyes locked on his. I will show no fear. He asked for the truth, and I told him.

"Talk about mood change," states Xander, in an attempt to lighten the mood. Once again, he proves to be different—the cool vamp.

I lower my head and take a moment to hold my emotions in check.

Xander slowly approaches me, only stopping an inch away. "I'm not allowing you to die, Claire." He tips my chin up with his finger. "I will never allow anything or anyone to hurt you again. Now that you have told me you want freedom, tell me how else you can achieve it. Death is not an option."

Teary-eyed, I look into his eyes filled with emotion. "I honestly don't know, Xander."

He releases me and walks away, leaving me with my own thoughts.

I feel bad for saying mean things about his kind. Xander is truly the kindest person. He didn't deserve my foul words.

He returns with a fitted long white dress with delicate lace features and a nude silk slip underneath to appear as though I'm naked under the lace.

"First you must look the part." He smiles from ear to ear. There goes that dreamy, pearly white smile. "And then we can play my favorite game." He pauses, just for a second. "We are going to play chess."

# CHAPTER TWENTY-FIVE
## A Mural of Tales

When we first walk into the library, I stop right in my tracks and go rigid. The view takes my breath away. Rows and rows of books placed in beautiful and tall oak bookshelves are all around me—not to mention the several gold globes, fancy gadgets, and ancient artifacts. It's a room filled with antique treasures, and I'm totally stunned; even more so when I look up and find myself staring at a vaulted ceiling with a mural that depicts different events throughout history. The artist did an amazing job. He or she truly took the time to create and tell the stories in great detail.

There's portraiture of a very fair, fiery red-headed woman. She is wearing gold armor and a golden crown while slaying her attackers with a golden sword. She is a queen, fighting alongside her men. They conquer their enemies by an ocean that holds at least a hundred ships. The queen is victorious; her crown is secured.

There is another story on the left side of the arch. It's about a man who fights with great skill, yet in the end, he is defeated on a smoky battlefield and is left to bleed to death. He has inky-black hair and chilling ice-blue eyes that are strikingly similar to Xander's icy irises. Over the top of the man is a boy with skin as white as snow, glowing red eyes, and sharp, pointy fangs. The boy isn't a boy at all but a vampire in his true form. His fangs are plunged into the human man's skin, leaving a trail of red blood in his wake.

I study the green paint that is used for the grass. It smears faintly with the red that creates blood. The artist painted the perfect picture with a swish of his paintbrush, somehow managing to express the pain that came along with this story.

My favorite part of the mural is the one I can relate to the most—the Awakening. This portion of the painting puts the reality of my species on full display.

A beautiful girl with chestnut hair and coffee-colored eyes is the most-attractive female I've ever seen. There is something wild and gentle about her, blending together as one. She is standing over top of a man. She is holding his heart and suddenly crushes it, and red paint slowly drips down. The man stands to his feet and walks into a room of four scary vampires and a raven-haired man who is sitting on a throne. He leaves with another man on a horse and eventually meets up with six more. The men ride together on the day when the sun is covered. They take millions of humans. They rip seven men's heads off after torturing them for countless days. I'm able to quickly identify the men with no heads. They were our human world leaders.

As the story goes on, you see humans painted with various colors. Their offsprings—my generation—are born in silver chains. Humans running for their lives are blended with Irish-green and electric blue paint. The moon blocks the sun, burning yellow, and jet-black ink swirls to life—an eclipse.

A cage of werewolves and other creatures are the highlight of the story. They are all locked away. The eight vampires kings, with smiles on their faces, are the ones holding the keys.

My emotions run wild, and my heart rate increases by the second. The detailed colors bring each story to life. I can feel the mood behind the brush, the feelings of the artist. There's a deep connection. I can't explain it, but it's there. I know for certain the artist was excited, thrilled, and satisfied while painting the Awakening portion of the mural. Each stroke of my species's downfall brought forth happiness. That fact gives me chills.

I shake my head and continue to admire the work of art. The sun shines brightly throughout the room, its golden light beaming through the glass.

To be honest, the artist did a fantastic job of capturing the viewer's attention. The blend of colors running together forms a horrific reality that captivates me. Every painting makes me feel as if I lived during those times and experienced each story with my own eyes.

"I'm sorry to be the bearer of bad news, but most vampires are not affected by the sun," Xander says quietly, extending his hand into the ray of sunlight.

"I'm aware." I sigh, drawing in a deep breath.

I figured that out long ago. Some myths are just myths. Sunlight doesn't hurt all vampires, neither does garlic. I once tried to use the golden light against one of my teachers back at school. Who would have thought that one simple miscalculation could cause me so much?

Once upon a time, I longed to feel that golden ray of light beaming down onto my skin since the teachers at our school rarely allowed us to soak up vitamin D. They kept us caged like animals, leading me to believe that they were afraid of the sun and that the myths were true. (Some of them are, but not all of them.)

I wanted my freedom, and I felt like the sun was my chance, so I used that to my advantage. Well, at least, I thought I did. I snuck out and spent a day in the sun. I tried to escape using the sun as my protection, but that was the day I lost it all, the same day I lost my innocence. It was the first time reality really sank in. The day I lost a part of myself was the day I decided to die, because that had to be better than living under their rule.

That was the day I've been trying to forget for the past four years.

I close my eyes, forcing the images out of my head. *Please, go away. I don't want to remember.*

165

"If the sun is not your interest, what is, brave one?" Xander asks, thankfully staying out of my head.

I turn to face him with a forced smile. "The painting," I say shyly, leaning my head back to view the mind-blowing piece of art once more.It's really amazing. I could stand here and look at it all day."

Xander crosses his arms behind his back. "It took the artist three years to complete one side of the mural, another five years to start on the other side . . . twenty years to finish the mural completely," Xander informs, as he admires it alongside me. "He would always say that something was missing, not enough red or not enough blue. He spent countless hours to perfect his craft, and I must admit his hard work pays off."

"Who?" I turn to face him. "Who is the artist?"

Xander's lips curl into that devilish smirk.

Oh, God, I hate that smirk.

"I'll make you a deal. If you beat me in a game of chess, I will tell you."

*Okay, that should be easy enough.*

Boy was I wrong! Beating Xander in chess is a lot easier said than done.

Now, when you think about chess, the first thing that comes to mind is a little board and two players, but that's too boring for the vampire king of Antarctica. When Xander plays chess, he believes it is a real-life game. His idea of chess is a life-size chessboard with mega chess pieces. They are so big. I probably could ride the horse.

It doesn't stop there. Nope. It only gets better. The pieces move with a tap, and when you make the wrong move, they die, like boom! They explode and disappear, only to reappear on the sideline to remind you of your epic failure. For the past four hours, I have been too familiar with that feeling of defeat.

"Pay attention, Claire. Your pawn is on the fourth space. Your entire strategy is off."

166

He's been saying this over and over although we just started. I move left, he says it's a wrong move. I move right, he knocks my pawn over.

"You must learn how to move your pawns," he reminds me for the thousandth time. "Correctly!" he yells.

His pawn is on the fifth rank. I move my pawn two squares in a single move, then—boom!—he captures my pawn, and the feeling of failure is back again.

*I really think he is taking advantage of me. That's right. I think he's cheating.*

"I'm not cheating. You just make it too easy. If you place your focus on the game, you may actually get somewhere."

He invades my privacy once again.

I run to his side of the board and kick his queen square in the face. "Pay attention to that, sucker. Checkmate!"

Now, he gets some of that failure juice.

"How about we take a break?" He laughs, jumping off the chessboard.

"How did you get a life-size chess set by the way?" I ask, like seriously. "And how the hell does it move?"

"Aurora." He disappears into one of the many rows of books.

*Who is Aurora?* I think, making a mental note to ask him.

I look around the library once more, intrigued by the grandeur of it. I get lost in thought and don't even realize when Xander comes back, or that we have gained company.

"What are you doing here, Nicklaus?" Xander queries. "I didn't expect to see you for some time."

"I was just admiring the view," responds Nicklaus, stopping everything in the room.

The universe freezes as his eyes lock on mine. We are chained in place as we stare at each other. He is all I see at the moment. The fire in his eyes is telling me I have his undivided attention. He is just as beautiful as the mural overhead. He is so tall,

167

muscular, and lean—cut to perfection. Every time he walks into a room, it goes still. The couches, beds, lamps, and now even the books seem to go into hiding. The power that radiates off him is intimidating. I have never felt anything similar to be able to describe the feeling, but something is different about him, or about us. King Nicklaus has always been attractive to me. Which vampire isn't? However, this feeling is new, strange, and frightening.

I run my tongue over my lips like I'm about to sink my teeth into a slab of juicy meat. King Nicklaus is wearing black slacks—which do little justice to hiding his toned and muscular legs—and a white T-shirt that fits him like a glove, hugging his well-defined six-pack (filet mignon indeed). He has never seemed to look so freaking good. I can't take my eyes off him.

He smiles, revealing his straight white teeth and pointy fangs.

Now why did he have to do that? My heart races as vision of the two of us in his soft silk bedsheets making sweet passionate love in a dance of sex tango rushes through my head like a flood.

*What the hell! Snap out of it, Claire, right now! What has gotten into me? This is not our first meeting. I have seen this man for plenty of occasions. Yes, he has always been hot. He has always appeared to be dangerous as well, of course, so why the hell am I dreaming about snatching off his pants or running my fingers down his well-crafted chest and screaming his name over and over for the entire world to hear? Why, why, why?*

*Freak! Snap out of it, Claire, right freaking now! He can read your thoughts, remember? Earth to Claire, come back to reality.*

I finally draw the strength to turn away from King Nicklaus. I desperately hope and pray that he didn't read my mind. But all my hope is gone when his lips curl into a sheepish grin, followed by a look of amusement. Clearly, he is holding back his laughter. His actions tell it all.

*The assh\*le was in my head. Freak, freak, freak!*

My cheeks become hot and begin to burn bright pink.

"Now that you two are finished eye-f*cking each other," says Xander, adding more to my embarrassment, "what can I help you with?" He turns to face his brother.

King Nicklaus smiles charmingly. "Your governor has arrived. Also, I came for my chosen."

My heart beats frantically.

*I cannot be around him with my mind scrambling, absolutely not. Hopefully, Xander will find a way to help me.*

"Very well," replies Xander, switching his focus to me. "This is for you. When you have free time, I suggest you read this." He hands me a book titled *The Vampire Studies*.

*Oh great.*

"I promise, it is not as boring as it sounds," he adds, reading my mind. "Once you're finished with this one, you can start reading *The Studies of the Supernatural*. I shall have my chosen deliver it to your room."

*Now, why would you do that?*

"Thank you." I choose to voice a different response, not wanting to sound rude.

Xander smiles and takes a bow before making his departure.

# CHAPTER TWENTY-SIX
## You're Burning Me Alive

My palms are sweaty, and my heart rate increases the moment Xander steps out of the room, leaving me all alone with this sex god.

"Why are you so nervous?" King Nicklaus takes a step forward, and I take a step back. "Your heart is beating loud enough that it could pop my eardrums."

"Uh, I'm not nervous . . ."

He doesn't need to know the effect he has on me. Gosh, can a girl catch a break?

"Really? It seems like you are. Your heartbeats say you are."

"I-I am not. I'm fine," I quickly lie.

Why does it matter if I'm nervous anyway?

"Hmmm, your palms are dripping with sweat."

"Oh. Um, Xander and I were playing chess. It's a game of great thought."

"Most certainly. It takes a great mind to excel in chess, just like it takes a lot of skill to read another person's mind. And your mind is screaming how nervous you are."

*Freak, he's caught me there. Ewww, why does he have to be a mind-reader?*

"I can still hear you, you know?" He winks.

*Gosh, that's so annoying.*

"So, we have three days before we journey to North America," he changes the subject.

*Thank God!*

"As my chosen, you will be with me at all times. That means sometimes you may be placed in dangerous situations."

*Danger? Ha! I laugh in the face of danger. Haha.*

"Claire, this is not a joke!" he snaps. "I have declared war against another barbaric species." His voice is low, dangerously low. "They will rip your heart out with their bare hands and feast on your liver while your heart takes the last beat. Werewolves are wild and dangerous. They will kill you. This"—he taps my heart with his finger—"will be theirs to do with as they please if you don't take this matter more seriously," he warns, giving me chills.

"Okay," I respond quietly. I can no longer hide how nervous I feel. Okay, I may be scared, shaking-in-my-boots scared, but not of werewolves. I'm not a punk. It's his tone now that's scary. Well, maybe I'm a punk when he's involved.

"I won't let anything happen to you, Claire." He takes another step toward me. "You must be able to defend yourself. If opportunity presents itself, you must know how to fight. That way, I'll feel better."

King Nicklaus makes me feel all bubbly inside. His words send another wave of icicles to erupt inside my heart and explode into my core. His words make me feel special and confused—very, very confused. Why would he care about me? I'm just a slave, his chosen. There's nothing special about that. He shouldn't care, and it shouldn't matter if I'm alive or dead because I can be replaced quicker than any werewolf could rip my heart out.

"I'm going to train you." He takes another step forward.

Now we're only inches apart—oh geez, I'm going to explode into a million and one pieces.

"I will teach you basic defense techniques, like how to throw a punch and dodge an incoming attack. By the end of our lesson, you will be able to handle yourself well enough. I'll make sure of it." He tucks a loose strand of my hair behind my ear and then runs his hand down my head, softly stroking my golden waves.

Whoosh, I'm suddenly on fire. Did somebody turn up the heat? I'm now drenched in sweat, my heart pounding. I'm one hundred percent certain his eardrums pop. The close proximity of our bodies is making me lose focus. I'm jello. Nope, scratch that. I'm a roasted marshmallow, hot and ready to be the center of this vampire s'more. He's the Graham crackers, ready to sandwich me in. Oh my God, someone please come and save me.

He turns and makes his way to the door, providing me with much-needed space before I pass out from a hot flash.

I wipe the sweat from my forehead. Yup, it's that serious.

*I may be a little extra, but this vamp is really that hot. I'm sure he can hear my thoughts loud and clear.*

"My guards will be in shortly to walk you to our chambers so you can get changed, then to the training arena."

*Our chambers?*

"I'll be there right away," King Nicklaus adds, obviously ignoring my thoughts. "Then we shall start with our first lesson. Don't give them any trouble," he instructs, his tone leaving no room for arguments.

I nod, only because I'm incapable of speaking. I can still feel his fingers running through my hair. My voice box has disintegrated. He doesn't comment on it, thank God!

I'm not sure I can still handle hearing that deep intoxicating voice of his. I may do something stupid, like jump in his arms and officially melt there.

*Oh gosh, Claire get it together. Ugh, I'm super pathetic.*

He watches me for a while longer before taking his leave. Those eyes—his piercing, icy eyes—are swirling a shade of deep-sea blue. I admire them as he quickly slips out of the door. That beautiful midnight-blue color makes my blood boil and my body blaze like an inferno, burning me alive and drenching my soul.

*     *     *

NICKLAUS

When I walk into the room and see Claire standing under the sunlight in that long white dress that hugs her tiny, curvy frame perfectly, it takes every ounce of my self-control not to pick her up in my arms and give in to my body's true desire. I want her so badly. I want her more than I've ever wanted another creature's blood. She is driving me crazy, past the point of insanity. The worst part of it is she isn't even doing anything special. Just one look at her has me speechless. I feel like a human boy crushing on his high school teacher. I'm hooked!

Xander is laughing at me. I can hear his thoughts. Of course, he refuses to block them. He wants me to know he's fully aware of the effect Claire has on me. And judging on the increase of her heart rate, she feels the same way.

After telling Xander about his governor's arrival and admitting to him and myself that I came for her, he leaves us alone without a second thought. I notice he is preparing Claire mentally for her life as a royal. He believes we can make this work. He has faith in her. I want to have faith in her as well. Maybe one day I shall.

Claire is special. She has changed me without even trying. If she can make my frozen heart form a beat, there's no telling what she is capable of. If only she had been born a vampire, she would make a strong trueborn queen. Claire is courageous, beautiful, kindhearted, headstrong, and brave. If only she could protect herself, she would be a force to be reckoned with.

Who am I kidding? She is already a force of nature. She just needs to be trained properly, and I'm going to be the one to do that.

Claire's thudding heart disrupts my train of thought. She's nervous. I can see sweat beading in her tiny little palms. She is so

173

fragile, sort of like a porcelain china doll that brings me back to my current thoughts.

We are going to North America, and I still have my worries. What if a werewolf attacks us? What if something happens to me? She would be in the outside world alone. I must train her.

The thought of something happening to her scares me sh*tless, enough to destroy me. It causes a fire of raw emotions to roar up and burn me alive.

I inform her about her training after teasing her about how nervous she is. I can't help myself. Claire makes it almost impossible not to tease her. I enjoy teasing her, maybe a little too much. I love hearing her heart pound—beating louder by the second—and the way it skips a beat with every step I take.

The golden color of her hair shines brightly as it blazes under the sun, highlighting her rare and radiant green eyes that are enhanced by her long, full lashes. Her beauty is bewitching. Everything about her is rich and fierce, and magnificent. She looks like a queen. Her beauty sets the room on fire just by standing in the center of it like a devouring, radiating light ablaze with orange and yellow.

I want to stroke her hair and trail kisses down her milky skin. The thoughts running through her mind create a wildfire that spreads throughout my body, burning me alive and begging me to capture those soft, full red lips. I want to give her what she wants right here, fast and hard, but I can't. I'll have to settle for just a touch.

I reach for her, nearly losing it the moment I trail my fingers through her silky, soft hair. I need to put space between us before I give our bodies exactly what they want.

*Oh f*ck her sweet and naughty mind. I can't concentrate. I don't know how the hell I'm going to last. I need to go now.*

After mind-linking with her new guards and telling her not to give them any trouble, I jet. I have to. My control is slipping, but not without looking at her one more time.

174

*F\*ck! I think I just . . .*

The volcano erupts inside my pants. How f*cking great!

*Come on, man. I have turned down countless trueborn vampire women walking into my room naked and begging me to allow them just to taste me, only to explode because I touched her hair? What am I, ten? The f\*cking irony.*

I walk in the hallway with my head down. I pass some soldiers, and it really is a walk of shame. I have never been so embarrassed in my entire existence.

*     *     *

After taking a shower in Xander's chambers, I quickly get dressed.

*"Have you picked up my chosen?"* I mind-link with Astrid. She's one of my highest-ranking lieutenants and one of the vampires on Claire's new security detail who knows her sh*t.

*"Yes, Your Highness. The human is talking about how much the vampire race sucks ass. Excuse my French. I believe she is purposely attempting to get under the commander's skin after ignoring her request to stop at the kitchen."*

Now, that makes me chuckle. Commander Vlad has been assigned to her as well. They are the real deal. Leave it up to my little firecracker to give them a hard time, especially after I told her not to.

Vlad and Astrid have been ordered to discreetly guard her when she's in the slave quarters and then walk her to different locations when Xander and I are unable to do so. She will hate it. However, I'm not leaving anything up to the chance. Cyrus's interaction with Claire has taught me a great deal. I figured his ulterior motive. He always has a reason for doing something that can frighten Claire. I will never admit to him that Claire means a lot to me, and he knows it. He must have already realized. He sent me a message without really saying anything, secretly looking out for me like he always does. That's just how he is.

*"Stop at the kitchen and allow her to eat,"* I instruct.

*"But, Your Highness—"*

I growl. I don't like to hear buts. My word is final. Only a few get a chance to question me, and my soldiers are none of them.

*"My apologies, Your Highness."*

I'm sure she drops to her knees at that very moment. I can imagine Claire's facial expression right now as she watches Astrid's action—priceless.

*"I did not mean any harm,"* she continues. *"My only concern is the human's safety."*

*"What do you mean? Isn't it why I assigned the two of you to her?"*

*"Lady Gwen and her guest Master Azazel are in the west-wing kitchen."*

My vision is tinted red. My temperature rises. Master Azazel is the pervert that raped Claire. Xander publicly whipped him and told a crowd of vampires why he did it, making it impossible for me to just kill him on the spot. I'm the king. I can kill who I want when I want, but Xander's slip of control saved Master Azazel's life. I stopped Xander just for the sake of appearance. I'll dispose of Master Azazel when I get the chance. Until then, I need to keep Claire far away from him.

*"Take her to my private kitchen and order the chef to cook whatever she wants."*

*"Yes, Your Highness."*

# CHAPTER TWENTY-SEVEN
## Mr. Meany and the Little Old Lady

CLAIRE

King Nicklaus's guards arrive, one female vampire and one male vampire. Neither of them is very friendly, but at least the female has enough manners to introduce herself.

Lieutenant Astrid is very attractive, just like the rest of the leeches. She has long dark-burgundy hair and stunning greenish-hazel eyes. She looks like she can kick someone's ass. Yup, she's a tough one, but there's no fear in my heart. Astrid is a beauty, sure. No big deal. Show me a vampire that isn't. I, for one, have learned my lesson with these bloodsuckers. Everything that glitters is not gold. In other words, looks can be deceiving. I guess it's safe to say I really don't fancy Astrid that much.

The other vamp doesn't tell me his name. He's also extremely attractive—tall, lean, and fair. He has blond hair and a face carved to perfection. He is a lean, mean, blond fighting machine. This man looks dangerous—and an assh*le, a big giant assh*le. I've chosen a name for him: Mr. Meany. I really don't fancy him either. Stupid leech refuses to allow me to stop and get something to eat. Mr. Meany chooses to ignore me, so I'm going to have fun annoying him. See how that works. He's playing an assh*le, and I'm playing a jerk.

Did I mention how good I am at getting under people's skin? Well, if I didn't, I'm here to tell you I'm the best.

"Your race sucks," is my first insult, and it's only the beginning. "Vampires suck ass." I smile brightly from ear to ear.

I might be annoying Astrid as well. She has been caught in the crossfire, but I don't care. Oh well, Mr. Meany started this. I shall finish it.

"What's a vampire's favorite soup?" I look directly into his eyes.

Mr. Meany has a lot more patience than the others I've encountered, surprisingly enough.

He continues to ignore me.

"Scream of tomatoes," I quip.

Neither one of them laughs, but I do. I'm cracking the hell up.

"Why do vampires scare people?" I move my eyes back and forth between the two of them. "Any takers? Come on, one of you must know the answer."

Again, they remain silent as they walk beside me through the hallway like zombies. That's exactly why the answer to my question already has me rolling on the inside.

"Okay, I'll tell you. Vampires scare people because they're bored to death." I burst out laughing. "Get it?" I laugh hysterically. "Bored to death."

Obviously, they don't get it. Mr. Meany keeps on walking silently while twirling a pocket knife in his left hand. Astrid, on the other hand, seems to be lost in thought. You would think she's talking to herself the way her eyes close for a second and then open. You would think she is measuring something out in her mind, or should I say, she is measuring me out in her mind? I don't miss the curious glances she shoots me every once in a while. She is weird.

I laugh so hard that I almost pee myself. Seriously, I'm dying. Oh boy, this is going to be a long walk for both of them. I have more than enough vampire jokes to last them a lifetime. Mr. Meany is in for it.

Astrid stops in her tracks, then bows down. She seems worried. Her entire body tenses, and her head is so low that it almost touches the floor.

*What the hell! Is she praying? I have been told I can be extremely annoying but not that annoying, not enough to make someone drop to their knees and pray.*

Mr. Meany suddenly stops walking as well. His body goes still like a statue. He doesn't move or flinch, or even breathe. I wave my hand in front of his face just to see if he is still alive. Mr. Meany doesn't respond, not with words at least. Nope. He is frozen, but his eyes turn red as he stares directly into mine, daring me to try that again. There is something lethal and threatening hidden in their depths.

*Okay, so I guess I'm taking things a little too far.*

I cross my arms over my chest, refusing to meet his stare at the moment. He straightens me right up.

Astrid stands to her feet and stares directly at Mr. Meany. I can tell with their facial expressions that they are having a private conversation. It's weird—the way they communicate without actually speaking out loud. I have been around enough leeches to be able to identify when they are doing it. I wonder how they do it. Maybe I will have a better understanding when I read *The Studies of Vampires*.

Xander and King Nicklaus are the only vampires I've met that can read my mind. I wonder what's the story behind that. Hmmm, maybe it has something to do with their being brothers.

My mind starts to drift. King Nicklaus's glorious body and the feel of his hands running through my hair completely take over. Suddenly, he is all I can think about—his charming smile, the beautiful shade of his piercing eyes, his well-defined frame, and his long and thick half-smoke that was poking me through his pants.

Oh my God! King Nicklaus's perfect body completely floods my brain, washing away any of my other thoughts and making me . . . How should I say this? Making me . . . Hmm. Okay, you know how the kitty in the middle feels right about now.

"This way, human," says a dark, deeply masculine voice beside me, bringing me straight back to dry land.

Mr. Meany and Astrid are both waiting for me. They exchange a look, then Mr. Meany leads the way. There is something in the way they stare at me that places me on edge. It's strange.

Astrid continues to look at me, as if trying to figure me out or trying to figure something out, and I don't like it. She is slowly making her way to my jeepers-creepers list.

We pass through a red door, walk down a flight of stairs, and enter another door. We repeat those actions for about ten minutes until Astrid finally stops in front of a blue door.

*Thank God! My legs are cramping.*

She inputs a code and then we all step into a pad. Instantly, my heart skips a beat. When I said that the mural in the library was beautiful, it was beautiful. However, this artistic pad makes that breathtaking, colorful work of art fade into the background like it's nothing but black-and-white scrap. The walls pop to life, literally, each telling a story that goes into another story and another story. Everything is bright——pink, striped, yellow, and blue walls that host neon lights. There are even statues made of beer cans, full of life and so cool. There are also portraits of different people from different times. They weren't painted to life but were captured from many various angles, which is a unique type of art. I love it! I have never seen anything like it. I'm completely lost for words.

We enter a room with a sliding glass door, and my stomach quickly comes to life when I realize it's a kitchen. I nearly squeak and jump for joy as Astrid directs me to sit down, and I follow her command with no complaints. I'm starving. If following their orders gets me food, so be it.

She leaves the room, and when she returns seconds later, I nearly faint. She comes back with a woman, not just any woman. She has silver hair and silver-cerulean eyes that are oddly similar to King Nicklaus's, only a little lighter in shade. She has wrinkled skin, proving that she has lived a long time. This woman is human and seems to be my elder.

Then everything around me darkens.

\*       \*       \*

The smell of pancakes and strawberries invade my senses, waking me right up. I rise from the godforsaken red couch, only to be met by the woman responsible for my fall into darkness. Mr. Meany and his sidekick are here too. They don't really matter because I'm used to seeing leeches. However, meeting an older human woman is something I don't get to experience every day.

"A little birdie told me that you like pancakes," the older woman begins, her voice warm and gentle. She hands me a plate full of pancakes topped with thick strawberry syrup.

It doesn't take a rocket scientist to figure out which little birdie chirped.

"Eat, child. You must be hungry," she gently commands.

Of course, I'm hungry. I would have licked this plate dry by now, but she is distracting me. I have never seen a human over the age of thirty. That's our expiration according to the Awakening standards, unless you're a breeder, then you might get lucky enough to reach forty.

I steal one more glance at her before diving into the fluffy cakes of wonderland. She watches me, studying my every move like I'm the mysterious one. It's strange. She's the elder, and I'm just a typical human. I should be the one studying her.

"My name is Nannie," she speaks, after a while of silence.

How fitting? She looks at me as if she's waiting for me to introduce myself as well.

When I remain silent, she continues, "Oh good heavens, child! I'm not Xander or Nicklaus. I cannot read your mind. You must communicate with me by using your mouth."

I drop my fork, not because she knows about their talents. That's easy. I'm sure a lot of people do, but she specifically call them by their names, both of them—not king, master, or sir. She has stated their names loud and clear.

"Who are you?" I ask because I can't hold it any longer.

She smiles, then hands me a cup of juice. "I told you I'm Nannie.

"The real question is, Who are you?" She takes a seat across from me.

Nannie is a pretty old woman with a motherly smile and soft, bright blue eyes that captivate me. I avert my eyes from her and focus on the pop art behind her. I realize it's a picture of a younger Nannie. She was stunning, drop-dead gorgeous just like the Nannie who is sitting in front of me.

Having finally decided to answer her, I clear my throat. "My name is Claire. I'm King Nicklaus's chosen."

She leans over and hands me a napkin.

*So much hospitality. Wow! It's nice to meet this unique woman.*

"You're so much more than Nicklaus's chosen, my dear." She pauses just to smile widely. "So much more."

I take that as a compliment, so I return her smile. It's hard not to. Nannie has this natural warm energy about her that makes you want to hug her and never let go. I'm intrigued, and fascination often brings questions.

"How are you still alive?" I query, sounding just as crazy as I look.

*Oh my God, seriously? I don't just say that out loud.*

Nannie doesn't seem taken aback by my question. She looks like she is holding back laughter if anything.

"I was wondering when you were going to ask that dear."
She softly giggles, then turns to face Mr. Meany and his sidekick. (I
forgot they are even here.) "Can you two give us a second?"

They nod and leave, just like that. I have never seen leeches
take instructions from a human, let alone follow a command.

Nannie turns to face me. She doesn't say anything, but she
does flash a smile.

*I would add her to my jeepers-creepers list if she were a leech, but she's
just a sweet, old woman, I think. What if she really isn't? I mean, older
humans are extinct.*

And then it hits me.

*This must be a trap! Okay, I can't take it anymore. Curiosity is not
going to kill this cat. I need answers right now. Nannie will not fool me any
longer.*

"Listen here, lady. You're going to tell me what you are and
who you are this very instant," I command her.

"Aww, there it is! I was wondering when the fire in your
eyes would reveal itself."

"Who are you?" I ask again, ignoring her previous
statement.

"Oh dear, you are a little feisty one, aren't you? No wonder
you caught his eye. You are perfect for each other."

*Oh Lord, here goes another riddle. She is acting like Xander. Hmm .
. . interesting. Maybe I should try a different approach.*

"Who are you to them?"

She raises her eyebrows in response, not expecting that at
all.

*Checkmate! Xander's chess lessons may actually be paying off. Look
at that.*

"Tell me!"

"I'm their niece."

*Niece, how?*

"That's impossible! That's the best you came up with?"

*She must be crazy.*

183

"Oh dear, I wish. My imagination is not that grand. Unfortunately, I wasn't blessed with the family's characteristics; my mother was. She was very artistic just like Uncle Nick."

*I knew it. She is crazier than I thought, a f\*cking lunatic. Not only does she believe King Nicklaus is her uncle, she even called him Uncle Nick.*

"Your imagination may be grander than you believe," I confess, because seriously this lady is coo-coo.

"Enough about me, darling." She ignores my statement completely. "Tell me more about you." She flashes another sweet smile. "I always knew who Nicklaus's beloved would—"

"Nannie," a deep, husky, hypnotizing voice cuts in, gaining both of our attention.

Nannie turns. "Hey, Uncle Nick. We were just talking about you." She flashes that award-winning, granny apple smile.

Love and adoration travel between them, warming my heart completely. She looks at him like how a daughter looks at her father, and he looks at her like how a parent looks at their newborn. I quickly figure before he can even say she was telling the truth. They are family. Somehow, it's kind of strange. She has to be at least seventy whereas he looks no more than twenty-five, which makes me wonder. How old is he really? I mean it's obvious he's older than twenty-five. The Awakening happened over a hundred years ago.

He kisses her softly on her cheek and then places his full attention on me. "Are you ready to train, Claire?"

*Oh f\*ck, I forgot about that.*

184

# CHAPTER TWENTY-EIGHT
## Training

Once King Nicklaus has commanded Mr. Meany and his sidekick to stay here with Nannie, he then takes me out of the artsy pad and away from sweet ole Nannie. He's acting like the mean big fighting machine, annoying me to no end. I like Nannie, and I like that little artsy pad. I'd much rather be there, eating pancakes all day with her instead of training and getting my ass kicked.

Nicklaus also forces me to go to the gym, but working out has never been my thing. I hate it. Physical education was another epic failure of my time in school. Okay, it's a lie. It really wasn't, but I don't want to train with him. He's the king of all vampire kings. He's scary.

Walking behind King Nicklaus's tall, lean, and muscular frame has me tripping over my own feet. He does stuff like that to me. He makes me feel so nervous.

*Oh God, I'm so pathetic. I need to distract myself. How about counting to ten? Okay, that should work. Yeah, that should take my mind off his rock-hard body.*

*One, two, three, four, five, six . . . The number six . . . just like his sexy, well-defined six-pack . . . where I want to run my tongue down.*

"Oh my God, his abs are on full display! How can I focus when his body is screaming 'come lick me'?"

"You said that out loud you know," King Nicklaus says with a chuckle, making my face feel like it's been set on fire. He stops in his tracks and turns to face me. His eyes resemble the deep blue sea, and on his handsome face is a fierce and hungry look.

The air around us shifts, forcefully pulling our bodies into each other, begging us to become one.

*F\*ck! It's gravity, or maybe it's just my imagination playing tricks on me because that's secretly how I want it to be.*

"Do you like what you see?" King Nicklaus asks, licking his very scrumptious-looking lips.

*I want to taste them. They look so rich and appetizing. Ugh, what the hell is going on with me? Every time I'm around him, I act like a dog in heat. Gee, even when I'm not around him, I still think about him and act like a dog in heat. See? That's not normal. He must have done something to me.*

"You did something to me, didn't you?"

"I didn't do anything, Claire. What you're experiencing is called a bond. It pulls us to each other. The universe wants us to be together . . . My blood lingers in your system. It shouldn't last too much longer. You're human."

*Wait. Huh?*

"What do you mean by your blood being in my system?"

"I fed you my blood when you were too weak to eat."

*He did what?*

"You did what?" I take a step back, surprised.

"You don't have to ask the same question twice. I can read your mind, remember?" he says. "Once a human is given vampire blood, they may become addicted. It's rare but not unheard of. Typically it happens when a vampire and human form a bond or when a human belongs to a vampire."

"I don't belong to you. I may be your slave, but I'm not an item or anyone's property."

"Oh really? What do you think being a slave is, Claire? You're my chosen, that's why you feel what you feel," he replies, lying through clenched teeth.

*I know he's not telling me everything. I can feel it. Being his chosen has nothing to do with anything. He is keeping me in the dark, just like*

186

*Xander. Hmm. Maybe I should try another way to get the truth out of him,* *like a trick question just as Xander taught me. "When one pawn doesn't work,* *use the other one." Nannie wasn't expecting it. Hopefully, King Nicklaus isn't* *either. Speaking of Nannie . . .*

"How is Nannie related to you," I ask, changing the subject.

"She's not." He continues to walk, and I follow. "Nannie is related to Xander. We have different fathers. She is a descendant of Xander's father. She's a human, just like Xander was once before."

I'm stunned, almost dropping to the floor. His face lights up—my facial expression amuses him.

"Unlike Xander, I was born a vampire. My father is a trueborn vampire. I turned Xander many centuries ago when I found him dying on the battlefield. I was nothing but a mere vampire boy at the time," he explains.

I stop in my tracks. *Vampire boy . . . the battlefield . . .*

"The mural! You're the artist that painted it, aren't you?" I ask in amazement. It's obvious, but I still have to.

The mural was painted with lots of raw, real emotions. It's as if the artist had lived through each story before he painted it alive. King Nicklaus is the beauty behind the brush.

A genuine smile stretches across his face. "You're smarter than you realize, firecracker," he states, his voice low and husky. He stops and pushes me against the wall, making my heart rate increase by the second. He gently cups my face with his talented hands, melting my heart completely.

"Why are you telling me this? I'm your chosen, not your friend. Vampires don't tell their secrets to their slaves."

He leans in closer—too close—bringing his face directly in front of mine. Right now, all I can think about is his lips touching my own. Right now, I can see in his deep, dark ocean-blue eyes that he also wants to taste my mouth. He parts his lips, and I brace myself. I know this is going to be the moment of a lifetime that I shall cherish for the rest of my human years.

"Firecracker," King Nicklaus whispers. His cool, minty breath breezes onto my lips, then a force filled with chills travels through my veins. "Every inch of your body belongs to me. Your plump and delicious lips belong to me, and so do your vivid green eyes. The fluttering in your heart is caused by me. Before I command you to forget the rest of our conversation, I want you to remember one thing: you belong to me."

His words leave me in a trance, as though I'm in la-la land. His juicy lips are so close to mine, basically calling my name. I can taste him, can't I? He said I'm his, so that also makes him mine, right? I don't know the answer to that question, but I do know I'm going to taste him.

I lean in—almost there—his ruby-red lips just an inch away.

"Claire," he whispers, his voice so compelling.

"Huh? Yes? You called me?"

He smiles. "Forget everything that we have discussed until I tell you to remember it. Forget all about Nannie."

*     *     *

I'm currently getting my ass kicked big time.

"Again!" King Nicklaus yells after I fall flat on my ass for the thousandth time.

He's attempting to teach me how to anticipate an attack, and of course, it's an epic fail. I'm a lover, not a fighter. Well, okay, that's a lie. The truth is I just don't want to go up against a tall, scary, magnificent bloodsucker like him.

I pick my face up off the ground again. My eyes meet Xander's, and I notice Mr. Meany and his sidekick walking into the room. Now all three of them are watching me and then— swoosh!—the wind rushes around me, and I'm back on the ground again. King Nicklaus trips me up, knocking me flat on my ass before I even have a chance to stand up.

"Never allow anyone to distract you!" reprimands King Nicklaus.

"Yikes! A warning would have been nice."

Our spectators burst into a fit of giggles, including Xander. He's such a traitor.

I get to my feet. Seconds later, King Nicklaus attacks again—smack! God, that hurts.

He told me when we just started he would send smacks instead of jabs because he didn't want to break anything on my body. At first, I thought, *Aww how sweet. He doesn't want to hurt me.* That's until he sends an open-hand strike my way, knocking the hell out of me. His hand collides with my skin with a resounding crack and leaving me with my first official purple bruise. Now, I think differently.

Three hours later, over a million and one purple bruises now cover my body. I should have known better. Being sweet is the last thing on the vampire king's mind. He's a war god and would rather make his enemies experience a slow death—he's smart.

He has been torturing me, and now my body is sore from head to toe. Sweat is pouring from my pores like rain as I gasp for air. On top of that, I have to look at his body drenched in sexiness. Now that's real torture.

*Focus, Claire,* I keep telling myself.

I know he expected me to give up a long time ago, but Claire the Human isn't a quitter. Nobody likes a quitter, or at least that was what Xander said when I tried to quit the game of chess.

"Stop relying on your sight. You have other senses, Claire. Use them," advises King Nicklaus.

Right. Whatever the hell that's supposed to mean, but these brothers and their riddles are starting to give me whiplash.

All of a sudden, the wind shifts around me, and the ground catches my butt again.

*When did he move? He doesn't want me to rely on my sight, but he gets to rely on his vampire skills. Hey, that's not fair!*

189

"Life's not fair," he chastises me, utilizing another vampire skill of his.

*Great. That's just perfect.*

Mr. Meany decides to put his two cents in. "Maybe you should take her sight away. She would have no choice but to depend on her other senses."

*Oh, so he does speak. Wait, what? Is he suggesting what I think he is? Surely, he is not advising him to blind me. Oh no, no, no. He has lost his marbles! How would King Nicklaus blind me anyway? Would he cut out my eyes, drain my eye sockets, burn my eyeballs, or something worse? Oh hell no, I think not.*

"Nobody asked for your opinion, Mr. Meany!" I blurt out.

"You're childish," he spits back.

*So?*

"Again, no one asked for your opinion," I respond venomously, finally picking myself up off the ground.

Xander lets out a hearty laugh. "That's my girl." He applauds, earning a growl from his brother.

"You're right," King Nicklaus says, his eyes scanning Mr. Meany and then Xander before stopping on me.

"Who's right?" I ask.

He does not answer. His silence is scarier than the predatory look that lingers in his cold stare. In my peripheral vision, I can see Xander's facial expression, and it doesn't look too happy. I can tell something isn't right.

I try to break eye contact, but I can't. King Nicklaus won't let me. His eyes won't allow me to look away. My eyes are locked in place, chained to his. There is no escape.

Suddenly, I feel a tugging sensation inside my mind, followed by white noise.

"Sight."

I hear him murmur. My heart skips a beat and then everything around me goes black, pitch black. I scream bloody murder and place my hands over my eyes to make sure they're open.

"I can't see! I can't see, you bastard! I can't f*cking see!" I scream too loud that I'm sure I can be heard several miles away. I sink to the ground, my hands still covering my eyes and my heart slamming against my chest. I have never been so afraid in my eighteen years of existence.

"Nicklaus."

I can hear Xander whisper, but to me he sounds so loud like he's yelling in my ears. I start to go crazy, nearly clawing my eyes out.

"You're scaring her!" Xander shouts.

I throw my hands over my ears. He's excruciatingly loud.

*"Relax, Claire."* King Nicklaus's voice appears inside my head, then instantly my body goes limp. *"Listen. Don't think or speak. Just listen."*

I follow his command. For once on my own, I listen. I hear the sound of water dripping from the ceiling. I hear a bee buzzing by the open window and the air swooshing around me. I can feel some movement on my left side—it must be King Nicklaus—so without thinking, I slide my leg out as fast as I can. It connects with his leg, and he tumbles down. Instantly, my sight returns.

"Well done, Claire!" praises Xander.

The room explodes with applause. Even Mr. Meany claps with them.

*OMG, I did it! I did it! I may have had to be blinded to do it, but I did it! How the hell did he blind me anyway? I'll ask later. The only thing that matters is I knocked him on his ass. Speaking of which, where the hell is . . . ?*

Suddenly, the wind shifts around me again, and my moment of glory quickly comes to an end. King Nicklaus smashes hard into me, crushing and completely covering me.

*Darn it! Can't a girl enjoy her victory without being crushed to death?*

Applause turns into laughter.

*Gosh, how quickly did I fall?*

191

King Nicklaus laughs, the vibration of his chest shaking my whole body. His muscular frame is a rock against my skin. His upper body is not the only part of him that's hard but also his half-smoke that's poking through his pants and barking at my kitty.

Xander laughs hysterically, and my face immediately bursts into flames. That's freaking embarrassing.

I stare into King Nicklaus's face, thinking that he's sharing my embarrassment. Unfortunately, he isn't. He is smiling wolfishly instead. He likes this position. In fact, the look on his face tells me he loves it, and he most definitely enjoys this.

I try to wiggle myself from underneath him, but he refuses to allow me to move away. I can feel his chest rising and falling, his hot dog growing harder as it pushes into my bun.

"Good job, Claire," he huskily whispers in my ear.

My entire body goes still. He, again, has me locked down— chained—just like he did moments ago.

*Wait . . . This f*cking leech took my vision. He blinded me.*

"King Nicklaus," I say his name seductively while running my hands through his hair.

He releases a growl, and his eyes turn pitch black once more.

*Just like my sight when he blinded me.*

With that new thought, I decide to make him pay for what he did. I slide my leg up quickly and smash my knee into his penis as hard as I can. "Never allow anyone to distract you!" I chastise him, and I bet he wasn't expecting that.

# CHAPTER TWENTY-NINE
## Creepy, Creeper, and Creepicious

I have seen deer caught in headlights, literally? They are so surprised that they cannot move. Their eyes bulge. You would think they are owls sitting on a branch only to hop away. A vampire getting their nutsack kicked is no different. First, they freeze, then their whole body goes still and stiff and then their eyes widen like an owl's. Finally, they let out a very loud bawl or blat sound as if they were dying.

That's exactly what happened to King Nicklaus. It was classic—no, it was epic. Let's just say he was pissed. However, before I could fully revel in my victory, Xander swooshed me out of the room, like my knight in shining armor. He's no fun.

Now I'm in the slave quarters reading *The Vampire Studies*. I must admit, Xander was right. It really isn't anywhere near as boring as it sounds, unlike the garbage heroic vampire stories the academy likes to feed our brains. This book tells the truth. It doesn't paint vampires to be heroes, villains, or monsters. What it does is explain their history, society, and culture. I'm intrigued, and to be honest, I cannot put it down. This book contains true knowledge, and one thing I agree with is that knowledge is power.

So far, I have learned that there are a total of seven vampire houses—House Ettore, House Akeldama, House Throne, House Athan, House Baldassare, House Marku, and House Vlad—

and each vampire king is blood descendant of a powerful vampire house. Only one of the kings is not a trueborn vampire.

King Nicklaus is from House Vlad, the royal and the most-powerful family of them all. According to the text, his family is victorious. They are legends to the other vampire houses. Each and every house worships the ground House Vlad walks on. They originated from a place called Sighişoara, Romania, although they have lived in places such as England, Italy, and Egypt. They'd relocated many, many times before they finally decided to settle in Cyprus, an island surrounded by three continents—Europe, Asia, and Africa—which the vampires call the circling kingdoms. I remember the kings speaking about the circling kingdoms during their royal tradition the Feast of the Brothers.

Speaking of traditions, according to the text, every one hundred years, the vampire houses come together to host a Massacre Ball, a blood gathering. It is on this occasion that they discuss the well-being of their futures. The last ball was when the Awakening was orchestrated. Every house agreed upon the course of action that led to the slavery of my race—just perfect! King Nicklaus was the one who led the attack.

Actually, the book states that descendants of the Vlad family have always led the vampires in battles against other supernatural creatures, or in my case human species, and they win just about whatever war they fight. Vampires believe that if other houses go to war without the House of Vlad's blessing, they will lose, terribly. They call this the curse of the Vlads.

It's weird. Honestly, I think it's just a bunch of superstitious bullcrap. Like come on, one family cannot determine whether they can win or lose a war. In my opinion, the House of Vlad has only instilled this fear into other vampires so they can hold on to their power and secure the crown.

I've also learned there are four council members selected by the houses every two hundred years. These council members set rule books, and whatever they say goes. The only person that can overrule them is the overseer of the vampire race, and usually it's a direct descendant of the House of Vlad. King Nicklaus's father became the overseer after he passed the throne down to his son. His new title is King Father Apollyon, and this book makes it very clear he is a wicked and malicious king. His daughter and King Nicklaus's sister, Princess Daniela, is next in line to be the overseer.

See? What I mean is their family name alone holds true power.

I've even learned that trueborn vampires pass their powers to the ones they turn, and that all trueborn vampires are born with their own specific powers. Some can read minds, compel people, and even pick up on others's emotions. The list of trueborn vampires goes on and on. However, the House of Vlad's decendants are always born with unique powers. They aren't listed, and I'm guessing it's for a reason—just in case the wrong person gets their hands on this book.

After the Legend of the Awakening—well, that's what the book lists the Awakening as—laws of vampires changed completely, and no one other than a person born or turned before the Awakening should know the secrets, which means I probably really shouldn't have given access to this book. Why did Xander willingly allow me, though?

Legend has it that some vampire fell in love with a human and declared she was his beloved and immediately requested the council's blessing to turn her immortal. The council granted his request, but on the day the human was supposed to be turned was the day the vampire community suffered a terrible fate. The human was actually also in love with a lycan who hated vampires with a burning passion, but she betrayed him, so the lycan—along with many other supernatural creatures—attacked the event and killed millions and millions of vampires. Children, women, and many other innocent vampires were slaughtered. The lycans didn't show mercy, and neither did the vampires when they retaliated, making the human girl's entire race suffer to this day.

I figure that this is the same story, about a vampire and a human, as the one Mecca told me. There are always two sides to it and then there's the truth, and I can't help but wonder what the truth holds. My entire species has been suffering because of whatever happened.

I sigh deeply and roll off the bed. I've had enough of vampire history for today.

"What are you reading?" asks a female voice from behind me.

I quickly throw a cover over the top of the book before turning around to face no other than Mr. Meany's sidekick—the last person I expected to see.

"*Slave Cooperation,*" I lie, figuring it is best not to tell her the truth.

The book states in bold black ink that no other species should know anything about their history.

Sidekick Astrid tilts her head to the side, her eyes rapidly flickering around the room. With a weird look on her face, she saunters into the center of my room—Jadis's room—that I currently inhabit, then she looks at me exactly how she did earlier during our walk into the artsy pad. Jeepers freaking creepers!

"Why are you here?" I am unable to stop the words from rolling off my tongue.

"I came to escort you to the slave quarters for dinner." She brings her head up straight. The king orders. He would like to make sure you're fed before your journey to North America."

*Oh right! I forgot about our upcoming journey to the continent I thought I have officially escaped from. It used to be the land of the free. What an irony!*

I do not respond. I just enter the walk-in closet and search for something to wear. Even though I'm a little curvier than Jadis, I'm still able to squeeze my fat ass into her pair of leather jeans and pull a black V-neck over my head. Honestly, Jadis has kick-ass fashion sense.

I head for the bathroom. I throw some water in my hair to make my waves come back to life. Once I've finished, Astrid opens the door for me and leads the way. She's also wearing leather pants and a black tank top, which suddenly makes me feel like puking. I didn't intentionally mean to dress like her, and the fact that I did kind of bothers me.

"I sense you don't like me." Astrid looks over her shoulder and gives me that creepy look of hers. "You know your heart rate is an indicator whether you're lying, right?" She stops in her tracks. "I know you were lying about what you were reading. If my powers didn't reveal the truth, your racing heart did." She continues to walk. "I suggest you practice keeping it steady at all times. I can help you with that if you want me to."

"And why would you help me?" I rasp my eyebrows.

Vampires don't help humans—that's just a fact—especially someone like me. If I have to be truthful, the idea of Astrid offering help rings creepy bells. She puts the capital *C* in *creepy*. I don't trust her. I'm already tired of all these vampires suddenly wanting to train me for whatever reasons they see fit. I'm officially overtrained, exhausted. My day of training was extremely hard.

"Not all vampires are pure evil, human. Even if I don't particularly favor you, it's my job to protect you. Without learning how to control your fear when caught in a lie, you will forever be an open book. And that will place you in unnecessary danger. I'll talk to the king about my offer. At the end of the day, he is the one who controls what you must do or musn't."

"Your king doesn't control sh*t. Let me make things clear. Just because you follow his orders like the creepy, little, flunky sidekick that you are, that doesn't mean I do too."

She stops and turns to face me. "Oh really?"

"Yes really, and I accept your offer of my own free will, not because he wants me to or because you think I should. I accept your offer because that's what I want to do." I shove right past her as I make my way to the slave dining quarters, fighting the urge not to kick her in the crotch.

I really don't like Astrid. Actually, I've made up my mind: I despise her. However, if she can teach me how to control my heart rate, then that's better for me. I can use that to my advantage. And if she wants to teach me to deceive her race, only a fool will decline that opportunity.

I look over my shoulder and catch her smiling. Astrid the Sidekick has officially become Miss Creepy.

*     *     *

Dinner at the slave quarters was typical and uneventful besides the fact that Victoria was shooting daggers at me the whole time. That's not anything new, though. I hope Xander decides to leave her behind.

Being forced to go back to North (freaking) America is already bad enough. What makes it worse is I have to travel with Victoria. Why does fate get so damn cruel?

Miss Creepy walks me back to Jadis's chambers and informs me that the king gave her his permission to train me. She just becomes weirder and weirder by the second. For one, she didn't leave my side the entire time and watched me like a hawk— and how the hell was she able to persuade King Nicklaus? For two, she kept staring into space every so often. Creepy, creepy, creepy.

I immediately dive into bed and search for the book the moment I walk into into Jadis's chambers. To make my day creepier, the book isn't there anymore. I know I put it there, and Miss Creepy ensured me that no one is allowed to enter my room.The king orders," I quote. I also know for a fact that King Nicklaus and Xander are attending another meeting with Xander's governors, so who the hell came in?

I retrace my steps before dinner, and still nothing.

*Okay, maybe Miss Creepy's nosy ass did some creepy vampire sh\*t and took my book when I was changing. Yup, she is dead. I'm about to scream her name through the halls and give her a piece of my mind.*

I'm about to do what I've planned when I see my underwear from this morning sitting by the bathroom door.

*Wait, I left it in the clothes hamper by the closet. What the hell!*

I decide to walk over to the bathroom, only to come face-to-face with glowing bright-green eyes. I find the book, and the culprit. I'm about to scream when in the blink of an eye, my intruder covers my mouth with his hand. My heart rate increases. I struggle to fight, but it's no use. He is stronger.

"Stop moving now before I stick my dick back up into you so fast and hard that you won't be able to move ever again."

# CHAPTER THIRTY
## Sick and Sadistic Piece of Sh*t

NICKLAUS

Xander and I are in a meeting with his governors, and I'm bored—officially bored as hell. I just want to be with Claire and watch her curvy body as she trains, but duty calls. We have to meet with the governors before we head for the northern kingdom.

Governors are responsible to govern and protect a kingdom when the king departs. They aren't descendants of the wealthy houses, but they come from respected houses that have shown nothing but undying loyalty for the wealthy house of their assigned kingdom.

Count Cloven and Duke Aldon are Xander's governors. Count Cloven's ancestors had been loyal companions of my ancestors for decades. His father was my personal guard for over a hundred years. Count Cloven had protected Xander during his human years. If it hadn't been for him, pretending to be a human companion, Xander would have died during his life as a human. Because of that, he earned his place to govern my brother's kingdom.

Duke Aldon is quite unique. He was Xander's human best friend. Xander almost killed him when he was first turned. My brother came to me with the dying boy in his arms and begged me to turn him and save his life like I had saved his a couple of days before then. Granting his wish, I turned Duke Aldon into an immortal.

Duke Aldon was so gracious. He swore to protect me and give his new life for me if time presented itself. As he grew older, he became Lieutenant Aldon. He kept his promise when he risked his life to save mine about a hundred years ago. My father rewarded him handsomely—Lieutenant Aldon became Duke Aldon, the first turned vampire who has been honored to be called a lord. He was adopted by the House of Vlad and has been considered our blood. Apart from Xander, he is the wealthiest and most-powerful human turned into a vampire that has ever existed.

So for the last eight hours, we have been discussing plans, war strategies, and a bunch of boring BS when all I want to do is get back to Claire. I need to get back to her. Besides, she has to be punished for pulling that little stunt earlier. My balls are still tingling, and the urge to allow her sweet juices to ease my pain only grows. Honestly, the craving to explore every inch of her body becomes stronger by the second. I miss her.

The mood in the room is full of good vibes. We are all family here. Claire should also be here. She should be sitting right by my side, taking her rightful place as my queen. Unfortunately, that will never happen. I care too much about her safety to even consider allowing that to happen.

I take a sip of the blood and force myself to swallow the bitter content. No one's blood can please my taste buds anymore ever since I tasted Claire's sweet, intoxicating, and honey-laced blood. That's the only taste that can satisfy me now.

I can't take it anymore. I'm going to go see my little firecracker.

"Nicklaus," calls Xander, "do you agree?"

Agree to what? Honesty, I wasn't listening to anything they were discussing.

I nod and wave my hands dismissively, finally deciding to listen.

"Now that my brother is actually listening," Xander says with some irritation in his voice, making the others laugh, "does anyone have any concerns or perhaps anything to add?"

Xander knows me too well.

"How should we handle the hunter problem? There have been numerous reports of suspicious activity," speaks Count Cloven. "There are also rumors about a so-called trueborn huntress queen. I know we don't necessarily entertain rumors, but with all the suspicious activity and different reports about hunters settling in our kingdoms, surely you can understand my concerns."

"It is true. There is a trueborn huntress named Isis. She is said to be a direct descendant of Maddox Hunter," Xander reveals. "She is his great-granddaughter, which means that she is the heiress to the hunter throne."

"And when did you make me aware of this?" I snap. "Our people's safety is in jeopardy as long as that huntress b*tch breathes. The war between us and the dogs will mean nothing if what you say is true, so killing that huntress is far more important than anything else."

"She is no threat, Nicklaus. I have been monitoring the situation for a while now."

"It'd better be," I warn.

"I promise you she will be eliminated the moment she decides to side with her race," is Xander's response.

Hunters are nothing but humans with a tad bit of speed, brains, and strength. A trueborn hunter is an offspring of a trueborn vampire and hunter. Mixing species is never good for anyone, which is another reason why I cannot claim Claire. If she decides to remain human—I'm all but certain that she will—our offsprings will be dhampirs, who are ten times more powerful than trueborn hunters.

Creating a trueborn hunter or huntress, or dhampirs, had been forbidden way before the Awakening. If a vampire's beloved refused to be turned, they were sterilized immediately, sealing their

202

childless fate. Honestly, that was the easy way out because having a dhampir as a child would have been far worse, for they are the deadliest supernatural race to ever exist.

"I said you have my word, Nicklaus. Do I need to remind you I'm the one who helped track and kill Maddox Hunter? I can handle his offspring. I have done this for decades now, so trust me when I say the girl is no threat."

He's right. Xander has proven time after time he is more than capable of dealing with that species.

"You know the dangers. There is nothing else to discuss," I say.

"With that new information, my concerns have increased. How should we deal with that problem, Xander?" Count Cloven asks again. "I understand well that you have everything under control, but you shall be absent."

"Good point. The girl and her human sister have settled on Elephant Island. I have sent a spy to watch them, and she has killed any hunter who may have come in contact with them to reveal that the rumors are true." Xander stands. "My spy has been instructed not to engage with the girl and her sister," he goes on, walking toward the balcony. "The hunter doesn't know about her heritage, and I intend to keep it that way."

"So how can you be sure she is a direct descendant of Maddox Hunter?" questions Duke Aldon.

It's very rare for a trueborn hunter to not know their heritage. They are considered the Vlad family in the hunter world. Hunters would die to protect that girl. Every species around the planet would die to protect her as she can be their savior.

"I was there when she was born." Xander turns to face me, knowing he has officially pissed me off.

We share everything, so why the hell didn't he share this with me? What is he hiding?

"She clearly is the daughter of Madelyn Hunter. Even without having this critical piece of information, by just one look at her, you would know."

I clench my hands into tight fists and stand to my feet immediately. I am just about to punch Xander right in the face when a rush wave of pain knocks the wind out of me. I crouch down, my hands over my stomach.

Xander is the first to come by my side, followed by the others. "What is it, Nicklaus?" he asks.

Another shot of pain hits me, then another.

When vampires bond with their human beloved, they can feel their emotions, and sometimes even their pain. I'm a hundred percent positive that I'm feeling my beloved's pain. I need to get to Claire.

*     *     *

CLAIRE

"Stop moving now before I stick my dick back up into you so fast and hard that you won't be able to move ever again."

My entire body goes limp. I'm disgusted—appalled. Just listening to his words makes me feel nauseous. I know for a fact his words aren't a threat, but he will take me by force if I don't follow his command.

He runs a sharp nail down my skin, and it leaves a shudder in its wake.

"Please . . . don't."

That's all I manage to say, but it only seems to do more bad than good.

"Your pleas are even sexier than I remember." He gently squeezes my nipple and turns me around to face him. His evil green eyes travel up and down my body. "I love your silence more, the way you quietly take every inch of my dick. Never once did you try

204

to fight me when I entered your precious jewel." He brushes his finger against my lips.

I jump in response. This sick, sadistic piece of sh*t has the audacity to moan! I try my hardest to stay still as I remember his threat.

"You have no idea how many times I've dreamed about having you again and tasting your sweet and intoxicating scent." He lowers his head and places his lips directly in front of my ear. "And I beat my dick after each and every dream."

Gross, he's sick and crazy!

He brushes his vile and disgusting tongue against my ear. I hold back the urge to scream, an unpleasant chill traveling throughout my body.

"You want me, don't you?" he asks, sounding crazier than I thought.

This vampire is far past sick. He is insane.

I try my hardest to remain quiet and follow his command. However, my control slips and alters with each passing second.

"Tell me you want me, sweet Claire," he demands.

I don't know if it's the pet name or the fact that he has said my name, but I can no longer fight it. My control is officially gone. I take a step back, bracing myself to make a run for it while the sick and sadistic piece of sh*t's eyes glow brighter with excitement.

"I belong to King Nicklaus," I tell him, as I take another step backward.

He bursts out laughing, sounding like a dying hyena. "I'm Master Azazel, sweet Claire." Here he goes with the pet name again. "It's my job to punish slaves who act out of line. I can do whatever I want with your body, and your master would most likely reward me for it."

I allow his words to sink in. Now I start thinking about it. King Nicklaus was the one to stop Xander from whipping him at the auction. I remember King Nicklaus saying there is no law that forbids a vampire from raping a human. I hate to admit it, but this piece of sh*t may be right. No one will save me. King Nicklaus doesn't give a hell about what is done or what happens to me. I'm on my own.

One look into his evil eyes confirms what I'm thinking. He's right. There will be no consequences for him taking me.

Just when I'm about to give in, Xander's words appear inside my head. *"It is a crime to rape a human who has not been auctioned off and classified."*

That's right! No, the master can't punish me unless I break a rule.

"I haven't done anything to deserve a punishment," I remind him.

He gives me a big and creepy smile, his fangs now poking through his top lip and his evil eyes glowing brighter. I can't shake the feeling that he knew I was going to say that.

"Sweet Claire"—he chuckles, placing himself right back in front of me—"do I need to remind you that humans are absolutely forbidden to learn about vampire histories?" He throws the book, *The Vampire Studies,* onto the floor.

The sick and sadistic piece of sh*t then pulls me and buries his face into my neck. We are close now, so close that I can feel his hot breath and smell the metallic odor that beams out of his pores.

"Please don't," I plead again, sounding defeated.

"I already told you that I like you better silent," he says, unbuckling his pants. "But because you insist on talking, I will have to silence you in another way."

I start to panic, and my body goes into shock when he pulls down his pants.

*No, no, no! This isn't going to happen again.*

The sick and weak piece of sh*t roughly grabs me by my left arm. Adrenaline must be kicking in because I start to fight. I kick my leg out, and my foot collides with his manhood. Just like King Nicklaus, he resembles a deer caught in headlights, surprised and stiff. He crouches over in pain as expected, and that's when I make a run for it.

I'm almost there, inches away from the door, when he pulls me by the hair and slams me into a wall. My body crumples as I slide onto the floor. Seconds later, he jabs his powerful hand into my stomach, knocking the air out of my chest.

"You see, I was going to take it gently, but you just had to act like the stupid little b*tch that you are!" he growls. He slams his hand into my side, breaking my ribs in the process.

I howl out in pain.

"Does that hurt, baby? Don't worry. I'll ease your pain, just like you're going to ease the pain that you caused."

Without warning, he grabs a handful of my hair and shoves his manhood in my mouth. I can feel his full length in the back of my throat as he rams in and out of my mouth, the sound of his moans covering my ear-splitting screams. He continues his assault, slamming and ramming at a fast pace.

My vision is already blurry when he begins to slow down. I can feel he is close to erupting, so I gather all my strength. Just before he releases his seed, I bite down onto his dick with so much force that I draw blood. He yanks his manhood back, his screams of pain filling the air.

I try to pull myself up off the ground. The pain I feel is unbearable. I gasp for air while coughing up blood, then everything around me goes dark.

# CHAPTER THIRTY-ONE
## Predator

NICKLAUS

I rush to get to Claire, the air around me rustling. Whoever caused my beloved—my queen, my everything—pain shall die! I can feel and hear the others following behind me. They're not fast enough to reach me before I end whoever dared to touch her. The sound of someone screaming makes me pick up my speed.

The moment I arrive in front of the chamber, my body comes to a complete halt. Under any other circumstances, I would be bent, jeering and laughing my ass off at the scene before my eyes—the last thing I expected to see.

I'm met by Master Azazel, who is screaming at the top of his lungs. His pants are hanging low, his head is held back, and his eyes are blazing red. He is covering his manhood with his hands, a puddle of blood trickling down his legs. His blond hair is dripping with sweat, and his face is colored in pain. Then I see Claire, covered in vomit and lying in blood on the ground. She is unconscious.

It doesn't take me long to put two and two together. Mr. Azazel forced her to perform the unthinkable—he placed his manhood in her mouth, and she bit it in return.

Since day one, my beloved has proven that she does not tolerate disrespect in any shape or form. She has always proven she

208

has a backbone. That's my girl, and I have never been more proud. But what type of beloved would I be if I didn't finish the job?

My now red eyes zero in on my beloved's attacker. All I can think about is ending him for good. His blood is mine to take. He shall suffer the most-painful death imaginable, and I shall be the one to execute the task. I shall be the one to end him.

My chest feels heavy as the predator claws his way out of me. Fire burns within me and rushes throughout my body like a tidal wave. My chest is ablaze, the monster inside me ready to be released.

Master Azazel goes visibly still. The antelope finally notices the lion's presence. He begins to speak, but I cannot understand a single word that leaves his mouth. All I can see, hear, and think about is his heart, with blood oozing out of it and onto my hands. I can taste it in my mouth as I imagine his lifeless eyes after I rip his body apart, limb from limb.

My vision is dripping in blood—deep, deep scarlet-red blood. The predator has taken over completely, and now I'm nothing but the barbaric monster I'm known to be. My hunt is about to begin!

My first step is slow, very slow, just in case his body alerts his mind of the danger he has placed himself in. I hold back the monster inside me just a little. If I give him his way, the bastard's death will be fast. A quick death is too good for Azazel. He needs to suffer and beg me to end him. I wouldn't have it any other way.

His once red eyes now glow green—aww, he senses the threat—and a new emotion starts brewing in the atmosphere. I can smell fear as it swirls in the air. I take a deep breath in. Claire's scent travels through the air as well, slightly calming my monster.

My second step is calculated. I carefully watch my prey as panic whirls in the center of his fearful eyes. I'm sure that if his heart could beat, it would be pounding—sounding the alarm. His survival instinct shall kick in soon, and I want him to fight back, just like Claire had to fight back. I want him to plead with his superior, but not that it matters because he is done for nonetheless.

To remain calm, cool, and collected is my third step. In fact, my monster has calmed completely. We are on the same page; we both agree that making this weak creature suffer would make the kill exciting.

I run my tongue over my fangs that have been throbbing for his blood.

Master Azazel takes a step but slips and lands in his own puddle of blood. He quickly stands back up, and I can tell he is going to make another run for it.

Good. I want him to. I welcome the thrill of the chase. The hunt shall be full of fun. What he doesn't know is he won't make it out of the door. This room shall be his final resting place.

"My king," he begins, "please give me the opportunity to explain myself. The human had broken the rules, so I issued the punishment in your favor."

*Pounce, pounce, pounce* . . . That's all I can think about.

The closer I get to him, the more the excitement of the hunt seems to increase. He pleads more, and another tidal wave of fire rushes inside me. The thrill of tasting his blood that shall come delights me.

*Pounce, pounce, pounce* . . .

I'm almost there. I swear I can hear his unbeaten heart start to beat. *Pound, pound, pound* . . . That's how it sounds.

He bolts!

"Aww, not so fast, Azazel." I grab him by the back of his neck—such an easy catch!—not giving him a chance to move even an inch. "Now tell me, Azazel, what have you done to my Claire?" I hold him high into the sky, my bare hand around his neck.

I remember Claire's pain that knocked the wind out of me. I remember what followed shortly after. I remember the fear that this weak piece of sh*t caused Claire as it flushed through me like a bucket of cold water.

I dig my sharp claws into his neck, crushing his windpipe like he crushed her ribs. "I'm going to enjoy this," I tell him.

The sound of his voice is music to my ears as he continues to beg and plead for his life like the weak and pathetic little b*tch he is. Have you ever heard a mute man scream? That's exactly what he sounds like when I crush his voice box completely, no longer holding the monster back that is ready to shed some blood. I should have ended his life at the auction. This is my fault!

I throw him into the wall, and his back snaps and cracks. I do it to his body over and over until he is nothing but a loose bag of bones. Next, I use my claws to leave open gashes down his face. The blood flows out by a gallon, cascading down his skin. Still, the wicked, menacing monster inside me is not satisfied. He wants more blood. He needs his blood.

I sink my fangs into Azazel's throat and rip off his flesh, at the same time holding myself back from tearing him piece by piece. The taste and scent of his blood send my dark and barbaric side into a bloodlust frenzy. Even though he cannot scream, I know he's screaming as I can feel his throat vibrate. I'm going to drain him. He shall die!

All of a sudden, a cool hand firmly grips my shoulder. "Nicklaus that's enough," says a voice I can't seem to recognize at the moment.

I growl, warning the newcomer away.

"Xander, stop him! He's going to kill him," shouts another voice while I continue to drain Azazel. I won't stop until I have every ounce of his blood.

"He's already dead!" a cold and malicious voice exclaims.

Another monster is close by. I can feel him rising on the horizon. My prey is no longer struggling. The smell of his blood hangs in the air as his life is slipping away in my very hands.

"Get the girl," orders a voice.

Another smell invades my senses, hitting me fast and hard like a breath of fresh air.

211

*My beloved.*

Claire's bewitching and delightful scent calms the storm and locks the monster away. Instead of seeing red, everything around me turns black and white and then to vivid shades. I'm drenched in blood from head to toe.

I drop Azazel's limp body onto the floor. He's still alive but barely hanging on. Claire's body is tossed into my hands. Its warmth is my consolation and serenity, her soft moans music to my ears.

After what seems like forever, I start to notice the others who are in the room. Xander is standing by the door like a statue. His eyes are on fire, and his body is visibly stiff. His monster must be fighting to take full control.

"The girl needs blood," Aldon calmly speaks. He takes a single step, careful enough not to set me back on guard.

I slice into my skin with my fangs. Claire moans again. She can smell my scent. I place her soft lips onto the cut, allowing my blood to pour into her mouth.

"My king, are you sure you want to feed the girl? I can feed her with my blood. No human should be allowed to taste royal blood," Count Cloven states.

I growl in response. "Her name is Claire and don't speak about her in such manner. I'm the only vampire that shall feed her. She is mine."

Cloven's and Aldon's eyes shift completely to Claire and then back to me. The two share a look, then nod in understanding. They now know that Claire is my beloved without further explanation.

Claire continues to sup my blood like it's her last meal. Once her body has completely healed, I softly push her mouth away. She inhales deeply and buries her face into my chest. She knows she is safe. She should have never been placed in danger. Her body should have never been degraded. He shouldn't have been able to come anywhere near her.

"Bring me Lieutenant Astrid and Commander Vlad," I demand.

There shall be hell to pay.

Cloven disappears, leaving Xander and Aldon.

"And what should we do with him?" asks Aldon, holding that pathetic scum by the neck.

I place a gentle kiss on my beloved's forehead. "Xander, take Claire."

He immediately takes her out of my hands, and she softly whines. I fight the urge to bring her back into the safety of my arms.

Xander senses my struggle. "She is safe. You have my word."

I watch him leave the room with my love safely tucked into his arms. Jealousy hits me hot and strong, but I know now isn't the time. I must finish dealing with Claire's attacker.

"Bring him to me!" I order.

Aldon hesitates at first.

"Brother, this bag of sh*t deserves death. He should be prosecuted without trial," he finally says, using his tone of reason. "However, that's not our way. He comes from a respectable family, which means he has the right to request trial. If you kill him without that honor, the council will demand consequences."

"F*ck the council!" I growl. "This is not his first attack against my beloved. He shall die!"

"She is not claimed as your beloved," he points out. "Furthermore, your emotions are clouding your better judgment. His disappearance won't go unnoticed as he is a representative from Lady Gwen's house. She would demand to know his whereabouts."

"F*ck her too!"

"Please listen to reason. I have never steered you wrong."

I growl in frustration. I hate to admit it, but he's right.

Our laws were created for a reason. An attack against the king's beloved is an act of treason. However, only a handful of people know that Claire is my true beloved. Even if I brought Master Azazel to trial, he would win. My beloved will never get fair justice because of the stupid laws I made.

"You're right." I make my way over to Aldon and the piece of sh*t. "He shall keep his life until I find a way to take it once and for all. But he cannot roam freely in my kingdom or any other kingdom." I yank the pathetic creature out of Aldon's hand. He is still out cold, but his vampirism has already started the healing process. "Master Azazel is under arrest. If anyone asks why, tell them to take it up with me."

Aldon nods in agreement. Quickly, he takes Master Azazel out of my hold, knowing that the predator inside me may change his mind and take his life at any time.

I walk toward the door, struggling to control my monster. Master Azazel is getting off too easily. I turn to face Aldon one last time as he drags him out of the room. Having decided that I'm not satisfied with the outcome, I make my way over to them. Aldon freezes as I grab onto Azazel's manhood and squeeze it so hard that blood starts to pour out of it. Azazel's eyes shoot open—just in time for the grand finale—as I yank his manhood out of its socket. Somehow managing to find his vocal cords, he screams so loud that I can imagine the windows busting out of the entire palace.

"There. Now you can take him," I tell Aldon, as I finally make my exit.

# CHAPTER THIRTY-TWO
## It's Getting Hot and Spicy

I reach my private chamber seconds later, still struggling with controlling my monster. He wants the blood of that pathetic excuse of a vampire, but he can't have him.

The first thing I hear when I step inside is Claire's steady heartbeat. She is still asleep. I can sense that Xander is upstairs with her. He is the only one besides Claire's private guards that has access to my wing. Nannie is also here. She's in the kitchen, most likely making Claire some pancakes. My beloved loves pancakes, and I don't understand why. They are such terrible-tasting things.

Everyone has already been waiting for me patiently when I head downstairs after taking a shower and cleaning myself up. Count Cloven and Duke Aldon are sitting on the couch. Xander is leaning against the wall, holding a glass of blood. He is still very angry.

Lieutenant Astrid and Commander Vlad are both on their left knees, heads bowed down and backs straightened.

"You may rise. There is no need for pleasantries. Let's get straight to the point." My eyes rake over the both of them. My monster is already at the surface. He wants the blood of Claire's attacker and the ones that should have been there to protect her.

Master Azazel may be protected by the law, but Lieutenant Astrid and Commander Vlad broke it. They defied my command and didn't follow my direct orders. Now, nothing can save them.

The moment Vlad stands to his full height, I am in front him. I grab the base of his neck with my bare hand. "Explain yourself."

There is absolutely no reason he could have failed protecting my beloved. He is the best of the best. I assigned him to protect Claire because of that particular reason. So he doesn't know who or what Claire is to me? Regardless, an order is an order. As a commander, it is his job to follow that; it is his job to carry it out even if it costs his life. He's a disappointment.

"Forgive me," says Vlad, his eyes fixed on the floor.

He knows better than to look me in the eye. At this moment, he is my prey.

"I was communicating with the comrades in the northern kingdoms. There was another attack. The dogs issued a direct attack on King Cyrus's palaces, and many were dying. The intelligence team requested to speak with me. Once I became aware of how big the threat our armies were facing, I summoned Lieutenant Astrid. She was the only one on our team who came face-to-face with lycans," he continues.

"Lycans?" I drop him to his feet.

Cyrus mentioned once that werewolves and lycans had teamed up. Even so, a direct attack on the northern palace is a declaration of war.

I turn to face Cloven. "Is it true?"

He answers with a single nod.

"Very well, then I grant forgiveness to the both of you."

"However, if this ever happens again, I myself shall end you," Xander pipes up, warning them with cold and piercing eyes.

They both bow and accept his words with no argument. One thing is clear: Xander will take action behind his threat.

"The new moon is in three days," informs Xander. "Are we prepared to depart?"

"Yes, but we are leaving at once. I will not allow my dear friend to continue to fight alone," I respond.

216

Everyone stands up and bows, then gets straight to their tasks.

It's time to take a trip to North America.

*     *     *

## CLAIRE

My throat hurts. It burns so badly, and I don't know why. I can't shake this god-awful taste on my tongue. Other than that, I'm very comfortable while I'm covered in warm, silky (and muscular) comfort. It feels so good.

I move in a little closer—heavenly! Ummm . . . I have never been this comfortable in my life. With the exception of my throat tingling periodically, I'm content.

A smooth, cool surface touches my ribs, and I instantly flinch. An image of somebody's strong hand colliding with my body invades my memories. Replays of recent events flicker in and out of my mind like a movie: the training, the dinner, the book, and me being attacked again for the thousandth time and violated for the millionth time.

Oh God, I feel sick. I roll over in the very moment vomit erupts, explodes, then pours out of my mouth. My eyes snap open as I feel a soft hand tracing circles on the back of my neck. The pounding of my heart increases tremendously.

*Where am I? Who the hell am I with?*

Starting to panic, I release a high-pitched scream. I can't see, think, or hear clearly as my body is being attacked by my mind—the images of that leech forcing himself down my throat, the wicked glint in his glowing green eyes blazing with pure evil, and his touch and the brutal force he used to get his way!

I scream and scream and scream as loud as I can.

*"Shh, calm down, firecracker,"* comes a soft voice inside my head.

217

I continue to shake, losing focus. I know that voice.

*"Calm down. You're safe. I'm here, Claire. No harm shall come to you."*

I instantly relax, and that's when I realize I'm on a bed, someone's bed. The stench of my own vomit invades my senses.

"Claire, you are safe."

"Where am I?" I jump out of the bed.

King Nicklaus holds his hands up carefully and points down to the puddle of vomit that's one step away from my feet. My eyes scan the place. I don't recognize my surroundings. We are in a really small room—smaller than the ones I have grown used to waking up to—with simple but elegant decorations. In that very room is a small black bar filled with many alcoholic beverages. It has a big flat-screen TV mounted onto the wall. There's also a small closet—extremely small—so there's no way we are in a room that's inside the king's home.

Once the tiny oval window comes into view, my suspicions are confirmed.

"We are flying," King Nicklaus tells me, reminding me of his presence. "We are on a plane of course, well, my private jet." He slowly rolls off the other side of the bed, then enters a door I didn't realize was there.

I stare into space, and clouds in the pitch-black sky seem to pass by.

King Nicklaus returns seconds later with a cleaning bottle and a rag in his left hand.

My eyes trail down to my puddle of puke.

Oh right. I forgot about that.

"We are on our way to the northern kingdom." He bends down right beside me, and I nearly lose my mind. He sprays the cleaning chemicals and starts to clean up my mess—my puke.

"You don't have to do that. I got it."

218

"Nonsense," he says, scrubbing up *my* mess. "If you want to brush your teeth, you can use the bathroom. I left you a toothbrush on the counter sink."

"Bathroom?"

"Yes." He holds his free hand out toward the direction of the door. "That's the bathroom. There is also a washcloth on the counter just in case you need to wash your face."

Wash my face? Oh right. After what I just went through, I'm sure I look like a rabid animal.

Without further questions, I make my way into the bathroom. I don't even get a chance to view my surroundings. I'm caught off guard by the first thing I see—my own reflection. It's me but not really me. I mean I look like myself, but at the same time I don't. In the past couple of weeks, my hair has grown faster than usual. From the looks of it, it is now a few inches longer. It's full of life, and its color is now extremely bright, sort of like the beaming rays of the sun.

My green eyes are brighter as well and are more vivid, electrifying, and intense. They remind me of two tiny emeralds. My usual tan skin is now a little pale, which just makes me look more alive—believe it or not. It is also clear, not even a scar in sight. My breasts feel heavier, perkier, and rounder. They look great, really freaking great! I swear my boobs have grown from a *C* to a *D* cup. Wow, I'm beautiful! I mean I have always been beautiful, but gosh, I'm hot.

I pull up my shirt to search for bruises. That weak piece of sh*t punched me in my ribs, and even though I don't feel pain, I'm sure he left a bruise. Well, I thought he did, but my skin looks flawless. There is no purple bruise, and there are no black marks.

"I healed you," says King Nicklaus, startling me.

I didn't even hear him come in.

He squeezes his way over toward the sink. The bathroom is so small, so we are basically forced to be side by side. When his warm, soft skin brushes against mine, I can't help but shiver. It feels so good that it's scary.

King Nicklaus runs some hot water over the washcloth, the steam from it floating in the air. Suddenly, this tight confinement of a space feels hot, extra spicy. Then I realize for the very first time I'm wearing a cream cashmere sweater and some matching cream leggings instead of the black V-neck and leather jeans.

"Who dressed me?" I ask, hoping and praying that it wasn't him.

"Xander's chosen." He tightly squeezes out water from the rag. "She was the closest female slave available. She was also told to clean you up."

Strangely, his statement makes me smile from ear to ear. I know most people would feel uncomfortable with their enemy being the one to change their clothes, but I'm not that person. Honestly, it kind of feels good to know that Victoria Uppity Ass was the one forced to clean me up. I know for a fact that I got under her perfectly flawless skin. Trust me, she's not used to playing the errand girl. I can't wait to rub it in her face and say, "Hey, Victoria, why don't you wipe my ass?" or "Hey, red-headed she-devil b*tch, come over and brush my hair." Oh torture at its best.

"Why are you grinning like a Cheshire cat? Don't tell me that human-saving Claire is stepping over to the bad side?" He takes a step in front of me and boxes me in. He flashes me a deep, dark, and seductive smile.

I think I might faint. After a second of him, me, and the good ole bathroom of steam, I take a single step back. It's getting hot in here. My palms are sweaty, and my knees feel like jelly. To make matters worse, his hard abs are on full display.

"Hmm, is that mine?" I look at the warm rag.

He wrings it out one more time, allowing water to drip onto the floor, then he gently trails it down my face. The skin-to-skin contact gives me another round of chills.

220

"You deserve to be waited on, Claire," he tells me, his voice dark and wicked. "The world should cater to you."

I'm so lost in his touch that I can't even question his words. When he removes the rag from my face, I literally almost whine.

King Nicklaus walks out of the door shortly after I start brushing my teeth. The toothpaste is heaven to my tongue. Feeling refreshed, I then follow after him.

"What's your poison?" he asks, as I settle down on the bed.

I don't answer him right away. Instead, I focus on him pouring some liquid and then some red mixture into a glass—gross!

I believe he just spiked his drink with . . . Yuck, I think I'm going to be sick again. I don't drink, but I do know that a Bloody Mary is not my thing.

I scrunch up my nose in disgust. "Toxin-free?" I turn to face the small window. Anything is better than watching a vampire drink a blood-infused alcoholic beverage.

"Virgin then," he responds, making me flinch.

Just hearing that first word makes me think of why I'm not a virgin. With one single word, I retreat back to a dark place. I may be a lot of things but being a virgin is not one of them.

The bed sinks as King Nicklaus lowers his tall frame down right next to me. "My apologies, Claire." He places his drink on the little nightstand.You know, I noticed how you scrunched up your nose at my drink," he says. "Do you want to hear a secret?" he asks in a playful tone.

I can tell he is attempting to lighten the mood, and I'm beyond grateful.

He flashes that award-winning Cheshire-cat smile—that smile that reaches his eyes and reveals his pearly white teeth. Yup, that one.

"I'll be honored." I respond, purposely sounding overexcited. I put my hands over my heart and bat an eye.

His smiles flip upside down, turning into a childlike frown. He gets me just fine, doesn't he? I can't help but laugh, and surprisingly he joins right in.

"No, seriously, would you like to hear a secret?" he asks again in between fits of laughter.

When I don't answer and continue to laugh my butt off, King Nicklaus decides to tell me.

"Vampire blood has healing powers, Claire."

"Dun, dun, dun. Is that the big, bad secret?" I joke, still laughing my ass off. I'm actually rolling. I have no idea why it's so funny, but it is.

King Nicklaus has stopped laughing. "No, it's not, Claire." He pulls me onto his lap unexpectedly, and before I have time to react, he says,The secret is I gave you my blood to drink, twice now."

I start to fidget, his words really not registering.

"You gulped down the substance both times and moaned from the taste," he continues.

I'm lost for words, but I have one for him: crazy. He has gone insane.

Just when I'm about to tell him he has lost his goddamn mind, his lips crash into mine.

# CHAPTER THIRTY-THREE
## French Kiss

His soft lips are like a feather tickling my skin; they are steam that rises to the air from a cup of morning coffee. And his wicked and savory tongue is like warm apple cider, providing a sweet spice to coat my very own.

My taste buds explode, and each and every sensation blends in perfect harmony as our tongues tango passionately. His mouth latches onto my bottom lip, sending my body straight to hell and burning me whole before bringing ice water to freeze hell over. I'm set on fire and frozen alive together at the same goddamn time.

He lifts his right hand, only to place it onto my inner thigh. I moan as he squeezes it while deepening the kiss—our kiss, the French kiss that King Nicklaus and I share.

My moan must have sparked something inside him because suddenly he starts to gently suck on my bottom lip. My mind forms another word: inferno—a large fire wildly spreading through my entire body, dangerously breaking the rest of my self-control. That's exactly what seems to be happening inside me.

I devour his lips, sucking, tasting, and licking them. Oh my God, they taste so good! He returns the favor by sucking, tasting, and licking my own tongue. We are at war. Our tongues are fighting against each other, battling for control. The kiss is hot and demanding yet cold and isolating. Nothing around us seems to exist right now. It's just me, King Nicklaus, our lips, and our tongues.

There is nothing else in this entire godforsaken world matters at the moment.

I roll over on top of him, ready and hungry. He slightly lifts up my cashmere sweater with his left hand to grip my waist, and my mind goes haywire with the skin-to-skin contact. The feel of his fingernails digging into my skin sends a tidal wave of need and want to surface in the center of my core. Desire is stirring in my blood as his hungry tongue travels to the back of my throat. I open up my mouth wider, finally allowing him to take full control.

Oh, now why did I do that?

The feel of his tongue down my throat and his hands touching my bare skin makes my heart, mind, body, and soul explode.

He pulls away, breaking the kiss and leaving both of us breathless. My lips are swollen.

"Claire," he breathes, capturing my heart with his eyes, "I have waited a thousand lifetimes to taste your lips."

Once again, he holds me captive with his mouth. He doesn't take his time anymore or fight with me for control. He does it hungrily, kissing me hard and strong. He's an artist painting a story with his lips, and I can feel his raw emotion traveling inside my soul from the tenderness of his kiss. I know he means every word he utters. His actions speak louder than his words. His kiss says, "I need you" in English, French, and Russian. His hunger is pulling me underneath, adrift, and I'm sinking.

When he takes his lips away, I whimper like a child who has lost their favorite toy. Oh, I have never experienced this before. My heart is in his hands, and my soul has been transferred into his heart by the touch of our lips. He unbuttons his dress shirt seductively, the look in his eyes telling it all. I know exactly what he's going to say before he even says it.

"Take off your clothes, Claire," he demands.

I follow. In this moment, I'll follow his every command.

Slowly, I pull off my sweater and hesitantly pull down my leggings. I start to shake, feeling nervous under his watchful stare. My reflection is drowning in his irises. I cannot breathe. His eyes are like smoke suffocating me.

Once I've undressed, he slowly drinks in my features. He's hungry. He is hungry for me. I'm wearing nothing but my undergarments, and I have never felt this bare, so naked. He pushes me back onto the bed, and my heart pounds faster. I'm far from a virgin, but I never gave anyone my body willingly. This is different.

He pins my arms over my head, and adrenaline flushes through my veins. He stares at me, his eyes full of lust, passion, love, and devotion. However, in the back of his beautiful irises I can see his predator lurking, his inner monster surfacing.

I place my focus on his glorious chest, secretly gushing over his well-built frame. He unbuckles his pants, and I can hear his belt jingle.

*     *     *

"But because you insist on talking, I will have to silence you in another way."

I start to panic, and my body goes into shock when he pulls down his pants.

*No, no, no! This isn't going to happen again.*

The sick and weak piece of sh*t roughly grabs me by my left arm. Adrenaline must be kicking in because I start to fight. I kick my leg out, and my foot collides with his manhood. Just like King Nicklaus, he resembles a deer caught in headlights, surprised and stiff. He crouches over in pain as expected, and that's when I make a run for it.

I'm almost there, inches away from the door, when he pulls me by the hair and slams me into a wall. My body crumples as I slide onto the floor. Seconds later, he jabs his powerful hand into my stomach, knocking the air out of my chest.

"You see, I was going to take it gently, but you just had to act like the stupid little b*tch that you are!" he growls. He slams his hand into my side, breaking my ribs in the process.

I howl out in pain.

"Does that hurt, baby? Don't worry. I'll ease your pain, just like you're going to ease the pain that you caused."

Without warning, he grabs a handful of my hair and shoves his manhood in my mouth.

*    *    *

"Nooo!" I scream at the top of my lungs. My body visibly starts to shake, and hot tears trickle down my face as my back hits the wall. Every touch and every vile and monstrous act that leech performed on my body surface in my consciousness. I feel a deep sense of shame as I'm reliving my past, of which I'm a prisoner; I'm chained to it.

"Claire." King Nicklaus pulls me into his arms. "Firecracker, it's me. I'm here. Please come back to me."

I kick, shout, and desperately attempt to get away. "Nooo! Please, don't touch me. Please, no . . . Leave me alone!"

He ignores my screams. He lifts me up into his arms and cradles me into his warm chest. I allow him to rock me and place gentle kisses on my forehead. My body goes numb. His kisses calm me down. He is my comfort.

"I will never do anything you don't want me to do," he whispers in my ear, his voice full of raw emotions and his tone calm.

I cry, releasing all my pain on the beauty of his rock-hard chest. He pulls me in closer, and I feel secure in his arms. He softly strokes my hair with his fingers. I close my eyes and breathe in his clean, crisp, and fresh scent. His natural aroma blends perfectly with his rich and elegant cologne. My eyelids start to feel heavy. I'm in love. I feel at peace.

*     *     *

"Claire, wake up." King Nicklaus's soothing voice invades my eardrums. "Claire, please wake up. I would like to talk to you before we enter the northern kingdom."

I roll over on my left side. King Nicklaus's beautiful, stormy, unapologetic eyes meet mine and pierce my soul.

Argh, I would never get used to these mind-blowing orbs.

He drapes his right arm over me and gently places his chin on top of my forehead. We are wrapped as one in an intimate position, tangled together under the silk sheets.

"Yes, King Nicklaus?" I yawn, still half-awake.

"My name is Nicklaus, Claire," he says, his tasteful lips curving into an attractive smirk. "I would like you to call me by my name. However, if you insist on utilizing my title, so be it. You may call me King Handsome or King the Great, or King Sweet Kisser. Yeah, that's more like it. I like the last one the most."

I burst out laughing. "King of ass kissing!"

"Claire's ass-kissing king." He puckers his mouth and starts to make smooching sounds.

I can't help but roll my eyes. He is so childish.

"Seriously, Claire, please call me Nicklaus." He strokes my golden hair.

I love it when he does that. The feel of his masculine but soft fingers is like firm rose petals gently brushing through the roots.

I release a deep sigh. "Okay, okay, I'll call you Nicklaus even though I don't understand why it's such a big deal. You're a king." I point at his chest. I'm a slave, your slave."

"You're right. That's exactly why you have to do what I tell you to." He points at my chest, copying me.

I glare in his direction.

"So, Claire's ass-kissing king it is then?" he asks.

227

"Yup, that works."

"I bet it does." He laughs.

His laughter makes me smile. I love that sound and the way his silver-cerulean eyes glint with mischief during the process. He is mesmerizing—such a phenomenal catch.

"As entertaining as this conversation is, I didn't break your sleep just to discuss what you can or cannot call me." He flashes that devilish smirk.

Gosh, he is so goddamn charming. The vampire world should really make a law that forbids King Nicklaus from smiling, smirking, or grinning. It should be illegal.

"I'm sure." I look anywhere but at him.

Seriously, he really should be banned from smiling.

He uses his gentle but firm index finger to turn my face with my chin. His usual silver-cerulean eyes are three shades darker, resembling the deep blue sea. Staring at them puts my cheeks on fire and makes my heart race. King Nicklaus—oh, I mean my ass-kissing king—will always and forever have this effect on me.

"I would like to erase the memories that haunt you," he tells me, turning the mood from playful to serious.

"Haunt me?" I say out loud. "Wipe my memories . . . You can do that?"

Of course, he can. If he can control people's actions, read minds, and make a person lose their sight, why wouldn't he be able to wipe memories? The real question is, What else can he do?

"Have you wiped my memories before?" I ask.

He doesn't respond right away.

"Anything I have done has been to protect you, Claire," is his vague answer.

"And what is that supposed to mean, ass-kissing king?" I mock, using that ridiculous pet name just to get under his skin.

"You know exactly what it means, Claire," he says with a frown, rolling off the bed. "Sometimes, it's better not to know." He walks into the bathroom and closes the door behind him.

*Oh no, he doesn't . . . He will not get away with playing mind games. He will tell me what he did like a man—well, like a blood-sucking leech of a man.*

I stand up and bang on the door. "So what you're basically saying is you wiped my memory once before to protect me, right? If you already did some creepy vampire voodoo," I yell at him, banging harder, "why bother asking for my permission now? As a matter of fact, why did you erase some memories in the first place?"

I'm met by silence.

"Answer me, you blood-sucking leech."

He chuckles.

*Ugh. That deep, dark chuckle annoys me to no end.*

He opens the door. "Oh really? I was under the impression that my 'deep, dark chuckle' makes you smile." He winks.

"Stay out of my head!"

*Gosh. That's so freaking annoying. Can't a girl have a little privacy? My head equals my thoughts. Nicklaus is . . .*

"The best ass-kissing vampire king there is," he says, obviously refusing to stay out of my head.

I just can't win with him. I throw my hands up in the air in surrender and turn my back to him. I've decided I will not talk to him. Nope! Two can play that annoying game.

Before I know it, his two muscular arms already wrap around my waist, and he lifts me up in the air.

"Claire, say sorry."

*Sorry? Is he crazy?*

"Sorry for what? You're the one invading my privacy."

*Argg. Now, here come his magical lips, coating my neck.*

"Say sorry now, Claire." He continues to attack, trailing soft kisses.

When his wicked tongue travels on the base of my neck— oh boy!—I freaking explode.

"Sorry," I tell him.

*Gosh, he is so goddamn annoying.*

He attacks my neck harder and faster, so I guess my apology isn't accepted. "Say it again," he says.

*Oh my gosh. Someone save me.*

# CHAPTER THIRTY-FOUR
## The City That Never Sleeps

Right after Nicklaus finished his ruthless attack on my neck, the pilot announced we were landing. We are currently getting off the plane. Astonishingly high skyscrapers, a sea of eye-catching lights, and the one and only green lady with a green torch greet my eyes. We have entered New York City—the Big Apple, the Empire State.

This is called the City That Never Sleeps because vampires don't need to sleep. They can if they want to, but they don't need to. Hmmm, that proves my theory. Leeches are always awake.

The city is still as spectacular as it ever was. It was once filled with billions of humans from different walks of life. Now, it's filled with millions of vampires who carry their humans on a collar. These humans are their slaves, and they walk behind their masters, the leeches themselves.

I breathe in my first breath of city air. Fog appears, and white snowflakes land on top of my head. My fingers freeze.

I was told that New York City is always cold around this time of the year, but I think it is much colder now. I'm not just talking about the fresh air from the winter weather.

We make our way into an airport, and I see several other jets beside ours. There are vampires in black suits and glasses of the same color, shielding us from other views. I name them "men in black." They are serious, stone-faced men carrying weapons. You wouldn't want to mess with them.

When we step outside, sleek and matt black limos are already waiting for us—men in black (vampires) and black limos! If the king of vampire kings travels like this now, I could only imagine how he traveled when humans still roamed around freely.

Inside the airport, vampires acted like human servants. They practically bent over backwards, doing whatever King Nicklaus directed them to do. Well, he didn't actually direct anyone to do anything. He just looked at one of his men in black, who then looked at the vampire airport workers and instructed them to do certain tasks.

I have never been out in the vampire society, so I guess it's weird for me. When I think about a vampire-infested world, I think about gutted humans pinned to the wall. I think about creatures of the night walking around with faces painted in scarlet, not vampires working human jobs. I just didn't expect them to act so . . . so human.

Mr. Meany and his sidekick join us the moment we step out of the airport. They place a coat and umbrella on top of me, as if shielding me from the world, and it is another thing that catches me off guard. They behave like I'm the president's daughter, and they are my security detail.

Weird, weirder, and weirdos! What has gotten into these people?

We are on our way to King Cyrus's penthouse. I overhear the men in black talking about his palace in Canada that has been under consistent attacks, that is why the ruthless king is transported here.

Serves the jerk right. Karma is a big b*tch. That's exactly what he gets for scaring the life out of me.

The men in black are driving black *SUV*s. They are in front of us and behind us. There are also other limos in between the *SUV*s.

232

Nicklaus is holding my hand as we travel through the city. No one seems to notice or care that their king is holding his chosen's human hand in public.

I see many skyscrapers and countless lights that seem to blink as we drive by. I have seen pictures of this city's beauty, and so far, the scenery has lived up to my expectations. As anticipated, vampires and their human slaves watch the limos as we drive past. Some of them even stop what they are doing just to bow and drop to their knees. It's interesting.

"Are you enjoying the view?" asks Nicklaus. He gently squeezes my knees and rests his hand on my lap.

He is acting weird too. A chosen and their owner getting a little hot and heavy is not unheard of. However, it really shouldn't be happening, especially with me and the king. Displaying affection in public is strange, or maybe it's just my imagination running wild. Nicklaus probably acts like this with all his slaves.

"Are you enjoying the view, Claire?" he asks again.

Oh right, I forgot he'd asked me a question.

"Yes, King Nicklaus, it's really nice."

He raises an eyebrow. I can feel the disapproval rolling off him in energetic waves. The vibe goes from fresh to stale in a matter of seconds.

What did I say wrong?

I reevaluate my answer and conclude that it has to be the fact that I used his title, but he is the king. He couldn't have possibly expected me to call him by his name in public, could he? I may just be overthinking once again.

His jaw clenches as his grip on my lap tightens. I know now I'm most certainly not overthinking anything.

"What's my name, Claire?" he asks, gaining Mr. Meany's and his sidekick's attention.

Three pairs of eyes are all on me. The enormous limo seems to shrink as Nicklaus watches me closely, dangerously.

233

I place my focus back on the passing city lights. "Yes," I answer, my voice no more than a whisper. "I'm enjoying the view, ass-kissing king."

The sidekick bursts out laughing but with one look from her king, she immediately goes silent and returns to her usual stoned expression.

"Good. We are staying in Cyrus's penthouse," Nicklaus announces. "It was once one of the tallest buildings in the city."

"How tall?" I'm suddenly interested in architecture.

"Around 1,300 feet or so." He shrugs. "If I'm not mistaken, it was called 423 Park Avenue Condominiums before."

*Wait, what?*

"So, King Cyrus has a penthouse in the building?"

I saw pictures of that building in an old magazine at school. While growing up, I had always imagined life before the Awakening. New York City's skyscrapers always caught my eye, especially that one. There was something about the view that captivated me.

"The entire building is his penthouse," says Nicklaus nonchalantly. "If you prefer something more casual, we can stay in my old home."

"And where is that?" I can't stop myself from asking.

He flashes that award-winning smile but doesn't say anything further—such a tease.

The rest of our ride is quiet and peaceful, besides the fact that the predator, or the ass-kissing, continues to stare at me the entire time. The way he looks at me is unsettling and unnerving. It takes away a huge chunk of my peace, bringing forth distress. Anxiety rolls through my entire frame as I sense his predator lurking and on alert. For the life of me, I can't seem to understand why. I try my hardest to focus on the city lights, the buildings, the sea of people, and anything other than him, but I can't. My body seems to disagree with my mind.

His stare has its hooks in my soul. Lust and heated passion swirl in his eyes, holding me captive once again. King Nicklaus is practically screaming he wants to f*ck me, but honestly, so is my body. I want to f*ck him too. Gosh, I want those lips to devour me, those magical hands to explore my body, and those magnetic eyes to scream love instead of lust. I want him in a way that I will never be able to have him. I want him so bad that it's pathetic.

Out of the corner of my eye, I can see Mr. Meany and his sidekick watching us. I'm one hundred percent positive they can see and smell the arousal between us. It lingers in the air as our bodies speak their own language, not to mention how hard King Nicklaus is squeezing my hand. I think it's safe to say we have unfinished business. Actually, that's not safe to say at all.

*       *       *

We arrive in front of the building with a million windows and green beaming lights—423 Park Avenue Condominiums! The pictures I've seen did not truly capture the beauty of this building that seems to touch the sky. Down and up its entrance are well-manicured flowers, bushes, and even trees. Lined up on the side of the entrance is a crowd of vampires. I guess they are all here to get a glimpse of their king.

Back in the day, viewing a skyscraper in person was a part of many people's everyday life. In this day and time, it's a once-in-a-lifetime opportunity.

Seconds after the limo stops, the door opens and the men in black reappear, surrounding the entire vehicle. Flashing lights snap from every direction. Mr. Meany is back with the umbrella, dragging me inside. I feel like I'm a celebrity. Nicklaus follows closely behind me, holding up his hand to shield himself from the cameras.

When we enter the building, my eyes immediately travel to the arch, high ceiling, and extravagant crystal chandeliers and then

235

they land on the squeaky clean marble floor. In the center is a grand staircase, where many servants are patiently waiting. All humans, of course, stand with their back straightened and heads held down. There have to be at least one hundred males and females alike. At the top of the staircase stands King Cyrus.

"Welcome, my friend," he greets, his deep voice booming. "You've arrived earlier than expected."

"Of course," Nicklaus replies. "There is no way in hell we are allowing those dogs to get away with attacking a palace."

They continue their conversation as we walk up the numerous flights of stairs. My eyes linger on the many servants's faces I pass by. I study the males longer than the females since I have never seen a male servant before. The schools I attended housed only one gender, but I'd been told it may not be the case in other academies. I guess I'm just fascinated by them as Nicklaus's servants are all females too.

These male servants look like robots, so the sudden urge to wave my hand in front of their faces to see if they blink appears inside my mind.

*Hello, are you real? Blink,* I think to myself.

My fascination with them starts to burn out. Well, it's until one of them finally makes eye contact. He is smoking hot and appears to be in his middle twenties, around twenty-three or twenty-four. He has a face of a god. The color of his hair is somewhat similar to my golden shade, but maybe just a few shades darker. However, that's not what gains my attention. No, not at all. It's his eyes that resemble my very own. They stop me right in my tracks. I feel like I'm staring at the male version of myself in the mirror as we blankly stare at each other. His unique green shades really shock my soul.

Neither of us seems to want to break eye contact until a heart-dropping growl fills the air. It is so loud that I'm sure the entire building shakes. I turn in the direction of the growl. Nicklaus's glowing red eyes travel from me and then to the male

236

servant, literally popping out of his head. His fangs are on full display, and he looks way past the point of pissed.

Surprisingly, the male servant doesn't look afraid. A ghost of a smile graces his lips as he slightly bows his head. He doesn't bow to Nicklaus but to me. He must have a death wish.

*Oh sh\*t. Oh sh\*t. I can't be the reason another slave loses their life, not again.*

In the blink of an eye, Nicklaus is in front of us. I can see him yanking out the servant's heart before his hand even hits his chest. It's like déjà vu.

I quickly push the servant boy to the floor. "No!" I say firmly, holding out my arms to cover the servant boy—wrong move.

Nicklaus growls so loud, and the building literally shakes. His wicked and monstrous eyes drift from me and then to the servant boy. "You're dead," he announces, his voice dangerously low.

F\*ck! I think I've just made things worse.

# CHAPTER THIRTY-FIVE
## You Can't Talk Sense into the Senseless

"Commander," Nicklaus calls out.

Seconds later, two strong hands grip my left upper arm. Mr. Meany starts to manhandle me, roughly dragging me toward the top of the staircase.

"No, get the hell off me!" I yell in his big, mean face, attempting to break free. "Arghhh! I swear when I get free, I'm going to play ping-pong with your balls."

He doesn't budge, not even a bit.

"Asswipe! Jerk!" I mumble.

He still doesn't loosen his grip no matter how many names I call him. I see the slave boy shaking in his boots at this point, most likely pissing his pants, whereas Nicklaus cannot suppress the excitement in his glowing red eyes. He's circling the boy like a vulture circling its meal—a predator cornering its prey.

*This isn't happening. No, this can't be happening!*

We have just been in this building for less than five minutes, and within three minutes I've already had a poor slave sentenced to death. I don't get it. This must be some sick joke. What's the harm in looking at another slave? This is ridiculous, unbelievable, and completely absurd.

I continue my attempt to break free from Mr. Meany's iron grip. All the other slaves are now watching with horror-filled expressions.

"If you do this, I will never forgive you!" I yell as Mr. Meany pulls me up the stairs.

He doesn't say anything. Nicklaus doesn't even look my way either.

"You're a monster!" I yell again.

Mr. Meany continues to haul me up the staircase.

Nicklaus turns around to face me. "I know, firecracker." He smiles.

God, I hate that sick, beautiful, and sadistic smile. Okay, I'm lying. I love that smile, but seriously, who kills a slave because his chosen decided to look at him? This is some sick sh*t. It's barbaric, wild, and absolutely unacceptable!

*Thud, thud, thud.*

My heart is thundering in my chest, sounding like a beating drum—I'm so tired of hearing that goddamn sound. Everything goes in motion the very moment my two feet hit the top of the staircase. I feel like I'm watching a movie about a lion getting ready to pounce on a flamingo.

Nicklaus grabs the poor slave boy by the neck. All eyes are on them, but Nicklaus's eyes lock on mine. He turns the boy to face me, squeezing his windpipe so hard that I'm sure the boy is now mute.

King Cyrus says nothing. He seems rather amused, or tickled. Now I understand why he deserves the title Ruthless King. He doesn't even care that one of his slaves is about to be drained on his lobby floor. There's no pity or sympathy in his eyes. He's smiling instead, thrilled.

What type of man gets a kick out of another man's impending death? I know what kind: a sick one, sicker than sick!

In the next second, Nicklaus wraps his arm around the poor slave boy's neck and then sinks his fangs into his flesh. I can hear the human boy's skin as it rips. His screams fill the air, and his blood spurts out of his wounds.

My heart flutters rapidly as reality hits me. Nicklaus is really going to kill him. I can't believe I'm the cause of another soul to be taken from its body. I can't believe I have been so foolish, so stupid, and dumb. This is my fault. I let my guard down, knowing damn well that I'm dealing with a barbaric and unpredictable king. How can I allow this to happen?

My body starts to shake as guilt washes over me. I swear on my life I will not make the same mistake. Screw them all.

I look into the slave boy's eyes. "Please, stop! Please, Nicklaus," I beg.

Nicklaus only digs his fangs deeper, never once breaking eye contact with me. How can he be so cruel?

The boy's golden skin turns pale. I know he will be dead within the next minute. I can't watch this.

My eyes drop to the marble floor. It is squeaky clean in reality, but in my mind it's smothered in blood. My tears are flowing freely. My heart is breaking. My guilt is swallowing me whole.

"Your Highness, we have a problem," Mr. Meany speaks, catching me right before I fall.

I'm here, but at the same time I'm not. I can see and hear, but I can't feel. I'm officially numb.

The commotion from outside is loud. Seconds later, I hear someone burst through the front door, but I'm too afraid to raise my eyes. I'm lost in my own mind.

"What happened?"

"The dog got loose," is the last thing I recall hearing.

\*       \*       \*

The view is great. New York City lights shine bright like diamonds, glistening high above in the night sky as I stare out of the window in some room I don't remember entering. The last couple of hours has been a blur to me. All my emotions seem to be all over the place, and I'm too exhausted to sort anything out at the moment. Perhaps my mind has shut down completely. I don't want to know what's going on around me. I'm tired of this life and these monsters.

Someone knocks on the door.

"Claire," calls Xander. "Can I come in?"

No! I'm tired of him too.

Instead of telling him to piss off, I don't say anything at all. He takes that as an invitation and comes in. I continue to stare out of the window, pretending to be oblivious to his presence.

"My apologies for not getting to you sooner," says Xander with a concerned voice. "Are you okay? Have you eaten? I can get a servant to bring you something."

Oh, now he cares. Where the hell was he and why does it have to be a servant to bring me food? Why can't he since he cares so much? It's kind of funny how he was nowhere to be found when I needed him the most. He wasn't there when that monster attempted to force himself into me and when his barbaric brother added trauma to my already traumatized mind. The moral of the story is that one's words cannot be trusted. They say they care, but they actually don't.

"I'm fine. Can you just go away?" Right now I prefer to be left alone. I don't need anyone's pity or sympathy.

Xander takes a step closer. I can see his reflection in the window. The look on his face says it all. He isn't going anywhere anytime soon. Now that I don't need him, he's sticking to me like glue.

"Don't push me away, brave one."

I roll my eyes so hard. I'm surprised they don't get stuck in the back of my head. "How can you push away an invisible wall?"

"By smashing away the invisible barrier," he answers.

Of course Xander is the one to snap back with a clever remark. He is the king of wit.

I turn to give him a piece of my mind, but I'm left with my jaw dropped when I see a long claw mark on the left side of his face. All my anger fades at once. Without thinking, I run to him and jump in his arms.

"What happened to you?" My chest tightens with pain.

"Shh, brave one." He wraps his arms around me. "I should be the one apologizing to you. I wasn't here to talk some sense into Nicklaus. Please, forgive me."

"You can't talk sense into the senseless," I simply tell him, burying my head in his chest.

Xander is a giant compared to me, so I have to stand on tiptoes and try to hold my balance. I wrap my arms around his huge frame. I hate to admit that I needed this. I needed the comfort of a good friend. We both do.

"Brave one, I know you don't want to hear this"—Xander pulls away and studies my face for a while—"but I don't believe you should be too hard on Nicklaus about what happened."

I don't want to hear what he has to say.

"Can you at least promise me you will try to have an open mind?" he asks.

"Nope. Not going to happen!"

They say, "No question is a dumb question," but that was a dumb question.

"Claire," he calls, as I turn my back.

"Xander." I look out of the window.

He takes a deep breath. I can tell he is carrying the world on his shoulders, and for the life of me I can't figure out why.

"Did you finish reading *The Vampire Studies?*" he queries, changing the subject.

"Nope, something came up." I close my eyes. I don't want to think about that right now either.

"Hmm, I see. Do you have it with you?"

I nod in response. Someone had packed my belongings for my trip here in North America. I figured it was Xander, but once I found the book inside my luggage, I guess I was wrong.

"There's a chapter titled 'Blood Lust.' You should read it," he suggests. His tone makes it sound like a request more than a suggestion. He must be up to something.

"Are you going to explain to me why all of a sudden you recommend I read a certain chapter?"

"I think you will like it," he answers quickly, quicker than usual, confirming my suspicions. He really is up to something.

"And I expect that you're not going to tell me what happened to your face, are you?" I ask, although I already know the answer.

He doesn't respond. Now I'm the one asking dumb questions. Uh, Nicklaus and his brother are not the same in any shape or form, but they are both . . . unbelievable. You know what? I'm sick of the mind games.

I make my way toward the luggage, then start throwing out the items from it one by one. He wants me to read some stupid chapter. Fine. We can read it together.

I find the book in less than a minute, but to my surprise, he is gone.

*Typical of Xander.*

\*       \*       \*

Nine hours, five minutes, and fifty-nine seconds—that's how long I have been in this stupid room since Xander left me. To make matters worse, Mr. Meany and his sidekick are outside the door, guarding me like hawks.

I tried to go after Xander the exact moment I realized he left, but—boom!—came Mr. Meany. He's standing at the door right now with one hand pointed to the window. It doesn't take me long to figure out who sentenced me to prison.

I'm losing my mind. I'd rather be with the other slaves than sit in one place for however long King Monster determines is fit for me. It's not fair. I don't see why I'm incarcerated. He's the one who killed someone for no reason, not me. Argh! The only perk is they send lots and lots of food.

Astrid has been in and out of the room, asking if I want to learn how to control my heartbeat. Screw her too. I just looked at her as though she were invisible. I think she has decided to give up at this point. She hasn't been in here in a while now. I know I am acting childish, but oh, they treat me like a child, so I might as well act like one. Technically, I'm a child compared to them. For all I know, the sidekick can be three hundred years old or so.

Boredom strikes, so I follow Xander's advice. I take a seat on the windowsill and immediately attempt to locate the "Blood Lust" chapter, but to no avail because the book is so thick.

After ten minutes of searching for the chapter, I finally decide just to pick where I left off.

"The Story behind the Awakening." Nope, I had enough of that.

I flip through the page.

"Beloved." Okay, now this sounds interesting.

*A vampire has only one destined beloved. They are considered to be a vampire's other half—the most-cherished being in the world.*

I fight the urge to roll my eyes. How cliche can you get? I mean, I'm perfectly aware of what a vampire's beloved is, but this entry sounds cheesy as f*ck. Pardon my language, but it's done.

To make matters worse, I know plenty of slaves like Jadis, who fantasize about this ridiculous scenario. Don't get me wrong. She's a sweet girl. She just has a sick obsession.

*Like I have an obsession with Nicklaus's lips,* says the voice inside my head.

Okay, okay I'm being a hypocrite.

I continue to read.

*A vampire can decide to deny their destined beloved and choose to claim another. If a vampire denies their destined, they may risk their destiny. They have to be prepared for their destined to find a second-chance mate.*

"A second-chance mate," I repeat the last words out loud.

What the hell is that? I make a mental note to ask Xander about this later.

My eyes shoot to the door when it bursts open.

"Let's go now," says the sidekick.

Oh great, she's back for me. Some people will never get enough of blatant disrespect.

As soon as I open my big, sarcastic mouth to tell her to f*ck off, her eyes widen, and seconds later she is thrown into the wall.

What the f*ck!

My head snaps back to the door, and my eyes land on a tiny-framed woman with long jet-black hair that blends perfectly with her milk-chocolate skin.

"Mecca?" I am unsure if my eyes are playing tricks on me.

"Hello, human!" she growls fiercely. Her skin seems to glow, her yellow eyes sparking with light. She looks stunning. "I told you we shall meet again," she adds.

# CHAPTER THIRTY-SIX
## Hunting the Hunter Beast

Mecca is standing right in the doorway. Well, I'll be darned! She looks flawless, not a single bruise or scratch in sight. The wool blanket, the same blanket I loaned her a couple of days ago, barely wraps her body. Her long bronze legs—along with her kitten in the middle that most certainly needs shaving—are on full display. Mecca is almost bare, hairy but bare. Her hair is shinier than I remember. Wait a minute, why is it covered in blood?

Better yet . . . Why is she here? How is she even here in the first place? She looks like an avenging angel, basking in her hairy, bloody glory. She's a beast woman for sure. My gut is telling me that Mecca has been a naughty, naughty little she-wolf.

"You need to wash your hair," I tell her. "And, shave." I just have to add that.

She closes the door and sniffs the air. "And you need to take a bath. I can smell the cold-hearted king all over you." She tilts her head to the side. "Where is your leech king by the way?" asks Mecca.

Typical beast woman—she can't help but be that strange and creepy ole Mecca. Oh, how I missed her!

I rush to her side and give her a nice big bear hug, completely disregarding the fact that she almost has nothing on. Weird, I know, but don't judge me.

Her eyes widen, surprised obviously. Shockingly, she hugs me back.

"I missed you, Mecca," I confess.

Some icky blood drips from her hair and onto my skin—yuck!

Weird ole Mecca sniffs my hair. Her body goes stiff, more alert. "His scent is fresh. Where is he?"

"Huh? What are you talking about?"

"The cold-hearted king." She pulls away.

The cold-hearted king? I believe she is referring to Xander. I keep forgetting that's what people call him.

"I can smell him all over you. Where is he? How long has he been gone," she interrogates. "You smell like you took a bath with him." Her face crumples in disgust. This time she starts sniffing my entire body. She even bends over and places her nose dangerously close to my crotch. Oh my!

"Bad doggy." I push her back slightly.

Mecca looks at me like she wants to kill me. Oops! Wrong choice of words. Gosh, it's not my fault that she is so goddamn strange.

"I'll let that slide this one time, human," she growls.

I cross my arms. Here she goes with that *human* word. In her defense, I did just call her a dog. Oh well, I have no filter.

"I'll let that slide this one time, dog," I retort.

She growls again, but this time she sounds just like the wolf she is—deadly.

I lift my head and continue to stare directly into her bright, highlighted yellow eyes. I will not show any type of fear, beast woman or not. Mecca should know by now I'm not a coward, and she doesn't scare me.

Apparently, my actions amuse her because she holds back her head, laughing like the madwoman she is. There goes crazy ole Mecca again. I'm starting to believe she is bipolar.

"I apologize for offending you, brave little human. My sense of smell is not at its best right now." She takes a deep, sharp breath.

Right, so that's a good excuse for attempting to smell my kitty? Yup, she's a madwoman.

Her eye color returns to its natural amber shade. The city's beaming, glistening lights that illuminate the room shine down on her, highlighting her mocha-cream skin. I swear if I hadn't met Mecca in the dungeon, I would never believe she has been down there for over a hundred years already. Thinking of which . . .

"How did you get free?" I ask.

Her face creases into a lazy smile, and I can see the amusement flickering in her eyes as she turns to me. "I have to thank you for that."

"Me?"

"Yes, you! You helped me regain my strength. Those leeches, as you called them, had been starving me since day one. Everything changed when you spared me some of your rations. I'm forever grateful."

"Wait! Are you referring to the bread and water I shared with you?"

It couldn't possibly be. It was nothing but a piece of bread here and there. I'm sure even a werewolf, I mean she-wolf, needs more than that to regain their strength, especially one who has been starved and tortured for so many years.

Her smile deepens. "That's exactly what I'm referring to, and now I'm here to free you."

By sniffing me to death? Aww, how will I ever return the favor? I almost laugh out loud. Man, oh man, I crack myself up.

"A favor for a favor," announces Mecca.

This time I can't contain my laughter. Haha . . . very funny.

She looks at me suspiciously. "What's funny, human?"

Here she goes with that word again.

I'm still laughing, as she continues standing there.

248

Hold up. She must be serious. Mecca is crazier than I thought. We'll both as good as dead if we even try to escape. This is no problem honestly besides the fact that Nicklaus will drag me back by the hair and drain every slave before he finally decides to drain me.

"You must have a death wish," I tell her in between my fits of laughter.

"Do you doubt my strength, human?" She smirks.

Doubt? No. Think you're crazy, yes!

"Or, is it that you're content with your chains?" Now, she starts laughing. "I thought you were different, human. I was wrong. You're just like the rest of your kind, brainwashed and too afraid of their captors."

"Oh please! I'm far from brainwashed, and I'm most certainly not afraid of anyone."

She raises her eyebrow. "Oh, is that right?" she taunts. "Prove it! Come with me. I'm giving you the chance to get far away from your leeches. I'm offering you freedom." She leans in closer. "Come on. What's the worst thing that can happen? They'll capture us and decide to kill us. That shouldn't be a problem for you, right?" She taps her finger on her head. "If my memory is correct, which I'm sure it is, I recall you stating you'd rather die than continue to live the remainder of your life as the slave of the vampire leech. So you have nothing to fear."

She's right. I'd rather die.

"I just don't want others to die because of me," I admit. "Nicklaus has a bad habit of using others to try to break me."

Creepy ole Mecca laughs. "Nicklaus? Hmm. Aren't you just full of surprises? You don't have to worry about the other humans. The leech king, or Nicklaus, is occupied. Besides, my pack is on the way to free the other slaves. We're going to my old pack. You will be safe there."

Pack? Like a werewolf pack? Oh no, no, no. I'm not leaving these demons just to walk into the hands of another group of beasts. Wait, she just said they are on their way to free the other slaves. King Marcellus said something about a pack of dogs freeing slaves, and Mecca's pack does the same thing. How strange? Maybe it's just a coincidence. Nope, I doubt it is. That means her pack is already under the king's radar, so I'm not sure if it's that safe.

"It's really a win-win situation." Mecca smiles again. "They won't catch us. My pack will make sure of that."

An alarm goes off at the exact same moment—that doesn't sound too good.

"Times up, human. You must decide now," she tells me.

Oh crap. I don't know what to do. Should I stay or go?

I can hear war erupting outside the room door.

Mecca's eyes flash yellow. "Human, decide now!" she roars.

The sidekick groans from the other side of the room. Mecca and I both turn to face her. Mecca's eyes glow brighter as she takes a step forward.

F*ck, she is going to kill her. I don't like the sidekick, but she doesn't deserve death.

"Wait!" I grab Mecca's arm, and she snaps her head in my direction. "Let's go. I'm in."

"Don't tell me the famous, brave, leech-hating Claire has a soft spot for this particular leech?"

"I do not." I sigh. "We just don't have time for that. We need to come up with a plan. It's not like we can walk through the front door."

The noise from outside grows by the second.

Mecca shatters the window with her bare hand. "Hurry," she hisses.

OMFG! I know she is not indicating we are jumping out of that window. This building is around 1,300 feet or so. Hell no. This woman is insane.

"Are you crazy?" I ask.

Before I can further object, she rushes to my side, picks me up, and jumps.

\*　　\*　　\*

NICKLAUS

I lost control again. I was listening to that thinking about that filthy human doing indecent things with my beloved. I snapped. He should have been dead. Luckily for him, there are more pressing matters at hand. The dog b\*tch got away, attacking my brother in the process. She has taken me away from my beloved, stopped me from draining the boy, and touched Xander. I'm going to end her. She will die. I should have ended her when I had the chance. No worries, though. I'm in the mood to put a dog down. I just want to get back to my beloved. I miss her. I need to see her. I know she probably hates me right now because there are things she doesn't understand. I'll just have to make it up to her.

I'm still going to kill that slave. My beloved already believes he is dead, so what's the harm in getting rid of him altogether? Claire will forgive me. She can't resist me, just like I can't resist her. Before I can get back to her, I need to eliminate these beasts, starting with Mecca. I'll be damned if they continue to get away with their little stunts.

When Xander burst into the penthouse, he was drenched in blood. He informed us that the b\*tch had attacked him, and it infuriated us. A direct attack on a king, especially my brother, is punishable by death. The dog b\*tch will never go unpunished. That crazy dog has lost her mind. She knows she is no match for me. I'm going to torture every inch of her body, slowly killing her. I will break every single one of her bones, then heal her completely just to break her bones all over again. She will beg for mercy.

We just need to find the mutt first. That's exactly what we're doing now, searching for the animal. So far, we've had no luck. The stupid b*tch is smarter than we thought. I figured she will directly head back to her pack since we are close to their territory. Her pack members are the ones who have been stirring up all this trouble. I planned to use her as leverage to flush out the Alpha. She is the Luna after all, so they would be willing to die for her. That's exactly what will happen. They shall all die.

I have been outside the city gates for hours, looking for a single trail. She couldn't have gotten that far. I don't know how she'd managed to regain her strength.

"Nicklaus," calls Xander, as he gets out of the *SUV*.

I left him back in the penthouse hours ago so he could clean himself up and most importantly go check on Claire.

"Sorry for the wait. I needed to feed and regenerate. The dog was inches away from my heart."

His words only piss me off more.

I nod in understanding as we enter the woods together. I search the trees for the dog's scent while Xander checks the ground for footprints.

"Where are Cyrus and the others?" Xander asks.

"He is closer to the Northern Pack's border. I sent him to search some of the pack's villages just in case she goes there first. The others are closer to the penthouse."

"Claire is fine," he informs me. "Mad but fine. You've really f*cked things up. I feel like she isn't going to forgive you so easily this time, Nicklaus."

"We shall see." I wink.

I know my beloved is mad. My little firecracker has a soft spot for her humans, which bothers me sometimes. I get that she has a big heart, but in this day and time, her caring nature can also be her own downfall.

"Claire's attachment to her species is a weakness, Xander. I don't know how to break it."

"I don't think you should. Claire's kind and genuine nature is refreshing to me. It's like a breath of fresh air. In all my years of living, I have never met any woman from any other species that hosts such great qualities. She is brave, smart, and kind. She stands up for what she believes in and doesn't back down. She cares more for others than they do for themselves."

Xander is right. She truly is one of a kind, but her emotional attachment to others can make her vulnerable.

"I fear for her," I admit. "I don't want her to get hurt physically or mentally. She is too fragile. It bothers me that she will risk her life for another person. The lessons at the boarding school were designed to break humans like her. I don't understand how they didn't break her."

He raises his eyebrows. "One look was all it took for me to realize she would bend the rules and never break. Claire is a human who will really bring forth another awakening." Xander bends down to search the ground for footprints. "There's one more thing I notice," he says, moving some dirt aside with his hands. "I know you're going through blood lust . . ."

*"Your Highness."* Astrid's voice appears inside my mind. She is breathing heavily. I can sense her panicking through our coven link. Something is wrong.

*"They're here. We are under attack,"* she informs, without waiting for an acknowledgment from me.

I open my mind up completely. *"Get Claire out there now."*

A strong emotion of fear hits me hard. My body leans forward. My chest tightens, burning with scorching hot fury. I can feel the shift of my irises, matching my chest in color. My monster is taking full control. I've never felt this much rage. I know what she is about to say. I can feel it. There is only one reason why Astrid's fear seeps through my pores.

"Nicklaus, what is wrong?" Xander queries, his voice sounding distant.

*"Where is Claire?"* I ask Astrid.

Astrid's fear pours. Xander's body goes still. He is now mind-linking. I can feel his monster pushing through his own border, rising and making his presence known.

*"Where is Claire?"* I ask her again, this time using my power of command.

*"She took her,"* she answers in a whisper.

# CHAPTER THIRTY-SEVEN
## Thrilling Kill

My life flashes through my mind, different scenes flickering in and out in my head like a movie. I'm here and there, sort of somewhere in between, and it's a terrifying yet exciting type of thing. That's exactly what I'm experiencing right now as we fall at least 1,300 feet from the sky. My stomach drops, and I automatically release a scream. I don't know if I'm screaming out of fear or screaming because of the thrill. I have mixed emotions. Either way, the speed is animated and frightening.

My hands rise up into the air as Mecca tightens her arms around me. Her eyes are wide open, alert. She looks like a cat woman, which is quite interesting, with her being a she-wolf and all. She is basically the cousin of a dog.

Haha. Leave it to me to turn a life-threatening experience into a laughing matter.

The air pressure hits my face, smacking me back to reality. The speed, the height, the force of the wind, and the intensity of the drop make me scream louder. This is not how I imagined my life to end. I mean, sure this is totally a kick-ass way, but only a crazy person will actually go through with this.

Bingo, Claire! Mecca is the epitome of crazy. Actually, she's dangerously insane, which might also be an understatement. A mad maniac suits her best.

*When the hell is this going to be over? I swear to God this fall seems to have no end.*

As if on cue, Mecca's two feet hit the ground gracefully.

Gosh, this woman has doggy powers, catty eyes, and the techniques of a swan. Meanwhile, the human—and I mean I—is clinging to the animal woman like she is the air she breathes. I really, really, really want to choke her to death, but I don't think I can even manage to move. I'm still in utter shock.

"I can smell your fear, brave human," laughs Mecca.

Yeah, no sh*t, Sherlock. She just jumped off a freaking skyscraper with me cradled in her arms. I'm sure the entire building could smell my fear at this rate.

"It's not funny. You could have killed me! You're a psycho, lunatic, crazed, and deranged!"

She holds her head back, laughing her ass off.

See? That's exactly what I'm talking about. She is crazy!

"Relax. I was just having a little fun." She places me down firmly on the ground.

Relax? Oh, I'll show her relaxing right after I kick her doggy female nut. I don't care if she can't feel anything. She's lucky she is a *she* instead of a *he* because I would have really kicked her in the balls. That's my new signature move by the way.

Gosh, she really freaking jumped, and she still has the blanket wrapped around her. Even I must admit that's some cool sh*t.

Mecca smiles at me like she knows what I'm thinking, and I could only thank God she really doesn't.

"Just give me a warning next time," I tell her.

I focus my attention on my new surroundings. We are in a dark alleyway. It's a completely different world from the front of the building. There are no shining, glistening city lights. There is no entourage, and there are no beautiful vampires waiting to take pictures of you. It's silent, but I can still sense animals running by the trash cans. I believe I just saw a gigantic rat. Even my human

256

nose can smell the stench in the air. It's jeepers creepers creepiest! The chill in the air doesn't help the eerie vibe or feelings I cannot seem to shake.

Mecca responds with a nod and turns to scan the area. If she is frightened by our surroundings, she's very good at hiding it. Her nostrils flare as she sniffs the air. "This way," she says and then takes off, running into the darker part of the alleyway.

Of course, she goes in the direction where strange and weird things most likely linger during the night. She wouldn't be creepy ole Mecca if she didn't.

I throw my arms in the air and take off after her like the foolish human I am. My heart beats faster when I realize how far ahead she is already. "Mecca," I whisper urgently, hoping that no creepy thing pops up to strangle me.

I pick up speed.

I swear if this crazy she-wolf jumped from a sky-high building just to ditch me, I'm going to mentally smack myself.

"Mecca, come out. Come out wherever you are, doggy."

I do not care how mad she'll be at me. That's what she gets for trying to ditch me.

I can now see her shadow a few feet away from me. Some of the city lights shine down on this part of the alleyway, making it a lot easier to see. As I draw nearer, she looks stockier in the dark and her head appears bigger. My heart starts to go haywire as I get closer to her shadow.

*That's not Mecca. That's a man, a bulky man. And he is not alone.*

I stop right in my tracks, my heart pounding, hair raising, and gut wrenching. Basically, I'm scared as f\*ck.

The man turns to face me. He has wide eyes.

\*     \*     \*

NICKLAUS

We've made it back to the penthouse after a little over five minutes. My inner monster has taken over, alert and ready to kill. My chest is on fire, burning scorching hot coal. As soon as I breathe in the fresh scent of a werewolf, my entire body is drenched in the heat.

The first dog leaps into the air, and I slam my hand into his chest. I squeeze his heart and then yank it out with my bare hands. My vision is tinted red. All I can see or think about is the death I am going to bring to these dogs. They will all die.

I snatch out another dog's heart and then another, my hands laced with silver. Seconds pass and ten dogs have been put down, dead. They suffer the worst death. This is just the beginning. I will rid the world of their kind if it's the last thing I do. They took my beloved. None of them is safe.

I can sense Xander behind me. His monster is out, draining each and every one of his victims. He is taking his time to end them. He makes them suffer before he snatches their lives. It's one reason our enemies call him the cold-hearted king.

The scent of fear clings to the air as I make my way toward my next kill. It's a she-wolf, tiny and fragile. I run my tongue over my fangs. I can already taste her blood before I even bite into her skin. Her heart is beating so loudly, frantically; the closer I get, the louder it roars.

"Aren't you a beautiful little wolf?" I coo, the voice not my own. I flash a smile, making sure to reveal my fangs that will drain every ounce of her blood.

She takes a step back, and I take a step forward. I'm a predator, and she is my prey. I'm going to make this a painful kill.

"Please, don't," she begs. Her pleading is music to my ears—it's glorious. "I have a child. Please, please, please . . ."

"F*ck your child!" I yell, not giving a sh*t. I yank her by the neck and plunge my fangs deep into her throat. I can feel the vibration as she screams, but I can't hear a thing. Blood flows down my throat, tasting like heaven to my tongue. My bite to werewolves is like a silver bullet. It will take her life.

I gulp down the substance, and her body goes lifeless in my arms. I sling her aside like a rag doll and focus on my next kill. The sinister part of me has taken full control. My monster will not be satisfied until this entire penthouse is painted in dogs's blood. Men, women, boys, or girls—it doesn't matter—are all as good as dead in my eyes. None of them shall see the day. There are so many hearts beating wildly. I don't know who will meet their end next.

My red vision does a quick scan. Instantly, I come in contact with a golden-eyed beast. It's another she-wolf, but unlike the previous one, she is sizing me up viciously. She is a Wilde.

A Wilde wolf is supposed to be a very special dog breed, but they are still dogs after all.

This dog is big mad. I can see the monster glimmering in her eyes as they travel from the lifeless body of the dog I just drained and then to me. I can see the hurt, and here comes the rage.

She slams into me with full force. Unlike the other wolf, this one is trained in combat. She shifts into her wolf form and effortlessly lands on her paws. Her gray-and-white wolf is on full display, her bright golden eyes staring into my soul. She is not fighting to defend herself. She is fighting for revenge—good!—and so am I.

What she lacks in strength, she makes it up with technique. Her movements are quick, strike after strike. She must be high up in their ranks, a relative of the Alpha maybe. My monster is having fun, playing with the little wolf. He wants to see her skills. She isn't really a challenge, but she does move with beautiful force.

I kick my leg, hitting her right in the snout. She whines and whimpers, but seconds later she is back to attack. She pounces, and this time I catch her in my arms. I squeeze her body, breaking a few bones in the process. The little wolf screams in pain and turns back into a woman. Now, here comes the fun part.

"I'm going to enjoy tasting you," I whisper in a menacing voice. My monster is craving her delicious, sweet-scented blood.

Her heartbeat is steady. She doesn't seem to be afraid to die. That's even better. She won't struggle as I take my fill.

Right before I plunge into the side of her neck, I'm already knocked to the ground. My head snaps in the direction of my attacker. "What the hell are you doing?" I yell, as I stand to my feet.

"Sorry, I didn't know any other way to stop you." Cyrus holds his hands up.

"Why the f*ck did you do that?" My muscles flex, and the red haze begins to flicker in and out.

The sound of gunshots being released in the air stops Cyrus from responding. A wolf's howl of pain follows shortly. We have won. Bodies of dogs and some humans are all around me. My warriors must have drained them of their blood to regain strength. Xander is still draining a wolf on the other side of the room. It may take some time to calm him down.

I shift my attention back to Cyrus. "And why did you do that?" I ask again, my eyes now on the unconscious she-wolf.

"She is my chosen," he answers promptly.

When the hell did that happen?

"She is a she-wolf."

"I know," he says softly.

Well, somebody is having mixed emotions.

My attention shifts completely when a certain somebody makes their way down the stairs. It's Astrid, the vampire who has failed twice at protecting her charge. This failure will not go unpunished.

My crystal clear vision is once again painted scarlet.

Astrid drops to her knees at once and begs for forgiveness. Commander Vlad doesn't come to her aid this time. He looks at her with disgust. He knows like I know that her time will soon come to an end.

I make my way toward her, slowly taking my precious time to end her pathetic life. She lowers her head, submitting completely. The thrill of the kill is creeping up. My monster is back at the surface.

"You may rise," I command.

She stands but still refuses to look at me—she is a coward. My fangs descend, throbbing and ready to drain every ounce of her cowardly blood. Unfortunately for her, my brother beats me to the punch. Xander sinks his fangs into the right side of her neck. I plunge mine into the left, eager to have my fill. We drain her together, our fangs equally ripping and breaking into her skin.

She lets out an ear-splitting scream but doesn't fight. She knows it's pointless. She has no chance. The smell of her blood is intoxicating and excites me to the very end. Her fear adds to my thrill, and her screams even make my penis twitch.

Xander pulls away, allowing me the chance to end her. I take it, snatching her spine before I finally rip her heart out. She is dead.

My eyes moves back to the she-wolf who so foolishly attacked me. She is now awake, eyes wide. I can see her fear. Cyrus is standing in front of her with a sinister smile. He also loves the thrill of the kill.

"Let's go and finish what they started," I announce, loud and clear.

My soldiers become more alert, their faces fierce and eager. They want blood. They want their revenge. It's time to go get Claire.

# CHAPTER THIRTY-EIGHT
## Equally Measured Attraction

CLAIRE

I stare into his familiar and unique green eyes. I blink twice just to see if my mind is not playing tricks on me. It's him. His handsome heart-shaped face, his sun-kissed golden hair, and his bulky and muscular frame are right in front of me. The slave boy is here in the flesh, alive.

He flashes me a cocky smile.

*My God, he is most certainly here and well.*

"You're the last person I expected to see here," he says to me.

*I bet. You're supposed to be dead.*

"How are you here?" I ask, skeptically. I'm still unsure about this one. Maybe the creepy alleyway hosts ghostly figures.

His smile deepens. "I could ask the same thing to you." He runs his hands through his perfect golden hair.

Our physical resemblance is mind-blowing. Is it weird that I'm attracted to a man that can pass as my brother? Don't answer that. I already know how weird it is.

"The vampires were attacked by humans that turned into wolves. We took that as our chance to escape," he reveals, holding out his hand.

I look at the girl beside him as she takes his hand. She is also a pretty slave but basic. Well, I have seen better-looking humans before. She is about my height or shorter. Her pixie haircut does little to shape her narrow face. The warmth in her brown eyes is her best feature, but as I said, she is basic.

"Are there others?" I place my focus back on the golden boy.

"Yes. Some others escaped, but we split up once we saw the kings rush in."

"The kings?"

*Nicklaus . . . Oh crap, he is still here.*

"We must go at once," I say.

"What do we have here?" questions an oddly familiar voice from behind us.

I turn to face the one and only creepy ole Mecca. My hands tighten into two little fists.You ditched me!"

*Oh, she found a shirt. Now, look at that. What type of friend leaves her human friend to go search for clothes? I thought dogs are supposed to be loyal.*

Mecca stares at my golden boy. I mean the slave boy. I wonder if she even heard what I said. Her eyes drop to the two slaves's entwined fingers and then back to him.

"You look so much better with Claire," Mecca blurts out.

My jaw hits the floor. The golden boy blushes. His friend yanks her hand out of his grasp.

Ouch! I know that hurts.

Of course creepy ole Mecca releases a hearty laugh. "Come on, humans. I've seen some of my packmates go east of the city."

The slave girl glares. "Why should we follow you?"

"You can do what you want, human," Mecca replies with a growl. "I only care about Claire, so if you want to walk back into the hands of your captors, be my guest." She grabs my arm and pulls me to her.

My eyes lock on the golden slave boy's eyes. He seems to be contemplating. I can tell he wants to follow but doesn't want to leave his friend on her own.

The slave girl eventually follows, stomping her feet—how childish! The slave boy walks behind us.

*    *    *

We have been walking through the city for over an hour now. We use the shadows of the building as blankets, hiding and ducking whenever Mecca picks up a scent. Mecca said her packmates must be using undiluted silver in their weapons to mask their smell. I have no clue what that really is. Apparently, vampires are allergic to it.

Mecca comes to a complete halt, and now we are out in the open. Thanks to some abandoned vehicles that serve as our refuge. According to Mecca, we have to cross a bridge to get out of the city, and there is no other way out. Even my human eyes can see we are attempting an impossible task. There are black *SUV*s everywhere. The vampires have blocked off the bridge completely. The men in black are back in full effect, searching and waiting for any sign of a threat. It's an army of them.

"We're gonna have to swim across the river," Mecca speaks.

My eyes flicker to the river in front of me. The crazy woman is back.

"We are human. There is no way we can swim in there," mutters the golden boy.

Mecca gives me a quick glance, then smiles. I already know what she is thinking. The doggy loves to jump.

"I'll get each of you across, but you can't scream. The leeches have sensitive ears, although there's a small chance they will pick up on your heartbeats. We might get lucky, but if one of you screams, your death will be certain," she warns. She casts the men

264

in black one more look, then she says to the slave girl, "You're first."

"Why me? I want to go with Alec."

I gaze at the golden boy. *His name suits him. It's hot. Ew. Focus, Claire, he is taken. Stop being a slut. Stop being a slut!* I mentally chastise myself.

I'm acting like a teenage girl; or worse, a teenage boy with surging sex hormones. I'm starting to believe I have a thing for forbidden fruit—first a vampire king I know I can never have and now a slave boy who has a relationship with another slave girl. Talk about cliché. Yup, I'm officially the girl who wants what she can't have. How miserable can one get?

"Lover boy can't swim with you attached to his back," Mecca responds. "Besides, I believe lover boy wants some alone time with Claire."

Without another word, Mecca snatches the human girl off the ground and jumps in. I'm surprised the poor girl doesn't scream. Knowing Mecca, she is most likely smothering her to death. I don't think she likes the girl that much.

"I don't think she likes her a lot," says Alec, watching my face closely.

I nod. "I guess like vampires, they just don't have a liking for humans."

"Nonsense." He smiles. "They all seem to have a liking for you. The king almost drained me for just looking at you. Fortunately, his brother fed me his blood after King Cyrus explained to him why the king attacked me in the first place. And now the werewolf is sassing my friend because she believes we have a crush on each other. I'll say they all seem to like you."

"She-wolf," I correct him. "Wait! Did you just say the king's brother fed you his blood?"

"Yes," he quickly answers. "I'm alive because of him, and well, because of you. I don't believe he would have saved me if he wasn't aware of your fondness for me."

"What makes you think that? I mean, why do you think I am fond of you?" I ask, nervously.

A chill in the air drifts through my hair. It's strange how similar Alec's green eyes are to mine, like mirrors to my soul.

"Even a blind man can see the attraction we hold for each other," he admits. "I know you want me just like I want you. But you're his, aren't you?"

*His? Who is he referring to?*

My mind is spinning. He is right about one thing, though. I'm very attracted to him.

"I don't know who *he* is," is my honest answer. "But I know there is something between you and your friend."

"We have shared moments. I have also had intimate moments with many female slaves, but no one has captivated my attention"—he takes a step forward—"as you have."

My heart skips a beat. We stare into each other's eyes for a second.

"Aww, get a room!"

Our necks snap in the direction of the voice.

*When the hell did she get back?*

Mecca's glowing yellow eyes are filled with mischief. I have a feeling she really wanted us to have some quote, unquote "alone time."

"Let's go, Claire. It's your turn," she says with amusement. She picks me up and gently cradles me into her chest. "Are you ready? I'm about to jump in."

I realize she is doing exactly what I asked her to do: warning me. Maybe Alec's observation holds some truth.

Mecca doesn't say another word and jumps right in.

*     *     *

"Claire," comes a deep voice. "Wake up, beautiful."

"Nicklaus?" I call out.

266

"Sorry to disappoint you, sweetheart. It's Alec."

I force my eyes to open, and I jump to my feet. "What happened? I thought we were going for a swim."

Well, looking at the water soaking down to the ground from off my body, we, without a doubt, went for a swim. Alec is drenched as well. I don't see his slave friend or Mecca. I scan my surroundings. I notice it's completely different from where we departed. Trees covered in snow are as tall as skyscrapers here. The forest ground is white, wet, and frozen solid. This type of weather is not fit for humans. I'm shaking.

"The strong current of the river put you to sleep," Alec says. "Your friend went to search for something. She said there's a cabin a few miles from here. That's where we are going to take shelter in."

"Where is your friend?" I am still looking at my surroundings, but I can barely see anything. The wooded area is pitch black.

"She left her in the cabin. I believe she did something to save you because it took her a while to come back for me. Something about you needs her more."

"I shifted into my wolf form to save you," Mecca pipes up, appearing out of nowhere. Her amber eyes beam with delight. She is soaking wet, her hardened nipples poking through her shirt. "My wolf seems to like you, Claire."

Now that's weird. She is talking about her wolf—she-wolf—like it's another person.

"How did *she* save me? Of course she likes me. You love me," I tease.

Oh God, it's freezing. I get why Mecca is not cold, but Alec is acting like he is not even affected.

"Yes, *she*, Claire. My wolf has a mind of her own. I'm surprised she didn't attack you. We had been caged, and you needed body heat." She looks at me with pure amusement written all over her face. The river has completely washed away the traces of blood that once smeared her hair, and she looks even more flawless. Her skin glistens under the light of the full moon. She is in her natural habitat. It's obvious nature is a part of her.

"Here." She tosses a bag to me.

I open it, and it is full of human clothes.

*Where the hell did she get this from? We are in the middle of nowhere.*

"Good thing my packmates still leave clothes all around the woods. Hurry and change. We must go. We are still a little far from my territory. Plus, these woods are not safe," she tells us, as I make my way toward a tree for security. "Where are you going?" she asks.

"To change," I answer, indicating that Alec is standing right there.

She knocks her head back with laughter.

Geez, this wolf woman will always and forever be crazy and deranged.

"Oh, I think lover boy wouldn't mind watching you change, brave human," she teases. Although her voice sounds playful, I can hear that she really believes every word she speaks. "He was more concerned about you than his girlfriend or her whereabouts. What did he call you? Sleeping beauty? I think that's exactly what he said."

My cheeks are on fire, and so are Alec's. We look like flaming-hot twins.

"I was not," he states.

"Sure, you weren't," Mecca replies. "Hurry and get dressed. We need to make it back to his girlfriend."

*Right! His girlfriend.*

# CHAPTER THIRTY-NINE
## Bond Understood

The walk to the cabin is long and ice-cold. My feet are frozen solid like little icicles. Mecca has been very attentive to me, watching my every step. She has offered to give me a piggyback ride several times, and I nicely decline. I'm not a child. I can handle something as simple as hiking in the snow.

We have walked in silence for the most part, and once in a while, I steal a glance at Alec to see his similar green eyes. I feel bad we keep flirting openly with each other, especially with him having a girlfriend and all. I'm not that type of girl. Alec is smoking hot. Any woman would want him, but I'm not going to be labeled as a slave wrecker. Besides, he doesn't make my soul burn like the one and only Nicklaus does to me even in this winter weather. Just one thought about his pantie-melting silver-cerulean eyes is enough to make me feel warm inside. I miss him. I really want to turn around and run back to him.

I sound like a fool. I know a human who has waited her entire life to be free, only to willingly run back into the arms of her captor. I should be happy I'm running far, far away. Nicklaus is a monster—a mean, beautiful killing machine. He is wild and reckless. He holds no regard for human life or whatsoever. He is ruthless and barbaric in every way.

Even with all that being said, I still want him more than I want my freedom. I'm infatuated with his monstrous ways. It's sad but it's true. The vampire king has somehow placed his hooks in my soul.

My mind keeps wandering to the hot and steamy kiss we shared. I'm aware it meant nothing to him, but it was everything to me. No matter how mad I get, I will always remember how our two tongues felt together as one and how one touch of his gentle finger set my skin on fire. That one intimate moment together will always outweigh any bad moment we have shared. I'm addicted.

Mecca may have a valid point when she stated I'm brainwashed. I was once a human who despised humans for craving vampires, and now I crave the touch of the king of all vampires.

"We're almost there," says Mecca, as we walk down another frozen hill. "This journey would be a lot quicker if I shifted into my wolf form."

"Well, not all of us can shift into a gigantic dog," I remind her.

Geez, she doesn't have to keep making us feel bad because we are built to walk on two legs instead of four.

"You're right. You humans are not that cool."

Alec and I both roll our eyes. I guess that's also a human thing.

We continue to walk for another ten minutes before a small little cabin comes into view. The first word that pops up to my mind is: magical. The stars twinkle and the moonlight shines down on us from the night sky. The oak wood and lantern scream welcome. The ground is covered in a blanket of pure-white snow, and the pine trees surround the cabin like soldiers—tall, strong, and firm. It's beautiful.

"I'll go search for dinner," Mecca states. "Make yourselves at home. His girlfriend is still asleep," she adds, sounding amused, then she disappears into the woods.

It's obvious she is playing matchmaker. She seems to want Alec and me to hook up.

I choose to ignore her remark and make my way into the cabin when Alec grabs my hand.

"Can we talk?" he asks.

I nod and sit on the little wooden rocking chair.

"This place is *magical*, isn't it? I have never seen a place like this," he says.

"Yes, it is. That's exactly the same word that came to me."

We sit in silence for a moment before he starts the conversation back up. "So how long have you lived in the kingdom of the king of all kings?"

"I'm not sure. I was selected as his chosen, maybe a couple of months ago." I lift my head up to admire the beauty of the night sky.

Now, why does he have to bring up Nicklaus? He's making me miss him again. The twinkling stars remind me of his piercing, soul-snatching eyes.

Ew, I'm so pathetic.

"Was that when you met the werewolf?"

His question grabs my attention.

"She-wolf," I correct him. "Male wolves call themselves werewolves. Female wolves are called she-wolves. Their children are called pups. It's considered disrespectful not to address a wolf using their traditional titles. They don't like to be called anything but who they are."

"But you've called her *dog* several times," he points out, raising his eyebrow. "Isn't that what vampires call them to ruffle their feathers?"

"Yes, that's why I call her that." I study the wooded area briefly. "To ruffle her feathers, or should I say tail?" I laugh slightly. "But as you can see it doesn't work anymore. She is immune to my insults." I scan my surroundings once again.

*Mecca should have been back by now. I hope she doesn't ditch me again while I'm in the middle of nowhere.*

"Or maybe she is just drawn to your charm," he says with a wolfish smile of his own. "I know I am."

I stare into his unique green eyes that seem to sparkle underneath the night sky. With his perfect white teeth and tousled golden hair, this man is simply seductive.

"Did anyone ever tell you how bad of a womanizer you are?" I quip. "You're such a playboy. Your girlfriend is inside the cabin while you're outside, flirting with me."

He blushes. His eyes travel to the cabin and then to me. "I'm not trying to seduce you, Claire. I'm just telling you how I feel."

I take a deep breath.

"It's just you're not like the other slave girls I have met."

*Why does everyone keep saying that?*

"I have never seen a male or female stand up to a vampire or risk their life for another human. It's just unheard of, and it's sexy as hell," he adds.

Now, it's my turn to blush.

Mecca appears from nowhere. She throws some wood and a rabbit down. "Damn. It's so goddamn hard to find a nice and decent rabbit these days," she complains.

Alec and I roll our eyes in unison again. Leave it to creepy ole Mecca to appear out of thin air with an animal once used for magic tricks. How weird?

\*     \*     \*

After Alec started the fire and Mecca skinned the rabbit with her claws—jeepers creepers! All four of us, including Alec's girlfriend, sit by the fireplace in this cozy, dream-like little cabin home. The fireplace is ancient, but its roaring fire is burning alive.

272

The inside is just as magical as the outside. The cabin is small, with checkered curtains and old red furniture. It has a ladder in the middle that takes you to a tiny bed. The entire place is antique-looking, but it still feels like the perfect home. It's a completely different world from the fancy and extravagant vampire civilization I've grown used to. This cabin is so human.

*Nicklaus and the other kings will probably sleep on the forest ground before they take a single step inside here.*

I laugh to myself as I picture one of the kings making fire or sleeping on a grandma-looking couch. Just thinking about it makes me flash a priceless smile.

*Oh, stop! I'm doing it again. Get the vampire king and the life you escaped from out of your head.*

I take a bite of the rabbit and almost puke. I try my best not to show my disgust, but I fail.

"You don't like your dinner?" Mecca leans her neck to the side. "I didn't expect you to be a spoiled human."

I make a face at her. "Just because I don't like the taste of the rabbit, that doesn't make me spoiled. I'm not spoiled." I stick my tongue out at her. I may be a little childish, but I'm not spoiled.

"Sure, you're not."

"I'm not." I don't know why her words get under my skin.

Mecca sticks her tongue out right back at me. She is annoying as hell. Gosh! Stupid freaking dog.

"How old are you again? It doesn't look good for a she-wolf over the age of one hundred to do that."

Mecca shrugs. "The opinion of a mortal human doesn't bother a 250-year-old she-wolf."

Alec's girlfriend's big brown eyes widen. "Did you just say—"

"Quiet, human!" Mecca snaps. She sniffs the air, fur sprouting in her skin.

Something is wrong, very wrong. I can see her wolf clawing to escape. The last time she acted like this was because she sensed Xander.

*Xander! He must be near.*

I jump to my feet and shoot toward the front door. Within a second, Mecca turns into her full-fledged wolf form. She releases a deep, monstrous growl and leaps in front of the door.

This is the first time I really get to see her wolf up close. It's deep oak brown, and just like her mocha-cream skin, her fur looks so soft to touch. Her eyes glow bright yellow, reminding me of a full moon. They're big, bright, and beautiful.

I open the door slightly, and she snaps at me, her scary long canines inches away from my hand. Alec rushes to my side to protect me, but it only seems to piss her off more. She growls warningly, then rushes out of the door. Of course my dumb self chases after her.

\*     \*     \*

NICKLAUS

It has been almost twenty-four hours since I last saw Claire. My monster is on edge without her. I miss her so bad. We were able to track her through her scent, but it disappeared by the river. She must have jumped in. She is with the she-wolf and two other slaves.

Cyrus's commander stated that one of the scents she picked up was of the slave boy whose life I almost ended. The f*cking irony. My beloved is with some lovesick puppy that wants to hump her leg. It doesn't take me long to figure out who is responsible for it.

"You gave that slave boy your blood?" I approach Xander, my blood boiling with rage.

274

He is the only one who will risk crossing me, especially concerning Claire.

Xander ignores me. He continues to search the riverside for any signs of my beloved.

"Don't ignore me, or—"

"Or what, Little Brother?" He stands to his full height. "Yes, I spared the slave boy's life. Do you really think Claire would forgive herself if he died? She already took the blame for that slave girl you killed."

"I killed her to protect Claire, and I will do it again!" I yell, struggling to keep my monster at bay. He wants blood.

Xander picks up a rock and throws it. He is also struggling with his beast. "I could care less about how you feel."

Both of our visions are tinted red.

"Brothers!" Cyrus interrupts, as he rolls down the window of the *SUV*. "Commander Vlad has picked back up on the trail. He's in Northern Forest. He sees human footprints, and he also smells the stench of the were-b*tch."

Xander brushes past me without another word. The cold-hearted king wants to lose his head.

I release a sigh and enter the *SUV*. Cyrus's chosen is still out cold, balled up in a protective ball. The mutt passed out again when I pulled out Astrid's spine. She is a wild beast, so why the hell does she have such a low tolerance for blood? Now that's just ironic as f*ck.

Cyrus's eyes move from me and then to the girl. His stone-cold gaze is filled with a flicker of warmth. I know that look.

"She is your beloved, isn't she?" I run my hands over my hair.

The mutt's heart rate increases.

*Interesting. The little f*cker is really awake.*

"Claire is also your beloved, isn't she?" he replies in my native language Romanian. He doesn't want her to understand what he says.

275

I nod. I already figured Cyrus has put two and two together. There's no point hiding or denying the truth. I don't trust anyone completely except Xander, but Cyrus is my best friend, and I do know he values our friendship.

"When I raided one of the northern villages, I did what I do best. I killed with no mercy. I even set her hut on fire. I don't think I'll be able to forgive myself," he explains with guilt-filled eyes. "I almost killed her. I almost killed my own beloved."

"Don't beat yourself up over things you can't change, Brother," I advise, still speaking in our native tongue. "You didn't know." I look at my best friend's beloved. "She is a strong little wolf. She fought against me with great skill and without fear." I sigh deeply and take a moment to think over his half confession.

Cyrus is scared to admit who his beloved is to him because of her species, just like how scared I am to admit who Claire is to me. We are in the same boat, basically on the same sinking ship. He needs me just like how I need Xander. He needs someone to be on his side, on *their* side.

"Any she-wolf brave enough to go against me is okay in my book. I think I can learn to like her." I let out a heavy sigh.

"You can?" he asks, suspiciously.

I understand his doubts. Wolves and vampires are like water and oil. We just don't mix.

He rubs his hair with his hands. "I think you killed her sister. That's why she attacked you. I don't think she is much of a fighter."

"That's impossible. She is well-trained. All wolves enjoy the thrill of the kill. That's just their nature." I look out of the window. We are almost in Northern Forest. "I'll stay away until she heals. If I were in her shoes, I wouldn't be able to even imagine being around the person who took my sibling's life."

"Embry is different, and she will never heal." He places his focus back onto her.

*So her name is Embry.*

276

"She will never forgive me. To make matters worse, we are at war with her kind. They will end her if they find out what she is to me, she-wolf or not. Even our kind would want her dead. How can I protect her if she doesn't trust me, Nicklaus?"

"She will learn to trust you, Cyrus. You are a good man. I understand how you feel. I've been worried about Claire's safety since day one. Similarly, our kind will never accept her, but it doesn't matter to me at this point. I'd kill anyone to keep her safe. I vow to protect your beloved as well."

"Thank you, Brother. I also vow to keep your beloved safe," he assures me. "I think your little hotheaded beloved may kill me in the process. My adviser overheard Commander Vlad gossiping about how she handled Master Azazel. She was born to rule by your side. She's brave and beautiful."

I smile at his words. He is right. My little firecracker has balls of steel. She shows courage even in a room full of predators.

"What are you going to do about Lady Gwen? She won't allow you to claim your beloved in peace."

It takes me a while to answer. If Gwen finds out about Claire, she will go straight to the council.

Just thinking about the outcome makes my vision bleed red.

"As I said, I'll kill anyone to keep her safe," I tell him.

The *SUV* stops and my senses are on high alert. We are not at our destination, so I mind-link with our driver, but there is no response. I mind-link with some guards and still no response. I then mind-link with Xander.

*"How far away are you?"*

*"I'm right behind you,"* he quickly replies. *"Did you order the drivers to stop?"*

*"No, I didn't. Something is off."* I roll the tinted window down to check on the driver, and to my surprise, he is knocked out. I can see the road through the window. It's clear.

"What's wrong?" Cyrus questions, as he looks toward the front seat.

I ignore him. I open the car door and search my surroundings. Xander and Cyrus also exit the cars.

"Cyrus, take Embry to my safe house. The drivers have been put to sleep, and our guards may have been put to sleep as well."

"How? If witches are involved, we all should be affected."

That's true. We all should be affected if it's a sleeping spell.

We continue to scan the woods.

"I heard rumors about the lycan princess," Xander speaks. "They say she has magic."

"Impossible!" Cyrus and I comment in unison.

Xander shrugs and continues to search the woods. "We don't know what's been going on in their world."

The world of the wolves is a completely different ball game compared to what we are used to. The Awakening changed everything.

Embry's heart is beating louder by the second, and our heads snap in the direction of the *SUV*.

"You're right. Cyrus, take Embry to safety. Whatever is going on will not affect us. We will search for Claire, and we'll meet at my safe house. If any of the guards communicates with you, tell them to go to your safe house instead. Don't reveal your location to anyone unless you are one hundred percent sure they are trustworthy."

He nods and disappears.

I put my driver in the back seat and throw the keys to Xander. "You're driving."

He rolls his eyes. Claire has rubbed off on him. "Why were you calling that dog by a name?"

"I'll fill you in along the way."

# CHAPTER FORTY
## Fluent in the Language of Idioms

CLAIRE

I trip over my own feet as I make my way toward the front door. Alec also stumbles, following after me. His girl falls flat on her face as well.

Boom, boom, boom! It's a domino effect. It's about time we made it outside of the door.

Mecca is in her full-fledged wolf, dark and angry. She is standing by the edge of the forest, growling and snarling. She looks deadly. For sure I wouldn't want to be Xander right now. The logical side of me is screaming, "Run, duck, and hide." However, the idiotic side of me—yes, I do have that side—wants me to intervene. See what I mean? I can be very idiotic.

I use my hands to push myself to my feet and rush to Mecca's side. Her wolf gives me a warning growl as I approach. "Calm down, little wolf," I coo, holding up my hands in surrender.

She snaps at me in response.

*Oh, sh\*t! The wrong choice of words. Come on, Claire. You can do this,* I give myself a little pep talk.

"Okay, I'm sorry," I tell her. "Can you calm down, you big and bad wolf?"

Mecca stops growling.

*Great, I'm making progress.*

"Please," I plead.

She lifts her head up, and I swear her wolf just rolls her eyes.

What the hell?

I notice Alec and his girlfriend coming behind me. Mecca's bright yellow eyes shift to them. She growls again, making me want to get the hell out of her way like a coward—one thing that I will never be. I'm the complete opposite of it. I kick balls for a living and laugh in the face of danger, remember? Haha.

A twig snaps, and Mecca's wolf turns her head in the direction of the forest.

*Crap, crap, crap. It's about to go down.*

Seconds later, she jumps in the air, only to be smacked down by an enormous, real-life golden wolf. I'm absolutely stunned as the wolf digs its claws into Mecca's side, then bites down into her skin. My momentary shock lasts for only a second, and my stupidity goes into full effect.

I grab the first thing I can get my hands on. "Get the hell off her, you mutt," I warn, jumping right into action.

"No, Claire!" says Alec.

It's too late. I've smacked the golden wolf with a log. Yup, I'm that stupid.

She turns her snout to me and bares her big and scary canines, and of course my brave and stupid self just has to add fuel to the fire.

"You stupid mutt, stay the hell away from my doggy!"

The golden wolf lunges, but I duck. She gracefully lands on her four paws while I rush to Mecca, who is now howling in pain. She is back in her human form.

"Mecca! Oh no. No, no, no. This is bad."

Another twig breaks, and the next thing I know we are already surrounded by a pack of snarling wolves. They are not as big as the golden wolf, but the pitch-black one glaring at me is still scary as f*ck.

280

Alec is standing in front of me protectively, like a fool who's in love. A human defending another human against a pack of angry dogs is sort of cute, though.

The black wolf shifts into a human. "Mecca," he calls, then he runs toward our direction.

I throw the log at him. "Stay the hell away from her!" I shout.

"Get the hell out of my way, stupid human!" he retorts.

His muscles are flexing and his shoulders are broad, but I could give two sh*ts. None of them is coming anywhere near her. They will have to kill me first. I will kick their balls to death if they touch her, all of them. I don't care how yummy he looks . . . and my God, he is yummy. He has penetrating blue eyes and fair skin that contrasts with his dark features—dark hair and thick, dark lashes—and that's what makes him beautiful. His stare is cold, but he looks smoking hot.

"Make me, dog," I sass, "and I won't go down without a fight."

He knocks his head back, and laughter explodes out of his mouth. It reminds me of Mecca's laughter. I mean he's laughing like a madman. I guess it's a wolf thing. You know they say, "The apple never falls far from the tree."

"That can be arranged," he tells me, his eyes piercing. He turns at another wolf that is not pitch black—he may be dark brown—and not as big, but he still looks just as scary.

I can tell they are communicating. Out of the corner of my eye, I see the golden wolf staring at me. Alec is still standing in front of me. He says nothing, but his eyes tell another story. He will fight alongside me. At least that makes two of us. Meanwhile, his plain girlfriend is cowering away in fear. Ew, she is such a little wimp.

The other wolf shifts, turning into a glorious and tasteful-looking man. Dark and mysterious Mr. Hunky is drop-dead gorgeous, but he doesn't look better than Nicklaus in my opinion.

No one does. Although he is an eye-catcher, he can't compete with someone beyond compare.

I still feel the need to stress the fact that he looks good. His skin is flawless and tan. His eyes and mustache—hair included—are all warm and dark brown. His muscular frame serves him right, and oh my God his manhood! Well, it most certainly hangs, if you know what I mean. Oh, I forgot to mention that both of the men are completely naked.

Mecca whines softly. I switch my attention back to my lunatic friend. Oh poor crazy ole Mecca, look what they have done.

"It's okay, I'm here. I won't let them hurt you," I say.

Her lips curl into a faint smile. Leave it to crazy ole Mecca to manage to smile in a dire situation.

"We will not hurt her, human. She is our packmate. We only want to help her," Mr. Hunky speaks.

I scoff loudly. Some pack they are. "What type of pack attacked their mate?"

"A pack that didn't know who or what type of wolf she is," answers the black wolf man.

I can sense the irritation in his voice. Yup, he is crazy as they come, as mad as a hatter. How dare he show annoyance with me? His golden wolf friend is the one who attacked my friend. If he really cared, he would take it out on whoever the hell that is. Crap. What's the phrase? Off with her head or . . . ? It really doesn't matter. The moral of the story is they need to be mad at the golden wolf.

My eyes land on the golden wolf just in time to see her shift into a woman. She is damn sure beautiful and alluring. She can be a seductress. Her shiny honey-blond hair is so similar yet completely different from her wolf's golden fur. Her cold, absolutely mesmerizing "Irish Spring" green eyes are looking me up and down. Her presence screams power, radiance, and elegance. She walks with authority—head held high, shoulders straightened, and nose pointed in the air. She has to be their queen. That's the only logical explanation for her breathtaking aura.

Why the hell do all supernatural creatures have to be so striking? It's something the human world will never truly understand. Even Alec is smitten, caught off guard by the golden beauty. The poor boy bows the moment she is in front of us. For the first time since she shifted, I've noticed that everyone has been bowing their heads, including the pack of wolves that haven't shifted. The black wolf hesitates for just a second but eventually bows as well. She is definitely royalty. There's no doubt about that.

"Do you not know how to address your superior?" she asks, her eyes still fixed on me.

I guess she is attempting to put me in my place. Welp, I hate to be the bearer of bad news, but respect is earned, not given. I don't hold an ounce of respect for a foreign ruler playing the "kiss my ass" because I'm royalty card. Sorry but not sorry. She hasn't earned my respect, so she is clearly wasting her time.

I hold my head high, and now we are at eye level. Her stare spits fire while mine spits ice. She doesn't and will never intimidate me. Nicklaus doesn't even scare me despite being the king of all vampire kings. She will receive the same treatment. Try me, wolf b*tch.

Every one else around us may be sh*tting bricks, but I have never been a follower; I'm a leader. I'm brave and I damn sure won't bend or break for anyone.

She continues to stare, and so do I. Our staredown battle only comes to an end when Mecca releases another groan. My friend needs me. I don't have the time to keep on entertaining their quote, unquote "queen."

"I don't have time for this," I tell her. I bend down to help Mecca, who is burning up and shivering. Her eyes roll to the back of her head. "No, Mecca. Please stay strong, my favorite little doggy," I whisper softly, and several growls follow shortly after.

Who gives a f*ck?

The supposed wolf queen bends down beside me. "Sleep, Little Luna. Everything will be okay," she coos.

Mecca's eyes close at once, and her body goes still. She stops breathing, her skin pale and her body ice-cold.

"Nooo!" I scream at the top of my lungs.

Everything will be okay my ass!

My instinct is telling me to punch the golden wolf b*tch in her face, and that's exactly what I attempt to do, but then two strong arms wrap around my body. I try my hardest to break away from whoever the hell is holding me.

"Get the hell off me!" I yell fiercely, kicking out my legs in the process. "I'll kill you all, you untrained dogs!" I threaten, and several growls fill the air. "You all feral and wild beasts, I swear on my life I will kill you if it's the last thing I do!" All I can think about is putting every last one of them down forever. My chest is ablaze, my vision blurry. I have never experienced this much hatred in my life.

I feel a delicate hand rest on my shoulder. "Relax. Sleep now," says someone, then everything around me goes dark.

*    *    *

*"Firecracker,"* callls a sexy, deep, husky, and pantie-soaking voice.

I shiver. Water rushes from my kitty, and the rest of my body is on fire. There is only one man in this entire world that can do that to me. It's the king of all vampire kings.

*"Nicklaus, my ass-kissing king,"* I call out. I want to see his face—gosh, I really, really miss him—so I try to open my eyes, but I can't. It's dark all around me, as though I'm in a dream-like state.

*"Where are we? Why can't I open my eyes?"* I ask him.

He doesn't respond right away. It's quiet, too quiet. Maybe this is all in my head. I'm officially crazy.

*"I'm not with you."*

Wait, what? I'm so confused, my heart hammering in my chest.

*"Don't be scared, firecracker. I'm coming for you. I'll be there soon."*
My mind falls back into darkness.

# CHAPTER FORTY-ONE
## Putting Two and Two Together

NICKLAUS

We arrived at the Northern Forest just after midnight. We should have gotten here hours ago, but those bloody beasts used pure, undiluted silver smoke bombs. It didn't affect our strength, but it did slow us down. We couldn't afford to be at our weakest, so we decided to find another way around. I was actually surprised that those dogs used silver against us. Werewolves usually stay away from it because it is the one thing that can kill them, with the exception of a trueborn vampire or having their hearts ripped out. That just proves that Xander's theory is correct; we don't know anything about their world, and it is a huge weakness.

This marks forty-eight hours without Claire. All I can think about is getting her back to safety. I miss her so bad, and it hurts. This experience would be a lot more tasteful if I had marked my beloved. I would have been able to locate her instantly. My stupidity and blindness might cost Claire her life.

"What's bothering you, Brother?"asks Xander, as we make our way through the forest. His eyes scan the trees for any signs of threats.

My brother is a skilled fighter. He usually focuses on killing off the trueborn hunters, but he still is extremely skillful to fight against many other species including werewolves.

"Claire will be fine, Little Brother. Try not to worry so much."

"How can I not?" I ask, searching the trees as well and then scooping the grounds for any trails.

If I had controlled my inner monster, Claire would be in the safety of my arms. Now I may lose my beloved forever.

"This is my fault. If I hadn't lost my temper and hadn't locked her in that room, she would have been with us instead of being in the room when those dogs attacked."

"We both know that's not true, Nicklaus. You would have sent her away the moment you sensed danger. Your first instinct will forever be to protect your beloved. Some things are just out of your control, no matter how powerful you are."

I don't feel powerful.

"Besides, you can't control blood lust. We both know what it can do to you. I advise you claim Claire the moment we get her back."

I'm not going through blood lust. I have just officially lost reason.

"I'm not experiencing blood lust, idiot," I hiss.

When vampires have a taste of their true beloved's blood for the first time, some of them go through blood lust, which is extremely rare but is not unheard of. A vampire experiencing it will become completely enraged, blinded with jealousy, and unable to control themselves at times. Some say that the older the vampire, the more severe the lust is. This would be extremely bad in my case. Not only am I an older vampire, but I'm also immensely powerful. If I can't control myself, then there's no telling what will happen. My monster is vicious and bloodthirsty enough.

"First, you almost ended Claire's life from the first bite," Xander tells me instead of asking. "Then, you almost killed Azazel for touching her, not that I blame you of course, but I must point out that he is a representative from a respected vampire house. You could have started an intraspecies war.

"Lastly, you nearly drained a slave just for looking at Claire, so don't tell me I'm the one being idiotic because it's obvious I'm quite the opposite. You're in denial," he states, stopping me right in my tracks.

I take a moment to think about his observation. He has a valid point. Well, he has three, but he is missing a key factor.

"Claire has not accepted our bond. She doesn't even know who she is to me."

Xander may be talking from experience, but facts are facts. There is no blood lust in a one-sided bond.

All of a sudden, my head starts to hurt—physically hurt—and my frozen heart seems to beat as if I were a human. I can imagine this is what they experience when they have a headache.

Someone or something is trying to break through. I close my eyes, and Claire's beautiful, angelic face comes into view. I can't see her, but I know it's her. No one takes my breath away like the sight of my golden-haired beloved.

*"Firecracker."*

I can smell her arousal as if we were in the same room, and my mouth waters.

*"Nicklaus, my ass-kissing king."* She shivers. Her voice is like honey, thick with need and sweet as hell.

Damn, I miss this woman.

*"Where are we? Why can't I open my eyes?"* she asks.

I can hear the desperation in her voice. She is scared. My firecracker's heart is racing.

I take a moment to think this is how my bonded communicates with me. This is how vampires communicate with one another. For a human, it's actually impossible to do without the ritual unless their bond with their beloved runs deep and their heart yearns for their other half.

That can only mean one thing: Claire has accepted the bond, and she accepts me.

*"I'm not with you,"* I tell her.

288

Her heart is thudding in her chest, and my inner monster doesn't like her fear. I don't like her being scared.

I take a deep breath to calm myself down. She needs me, so I must stay calm. *"Don't be scared, firecracker. I'm coming for you. I'll be there soon."*

There is no response, and I can feel her slipping. Her human body is not strong enough to handle mind communication for too long. She's gone.

*"Nicklaus,"* Xander calls, attempting to break through.

We are behind a bush, and he's holding me protectively.

My eyes shoot open.

"What the hell . . . ?" he asks.

"Claire communicated with me."

"Well, I hate to be the one to tell you I told you so, but I told you so," he states.

I hear a sound of some movement from our left, making me instantly jump to my feet. I crouch down and allow my monster to take over. Xander's monster is present as well, and his power is booming at a mile radius.

In the blink of an eye, I am able to locate the new presence. I immediately grab it by the neck and knock it down. Observing his next kill with fangs bared, the clearer my monster sees Commander Vlad's face in front of him.

"Your Highness," Commander Vlad says, head bent down in complete submission.

I could have ended him within a second.

"I can smell the silver running through your pores, Commander," Xander speaks calmly, but there is a hard edge in his voice. "You were bombed, which is why your movements are so loud and sloppy."

I release Commander Vlad at once, and Xander leans over to give him some blood.

Once Commander Vlad has his fill, he stands up. "They made a fool out of me," he gravely admits. "It was a pack of

289

werewolves. They must have realized I was searching the forest for trails, so they set a trap inches away from Claire's footprints. I smelled her. I know she is close by," he informs. "The were-b*tch's blood filling the air was the only reason they didn't attack me, so I managed to escape but passed out seconds later."

"How are those dogs using silver without hurting themselves? Xander queries. "How could they use their weakness as a strength? We couldn't have possibly become that out of tune with the rest of the world, could we?" He seems to be talking to himself.

"They got immune to it," I respond.

"Why would you think that?"

"Because I've seen it with my own eyes," I tell both of them. "Cyrus and I were testing a theory, using different amounts of silver on the wolf b*tch, and it seemed it made her weaker by the day. However, when one of the guards attempted to rape her, believing she was too weak to fight off the deadliest attacks, he paid the price with his life.

"At first, I thought it was just pure luck. I still had my doubts and didn't think it was possible until Claire was placed in the cell with her. When she managed to escape, that's when I knew."

"And you just decided to tell me this?" says Xander, his voice filled with annoyance.

"I didn't believe it really mattered. Like seriously, who would intentionally harm themselves just to become stronger?" I argue. "Those beasts are more savage than we—"

"They're desperate," Xander cuts me off. "Those savage beasts are f*cking desperate, and they will do anything to win the war that's brewing on the horizon. If that's not bad enough, they have our queen. There's no telling what that dog b*tch figured out. She spent more than enough time around Claire. That b*tch knows Claire is your weakness, our weakness. That's most likely why she went after her."

"Wait, what?" asks Commander Vlad, looking at me. "Are you implying that your chosen is your beloved?" His eyes roll as something clicks in his head. "Of course she is. F*ck, we really are f*cked."

"It doesn't matter. What's done is done. You're right, Xander. I'm experiencing blood lust. Claire has accepted our bond."

"Then you should be able to locate her even without the claiming ritual," he replies.

"Commander, do you have any extra guns? They may still come in handy."

Commander Vlad flashes a smile. "I'm loaded."

\*     \*     \*

CLAIRE

I experienced my first wet dream. Okay maybe it wasn't my first, but my God, it was so goddamn good. Nicklaus's sexy, husky voice was inside my head. My panties are still soaking wet just thinking about it. God, it was heaven.

I'm just about to roll back over and conjure up sexier vampire lovemaking dreams when Mecca's face pops into my head, making me roll out of bed—I mean literally—and fall flat on my face.

Ouch! Damn, that hurts. I seriously need to stop waking up like this.

"Whoa. Cowgirl, take it easy," says an unfamiliar but familiar voice. Mr. Hunky wraps his muscular arms around me and helps me to my feet.

"Thank you."

"Of course, I'm your, ass-kissing king."

"What? Come again?"

*What name did he just use?*

"That's what you called me in your sleep."

291

The color drains from my face. "What else did you hear?" I ask. "Oh how freaking embarrassing!"

"Among other things. Don't be embarrassed. Even if you didn't talk in your sleep, I'm pretty sure even the mated wolves could still smell you." His eyes flash bright yellow as he smiles. "Delicious."

I don't want to know what that means. "Where are my friends, you pack killer?"

"Huh? What the hell is a pack killer?" He suddenly looks puzzled. His yellow eyes turn warm and dark. "Are you referring to what happened to the Luna?" He wiggles his brows with obvious confusion.

"Who the hell is Luna?" Now it's my turn to show confusion. "I'm referring to Mecca, my lunatic friend that your queen b*tch she-wolf knocked off!" I'm practically screaming at this point. "Where the hell are my other friends?" I can feel my ball kicking, power surfacing. He has no idea who he's dealing with.

"Brave little human," comes a voice.

*Wait . . . Mecca?*

My heart hammers viciously inside my chest as I turn to see my crazy ole friend. "Mecca!" I squeal with excitement and crash into her.

We most certainly need to stop meeting like this, seriously.

"I thought I lost you," I tell her, my voice sounding shakier than usual.

She knocks her head back with laughter. (Yup, it's most certainly crazy ole Mecca.) "It takes a lot more than a lycan bite to kill me," she brags.

*Lycan . . .*

"Hold up, she is a lycan?"

*So that's the reason they kissed Her Royal Highness. Mecca told me her kind believes that lycans are direct descendants of their Moon Goddess. What was her name, Luna or something? Wait, he called her the Luna. Oh my jeepers creepers!*

292

"Mecca, do these people think you're a goddess? He called you 'the Luna.' Didn't you tell me your Moon Goddess's name is Luna?"

My head spins. They worship crazy ole Mecca. They are all crazy, extremely freaking crazy—lunatics, complete bonkers.

Mr. Hunky and crazy ole Mecca laugh in unison.

See what I mean? If that's not crazy, I don't know what is.

"No, Claire. Humans are truly clueless. Those bloodsuckers may not have taken your courage, but they damn sure took your brain. Oh, where to begin? I told you once before I am not an ordinary she-wolf. Luna is our Moon Goddess, but the title Luna is also given to the Alpha's mate."

I still don't get it.

"Alpha Maddox is the northern alpha. He is also my mate," she states.

Ding-dong. Now, it all makes sense. No wonder they are laughing their butts off. I did sound clueless. Okay, well in my defense, I have lived in a vampire boarding school all my life, so beats me!

"Oh, I see," I tell her.

Mr. Hunky's eyes flash bright yellow. He is amused. Oh great!

"When do I get to meet this alpha of yours?" I look at the ground.

"You already have," she says, with that creepy she-wolf smile.

The door opens, and the black wolf guy steps inside.

This gets better and better. Not only did I just make a fool out of myself, but also this fool was in hearing range to listen in on my human mistake. Does a stupid human ring a bell? I hope not.

"Claire, I would like to properly introduce you to Alpha Maddox, the northern alpha and my mate," Mecca speaks, clearly trying to hold back her laughter.

My jaw hits the floor—drops!

293

Alpha Maddox's lips twitch into a smirk. He holds out his hand to take my own. "It's nice to properly meet you, Claire. My Luna has told us a great deal about your bravery and kindness. I'm forever grateful." He stares into my eyes for a long-drawn-out moment.

Mecca growls lowly, and he snatches his hand away in alarm. I, on the other hand, have grown used to her bipolar behavior.

"I'm Beta Rendell," Mr. Hunky pipes up, "but you may call me your ass-kissing king if you want. Any human who has the balls to attempt to hit the lycan princess can even call me a donkey, and I'll still answer."

My face burns. No, thank you. That name is already reserved for the hottest man—I mean vampire—I know, but Mr. Hunky is starting to be Mr. Charming in my book.

My stomach grumbles in response. The last thing I had was that nasty, filthy rabbit I barely ate.

They laugh together.

"Where are my manners? You must be hungry," Alpha Maddox says.

"Famished," I reply. "Please tell me you have anything other than rabbit."

"Hey," calls Mecca, "I'll have . . . you know . . . It took me longer than usual to hunt down that little creature."

It's strange seeing her standing beside her mate. She looks happy, really happy, and they look amazing together. Mecca has always been beautiful in my eyes. From our very first encounter, I knew she was a diamond in the rough. At least I thought so. I can see clearly she has always been a sparkling jewel. She was just missing her jeweler. She and Alpha Maddox do shine together, and I'm happy for her.

"Rendell, how about you take our guest to grab something to eat and then to see her friends? I'm sure they are worried about her," instructs Alpha Maddox.

294

*I totally forgot about Alec and his girlfriend. Darn it! How did I become distracted so fast?*

"Right. I'm sure Claire's boyfriend is worried about her," adds Mecca.

"Wait!" Beta Rendell exclaims. "They look more like siblings than significant others," he comments out loud.

*Not funny.*

I roll my eyes again. "He is not my brother or boyfriend," I tell them. "I don't understand why it even matters when that's no one's business."

Creepy ole Mecca bursts out in her usual laughter while both of the men also snicker beside her.

"Rendell wants it to be his business. Trust me." Mecca winks. "Now, run along, brave human. I'll see you later. It's time for the big bad wolf to make love to her mate."

*Yuck, she gives way too much information.*

Beta Rendell opens the door for me, then takes my hand. "Come on, let's go get you something to eat."

# CHAPTER FORTY-TWO
## Intro into a New World

The Northern Pack house is warm and full of life. Younger werewolves are walking around, laughing, and talking—unguarded. The children are running all through the house with no care in the world. Older she-wolves are in the massive kitchen, cooking and gossiping about who's mated to whom. At first, I felt self-conscious about walking into a kitchen full of wolves, but every single one of them offered warm smiles and talked about fattening me up. I felt welcomed, as if I belonged here even with my being human and all.

The place is sort of Utopia, a completely different world. They are so loving and carefree and are like one big family, which is completely the opposite of the savage beasts as they are rumored to be. You would think they're not even at war, like they didn't just bury so many of their kind. It's astonishing to say the least, and I am caught off guard. This isn't what I expected.

After breakfast, Beta Rendell offered to show me the rest of the pack house. I said yes because Alec and his girlfriend are still asleep, and Mecca is still doing God knows what with Alpha Maddox, who just told me about the world of the werewolves.

Beta Rendell takes his duty as a beta seriously. He tells me he spends most of his time traveling to their other territories. Werewolf packs have several around this mountain. According to him, before the Awakening—the Luna Blood Moon of 2081, as he calls it—there were a total of fifty packs in North America constantly at war with one another. Now only four are left: the Northern Pack, the Eastern Pack, the Western Pack, and the Southern Pack. Pack members who had lost their alphas joined in one of the remaining packs, so most wolves who live around the territories came from fallen packs. Alpha Maddox gave them their own settlement and still offers his protection and loyalty to this day.

It's amazing how these creatures who were once at war are now united as one. I have a newfound respect for the werewolves. I'm truly impressed. If humans were smart enough to come together instead of allowing another species to tear us apart, things would be so different. The werewolves are living proof of that theory. However, one thing I have noticed is that the hatred of the werewolves—Beta Rendell included—for vampires runs just as deep as the vampires's hatred for humans.

Beta Rendell has been asking me questions about my life as a slave, and it is kind of unsettling. The way he speaks about Nicklaus and Xander bothers me. I honestly can't blame him. Perhaps Mecca is right about me. The vampires may have lost the war of breaking my courage, but maybe they have my mind. I should be happy I'm surrounded by people that hate leeches. I mean this place is amazing, right? So why do I feel like a traitor?

"We're going to have a bonfire tonight in honor of Luna Mecca's return," says Beta Rendell, as we continue to walk down the hallway. He's giving me a tour of the wing dedicated to the long-lost Luna.

I still can't believe Mecca is a Luna. She's so crazy.

"It's a miracle she survived those monsters for all those years. She has always been strong, but damn."

My lips curl into a smile. That's exactly how I felt when Mecca first told me her story.

"Yup. Crazy ole Mecca is tougher than a box of nails. I'm glad she has returned to her mate. They look great together." I smile like a maniac.

"Crazy ole Mecca." He laughs, his eyes glowing yellow. "You really are something special. I have never met anyone that has the balls to call a Luna anything but Luna."

I laugh along with him. Beta Rendell has that effect on people. He is so hunky and charming. It's hard to believe he is a werewolf because he acts human. Well, they all do.

"They have always been perfect for each other. And no matter how long they had been apart, he refused to look for a second-chance mate," he says.

Mecca already told me that once a bond is broken from a wolf, they can accept a second-chance mate if the Moon Goddess allows it. Vampires can also have a second-chance beloved. Apparently, every species but humans can have a chance of finding love twice.

"What about your mate?" I ask. "Surely, she can't possibly be okay with you babysitting all day."

Beta Rendell's smile deepens.

These supernatural men are all so goddamn gorgeous, vampires and werewolves alike. Gosh! I swear I'm surprised I don't faint when we walk past the young wolves who are training. They are all hot with those sweaty muscles and abs, literally six-pack . . . eight-pack . . . ten-pack. Jeepers creepers! I'm sure the other human girls are in werewolf sex heaven, drooling as they walk by. Meanwhile, I can't get the bloodthirsty, bipolar, pantie-melting ass-kissing king out of my head the entire time. I know it's unbelievable.

"My mate was given to our goddess a long time ago." Beta Rendell switches his gaze in my direction.

*Given to his goddess? What does that mean? Oh no, he's not . . .*

"I'm sorry to hear that. If I had known about it, I would've never . . . I'm—"

"Claire, it's okay," he assures me, stopping in front of a balcony door. "My kind and your kind have both suffered enough from their kind. Before and after the last Luna Blood Moon, some things have just been out of our control."

I don't respond. Honestly, I don't know how to. Based on my observation, a mate bond is like the beat to the heart of these werewolves. They can't live without each other. The memorial hall dedicated to Mecca says it all. Alpha Maddox was never truly himself without her.

Beta Rendell is an amazing man. I know this even though I just met him. If this man is a shell of who he used to be before he lost his mate, that she-wolf had really won the lottery when they lived—bonded together.

"She was a lucky girl." I give him a faint smile.

His lips quirk into a half smirk. "I was the luckiest guy in the universe." He runs his hand through his dark hair. "I started to think my luck had run out until my wolf laid eyes on a golden goddess in the form of a human, who was willing to give her life for another wolf." Beta Rendell holds the balcony door open for me.

I take a moment to process his words. If I didn't know any better, I would think he has made a pass on me.

*Is it just my human mind playing tricks on me?*

I shake my head slightly and step onto the balcony. The enchanting view takes my breath away. The mountain is surrounded by a pure-white snow-frosted forest. The thick mist around us feels cool on my skin as I take a step closer toward the rail. I can see some wolves preparing for the bonfire.

Beta Rendell takes a step closer toward me. He seems afraid that I might fall over or something. He places his arm on top of the rail and leans over slightly, then flickers his gaze over to me. His eyes shift from brown to yellow.

I turn to face him completely. I study him without saying a word. Suddenly, his eyes return to their natural shade as he chuckles.

"You're truly remarkable."

299

I shake my head in response. Beta Rendell is starting to show his coo-coo side.

"You didn't show any fear in the presence of my wolf, Claire. It's one thing—to be brave for a crowd and to find the courage to save a person you care about. It's a whole different situation when you show no fear when you're alone, staring head-on into the eyes of the world's most-dangerous animal. You're truly remarkable. Somehow you managed to slip through the cracks those monsters attempted to stick you in. There's something about you, Claire. A human like you could change it all."

"Thank you," I say, not really sure what he is implying, but I can feel the sincerity in his words.

"No. Thank you, Claire. You make me feel . . ." He places his hand on top of mine. "Ouch!" He quickly removes his hand and shake it like it has been burned.

"Are you okay?" I ask.

"Yes," he responds, still studying it. "I feel like my bones were just crushed."

"Sorry. I didn't mean to—"

"You didn't do anything, Claire." He flashes me a soft smile. "Have you forgotten I'm the one who tried to touch you?" His eyes sparkle with amusement. "It may just be a charley horse." He continues to study his hand closely.

I tilt my head to the side.What's a charley horse?"

He bursts out laughing and shakes his head. His eyes flicker from brown to yellow. "You don't know what that is?" He lifts his thick and dark left eyebrow. "Have you ever been tickled before, Claire?"

*Tickled? What the hell does that have to do with anything?*

Suddenly, he starts to tickle me with his soft, bear-like hands. I burst out laughing. Some of the wolves below carrying the logs lift their heads up to stare at us, then they laugh along.

Beta Rendell picks me up off the balcony floor and tickles me harder. I throw my head back as laughter explodes from my lungs. Then out of nowhere, I see two red orbs staring at me. My neck snaps back as I jump out of Beta Rendell's hold.

"Claire, is everything okay?" he asks.

"Beta," a woman calls him.

I shift my attention back to the balcony doorway, and I'm met by a doll face, she-wolf beauty. She's tall and thin like a supermodel. Her dark hair is pulled into a high bun, her brilliant hazel eyes stealing the entire show.

"Farrah," acknowledges Beta Rendell.

They stare at each other for a long-drawn-out moment.

"I thought Beta Hunter already took you home," Beta Rendell says.

She doesn't respond. She switches her focus onto me, and I have her undivided attention.

"Where are my manners?" Beta Rendell questions himself. "Claire, this is Farrah Wilde, Alpha Maddox's oldest niece. Farrah, this is Claire, the human that saved Luna Mecca."

Farrah gives a slight bow. "Beta Rendell, can I talk to you in private?"

"About what?" He slightly grinds his teeth.

She turns to face me. "I will not discuss werewolf matters in front of a human!"

Okay, so someone doesn't like me. I mean it's not what she said, but how she said it.

I watch her emotionless face closely.

Beta Rendell's body goes stiff. "This human saved your uncle's mate. Show Claire respect."

Most humans will probably feel uneasy or uncomfortable, but I'm not that human. I bite my bottom lip and turn to face Beta Rendell. Somehow I can sense that his wolf is present, struggling to keep his control.

What is it between these two? I can't tell whether they are lovers or enemies, or both. The tension in the room is so thick that you could cut it with a knife.

I clear my throat. "It's okay. I want to go check on Alec."

"No, it's not okay," growls Beta Rendell. He narrows his eyes at Farrah. "We don't treat our friends like outsiders."

"And we don't treat our lovers like outsiders either," spits Farrah.

Oops, she has dropped a bomb.

Beta Rendell's wolf completely takes over. "This is not the time or place to discuss nonsense!"

"Nonsense!" she yells. "You have a f*cking nerve."

They start to bicker back and forth in a language I don't understand. Beta wolf's eyes are glowing yellow; Farrah's are a shining gold. Meanwhile, I'm in between the two, feeling so out of place.

I open the door, attempting to get the hell out of dodge.

"No, I'll take you." Beta Rendell walks toward me.

Farrah shoves past us as she makes her way out of the door herself. Again, I feel like I have just been sucked in between a lover tornado. I stand in silence to give Beta Rendell some time to calm down. His fingers turn into claws, his face dripping in sweat.

"My apologies, Claire." He releases a frustrated sigh.

"It's okay."

I really don't feel anything. I have nothing to do with their situation, and he has no reason to apologize.

"Come, I'll take you to the guest chambers so you can get ready for the bonfire," he offers.

\*     \*     \*

After Beta Rendell walked me to the room, I quickly took a shower and got dressed. Mecca had ordered some she-wolves to drop me off some clothes.

I'm wearing some black skinny jeans and a cashmere sweater of the same color. They even found me some black leather boots with cute, bulky heels. I feel like a ball-kicking heroine.

I stare at myself in the mirror, touching my lips. The last time I looked in the mirror was after Nicklaus and I shared that hot and steamy kiss. Just thinking about his sweet, seductive lips colliding with mine makes me shiver.

*I wonder if he's okay. I know the werewolves attacked King Cyrus's penthouse. I hope Nicklaus and Xander are safe.*

I laugh to myself. If I were with them, I wouldn't have to say anything at all. Neither of them knows how to stay out of my head. Gosh, I really miss them. I'm starting to become like one of those obsessed, typical human girls. It seems I'm infatuated with the vampire kings that take over the world. I know it's pathetic.

*Snap out of it, Claire,* I tell myself, closing my eyes. *You are better than that. You escaped without having to lose your life in the process. You're free. There's no need to look back. There's nothing or no one to look back on.*

I tell myself those exact words over and over as I stand in the bathroom, but for some strange reason my mind and heart refuse to accept my thoughts. I let out a deep sigh and focus on applying makeup. I fill in my brows, then put a tad bit of foundation on, just like how Jadis taught me. Oh gosh, I forgot about her. She is still in chains, most likely losing her mind and body in the Kingdom of Breeders. How can I ever be truly free while my first friend is still being held captive?

I grab the edges of the sink. My head feels like it's about to explode.

"What's wrong, brave human?" asks Mecca from behind me.

I turn to look at her. She looks beautiful, as always. She's also wearing some black skinny jeans and a black sweater. Her hair is curled and pulled into a nice updo. Her lips are painted scarlet.

"I'm fine," I lie, refusing to place my problems on her shoulders. "I'm just a little tired."

Mecca flashes a smile. "You're a bad liar, Claire."

"I know, but tonight isn't about me. It's about celebrating your freedom. It's about celebrating your return home." I drop down to one knee, just like how Beta Rendell showed me. "Welcome home, Luna." I slightly bend my head down in submission.

Mecca stands in front of me and pulls me back up from the floor. She gently lifts my chin up. "Claire," she says with a low growl, "you will never bow again for anyone. You are my friend," she reminds me, her eyes filled with raw emotions. "You are my equal." She pulls me into a tight hug, extremely tight.

"Ouch!" I pull away a little. "Mecca, I'm human."

She releases that beautiful, crazy ole laugh of hers. "My apologies, human. Now tell me what's bothering you."

I part my lips to say something but then decide to close them again instead. How can I tell my she-wolf friend I miss the same people that held her captive? How can I tell her I miss the same people who held me captive? I have never felt so weak.

Someone knocks on the door.

"Claire, can I come in?" asks Alec.

Mecca raises an eyebrow. "Oh, he knocks." She grins like a Cheshire cat. "Come in, human. You have about five minutes to make a baby."

My jaw drops. She hasn't just said that.

"No need to come in, boy," she tells him. "It's time to go." She walks over toward the folded clothes, then hands me a black fur coat. "Are you ready for your first bonfire, human?"

I nod, then follow her out of the door.

# CHAPTER FORTY-THREE
## Bonfire

My bulky leather boots crunch through the snow as we walk toward the bonfire. The ground, the trees, and the roof of the pack house are drenched in snow. The stars are shining above us, bright and alive. The night sky is a deep-blue color like the deepest, darkest sea. There's a chill in the air, but the flames from the bonfire roar to life, providing a little warmth.

Mecca's milk-chocolate skin glistens as she stands in front of the burning light. Her amber eyes that are filled with warmth glow along with the flames. Her sheer and long black dress clings to her body like a second skin. Her jet-black hair is still in the perfect updo, and some of her curls that hang freely blow in unison with the wind. Her natural habitat serves her right. She looks wildly beautiful.

I snuggle my face into the light-brown fur collar of my beautifully designed mink coat. Its silky fur provides extra warmth to my skin, and I'm grateful.

I stop to stand beside Alec and his girlfriend, Samantha. We are currently waiting for the other humans and lycan royals to arrive before they start the festivities. I'm not too excited about it. The golden wolf b*tch is still on my hit list, and most humans—except Alec and Jadis—always seem to hate me.

I sigh. *Claire, this is a night of new beginnings,* I tell myself. *This is Mecca's night, so try to enjoy it.*

Along the way, Mecca told me she ended her bond with Alpha Maddox twenty years after she was captured. That was over a century ago. She said it was the hardest thing she has ever done. She wanted him to be happy even though he wouldn't be happy without her. Alpha Maddox must have been heartbroken once she released their bond. He assumed she was dead.

I can't imagine living over a hundred years thinking that my other half was killed. I feel bad for him, for them. Alpha Maddox refused to search for a second-chance mate. He refused to move on. Mecca said he'd always told her that if the Moon Goddess called her home first, he would wait to go home to love again.

They will reclaim their bond tonight by a mating ritual.

Alpha Maddox is a man of his word. Mecca is the luckiest she-wolf in the universe. I wish them nothing but an eternity of happiness. They deserve it. I refuse to spoil that. I'm just a little moody. That's all.

The big bonfire is dancing wildly, growing taller by the second as the wind rushes around us. We are standing in front of the pack house. Werewolves from the other several surrounding territories and the Western Pack have also joined us. Alpha Maddox's brother, Beta Hunter, and their alpha—Luke—are also present. I must say they are both freaking, smoking hot. I mean, scorching hot. They are burning brighter than the bonfire. The heat I feel around them is unbearable. Gosh, these goddamn supernatural men, I can't take them.

According to Mecca, Beta Hunter is the father of Farrah— the she-wolf I met earlier. It's hard to believe because he doesn't even look thirty. His pack is here not only to celebrate Mecca's return and her union with Alpha Maddox but also to locate his lost daughter named Embry. Both packs will become one until she's found. They have officially declared war on King Cyrus, and it's sad that Mecca has to go to war too soon. She just returned home. She should be at peace, not preparing for a battle.

I know for a fact that Xander and Nicklaus will fight beside King Cyrus, that's why they came here in the first place. I'm pretty sure the other kings will also come to fight for him. It's going to get ugly, and I'm afraid for them all.

I try my best not to think about it and instead watch the western alpha and his beta from a distance. Alpha Luke has the most-usual eyes. His icy silver eyes, God-given face, and welcoming nature remind me of the younger version of Xander. Beta Hunter, on the other hand, looks extremely similar to his older brother. His dark features, extremely handsome face, and piercing blue eyes are just like his brother's. He gave me the cold shoulder during our introduction, and it sort of convinced me that the apple most certainly doesn't fall that far from the tree with the Wilde family. They are all the same—hot and cold. Apparently, the werewolf community looks up to them. Honestly, I don't see why, but who cares about what I think? I'm just a human.

The other humans have finally arrived. I watch their unfamiliar faces with no interest while Alec and Samantha rush over to them.

*At least some of their friends escaped. Jadis on the other hand . . .Oh my Jadis!*

I lower my head, attempting to get her soft features and gentle nature out of my head. I refuse to be a party pooper. Tonight is not about me. It's about freedom and second chances. It's not fair for me to be the Grinch. I should be grateful.

"Claire, is that you?" says a voice I really don't care to remember.

I lift my head. Victoria, the red-headed slut, is standing right in front of me.

*Screw not being the Grinch. This is not freaking fair. Jadis is still in chains while the vamp tramp is free. F\*ck the fates!*

I brush right past her, and yes, I bump her shoulder. This is the last person I expected to see, and I damn sure never want to see her face again. Stupid b\*tch.

"Wait, Claire!" She chases after me. "Claire, please wait."

I turn to face her.

*I'm not in the mood to play battle of the b\*tches, so if this redhead says the wrong thing, I swear things will get real.*

My eyes lock on Mecca, who is watching us from afar. Crazy ole Mecca's eyes flash bright yellow. That's my girl. She is trained to go, and I know for a fact she has my back, without a doubt.

"What do you want, Victoria?" I ask in a very hostile voice.

Her eyes drop to the ground. "Nothing. It's just nice to see a familiar face."

Victoria is wearing a black trench coat, red plaid shirt, black jeans, and some bulky black boots similar to the ones I'm wearing. Her red lips and flaming-red hair are a great contrast with her pale skin. She looks stunning, but that's to be expected. She has always been pretty. Her heart is really ugly, though.

I roll my eyes and walk away.

"I'm sorry, Claire. I'm sorry for everything. I was horrible to you. I will never be able to make up for it, but I hope you can forgive me."

"Now, why would I do that?" I turn back around to face her, placing my hands on my hips.

"Because tonight is about new beginnings, right? The other humans here speak highly of the golden-haired human, who was brave enough to stand up for another human slave." She smiles a genuine smile.

*What has gotten into this girl?*

"They say she stood her ground to save a human boy," she goes on. "The wolves have also been speaking highly of the golden-haired girl for saving their leader. None of us would be here if it weren't for that girl."

"I thought you were content with being a chosen. Why would it matter if you're free or not?"

"I have never been content with being a slave, Claire. I was just doing what I had to do to survive. I'm not that brave." She sighs. "I don't know how to stand up for myself, but I do know this. Any slave with that much courage deserves nothing but respect." Her eyes are filled with warmth.

I have known her since I was five years old, but never have I seen this side of her.

"With that being said, I want to apologize. The moment they spoke about the golden-haired girl, I knew in my heart they were tallking about you. I always envied your courage, the way you stood up against the vampires and other humans at school. I was always jealous that you could show no fear." She takes a deep breath. "But tonight is a new beginning for all of us, and that has a lot to do with you. So, thank you, Claire."

*Who is this girl, and what the hell did she do with my archnemesis?*

"Thank you, Claire, for showing courage when no one else did." She pulls me into a hug.

I'm completely lost for words—shocked.

\*     \*     \*

Tonight is a once-in-a-lifetime opportunity, and I'm deeply honored to witness and be a part of this glorious event.

The mating ritual was beautifully strange. Alpha Maddox and Mecca spoke vows my human mind couldn't process. It was something about the Luna giving them the power to become one again, which is obviously self-explanatory, but when they started to speak a foreign language, I could not fully grasp it. Their eyes began to glow, and they half shifted—they were halfway to becoming a human and werewolf, sort of between the two forms. Their hands and feet had claws, their bodies had little fur, and their eyes continued to gleam. It was creepy, and it kind of reminded me of the first time I met Mecca.

The ceremony was beautiful as expected until they humped each other in front of everyone and bit into each other's neck.

See what I mean? It was strangely beautiful. I had to turn away, refusing to watch the creatures doing the "humpty hump."

The mood is peaceful even with the privileged lycans being present. The golden wolf's aura most certainly gives off regal power and dominance whereas that of her parents, the lycan rulers, was triple stacks over. True to his title, Lycan King Luke screams "follow my lead." The crazy part is he hasn't spoken a word. He hasn't blinked, laughed, smiled, or even introduced himself. Just with one look and you'll know he's the king of these creatures. He's tall, strong, and handsome.

He seems bored—the way his stunning greenish-gray eyes don't show an ounce of interest and the way his full and luscious lips refuse to even twitch at the most-entertaining festivities that have been going on during this beautiful night. It's obvious he doesn't want to be here, the same with the lycan queen named Luna. She has thick, luscious dark hair pulled back into a high bun, exposing her flawlessly sculptured but unemotional face. Her thick and well-defined eyebrows enhance her cold, chilling green eyes that are so similar to her daughter's. She forces a smile every once in a while, but that's it. The only thing that seems to hold her attention is me. I have noticed her eyes flicker in my direction numerous times. She is watching me.

She raises her thick eyebrow when I stare right back at her. Finally, she looks away. I have a hunch she doesn't like me, but I'm completely unbothered. Like seriously, who cares? She might as well join the . . . club

Many different wolves are now giving speeches and their blessing to Mecca and the Alpha in their union. An older she-wolf is passing out hot chocolate around us, humans, while the children of werewolves are heating up marshmallows that will go well with their chocolate and Graham cracker dessert. This is truly a completely different world.

Mecca makes her way towards the front of the bonfire. Her eyes flicker in my direction. She looks so happy, and my eyes start to water. I'm really happy for her. Her happiness is my happiness.

She clears her throat. "First things first, I want to thank everyone who came to celebrate our union, peace, and my homecoming."

The crowd bursts in shouts of joy, whistles, and I'm sure I just heard a few wolf howls.

Mecca stares at me. "I want to thank someone special and very dear to my heart. As most of you already know, I wouldn't have had the strength to make it back here if it hadn't been for this brave little human." Her eyes glow that fascinating shade of yellow.

I'm aware that her wolf is present.

She walks over in my direction. All eyes are on us, but hers are locked on mine. "Claire." She holds out her hand to me.

I walk closer toward my friend and the bonfire, the festive and pleasant smell of the burning wood invading my nostrils. I accept Mecca's hand without hesitation. It's crazy how close we have grown in this short period of time. I feel safe standing beside her. My bond with the crazy ole she-wolf is not easy to explain.

"I once told you there was something about you," she says. "For the life of me, I couldn't place my finger on it."

Alpha Maddox, who is holding an oak box with little wolf carvings on the front of the case, steps beside her. The lycans, western pack, and the other wolves watch us with great interest. My heart is hammering, racing, and pounding a million beats per second. He opens the box slowly, revealing an astonishing piece of jewelry with a gorgeous and gigantic pear-shaped emerald pendant surrounded by pave-set diamonds. It glistens the very moment he holds it in his hand.

The crowd breaks out in chaos. There are audible gasps, shouts, and even some wolf growls.

"What the hell do you think you're doing?" says a heart-wrenching voice.

311

There is so much going on around me, but my eyes are glued to the pendant. I can hear things, but no matter how hard I try to turn away, I just can't. I'm stuck, lost in a trance. The diamond is calling to my soul, and the emerald feels extremely close to my heart.

Alpha Maddox is arguing with someone. I don't know who. I don't also recognize the person's voice, then I feel Mecca gently put her hand on my shoulder, as if she's protecting me from something or someone.

Seconds later, I notice the pendant being placed around my neck. The cool and fine feel of it is ice on my skin. My heart starts to beat wildly, and everything around me slows down in motion. The lycan king is now in front of me. His eyes are pure gold, burning hot rage and spitting angry fire. He attempts to snatch the pendant off my neck, but he howls in a fit of pain the very moment his hand comes in contact with my skin.

A surge of power rushes through me like a gust of wind.

"Turn around," says a deep and familiar voice.

The air seems to sizzle, zapping like lightning. My body becomes like mush. I turn to face him. My ass-kissing king and a group of unrecognizable vampires—the men in black—have returned.

"Come to me," he commands, but my feet don't move a single inch.

"Vampires!" someone calls out.

All hell breaks loose. Nicklaus holds up a silver item. From afar it looks like . . . It's a gun! He is holding a gun, and he is aiming it at Mecca.

Suddenly, my mind goes blank.

*     *     *

*"Are you just going to leave the beast woman there?" I raise an eyebrow.*

*He bursts out into another fit of laughter. "I've already sent some guards to take her back to her cell."*

*Wait a minute, the beast woman is alive? That's impossible. He snapped her neck. I saw it with my own eyes. It made a crunch sound—snap, just like that.*

*"It takes a lot more than snapping their neck to kill a werewolf, especially one as strong as her. The only way is to shoot them in the heart with a silver bullet," he answers my question. He has once again invaded my privacy.*

*"What do you mean by 'one as strong as her'?"*

\*      \*      \*

"Nooo!" I jump in front of Mecca at that exact same moment Nicklaus pulls the trigger.

# CHAPTER FORTY-FOUR
## Attack

NICKLAUS

*Before the attack*

Out of a sea of many faces that will gladly end me, my unbeaten heart only drops for my firecracker. She is standing proud and tall in the middle of the crowd with her shoulders pulled back, head held high, and chin pointed toward the air. She is showing no fear. You would think this human girl is the true superior. She is the beauty surrounded by beasts.

I'm standing a great distance away, and I can see how many of the wolves, humans, and lycans are watching her in awe. They are fascinated by my beloved. Her stance alone screams power. Her etiquette is better than that of the princess and queen of savage beasts put together.

The lycan queen is watching her even more closely. I can tell she is impressed but at the same time threatened by Claire's defiant nature. Every time her cold green eyes lock on my firecracker's soul-snatching green eyes, Claire holds her stare with a wicked glare of her own. Whenever the lycan queen raises her beastly eyebrow as a response to Claire's actions, my firecracker raises her delicate eyebrow right back at her, mocking her. It's extremely entertaining. If I know anything about the queen of savage beasts, it's the fact that she doesn't like to be challenged. However, Claire is someone who challenges even the world's most-dangerous predators.

Pride beams through me. My queen fears no one or nothing.

"Look at her," Xander speaks, sounding extremely proud.

"There is nothing else to look at," I reply.

It's true. Claire takes the cake, every time. I have been around for a long time—a very long time—but she's the only person who has ever had my sight hooked with one glance, piercing my soul with one look. She has me fall head over heels in love with her. She's my blessing after centuries of storms. She is the air invading my lungs. I need her more than I need blood, although it's the only thing that keeps me alive.

"What is your command, sire?" asks one of my men. They caught up with us hours after we met up with Commander Vlad.

Apparently, the magic of the princess of savage beasts isn't that strong. We have been here for a while, watching their every move. I have seen Claire multiple times since my arrival. I've been watching from the shadows, patiently waiting for the right time to strike. It doesn't take me long to realize they are preparing for a festival. The queen of the dogs is back. Of course they are celebrating. All hail the queen of ticks and fleas—disgusting mutt! Tonight is the night I'm going to kill that b*tch. She's going to be put down once and for all.

Everything has been going smoothly according to plan, except for the fact that I almost blew our cover. It was when I saw the dog beta placing his filthy paw on my beloved's treasured hand. My vision was quickly tinted red, and the next thing I knew my mind was already crushing his bones with my power. Xander came to save the day, as usual, but not before that feisty and alert beloved of mine made eye contact with me. She's truly very attentive to be a human, strangely enough.

She didn't react. (I don't think she trusted her intuition.) The wolves standing right beside me weren't able to detect my presence. Stupid mutts! I was right under their noses.

"Kill them all," I command, facing my soldier. "Spare no one except my chosen."

We still haven't told everyone that Claire is the rightful queen. I trust only a few with that piece of critical information.

"No, capture as many humans as possible," Xander pipes up. "We will need blood to regenerate. Try not to drain them. They may come in handy on our way back to the city."

The soldier turns to face me, and I nod in approval and dismiss him.

This festival of theirs has truly made this operation a piece of cake, thanks to the smell of burning wood. They can't sniff or detect us. We have been keeping a great distance. I only came close to check on my beloved. It was easy because I hold the power to make many dogs turn blind eyes. However, things started to become difficult when those savage lycans arrived. They are all idiots, except the princess of the beasts. She truly has magic, and it's *almost* impressive—almost! I know they don't think we would just allow their assault to slide.

"It's going to be too easy," says Xander, as we walk into our positions.

"I was thinking the same thing. At least one thing is certain. They don't know who Claire really is to me. If they did, they wouldn't be allowing her to roam around so freely."

"I don't know, Nicklaus. Why else would the dog take her? It's the only logical explanation unless—"

"Unless we are missing something."

Xander stops in his tracks. "When I took Claire out of the dungeon, she was acting different. At first, it seemed she was afraid of me."

I almost choke on my tongue. My firecracker is not afraid of anyone.

316

"I remember her telling me"—Xander turns around to look at the she-wolf b*tch—"that Mecca is interesting." He turns back to face me.

"Yeah, and I recall Claire calling her beast woman, but that still doesn't explain."

"It does." Xander's eyes flash crimson. "She called the mutt by her name, Mecca."

My eyes open with a new light. "She told Claire her name? That could only mean—"

"That she is fond of Claire," Xander says. "She possibly even likes her."

"The guards found a blanket I sent down for Claire in the mutt's cell," I point out. I didn't think anything of it, then it hits me. "That's how she was able to attack you! Claire must have been feeding her, sharing her rations." My blood starts to boil.

"Don't get mad, Nicklaus. Claire didn't know any better. Helping others in need is in her nature. That's one characteristic that will make her a great queen."

This is why our family never loses a war. We are skilled thinkers—crafty—and Xander's mind alone is a big asset.

My red vision zeroes in on the b*tch. "I'm not mad at my beloved for helping that mutt. I'm mad at that mutt for using my beloved to get to my brother."

"Agreed," he says. Red bleeds in his vision as well. "Speaking of which, you are going to claim Claire at once?"

My brother seems to be telling more than asking.

"My business with my beloved is my business. You should be worrying about finding a second-chance mate and claiming her."

"Claire's safety and well-being are just as much as my concerns as they are yours, Nicklaus. The only way to truly protect her is to turn her. Claire's life will always be in jeopardy until you do so."

He's right but wrong. Claire's safety will always be in jeopardy whether she is a human or a vampire. There will always be

317

a bounty placed on her head, may it be from vampires, wolves, or any other supernatural creatures. At this point, no one will accept us to be together. Even the hunters will be disgusted by our union. Too much damage has been done for anyone to accept it.

Based on my own evaluation and some eavesdropping, my little firecracker has made a name for herself. Humans and wolves speak highly of her, which means changing Claire will do more harm than good. The word will spread, and it can lead to an uprising by all species. I can't do that. To make matters worse, I don't think I can claim her without losing control. I may end her. My lust for her blood is too strong.

Claire may have accepted our bond, but she will never accept to be turned into a creature she calls a leech. Claiming her is just the first part of the transition. She will still have to accept and acknowledge the bond completely to transition into immortality and become my true beloved. If I know my beloved well enough, and trust me I do, she will fight until her last breath to hold on to her humanity.

"If what you say is true, about the mutt taking a liking to Claire, then that will make her the guest of honor," I tell him, changing the subject. "The mutt will give a speech and then present a gift. That's when we shall strike."

I mind-link with my men and instruct, *"Hold off. I'll give you the signal when it's time to attack."*

"I thought you wanted to be on the outskirts to take Claire to safety." Xander raises his eyebrow. He knows me all too well.

"I'm still taking her to safety, and I'm going to kill that b\*tch in the process."

\*       \*       \*

CLAIRE

Time seems to stop as the speeding bullet travels in our direction. I can see it coming, literally coming our way. I'm in front of Mecca. Alpha Maddox is standing on my left side while King Luke is on the right side of Mecca. Both Mecca's and Alpha Maddox's eyes are glowing yellow whereas the lycan king's are glowing gold.

It's crazy that my human eyes can actually see the speeding bullet seeming to curve as it gets closer toward us. I know it has only been a second, but to me it feels like it's been hours. The bullet is inches away from me and is about to hit me straight in the heart.

I feel Mecca attempt to move me out of the way, but her mate pushes her to the ground. My skin starts to tingle, my heart continues to pound rapidly, and my neck suddenly itches.

"No, I will not die like this. Stop, stop, stop!" I scream.

A bright, electric emerald green light flashes, then an unknown force knocks me to my feet, and the bullet falls right in front of me—just like that. I pick it up, but the burning silver metal is too hot, making my index finger feel like it's about to fall off.

"F*ck," I say, dropping the bullet. "What in the world?"

Instantly, the fighting begins.

"Sleep," states someone who is standing right beside me.

I turn my head to see the golden wolf b*tch. She speaks, and suddenly one of the men in black that is inches away from me sinks to his knees.

"That's for saving Mecca," she says to me. She shifts into her golden wolf form and then takes off.

*How the hell did she get here that quick?*

I look at the crowd of chaos. Wolves are shifting. The men in black are charging as the fire behind me roars viciously, carrying the smell of burnt flesh and blood in the air. Mecca also shifts into her full-fledged wolf form. A man in black closes in on her, then knocks her, but she manages to take him down. Her claws and massive teeth plunge into his neck, ripping off his head in the

319

process. The pure-white snow is now painted crimson—like a murder scene.

Alpha Maddox's big black wolf is fighting doggedly beside Mecca. With one bite, his claws and scary sharp teeth rip off the heads of two men in black.

I search the crowd for anyone else I can recognize. It's hard to tell with so many wolves and men in black killing each other off. My eyes then land on Beta Rendell, whose dark-brown—almost black—wolf jumps in midair just in time to save the she-wolf Farrah. He lunges at one of the men in black and pulls out the vampire's spine with his sharp teeth.

Now, that's just disgusting!

Farrah turns into a big light-gray wolf of her own and rushes over toward another massive wolf of the same color. The enormous creature is already fighting off three men in black by himself. I assume it's her father from the way she's rushing to his rescue even though it's not like he needs her help.

I can now see why the Wilde wolves are legends among the werewolves. He exceeds beyond expectations. He moves so fast. (I'm not sure how my human eyes are actually detecting him.) One second he's ripping off a vampire's head, then the next his big claws are already digging into a vampire's stomach and snatching their intestines out in the process. It sort of reminds me of the video I used to watch in school, of our world leaders being killed. The only difference is that his torture lasts for just a second. His kills are also clean and well-executed. Clearly, this wolf is the true monster.

I can hear the fire sizzle behind me. My heart races and the hair on the back of my neck stands as a sudden eerie feeling rushes through me. Something inside me is begging me to turn around. Call me crazy, but I follow my intuition, and that's when I see him. My eyes zoom in on Nicklaus. It's truly amazing how we are standing on a ground full of blood-smeared snow, falling trees, and dead bodies while the man behind the attack is still untouched. He doesn't even have a scratch. He is wearing a black sweatshirt, some black combat pants, matching black combat boots, and a black beanie.

Gosh, this man is dressed to kill—and he also takes hearts, literally.

King Nicklaus appears out of nowhere, just like the lycan king, who is now roaring and howling directly beside me. Come on, how the hell do these lycans keep doing this?

Everything goes in slow motion again before my very eyes. The lycan king shifts into an enormous and scary silver-haired wolf with mesmerizing fur that's almost hypnotic to look at. He jumps into the air, seconds away from pouncing on the king of all vampire kings.

My heart drops for only a second, then my instincts once again take over. "No, stop!" I shout.

A bright, electric emerald-green light flashes once more, and an unknown force stops him in midair. I feel a gentle hand on my shoulder before my mind has time to truly process what the hell has happened. An electric current zaps inside me, sparking all the way down to the center of my core. I feel like I'm on fire as the burning hot sensation speeds through my windpipe and then bursts out of my lungs. I place my face against a rock-hard surface, and instantly the chill of the midnight air seeps into my bones. The wind ruffles through my hair, and my skin continues to sizzle—zap, zap, zap—chilling, cracking sizzles while I'm being cradled and rocked.

I release a moan. I'm cold but at the same time so warm, feeling extremely safe and secure. The shouts and screams from the crowd and the smell of blood, fire, and fear are all starting to fade away. It's quiet, very quiet. I know for a fact I'm no longer standing where I was a second ago. I know for a fact I'm being ushered and carried away from the pack house. I'm no longer with a human, werewolf, or lycan. I'm with him. He is holding me close to his chest. No one's touch has this sort of impact on me. The skin-to-skin contact makes me feel extremely hot and bubble on the inside although it's so cold and damn near freezing on the outside. I know it's him.

The wind stops rushing.

"Firecracker," calls my one and only ass-kissing king. "Open your eyes," he says, his voice cracking in between words.

I'm too afraid to see him again. I still don't want to look into his soul-piercing eyes. I'm petrified to see those thick and long eyelashes and perfectly carved lips. I'm terrified that I might want to kiss him and taste him again.

I squeeze my eyes tighter.

"Open your eyes, Claire."

This time he is commanding me, but my eyes won't lift. They are practically glued shut. Nope, I'm not looking at him.

Seconds later, I feel those beautiful lips smash into my own. I moan. Magic pricks, seeps, and travels through my bones. With a single taste of his tongue—boom!—the fire burns; the ice freezes. Together our lips and tongues feel frozen solid but hot as hell. I'm suffocating, gasping for air inside my mind.

His fingers run through my hair at the same exact time as my fingers travel through his silky pitch-black hair. This is exactly what I was so afraid of. His kiss and his touch are enough to take over my mind. He's completely brainwashing me, with effortless pressure. He won. He has taken my mind, body, and soul.

"Claire," his husky voice whispers, as he bites down onto my bottom lip. "Open your eyes now."

My eyes open, and as expected his pierce straight into my soul. I don't see a single tear, but they seem to be watery as though he was crying. They still place their invisible hooks inside me before they snatch my soul out of my body to enter his, taking it as his own. We become one. In this moment I know this vampire is mine. He belongs to me. I'm his beloved—of that I'm sure.

# CHAPTER FORTY-FIVE
## Stake Your Claim

How can a person look into your soul through your eyes and snatch it away from you? I will never know, but he does it every time. My eyes are like open doors, inviting him in, while his are like an open book to a never-ending story.

I stare into his soul-snatching eyes. How could I miss what is right in front of me? It's obvious I long for him. Right now, it's just me and him. Nicklaus plus Claire equals us. His face is expressionless—masked—but his eyes tell an entirely different story. He is in pain; he's hurting. I can see it. I can see his soul. I could stare into them for the rest of eternity.

*Eternity? I'm human. We don't live that long, but he will. He lives forever. How can I give him my heart freely, knowing that he will remain this beautiful while I will eventually become old and wrinkled? That's if I live that long. A dog's lifespan is longer than that of a human these days. Is that why he hasn't claimed me as his true beloved? It makes perfect sense. That must be it, but I still deserve to hear it from him.*

"Put me down now," I demand.

His body goes stiff. "Claire, I'm sorry. I didn't mean to." He looks adorable, like a panicky human boy instead of the bloodthirsty monster that he really is.

A strong urge to run my fingers through his silky hair and kiss his sweet and tasty lips rushes through me.

*Gosh, he's so distracting. No, no, no. He's not getting away with this one. The least he can do is tell me the truth.*

"Who am I to you?" I ask, refusing to waste another second.

His jaw drops. I'm sure his heart has stopped beating as our eyes lock. He definitely wasn't expecting that one.

"What do you mean? You're already aware I selected you to be my chosen."

*My chosen your ass! If he really thinks I'm going to believe that bullsh\*t, then he is crazier than I thought. How long is he going to keep this from me?*

A pulling sensation invades my mind. It tickles but nothing more. Nicklaus's piercing eyes widen.

*Yup, motherf\*cker, you're caught. I got you.*

"Brave one," says another voice.

I quickly jump out of Nicklaus's arms and smash into Xander, who holds out his arms and catches me.

*Gosh, I miss him. I miss them.*

Nicklaus watches us warily. "I can't read her mind. They did something to her," he says. He's talking to Xander, acting as if I did not even exist.

"Who are they?" I pull away from Xander. I'm not dumb. I know he's talking about the werewolves, but still . . . "They did nothing. You, on the other hand, tried to kill my best friend, and you have been lying to me."

Both their eyes flash crimson.

"That dog isn't your friend," Nicklaus responds.

"Oh yes, she is." I make my way back over to him. "Just like I am your—"

"I can't read her mind either," Xander cuts in. "What happened?" His eyes shift from me and then to Nicklaus.

The two are doing some creepy vampire thing, most likely reading each other's mind. Nicklaus's eyes grow bright red by the second while Xander's are bleeding, burning, and blazing crimson.

They both look pissed. Nothing good can come from two big, broad, and pissed vampires.

Xander is the first to break eye contact. "Commander Vlad has arrived. We need to go now."

Nicklaus quickly scoops me off the ground, quicker than one can say, "I do." I can feel the angry heat waves seeping out of his pores. He's really, really angry, and it kind of bothers me. I don't like seeing him like that.

Wait, what am I talking about? Who the hell cares if he's angry? I'm acting whipped.

*You are whipped,* says my inner voice.

I want to confront Nicklaus, but I don't want to add fuel to his already blazing fire. I'll give him a moment to calm down. I think it's for the best.

We are running through an ice-frozen forest, but all I feel is him. He speeds like a race car, the wind rushing around us. I put my left hand over his heart. It's not beating, but mine is pounding loud enough for the both of us—we are one. He places his chin over my head, and I have to stop myself from purring. It feels so good. He doesn't have to do much. Just one touch is all it takes. Jeepers creepers! I'm officially buttercream whipped.

Nicklaus stops and slides into a black *SUV*. He moves so fast. One minute we were running, the next minute I'm already sitting on his lap, my hand still on his chest. His piercing eyes are once again locking me in chains. I can't move.

Xander climbs in and slams the door shut. The car speeds off at once. Oh God, I think I'm going to be sick. My stomach can't take all this unearthly movement.

"Are you f*cking stupid?" Xander shouts.

I knew it. He's pissed.

"You could have killed her."

"Remember who you're talking to," replies Nicklaus.

How can five words sound so dangerous, menacing, savage, threatening, heart-wrenching, and cruel?

Xander doesn't have to remember who he is talking to because I do. Nicklaus is still the world's most-feared and most-dangerous predator. I won't ever forget it. Never.

Something unnerving, wicked, and cold flashes through Xander's silver eyes as he shoots daggers at Nicklaus, reminding me of his reputation as the cold-hearted king. "I know perfectly well who I'm talking to," he says. Anger, hurt, and pain seep through him like water gushing through cracks in the wall. His body is dangerously still, his eyes flickering different shades of red.

Nicklaus's grip around my waist tightens. This is going from bad to worse in a matter of seconds.

"The spoiled and pathetic vampire, who almost killed his—"

That does it. Nicklaus lunges at Xander, knocking me over in the process. I manage to pull myself up as quickly as possible despite the gravity of the moving car. The two are like animals locked in a cage as they fight for their lives. Have you ever seen two lions fighting? It's petrifying—sharp teeth, massive claws, and a lot of blood!

Everything around me goes in slow motion, and my heart is hammering in my chest.

Xander's fist slams into Nicklaus's face while Nicklaus's knee collides with Xander's jaw.

I'm torn. Xander is like the big brother I've never had. Nicklaus is my . . . My skin starts to tingle, and my neck is burning scorching hot red rage. "Stop!" I scream at the top of my lungs.

A bright, electric emerald-green light flashes again, and an unknown force sends me flying. The vehicle stops with a thud as my back slams into the car seat. A buzzing white noise rings loudly inside my head and then it all goes dark.

*     *     *

NICKLAUS

My blood is boiling. Xander's words sting like a queen bee. I try to control myself for Claire's sake. She has seen enough bloodshed to last a lifetime. She doesn't need to see Xander and me at each other's neck. I grip her tiny little waist in an attempt to calm my monster down, but with each word, my control alters. My monster starts clawing, slowly easing to the surface. My fangs throb, itching. Someone wants to come out and play. Brother or not, Xander will learn his place.

"The spoiled and pathetic vampire, who almost killed his—"

He's dead. He will pay for his disrespect with his life.

I smash my fist into his face, then plunge my fangs into his neck. Sweet-tasting blood drips down my throat, edging my monster on. Xander yanks me off him and sinks his fangs into my skin. My knee hits his jaw, and his fist collides with my face.

"Stop!" Claire screams.

A bright emerald-green light blinds me, an unknown force holding me in place. Commander Vlad's foot works on the brakes as Claire's back slams into the car seat. Her eyes flutter shut, and blood starts trickling down the side of her face.

My stomach drops. I rush to her side, then place my hand on her head at the exact same moment that Xander's hand touches her heart. The red tint in my vision washes away. The air is knocked out of me. I'm empty—a hollow surface. All I can see and think about is Claire. She looks broken.

"What the f*ck was that?" Vlad swings the car door open. "What happened to Claire?" he asks, his voice sounding unusually concerned.

Xander's finger trails from my firecracker's heart to her collarbone, and jealousy stirs within me and swallows me whole.

"Don't touch her!" I hiss. Crimson red slowly bleeds into my vision.

Xander's neck snaps. "Drink from her now."

It's tempting, so tempting.

327

"Drink now, Nicklaus!"

I want to. I want to run my tongue over her soft and delicate skin. I want to sink my fangs into her very soul.

The wind blows in her scent. That sweet, honey-dipped, intoxicating scent is now driving my monster crazy. Lust spreads through my entire body as I'm fighting even harder to keep him caged. I want to claim every inch of her body. I want to thrust my cock into her very core, going deeper and deeper inside her treasured jewel as I get my fill.

"Claim her, before I do!" roars Xander.

"You shall die! She is mine." I snatch his hand off my beloved.

A vampire lost in blood lust can take down an entire army in seconds.

Xander raises his hands slowly. "I know she is yours, but if you don't claim her, you will lose her," he cautiously states.

"I might kill her," I speak through clenched teeth. My dark and vicious side doesn't care about that right now. He wants her. We are craving to taste that sweet, flowing blood.

"You won't," says Xander, his eyes trained on her neck. "The emerald won't allow any harm to come to her."

What emerald? My red vision snaps in Claire's direction. How did I miss it? The emerald! That emerald I never thought I would ever see again is hanging delicately from her neck. The fascinating piece of jewelry is glowing brightly, edging me on to stake my claim. I can feel its energy pulling me, wanting me to take her soul, to claim her.

Claire's heart starts pounding, knocking me right back to square one.

"Drink, Nicklaus." Xander's voice is no more than a whisper.

The intoxicating smell of her blood consumes me whole, and without warning, I dive in. My fangs sink into her feather-like skin. Her body is mine to claim next. She moans. She is inviting me

328

in. My firecracker wants this. Her arousal is floating, her essence dripping.

Everything around us ceases to exist. Sweet honey hits my tongue, and my vision bleeds with crimson red. I'm satisfying my monster's craving as we take our fill. The deeper I sink my fangs into Claire's flesh, the louder she moans and the more I lose control. I let go completely, allowing my sinister side to take over. He stakes his claim, taking what belongs to him. He releases our venom inside her, and I can feel her pure-white soul being tinted with pitch black. However, my firecracker is fighting back. My monster is struggling to claim her. He is trying to make her submit, but she refuses to. She is fighting with all her might. Her soul won't accept anything but equality.

I have no idea how long I devour her sweet-tasting essence. I'm locked in a cage inside my own mind, only to be released when her heart rate starts to slow down. Then suddenly, she's yanked out of my arms. My head spins and the red haze slowly disappears. Pain soars through me. I lift my head to see Vlad standing behind Xander, holding Claire. Xander is blocking them from full view, his eyes drenched in red. He is crouched down as if preparing to defend her with his life if he needs to.

Claire's blood drips from my chin to my clothes. I wipe some of it off my face and take a deep breath. I can hear her faint but steady heartbeat. She's okay, thanks to them. I can feel our bond soaring, spreading, and growing. Our souls are being tied as one. I have claimed what is mine to claim, and she has claimed what's hers.

Claire whimpers softly, slowly coming to awareness. I look at her, feeling disgusted with myself. My vision starts to bleed once again. I could have killed her. She's hurting because of me.

"Nicklaus, you have to calm down. She can't handle your emotions," advises Xander.

He's right. Claire can feel me like I can feel her. She is too weak to handle my demonic side.

329

"Sire, we have to leave at once. My men have contacted me. Some of the werewolves are picking up on our trail," informs Vlad, cautiously. "Our men are going to hold them off as long as possible."

"Let them come. I will kill them all!"

"With all due respect, Your Highness," Vlad says, on edge, "the queen is in no position to fight."

"He's right," adds Xander. "We must get her to safety."

My half-asleep beloved is in pain, and it's adding anger to my already raging monster. He can't stand to look at what he's done—what we have done. I have to go before I lose full control.

"I'll distract them. Take Claire to my safe house. I'll meet you there," I hiss, then take off.

# CHAPTER FORTY-SIX
## Claimed

CLAIRE

I feel a soft hand stroking my face, and I know it's him—I can get lost in his touch. I can also hear someone say something. I don't know who. They are talking about me. The pendant is burning my skin, so I try to bring my hands to my neck, but I can't move at all. I can't even feel my limbs.

*I must be dead! Is this death? It can't be. How did I die?*

The bickering around me grows louder, but I cannot decipher a single word. Suddenly, the pendant hanging from my neck squeezes tightly, sucking the little air left out of my lungs and taking the life out of me. My soul is being ripped out of my body, and death is knocking on my door.

In the next moment, I feel him. Nicklaus, my savior, comes to my rescue. His hands are like fire and ice. His touch—so hot yet so cold and inviting—is the air to my lungs, bringing me back to life. My heart is pounding. I want him. I need him. I can feel my soul calling to him, screaming and begging for him to take me as his. Razor-sharp fangs then plunge into my skin, giving my body, mind, and soul exactly what they want—him. His lips suck on my raw skin, and sparks of electricity rush straight to my core. His fangs dig deeper, and I moan my climax at its highest peak. My kitty is throbbing, wishing so badly that his sweet and seductive tongue makes its way down there. His soft lips are devouring me whole. My life force is his to take.

I want more. No, I need more than his touch and his pleasure-filled tongue. I need him all over me, inside me, taming and claiming me for once and all. I belong to him in every single way possible. I'm his light in the darkest room.

I moan louder, and I can feel his sinister side take over completely. He is exactly what I want. The monster's tainted touch is pulling my soul, dragging it. He doesn't disappoint. He provides my body with exactly what it wants. His demonic side is devouring my soul and attempting to force it into submission. He is sucking the light right out of me, like thick black smoke invading a white room. I can't breathe. I feel every inch of his wickedness inside me.

My body goes into a panic as pleasure is slowly replaced with pain. It hurts so bad. My soul is slipping, and the bright and pleasant world is turning dark, unsafe, and unreal. I feel his presence in and out of me, then reality starts to kick in: Nicklaus is staking his claim, attempting to tame, break, and control me. And the temptation is extremely hard to resist. His presence is corrupting my mind, body, and soul little by litlle.

*Nooo!* screams my consciousness. *Don't let him win. He can have my body and live in my heart, but my mind is my own. He must take me as I am.*

My soul is marinating with his own. It's a battle between good and evil, wrong and right, and dark and light. Only one can win. I refuse to allow him to take my humanity. He is the king, but I am meant to be his queen. We shall rule as one. Our souls are one universe. They must become one. They must coexist.

The pain becomes unbearable, but I'll fight against his dark hold no matter what. I'll fight to my very last breath. No pain lasts forever.

The world stops and fire explodes, then ice water freezes hell over. My heart drops as the world is ripped out of my hold.

After what feels like an eternity and a never-ending battle of strength, Nicklaus finally caves in. Our souls entwine, connect, and become one.

* * *

My mind is fully awake and alert, but my body is in a dream-like state. I can hear and feel everything that's happening around me, but I can't see, nor can I speak. It sucks. I do feel extremely weak but at the same time so strong like I've never been. I try to give myself into the darkness, but my mind refuses to take a nap, so I start to count sheep and think of peaceful things.

Arg! I do not have any luck.

Eventually, I allow my mind to drift and think about whatever it wants to. It wanders to him, of course. I think about his hot and cold touch, then his warm and cool lips. I know he is not here, but it feels like he is extremely close to me. Physically, he has been absent for over three hours now, but his presence is right here, right inside my mind. I know that sounds weird. It's just one of those things you have to experience first in order to understand it.

"She doesn't look any different."

I hear King Cyrus say, sounding concerned—shockingly enough.

"Are you sure?" he asks.

"I'm positive," Xander replies. "He has claimed her, but she hasn't fully accepted immortality. Her body is currently going through the transition. Only Claire can decide the outcome."

"Why does the pendant work for her? It's strange she can use its power."

"It is indeed strange. Marcellus is almost here. He has dealt with a lot of witches, so maybe he can explain it."

"Xander, how about you just contact Aurora?" King Cyrus suggests. "She's the one who granted the pendant to your beloved before."

"Aurora will kill me on sight, fool. How about you ask her?"

"Why is Claire's heart rate so low?" someone asks. (Mr. Meany, I think.)

"She's technically still human, so her body doesn't heal quickly. She needs his blood to fully regenerate," Xander responds.

*Wait, blood? Is he talking about me? What the hell does he mean when he said I'm technically still human?*

"Her body will reject anyone else's blood except his."

"Luckily for us, we are in his safe house," another voice speaks.

Someone touches my head and slightly parts my mouth. A warm, cinnamon-tasting liquid then rushes down my throat, hitting my senses hard and strong. My eyes pop open. Everything is bright around me; everything looks bright, almost white.

I squeeze my eyes, only for the white to be replaced with vivid, vibrant colors. I can hear a mouse's squeak like a yell in my ears although I am actually not anywhere near it, which is strange. My sense of hearing must be heightened as well.

Other voices hit me, and there's so much noise—too much for my sensitive ears to take in. I shake my head as the voices turn into loud, beeping white noise. I can also smell damp earth and wildflowers. Their potent fragrance mingles with many others but still stands out like a sore thumb. I take a deep breath and almost choke when too many mixed fragrances invade my lungs. My mind starts to work of its own accord, taking full control. I close my ears off with imaginary earplugs to stop the annoying, squeaking sound.

Seconds later, I learn how to lock and block other noises, which I quickly realize are other voices. I close off my lungs in the next moment, but what's just creepy as hell is I can still breathe in air.

334

Finally, within maybe two seconds later, my bright, vivid, and extremely clear vision locks on them; they are all watching me, as if waiting for me to pounce. Xander's icy gray eyes are drenching me in like we officially meet for the first time. His expression is cold, but I can see straight through his facade. The warmth and love he has for me sparkle in his irises.

King Cyrus seems curious and mildly intrigued but also on edge. The ruthless king seems scared. On the other hand, Mr. Meany looks mean as always, but his eyes hold odd concern for me. Something is extremely strange about his stare.

"Claire," Xander begins, "how do you feel?"

The smell of butterscotch, honey, and thick maple syrup invades my senses, washing all my troubles and questions away.

"Pancakes," I say.

King Cyrus raises an eyebrow and turns to face Xander.

"Pancakes," repeats Xander, slowly.

"Yes, I smell pancakes. I'm hungry." I stand up and follow that glorious smell. My taste buds are jumping as my nose leads the way. I'm particularly drooling.

When I walk past a room, the smell of damp earth and wildflowers stops me in my tracks. That's when I realize I'm in another unfamiliar house that's fit for royalty.

*Go figure!*

I start to debate with myself whether I should follow my nose to the pancakes or see what's behind the door.

*Pancakes or the door? Take your pick, Claire.*

I place my hand on the doorknob.

"Claire, what are you doing?" Xander walks down the stairs.

My eyes meet King Cyrus's tinted-red ones, and everything goes in slow motion. King Cyrus starts to run, but in my eyes he is just walking. I slide out my left foot just in time to clip him up. I open the door to get inside the room, and as soon as I slam it shut, hazel eyes greet me.

335

NICKLAUS

I hate leaving my beloved behind. She looked so broken and bruised, and it was all my fault. I need to keep her safe. These dogs are a threat to her.

I met up with some of my men four hours ago. I'd ordered two separate attacks to keep the wolves busy—one directly on the Northern Pack's territory and the other on the northern town of Vermont. King Cyrus's raid on Quebec went extremely well, so why not attack more lycan-protected towns? Those beasts started it; I'll finish it.

All I can think about is Claire, and it's driving me crazy. I can feel her inside me. I can still taste her honey-laced blood on the tip of my tongue. After I finish these dogs, I can make my way back to her. This issue is now a full-fledged war. I'm positive the council is now aware of the threat and would want it to be eliminated.

I'm currently at one of the base camps that Cyrus set up, but Claire's fragile body still refuses to leave my mind.

"Your Highness," calls Commander Ravana, Cyrus's best soldier. She's stepping in for Commander Vlad. "Both of the attacks were a success. It should take the wolves at least one moon to rebuild and issue an attack of their own."

I nod in approval.

"King Marcellus and Count Cloven are en route. They should meet us back at your safe house."

As expected, the council is aware. It's the only reason why Count Cloven will be present.

I wave my hand in dismissal. That's all I needed to hear. Finally, I can make my way back to Claire. I want to spend some alone time with her while she's transitioning. I have the perfect place.

I get out of the tent, more than eager to get straight to Claire.

"Also, we have captured the were-b*tch that attacked King Xander, along with two other humans," she adds, stopping me right in my tracks.

"Bring them to me!" I command.

The moment my men walk in, my chest is ablaze. The wolf b*tch's scent awakes my monster completely. She and some other humans who escaped during the raid on Cyrus's penthouse are being shoved into the tent. Crimson red completely bleeds in my vision. I can feel Claire's presence inside my mind. My little firecracker has already learned how to communicate with me, and it's really no surprise. She has communicated with me before in her dream state. She knows now how to instantly access our bond.

The wolf b*tch's eyes glow yellow the moment I come into view. She releases a low growl. Her wolf is present.

Good! I want her wolf to fight for her life.

"Welcome back, Mecca," is my greeting, and my fangs descend.

# CHAPTER FORTY-SEVEN
## The Wilde Wolf

CLAIRE

My green eyes land on someone's hazel eyes.

Judging by her now highlighted yellow or more like bright-gold eyes, it's a she-wolf—the source of the damp earth and wildflower scent that is now way more potent inside the room.

King Cyrus is slamming his body into the door.

*Why is he acting like that? Who is she?*

"Who are you?" she asks me the question I want to ask her. "You smell like their king."

I don't know if that's a compliment or an insult, but seeing the frown on her face, I'm guessing it's the latter.

I raise my eyebrow in response. "You smell like a flower tossed in the dirt, but hey, I'm not judging."

She smiles. "I have never met a sarcastic human before, but then again, I haven't met many humans."

"I get that a lot."

King Cyrus finally bursts into the room, knocking the hinges off the door in the process—typical vampire. Xander and Mr. Meany walk right in beside him. The cute little she-wolf's eyes are fixed on King Cyrus.

*I know that look. That's the same look that Jadis gives King Cornelius. Interesting.*

338

"It's not safe for you in here, Claire," Xander tells me. "You shouldn't be roaming where the wild things are."

"What the f*ck is that supposed to mean?" snarls King Cyrus, making the situation even more interesting.

"You know exactly what the f*ck I mean. Claire is too valuable to be placed in a room with the untamed and untrained."

"F*ck you!" King Cyrus spits, his eyes now red. "You would know all about the untamed and untrained, wouldn't you? All hail the cold-hearted king that fell in love with the lycan's human wh*re th—"

Xander smashes King Cyrus into the wall with a loud bang.

This is déjà vu. I'm starting to realize that none of the kings can be together in one place for more than five minutes without trying to kill one another.

King Cyrus wraps his hand around Xander's neck and flips him into the wall, and they start to wrestle—fangs bared and muscles flexing.

Honestly, watching them grapple like two human boys is kind of entertaining, but I can tell you it is way less frightening than the fight between Xander and Nicklaus earlier today. Now that I'm thinking about it, what the hell exactly happened by the way? I remember them fighting, then it went blank. I remember the feeling of Nicklaus feeding off me before it went blank again. I think I'd still remember the feeling of Nicklaus taking my blood even if I was in a coma. It's that good.

Noise from the left side of me forces me to focus my attention back on the two kings behaving like peasants. Mr. Meany places a protective hand on my shoulder while staring at the little she-wolf. I don't understand why they are acting like this. First of all, I'm a slave, nothing more and nothing less. Well, I'm Nicklaus's slave beloved, but I highly doubt Mr. Meany knows about that.

The she-wolf looks as if she is damn near pissing her pants instead of attacking me. The only thing wild about her is her beauty. She is gorgeous and tall, maybe around 5'10 or 5'11. I believe it is the average height of most she-wolves. They all look like supermodels, or how I imagine a supermodel should look like. If they were humans, they would have no problem being selected as chosens, especially her. She has waist-length dark-brown hair and a face of a porcelain doll. Her hazel eyes are brilliant and familiar. She looks wild and exotic but at the same time soft and delicate.

Most of the other wolves would be jumping for joy or howling upon seeing two vampires trying to kill each other. Their eyes would be filled with amusement. For a short period of time that I have been around werewolves, even I figured out they live for action and blood, specifically vampire blood. They are all lunatics, but not this she-wolf. She appears she'd rather run and hide than engage in a fight, not acting like the typical crazy ole she-wolves I have met. She does look oddly familiar, but I'm pretty sure she wasn't there at the pack house. You won't forget a face like hers; that's for sure. It brings me back to my original question, Who is she? I feel like I'm missing something big.

Her brilliant hazel eyes flash golden seconds after Xander's knees hit King Cyrus in his gut.

Now, this is really, really interesting.

She takes a step forward, and I'm certain she is going to pounce on Xander. But she doesn't. This she-wolf is just full of surprises. She takes another step—dangerously close to the fighting vampires—then throws herself at their feet unexpectedly, bowing to show submission.

My jaw hits the floor. No creature with wolf blood would ever show so much respect to vampires. No one.

Her action doesn't go unnoticed at all. Xander and King Cyrus stop fighting at once. Xander's face resembles my own—stunned—while Mr. Meany's usual unemotional mask drops for only a second. King Cyrus looks ten times more pissed and dangerous than he was ten seconds ago, his eyes on her as he moves toward her with the elegance of a predator.

"You," he growls, bringing her to her feet, "don't bow for anyone!"

She challenges his statement with one word: "Why?"

King Cyrus's eyes flash bright red, brighter than I can ever imagine, and before I know it, he disappears—just like that.

Now, that was quite a show.

The she-wolf's shoulders slump in defeat, and her eyes start to water. Xander and Mr. Meany look extremely uncomfortable.

Oh, I think I'm starting to see what's going on.

"Can we have some time alone?" I ask.

Xander looks at me. His eyes are back to their usual icy gray shade. "That's absolutely out of the question," he says. His words are cold and full of venom, and I don't like this side of him one bit. "You will not be left alone with the likes of her."

The she-wolf flinches and drops her head as though it could make her invisible.

"And I will not be told by the likes of you who I can or cannot be around with!" I spit.

He is dead wrong. What has gotten into him?

Xander makes his way in front of me, his eyes blazing. I stand my ground and burn him with my stare. He stands proud as he towers over me with his muscular frame. Mr. Meany's body goes stiff beside me, indicating that he will protect me against anyone. However, there is no need. I'm a big girl, and I damn sure can handle myself.

Xander tilts his chin. He's also a king in his own right, but even with me already knowing this, I still don't give two sh*ts. Suddenly his lips curve into a smirk. "Checkmate!" he says, then he leaves the room.

I should have known.

I look at Mr. Meany, and he nods and leaves as well.

Relief floods the she-wolf's face as she slumps down onto the floor.

"Xander is not really that bad," I begin, regaining her attention.

She looks at me curiously, her hazel eyes studying me carefully. "I don't think any of them are."

Again, this girl surprises me. Xander's insults were extremely harsh, but they only seemed to offend me more than they offend her.

"I'm a wolf. They are vampires. Our kinds have always been on edge around each other, so I understand why he reacted that way with me. What I don't get is why they are so overprotective of you, or why they would even take orders from you. You're just a human." She pauses. "No offense."

"None taken." I shrug. "They know I have ball-kicking superpowers, and that I will kick their asses," I tell her, in an attempt to make her laugh.

It works. She giggles slightly. Her soft nature reminds me of Jadis. She will love her. She will have a fun-filled day braiding her hair and playing dress-up with this girl, or more like dressing this girl up.

"So I guess that would explain why they are afraid of you. No male human, wolf, or vampire wants to get their balls kicked."

"Yup, ball kicking at its finest." I take a seat beside her.

She seems surprised but doesn't react. Her wildflower scent is more potent now. It's refreshing and peaceful. She looks out of the window, clearly lost in thought.

My mind wanders to Nicklaus. I miss him. I can feel his presence lingering inside my mind. I don't want to seem cliché, but his arrival is highly anticipated.

"Embry," the she-wolf speaks, knocking away my train of thought. She turns and holds out her hand for me to take. "I'm Embry Wilde."

"My name is Claire." I shake her hand briefly, and she gives me a faint smile.

*Yes, her name suits her. Embry Wilde. Wait, what? Embry Wilde is the she-wolf Mecca told me about! She's the one they've all been searching for and the reason why the werewolves officially declared war against King Cyrus. King Cyrus . . . OMG! Now, it all adds up.*

"You're his beloved, aren't you?"

Her hazel eyes bulge. They look so familiar. They are the exact same shade as her sister's. Now that I'm looking at her, I don't understand how I was not able to quickly put everything together. They look just alike, like twins.

"Yes, he is my mate," she whispers. Her shock turns into defeat.

I frown. I don't get it. Wolves are supposed to kiss the ground their mates walk on. Even her uncle was willing to wait until death to return to Mecca, but this girl doesn't seem too happy about finding King Cyrus. Maybe that's it. It's King Cyrus, the ruthless king. However, she is a Wilde. They are just as ruthless, trust me. Her father is a true beast. I have seen him in a battle.

"But I'm a Wilde. My people will never allow it. Plus, he won't even acknowledge it," she says, talking more to herself than me.

Xander walks back into the room. I give him the stink eye, then the smell of butter and maple hits me fast.

*Pan-f\*cking-cakes!*

My mouth waters, and my stomach growls on cue. The sound of the plate as Xander places it in front of me makes me jump. With all this new information, I must have worked up quite the appetite. Okay, that's a lie, and maybe I'm being a little overdramatic because with or without new information, I'm always hungry for pancakes.

Embry's stomach growls as well.

*Great! She likes pancakes too. Hopefully, this will make her a little better.*

All of a sudden, I start to feel light-headed, and it doesn't go unnoticed.

343

"Claire, what's wrong?" Xander turns to face Embry. "What did you do?" he snaps.

"Don't talk to her like that," I sneer, looking directly into his eyes.

Mr. Meany and King Cyrus rush inside the room the moment my body catches on fire. My chest is ablaze, my blood boiling and the entire room bleeding crimson. Unexpected anger, hatred, and rage flood through my veins like my own blood. My eyes flutter shut. I try to open them, but I can't. It's just like how it was before. My mind is fully awake and alert, but my body is in a dream-like state. I can hear and feel everything happening around me, but I can't see or speak.

"Something is wrong," Mr. Meany says.

"It's the claim!" King Cyrus gasps. "She's feeling his emotions."

I feel him move beside me, most likely closer to Embry.

"But how?" asks Mr. Meany. "It's too soon."

"She communicated with him before in a dream-like state," Xander responds.

I have absolutely no idea what they are talking about, and the pounding in my head only makes it difficult for me to even try and understand what they are saying. The pounding grows harder, my head spinning. The taste of displeasure and disgust is on the tip of my tongue, a dreadful feeling smacking me in the gut. I try to shake it, but no matter how hard I try, I just can't.

Mr. Meany is right; something is wrong—really, really wrong.

"Claire," Xander calls. He places his hand on my shoulder. "I know you can hear me. I promise it will be okay, but I need you to follow my directions." His voice is gentle, and his touch calms my nerves a little. Open your mind completely and search for the person that makes you feel the safest."

*Nicklaus. I'm safest with him.*

# CHAPTER FORTY-EIGHT
## The Battle of Power

NICKLAUS

"Also, we have captured the were-b*tch that attacked King Xander, along with two other humans," she adds, stopping me right in my tracks.

"Bring them in," I command.

The moment my men walk in, my chest is ablaze. The wolf b*tch's scent awakes my monster completely. She and some other humans who escaped during the raid on Cyrus's penthouse are being shoved into the tent.

Crimson red bleeds in my vision completely. I can feel Claire's presence inside my mind. My little firecracker has already learned how to communicate with me. It's really no surprise. She has communicated with me before in her dream state. She knows how to access her bond instantly.

The wolf b*tch's eyes glow yellow the moment I come into view. She releases a low growl. Her wolf is present.

Good! I want her wolf to fight for her life.

"Welcome back, Mecca," I greet her, and my fangs descend.

\*　　\*　　\*

Claire's presence is no longer inside my mind. I can still feel her soul attached, but it's more like a ghost of her presence. She's not aware of my actions at the moment, and I don't want her to know this side of me.

I close my mind off completely, making sure she can't break through. Commander Ravana throws the dog directly in front of me, then another comrade of mine holds the wolf b*tch in place on a silver leash.

I'm no fool. I know silver doesn't have any effect on her. She was only captured because she wanted to. She most likely was under the impression that Claire was with me.

My crimson-red vision zooms in on her two toys— Xander's chosen b*tch and the slave boy that was attracted to my beloved, the slave that got away. How great? He can also meet his end once and for all. His face is bloody and his body has numerous fang marks up and down his skin. The stupid human boy really attempted to fight against my monster, and for what? All in hope of finding my beloved? He should have run far away from here. Now, he will die as a consequence of his stupidity.

I lock my eyes on Xander's chosen b*tch. I'm surprised this selfish b*tch would risk her life for the dogs's cause. She lowers her eyes in submission. She is perfectly aware that I'll end her before her frantic heart skips another beat. She'll be drenched in scarlet from her red hair all the way down to her black combat boots—a bloody mess.

I control the urge to laugh in her face. How dare she? She should know better than to bite the hand that feeds her.

I give Commander Ravana the signal to handle her. I may be a monster, but being a woman beater is not one of my traits, unless you are a wolf b*tch. However, they are not human; they are animals. That's a major difference.

They all attempt to break free as the commander draws closer. Ravana's natural hazel eyes flicker violet as she sends her first strike at the b*tch's face, easily leaving a purple bruise. The chosen wh*re doesn't make a sound, adding to my surprise.

Oh, someone is trying to be brave.

I nod and Ravana strikes her again. This time the b*tch spits out blood but still holds back her urge to scream.

Mecca releases a growl.

I smile in her direction. "Don't worry, doggy. You shall have your time to play."

Her already yellow eyes glow brighter.

"Someone is anxious," I taunt.

She spits at my feet. The dog has always been rebellious, stupid, and full of defiance.

"Leave her alone, leech," the foolish slave boy snarls.

I'm in front of him faster than he can blink. I plunge my fangs into his neck, not caring about damaging any flesh. This causes the wolf b*tch to scream and shift into her wolf form. I release the nearly drained boy and give her my undivided attention. She viciously claws at the chain to break loose. Leave it to Mecca to find a way to endure pain and lessen it. That's exactly why it was so fun finding many ways to torture her—breaking her bones, using different chemicals repelling to her, and plunging different amounts of diluted silver into her veins.

I have to thank Cyrus for that one. He has always been great at coming up with ideas that don't pop into my head automatically. He once pointed out that the were-b*tch depends on her sense of smell more than her other senses. I don't know why I didn't realize that before. It is the most-developed sense of a dog. They have great olfactory memory.

With that thought in mind, I walk over to the table in the corner. I've directed my men to utilize acanthite with ammonia to help hinder the other dogs's sense of smell. This trick is proven to be of great use.

Their Luna has been a really good guinea pig. Her growls only become louder when I dip the rag inside the container of mixed chemicals. She is perfectly aware of the effect and harm it shall cause her. Taking away their sense of smell is like losing their sight. They can't see without it.

Commander Ravana kicks the chosen wh*re on the side of her head, knocking her out. The smell of her blood makes my nostrils flare. I love the smell of my enemy's blood. My monster is clawing to have his way with her next. If it weren't for Claire, I would allow my men to handle her, but after experiencing the trauma with someone I love firsthand, I will never tolerate that type of torture again. I'm disgusted that I allowed myself to pass that rule. No one should experience this.

Fire spurts through my body as I think about it. No worries, I'll take my frustration out on the wolf b*tch. My mouth starts to water, and my monster claws harder.

*Come on, wolf b*tch, break free.*

She doesn't disappoint. She breaks free and plunges her claws into one of my men, ripping his head off in the process before pouncing in the air. Commander Ravana intercepts her, wrapping her arms around her tightly and slowly crushing her bones. My personal guards run into the room, ready to end her. I hold up my hand, refusing to allow any interruptions. There is no need to add more to this party.

I viciously sink my fangs into her throat, and the sound of her growls fills my ear. I spit out her foul-tasting blood. I never enjoyed feeding on her. It always tasted more bitter than most dogs's blood.

She manages to scrape her claws across the face of Commander Ravana, who quickly hunches over in pain and drops the beast. The dog b*tch lands onto her feet and bounces back into the air before slamming her body into mine. My guards growl, but they won't dare to intervene after a direct order from me not to.

I wrap my arms around the wh*re's neck, completely cutting off her air supply. She squirms around, attempting to lunge her claws into my side but is unsuccesful. I plunge my fangs into

348

her throat and sink my claws into her side in retaliation. She whines and starts to panic as the fire burning inside me only grows fiercer and is more disastrous.

It pleases my inner monster. I allow him to have some fun biting down deeper into her throat. The silvery, salty taste of her blood fills my mouth while she howls and howls until she starts catching her breath. She begins to twitch, and her body temperature drops drastically as she shifts back into her human form. She's not dying, but she is close to losing consciousness. A trueborn vampire can end a werewolf with their bite, but the Luna and Alpha must be killed with a silver bullet to the heart for a permanent kill. I won't let her off this easy. She will suffer. My playtime has just begun.

I throw her limp body onto the floor. Commander Ravana stands to her feet and latches onto the chosen wh*re. She buries her fangs into her flesh, causing screams to once again fill my ears. My vision bleeds brighter as her heartbeat slows down. This has been a fruitful day.

The wolf b*tch is barely awake. I snatch her by the hair and throw the rag into her mouth. She gags and vomits from the chemicals, and her body starts to hyperventilate. Her heart beats rapidly as she releases ear-splitting screams while clawing at her own skin like the beast she is.

Yes, this has indeed been a prosperous day. The chemicals mixed together will poison the dogs. It's extremely effective in inflicting pain that even her mate can feel that. We hadn't tested this theory, but thanks to our success today. We have plenty of lab rats to test it on.

"Ravana," I call out, right before the chosen wh*re's heart takes its last beat.

She's not dead yet. However, that will change soon. All their deaths will be by my hands. My monster wouldn't have it any other way.

Ravana drops the girl at once. "Yes, sire."

"Hand me the gun," I order.

She eagerly follows my command. What an honor to be the one to hold the gun that will rid this b*tch of life! The dog is still clawing at her skin—deranged—while the slave boy's heart rate picks back up, indicating he is coming around to awareness.

Perfect. I want him to witness the grand finale.

All of a sudden, my head starts pounding. I can now sense it's Claire trying to break through. It's her form of communication with me. I don't know why I was unable to put it all together the first time around, when she is the only person in this universe who can cause me mental pain.

She will never approve of what's about to go down, so I decline her request to enter my mind. My head pounds more heavily, which means she is trying harder. We play this game with each other back and forth. She refuses to back down. I'm perfectly aware of how much pain she experiences every time I shut my mind off to her, so I eventually let her in.

I close my eyes, and Claire's captivating face comes into view. Every single time I lay eyes on her, it's like seeing her for the first time again. Her beauty is enchanting, bewitching, and alluring.

*"You need to stop now, Nicklaus,"* she demands, getting straight to the point.

Her words catch me off guard. She shouldn't pinpoint my action this soon.

The emerald of the pendant hanging from her neck glows brighter. My skin starts to tingle while Claire's heart beats frantically. My neck begins to itch the very moment she places her hand on the precious stone. She's going to command me; I can feel it. I wonder if the pendant has anything to do with her accessing her powers that shouldn't be accessed until we are completely blended.

*"Firecracker,"* I call, the tone of my voice compelling.

She scrunches up her nose, her electrifying green eyes fixed on me.

F*ck, she has caught me.

350

*"Don't try to use that vampire voodoo bullsh\*t on me,"* she snaps.

I'm completely lost for words. This girl has always surprised me in a way not even my own mother can. This woman has performed every impossible task placed upon her. She is the epitome of power.

My neck continues to itch. I notice the emerald glowing brighter along with Claire's eyes . How she manages to wield the power of the precious stone is truly extraordinary.

*"Earth to Nicklaus."*

Her honey tone brings me back to reality. Usually, I do not easily get distracted unless she is involved.

*"You can't kill Mecca. She is my best friend, and boyfriends don't kill their girlfriend's best friend."*

My monster doesn't like her verbiage concerning the wolf b\*tch , but he is thriving on the title she has used to label our relationship.

*"Boyfriend,"* I reply. I can imagine her face catching fire. *"I'm far more than your boyfriend, firecracker,"* I tell her, perfectly knowing the effect I'm causing to her body. *"I'm the gasoline that's poured onto that burning inner flame that you hold inside your soul,"* I whisper, seductively and extremely low.

Her arousal floats freely once again, as if we were in the same room. I inhale the mouthwatering scent I can't wait to taste. Tonight is the night I'll finally claim her body once and for all.

*"If you really feel that way,"* she says, *"you will grant me this one favor. Please, spare Mecca's life."*

My monster growls. He doesn't like her questioning our loyalty or even considering we feel anything but love for her.

I can see her fight the urge to roll her eyes. Dream-like state or not, Claire shall always be Claire.

*"Don't do that,"* I warn her.

*"Don't talk to me like I'm anything but you're equal,"* she retorts.

I fight the urge to smile at her words. As I just stated, Claire shall always be Claire, my firecracker. I wouldn't accept or expect anything else.

*"I'm still your king, so my words are final."*

I'm sure my response irks her to no end. I bet her chest is now blazing with unconcealed rage.

I allow myself to feel her emotions. As expected, intense anger travels down my spine.

*"I could care less if you were my creator,"* she spits. *"I am your queen. A king is nothing without his most-valuable player. Don't test my patience, Nicklaus,"* she speaks, like the true queen that she is. *"I'm asking you as your partner, ally, and most-trusted adviser to spare my friend."*

Pride runs through me. My true beloved has always shown courage. She has always stood out like a needle in a haystack amongst her species—a really shiny and pretty needle. She has never communicated like the ruler she was born to be, but now she understands how to move on the chessboard without being stopped. It's fascinating.

*"I'll make you a deal. Three of your friends's lives are in my hands. I'll give you the option to save one."*

*"I will not do such a thing,"* she speaks through clenched teeth.

I can feel her slipping. Her time is coming to an end. The physical pain her body currently enduring is taking its toll on her. Xander had better give her my blood at once.

I take a moment to think. I want to rid the wolf b*tch with everything in me, but I don't want to cause my beloved any more pain. She has gone through enough.

*"Your wish is my command, my queen. You have my word. No further harm shall come to any of your friends."*

# CHAPTER FORTY-NINE
## His Side

CLAIRE

My mind goes completely blank. I lost the connection. My human body could no longer endure the pain. Disappointment consumes me whole.

Xander told me he would give me Nicklaus's blood the moment my body broke down. His directions were crystal clear. I had to drink every drop of it. That's exactly why I gulp down the substance the moment I feel the cup being placed onto my lips. King Nicklaus's blood is actually quite tasty, but I refuse to admit that out loud. It's just too creepy.

My eyes flash open when I swallow the last drop. I can feel his blood regenerating every inch of my body, and I'm completely refreshed.

It's just Xander and I. He most likely demanded the others to leave so that he can concentrate on aiding me through the connection. I lost track of what was going on around me when I officially entered Nicklaus's mind. He tried his best to keep me out, but I refused to give up. I would break through the threshold even if doing it could cost me my life.

Xander warned me to back down, uttering things like I had a death wish and how repulsive I was acting. Oh well, I used his own words against him (nobody likes a quitter) right before

Nicklaus granted me access to his mind. The last thing I remember hearing from Xander was a growl when our minds departed from each other. His appearance says he is in a better mood, but his tone tells another story.

"Are you okay?" he asks.

"Just peachy."

"Good, because you were seconds away from losing your life!" he roars, his eyes crimson red.

I shrug, adding fuel to an already filled tank.

Xander smashes the chair beside me, and tiny pieces of wood fly around the room. "Do you have any idea what would have happened if you had died? How reckless could one be?"

I stand to my feet. "Nicklaus left me no choice. He was going to kill Mecca. What was I supposed to do?" Surely you didn't expect me to just let her die."

"That's exactly what you should have done." He makes his way back over to me in a flash.

"If I had known she was the reason your mind attempting to reach out to him, I would have never provided you with instructions to reach him."

"Welp, you did." I cross my arms.

"I instructed you to pull back the moment you would feel even the slightest bit of pain, but you didn't listen, now did you?" he asks a pointless question.

Duh, it's obvious I didn't or I would have never broken through.

Xander moves back over toward the couch and smashes a lamp into the window. He is extremely pissed, but I know he will never hurt me.

Mr. Meany rushes into the room the exact moment the glass shatters. The air whooshing around me makes me light-headed. Abruptly, the room stops spinning, and my eyes zero in on the place where I was previously standing. Tiny pieces of glass are now scattered in that exact spot.

"You're nothing but a weak-minded human, and you can't follow simple instructions."

The air is knocked out of my lungs, the world shifting around me. Tremendous pain pierces straight through my heart as soon as he finishes his sentence. He then zooms out of the room before I can respond. My breath catches in my throat, my vision blurring. Typically no one's harsh words about me being human can hurt me, but Xander's words cut me deeper than glass could ever do.

I stumble back, seconds away from hitting the floor.

Mr. Meany catches me, preventing the fall. "He didn't mean that, Claire," he says.

For the first time in my life, I cannot form a word; I cannot speak at all. Without thinking, I run out of the room inhumanly fast. I can hear Mr. Meany behind me, but I manage to lose him within a second.

\*     \*     \*

The rose-pink and lavender lights of dawn slowly rise on the horizon. The fascinating shades blend together perfectly in the early morning sky, leaving paint stain along the middle of the water. How beautiful the clouds are as they are reflected in the lake! I don't know exactly where we are on the continent of North America, but the view here is extraordinary.

I breathe in my first breath of morning air—it's refreshing. The chilling wind from the mountain whisks around me. Usually, I would be freezing to death, but for whatever unnatural reason, the cold no longer affects me. In fact, nothing that should affect a human seems to have an effect on me at the moment. I appear to be inhumanly fast and freakishly strong. I have no idea if it has something to do with whatever has happened between me and Nicklaus or with this goddamn pendant that periodically burns the flesh of my neck. I guess that's another thing my human mind can't

355

comprehend. It really doesn't matter to me at this point because I'm emotionally drained.

I've been sitting by the lake for two hours or so. Nicklaus invaded my mind the moment he was alerted about me taking off. At first, I didn't want to grant him access and then I remembered the physical pain I endured when he didn't allow me in. When his mind connected with my own, I was sure he would demand that I return. To my surprise, he didn't. He understood I needed a moment alone, but of course with the condition that I stay close to the house. He refused to leave me until I agreed. Eventually, I gave in and promised I wouldn't drift away too far. He assured me he would come to me as soon as possible and that my new pets are coming with him. It took everything out of me not to argue with him about calling my friends pets. I don't even know who's with him besides Mecca. I guess I'll find out soon enough.

The fresh smell of burning cedarwood and expensive cologne invades my senses for the seventh time. I'm aware that Xander has been present with me for quite a while now, watching from the shadows right behind the resting pine bush on my left side. He hasn't spoken, but he's here. He smells extremely similar to his brother, although his hint of cypress aroma gives him his own distinctive scent. He smells spicy and masculine. I don't understand how my sense of smell has enhanced so vividly. I guess that's another thing my human mind can't possibly grasp—another thing to add to the list of the weak traits of humans.

"Brave one," Xander finally speaks.

I make a face upon hearing the nickname. He has quite the nerve.

"I know you're upset with me, but please allow me the chance to explain." He comes directly from behind the sleeping pine bush as expected.

I almost laugh out loud. It's so interesting how right on my sense of smell actually is. Go figure.

"Here," says Xander, as he drapes the light-brown mink coat Mecca gave me the other night over me. I'm surprised it's not stained with blood. "I wanted to give you this a while ago, but I thought you needed some space. It's a nice coat by the way."

I nod. I wonder if he was going to say the same thing if he knew who gave it to me.

"Even though it smells like dogs," he suddenly jokes.

*So he is aware. Hmm.*

"Thank you," I tell him, putting the coat on.

He lowers himself right beside me and then stares at the lake quietly. The mood is peaceful. He appears calm, a lot better than he was a few hours ago. We sit in complete silence for a while, enjoying the cool and calm atmosphere.

Xander sighs. "A long time ago, I met a human named Isabella," he begins, seeming to be lost in his own thought. "Bella for short. I've always been attracted to blond, slender, light-eyed, and well-behaved women. There's nothing wrong with women without those physical characteristics. However, that was just my preference," he goes on. "Bella had chestnut-brown hair, coffee-colored eyes, and was curvy in all the right places. She was anything but well-behaved and untamed. Astonishingly enough, she took my breath away at first glance. There was something wild and gentle about her, and it captivated my soul."

His words spark something inside me, and the mural filled with stories flashes inside my head. I remember thinking of the exact same thing when I saw the woman with chestnut hair and coffee-colored eyes. She was the most-beautiful woman I've ever laid eyes on. She was also the woman who started the Awakening. She was the one Mecca told me about—the human that crushed a vampire's heart, the one . . . Oh my God! Everything starts to add up.

"It was you!" I gasp. "You're the vampire that started it all."

He doesn't respond. He doesn't have to. His face tells it all.

357

"Bella was my beloved." Xander wipes away the tears forming underneath his long eyelashes, breaking my heart instantly.

Xander has never seemed to be so vulnerable, but now his fascinating silver-gray eyes are filled with an intense amount of pain. His flawless, clear, pale but somehow well-tanned skin looks wrinkled. He looks fragile and so . . . so human. Never in a thousand years would I've ever expected to see this side of him.

"She tainted my dark soul pure . . . touched it and made my silent heart skip frantic beats. Bella was pure. She plagued my mind completely, bringing forth my humanity, and she wielded the power to warm my cold heart." He places his glassy stare back onto the lake. "She saved me," he says, rendering me speechless.

I don't understand. If all that is true, then why does the picture paint a different story? Why does everyone else have a different view? Why did he enslave her entire species?

"I rejected her. I was afraid to love again. I was a coward," he reveals, his own disgust at himself in his voice.

Not knowing what to say, I remain silent and allow him the chance to let it all out. He needs to.

"Back then, a vampire could bond with their beloved from other species, but it was often frowned upon," he explains. "I'd been a disappointment to my mother. She had always hated my guts, so I tried my best to please her."

I remember Xander's interaction with his mother. She didn't seem to fancy him that much.

"She was blessed with a second-chance mate," he continues with a deep sigh.

It reminds me of what I read about second-chance mates in the book he gave me.

He stands up and wipes away his tears with the sleeve of his dress shirt. "Your friend Mecca was her best friend. We had all been great friends until she met him."

My heart starts beating frantically. I take a moment to collect my thoughts and then everything that has happened so far replays like a movie. I can't believe I missed all the clues: Mecca's hatred for Xander, and vice versa. The picture has been painted crystal clear, right before my very eyes. How could I be so naive? How did I miss what has been right in front of me? Mecca? Xander? I'm so foolish.

"King Luke of the lycans was her second-chance mate."

His words literally knock the wind out of my body. Abruptly, the pendant around my neck tightens, completely cutting off my air supply. My skin tingles, the hair at the back of my neck standing. Xander instantly places a gentle but firm hand onto the pendant. It burns through his flesh like acid, but he refuses to let go. For the first time, I feel a new presence. The pendant hosts extremely wild and powerful presence. I close my eyes, only to be met with coffee-colored eyes that then disappear so fast. She is gone. My eyes snap open, and Xander comes back into view, looking like he's seen a ghost.

"Are you okay?" I take his burnt hand into my own.

He shivers from my touch and closes his eyes. I give him a moment to process what has happened. F*ck, even I need that moment too.

Seconds later, Xander opens his eyes and takes another deep breath.

"This was her pendant, wasn't it?" I ask the obvious.

He nods.

That's why the lycan king reacted so harshly at the bonfire. Yes, everything makes perfect sense, but there are still some blind spots in this story.

I fight the urge to ask more questions although I really want to know the rest of the story. Xander needs time to recover from whatever the hell just happened. I'm not going to force anything else out of him. It's not my place.

"My brother is . . . Well, my brother is more like me than you think. He lives by a certain code. He doesn't follow his heart and is more scared to love than you can ever imagine. He places

359

our people before anything. However, he cares about his father's judgment even if it stands in the way of his happiness. And I cannot let that happen, not when you are involved.

"I won't allow history to repeat itself. I shall right my wrongs. That's exactly why I snapped at you last night. I was scared that he would lose you. I was scared to lose you, Claire."

"I understand. I understand everything." I wrap myself around him, openly embracing him completely.

He may have done some terrible things in the past, but we all make mistakes. Xander is the most-genuine vampire I've ever encountered. He has done nothing but protect and guide me in this journey. I refuse to turn my back on him despite his past. I'll never hold a petty argument against him. He is my friend, protector, one of my greatest allies, and my most-trusted adviser. He's my brother even without the bond of blood, and I love him.

# CHAPTER FIFTY
## Time to Taste

NICKLAUS

I am back at my safe house a little after sunrise. I take a moment to view the grand lodge surrounded by nature. It's a majestic estate sitting on ten heavy, snow-covered wooded acres in the middle of a place that was once named Revelstoke, BC.

This safe house is just a short walk to Lake Revelstoke and is hidden in the center of the mountains. The ten-bedroom (approximately 26,700 square feet) timber-framed stone home was my gift to Xander and his late beloved. This was their escape from the cruel and judgmental outside world. This place sparked a little hope amidst their doomed, predestined, star-crossed love. It was truly tragic. I wonder if one day Xander shares his story with Claire. It would help her understand a lot of situations she has experienced.

I heave a deep sigh. It's not my place.

The moment I step into my home, relief floods through me. It has taken me much longer than expected to get back to my firecracker. I had to make a few stops to ensure the safety of her new pets. It would be dangerous to bring them back to the estate or leave them in an unguarded place, so I decided to leave them in a cabin a few miles back. Commander Ravana agreed to stay behind with a few of my men to protect and keep a watchful eye on them.

Commander Ravana's witch heritage has proven to be handy when it comes to keeping the dog at bay.

I plan to take Claire there for a visit prior to our return to my kingdom. It's extremely important that we spend some quality time together before I jump back into my role as king of all vampire kings.

Count Cloven and Marcellus have already arrived. I can smell them the very moment I walk through the door.

"Your Highness," greets Commander Vlad, bowing to show his respect.

"You may rise," I say curtly.

I'm not in the mood to play king. I just want to get to Claire. Her honey-laced scent lingers in the air. She must have passed through not too long ago. I thought I would have to carry her back into this estate. She's extremely stubborn. She would never have stepped another foot inside here without speaking to Xander, who must have grown the balls to apologize to her after our last communication.

"The King of Europe and Count Cloven have arrived. They've requested to meet with you at once," announces Commander Vlad.

My body freezes beside him. Count Cloven wanting to get straight to the point is expected, but Marcellus doesn't take anything seriously. Usually, he would want to settle in and plunge his fangs into one of my servants's necks before even the meeting starts.

Their scents still hang strong in the air, which means they just arrived around dawn. I'm also not in the mood to play politics or deal with anything other than my beloved. I just want to lie down with Claire. She's all I want.

"They are in your study along with King Cyrus and King Xander, awaiting your arrival," Commander Vlad informs.

"The servants have prepared breakfast, and Claire has offered some of her blood after overhearing some of the humans whispering about your whereabouts."

I smile at that. She has taken on her new role almost immediately. God, I seriously need to get a grip. Every one of my thoughts leads me back to her. I'm obsessed.

"I'll be in shortly." I head up the stairs to locate that beloved of mine.

"They have been quite frank about how urgent it is to meet with you," he states.

"I said I'll be in shortly." I end the conversation once and for all. I don't care if the world is going to sh*t. Right now, I need Claire—the only one that matters.

I make my way to my beloved. Her scent is stronger in the west wing of the house, my private wing. It's the area I used to utilize perhaps over a century ago. When you have lived as long as I have, it's easy to lose track of time.

My monster viciously claws to be freed the moment I step into my room.

Admire her forever, love dearly, and treasure her for eternity—these are exactly how I feel each and every time my eyes land on her delicate frame.

I greedily draw in a deep, sharp, and hungry breath, basking in the glory of that delicious scent of hers. She is lying on the bed with nothing but one of my dress shirts. It exposes those perfectly toned and sun-kissed legs—no undergarments, barely covered, freshly showered, and groomed to perfection. The morning sun shines brightly, highlighting her flawless, milky, soft skin. She's glowing underneath the light.

I'm still in love with how peaceful she looks during her slumber. My vision is now tinted a deep sea-blue shade, possibly almost black, due to the strong emotion of lust now dancing inside me. I battle against my monster for control, burying and locking the savage demon away deep down inside me. I refuse to allow him to have his way with our beloved. If he has his way with her, I'm almost certain her body would be sore from lovemaking for the rest of eternity. We both want to claim her mind, soul, and body. However, I know we have to be gentle and patient with her.

I was almost certain that last night was the night, but on my journey back here, I thought about everything she has experienced as a slave. Her body has been degraded, and I don't want to be the cause of such horrid memories to resurface.

When we shared a kiss, I saw firsthand how traumatized Claire truly is, and yet on the outside looking in, one would see nothing but a strong-minded human girl. She is brave and extremely powerful. Despite this, I can see right through her that she's hurting.

Without her pain and those horrific experiences she has gone through, she wouldn't be the courageous and strong woman she has grown to be. Her suffering has aided her courage. Her past has molded her to become the queen she has always been destined to be. I will not take that away from her. I will repair the damage without my powers, no matter how tempting it could be to use them. Claire's traumatizing story shall be another human girl's cure. I'm changing a lot of laws the moment I get back to my kingdom.

If I have to wait another lifetime to tame her God-given body, I will. If she decides I shall never receive the opportunity to explore its wonders, I won't hold it against her. Every inch of her belongs to me, but it's still up to her to give it away freely. For once, I won't take what I want even though that's all I can think about.

I have been standing on the threshold of the room for a while now, just admiring the breathtaking view of my sleeping beauty—a view I wouldn't get tired of watching as long as I live. If she was aware of what I'm currently doing, she would add me to her jeepers-creepers list. Yes, my little firecracker is quite the comedian. I have listened in on many of her humorous thoughts flowing within that pretty little head of hers. She's hilarious.

The sudden urge to kiss her and cuddle with her rolls around inside me. I want to slide in bed with her and run my fingers through her hair. I want to taste her honeysuckled center for hours. Just hearing her soft and moans makes my shaft go rockhard. It's now poking through the confinements of my combat pants.

I rush into the bathroom connected to the room to take a shower. I try my hardest not to indulge in self-pleasure as I quickly clean myself up. The stench of the dogs clings to my skin. It's an extremely disgusting scent.

I wrap a towel around my waist tightly, my member once again poking through. "F*cking fantastic," I groan to myself, as I walk toward the closet.

Claire is still sleeping peacefully. She moves right before I enter, gaining my attention. She rolls over, slightly opening her well-toned legs and providing me with a slight view of that nice and juicy pink part of her body that makes her a woman. I force myself to look anywhere but at her. I'm going to lose control. I can't do that. I must show strength.

My eyes drift to the nightstand beside the bed and zero in on a wine glass filled with my blood. I know Xander gave some of it to Claire to help her body recover from the dream state. I'm not quite sure if the emerald could prevent her from going back into a lustful state. The last time that happened, it took every ounce of self-control to refrain myself from claiming her body. Now that we are claimed, I don't believe I can stop myself. If she asks me to entertain, I'll do it.

I need to get out of here before I perform multiple pleasured-filled tasks on the sweet little body of hers.

The morning air blows through the window, carrying along a sweet-tasting scent. My nostrils flare widely as I draw in the first whiff of her sweet, warm, lightly-laced, honey-filled arousal. My monster awakens. I grip the side of the closet door, distancing myself as far away from the bed as possible, my vision now completely black. He wants her more than he has ever wanted just a single drop of blood. This is torture.

Somehow, I almost muster the strength to walk away when she opens her eyes.

*    *    *

## CLAIRE

The cool morning air whisks in the fresh vivid, aroma of expensive cologne and burning cedarwood.

My eyes lock on the monster side of my ass-kissing king. His rock-solid and well-maintained chest is on full display. He's wearing nothing but a towel. His half-smoke is poking through, desperately begging for release. I forgot how gigantic he is. Oh my! I suddenly feel a little light-headed. I don't know if it's coming from him or . . . No, it's coming from the view of him.

He takes a single step back. "Get out of here now," he growls in a warning tone.

I am confused about what's going on until I look deep into his almost pitch-black eyes, drenching and devouring my body whole. I then realize I forgot to put some undergarments on, and my kitty is roaring around freely—such a tease.

He's an extremely powerful vampire, known to be the world's most-dangerous predator, while right now I'm the world's most-vulnerable prey. As my heavy eyes stare into the monster's eyes, all I can think about is to get tamed. I want him.

"I said get out of here now," he says bitterly, adding fuel to the now scorching fire.

His tone leaves no room for arguments. It is a command, not a suggestion. I should follow direct instructions from my ass-kissing king, but the problem is I don't want to. I know he is fighting for control with his monster. I can feel it, and I want him to lose.

366

His grip around the arch of the door tightens, his eyes growing darker by the second. Nicklaus is losing, but he's still a king. He wouldn't go down that easily, unless I provide aid and come to his monster's defense.

I decide to take advantage of one of my best qualities—defiance. I arch my back, acting like I'm going to follow his command, only to unbutton his dress shirt, slowly. Then I slightly open my legs, perfectly aware that my womanhood is now on full display to allow him to view the center of my slick folds.

His body goes dangerously still as he watches me closely with great attentiveness that only a mighty predator would possess, greedily drenching me with his dark stare and lust-filled eyes. He wants me just as bad as I want him, no matter how unexpected and sudden it is. In this moment, at this exact time, we both want this. I don't know what's gotten into me. I have never behaved in such a manner, ever. We barely knew each other, and now we are claimed, going through some creepy vampire beloved transition.

I partially open the door to my bed—well, his bed. Either way, I'm inviting him in without shame. Maybe it's because he has caught me off guard with the perfect view of his muscular, God-given body; or maybe it's because as I stare into his now deep sea-blue eyes, all I can think about is diving inside. I don't know what it is. Truth be told, I'm thinking too much. It doesn't matter. My patience is running extremely thin. F*ck his self-control. I want him right now inside me to fill me with every single inch of his long and lengthy manhood. Right now, I'm lost in his stare—that stare that makes me feel all jittery and nervous inside; the kind of stare that sends tiny little icicles to prick me as it travels down my spine. The King of All Vampire King Nicklaus's dark, dangerous, and lustful stare is the one to blame for making my juices flow freely and race down my legs like a wildfire. Except his nostrils that flare widely like they can smell each drip of my essence, no part of his body is moving.

After what seems like a passing lifetime or a century, or maybe eternity, he finally takes a step, eyes focusing on my kitty. His nostrils are now wider than an elephant's ears. He takes another step, but this time his eyes study my face.

I try my best to look seductive, calling his soul to mingle with my own with just a stare. I softly bite down onto my lip, and that one single action does it. Just one single motion breaks his self-control. His monster is free, and within a breath, he moves with such grace, showing me exactly why he is called what he's called—the world's most-dangerous predator. He pounces onto the bed in the blink of an eye, slowly drenching in every detail of my naked frame. Without hesitation, he then snatches his shirt off my body. He covers me with his muscular frame and places his manhood by my slick folds the very moment his magical hands touch my body. I moan as the heat wave starts to rise. He cups my breast, then sucks and tastes my now hard nipples, forcing the heat wave to explode. His cool lips touch my lukewarm skin within a heartbeat, shooting the heat wave straight up my spine. I moan louder as he trails cool kisses along my skin, leaving a spark with each peck.

I moan out his name. His fangs descend and then they gently bite down without breaking a kiss. He sucks and feasts on my flesh, taking his precious time to enjoy each and every spot. His cool tongue licks all over me like I'm his favorite icing, and I moan a sigh of bliss.

He spreads my legs apart with his powerful hands and gently rubs all over my heat. He slips one single finger into the center. "You're so tight," he says, as he pulls his finger out and places it in his mouth.

My eyes widen the moment he dives in. He doesn't waste any time. He provides my body with a volcano of pleasure just with the first sweep of his tongue. His lips then latch onto my center. He makes sure every bit of my heat is placed into his mouth.

Oh my God! I can't think. I can't speak. All I can do is scream at the top of my lungs as he slowly and carefully sucks and licks my womanhood. He drinks every ounce of my essence and moans from the taste.

I have never experienced such pleasure, ever! And just when I thought this was the best I'll ever have, a tingly sensation starts to arise, anxious to break free. I wrap my legs around his face, locking him in. Somehow he pulls me on top of him, never once removing his tongue from my super soaked heat. Instincts take over, and I start to move back and forth, rocking gently over his face. He grips my ass with his hands, but he doesn't stop his rhythm, continuing to move his tongue with a steady and pleasure-filled beat.

He smacks my ass the moment the tingly sensation reaches its highest peak. I scream so loud as my juices flood through me and are released onto his now inhumanly fast tongue. He holds onto my hips firmly, refusing to allow me to move and never once stopping the movement of his flicking tongue—encouraging me to release as much of my juices as possible.

The very moment the flood comes to a stop, I fall back onto the bed with a carefree body. My eyelids feel heavy, then they flutter shut.

# CHAPTER FIFTY-ONE
## Time-sensitive

NICKLAUS

Even after I take another shower, Claire's essence remains on me. It clings to my body like a second skin. Just thinking about it makes me hard again. I'll hold on to the memory of her sweet, tasty arousal to the end of time. Her taste—sweet like candy—has satisfied my monster for a moment. We shall never be completely full as long as her honeysuckled dish is being served.

Based on Claire's reaction, I can tell she has never been pleased during those dreadful sexual encounters she has experienced. I don't think she had ever felt a climax until I explored her delicious and precious jewel with the tip of my tongue. I'm almost positive I'm the first and only person that has tasted her cum. In fact, I'm positive I'm the only one who has caused her to have an orgasm, and I shall be her last.

With that thought, I freshen up and quickly leave the room. I'm extremely eager to get this meeting over with, just so I can get back to exploring that God-given body of hers.

Xander is sitting in a chair placed directly in front of the entryway of the west wing. He seems to be lost in his own world as he looks out of the window. I knew he was here. I picked up his scent the exact moment Claire's body gave in—that delicious beehive of a body that's filled with the richest honey. She hosts the most-expensive honey that money can buy.

Xander hasn't noticed I exited the room, which is strange. Something must be bothering him. It's not like he does not pay attention to his surroundings. He's a powerful vampire, almost as powerful as me.

My vision zeroes in on him. I notice his eyes don't hold their usual warmth and his lips aren't anywhere close to a smile. I know Xander overheard my little tasting session. If this were any other time, his eyes would be bright, and I would want to knock a smirk off his face. His unusual behavior doesn't flash warning signs, but his body does. It goes stiff the moment he senses my presence.

Xander stands up. "Pardon my intrusion, but I thought it would be best if I should be the one to tell you."

Something is really off. He has never given a f*ck about interrupting me, and he damn sure doesn't apologize for anything. He doesn't even properly address me or utilize my title, not that it matters. He is my brother, so he can do that.

"Tell me what?" I ignore his strange behavior. I don't know why he is so upset, but right now I don't have a care in the world. Nothing can destroy the eternity of happiness I have finally found.

That reminds me that I need to speak to Claire about accepting immortality. Hopefully, she agrees. She has to.

Xander clears his throat.

Oh right! Back to the current task at hand. F*ck, I'm acting like a lovesick puppy.

"We have been summoned," he speaks through clenched teeth.

"We have been summoned," I repeat in a low voice.

Summoned? It hasn't happened in over a century since my father officially abdicated the throne.

It takes a second for his words to sink in, and when they finally do, my hands clench into tight fists. A tidal wave of exasperation and anger seeps through my pores. Only one soul in this universe is powerful enough to summon me—my father! Who the f*ck does he think he is? How dare he? I'm the king of all kings. That bastard of a man irks my existence to the very end.

"How much time do we have?" I cut straight to the point.

"Your father has demanded an audience at once," answers Xander. "All of us are required to attend."

"Of course we are!" I snap.

A summons for one king extends to all kings. No wonder Marcellus wanted to speak to me. He knew this is no game. I expected certain casualties once the council learned I'd declared war against the dogs without their approval, but I never expected this.

"No, Nicklaus, you do not fully comprehend what I'm saying!"

The air in the room shifts in a matter of seconds. Xander's words confuse me.

"Enlighten me then," I state, struggling to keep my monster at bay. I'm certain that whatever my father requested is unreasonable. That's just what he does.

"The summons was issued to all eight kings . . ." Xander says languidly, as if the weight of the world were on his shoulders.

I place my hand on his shoulder, encouraging him to continue.

"The summons was issued to all eight vampire kings and the chosen of the king of all vampire kings."

His words knock the wind out of my stomach. My vision starts to bleed as a ton of negative emotions weigh me down like ten pounds of bricks are being placed onto my back. My grip on Xander's shoulder tightens. He continues to stand there, holding me in place to keep me from falling. Apprehension cracks through my ice-cold skin like the first strike from a brand-new whip. I shake my head as I try my hardest to take Xander's last words off my mind.

"What are you implying?" my monsters queries. He is no longer buried deep down inside me. He is fully awake, alert, and ready to spill blood.

Xander removes my hand carefully. I know he is barely detaining his own monster, but he is aware that my monster has freed himself.

"Brother," he says with caution, "you need to calm yourself at once." He sighs deeply. "We don't know the reason why he summoned Claire."

With a monstrous growl, I pick up the chair and smash it into the window. Tiny pieces of glass shatter and fly freely all around the west wing. I go on a complete rampage, throwing and breaking anything my claws could get on.

Xander doesn't interfere. He allows me to release my rage and frustration. My emotions are haywire, my judgment is cloudy, and my monster is craving to sink our fangs into anyone.

Suddenly, Xander's body goes stiff and his eyes travel to my bedroom door.

Claire's heart rate picks up speed. My beloved has awakened. I can feel her trying to invade my mind and understand my thoughts in the process. I block her off, slamming the door to my mind and emotions shut. My sensitive ears then lock on the sound of her heavy footsteps as she makes her way to the bedroom door. She stops for a second and then changes her direction, heading toward the closet. I can detect she is putting clothes on.

Once dressed, she turns back around to make her way out of the room. The door opens and my bloodshot vision centers on her mesmerizing green eyes. Time slows down as we stare at each other for a long while. Without warning, I jump out of the busted window.

\*     \*     \*

CLAIRE

My breath hitches, forcing me to jump out of my sleep and gasp for air. A ton of negative emotions slams straight into my chest like a car crash and then like a door, it shuts. It takes me a second to fully awaken to pinpoint the exact source. There's only one person in this world that can take my breath away.

"Nicklaus," I whisper to myself. I hop out of the bed and then rush toward the bedroom door, only to come to a complete halt the moment my mind realizes I'm completely naked, even more naked than a newborn baby that's fresh out of their mother's womb—no underwear, no bra. I'm not even wearing Nicklaus's dress shirt.

The aroma of burning cedarwood and expensive cologne lingers on me like a cloud of thick smoke. That's when I realize that his intoxicating scent is more potent on the other side of the door. It's blending with a hint of cypress, indicating that he is only a few steps away. He is not alone; Xander is with him.

I rush to the closet and throw on the first thing my hands grab. I pull one of Nicklaus's V-necks over my head, then put on a pair of one of his washed-out jeans—which sags loosely on my tiny frame.

I get out of the bedroom, ignoring the fact that I look like crap. My eyes instantly lock on Nicklaus's bright, vivid, and glowing red eyes. I'm used to vampires's eyes turning red, especially when Nicklaus is brought into the equation, but I have never witnessed anything like this. The sight of him completely shocks my soul. His entire eyes bleed different shades of red. His irises and lens are soaking scarlet. His pupils dilate, yet they somehow manage to drip crimson. And his corneas are bleeding ruby red. Good God.

Our eyes have stayed locked in place for a long-drawn-out moment until he decides to finally release me from the hold and unexpectedly jumps out of the window. Without thinking, I rush at an inhuman speed and follow suit. I can hear Xander screaming.

I land gracefully, surprising the f*ck out of myself. My moment of shock lasts for barely a second as a blurry figure—

Nicklaus— running faster than the wind is now a few feet ahead of me.

Once again I take off in an inhuman speed. He moves faster than lightning, whooshing past the twenty snow-covered trees. Somehow, I manage to keep up with him, embracing the cold wind as it whirls fiercely around me. I chase after him like I'm running for my life. He's only a few feet away, giving me the push to run faster than I would have ever thought my body could manage.

I can feel someone also running after me—after us—but we lose them within a second. Maybe they realize it is a bad idea to chase after another man's beloved who is dead set on hunting him down. Right now, Nicklaus is the only one that matters. No one will stand in my way.

I feel an unfamiliar wicked presence within me as I pick up speed, snow crunching underneath my bare feet. We bolt up a steep hill, and now I'm only seconds away from catching up with him— he's so close. I can almost reach and touch him. A foreign instinct takes over, and I leap into the air. I land directly onto his back, and Nicklaus slightly stumbles but catches me without stopping.

He continues to move with me while I cling to his back for dear life. I lock my legs around his waist after he somehow places his arms underneath them. His sharp claws dig deep into my skin, but I don't complain.

The wind smashes straight into my face like a ton of bricks as he speeds up. Nonetheless, I enjoy the rush of the wind. I welcome the thrill that comes with my piggyback ride. I can see everything perfectly clear, and around us seems to be in slow motion. We pass flying birds and deer that appear to be running extremely slow. It's amazing.

Nicklaus continues to run up the mountain with no signs of slowing down. I rest my head on his shoulder and bury my nose in the crook of his neck. Shivers travel down my spine as I take in his rich, seductive, and mind-blowing scent. There is no denying he is the best thing I have ever smelled, and his tongue is damn sure the best thing I've ever felt. Just thinking about it instantly makes me wet.

He continues to run at an inhuman speed for what seems like forever. I feel his monster slowly sinking deep inside him. Then all of a sudden, his running turns into a steady jog before he comes to a complete stop. My head is still on his shoulder. It feels so good.

The stunning view of an ice-covered lake spreading for miles underneath us greets my eyes as soon as I lift my head. This type of scenery can only be seen from the highest point of the mountain top—our exact location. We're surrounded by tall, snow-covered trees that seem to nearly reach the sky. The morning sun shines high above our heads, providing not an ounce of warmth. Then it dawns on me that I must be freezing to death, but somehow I'm not. Actually, I'm numb.

Nicklaus puts me down onto the ground, my bare feet touching the ice-cold snow. I'm still numb, strangely enough. It's like my body doesn't know how to tell whether it's too hot or too cold.

"Why am I not freezing to death?"

He chuckles. "Vampires don't get hot or cold." His beautiful cerulean eyes meet mine head-on.

I find myself almost lost in his stare until I actually catch on to what he has said. "But I'm human," I breathe.

He doesn't respond right away. Instead, he places his attention on the ice-solid lake and takes a deep breath. I allow him to have a moment to himself. Obviously, he needs some time to think. I don't understand what he meant by "Vampires don't get hot or cold." With their having superpowers and living for a long time, it should make sense. Surely, they don't experience hypothermia or heatstrokes, but still.

What does that have to do with me? I'm just human. I know I'm not acting like one, with my sudden abilities to run faster than a cheetah and pounce like an animal or have newly enhanced senses, still I'm human, right?

"I'm not turning into a vampire, am I?" I blurt out.

"Would it be a problem if you were?" he casually asks, his attention still on the lake.

It feels like a tricky question.

"Will it be a problem if I'm not?" I ask back, utilizing reverse psychology.

Nicklaus just simply grinds his teeth. I take a seat on the ground and decide to enjoy the beautiful view alongside him. My hands can't help but draw patterns in the snow. It's really fascinating how the snow doesn't really feel like snow. It feels like nothing.

I continue to think about his question. Nicklaus seems to be lost in his own thought. I can tell—well, I can see—something is bothering him. I wonder if it really is going to be a problem, with me remaining human. Is that why all his emotions are all over the place? I know we are bonded somehow, but I really don't understand what that means and what that means for us. For some reason, it takes me back to how my life had been like before I met him. All the other girls at school would have killed to be turned, literally. They used to fantasize about gaining the attention of a vampire, becoming their beloved, and living happily ever after, forever. I, on the other hand, didn't. All I wanted was to escape even if that meant I had to die. Funny how becoming a vampire means that my heart will no longer beat, so technically I'd be dead.

After five minutes of silence and the both of us having been lost in our own minds, I finally answer, "All I ever wanted was to be free," I tell him quietly, gaining his attention. "Free from chains. Free from bondage. Free from the constant judgment of my own species because I refused to think like I was told to think." My voice starts to break, my tears flowing freely.

Nicklaus's body freezes as he sits down beside me. He takes my hands, then holds them tightly as if I could disappear

377

before his very eyes. He seems afraid. I can feel it. Whatever type of bond we share, it's wide open. His emotions are like words, loud and clear. I'm also afraid that if I speak about my past, it will come back to take me; that if I tell him I don't want to be a vampire, he will be the one to officially break me. I'm just as scared to lose him as he is to lose me.

Somehow, I manage to speak my truth: "Free from the disgusting teachers that took my body however and whenever they pleased, making me do things that no soul on Earth should have ever been forced to do. When they realized they couldn't break my mind, they decided to target my body. One way or the other, all the vampire teachers were dead set on breaking me."

His eyes flash crimson, but he remains quiet, and I'm thankful. Right now I just want to speak freely. He continues to hold my hand, giving me all the encouragement I need.

"All I ever wanted was to be free from eighteen years of nothing but hurt and pain, so I suppose it won't make a difference if I do or don't become a vampire. At least I'll be free." I wipe my tears. "That still doesn't mean that I'm sure I want to, but I'm certain I do want to spend however long I live with you," I confess. "You saved me and taught me that anything is possible. You showed me how it feels to love and be loved."

Without warning, his lips crash down onto mine. A million electric shocks travel up my spine, followed by a million icicles. Then comes the heat, burning my soul. We kiss each other long and hard, and I know it is the best kind of freedom.

Once we finally break apart, we are both breathless. He lifts my chin, his hand soft like a feather against my skin. His mesmerizing eyes are staring into the center of my soul.

It is tempting to become a vampire if it means I'll spend the rest of eternity with him. To be honest, eternity doesn't seem long enough, and it will never be enough time with him, vampire or not.

"You're not turning into a vampire, firecracker," he finally speaks. "You are claimed, but only you can truly accept immortality. I will have to turn you, but if your heart, soul, and body aren't in accord with it, my venom may kill you if any part of you decides to fight against the change."

I lean my head to the side. "What do you mean?" I ask quietly.

He looks at our entwined fingers, the light from the sun reflected down onto his hands. I don't think any part of me will be able to fight against this—fight against being with him. When did we become so close?

He stares at me again. "There is much we have to discuss, firecracker. Unfortunately, right now is not the time." He runs his free fingers through his hair.

I hate how tired and stressed he looks, and it bothers me.

"There isn't enough time to go over everything. I have to deal with something," he adds.

I nod in understanding. We sit in silence for a little while longer, enjoying the view and each other's presence.

He takes a deep breath, then stands up. His vivid cerulean eyes shine brighter underneath the sun. "We don't have time to go into detail, but I will say this"—he takes my hands and pulls me to my feet—"you will never be placed in chains again. You are free and will remain free for the rest of your life, even if the rest of your years is spent as a human. I'll never allow a single soul to hurt you, bring you pain, or place chains on you ever again."

His words melt my heart, and I try my best not to break into tears. How can I not want an eternity with him? I would want him forever.

# CHAPTER FIFTY-TWO
## Time to Talk

NICKLAUS

We got back to my estate around noon. Claire kept bugging me about taking her to Cyrus's beloved. She talked about how much she loved her scent, and it annoyed me to the very end. She shouldn't like anyone's scent but mine.

I told her no, and of course, she wouldn't have any of it. My manipulative little firecracker started complaining about me not allowing her to see her dog, Mecca, and then she went on giving me hell about her needing some girl time. Left with no choice, I promised to take her to go see the dog tomorrow. However, I made up some bullsh*t about Cyrus and Embry being occupied, so she would have to wait for a while, and she seemed to believe me.

I don't know how my clever beloved figured out that Embry is Cyrus's beloved, but she did. She's just too goddamn smart for her own good. Luckily, my excuse worked out in my favor—she caved in. I don't want her to spend time with anyone. She doesn't really need to. She has Xander and me, and we are all the friends she needs. Still, I really have to take her to see the dog tomorrow, mostly because she will kill me if I don't.

After I ordered Commander Vlad to come to stand guard and ensure that Claire was comfortable, I commanded some servants to bring my beloved lunch and a change of clothes. I also ordered one of the men to collect her belongings from Cyrus's penthouse. I had forgotten to bring them, and that's another thing she was pissed at. She told me she couldn't just walk around in my clothing all day. And why not? She looks good on my clothes, even better with me although she disagreed.

She commanded one of my men to bring her *The Vampire Studies*. She's such a bossy little queen. She was very adamant about learning everything there is to know concerning vampires. I remember her saying, "How can I lead a race if I don't know their true past?" I've never been so proud. She's going to make a great queen.

I'm currently making my way to my study. I mind-linked with Xander a while back and told him we all shall meet this afternoon, so they should be in soon. Once I enter my studies, I start to prepare for the meeting. Usually, I don't postpone meetings, but under this extreme circumstance, it is clear I need time to calm down. I need Claire. She is my peace and calm before and after every storm. Now, I have to figure out how to protect my peace. I know my father has an agenda for summoning her, and the only logical explanation is that he is aware of what she is to me. It's the only reason why he would summon a human. What I don't understand is how? I have been extremely careful of hiding the fact that she is my beloved. Only a few know the truth, and they would all rather die than betray me. Loyalty is everything among vampires, that's why it's such a mystery.

What am I missing, or rather who am I missing? How did he figure it out? I guess we shall find out sooner than later. The biggest challenge is how I will protect her. For sure, they will demand her head. Make no mistake, I shall fight for her life even if that means giving my own in exchange for hers. I know even that won't still be enough.

Now that we are officially bonded, my father and the council will hunt her down, even if I'm eliminated from the equation. Claire is a threat to the entire awakening. She can change

381

things that have been our normal for over a century. That's exactly why we made a law prohibiting us from mating with humans in the first place. The Awakening would have never been successful if we had continued to mate and bond with them.

Claire is such a big threat, especially now that she shares my powers and shall be crowned as queen. Even if she is turned, I believe in my heart and soul she will be against keeping humans in chains, and there's no doubt about me giving her whatever she wants. I don't give a f*ck about who doesn't like it.

I remember Claire wants pancakes, so I quickly mind-link with one of my men and order them to go get more pancake mix and flour. I hated the look on Claire's face when I told her the cooks were out of pancake mix and the main key ingredient of making it.

That's not going to happen again. Whatever the queen wants, she shall get it. As I said, I will give her whatever her heart desires. That's how beloved bonds work. The council knows, and so does my father. They will never accept that, though.

I really have no idea what's going on with Claire, which makes matters worse. When she asked me on the mountain if she was turning into a vampire, I could have sworn my heart started beating. I played it cool, behaving as if nothing was wrong and flipping the focus onto her by answering her question with a question. In return, she burst into tears, breaking my heart in the process. I didn't mean to be the reason for such dark memories of hers to resurface. I was too afraid to tell her the truth.

It's true we are officially claimed, so she should share some of my powers. Her senses are expected to enhance, and it's not strange that she can run like a vampire or be as strong as a vampire. It's just extremely rare that it's happening so soon, but it is not unheard of. The mysterious emerald also gives her gifts of her own. I don't know the exact intent, but I know the gemstone was crafted by the most-powerful witch of all time—Aurora. Only she knows what it can or cannot do. She can also explain how Claire is able to wield its powers. Too bad she won't explain sh*t, not when Xander and I are involved. She hates us with a passion, thanks to Xander. He's the reason why many powerful women hate us. He is called the cold-hearted king for many reasons, and one of those is his being a womanizer. He breaks the hearts of others with no remorse. Perhaps he is remorseful, but it does not matter. We have bigger problems at hand, and they all involve my beloved.

I think I felt a wicked, dark, and dangerous predator in my beloved. I recognized it during our run, with her on my back. This is nearly impossible, especially when you consider the fact that my venom hasn't been placed inside her body. Plus, she hasn't accepted immortality completely, which is the only way for her to complete the transition. So that makes things strange, and I have to tackle all this f*cking odd sh*t while dealing with this summons. I really need to figure everything out. I've been sitting at the conference table for about ten minutes now, trying to do just that. Claire has really flipped my world upside down.

"Brother," calls Count Cloven. He is the first to enter the room.

I stand to greet him with a nice, brotherly hug.

He pats my back. "Xander has already told us that he has passed along the news," he says, pulling away.

I nod in response.

We both take a seat, and now we are sitting in silence when one of the servants walks into the room and places a glass of Claire's blood in front of me. She puts some other blood and refreshments on the center of the table before she takes her leave. Count Cloven's naturally crimson eyes study the small glass filled with Claire's blood, then they travel to me.

"First, I want to apologize for abandoning my duties without permission. I just thought it was best that I should deliver the message."

"There's no need to apologize." I take a sip of the blood.

383

I know he only left Xander's kingdom to personally tell me we have been summoned. I suspect his father was the one who gave him the heads-up. As I stated before, our ancestors had a long history of companionship. Count Cloven is one of my most-trusted advisers, and his father is like a second father to me.

"I expect that Duke Aldon is aware as well?" I put the glass down.

He nods. "Yes, I informed him the moment my father contacted me. Duke Aldon requested permission to attend the meeting with you," Cloven informs, and it confirms my suspicions.

"I'll return to the far southern kingdom as soon as the meeting is over and then he will meet you in Romania. We believe he will be able to smooth things out with your father if need be," he states.

I doubt it, but I do understand why they would think that. Ever since Aldon saved my life, my father has been favoring him. He also wants him to claim my sister as his beloved. Typically with Aldon, things would go swimmingly. However, this matter isn't that simple.

Count Cloven places his attention back onto the glass. I know he can smell Claire's milk-and-honey scent.

"I think we both know nothing would smooth things over, not when Claire is placed into the equation. The council will most likely demand her death on sight, and no one can stop it," I tell him.

"You know that your father will never allow any harm to come to you." He shifts his focus back to me.

"And I will never allow anyone to harm her."

"Understood." He sighs. "So, that human . . . Claire, is it? She really is your true beloved, huh?" he asks, seeming to be talking to himself more than asking me.

I understand his doubts. Who would have thought the beloved of the king of all vampire kings is a human? A defiant and bold little human at that! I have no doubt she is disobeying me at

384

this very moment. I can bet on my crown that she went to go search for Embry. She wouldn't be herself if she didn't.

"It's something else," he speaks quietly. "As a result of the summons, a background check was done on your beloved. My father was the one who was sent to Australia to locate her files."

It makes sense. If the council is aware that she is my beloved, they will rid anyone related to her out of spite.

"The thing is your father made it very clear that no one is supposed to know about it," he says.

Now that piques my interest. If the council is aware of who Claire is, then why would my father want to keep it under wraps? What is he up to?

"Another interesting thing is my father was unable to find her file."

"What do you mean?" I ask.

I saw Claire's file before I went to the academy, so it does exist. Now that I think about it, I didn't really see any information about her early life. Usually, the school leaves little notes.

"He found her case file from the school, but that's it," he tells me. "Have you searched her heritage?" asks Cloven.

"No. I intended to, but the war with these dogs distracted me."

Xander and the others walk into the room, ending our conversation. They take their seats.

"Looks like the king is finally ready to address his loyal subjects," Marcellus speaks, being the first one to irritate me as usual. He has a thing about getting under people's skin.

The other men exchange annoyed looks.

"Shut the f*ck up Marcellus," spits Cyrus. "Now isn't the time for your bullsh*t."

"Of course, it's not. We have more pressing matters at hand, like why the f*ck are we being summoned?" Marcellus leans back and places his feet on the table.

Count Cloven's red eyes glow brighter. He's not used to this behavior. On the outside looking in, you would think Marcellus is being disrespectful. I, on the other hand, have been Marcellus's friend for centuries. He's just a douchebag. He can't help it.

"Agreed," I casually respond.

Xander rolls his eyes, obviously still in a bad mood.

"Why would your father all of a sudden summon us?" asks Marcellus.

He's the only one in the room who doesn't know about Claire, so of course he's the one who has the most questions. The other vampire kings are probably wondering the same thing.

"And why would he summon your chosen? What's going on, Nicklaus?"

"Don't forget who you're addressing," I warn.

The f*cking douchebag smirks.

"I think the most-important question is what we are going to do about the dog problem," Cyrus responds, attempting to place the focus on anything other than Claire.

Xander raises his eyebrow. He must have realized that too. "The last attack, the one I led, shall keep them busy for at least one passing moon. That should be more than enough time to deal with the summons and return."

"They want you all to be in Romania at once," Count Cloven states. "Everything is already set up for all of you to depart."

"No, we need to settle things in our kingdoms first before we take off to Romania," Xander replies. Send word that we shall be there within a week."

"I'll contact my father at once. I'm sure he can buy you all some time, especially when you consider the constant attacks from the werewolves," Count Cloven states.

"That's only if the council isn't pissed at us, coming over here in the first place. I wonder if that's the reason for the summons," Marcellus says. His eyes travel to my glass of blood, and they start to swirl with curiosity.

I am about to take another sip of my drink, only to place it back down, acting as if I didn't see right through his charade. I recognize his suspicions, but it really doesn't matter. I'm his king. He won't dare to challenge me if he wants to keep his life.

"No, that doesn't make sense. I mean we can't dismiss the key fact that your father summoned a human," he says, still fishing. He's playing a dangerous game.

I grip the table, trying my best to contain my emotions. However, my patience is running thin.

"Drop it, Marcellus," Xander speaks up. "It's none of your goddamn business why Claire was summoned."

"Ah-ha . . . there it goes." Marcellus stands up. "There is some deeper meaning behind the summons."

My monster is now on the horizon.

"I'm guessing"—he turns to face me—"it has something to do with you since Claire . . . is your chosen, isn't it? And let's not forget that your brother just called a human by its name," he continues.

That does it. In the blink of an eye, I'm out of my seat, smashing him into the wall. My hands are now around his neck, my vision painted blood.   "Do you want to die?" I growl low, extremely low. "I'll end you."

He raises his hands in mock surrender. "Come on, Bro. I was just kidding around. Geez. Get your panties out of the bunch."

I growl in response.

"Just kidding, just kidding. You know I got your back. You're my big brody."

Marcellus has a thing about using modern words. He thinks it makes him cool—f*cking clown!

I throw him across the room with little effort, then straighten out my leather jacket and make my way back to my seat.

"This isn't the time for games, Marcellus," I tell him as he stands to his feet. "Meeting adjourned. I don't have time for this sh*t."

Without question, everyone leaves except Xander.

"You know, Nicklaus, all the kings will have questions about Claire," he begins after waiting for a while. "We need to know who will remain with us and who will turn against us."

He is right.

I take the last sip of Claire's blood, allowing the taste of milk and honey to calm my nerves. I twirl the empty wine glass around my fingers. "I'm aware. What should we do?"

Xander walks toward the window. He's wearing an all-black suit, nice and clean. For the first time in a while, he looks like himself. He's doing it—thinking about a master plan. "A feast," he suggests.

I put my glass on the table. "A feast? What the f*ck would that do?"

He crosses his arms behind his back. "Call for a feast and introduce Claire as your beloved, then we shall get the answers we seek."

I think over his words. He's right, which seems to be like always.

"I'll do it at once," I respond.

The other kings won't think anything of it. They most likely are hoping that I call for a feast so they can figure out what's going on.

"There's more," I say.

Xander turns to face me.

"Claire's file is missing. I need to locate it before my father does, and I sensed another presence in Claire. That felt like our presence."

"Impossible," Xander remarks. "You know like I know she's nowhere near ready. You haven't even given her your venom, have you?"

"Of course not!" I growl. "I wouldn't do that unless I'm one hundred percent certain she's ready. I suppose it has something to do with the emerald."

Xander frowns. "Maybe. There's only one way to find out. It's time to talk with Aurora."

"We don't have time for petty disputes with the witches, Xander."

"No, we don't, and I'm sure she will try to kill me on sight. However, she's the only one who can tell us about the emerald. I guess I just have to right my wrongs."

I burst out laughing. "Good luck."

# CHAPTER FIFTY-THREE
## Time to Think

CLAIRE

Nicklaus left me in the room about ten minutes ago to handle some official vampire business, and I am alone and bored out of my mind. Well, Mr. Meany is here. He is watching me like a guard dog. This is nothing new, except the fact that his sidekick is missing. I haven't really seen her around, which is odd. He wouldn't have a sidekick without someone actually hanging at his side.

"Where is Astrid?" I ask him.

He responds with a stony stare. His face doesn't give anything away. I'm just about to crack one of my legendary vampire jokes when someone knocks on the door. The smell of sugary, buttery syrup invades my nostrils.

*Pancakes!*

I jump off the bed and answer the door quicker than Mr. Meany can blink. Actually, he never blinks, but you get the picture. The human girl who collected my blood five minutes ago walks in with a tray full of pancakes that are drenched in warm and thick maple syrup. My mouth waters, and I have to restrain myself from kissing her.

The cooks told us we were out of the ingredients for pancakes, which was nerve-wracking as hell. I can't live without pancakes. Just check my record. I'd be willing to die for this sugary breakfast cake.

After giving the human a polite thank-you, I dive right in with no remorse. Mr. Meany watches me devour my food like a starved girl. Of course, he doesn't show what is inside his head—not that he needs to—but it's obvious he thinks I'm behaving like a pig. I can see the judgment in his mean big eyes. Oh well, I think he behaves like a gorilla twenty-four seven. Whatever, I'm not judging.

Once I finish eating the best creation in the entire world, I lick the syrup off my fingers and place the empty plate down on the nightstand. My eyes scan the room, searching for something to do. Unfortunately, I find nothing. Boredom strikes once again.

What's a girl to do when there's nothing else to do?

An idea pops into my head, and it smells just as good as the pancakes I've tasted: Embry. I love her natural scent, not in a creepy way, like I'm sure it sounds. It's more like the-best-perfume-in-the-world type of way that you want to spray back on your body the moment the fragrance stops lingering on your skin. I know it's weird, but that girl really does smell that good.

Gosh, I need to behave. I wouldn't want to place myself on my own jeepers-creepers list, now would I? No, I wouldn't, but I really like her scent. Plus, she seems nice. I can't believe King Cyrus is her beloved. It's ironic because he's a barbaric king that wolves hate with a passion whereas she's the strange, not-so-crazy she-wolf. She's an angel while he's the devil's son.

Welp, I really don't have any room to speak. I'm a human who happens to be the beloved of and bonded to king of all vampire kings, who most certainly is the devil, so does this kind of make me the devil's wife? Well, actually, that makes me the queen of all vampire kings, I think.

I break into a fit of laughter inside my head. Now I know I used that queen bullcrap when I wanted my way with Nicklaus, but I'm far from anybody's queen. Who would take me seriously?

*Claire the Queen of All Vampire Kings. Claire the Queen of All Leeches. Claire the Queen of All Bloodthirsty Monsters. Claire the Queen.*

Haha. I wouldn't dare to say that out loud. They would hang me and then hang themselves just because they lived to see the day that a human would so boldly state she's their queen. Oh, I'm going to say it out loud just to get under Mr. Meany's skin. Okay, I'm officially bored to death. Haha. Bored to death, get it?

"Commander Vlad," I call out.

He looks at me suspiciously, probably not missing the fact that it's the first time I've actually said his name. Oh boy, this is going to be fun.

"Nicklaus told me you are here to protect, serve, and provide me with anything I need."

He raises his eyebrow in response, nothing else. That's it.

"He also told me that I'm your future queen, and you have to obey my every command," I brag in my Dr. Evil's voice, seeking a reaction.

Surprisingly enough, he doesn't react at all—no scary red eyes, no flash of his monstrous fangs, and no frightening growl. There is nothing—nada, no reaction. He just returns to his usual, unemotional facial expression, which only annoys me to no end. It sucks big time. Gosh, he's no fun. Should I try a different approach? He hates it when I crack my vampire jokes.

"How about you go bother your dog friend since you're so bored?" Mr. Meany suggests.

My head snaps in his direction. Oh my God, he speaks! Maybe I'm a little overdramatic. I've heard him speak before, but he's never tried striking up a conversation with me. Why didn't I just think about starting a casual conversation with him? Hmmm. Why didn't I? Oh right, I know why: because that would be boring, and I'm already bored to death like him. Haha. I'm childish.

"Why do you have to call all werewolves dogs, leech?" I flash an innocent smile.

"Why are you trying your hardest to get under my skin?"

392

*What do you think?*

"Uh . . . because it's funny."

Commander Vlad lets out a slight snicker.

Wow, he can laugh too? That's mind-blowing.

"Seriously, Claire, would you like to go see your friend?"

He earns a wide-eyed stare from me.

Is he serious? He really would take me to go see Embry without a fight? Wow, this is new.

"You will do that for me?" I ask. I mean it's already set in stone that I'm most likely the biggest drama queen in history, but seriously, this is major progress.

His lips curve into a half smile, his head tilted to one side. "Why do you seem to be surprised? I'm here to protect, serve, and provide you with whatever you need, remember?" He pauses for a second. "Right now, you need to go drive someone else crazy, anyone other than me. Why wouldn't I take you to go bother your friend?"

If my eyes were wide before, they might have popped by now. Never in a million centuries would I expect Mr. Meany to be anything but mean. I don't even know how to respond. I'm lost for words.

I must have gone into some type of shock because he is already waving his hand in front of my face—I did not even notice him walking toward me. That brings me back to reality real quick. He's taking a play out of my own book.

"Hey, don't pull it on me. I think I'm rubbing off on you," he states. Commander Vlad puts his mask back on, turning back to Mr. Meany, as we walk out of the door.

Bipolar!

\*     \*     \*

It wasn't hard to find Embry. Our noses basically led the way. Her potent and distinctive scent is really hard to ignore.

393

As we were on our way, Mr. Meany explained that all creatures, including humans, rely on their senses. He said the main difference between humans and supernatural beings is that the latter's senses are more enhanced and are used for more than touching, tasting, seeing, smelling, and hearing.

I didn't understand what he meant. Luckily for me, Mr. Meany is not being so mean today. He broke everything down, giving examples. He said we humans use our ears to listen, which is normal and totally expected. However, some supernatural creatures have learned how to use their ears to see, kind of like an echo which allows them to analyze their surroundings by the way sound reflects off objects around them. It does make a lot of sense if you think about it.

According to him, many supernatural creatures like werewolves and lycans depend on their sense of smell much more than on their other senses, which explains why Mecca is always sniffing. Apparently to them, they can find food, communicate, and sense danger through a scent. Vampires also utilize their sense of smell to locate their mate and even others.

The first thing I notice the moment we find Embry, before we are even in plain view, is her flaring nostrils. It proves that Mr. Meany was right.

Embry's eyes glow that unusual shade of gold. A dreadful expression seems to plague her delicate features, only to completely disappear when her eyes land on me.

It's not the season for flowers to bloom, but Embry's unique scent of wildflower and damp earth makes it seem like spring. The white bed of snow covering the ground and the tall oak trees surrounding us host their own type of earthly beauty—it's enchanting. Embry is an enchantress herself. She does look like a porcelain doll with her natural cherry blush, snow-white skin, long dark-brown hair, and big hazel eyes. She is blessed, and I know for a fact that it runs in her family. She is wearing an oversized black turtleneck, a long black trench coat, and some oversized black biker

394

jeans. She is dressed to impress in her beloved's clothes, just like me.

"I'll be sitting there." Mr. Meany points to the tiny house that's inside the garden. "Just remember our talk about my kind having greatly enhanced senses," he reminds me.

I roll my eyes.

*Yes, Dad.* I wanted to say but somehow held my tongue. He's been nice today, so I guess I should be nice too.

"Are you okay?" Embry asks the moment Mr. Meany walks into the house. "I was worried about you. King Cyrus wouldn't allow me to go see you. He kept saying you were occupied."

*Occupied? Hmm. Nicklaus told me that Embry and King Cyrus were busy. It looks like the kings were the only ones who were really occupied . . . with lying and trying to keep us apart. Asswipes. Nicklaus has some explaining to do.*

I can understand why King Cyrus would want Embry in the safety of his room. Everyone else acts like she's some wild animal that's ready to pounce.

"Yeah, I'm fine," I answer slowly, taking a seat beside her.

The real question should be, Is she okay? No matter how pretty she is, it's almost impossible not to see how stressed she looks.

Embry stares at me with those big hazel eyes of hers, then she suddenly scrunches up her nose and makes a weird face.

"Do I smell?" I take a sniff of my fur coat. At least, I have one piece of clothing on that actually belongs to me.

"Oh God, no," she quickly answers. "I'm sorry. I didn't mean to offend you. It's just you smell like their king, mixed with an unfamiliar scent and a very familiar one. I just can't place my finger on it." She releases a frustrated sigh. "I believe it's your coat," she says a second later. "Where did you get it from?"

"Mecca," I answer.

Oh, now I understand. Embry's uncle is the alpha of the Northern Pack. She is familiar with them, so she must have recognized Mecca's scent.

"Who is Mecca?" She quirks her thick eyebrows.

I stare at her, wide-eyed.

*Who is Mecca? She is the craziest she-wolf of all time. I am sure she knows her. Plus, Mecca is the mate of her uncle, who has an entire hallway dedicated to her memory. How can she not know?*

I think over my own question.

*Oh right, I almost forgot she had been taken away from her family, most likely before Mecca returned.*

"When were you taken, Embry?" I ask after a while.

She breaks eye contact.

Now I feel bad. It's obvious she is still struggling with everything that's going on. I can see it all over her face, almost like I can see what's inside her head. "You don't have . . . to answer. I understand."

"No, no, no, it's fine. It hasn't been that long, not even a full passing moon." She sighs.

I really feel bad. Whatever pain she is experiencing is still fresh.

The supernatural community uses moons to make reference to time. One moon equals one month. At least, the academy taught us something. How to tell time was probably the best lesson the school had to offer.

"I just miss my family." She clears her throat after a few minutes of silence. "I'm worried about them. My father and I didn't really leave on good terms, and my cousin needs me now more than ever, especially after . . ." she trails off. Visible pain suddenly crosses her features.

Embry reminds me of Jadis right now. So much pain from her past is on her shoulders. This is proof that humans are not the only ones suffering because of the way things are. So much needs to change.

"I met your dad, and he seemed pretty nice," I tell her, lying through my teeth.

*He is far from nice.*

Embry's face brightens. "You know I can tell when you're lying," she responds with a giggle. "Your heartbeat picks up when you aren't telling the truth. I didn't really need to hear it. I have known my father for a century now, and he's far from nice," she admits, taking the words right out of my head.

"You caught me there." I release a small giggle of my own.

*Mr. Meany and I just had a conversation about their heightened senses. How stupid can I be?*

"I did get to meet him, your father, and I can assure you he is fine," I tell her, not wanting to sound like a complete liar.

Actually, he is more than fine. The last time I saw him, he was drenched in his enemies's blood. He was lethal.

Embry stares at me skeptically, then she gives me a look of utter shock. "That wasn't a lie," she says, as her eyes travel to my fur coat. "That's why you smell so familiar. Someone from my uncle's territory gave you this coat."

"Yes, I told you. Mecca gave it to me. She's a good friend of mine and your uncle's long-lost mate."

Embry's big and bright hazel eyes widen. She jumps up off the bench. "So she did make it home safely. Thank Goddess. She had been missing before I was even born. Prior to my abduction, my brother had told me she was on her way home. I often wondered if she ever made it."

*Wait, did she just say before she was . . . ?*

"Is my sister okay? Have you met her? How is Celine? When did Mecca return? How do you know her? Have you met my aunt?" she asks.

At this point, I don't even believe her own questions are registering inside her head before they come out of her mouth.

"Whoa, whoa, whoa. Slow down." I hold my hands up in mock surrender. "I'm only human, remember? I can't pick up on everything so fast."

She frowns. "Oh right. Sorry. I just really miss them." She flashes me an apologetic smile.

"They miss you too. They even declared war against the vampires just because of what happened to you."

"They did what?" she speaks quietly. A look of horror shoots to her face like a gun.

*What did I just do?*

Call it a sixth sense or something, but I can see, hear, and feel the panic attack coming before it actually arrives—which is extremely weird. She's a wolf for Luna's sake!

"There was an attack," I tell her. My nearly enhanced, sensitive ears decide to go into overdrive and pick up on her booming, racing heartbeats.

"Who attacked?" Her voice is now extremely low.

My mouth closes instantly. Something inside me screamed that I had to shut my big mouth, but it's too late.

Her entire face turns red, and her bright eyes widen. They flicker from gold to hazel, to gold again, and then back to golden hazel. She brings her hands up to her chest and starts to gasp for air.

*F*ck.*

"Oh God! No. Embry, breathe!" I jump to my feet, then place my hand on her back.

Commander Vlad appears in the blink of an eye, yanking me behind him. "Get out of here, Claire." He crouches down, preparing for a fight.

"Nooo!" I scream, jumping in front of Embry.

It's not her fault. It's mine. I just had to open my big mouth. Stupid, stupid self.

Embry pushes me into Mr. Meany, and he growls in response to her action. She crouches, releasing a cry of pain. My

398

eyes grow wide as I watch her wolf struggle to take over. Pearl-white and gray fur pokes from out of her hands that soon turn into paws. She growls low, showing her scary canines.

My head starts pounding. I can feel Nicklaus attempting to break in, but I push him away. I focus all my attention on Embry. Her once hazel-and-gold eyes are now pure golden. Her clothing is drenched in sweat, and her waist-length dark hair is turning silver-gray. She screams louder, her skin looking more transparent. Her wolf seems to be almost breaking free. She is somehow stuck between half human and half wolf, and it is certainly the scariest sh*t I have ever seen—even scarier than Mecca's turning, which was already downright frightening.

King Cyrus appears. He is with two other vampires I don't have time to fully analyze who. Panic and shock settle on King Cyrus's face the moment he sees Embry. He attempts to touch her. It only earns him a growl and a snap of her canines at his hand, forcing him to take a step back.

Embry's entire body is now bent over, spots of gray fur visible on her arms and neck. She's attempting to control her wolf the best she can, but her inner beast is demanding control. It's evident she's experiencing intense pain, torture, and excruciation—it breaks my heart.

*What's happening to her? What have I done?*

Her bones make a clenching sound. Her suffering, unbearable and heart-wrenching, becomes my own. She screams in the next second and fall to her knees before her entire body goes still.

"Embry," I call to her, my heart racing, drastically.

Her head snaps in my direction. She stands to her feet, and that's when I see it. The battle for control she was attempting less than a second ago is long gone. She has lost it. Her wolf has taken over completely. She is still half-fazed, her golden eyes cold and dark.

All the others are now preparing for a fight while Embry's wolf is sizing them up, daring to attack them. King Cyrus is the first to lunge, but she dodges and then she swings her claw out, scratching his left arm in the process.

One of the vampires I now recognize to be King Marcellus steps forward, studying his prey.

King Cyrus's neck snaps in his direction. "Stay the f*ck out of this!" he growls, still struggling to gain hold of his deranged beloved.

The other vampires stand still, allowing him to take full control for now as they tangle in a passionate dance of anger, love, and hurt. The way she moves with grace of a predator reminds me of her lethal and well-trained father. King Cyrus is not fighting, only attempting to contain her, but she is too fast. She sends strike after strike. Crimson-red blood smears across his chest.

Hot rage sears down my spine, and I shiver. That's when I feel him; he's close. Nicklaus is coming, bringing a mesh of fury with him.

My inner voice is screaming at me once again, *Stop this! Stop this fast. Think, think, think. His presence will only make things worse. I know it. I can feel it.*

The scent of expensive cologne and burning cedarwood floats in the air. Embry stops her attack on her beloved at once, her eyes shooting to the door.

"Embry," King Cyrus calls.

In the next second, Nicklaus comes into view, and Embry turns into her full-fledged pearl-white and gray wolf.

# CHAPTER FIFTY-FOUR
## Time to Protect

Embry's wolf pounces in his direction. I lunge and catch her silver-gray wolf in midair. We land on the snow-covered ground with a loud thud. I don't feel anything, my senses fully alert. Embry's wildflower and damp earth aroma that is now more potent than when she is in her true form invades my senses. She stands on four paws while I pull myself up off the ground in inhuman speed, only to crouch down into a defense position and wait for her to make her first move.

My eyes drift to Nicklaus. His own eyes shoot fire, ash, and sizzling hot coal.

"She lost against her wolf!" shouts Xander from behind me.

A chilling silence lingers in the air as everyone watches Embry intensely.

"You promised," says King Cyrus, then he steps closer toward her. "Allow me to calm her down."

Embry snaps her monstrous jaws in Nicklaus's direction. Her wolf makes her intentions extremely clear. She wants him, his blood.

*"Keep everyone out of this."* I enter Nicklaus's mind.

*"Are you f*cking crazy?"* he snarls.

My eyes are now on Embry, but I know for a fact his eyes are glowing bright red and are centered on me.

"Don't intervene!" I shout out loud, in a voice that is not my own.

An audible gasp bounces off the trees, confirming that the voice is very much not my own.

"Please, Nicklaus. Embry is your best friend's beloved. Please!"

I can sense his dilemma and frustration over my words. He's struggling to control his own monster that is clawing inside his chest. I can also sense worry rushing through his emotions, not only for me but also for Embry and King Cyrus. He doesn't want to hurt either of them.

*"She attacked you,"* he hisses inside my mind. He seems to be battling with himself.

*"She was going for you, not me. Please, Nicklaus. Give me a chance to calm her down."*

*"You're f\*cking human."* His words boom inside my mind.

I tune the rest of his words out and pay attention to my surroundings. In my peripheral vision, I can see everything going on around me. King Cyrus is now in a threatening stance, ready to take out whoever dares to touch his beloved. He will protect her as he should—even against his own king, if that's what it comes to. I can feel Xander's deadly and dangerous presence. He is ready to kill anyone he deems to be a threat to me. Commander Vlad's blazing red eyes are also extremely hard to ignore.

I have King Marcellus's undivided attention. I can sense his monster's wickedly delightful soul as they watch the scene unfold with unconcealed interest.

The other vampire I have never seen before is also watching me with a curious red-eye stare. King Cyrus will fight to the very death against all of these men to protect his beloved. I know he will.

My beloved will do the same to keep me safe, but they shouldn't fight against one another. We should all be united, fighting side by side.

My attention zooms back onto Embry when she starts to circle me. Her silver-gray wolf is flawless, just as beautiful as the human caged inside her.

I stand to my feet, and Nicklaus's body tenses behind me. "Embry, I know you can hear me. I don't want you to get hurt," I coo.

Her wolf growls.

*Okay, now that didn't go too well. Think, think, think.*

We circle each other, and the others watch us intensely. My skin tingles as the pendant hanging from my neck draws forth its now familiar power. I push it back in, refusing to allow the powerful magic to have its way. I can do this without actually hurting her. I know I can.

I can tell my beloved's impatience is running extremely thin. He is still struggling, attempting to figure out the best course of action to take. I can feel his monster thinking for him, slowly but shortly taking over. He looks at Embry's wolf and sees a threat. His monster doesn't know logic.

My own dark and menacing presence lingers in the back of my mind. It is watching, waiting, and searching for the right time to strike. It is dying to make itself known, silently whispering inside my mind to give it the opportunity to take over. It's weird how it feels like it's another person living inside me, but somehow I know it's a part of me—darker and more dangerous—with a mind of its own. It wants to take control, but I won't allow that to happen.

I stare into Embry's eyes and see no sign of that sweet and fragile human girl.

*She is lost inside her own mind, caged by her own wolf.*

Nicklaus grinds his teeth. *"I'm sorry Claire,"* he says inside my head.

I give him a penetrating gaze.

"She is lost inside her own mind!" he says out loud, speaking the exact words I was just thinking. His eyes travel to King Cyrus. "Brother, I'm sorry. I hope you can forgive me."

"Nooo!" King Cyrus's growls savagely.

The exact moment I shut everything out around me, my heart starts to thud. My skin also tingles, and my neck suddenly itches as the familiar but foreign feeling rushes through my body. And before anyone could move, an electric emerald-green light flashes out of my hand, knocking everyone—except Embry—off their feet, pinning them in place. Ear-splitting growls fill the air. Unfortunately, I don't have time to pinpoint who growls the loudest.

Embry rushes toward me. Once closer, she pounces in the air. I duck just in time, making her miss me. Thankfully, luck is on my side. I swiftly sweep my leg out, and she stumbles over a branch and then falls onto the ground. I can feel the power of the emerald rising and Nicklaus's desperate attempt to gain control over his body. I get to my feet, my mind searching for a game plan.

*Focus, Claire! That's the only way to prevent bloodshed.*

With that thought, I pounce on Embry, knocking her to the ground. She claws at me, but I move faster and somehow manage to pin her down. She growls threateningly as I gently but firmly hold her neck down in place. She continues to shake violently under my tight grip. She is stronger than she looks, much stronger, so she shakes me off with ease.

*Ugh.*

She plunges her sharp claws into my calf, and pain chars across my left lower leg.

*F\*ck, my luck is running out.*

She digs deeper. Everything around me is in slow motion once again. My heart is pounding, skin tingling, and my neck suddenly itching. Embry's monster drags her massive claws through my skin, digging a little deeper. Intense pain sears through my leg, and the world seems to stop. Instincts take over once again as I reach out my hand to touch her.

"*Cessabit* (Calm down)," I speak in a language I don't understand. "*Derivare, parum lupus* (Shift, little wolf.)"

Bright emerald-green lights flash out of my hand and spread through Embry's entire body, covering her whole. Her pearly-white and silver-gray fur changes to snow-white skin.

The world then goes blank.

\*       \*       \*

"Firecracker."

His voice is the first thing I hear. I open my eyes and stare into his own teary ones. "What happened?" I lift my body up to see we are now in his room. I feel like I just had the best sleep of my life, and now I am ready to run a marathon, if that's what the day brings forth. I feel good.

Nicklaus is sitting on a chair that wasn't here before. He is wearing dress slacks and a black silk dress shirt that is unbuttoned all the way up, providing me with a view of his carved-by-a-god, muscular chest. He looks like hell, his one hand running through his pitch-black hair while the other gently stroking my left hand. A glass of untouched blood and a bucket of soapy water are at his feet. He's staring into my eyes like they are the center of his world, looking defeated—like a pirate forced to bury his most-valuable treasure.

I reach out my hand to touch his face. "Why do you look so sad, my ass-kissing king?"

He remains silent.

I try to enter into his mind, but it is closed off, shut like a closed door. I don't know how to break through his barrier without proper guidance.

*How did we get here? I can't seem to remember anything past Embry and me chitchatting in the garden this afternoon. It's a little troublesome. Nicklaus must have done some freaky vampire thing. That is the only logical explanation.*

"Did you do some vampire voodoo crap on me again?"

405

My question causes his lips to twitch into a half-smile—there goes my ass-kissing king.

"I wouldn't be able to use my vampire voodoo even if I wanted to." He releases a frustrated sigh.

"You just did."

He doesn't respond but starts rubbing soft circles over my hand. He doesn't blink. He refuses to remove the hooks his eyes placed inside my soul.

I break eye contact and attempt to get out of bed, but he stops me.

"You need to rest, Claire."

"Are you kidding me? I feel like an energized bunny. What time is it anyway? It seems I slept all day." I pull back the covers and make my way out of the bed.

That's when I see three large beast's claws tattooed onto my skin.

"Jeepers creepers! What the f*ck is this?"

Nicklaus flinches at my reaction and hurriedly places me back into bed before I have the chance to actually get out of it. My skin is tattered. Swollen red marks run from up and down my left leg, and three large purplish claw marks are on my calf. I don't feel an ounce of pain. I wouldn't even have known they were there if it weren't for the visible proof in my flesh.

I stare at my leg, wary.

Nicklaus places his hand gently on the side of my injured calf and kisses it softly before pulling the covers back over my body. "You need to rest, firecracker," he speaks softly. "Your body has been through a major trauma."

*You think!*

"Can you please explain to me what the hell is going on?" I ask, slightly raising my voice.

*Why can't I remember? The wounds are still fresh. They most certainly cause intense pain. I should feel pain now.*

After making sure I'm in a comfortable position, Nicklaus sits back in the chair. He stares out of the window for a long while.

"You were attacked," he finally says. His eyes hold the pain that my leg doesn't feel. "Cyrus's beloved attacked you."

*Who, Embry?*

"No way! Embry is not like that."

"That's your problem!" he snaps. He stands up. "You're too trusting. You continue to place yourself in danger, willing to give your life for others you don't know anything about."

Multiple footsteps can be heard as his voice gets louder.

"Claire, Embry is a she-wolf you willingly provoked in some idle attempt to save me. I'm a vampire. I don't need your f*cking protection!" he yells.

*What? I'm so lost.*

"That Mecca b*tch is a she-wolf. You also willing jumped in front of her when a bullet was flying in her direction. She's a dog! She doesn't need you to f*cking save her." His eyes flash violently with each word that comes out of his mouth. "You're a f*cking human. Why the f*ck don't you get?"

His words send bullets to my heart.

"And you're the one who pulled the trigger," I remind him.

*How dare you?*

Nicklaus releases a spine-chilling growl. He picks up the chair and throws it, sending it flying across the room. It slams into the door, leaving a large hole.

Xander, Commander Vlad, and another vampire rush into the room, their eyes bloodshot red.

"Nicklaus," calls Xander warningly from behind him.

Nicklaus's blazing red eyes move in Xander's direction. "Don't Nicklaus me," he hisses. "She wants to know what happened, so tell her! Tell her!" he screams. "Tell her how her foolish and reckless behavior left a permanent scar that my blood won't heal." He turns back around to face me and then stalks back

407

to the bed. "Tell her how her immature mind almost cost her her f*cking life."

Nicklaus's eyes are filled with raw emotion and so much pain. Disappointment and hurt are visible on every inch of his beautiful face.

"Tell Claire how her foolish little stunt made her heart stop beating, forcing me to give her my venom," he adds.

"What?" I shoot up.

*What is he saying?*

Wordlessly, he walks out of the room and leaves me.

# CHAPTER FIFTY-FIVE
## Time to Bathe

Xander explained everything after Nicklaus angrily stormed out of the room.

Apparently, Embry went apesh*t in the afternoon, trying to control her wolf. Xander told me that if a werewolf denies their inner beast the opportunity to shift when it needs to, it will fight for control. And if the human loses the fight, they go apesh*t, which is exactly what Xander said had happened to Embry.

It's crazy, right? Xander thinks that Embry's inner wolf was controlling her mind and body. Her inner wolf overpowered her human.

He said there have even been cases when the wolf takes full control of their human for the rest of their lives. Xander doesn't understand how or why it happens. He just knows it can happen.

He also told me that I somehow achieved the impossible, freeing her from her wolf's hold. However, it came with a price—my life. Nicklaus saved me by giving me his venom. He *attempted* to change me—key word: attempted. He gave me his venom in hopes that my body would accept the change. Now here's another mystery. I rejected the turn, and miraculously my heart started to beat again. It beats slowly and faintly, but it still beats. I'm still human for now, which is alarming.

Xander said he had never seen anything like it, ever! They all are freaking out, which is why I'm in prison. I am detained in

Nicklaus's room and on bed rest, under strict surveillance by none other than Mr. Meany. Nicklaus somehow found a vampire doctor to run some test on me as though I were a lab rat.

Xander left a couple of hours ago. He went to make sure that Nicklaus and King Cyrus don't rip each other's head off. Judging by how long he has been gone, that must be a nearly impossible task. He assured me that Embry is safe, but Cyrus took her away when I was sleeping. No one knows where he took her.

My mind is spinning. I must admit I am worried. Who wouldn't be, really? I could have died, right? Let's not forget, though, that out of nowhere I was able to access some foreign power that basically helped me achieve the impossible. No one understands how or why I wielded such power. I mean, come on. Nicklaus and Xander have been around for centuries, I think.

This brings me to worry number three. They have been around for a long while, and even they can't seem to explain what's going on with me—how I died and then somehow came back to life without becoming a vampire. I'm a freak of nature. Am I even human? I feel like I'm some unknown species.

Nicklaus is still pissed at me. He has been checking on me, going back and forth to make sure I'm still breathing, eating, and on bed rest. But it seems like I'm more of a prisoner instead. He leaves again without even sparing me a single glance, not that I want him to. I'm just as pissed as him.

Okay, that's the half-truth. I am pissed, really pissed. I'm upset with him for lashing out at me. Even though I do understand why he did it, I can't help that I feel the need to save other people, just like he can't help that he needs to sink his fangs into them. Regardless, I deserve his comfort. I need him to tell me it's going to be okay. I don't think it's fair that he is acting as if I didn't exist at all. It kind of hurts.

Okay, that's another half-truth. It actually hurts a lot more than I care to admit.

That's all I can think about. My own thoughts are driving me to the brink of insanity. I've been lying in bed ever since Nicklaus snapped, and that was last night. I don't have the energy to move, but I'm tired of lying in my own prison, so I pull myself up and get out of bed. It's early morning—a new day for a fresh start, hopefully. I'm going to see if Nicklaus is still going to take me to see Mecca. I don't think he will, but trying won't hurt. I miss her, and I need to make sure she is okay.

I want to relax, refresh myself, and regenerate. I think I'll feel better after I've cleaned up. Besides, I'm dying to get out of these blood-stained clothes. The vampire doctor refused to allow me to change them even when he finished running a blood test, which was all goddamn night. He didn't even let me use the potty. He placed some tube in my kitty that magically collected my urine.

Gross! I'm going to take a long bath and just relax.

Mr. Meany is still here. He had watched the doctor from the couch like a hawk, making sure he didn't leave a single scratch on my heavily guarded body. I tried to speak to him, but he ignored me; we are back to square one. He's lying on the couch, getting lost in his own world—which is what I'm about to do. I'm closing the bathroom door to be lost in a world of my own. I don't really think I am actually stepping into a new world, but that's exactly where I am now.

The bathroom is stone gray like the bedroom. A squeaky clean glass shower, maybe big enough for three people at most, is sitting to its left side. However, that's not what catches my eyes. No, not at all. It's the bathtub—or should I say square tub?—that is big enough for me to swim in. It is directly in front of a big square window overlooking the perfect view of the snow-covered ground, trees, and mountaintops. I can see the gray mist in the sky and enjoy the beauty of the mountain in the early morning. The stunning nature takes my breath away. The tub is most certainly fit for a king, and queen if I must add.

I am anxious to get inside. I start to run some warm water and some of the bubble baths I just found underneath the sink into the tub. The bottle looks ancient, but the fragrance of honey is still freshly reserved. I even found a bottle labeled *bath milk*, which piqued my interest because I'd never heard of milk being made for a bath. I guess there are just a lot of things I don't know.

I sigh.

That's expected, considering my upbringing. To be honest, I've never seen or used a bubble bath until now. The academies we attended weren't that grand, and they damn sure didn't hold items of luxury—well, at least not for humans anyway. We are not that important.

Here come the thoughts about Nicklaus.

*He makes me feel important. How long is he going to stay mad at me? I miss him. Oh God, Claire, stop acting so goddamn clingy.*

I should smack myself back to reality.

Desperately seeking to change my thought pattern, I sit on the edge of the tub and pour both liquids in the steamy running water. I watch with fascination as the honey-smelled liquid turns into bubbles while the milky one turns the water from clear to milky white.

There is a button built into the tub. "Activate jets," I read the words out loud.

*What's that?*

Curiosity kills the cat, and I push the button. I flinch as the milky-white water starts to roar and bubble of its own accord.

"It's a Jacuzzi tub," Nicklaus's husky voice says from behind me.

I didn't even hear him come in. I turn to face him. "Huh?" I ask, most likely sounding exactly how I feel—clueless.

"The tub is called a Jacuzzi tub."

I nod. "Oh cool."

*Really, Claire?*

That's all I could come up with. Like what am I, ten?

His lips curve into a smile.

*Gosh, that beautiful, sadistic smile. I just want him to kiss me
already, then we'll make up. I'm whipped. I know.*

"So I take it you're no longer mad at me?"

*Please, don't be mad. Please, don't be mad.*

"No, I'm still mad," he says to me. "That's why I'm here.
It's time for your punishment."

"Punishment?"

"Punishment," he repeats casually.

Call it a hunch, but I think I'm going to like that
punishment.

My eyes momentarily sweep over him. He's wearing a black
turtleneck sweater, a nicely tailored gray trench coat, and an
expensive pair of black designer jeans. The silver watch on his left
wrist must also be expensive. His jet-black hair is nicely slicked
back—the style provides the perfect view of his extraordinary
cerulean eyes.

*He's so handsome. I'd rather he punished me naked.*

"Do you like what you see?" he teases, as he leans on the
door frame.

I smile. Nicklaus knows I do like what I see. I remember
the first time he asked me that question. He still has the same effect
on me as he did the first time we met, and he knows that. He is a
cocky, arrogant man.

I love it. This arrogant teasing behavior turns me on. That's
most likely why he's doing it. He is the type of man that wants a
woman to drool and drop to their knees to beg for forgiveness. I'll
drool, but I'm not dropping down and begging for anyone. Instead,
I'll bend over backward and do a backflip and a split on top of him.
I'll do anything for him. There is no point in continuing to live in
denial. I got it bad.

He walks over toward the tub and dips his right hand into
the water. His eyes linger on the water for a second, then he speaks

again, "I see, you have found my personal stash. I've always fancied the smell of milk and warm honey." He stares at me. "Always."

"Yeah, it smells nice." I turn off the bathwater. The beacon of heaven is calling for me to dive in. "I never used bath milk," I admit. "The view is amazing by the way."

"Yeah, it is," he says, without breaking eye contact. He raises an eyebrow, as if lost in thought. "You never used bath milk?"

"No. I didn't even know bath milk exists."

His lips curve into a mischievous smirk. "I could have given you a milk bath, honey," he teases more, wiggling his eyebrows.

My face is set on flames. Now, why do I feel like his words have a deeper meaning?

I lower my head, suddenly feeling breathless. His beautiful stare always puts invisible hooks into my soul, always.

"I have all of my bathtubs placed by a window in most of my houses around the world," he tells me, changing the subject. He turns off the heat.

"How many houses do you have?"

What I should be asking is, Why do you like to take a bath in front of the window? But that would make me a hypocrite because I'm dying to have a bath in front of the window too.

"A lot," is his vague answer. "I usually take a bath before painting. Studying different landscapes helps me prepare and clear my mind."

"You paint? I didn't know you have an interest in art."

He sits down right beside me. "You know more than you think, firecracker."

Again, I feel like his words have a deeper meaning.

Deciding to ignore my hunch, I place my focus on the beauty of the early morning. We sit in silence and enjoy the view for about five minutes, then somehow, one of his magical fingers makes its way to my hair. Nicklaus tucks a loose strand of hair from

414

my messy bun behind my ear, sending a sudden chill traveling through my entire body. His finger lingers behind my ear for a while before it travels down the side of my neck.

His touch is always a work of a skillful artist. I don't know why I even doubted that he is capable of making a piece of art. His touch right now is proof he can create a masterpiece with or without a paintbrush.

He leans over, bringing forth an invisible force to send shivers down my spine. He places his warm lips dangerously close to the base of my neck. "Art is a form of expression," he whispers. His warm lips are now close to my ear, his minty breath fanning the base of my neck.

"Art speaks the colorful language when dull words are unable to explain the intensity of the moment. A paintbrush can paint a vivid picture of the six identified basic emotions." He plants one sweet kiss on my neck.

It feels so good, so very good.

"But the mind of the artist is what truly holds the story," he continues, now nibbling on my ear.

*Good God.*

He nibbles, sucks, and tastes with that skillful, warm tongue of his. Delightful memories of all the wonders it can bring surface. He most certainly is an artist creating pleasure-filled memories with a swift of his silky tongue.

I moan, the soft beating of my gentle heart picking up.

"Take off your clothes, firecracker, and I'll show you how good I am at creating art."

I gulp. The rational side of me is telling me to take my clothes off while the not-so-rational side is asking me to do the same, so I'll obey.

I stand in front of him and start to follow his command. First, I lift his oversized shirt over my head. There's no point in playing shy. He has seen everything there is to see on my body. I want him to capture it, and that's exactly what his brilliant cerulean eyes are doing. They glow brighter than usual as they take me in.

Nicklaus studies the necklace around my neck and then slowly ranks my entire upper body, drenching me in heat and burning me with his lust-filled stare that seems to linger longer than usual as he patiently waits for my next action.

I unclasp my bra extremely slowly, and an animalistic growl purrs from his chest as a response to my teasing. His eyes are scouting every inch of my body, and I can very much imagine him bathing me in his own man-made milk.

"You're moving too slowly," he complains, his facial expression primal and raw. His desire speaks clearly without actual words.

I can see him creating a masterpiece with a single touch of his gifted hands. I now understand what he meant when he said the artist's mind holds the story. His eyes are painting it—a vivid and visual one.

He wraps his muscular arms around my waist, providing my body with the hot-and-cold effect his touch always brings and chasing all my worries away as he pulls me into him.

"I told you to take your clothes off," he whispers.I meant all of them."

My heart beats profusely inside my chest.

Nicklaus places his warm and gentle lips in the crook of my neck before he starts to nibble and suck on a certain spot of my skin—my spot, that spot that makes my juice flow freely. He takes a very deep breath and then runs his silky tongue up and down, tasting me. Up and down he goes.

"Nicklaus," I moan, no longer able to hold it back. "God, it feels so good."

"I'm not God, firecracker."

Did I just say that out loud? I did say that out loud.

"I'm the artist that's going to take my time painting on every inch of your canvas," he says, "starting with my tongue."

Oh my God, I can't think. The warmth of his lips and the frost of his minty breath—they're too much to take.

Then he stops, taking all away. His body tenses up behind me. "I've got to go, firecracker."

*What?*

"You are not serious!"

He groans and releases me. "I'm sorry, my queen." He walks toward the bathroom door. "I am . . . I will make it up to you. I promise."

"You make promises you can't keep," I mutter under my breath.

He's back in front of me before I can even blink. "Take a bath and relax. I'll take you to go see your friend when I get back and finish what I just started after that."

"Really?"

"Really, Claire. I always keep my promises."

# CHAPTER FIFTY-SIX
## Time Is Ticking

NICKLAUS

Leaving her half-naked in the washroom was the hardest thing I've ever done. My penis is still suffering the consequences. Right now it's as hard as a f*cking rock. I try my hardest not to run back there and plunge it into her sweet-tasting slick folds. This is f*cking torture; she is f*cking torture. I am hooked.

Xander constantly attempted to communicate with me while I was enjoying the amazing view of Claire. I assumed he was cock-blocking. Turns out he wasn't. The doctor found something interesting in Claire's blood samples. Hopefully, we can finally get some answers.

Doctor Regus usually treats vampires in New York City. I didn't think that bringing him, an outsider, into our situation was the best route, and neither did Xander. Count Cloven was the one to have actually persuaded me to get him involved. He pointed out several times that Claire's heart barely beat. Now it is even sometimes hard for my sensitive ears to pick up on it.

I need to figure out what's going on with Claire as soon as possible. We still have to deal with the summons, and I need reassurance that she is healthy before we travel to Romania. Time is ticking. I know my father will hunt us down if we don't make it there by the end of the week. He will hunt us to the ends of the earth if that's what it takes. He is a dick.

I'm still agitated that he and the sh*thole of a council even had the nerve to summon me as if I were some typical commoner. Hell, I'm their f*cking king, if you want to be technical. The only reason I'm entertaining the summons is because Claire is involved. As king of all kings, I'm the only person who can say, "F*ck the summons, I'm not coming." Claire and the other kings, on the other hand, cannot. My beloved will be killed on sight if she does not present herself. The other kings can be punished too. I'll never let that happen. They are all my brothers. I refuse to allow my father to place his hands on any of them. F*ck, I hate that man with a passion.

I walk past my men who are standing at my oakwood office door, not sparing them a single glance. The doctor is sitting at the end of the table, fidgeting with his gown. It's quite clear he is nervous.

Xander, Marcellus, and Cloven are already seated and are having a casual conversation. It pains me that Cyrus is not here to figure this out alongside me. Things got pretty bloody between us last night, but in all honesty, I can't blame him. If he tried to take out Claire, he would be dead. I don't care how many centuries we have known each other and how close we are, but Claire comes before everybody, so it's completely understandable that Cyrus feels the same way about Embry. Her wolf has every right to hate me, but I just couldn't allow her to accidentally hurt my beloved during her deranged state. She may be a sweet human, but a wolf is a wolf. They kill with no mercy, especially when their wolf takes over. That was just a chance I wasn't willing to take. Claire is too important.

The others continued to converse until I take my seat. Xander's unemotional gaze falls onto me. He's waiting for me to dismiss the others, or more like Marcellus, but I am not going to do so. He will find out the truth sooner than later, so f*ck it. I will no longer hide who Claire is to me. I am ashamed of nothing. My

419

beloved is the future queen, whether they like it or not. No one can stop it. She will make a way better queen than any of the respected women of our bloodline. Anyone who disagrees can f*ck off and die.

I place a timer down on the table and look at Doctor Regus. "You have ten minutes to explain what you have found," I tell him, starting the timer.

Marcellus snickers underneath his breath while the others are paying attention to the doctor as he gulps.

"Nine minutes!" I growl.

"My apologies, my king," he says, rising to his feet. He makes his way toward the front of the office and pulls down the projector screen we use for presenting war strategies. He quickly taps on his laptop and an image appears on the screen. "This is the human girl's blood cells I collected," he begins.

I turn to study what he is presenting. I don't know that much about science, but for the looks of things they seem normal.

"From first glance, they look normal," he says, confirming my theory. Then he zooms in the image.

My eyes bulge, and I hear a gasp from someone behind me.

"If you look closer, you can see they are far from normal," Doctor Regus goes on. "Claire's cells have black outlines around the surface. Royal vampire blood cells are black with specks of silver, normal vampire blood cells are black, and human blood cells are red, which means—"

"She is a dhampir," says Count Cloven skeptically, taking the words right out of my mouth.

"That's impossible," Xander argues. "The institute where she was educated would have reported her the moment she stepped foot in the school."

I rub my chin. Xander has a point. The institute is required to collect blood samples of students every year and have those sent to the lab to be tested. It's one of the ways how we select our candidates as breeders and bleeders. I know for a fact that Claire

420

was tested more than usual. The school requested she should be marked a bleeder. They wanted her dead. Claire's case would have been discovered years ago. There is no way anyone would have overlooked it.

"Furthermore, a dhampir's blood cells have several specks of vampirism," adds Marcellus.

We all turn to face him.

How the f*ck does he know that?

"What?" says Marcellus with a shrug. "I had my experiences with dhampirs, before we eliminated their species altogether. Where do you think I got the idea of hosting the games?"

I shake my head and turn back to the doctor. I don't understand his logic, and I don't think I want to.

"Which brings me to my next slide." Doctor Regus clears his throat. Small drips of sweat—too small for the naked eye to see—are forming on his forehead.

My eyesight is far from naked. He is extremely nervous.

"Why are you so nervous?" I ask him before he turns to the next slide.

Something is off about this doctor. It is typical for commoners to be on edge around us because they are basically humans when you compared them to royal vampires. Even so, they are still drawn to us and tend to even get obsessed with us. Lower-level—or should I say, low bloodline vampires?—can't help serving us, higher-level vampires. It has been that way since our creation. They typically act nervous when they feel like they have wronged us or if they have offended one of us.

The doctor's shaking hands and the sweat dripping on his forehead tell me he did just that. He is putting my monster on edge; he doesn't trust him.

Doctor Regus wipes his forehead. "My apologies, my king. I've just never been in the presence of royalty."

421

I nod in understanding. That makes sense, and I hope that's the case.

He flicks the next slide. "King Marcellus is correct. Blood cells of dhampirs usually have several specks of vampirism. This human girl's cells have nearly invisible specks of vampirism that are growing rapidly." He flicks another slide.

"I collected some of her blood every two hours, and each time a different speck was formed," he continues, flicking the slide again (and we all watch with great interest). "The human girl is certainly a dhampir," Doctor Regus spits with venom.

My monster is now present. We don't like his new tone. Xander and the others, including Marcellus, growl from behind me. They don't like his tone either.

"Do not forget your place, commoner," Marcellus speaks before I get a chance.

Someone is forming a liking to my little firecracker. I see.

Doctor Regus bows. "My apologies, my king," he responds with caution.

"Finish what the f*ck you were saying!" I spit. My monster is now on the horizon. I don't have time for this sh*t.

The doctor is slowly bringing forth my more festive side. My vision begins to tint crimson.

Xander is oddly quiet. I guess he is struggling to contain his own monster at this time.

Doctor Regus stands up quickly. "The girl is most certainly a dhampir."

"You already said that," I say, holding back a growl. "Get to the point! What did you find out? What is your proof?"

He zooms in the image and then walks over to the screen. Tension is obvious in his entire frame. I think someone has a death wish.

Doctor Regus points at the screen, at a tiny silver fleck of vampirism inside one of Claire's blood cells.

I jump out of my seat and make my way in front of him. "What the f*ck is that?" I know what it is, but that is just f*cking impossible. This slide indicates the unthinkable.

Doctor Regus is shaking.

Is this the reason why he is so nervous? Is he f*cking with me, with us?

He shrinks back. "The girl has tiny specks of royal vampirism," he whispers, almost inaudibly. "I noticed that it became more visible after each blood sample I collected."

Xander is now beside us, studyingthe slide in silence.

"The vampirism is like red blood cells," Marcellus states, standing up.

When did he become a f*cking scientist?

"What the hell are you doing in Europe, dissecting humans?" I make a face at him.

"Well, I did host an event of the sort if you must know." He smirks.

Doctor Regus hesitates before he walks back over toward his laptop. "King Marcellus is correct again. The human girl's specks of black and silver blood cells are growing rapidly," he states in a low voice.

My eyes move along with each slide he flicks at a rapid pace. Each one shows the specks growing. I've never seen anything like it.

"Which means that the human girl isn't a human girl, well kind of. She is half-human and half-vampire," Doctor Regus reveals, still moving the slides. "She wasn't born a dhampir based on my evaluation—"

"Dhampirs are born, not created," Marcellus interrupts him.

"She was bitten by a royal," he responds. "That's how the human girl vampire side was first created."

"Impossible," I tell him.

423

"However, it's the only thing that adds up. Someone attempted to change that human!" he spits. His disgust of the situation is evident. The fool can't hide his emotion even if his life depends on it, which it does. "Somehow the human managed to fight off halfway through the transition. It's truly remarkable, but it needs to be reported to the council at once."

The fool's time is up. His foolishness will cost him his life.

My crimson eyes travel to Xander, whose eyes are bleeding as well. Good, we are on the same page.

Count Cloven is taking a sip of his blood with no emotions on his face whereas Marcellus is smiling from ear to ear.

"So what are you suggesting, Doctor?" Xander asks, now in front of him.

Doctor Regus cowers away, his lips quivering. "I-I didn't . . . m-mean to offend you. P-please . . . forgive—" His hands go up in the air in surrender.

I shift my focus back to the screen. My mind is elsewhere—with Claire. My firecracker is one of a kind, truly extraordinary.

The doctor is still pleading for his life behind me.

"Stop playing with your toys," growls Marcellus, sounding excited.

Oh yes, the doctor is still alive.

I turn to face Xander. He now has the doctor by the neck, dangling the commoner in the air. He stares at me, his eyes filled with the excitement to kill. I nod in approval. He can have his life. I don't want to get blood on my attire. Claire and I have a date.

The timer goes off. Marcellus crushes the device in his hand.

"Time is up," I hiss.

Xander lets out a spine-chilling growl and plunges his fangs into the right side of the doctor's neck. Blood gushes from it and down to Xander's mouth. The doctor attempts to scream, but

Xander swiftly pulls out his spine and then tosses him to the floor. Blood oozes out of his throat. He is lifeless.

Impressive! Xander killed him within a second.

"Indeed," I say, my focus back on the screen. "Dispose of any evidence and have Commander Vlad search his laptop, just in case the doctor has sent anyone what he discovered. I want all he has contacted in the last twenty-four hours to be dealt with. We cannot afford this critical information to be leaked." I turn to face them, and they all agree.

"I'll do some research about dhampirs. We need to be sure as this has never happened before and figure out what this turn even means for Claire's overall health. We should also host the dinner sooner than later. We need to know who will remain loyal to you," Xander speaks.

"Especially before we answer the summons. If the council figures out her condition—"

"I pledge my loyalty to you and the half-breed queen," Marcellus cuts me off, earning a low growl from me. He chuckles. "Just kidding, but seriously the queen has my loyalty. Anyone who can spit in your face and go head-to-head with a dog is good with me."

"So is with me," Count Cloven adds. "Wait, she spat in your face?" He laughs, and we all laugh in unison. "She does have balls."

"Yeah, she does. But there are still things that don't add up," says Xander. "Claire's files are missing, not to mention the fact she can still wield power from the emerald. Now that I'm thinking about it, I believe the emerald may be the reason why her body didn't accept the turn."

"It does make sense," I tell him. "I don't know much about the mysterious emerald, but I do know the person who possesses it can call on the power to prevent certain things from occurring."

"The queen may have somehow accessed the power when she was unconscious," suggests Cloven.

"Or maybe the emerald refused to allow the queen to fully complete the transition," Marcellus guesses.

I hold back a smile. My firecracker has gained the respect of a royal and my most-trusted adviser without a proper introduction. She is extraordinary.

"Both of you have good points," I say. "The only creature who can reveal the truth is Aurora, but we all know that she will never—"

"Speak for yourself," Marcellus cuts in again. "I may not have access to Aurora, but I do have access to one of her seven daughters. Circe's hot ass loves my awesomeness." He smirks.

"Mingling with witches is not good for your dick," I tell him. "You should know better."

"It's worth the ride." He wiggles his eyebrows. "I'll reach out to her before the feast. Maybe she can meet us in your kingdom or even in Romania."

"You do that," Xander and I speak in unison.

Cloven's lips curve into a smirk.

"Of course, of course, I will risk my dick for our queen, but I do have one condition," Marcellus states.

I hear Xander sigh. He hates Marcellus's games.

"Of course, you do Marcellus." I make my way to the door. "Enlighten me."

"You know, it's really a simple request. I just want a proper introduction with my queen."

Cloven spits out his blood, and Xander rolls his eyes.

"Done," I assure him. "But it will be later. I've promised Claire that I would take her to see her pets. I also have some other things planned."

"Are you sure that's a good idea?" Xander asks, right before I make it to the door. "Claire's scent is different. Surely, the dog will notice it."

"She has a pet dog?" Marcellus queries. "She is f*cking lit!"

"What the f*ck is lit?" I ask.

426

"Oh come on, man, you are not that old."

Everyone laughs at our little inside joke.

"No, seriously, good point!" I tell Xander. "But you know Claire. She won't rest until she knows the pet is okay."

"Have the commander deliver the other pets instead. Maybe we can tell them to explain that the dog has chosen to return home instead of tagging along with them to the safe house."

I rub my chin. "That's a good idea. We can keep her in prison until the dog finally dies. I gave my word that I wouldn't let any harm come to her. A natural death is more than that dog deserves, but Claire's happiness comes first."

"Dude, you're whipped," Marcellus comments.

I flip him off as I walk out of the door. I don't know why. I really should have taken that as a compliment. I am Claire's ass-kissing king after all.

# CHAPTER FIFTY-SEVEN
## Alone Time

CLAIRE

I step out of the magnificent Jacuzzi tub, feeling relaxed, refreshed, and renewed. My entire body is humming in blissful harmony. My eyes land on some neatly folded clothes placed on top of the toilet seat. I smile to myself, knowing who left them there for me. I smile harder upon realizing that they are actually my belongings. They're nothing too much or too fancy—just a light-gray turtleneck, a full bodysuit, and a set of matching black lace bra and panties. I'm just happy they are mine. Well, technically Nicklaus purchased them for me when I first arrived in his kingdom, so they actually belong to him.

I have gotten dressed. My already bright smile shines sunlight when I spot the book Xander encouraged me to read. It's left on the bathroom sink. Nicklaus's first promise has been fulfilled. This man doesn't understand how much little things mean to me. Oh gosh, I can't get him out of my head. I've been thinking about him ever since he left. Every time I think or see anything, my thought patterns lead right back to him. Hopefully, some reading and fresh air would help me get him off my mind. Yes, that's it! That's what I need.

I grab the book and make my way into the room. I find Mr. Meany half asleep on the sofa that's on the other side of the room.

He looks exhausted, which is expected. His eyes were practically glued open all night as he watched the doctor evaluate me. Whenever the doctor poked a needle into my flesh, and I uttered a single ouch, Mr. Meany was in front of him in a flash with angry eyes. Also, whenever the doctor pulled out some strange tools and examined some parts of my body, Mr. Meany would rudely question him.

I feel guilty he was left to babysit me and the doctor. Vampires don't have to sleep, but from what I've noticed, they do enjoy having wind-down time.

Mr. Meany has been resting on the sofa for over sixteen hours now. Surely, he wants to be in the comfort of a bed, not that the sofa looks uncomfortable. However, a sofa is a place to sit on.

I glance at the clock on the wall above the sofa. It's *7:05 AM*. Mr. Meany has indeed been confined to the sofa for over sixteen hours. I woke up around 2 PM after the incident yesterday, and he has been here ever since Nicklaus stormed out. That's a long time to play guard.

His usual pale-blond, slicked-back hair is now a shaggy mess. His eyes are half-closed, and his left pant leg is rolled up halfway. He reminds me of how I used to look during one of those boring lectures back at school. Nicklaus reminds me of that as well when he is doing any one of his royal duties. He always seems bored. Unless Xander is around, then Nicklaus acts like a class clown—playful and entertaining.

I'v been standing in the same spot for about five minutes, just thinking about all of the faces Nicklaus makes.

"Why are you looking at me," Mr. Meany mumbles, getting up.

Ugh, that's a good question. Why was I looking at him? Oh, I know why. I got distracted, thinking about Mr. Meany looking exhausted, and when I began to think about Nicklaus, I only ended up thinking about him more.

I do not respond. I place the book down on the dresser and make my way inside the closet. As expected, all my belongings are neatly hung and folded on the left side.

A king will do everything on his left side until he finds the one who is meant to sit on that side. Butterflies erupt in my tummy, and a small smile tugs on my lips. Thinking about that little piece of information makes me feel all warm and bubbly inside. Nicklaus's expensive cologne and burning cedarwood scent are a lot more potent inside this tight confinement of space.

I run my fingers along his many clothing items. They are all crisp, clean, and organized. I put on his tan-gray and white sweater. It is big on me and hangs down past my knees. I smell the sleeve of the clothing, and my kitty instantly purrs from the extremely strong scent.

After sniffing Nicklaus's sweater to death, I grab a pair of gray sheepskin boots and start working on my hair. The ends of it are still a little damp, so I make a loose fishtail braid with my golden waves. Once done, I look at myself in the full-body mirror and can't help but realize how much I am glowing.

When I exit, I find Mr. Meany standing by the window with a glass of blood in his hands. The sweet aroma of burnt oranges and spices invades my nostrils as I make my way to the sofa. My stomach grumbles in response, gaining Mr. Meany's attention.

He raises the glass in my direction. "Hungry?" he asks, speaking to me like he didn't ignore me the entire time the doctor was sticking me to death yesterday.

He is so f*cking bipolar. Welp, there's no need to hold grudges. He can't help himself. His name is Mr. Meany for a reason.

I wince in disgust. "I'll pass."

He nods. "Only the king's blood would taste appealing to you anyway."

Yes, only the king can do a lot of things to me. Right now I need his lips to satisfy my hunger because that's exactly what I'm craving. I am hungry for him. Oh gosh, I miss him. All my thoughts keep traveling back to him—Nicklaus, Nicklaus, Nicklaus.

"But you are hungry," says Mr. Meany, looking amused.

"Yes. Hungry for Nicklaus."

His eyes widen before I realize what I've said out loud.

I clap my hands over my mouth. I flush red with embarrassment, looking anywhere but at him—humiliation at its finest I tell you.

"On that note, I'll go fetch the servant assigned to cook for you," Mr. Meany tells me, barely holding back his laughter.

*Yeah, you do that.*

I hear him take a sip of his blood before he walks toward the door.

*Urgh! Please, please, please . . . Please make him forget that awkward moment,* I pray inside my head.

"King Nicklaus's pancakes," he teases.

Failed prayers. Haha. How funny!

I grab a pillow from the sofa and throw it at him.

Mr. Meany explodes in a fit of laughter. "No, seriously, would you like pancakes?" he questions awkwardly, obviously trying to be funny.

Pancakes are all I ever want, and he knows this.

"With chocolate chips," I answer, now burying my red face in the couch.

"That's new." He walks out of the door, his laughter filling the hallways.

Embarrassing!

Sighing, I sit down and then turn to look out of the window. The sight of the beautiful bed of snow seems to be the only thing that takes my mind off him. It's beautiful, fresh, and inviting. I open the window and stick my head out just to feel the breeze. I wonder if I am allowed to explore the estate grounds, or if I'm going to have to sneak out. It would be best just to ask Nicklaus to take me out instead of stirring up more trouble. He

431

seems to be under a lot of stress already, so there's no point in adding extra to his plate. Asking for permission to go outside won't hurt, will it? I mean it wouldn't kill me, right? All I have to do is ask nicely. Who am I kidding? I wouldn't die from embarrassment if I asked for permission. Nicklaus would still probably say no and most certainly believe I am sick, but the snow is way too inviting to accept no as an answer.

I always wondered what it would feel like to have a snow day. Maybe Mecca and I can go out in the snow when Nicklaus takes me to go see her today. I wonder where he is. What is taking him so long? Gosh, the thought of him slowly creeps its way back into my head. Missing him when he is not around is just one of those things I am going to have to get used to. My alone time most likely consists of thinking about him.

Soon enough the smell of expensive cologne and burning cedarwood fills the air, giving me butterflies inside again.

*Darn it, that smell is another reason why I can't stop thinking about him.*

Seconds, later Nicklaus walks inside, brightening the room with that amused smile of his. He is carrying a tray filled with a plate of chocolate-chip pancakes and eggs and bacon. There's also a cup filled with dark-red juice. The smell of the food and the sight of him make my mouth water.

"I heard someone is hungry," he teases as if he knows what I'm thinking.

*Hungry for you and pancakes. When am I not?*

In a flash, he is right in front of me and places the tray on the coffee table. He moves so fast. I'm surprised he doesn't drop it.

Before I have a chance to speak, he's already sitting right beside me and devouring my lips, hard and fast. His kiss completely satisfies my hunger and settles my craving to taste him. His hands make their way to my hard nipples and squeeze them gently. His hot-and-cold touch and the feel of his warm and juicy lips are exactly what I needed. I needed him.

432

His minty and savory tongue runs over my now swollen lips, anxiously demanding more access. I grant him, and he wastes no time accepting my offer. He hungrily devours my tongue with his pleasure-filled one, taking every inch of my breath away and sending a volcano of shivers to cover me whole. I am speechless.

He slowly pulls away, and a whine escapes my throat.

We both gasp for air. The kiss only lasted for a little over a minute—short and sweet—but the feeling of our lips blending together will always be imprinted into my memory. Every one of our kisses will forever be in my heart, mind, body, and soul.

"Someone missed me," Nicklaus teases, still fighting to catch his breath. His chest matches my own, moving up and down.

"Someone missed me," I tease him back in between my own struggle for air.

"Every second, minute, or hour of the day, when I'm away from you"—he takes my hand—"I will always miss you."

He plants a kiss onto my skin with those mouthwatering lips of his. "Being apart from you for even a second is torture," he tells me, making my heart skip a beat as he pecks my hand again with those goddamn most-delicious lips. "It does help to know that you miss me too, starve for my touch, and are just as hungry for me as I am hungry for you." He flashes his beautiful, sadistic smile.

Oh God, save me from the electric current that is flowing through my blood. Save me from him. I can't breathe.

We stare at each other for a long while in a self-imposed trance.

Finally, I somehow break eye contact, and he gently places my hand down onto my lap. I look down at it, but I know his eyes remain locked on me.

"You look good in my sweater," he begins.

I know he has a smug look on his face even though I am not looking at him. I lift my head up, only to come face-to-face with smugness on his handsome face. This man has no idea what he does to me.

433

Nicklaus is the one to break eye contact this time, then he leans over to grab the plate filled with delicious breakfast food. I watch him as he carefully cuts the pancakes into triangles and then stabs a piece with the fork.

"Here, firecracker, you need to eat." He holds the fork up toward my lips.

I take a bite and moan. The rich dark-chocolate chip and sweet maple syrup are pure happiness to my taste buds.

His body stiffens, and his eyes darken. For a long-drawn-out moment, he stares into my soul before he continues to feed me nice and slow. Occasionally, he stops to wipe my mouth with a napkin or allow me to chew my food. It is very entertaining and extremely adorable. A creature whose natural instinct is to feed on a human is actually feeding a human. How cute? The fact that I'm blushing the entire time is not helping.

"You're easy to please, firecracker." He feeds me with the last scoop of eggs.

I take my time to enjoy the tasty, cheesy scrambled eggs. Once finished, I sigh in pure happiness and fulfillment. "And you know the way to a girl's heart." I grab the glass of dark-red juice. The aroma of cedarwood, fresh berries, and a hint of cinnamon invades my senses.

Nicklaus watches me intensely as I take a sip of the tasty drink. It's kind of sweet and slightly tart, but both the tastes balance out together. I like it a lot. No, that's an understatement. I love it so much.

I moan and my eyes roll in the back of my head from the unexpected blissful taste. Nicklaus's intense cerulean eyes darken like the deepest sea. I love it when they change to that shade. They spark something inside my soul and make moisture trickle down my legs.

Excitement travels through my entire body. Suddenly, I go into some sort of frenzy as I continue to moan, gulping down the tasty drink. Once finished, the frenzy stops. Nicklaus hesitantly takes the empty glass from my hand and sits it onto the tray without breaking eye contact. I lick my lips. The sour-sweet taste lingers.

*Ummm, so good.*

I inhale deeply, attempting to get the thought of the taste out of my mouth, head, and body. It's so good that my entire body sizzles with joy.

Nicklaus is still watching me, studying me in silence. "You like?" he asks, his eyes still dark and his voice so low and husky.

*Like, like, like! Oh, my taste buds are far past the point of liking.*

"Yes. Thank you," I breathe. "The food was delicious, and the juice was the best thing I've ever tasted. What was that?"

Seriously, I think I'll prefer the juice to pancakes any day, and I love pancakes.

He smiles.

*Aww, here goes that freaking, pantie-wetting smile again.*

"Oh really?" His smile turns into an extremely handsome, cocky smirk. "That was all me, firecracker." He turns his eyes toward the window.

It seems as if he is referring to his blood, which confuses me because I have tasted it. I'll admit it is good, really tasty. I may even say it's appetizing, but that drink was heaven in a cup.

"I don't understand," I voice my confusion out loud.

He looks at me but doesn't speak right away, which is strange. His cocky and teasing demeanor completely disappears. He exhales heavily, his eyes wandering back to the window. "I didn't think about how you were going to react until I just watched you drink my blood," he speaks after some moments of silence.

*Oh, so it is his blood. What did he spike it with? Whatever it was, it damn sure gave an extra kick.*

"We need to talk, Claire," he says quietly, suddenly looking very thoughtful and worried.

I frown.

*How did we go from him feeding and watching me as though he wanted to rip my clothes off to this? What did I miss? He has given me his blood countless times already, so I don't get it.*

"My blood tastes different because you have changed."

*Changed?*

"The doctor figured out what happened during the turn."

*Turn? Okay.*

"So what did he say?"

Nicklaus's eyes are now boring holes into my own, their usual cerulean color now a glowing neon blue. I gasp at the sudden change. I haven't seen them turn to that shade before. They are beautiful, electrifying, and intense.

He hesitates for a second. I can tell he is calculating his next choice of words.

After what seems like an eternity of complete silence, he finally speaks, "He confirmed you are no longer a human."

# CHAPTER FIFTY-EIGHT
## The Time of My Life

He takes a deep breath. "Well, he confirmed you're only half-human."

Not human? Half-human? So, what the hell am I then, a half-ghost? My heart beats like I'm human. I look pretty much like a human. Well, I look better than I've ever looked in my opinion, maybe a little prettier. My body seems too toned, but that's normal for humans. All humans tend to look better after puberty. My heart did stop, and Nicklaus was pissed because he thought I was dead, so that brings me back to point A—am I a ghost?

"So what am I then, a ghost? In the half?"

Nicklaus's glowing neon-blue eyes flicker back to their regular shade of cerulean. The serious vibe he has given off quickly shifts back to legendary humor. "A ghost," he jokes, holding back his laughter. In a half? I told you you're half-human, and the first thing that came to your head was that you are a half-ghost? I don't even think half-ghosts exist, baby."

*Oh yeah, they do. What else do you call a person who comes back from the dead and can still be seen and touched?*

Instead of elaborating on it, he bursts out laughing. Can you believe that? He is laughing at me. The king of all vampire kings has checked out, and here comes the human boyish behavior. He is laughing so hard that he loses his breath. Meanwhile, I'm looking at him with my face balled up, trying my best not to karate-kick him. This is not a laughing matter.

"I don't think this is funny." I cross my arms over my chest.

"Yes, it is." Nicklaus keeps laughing like a maniac.

"No, it's not."

"Yes, it is."

"No, it's not!"

"Yes, it is," he says, with his hand over his stomach.

I'm surprised he hasn't fallen off the sofa at this point. Immature dick. Aaahhh!

"If I'm not a half-ghost, what the hell am I then?" I jump up off the sofa. "Where the hell is that doctor? I'll ask him myself."

I may sound a little crazy, but who can blame me? First, he gets all serious and says I'm not a human, then he adds I am a human in the half, whatever the hell that's supposed to mean. Next, he starts laughing his ass off while looking at me like I were crazy. I'm not the crazy one; he is!

"You're crazy!" I yell at him, walking away.

"Only for you, baby." He follows behind me.

As expected, he is already in front of the bedroom door before I even reach it. "The doctor is pretty much useless at this point, firecracker."

"How so? You know what? That doesn't even matter because apparently you are useless too!" I snap, sending an evil glare his way. I try to make it around his well-toned and muscular frame, which might be deemed mission impossible.

I move to the left side, and he takes a step left. I move to the right side, and he takes a step right.

"Arghhh! You're ridiculous," I tell him, finally giving up.

He doesn't respond. He just stands there with this smug look on his face, annoying me to no end.

"What am I, Nicklaus?" I ask with a shaky voice. I lower my head. I feel like crying. I don't know why. I just do. Gosh, I never cry. What the hell is going on with me? "What's wrong with me?" I mutter.

Nicklaus places his finger underneath my chin and lifts it up. "Nothing is wrong with you, firecracker. You are just going through what we vampires call a transition. At times, you will act a little overdramatic, like now, and bipolar."

Dramatic? Bipolar? He has a f*cking nerve.

"Why would I be going through some freaky leech transition?" I yell, throwing my hands up in the air. I make my way back to the sofa and take a seat.

Urgh! He is ridiculous. I hate it when he talks in circles.

Nicklaus sits beside me. Unexpectedly, he pulls me closer to him and then places me down onto his lap. And I'm the bipolar one? He just insulted me, and now he wants to cuddle within three seconds?

"Your inner monster is attempting to find its way," he finally reveals.

Huh?

"There is a darker part growing inside you. It started when we first bonded, sort of like how an embryo is implanted in your uterus."

"What? In my uterus? I'm not carrying your baby! I mean, is that even possible to carry a vampire baby?"

He bites down on his lip. I can tell he is trying his hardest not to laugh. There is some amusement and mischief hidden in the depth of his eyes.

"It is highly possible for you to produce me an heir," he whispers dangerously close to my ear. "And one day you shall."

My heart stops beating altogether at his words.

"When we have our child, and trust me we will, they will be the spitting image of their mother. He or she will be half-human and half-vampire just like their mother," he tells me.

I take a moment to process his sweet words, then out of nowhere, they hit me hard.

439

*Half-human and half-vampire just like . . . OMG!*

I give him a wide-eyed look. "Wait! Is that what the doctor thinks I am? Half-vampire, half-human that's not possible."

"That is very much possible, firecracker," he casually states, not once breaking eye contact. "A child created from a human and a vampire is called a dhampir."

"Dhampir," I repeat.

"Yes, a dhampir." He takes my hand.

"How can I be that? My parents were breeders . . . I think." I lower my head, becoming lost in my own thought.

*I don't know who my parents are.*

"Claire . . ."

*No human born after the Awakening does, with the exception of Jadis. Her story is different. She is special.*

"Claire . . ."

*F\*ck, vampires really screwed us up. I'm screwed up. I don't even know my own species. What the hell is wrong with me?*

"Firecracker, talk to me?" He places his finger underneath my chin. "Let me know what you're thinking. I know it's a lot to take in."

I sigh deeply. "You think."

He releases a frustrated sigh of his own as he removes his finger. I know I'm being difficult, but who can blame me?

"I'm confused. I just don't understand which of my parents is potentially a vampire? I just don't understand what this means. But I guess it is expected, considering the fact that I don't even know who my parents are."

"No, firecracker, you weren't born a half vampire. You were created. The doctor found growing vampirism specks in your blood samples," Nicklaus says, a look of understanding on his face.

"I still don't get it."

He knows darn well I didn't do well in school.

"It's complicated," he quickly explains.

Ugh, that's not really reassuring.

"Xander and I are still trying to figure everything out." He squeezes my hand lightly, then turns to face me.

I take a moment to evaluate him. For the first time, since we started this conversation, I can see he has seemed to be just as lost as me.

"Don't waste time worrying about things you can't understand," he tells me.

Who is he fooling? Even he does not appear to understand it—his goddamn self.

"So, what you're saying is I miraculously became a blood-sucking leech?" I groan. I sit up and place my head in my hands. "And you don't really know how."

"A half blood-sucking leech," he corrects me.

Right, like that's any better.

"And now we are bonded for the rest of eternity. I'll live forever like you?" I ask him. "With you forever, right?"

I feel his body stiffen underneath me.

"Does that bother you, firecracker? Don't you want to be with me forever?"

I pull my head up to stare into his eyes. They are so beautiful and full of unspoken emotion. He looks so adorable with his face balled up into a boyish frown.

"Of course, I want to be with you." I cup his perfectly beautiful face with my hands. "For the rest of eternity. Who wouldn't really, Nicklaus?"

His frown turns into an award-winning, cocky smirk—that beautiful, sadistic smirk. "Good." He leans in closer, extremely close that our faces now only inches apart. "Because I will never let you go, Claire. Never. You are mine." He brushes his warm lips against my own, then he softly bites down onto my lower lip with his fangs.

I immediately release a soft moan, and the hot flame that always comes along with his touch burns brightly.

"You will spend the rest of your existence having the time of your life with me." He bites my lip harder.

My mind is abruptly filled with images of how wonderful my life will be—the passion, the heat, the chills, and the thrill. Every day will most certainly be the best day of my life as long as it's spent with him. Our connection is like an addiction, and I'm certainly hooked on it.

Nicklaus stops, and I almost cry. Gosh, why am I so damn clingy? Maybe it's some weird side effect of the changes my body is experiencing.

"Let's go, my love," he speaks, bringing me back to reality. "We have a big day ahead of us."

"Yes, we do," I squeal excitedly, hopping off his lap. "You promised to take me to see Mecca!"

His entire frame tenses. "Your pet dog decided to return home."

"What? When did this happen?" I ask skeptically.

Mecca wouldn't leave without saying goodbye.

Nicklaus stands up. His body is now relaxed, but his face screams worry. "I sent Xander to pick up your pets, and Mecca demanded she should be released. So, I told Xander to just let her go. But your other pets are on their way."

My other pets? Nicklaus, the king of all vampires kings, let a she-wolf he imprisoned for over a century ago out? Nope, that doesn't sound right.

"Nicklaus, that doesn't—"

"Shhhh, my firecracker. We can talk more during our date."

"Our date?"

He gently pecks my lips. "Yes, a date." He flashes a charming smile. "Are you ready to have the best time of your life, firecracker?"

I smile and nod in response.

You're damn right. I'm ready!

442

*     *     *

I haven't seen a kid in a candy store, but I expect them to be smiling from ear to ear. I expect that their eyes will pop out of their heads and flicker all around. They'd be wondering where to start first. I expect that any child will probably jump excitedly the very moment they walk through the door. I expect an epic reaction, similar to the one I'm experiencing right now.

I'm beyond the point of ecstatic. We've been out here for at least four hours. Nicklaus has exceeded my expectations of a dream date. We rode around on a machine called a snowmobile, traveling up and down the mountain at full speed and doing a lot of sightseeing. The entire experience was freaking awesome!

We also went ice-skating on the frozen lake. Nicklaus had saved me from falling on my ass several times. He picked me up in the air and twirled me around, making me feel like a princess—his princess. I loved it. I was so excited as we were gliding on ice while I was holding his hand. He was extremely careful and patient with me. I didn't think it could get better, well until now.

"Firecracker, your snowman looks like a devil."

"Oh really?" I raise my eyebrow. "I'll name him Nicklaus."

We are having a snowman contest. The winner gets to pick what we're eating for dinner. I want pancakes, but he wants some fancy food of which name I can't even pronounce.

"Then he most certainly is a devil," he jokes, flashing a sexy grin.

We continue to build our snowmen in peace. This is the quietest Nicklaus has been all day.

"You know, I always wanted to have a snowball fight," I say.

He doesn't even spare me a single glance. "Don't you even think about it," he warns.

443

"Aww, come on. It would be fun. I'll be the ice-queen warrior and you'll be the evil king."

"I'm already the evil king, firecracker." He grabs a branch from the ground and gives his snowman an arm. "There is no need to pretend."

I sigh in defeat. He is right about that.

The sun is briefly shining through the thick mountain fog. The cool air rushes around me, blowing my hair all over my face. I'm officially obsessed with winter in the mountains. It's magical. I wish we could stay here forever, but it is nearly impossible due to Nicklaus being the ruler of the entire world. He told me we have to go back to his kingdom sooner than later. I don't know what to feel about that. I really like it here.

"Are you sure we can't stay here a little longer?" I ask him, bending over to pick up more snow off the ground.

Nicklaus wraps his strong arms around my waist, his minty breath blowing into my ear. "I'm sure, firecracker. Don't worry, there is a lot of fun in our kingdom," he whispers, sending invisible sparks to shock me alive.

"Like what?" I turn around and wrap my arms around his neck.

It's been like this all day. He touches me, and I melt. He kisses me, and I almost faint. He whispers into my ear, and I lean in. I'm officially in love.

"Let's see," he says with that flirtatious, mischievous glint in his soul-snatching eyes. "There is a stable filled with beautiful horses. You can pick any one you like."

"I've never ridden a horse in my life."

"Don't worry." He brings his lips closer to mine.

I squirm when I feel his horse of manhood poking against my belly.

"You will have private lessons tonight," he says. Oh my! His lips come crashing down, showing me all the wonders I would feel with his tongue later in my private horseback lessons with him. One, this is certain; and two, for sure we are on the same page.

"Get a room!" a deep, amused voice with an unfamiliar accent calls out, followed by a snowball slamming directly into Nicklaus's face.

Chunks of snow bounce off his skin and fly into my hair. Nicklaus's eyes flash bright red. He releases a low growl as we turn around to meet our unexpected attacker.

The first one is King Marcellus—I'll recognize that walking piece of art from anywhere. He is with an unfamiliar vampire with crimson-red eyes and skin as white as snow. Both are on top of the hill. The vampire I don't know is staring at King Marcellus in boredom.

Nicklaus is still growling while King Marcellus is standing in his glory, smiling from ear to ear. He looks very amused. "I told you I wanted a proper introduction with my queen." He makes his way down the hill.

*His queen? Who? Me? He cannot be serious.*

Nicklaus's eyes sparkle with wicked excitement as he casts his gaze onto me. He looks at the snow and then flashes one of his legendary, sadistic smile. "This is King Marcellus, firecracker."

I stare at King Marcellus, at the unfamiliar vampire, then back at Nicklaus.

"He is the king of Europe and a royal pain in my ass," Nicklaus quips.

*Oh, that explains his accent. He is British. Duh, Claire, you know that.*

"He likes to host a series of cruel games, and his mouth doesn't know what to say," Nicklaus continues.

The two vampires are only inches away from us at this point.

"This is Count Cloven." Nicklaus turns to face the other vampire.He is a very close friend of mine and one of my most-trusted advisers."

I place my focus on Count Cloven. He is now standing directly in front of me, watching me with unconcealed interest. I study him closely. I saw him once, when Nicklaus was going off about Embry going ape-sh\*t. And even then, I really didn't pay him that much attention. I don't know why, but Count Cloven is surely something good to look at. He appears to be in his early twenties, but I'm almost certain he's way past that. He is handsome, and did I mention he is dark and mysterious? His bright blood-red eyes do complement his pale skin.

Nicklaus releases a low growl, gaining my attention.

Oh, snap! I've just openly eye-f\*cked his friend.

King Marcellus mostly has realized what just transpired between us as a corner of his lips curls up into a smile. "He doesn't have the balls to dive in, half-breed queen," he teases.

Nicklaus's growl goes from quiet to monstrous, literally bouncing off the trees.

King Marcellus is unaffected by my beloved's behavior. "But I will. Other men's treasures are the rarest jewels," he adds.

Oops, he didn't just say that.

My eyes briefly travel to Nicklaus, and I'm almost certain he is about to rip King Marcellus's neck off at any moment. To my surprise, he doesn't. He actually looks wickedly delightful.

Count Cloven still looks bored. I've decided I really like his nonchalant behavior.

"Firecracker, do you still want to be an ice-queen warrior?" Nicklaus suddenly asks, completely catching me off guard.

My lips turn into a smirk. "Why? Yes, I do, evil king." I wink, catching right on.

The other two vampires are staring awkwardly at us, extremely clueless.

Nicklaus takes my hands and steals my soul with his eyes. "You can be whatever you want, my love," he says, making me smile from ear to ear. He gives my hand a gentle kiss. "Have your fun, my ice queen."

Without further warning, we dip down at inhuman speed and grab balls of snow.

"Snowball fight!" I yell at the top of my lungs, as we throw the snowballs at the two.

The vampires are taken by surprise when two massive snowballs slam directly into their faces. My snowball hits King Marcellus in the jaw.

I am about to enjoy my victory when he sends one flying back, and it smashes straight into my now reddened face. Unexpected laughter erupts from the other side of the field. I see Mr. Meany standing beside Xander, who is currently bending over and holding his stomach—his piercing gray eyes sparkling with happy tears. Next to him is a flawless, doll-faced redhead that looks like she is about to piss herself.

My eyes zero in on another familiar face. "Victoria!" I call out in surprise, then make my way up the hill at inhuman speed.

Victoria looks like a scared kitten, out of place and out of space. "Claire?" she says in disbelief.

I am close to getting where she is standing when another snowball hits directly the back of my head. I turn to face my attacker, and surprisingly, it's a vampire king, my vampire king. With a sheepish smirk, he holds up his hands innocently.

He didn't just do that! But the sneaky snickers coming from the other vampires tell me he just did.

I pick up a handful of snow and throw a wicked curveball in his direction, and shortly, more snowballs fly from every angle.

We all partake in the happiest, funniest, combative snowball battle of our lives.

# CHAPTER FIFTY-NINE
## Now Is Not the Time

We sit near the frozen lake, enjoying this wonderful winter night. The bright moon is hanging high in the star-filled deep-blue night sky. We're laughing and talking about our epic day in the snow amongst many other things. Mr. Meany has just started a small fire with a smile on his face. He sits down beside us and jumps right into the conversation, laughing his ass off like a teenager.

I never thought I'd live to see the time when Mr. Meany kids around like a human child.

King Marcellus or Cellus, as he begged me to call him, is cracking jokes. He is trying his best to get under Xander's skin. I officially like him. There is something inviting and charming about him. It's hard to believe this man cracking vampire jokes is rumored to be the malicious vampire king.

Victoria takes small sips of her hot chocolate while constantly watching her surroundings in fear. She has been nervous and shivering no matter how many times I reassured her that no harm shall come her way. I feel bad she is uncomfortable. She assured me that's it's not me but the vampires because she doesn't trust them, and I kind of understand. Victoria had always been the main course to the male vampire professors at school. They had always been welcoming toward her due to her angelic features.

However, not all attention is good attention, and she learned that lesson the hard way.

Now, that I think about it, Victoria looks different through my newly enhanced eyes. Her hair is a dull red instead of the cherry red I'm used to seeing. Her usual, flawless porcelain skin appears to be paler. She's still beautiful but naturally prettier. She even smells different. Usually, all I could smell around her was a sweetly sick perfume. Now the cinnamon-and-spice aroma is far potent. I can literally taste it running through her laced blood. I can also hear and see her heart pounding fiercely inside her chest. It's been a constant ringing sound to my sensitive ears ever since she got here. It's kind of uncomfortable for me. I feel like I'm going to pounce on her at any minute, so I've been trying to keep my distance.

I don't understand why she didn't just return to the village with Mecca. I asked her how she got back with Xander. All she said was they came back for me, refusing to really elaborate. She acted the same way when I asked her why she didn't return with Mecca. Her answer seemed somewhat forced.

Victoria has been eyeing the vampires strangely, most likely trying to comprehend why they are acting so carefree. Whenever they catch her staring, she places her gaze on anything other than them, especially Nicklaus. She is terrified of him. She even refused to join in our winter wonder war no matter how many snowballs hit her in the head. She has been on edge, and she shouldn't be blamed. She is in the presence of the world's most-dangerous predators. They might end her life within a second, not that I'll let that happen, but still, they could.

Victoria is oblivious to the fact that I could end her life as well. She doesn't sense the darker, dangerous, and more sinister side of me that has been clawing to be released.

Nicklaus constantly checks on me to make sure I have the monster at bay. He can feel the raw power flowing through my entire body, growing stronger by the second like it's his own. He understands I'm kind of wary of myself. He had to reassure me several times that I have nothing to fear, but he is wrong. I should be afraid; the intensity of my power is frightening. I can feel myself changing drastically. All of my senses are permanently amplified. I can hear and see clearer—even from miles and miles away—and smell a million and one different scents that come easier for me to identify exactly who or where they come from. My taste buds are also freaking fantastic—for example, hot chocolate always tasted creamy, rich, and warm with its chocolate greatness, but right now not only can I taste the creamy, warm, dark, and rich chocolate base, I can also feel the warm liquid that helps my body process nitric oxide that regulates my blood flow. I can literally feel the improvement in my gentle beating heart.

I love it. I feel invincible, indestructible almost. I've never been this satisfied in my life. Now I understand why the vampire kings are known to be the deadliest predators in the world. This kind of power screams dominance and demands compliance. This is where I'm supposed to be. Right now I am who I've always been meant to be, right here sitting beside my ass-kissing king as the rightful queen.

Count Cloven and Nicklaus are talking about anything and everything. It's obvious they are longtime friends. They seem to be lost in their own world, only stopping their conversation once in a while to ask us what we think about it.

Nicklaus kisses the back of my hand every chance he gets and rubs his magical finger through my hair every so often. He enjoys his time with all of us, and that makes me feel like the happiest person in the world. Sitting here while watching them all drink hot chocolate with plastered smiles on their faces completes me. I love their boyish smiles and the jolly atmosphere. I feel this weird connection with them all. Their happiness is my happiness. Their anger is my anger. Their pain is mine to bear. I don't understand it, but I do accept it openheartedly. All of these vampires are now my family. All of the vampire kings and their loyal companions around the entire world are a part of my family now. It's strange because I don't even know them all, yet I feel bonded to them. I feel the connection flowing through my veins; it is engraved in my bones.

Cold wind with a mixture of new scents blows around us all, then the lively mood becomes eerie within seconds. All laughter turns into collective growls of anger. I can't identify who or where the smell comes from, but my senses cling to one of the many distinctive smells.

I turn around and am met by many glowing red eyes as everyone, besides Victoria and I, stands to their feet. Victoria looks like she is about to piss herself. I want to comfort her, but I get distracted by an oddly familiar scent of pinewood and damp earth floating in the chilly night air. It reminds me of Embry. I close my eyes and take a deep whiff of the refreshing aroma. All of my senses suddenly go into overdrive—sharper—but they quickly adjust to the changes as the sound of massive paws running through the left side of the forest rings in my sensitive ears. It's louder than Victoria's racing heart.

It takes me two seconds to identify the mixture of scents and a second for me to tell that they, werewolves, are in a big group—pack. They are coming straight in our direction fast. It takes me one more second to realize that the one carrying the distinctive scent of pinewood and damp earth is a Wilde wolf. Without orders, the men start to prepare for the unexpected battle, pulling out guns and loads of silver bullets.

Where the f*ck did they even come from?

Some men in black surround me like I'm some weak wimp.

"Go scout the area," Nicklaus commands Count Cloven.

He nods and disappears.

"I'll go flank after him," Xander tells Nicklaus. "I don't smell lycan, but that doesn't mean the beasts are not here. We need to be sure of it."

"Agreed. If we get separated, you know where to meet me," responds Nicklaus.

451

Xander nods. "Take my chosen to safety," he orders one of the men in black.

Oh gosh, how could I forget about Victoria! The poor thing is scared out of her mind, searching her surroundings in panic. One of the men in black scoops her in his arms.

"Nooo! I'm not leaving Claiiire!" she screams at the top of her lungs.

"It's okay, Victoria," I tell her in a calm voice, attempting to get around one of the tall, hunky leech bodyguard boys. "I'll be right behind you."

I don't think she hears me, her screams covering my voice.

"Brave one, I'll see you soon," Xander says. He kisses my forehead softly and then disappears before I can even utter a word.

Out of nowhere, I'm off the ground and cradled into the warmth of Nicklaus's body, which lasts for only a second. As soon as we are back in front of the estate, his warmth is gone. My eyes search for the scenery. Men in black are rushing out of the gates, preparing to fight while the slaves are searching for cover. The stench of promised death and blood hangs thick in the night air. No human wants to be in the middle of a battle between supernatural beings. Things can get pretty ugly.

"Take Claire to safety." Nicklaus hands me off to Mr. Meany. "We have been compromised. I'll meet you at the other safe house."

"No!" I object.

"Like hell you are," says Nicklaus, the voice not his own. His vision bleeds scarlet.

I manage to get out of Mr. Meany's hold and fall onto the ground. "I'm staying here." I can see, hear, and feel Niclaus's monster on the horizon, waiting to escape.

"You're leaving now, Claire. It's too dangerous." He turns his back to me and starts to walk toward the estate.

Who the hell does he think he is?

452

I take a step forward, but Mr. Meany gently grabs my arm. I send him a warning glare, and he holds his hands up in surrender.

"Stop acting like a pussy," Marcellus taunts Mr. Meany, walking right up beside us. "Our king ordered you to take the queen to safety."

"How about you do it since you're so badass?" he taunts back.

They both turn to face me. I growl threateningly, and both of them take a step back. I ignore them and quickly chase after Nicklaus.

"They won't hurt me," I tell him.

"I know they won't!" Nicklaus snaps, stopping in his tracks. "No one will ever lay a single finger on you ever again, but you're still leaving." He walks over to Mr. Meany and hands him a set of keys.

Mr. Meany disappears.

"I'm not going, and that's that!" I yell, crossing my arms over my chest.

Nicklaus growls in response. Out of the corner of my eye, I see Marcellus grin.

"Brave one." Xander appears out of nowhere—gosh, they move so fast. "Please see reason. Now is not the time."

I roll my eyes and flick my middle finger in his direction. Marcellus and Count Cloven instantly snicker but then automatically shut up when Nicklaus gives them the side-eye. He carefully tugs onto my left upper arm and pulls me toward the driveway.

"You're too precious, firecracker. No one can know how precious you are to me. Don't fight me on this because you will lose," he says firmly.

"But I can help the Wilde wolves."

"I said no! And that's final."

The monster that has been clawing to be released abruptly breaks free. "Who the f*ck do you think you're talking to?" I snap

453

back, my chest ablaze with uncontrollable heat. The monster within me doesn't like to be spoken to in any kind of way. I'm his equal, not his f*cking slave. How dare he?

My eyes are bloodshot, my chest rising and falling—matching Nicklaus's own. He's pissed. So what? I'm pissed too!

"Her eyes," someone points out.

I don't know who. At the moment, my focus is on one person and one person only, and that's Nicklaus. We stare into each other's crimson-red eyes with no sign of either of us backing down anytime soon.

"I don't have time for this!" he spits. "This is not the time for your insubordination."

Insubordination? What is this, school?

I continue to stare at my stubborn beloved's eyes that are blazing redder by the second. Wrath and fury run through his entire frame, and I can feel his frustration and rage boiling in my own blood. He is right; I can't win this argument, at least not like this.

I cup his impeccably handsome face with my hands, then a tidal wave of electricity sizzles between us. "The Northern Pack, trust me, will listen to me," I calmly tell him. "Why spill blood when there is still a chance it can remain concealed? Why continue a pointless war?" I bring my lips close to his. "Why risk our men's lives for absolutely no reason?"

Someone breaks out into a slow clap, gaining everyone's attention. It's Marcellus.

"What?" He shrugs his shoulders. "You have to admit she has just spoken like a true queen." His lips curve into a smirk. "A half-breed queen," he adds, earning him a chorus of collective growls.

"They're getting closer," Count Cloven warns.

He's right. I can hear the pack quickly approaching. They are less than three minutes away. The men in black are spread out around our little group.

Suddenly, a black *SUV* pulls into the driveway.

*Sh\*t! Think, Claire, think.*

An idea then comes into my head. "Please. I can talk to Mecca. She will listen to me," I tell Nicklaus.

He and Xander share a quick glance. Before I know it, his soft lips are already smashing onto mine. His hard and desperate kiss takes my breath away, literally. "I love you, Claire," he whispers, as he breaks the kiss.

"I love you too, Nicklaus."

"I know. That's exactly why I have to do this."

Before his words register, two gentle hands are placed onto my neck.

# CHAPTER SIXTY
## It's Time to Act

Commander Vlad drove away with my unconscious beloved, after Xander snapped her neck. It may have been a little harsh, but it is what it is. We are all aware that shall be hell to pay when she awakes, and it's something I'm willing to deal with. Claire's safety will always come first, even if I've got to save her from herself. F*ck whoever has a problem with it.

We are behind my estate, standing in the middle of the field that's soon to be stained with crimson. My men are spread out all around us. Xander, Cloven, and Marcellus are close behind me. A wicked chill is in the wind, the crisp winter night air filled with bloody promises. The moon is shining, gleaming, and reflecting off the blanket of white snow. The sound of dogs running through the frozen forest is the only thing that hits my sensitive ears. The wolves are now less than one minute away. Apparently, we have underestimated this group of mutts again. I will not make the same mistake twice. This is the last night the Northern Pack will see.

"It's cute that the queen believes she can train her pets," says Marcellus from behind me.

"Shut up, Marcellus," responds Xander.

"You know how pissed she is going to be when she wakes up."

"Shut up, Marcellus," Cloven says.

"He's going to have blue balls for centuries."

456

"Shut up, Marcellus!" I finally snap.

He's a f*cking nuisance at times. Leave it to him to joke at a time like this.

The group of dogs slowly present themselves, vastly outnumbering us. They are spread out amongst the borderline of the forest. Most of them have shifted into their beast forms, their growls of anger and howls of encouragement ringing loudly in the midnight sky. Their anticipation to die is remarkable.

Scarlet clouds my vision as the pet Alpha and mutt Beta come into view. My hands grip tightly around my silver pistol, ready to shoot. The Alpha wastes no time and walks to the center of the field. He is still in his human form, his eyes glowing golden and his chest rising and falling. The puppy is obviously in deep anger.

"King Nicklaus," the pet Alpha speaks, "where the f*ck is my mate?"

Oh yes, the queen dog b*tch.

I walk through the protective circle of my men, and without order, they step aside. Within a second, I'm in front of the pet Alpha. "Ask my dick." I smile ear to ear, and he attacks.

\*     \*     \*

CLAIRE

My eyes pop open. I groan as I lift my head up. It's killing me, and so are my neck and back. My eyes scan the confined area, only to be met by a black-tinted glass. I'm in the back seat of a car that's speeding like a bat out of hell. Instantly, I realize which member of the bat family is driving. It does take me a little over a second to realize how I end up in the back seat in the first place, and that's when it all goes red.

"Stop the car!" I yell, kicking the window that separates me from the front of the car.

Commander Vlad doesn't respond. He speeds up instead, like that's going to save him. My vision floods blood, my entire body on fire. The constant disrespect from my guard, my most-trusted adviser, and my own beloved is intolerable. Untamable fury takes over, and the familiar power of the emerald starts to tingle again. It squeezes around my neck, taking the air out of my lungs. My skin prickles, my heart pounds rapidly, and my neck suddenly itches.

"I said stop the f*cking car now!" I holler.

The car window bursts, and an electric emerald-green light flashes throughout the entire vehicle. I fly to the other end of the seat, and the car comes to a complete halt. Scarlet fury, crimson animosity, and red rage are all I see, hear, and feel. I'm way past the point of livid. Sharp, razor-like fangs are now bared. I run my tongue over the new addition to my teeth. They are throbbing, ready to sink into something sweet.

I slam the door and find Commander Vlad already outside the vehicle. I tilt my head to the side. The feeling of betrayal is real. He looks at me, and that is all it takes. His bright red eyes widen in shock. I'm sure I look like an avenging she-devil who has just returned from hell, because that's exactly how I feel. He bows down, showing submission. However, it's too late. I grab a fistful of his hair and plunge my fangs deep into his flesh. His bitter-sweet blood runs down my tongue, burning the back of my throat like acid. Still, I continue to take my fill. His blood is payment for his betrayal. All of them shall learn their place. They shall all put respect on my name.

He doesn't fight back. He doesn't move, speak, plead, or scream. He accepts his punishment openheartedly. Once satisfied, I throw his barely conscious body in the middle of the road without a single ounce of guilt. The darker side of me has taken full control.

I crouch down and take a deep sniff of air. Many scents invade my nostrils, but I cling to the faint one—of damp earth. Although we are in the middle of nowhere, that particular scent lingers, indicating that the wolves are fairly close. Darkness consumes me whole, allowing my newly enhanced senses to guide me in the direction of the scent. In inhuman speed, I follow it deep into the dark forest, across the frozen river and then down a steep, snow-covered hill. The scent becomes more potent. A faint smell of burning cedarwood mingling with the aroma of expensive cologne follows.

*He is close by! Nicklaus has to answer to me.*

*   *   *

NICKLAUS

Xander intercepts the Alpha's attack, sending him to the other side of the field with a loud thud. "The Alpha is mine," his monster hisses. "We have unfinished business."

The other wolves charge. I hold my hands into the air, signaling for my men to hold their positions. The exact moment I drop my hands, they start to attack our enemies. The battle has broken out, and it is deadly. Lifeless bodies of vampires and wolves lie all around the field within seconds. My men utilize strategy number one: releasing silver bullets directly into the crowd of dogs.

I cock my pistol and then let those bullets loose into the air. The silver bullets plus my speed equals their deaths. A large number of werewolves drop to their feet. It knocks down their numbers from many to some. This victory belongs to me.

In my peripheral vision, I see a figure charging toward me—the beast princess. I should have known that b*tch is here, despite our senses telling us otherwise. My chest blazes with uncontrollable heat, and all I see is red. She leaps into the air, attempting to slam directly into me. My fist smacks into her jaw first, and the b*tch spits out blood.

"No magic, today?" my monster taunts.

"I don't need magic to end you," she snarls.

459

I throw my gun in response. "I'll play fair! Come get me."

With a roar, she shifts into a golden wolf and takes a big leap in my direction. I manage to evade her attack, but her claws briefly swipe at my shirt and tatter it, drawing blood. Right away she issues attack after attack, moving quick enough to dance with me. Unfortunately, she's too slow to tangle with a vampire king.

Lycans are usually a lot stronger, faster, smarter, and deadlier than a werewolf alpha, but the b*tch moves like a regular were. I realize that although she has magic, she lacks that typical lycan strength. Foolish!

With this new knowledge I decide to have some fun. I dodge her pointless attacks, and once bored, I issue a few of my own. Instantly, she is back in her human form. Crimson-red blood soon stains her honey-blond hair, and her once beautiful face is now covered in violet and blue bruises. The fool doesn't use use her magic against me. What is she trying to prove?

Finally bored, I pounce on top of her body, only to sink my fangs deep into her throat. She releases a pain-filled scream into the air, making me sink my fangs deeper.

That's right! Scream for me, b*tch.

My monster rejoices with extreme satisfaction, knowing that I am the one causing this searing pain. Her pulse is tingling on my tongue, her heart rate slowing down—she's almost done. She starts chanting spells, but it's a little too late. Her words are mumbles to my ears. Her life is fading in my hands. She is now seconds away from death.

Out of nowhere, another dog jumps onto my back and knocks me down, taking my kill. With little ease, I dislodge the unexpected mutt off me and send it flying into the ground. "Coward!" I roar, standing to my feet. My eyes lock on the dark-brown beast—the Beta. I can smell his stench a mile away.

The wolf b*tch somehow manages to shift. She is now standing on four paws, struggling with her footing. She growls low, indicating she wants more.

460

Pathetic! These dogs just don't know when to give up. Stupid b*tch!

At this moment, the blood of this princess beast is trickling down my face, and she wants more. I lick her blood off my lips, and the Beta stands protectively in front of her. I knock my head back, my laughter filling the air. They both want to die. Good! Two lifeless dogs are always better than one.

The eyes of the beast princess eyes flash gold.

\*     \*     \*

CLAIRE

My feet barely hit the ground as I follow the scent. It only becomes stronger by the second, pulling me in. The moonlight gleams brightly from the midnight sky down onto my skin. The closer I get, the stronger the aroma of burning cedarwood, damp earth, and blood grows. I'm almost there.

My nose leads me deeper into the forest, the stench of blood wafting around me. Distant war cries and the raging battle start to get too loud. I come to a complete halt. My sensitive ears have picked up on some movement from my left. I look around, searching for any unseen threat. I find none, but the strong smell of roses and damp earth tells me otherwise—it's a wolf, possibly a she-wolf.

"Reveal yourself," I call out, sniffing the air. "I won't hurt you."

A branch snaps from behind me.

"No, you won't," says a very familiar voice.

*Wait, I know that voice.*

I turn and come face-to-face with Mecca. My red haze fades at once as I lock my monster within me. "Mecca!" I call out.

She doesn't respond. She's standing on top of a log with her head tilted to the left side. She looks like a Greek goddess. Even

461

though she is covered in purple bruises and her skin is smeared with blood, she remains flawless. She is still wearing the same attire she was wearing the last time I saw her. She looks rough, but in my eyes, she will be forever beautiful.

She watches me intensely, her curious honey-colored eyes staring me up and down with great interest. Quickly, that curiosity her eyes hold turns into rage, followed by unquestionable hate. The atmosphere becomes uncomfortable. The fighting beyond the forest can still be heard. My eyes travel in the direction of the noise and then back to Mecca. I swiftly jump when I hear gunshots and cries of wolves.

"Mecca, we need to stop this attack. Why would you come back? Nicklaus said you returned home to your pack," I begin.

Mecca's creepy ole laughter fills the air. "So, that's what the king of leeches told you? And you so foolishly believed him!" she growls through clenched teeth. "I had to see it for myself."

"He gave me his word," I defend. "He said—"

"The word of a leech means nothing to me." She studies me from head to toe. "That's why I didn't take the northern king's word."

Northern king? What is she talking about? You know what? None of that matters. What I only care about is her safety.

"Mecca, I was so—"

"Don't!" she hisses, jumping down from the log. "Don't speak to me, leech."

Her words sting.

She tilts her head to the side and takes a deep sniff of air. My heart starts to break as I look into her familiar, glowing yellow eyes. My best friend may have just become my enemy. She no longer sees me for me. The cold gleam in her eyes says it all: I am nothing but a leech to her.

She starts to stalk me, taking one step forward. My inner monster begins to scratch my inner surface, creeping back onto the horizon and ready to demonstrate her strength. My monster doesn't

462

like to be challenged, and that darker side of me now sees Mecca as a threat.

I try my best to hold my monster at bay, but I am losing fast, and my vision tints bright red. Mecca lowers her guard, and I do the same. If she attacks me, she will meet her end.

"Don't do this, Mecca. I don't want to hurt you."

The voice is not my own. It's darker, much darker. My fangs are now on display.

Mecca knocks back her head, releasing her laughter. "Pity, because I am going to end you. Don't tell me the human Claire has more balls than the leech Claire?"

"I am still myself. I am still the same Claire, your human."

"Nonsense! The human Claire will never beg. I am going to end you, leech b*tch. You are no longer Claire."

Many more scents are carried in the wind. Mecca snaps her head to the left, and in the next moment, a chorus of growls fills the air. Wolves start to surround me, and seconds later, the lycan queen and king come into view.

The queen smirks, her eyes studying me. "Perfect! Now, I can end you."

"Try me, b*tch," I hiss, watching her carefully.

Mecca growls, bringing everyone's attention back to her. "No one will touch her," she declares, crouching down lower. "She was my friend. This is my kill."

The surrounding wolves, including the lycan king, growl in approval.

The lycan queen steps forward and is now in the middle of the both of us. "Very well." She looks directly at Mecca. "Your kill."

Mecca's bones start to crack, and her skin is soon replaced with dark fur. Before I can talk her out of this traitorous act, Mecca as a wolf then jumps.

# CHAPTER SIXTY-ONE
## Showtime

NICKLAUS

The beast princess and the Beta start to circle me. Whether they attack in a united front or one by one, neither is anywhere close to a match for me. They charge at the same time, but I manage to evade them both. The Beta jumps into the air. I quickly grab his neck and break it with one squeeze before throwing him across the battlefield like he is nothing but a mere rag doll. He is weak.

Argh! Pain emerges into my left arm when the beast princess unexpectedly latches her teeth onto my flesh. She shakes her head wildly from side to side while burying her sharp teeth deeper into my flesh. I flip my body, slinging her off me in the process. Before she hits the ground, I manage to catch her by the neck. Rage sears through my spine, and fire spreads through my veins as I watch my blood stain the pure-white snow. This b*tch has a death wish.

I jab my hand into her chest, ready to grab her beating heart—her life is mine. Out of nowhere, the Beta slams into me, once again saving the beast princess from meeting her end. His sharp claws and pointy teeth dig into my open wound, and more pain travels through my left arm. Somehow, the beast princess suddenly appears to my right side and follows his lead, burying her sharp claws and razor-like teeth into my right arm. I slam my arms together, making them bump heads and fall to the ground with a loud boom.

"Fools!"

My growl rings through the crisp winter air. I'm tired of playing games with them. This is finally their end.

I'm about to attack when the familiar milk-and-honey scent spreads through the field. My neck snaps to the east side of the forest. I become more alert, and my sensitive ears and smell pick up on three things: the scent of lycans and wolves in the wind, the sound of growls of excitement from the same direction of the forest, and most importantly Claire. I'll always recognize my beloved anywhere—her distinctive aroma and her barely beating heart. She's in the forest, surrounded by wet dogs and two or so monstrous beasts.

*     *     *

CLAIRE

Mecca pounces, sending me flying down with a loud thud. Immediately, she plunges her sharp claws into my shoulder, and intense pain shoots through my entire body. I bite down onto my lips to hold back the urge to scream while she digs a little deeper, my tears threatening to escape. Then, reality kicks in. My blood splashes onto the snow, and my heart feels like it's been ripped out of my body. Amidst the pain, I manage to wrap my legs tightly around the middle of Mecca's wolf form and squeeze down with all my might. This forces Mecca to release her claws and stagger back. I jump to my feet in inhuman speed while she lands onto four paws, changing her stance. She wastes no time and pounces again. My blood drips freely. The surrounding wolves roar loudly. She jumps. I punch her, slamming her in her snout, and she falls to the ground with a thud.

No, stupid, backstabbing b*tch. That's what the f*ck she gets.

I blink away my tears and study Mecca carefully. She is now circling me. Her deep oak-brown wolf coat glows underneath the full moonlight, her pointy and sharp teeth and canines bared at me. Her menacing snares overlap the growls of excitement of other wolves. She looks gruesome, more monstrous than I ever could have imagined her to be. I'm f*cking dead.

My own monster screams within me, refusing to allow anyone else to spill another drop of my blood. Uncontrollable anger and fear seep through my pores, stirring the wickedness within me to life. My monster doesn't like my fear. She won't allow it.

Without warning, everything around me goes red, and the too-familiar power of the emerald presents itself. My monster and the magic are finally in complete accord. They will learn their lesson; all of them shall learn who the real dominant species is.

The growls of approval, the lycan queen's laughter, and Mecca's wolf form circling me are all in slow motion. Having enough of the betrayal, doubts from others, and constant disrespect, I try to fight for control to keep my monster and the magic at bay. Bravery takes over, quickly replacing my fear. My roaring heart goes still as I surrender myself to the darkness, embracing my more sinister side and allowing the raw power of the emerald to be on command. The tie of friendship and devotion fades away; wickedness, darkness, and my immortal corruption come out to play.

*     *     *

NICKLAUS

My body instantly reacts. I grab one of my hidden pistols and shoot at the Beta and the princess beast. Some of the bullets hit either of their heads, and the others rip through their leg. I don't have time to evaluate who get hit where.

*The bullets won't kill them but will slow them down, so they won't be able to follow me.*

With that thought, I take off in the direction of my beloved. Xander, Cloven, and Marcellus must also have picked up on Claire's scent as I can feel the presence of their monsters running fairly close behind me. We follow the strong scent of my beloved deep into the east side of the forest. Some of my men are still alive and must be holding the other wolves back.

Sounds of bullets flying in the opposite direction confirm my theory. My men are preventing them from going after us.

The full moon is shining and reflected in the snow. During this period, wolves are stronger, and that thought alone makes me move faster than I've ever moved in my entire existence. I swear on my own life that if anything happens to Claire, the world would meet its end tonight. I'll drain every creature on this entire universe before finding a way to end my own life myself. No one gets to live if she dies—no one!

Xander's monster growls, knocking away my train of thought. "Do you smell that?" he asks.

We take a deep whiff of the air as we jump over fallen logs. "Claire's blood!" Cloven exclaims.

Along with blood are fear and pain. Not only is my beloved bleeding, but she is also scarred and her heart is breaking.

I unblock my emotions just to feel hers. Her pain becomes my own. And if my monster was furious, now he is way past the point of enraged. Some of my other men are catching up with us. My senses become more alert as we quickly approach the pack of raging wolves. Their growls of excitement switch to angry snarls. They can't see us, but they feel us. Unexpectedly, I slam into the ground, and before I know it, Xander and Cloven are already on top of me. I fight against them, managing to knock Cloven into

Marcellus, but Xander swiftly places my arms behind my back and pins me down.

"Be patient, Little Brother," his monster growls. "Don't allow your emotions to cloud your better judgment. We must utilize one of our war tactics: watch." He points in the direction of the forest.

"Get the f*ck off me!" I hiss between my throbbing fangs. "I know what I am doing."

He looks at me closely, then nods and releases me. We are now crouching behind some fallen trees, about ten of my men behind me. My sensitive ears pick up on the battle we left behind and the one right in front of us.

"They're here," says the lycan king b*tch, his eyes scanning the forest. "Find them," he orders, and two wolves start to search for us.

*Good luck!* I growl to myself.

We, vampires, are stronger, faster, and smarter when the sun is down. The moon hanging high in the sky brings forth more power. We consider nighttime our best friend, especially when we are in our true form. Other creatures won't be able to detect our scent unless we allow them. They can sense us but will be unable to pinpoint exactly where we are, even if we are right under their noses.

I signal two of my men to run toward the west side of the forest. This will distract the wolves. As expected, the moment my men make their presence known, more wolves are also ordered to go in that same direction.

Stupid mutts!

A monstrous growl fills the air, and my eyes zero in on my beloved. She looks beautifully horrific. To my monster's astonishment, she isn't showing an ounce of fear. She is the complete opposite—fearless. Her monster has been uncaged, taking control as she and Mecca circle each other. Now I understand her

468

pain. She feels betrayed. The wolf b*tch will pay for the act with her life.

What I wasn't expecting is the foreign power of the emerald. Rays of green light surround Claire while she is staring at her prey with an eye of a predator. Her body is in a defensive stance, waiting for the wolf b*tch to attack. Her predatory glare is watching the wolf b*tch's every move. I've never been so proud.

The wolf jumps and she ducks, making the wolf bang straight into a tree. The wolf b*tch bounces back onto her paws, but Claire quickly smashes her fist straight into her jaw. The wolf spits out blood and is becoming frustrated. It's obvious she expected this to be an easy kill, but Claire is utilizing one of the self-defense strategies I taught her during our training session. She is not only tiring the beast out but also making it lose its temper. If my beloved continues to use the technique correctly, the outcome shall be highly favorable. This will be an easy win for her.

When wolves are lost in a blood rage, they don't think; they just act. Acting without thinking against a newly turned vampire is a fatal mistake. Claire being a dhampir is far deadlier.

The wolf b*tch pounces again. This time Claire grabs her by the snout and flips her in the air, then quickly manages to clutch the b*tch's neck with one hand. The wolf b*tch tries to get Claire off her—wrong move! She only ends up giving my beloved full access to her neck. Claire's fingers extend to sharp claws as she squeezes down tightly, snapping the wolf b*tch's neck in the process. The wolf's neck twitches awkwardly, providing more access. My beloved takes full advantage of it. She grips a handful of the wolf's fur and then digs her claws deep into her flesh. The smell of the wolf's blood wafts around us before her open wound becomes visible. Howls of pain linger in the air, and the light from the emerald glows brighter around Claire. She is victorious.

I open up my mind to her so she can feel my presence, but she blocks me off.

What the f*ck! She couldn't have known how to do that. When did she learn to do it? I just felt her emotions seconds ago.

My monster quickly scans the others for their reactions, waiting for one of them to intervene. The lycan queen and king remain standing in place, their eyes glowing bright gold. The other surrounding wolves stare at the scene in disbelief. Mecca must have issued a direct challenge. That would be the only logical explanation why no one has intervened even if they could.

Claire throws the wolf into the closest tree in full strength and speed, and blood drips from the b*tch's snout. My beloved then kicks her in the left side, and the b*tch's bones crack. She kicks the wolf in the right side, and her head snaps in an awkward position.

Claire is playing kickball with the over-a-century-old wolf's body, completely mesmerizing me. The dangerous, cold gleam in her bloodshot eyes is turning me on. She moves with no fear, as though she is scared of nothing or no one—a beautiful sight to behold. She is showing the wolves she is the one who holds the strength. She is the true beloved of the ruler of the entire world, and she deserves to stand beside me. I've never been more sure of anything in my life.

Bruised and bloody, Mecca's wolf pounces back to her feet, wiping out one of her massive claws. Claire dodges the attack and swiftly kicks the beast in her open wound. My eyes travel to the lycan queen b*tch, whose eyes are now spitting fire.

"End this now, Mecca," she screams, "or I will."

Smoke seeps through my pores as fire burns within my entire body. My monster is not taking her threat lightly. Her blood is mine.

A trembling growl escapes my throat, forcing everyone—including Claire—to snap in my direction. The wolf b*tch takes Claire's distraction to her advantage. She charges in full speed, ramming her massive body into my beloved's fragile frame before I even have a chance to anticipate her next assault. My eyes land on the charging lycan king's silver wolf as he takes a big leap into the air, swinging his claws. I sidestep him, then latch my claws onto the left side of his form before throwing his body in front of my brother like a gift.

Xander's monster instantly lunges forward. (They also have unfinished business.) Claire's blood blows in the wind, gaining my undivided attention. The wolf b*tch has Claire pinned down by her massive body and then she plunges her sharp claws deep into mt beloved's skin. She pulls them out, only to strike again, digging a little deeper. Claire's screams pierce my ears.

I charge. In my peripheral vision, I see the Alpha of the Northern Pack. More of their wolves charge in their direction as well. The wolf b*tch releases a growl of dominance, indicating her win. She is ready for the kill.

I'm still a minute away, and Claire is just seconds from death. How can I make it there in time?

The wolf is about to give the final blow when Claire's cries of pain unexpectedly turn into a vicious sneer. And somehow she finds the strength to push her arms up, throwing the wolf in the air. Within a second, she is back on her two feet. She quickly charges in the wolf's direction, preventing it from falling with her bare hand. She rams her hand into the wolf's chest, then grabs the wolf's heart with it.

I'm almost there, but the Alpha beats me to the punch. He dives in the direction of my beloved, but Claire proves herself to be the real dominant one once again. That light from the emerald flashes, and the unknown force knocks everyone—including me—to their feet as she commands, "Submit."

\*     \*     \*

CLAIRE

471

This is my end. Mecca's claws are digging deep into my skin, holding me down into place—her sharp teeth are only inches apart from my face. Pain swallows me whole, and I can see and feel her going in for the kill.

My monster refuses to give up. My arm finds the strength to throw her off me. Before I can register what the hell has happened, I'm already on my feet, charging. It's like I'm here, yet I'm not. I can see, smell, and hear everything going on around me, but I don't have control over it. My monster has still control my body. I have to admit she is kind of badass—evil but a badass. Out of the corner of my eye, I can see Nicklaus running in my direction. As always, he barely looks like he has been touched, for now anyway. I can't wait to get my hands on him.

My attention drifts elsewhere when I see Alpha Maddox, Beta Rendell, and the lycan princess charging our way. The Alpha's intention is clear: to kill. That's the moment I feel my hand slam into the chest of Mecca's wolf form. No panic settles within me as her heart beats inside my hand, literally. I try to take control of my own body, but I can't. It's as if I'm in the back seat, watching my monster does as she pleases. She holds Mecca's heart in a firm grip, seconds away from snatching it out.

I know Mecca attacked me, but she is still my only best friend. This is wrong, so wrong. The worst part of it all is deep down, in the darkest part of my heart, I agree with my monster's actions. I understand the reason why she wants Mecca dead. She is a huge threat to us both.

I refuse to let my monster take over my mind. I call forth the power of the emerald that is flowing within me, pulling on its strength to guide me. Time seems to stand still. My skin starts to tingle, my heart continues to pound rapidly, and my neck suddenly itches.

"Submit," I growl in an unearthly voice.

An electric emerald-green light flashes and everyone around me drops to their knees before me. Mecca's wolf is also

472

kneeling even with me still holding her heart in my hand. Her once bright yellow eyes flicker to their natural shade of soft brown as she transforms back into her human form right in front of me, her heart beating frantically in my hand. I release her, and her limp body crumples to the ground like a bag of bones.

My heart is torn as I stare into the eyes of my supposed best friend. I feel like I am going to faint. This is so wrong on so many levels. All of this was uncalled for.

I am lost for words, so I allow my monster to speak for me. My head voluntarily tilts to the side, my eyes flickering from Mecca to the seas of bodies. Wolves, lycans, and vampires alike are kneeling and bowing before me. Even the king of all vampire kings is kneeling right beside me.

"This pointless war is over," I hiss.

They only growl as a response, unable to move.

I ignore their reaction and turn to face Mecca, who is still crouching down in pain. "I've saved your life, twice!" I spit.

"Three times," Nicklaus reminds me.

"Shut up!" I snap. I shift my focus back to Mecca. "I would have willingly given my life for you, and this is how you repay me?" My head is pounding, heart broken as I gently scoop her into my arms. "Watch," I order, and all eyes are instantly glued to my movement.

The wolves growl, and I can feel quite a few of them desperately trying to break free from my command—just like the king of all vampire kings. After I deal with Mecca, Nicklaus is next.

Alpha Maddox is also attempting to break free, but his fight is hopeless—I am also his superior. His bright golden eyes glow with the full moon, intensely watching my every move. His growls are full of animosity. I bend over directly in front of him and stare right into his angry eyes, challenging him. Nicklaus releases a warning growl of his own.

Ignoring him, I place Mecca's bruised and beaten body down in front of Alpha Maddox. "This is my peace offering to you and the rest of the wolves," I declare. "Mecca's life in exchange for peace."

"And who the hell do you think you are to propose such an idea?" he spits, still locked in place with his bright golden eyes wide open.

My eyes flicker in his direction. "Stand," I command.

His body obeys at once. His eyes flood crimson as he angrily

stalks behind me. It's clear he doesn't like that I can control him. Oh, payback is so sweet. What he does not know is this is only the beginning!

Nicklaus places his hand into my own. "Claire is my beloved, you stupid mutt. She is the queen of all vampire kings."

# CHAPTER SIXTY-TWO
## Timeless Night

NICKLAUS

Judging by the position of the moon, it's a few hours before dawn. We are now in my safe house. The lycan beast king, queen, and a few of their guards are sitting in chairs on the left side of my office desk. The mutt beta, Rendell, and a few of the Northern Pack members are sitting on the right side of my office. The Alpha and the rest of his pack are long gone. They took the wolf b*tch with them because she needed to see a healer. I'd refused to be the one to help lick her wounds. No matter how many times my beloved speaks of peace, the backstabbing wolf b*tch will never walk freely in my home.

Cloven, Marcellus, and Commander Vlad are also present, but Xander refused to sit in the same room with the beast king, and I honestly cannot blame him. The others are standing behind Claire and me, just in case one of these fools decides to attack. I am sitting at the head of the table, my beloved beside me—exactly where she belongs. The tension in the room is so thick you could cut it with a knife. The negotiations to form a treaty that we vampires, werewolves, and lycans shall agree upon have been going on for a couple of hours now. Every time we come close to an agreement, one of us finds a reason to disagree. Every one of us is looking out for the best interest of our own species, as we should.

Let's face it, the vampires and lycans or werewolves will never be in accord. They are and will always be beneath us. However, Claire disagrees. She really feels like we can all coexist in peace, and she is handling this situation with ease. She listens to each side with great interest and evaluates each peace document like she has been educated in the studies of governance, adding her unbiased opinions here and there. She is certainly meant to rule.

How have I been so blind? I should've claimed her as my beloved the very first time we met.

Cloven will stay in the northern kingdom to make sure the treaty is adhered to if we can ever come to some sort of an agreement, but right now it doesn't look that promising. The hatred among species runs deep, centuries-of-bloody-violence type of deep. No matter how powerful my beloved is, I'm unsure if she could right our wrongs overnight.

Count Cloven is also speaking on our behalf. Apparently, my beloved believes I don't know how to cordially communicate. Before we walked into the room she said and I quote, "Nicklaus, please remain quiet. Cloven should speak for the vampires because you really don't know what comes out of your mouth. Oh, and one more thing, Nicklaus, please try not to read their thoughts. No good will come from it."

Can you believe that? She thinks Count Cloven can handle this situation better than me, and that I don't know what I am supposed to say. Me? She basically stated I am incapable of demonstrating a simple dialogue without causing confusion. Just thinking about it makes me laugh to myself. She was right, especially her concern about me reading their thoughts.

It's becoming harder and harder for me to remain in control, and my patience is running thin. The Beta's and the lycan king's sexual interest in my beloved is driving me crazy. Both of them have been thinking about claiming her as their own since we stepped into the room. On top of that, Claire is still a bloody mess. Her wounds haven't healed even after I gave her some of my blood. The nurses managed to stop the bleeding, and Claire swore she felt no pain, but I'm still worried about her. I have no way of knowing how or what she really feels. She has mastered the art of blocking me out.

Xander was also unsure. That's another reason why he was more than happy to skip this meeting. Claire has been giving both of us the cold shoulder for the remainder of the night. I guess it's safe to say she is still pissed. There shall be consequences for our actions. Hopefully, my punishment is wickedly delightful. Any punishment she will inflict on me shall be like that.

I'm sitting here, staring out of the window and imagining how sweet my punishment shall be. F*ck the other bullsh*t that's going on around me. I've never been the type to fancy business meetings. It's good that Cloven is speaking for me.

"This is the final agreement," Cloven says. He places a document down in front of me, knocking away all my tasty daydreams.

"I'm not signing this until the other species sign it," I tell him, after going over the document.

"We have signed it, leech," spits Beta Rendell. "Get your head out of the clouds so I can get the f*ck out of here."

"Watch your tone," Vlad warns, coming to my defense. You are still and always will be beneath us."

The Beta stands up, his eyes glowing yellow. "I'll issue a challenge and show you exactly who is beneath whom."

"Talk is cheap," Marcellus pipes up.

They all start to bicker, and I just simply kick back. I'd rather listen to their bickering than having those god-awful thoughts about my beloved. I place my hands behind my head and lean back into my seat, my feet on the office table.

They got this.

My eyes flicker at the beast family at the left side of the table. They look bored as hell, at least the princess seems so. The queen's and king's eyes are locked on Claire, the rarest jewel in the room. The queen's face says the words her mind and lips won't dare to reveal: jealousy. Her husband's facial expression is quite the opposite. He is watching Claire like she is a piece of meat, his next meal, or the holy f*cking feast. His mind reveals those exact words.

I growl in his direction, and that stops the bickering at once.

Claire stares at me in confusion. She sighs and stands to her feet. "The treaty has been signed by all species but one," she states.

Oh right, I forgot.

I growl low, and the fool has the nerve to smirk. Claire places her gentle hand onto my own, calming me down immediately. She points to the document, and I quickly examine it. I must admit this one will benefit all species, but it's missing one thing.

"Union!" I state out loud.

"Union?" they all repeat in unison.

"Yes. A marital union in fact." I rise from my seat and walk over to the window.

"What are you suggesting, king of all vampire kings? Are you referring to marriage?" asks the lycan beast queen.

I turn to face her. "That's exactly what I'm referring to. Our species have hated one another for centuries. We have no reason to believe that one of us will hold up our deal unless we seal the treaty with a cross-breed union."

Audible gasps can be heard thoughout the room.

I focus my attention back on Claire. Her lips curve into a small smirk, but it's gone before anyone else notices it. She knows what I'm up to.

"No wolf or lycan will ever want to marry a leech," the lycan beast king speaks.

I roll my eyes. The beast dog is really starting to irk my nerves.

"Unless . . ." he says, regaining everyone's attention, "unless your queen will take my hand in marriage," he so boldly states.

His beast queen's eyes flash gold while my vision tints red. Within a second, I am in front of him. The beast king is now out of his seat. My hands are inches away from his neck.

"Stop!" orders my beloved, somehow squeezing her tiny frame in between us.

That's when I realize I am not the only one ready to end the beast king. Vlad is standing beside him as well. The lycan guards look uneasy. It's obvious they don't want to fight. They are now out of their chairs in a defense stance, but their eyes and minds reveal what their lips won't tell. They are petrified. The funny thing is their fear is not because of Vlad or me. No. They fear the one and only Claire.

My anger quickly shifts to lust when my beloved turns around to face me. This woman has no idea what type of effect she has on me.

She cups my face with her gentle hands and brings me down to her eye level. "My king," she whispers low but loud enough for all the other sensitive ears to hear, "I belong to you and you only. Behave yourself." She gives me a soft peck that makes the both of our bodies shiver.

I stare into her deep, electric green eyes and find myself lost in her stare. My red vision is long gone. I almost forget we have others in the room until Marcellus opens his big mouth.

"Damn!" he says. "Now that's hot as hell."

Claire shakes her head as Vlad and I make it back over to our side of the room.

"What my beloved was trying to say is we need a blessed and honored union," Claire announces.

I glare at the lycan beast king, who is staring at Claire with a smirk. Her eyes meet his head-on, challenging him.

That's my girl.

"The Wilde wolves are respected amongst the werewolves and lycans. Why not promise them to one of our kings?"

"With all due respect, Claire . . ." the mutt, Beta Rendell, speaks first, followed by a chorus of vampire growls.

Who the f*ck does he think he is, addressing Claire by anything but Your Highness? He has a death wish.

"My apologies, Your Highness," he states, quickly acknowledging his mistake. "However, werewolves will wait a lifetime for their mates. No wolf, especially a Wilde wolf, will accept such a union. Arranged marriages are not really our way."

Claire tilts her head to the side. "And yet you all arranged a mating between the youngest Wilde wolf and the lycan prince?"

This time the beast queen stands up. "That's different and none of your business," she snaps.

Warning growls, including my own, fill the room once again.

Claire keeps her cool. "You're right," she says, earning another warning growl from me.

What the f*ck does she mean she is right? F*ck the beast b*tch.

Claire rolls her eyes. "Your business is your business. I have no right to question your traditions." She shrugs her shoulders.

The beast queen smiles as she takes her seat, adding to my frustration.

"However, the vampires are my business," Claire adds. She walks over and takes the document from the table and holds it high in the air for all to see. "This treaty is my business, and I can promise you it will never be signed without the union of a Wilde wolf and vampire king." She rips the document slowly and then throws the torn pieces of paper onto the floor.

The lycan queen's eyes flash gold. "And which Wilde wolf do you want?" she asks.

"Embry," Claire nonchalantly answers with another shrug.

480

God, I love this woman.

The lycan king shakes his head. "Embry is mated, my love"

"Mind your f*cking tongue!" I spit, standing up.

The beast queen's eyes water, but she doesn't dare to utter a word. The b*tch has no backbone.

The beast king ignores me, and before he can continue, Claire beats him to it. "I suggest you take my beloved's advice. I will no longer tolerate your blatant disrespect."

The rest in the room fall into silence.

"My apologies, my queen," he sarcastically responds. "However, Embry is mated, and that is completely against our ways. The whole point of the treaty is to respect the ways, values, and traditions of each species, is it not?"

Claire sighs in defeat. "Of course, it is. If you refuse to bless and accept a Wilde wolf and vampire's union, what union will you bless?"

The king smiles unapologetically. "In all honesty, Your Majesty, that is not my call to make. Only the Alpha can give away one of his wolves."

Claire's patience is wearing thin. She is masking her emotions for all to see but me. I can see straight through her calm facade.

Now it's my turn to defuse the situation. "Very well. There will be no treaty without a Wilde wolf and a vampire's union. We have to return to our kingdom at once. My royal adviser will stay behind to discuss further negotiations."

"Why not you?" spits the lycan beast queen.

Claire's patience is gone.Now that's none of your business!" she snaps. "Please take your leave now. We shall be in touch."

They all stand to their feet at once and begin to take their leave. The mutt (Beta Rendell) parts his lips to speak to Claire, but with one look into my beloved's now reddened eyes, he walks out of the room without another word.

They all take their leave one by one except the foolish lycan king. He has been staring at my beloved for a long while, completely disregarding all our monstrous growls.

"By the way," he begins as he finally makes his way out of the door, "please tell your brother it was truly a disappointment that he was unable to attend. I was really hoping to see him."

I smirk. "Next time."

"Yeah, next time." Then he is gone, leaving Cloven, Vlad, Marcellus, me, and my extremely pissed-off beloved.

"Leave us," she orders.

With no hesitation, my men leave me alone with the devil—f*cking pussies!

"Would you like to explain to me what the f*ck that was about?" she questions, getting straight to the point.

I take a seat and relax, finally able to have peace of mind. "I don't want to talk about it."

This only angers my beloved more. She flashes her freshly new pearly-white fangs. Her eyes glow bright red, with a tiny hint of green, as her monster takes over her human form completely.

"At this point, I could give a rat's ass about what you want or don't want to talk about," she hisses.

Her monster believes I am scared of her. How cute?

My beloved has managed to instill fear in the hearts of millions tonight but not me. If anything, I am way over the point of turned on. Her rare power, newly awakened darkness, and desire to dominate all make my dick hard. I want her. In fact, my monster is now awakened and ready to put our naughty little beloved in her place.

The moment my vision tints red, she is in front of me. She moves in a well-crafted, seductive manner. Her nails, having changed into sharp talons, pierce my skin. "Tell me everything!" she hisses. That dark and dangerous tone of her powerful voice is music to my ears.

I grab her by the neck with a firm grip but gentle enough not to hurt her. "Or what, firecracker?" my monster retorts. He enjoys this, and so do I. My penis is hard as sh*t. I flip Claire's body around, swiftly making sure her ass is arched in the air before she regains her footing.

She moans the very moment her ass touches my hard shaft.

"Or what, firecracker?" my monster taunts yet again.

She shivers, her monster still very much present. She hisses and purrs at the same time without really saying a word, but I can hear her clearly. I can feel the darkness that's begging for me to take her hard and fast. Her monster is going to enjoy this. Claire is going to enjoy this.

I can feel her juices already flowing and soaking her pants. It's time. I want our first time to be soft, slow, and sweet. However, my monster disagrees. Claire's monster disagrees. Both of them want to battle for dominance, so why not battle in bed—or on top of the office table with the window wide open for anyone to take a peek? Judging by the new position of the moon, dawn is now an hour away, which means we have less than three hours to board my private jet.

Claire's moans knock my focus right back to her. The late moonlight glistens through the window, gleaming down onto her skin and illuminating her already infinite beauty. She is flawless in every aspect. Her beauty is the epitome of timeless. The love I feel for her is everlasting. The devotion and respect I have for her will last until the end of time. My feelings for her are abiding, permanently stained and tattooed into my soul.

My fingers trail down her silk skin. She moans again, sealing her fate once and for all. I rip off her pants and snatch off my crisp white T-shirt that the nurses put on her. She is still arched over, wearing nothing but her matching cream-colored lace lingerie set that reminds me of warm milk dripping down her honey-tasting skin.

CLAIRE

Nicklaus's body goes dangerously still behind me. I can feel his monster's fire gaze burning passion into my back. Out of nowhere, his warm and soft lips touch my bare skin. He kisses me slowly, but the chill from his minty breath lingers each and every time his magical lips part from my skin.

I shiver. My body's reaction to his touch is problematic, a difficult chemistry. I arch my back all the way over, bending a little further. His monster finally loses all self-control, and he runs his silky tongue all over my shoulder, only stopping to suck on certain spots of my bare skin. He then continues to devour my flesh inside his mouth. He unclasps or more like yanks my bra off my body, acting like the impatient king that he is. My lace underwear has disappeared, and I don't know how or when he snatched it off my body.

His hands run through my hair, and without warning, my head yanks back with a firm pull of his fist. I am not a rough-foreplay type of girl, but my monster is. She loves every second of his display of dominance, wanting to be tamed by him.

I cover up my moans. I'm wet as sh*t.

"Don't," he hisses, sounding gruff as his grip on my hair tightens. "Don't stop yourself from moaning, screaming, or pleading, firecracker." He continues placing gentle kisses on my skin.

My mind is muffled, my sexual frustration increasing by the second. His kiss, his grip, and his voice are nothing but a combination of sensual seductions. I am losing my mind.

"Do you hear me, firecracker," he whispers, as his fangs nibble on my ear.

My body trembles in response. Now, if I thought he lost control moments before, I was wrong. That reaction is his breaking point. His horse dick rams into me, and my slick walls are more than ready for him, opening of their own accord to provide him with full access to my core. I scream and he pounds harder in inhuman speed. Tremendous pain shoots straight into my abdomen, followed by a sh*t storm of pleasure. My monster takes over my body completely. She slams my ass back, squeezes my kitty around his horse and then releases. The rest of the God-given pleasure is automatic.

Nicklaus smacks my ass as he goes deeper. His husky moans fill the air, tangling with my loud screams. He rams in and out of me, and my monster throws it back. He is hungry for me as I am for him. His touch is timeless.

The raging hot fire mixed with the freezing ice storm runs throughout my entire body, then—boom!—it's a frozen inferno. He takes a fistful of my hair and pulls me back, never once stopping his attack on me. Strike after strike, I can hear him growl. Moments later, I feel his fangs sink into my shoulder. I scream but he continues to take his fill. Soon the intense pain fades away and is quickly replaced with great pleasure.

Nicklaus starts to trail soft kisses around the tender mark, hugging my heart and touching my soul. Without warning, I break free from him and sink my fangs deep into his skin, hungrily devouring his intoxicating essence. My world dramatically shifts into a fantasy wonderland—a universe where nothing exists but me and him. His beautiful dark soul is all I see, and his unbeaten heart beats within me. I can feel him inside me. I can see out of the eyes of his monster. I hear our monsters having a battle of passionate love, becoming one. He is me; I am him. We have officially claimed and accept each other all the way. The transition is over. From now on, our hearts, minds, bodies, and souls are one.

He almost whines as I release my fangs from his skin. "I love you, Claire," he whispers, his fascinating cerulean eyes filled with unshed tears.

I can feel his words seeping deep into my blood, body, and soul. "I love you too, Nicklaus." I wrap my arms around his neck, holding back my own unshed tears. I give him a soft kiss. "That's exactly why I have to do this." I snap his neck before he can react.

# CHAPTER SIXTY-THREE
## Just My Luck

CLAIRE

I rush back into our chamber, careful not to draw too much attention to myself and still quick enough to make it there within three minutes. I manage to evade everyone except a few servants here and there. My eyes travel to the window as soon as I step into our room. The extraordinary scenery takes my breath away. I take a moment to enjoy the view of the beautiful sun hovering over the snow-coated mountains in the early, misty winter morning. My eyes scan the land full of flawless, pure-white snow as I take a step closer toward the window. Just a few hours ago, bloody and lifeless bodies were scattered all over the place, resembling a mass murder scene. If I hadn't witnessed the scene with my own eyes, I would have never believed it. The snow around the estate is now untouched and unsoiled. It's refreshing, and I'm going to miss this. Hopefully, we can visit this place often.

I didn't know we are leaving until Nicklaus announced it during my failed attempt to have the three species make peace. I didn't want to question him in front of others. I'm strong, but he is still the king—my king—and I refuse to allow anyone to use our bond as a weakness against him. If they are going to find peace, they will have to learn how to respect one another. They will have to forgive the wrongs they caused the other species in the past and move forward. They have to let go, all of them, and I am going to lead by example. So, off to see Mecca I go—well, hopefully. I don't know how to get back to the Northern Pack because I can't drive. I'll think of it once I make it out of the estate.

I still can't believe Mecca tried to kill me. In this short period of time of knowing each other, we have been through so much. For Christ's sake, we were incarcerated together. That has to amount to something, right?

I start to fiddle with the powerful pendant that hang from my neck. My mind drifts back to the moment when Mecca gifted me this extraordinary present.

*"I want to thank someone special and very dear to my heart. As most of you already know, I wouldn't have had the strength to make it back here if it hadn't been for this brave little human."*

*No one has ever thanked me for anything. Xander, Mecca, and Jade are truly the only friends I've ever had. I don't think I can lose any of their friendships, ever.*

With that thought, I rush into the bathroom and take a quick shower. Although I'd prefer to take a long and well-needed bath, I just don't have the time for such luxury.

After showering and getting myself together, I make my way back to Nicklaus's office. I need to confirm if he is still knocked out. That's the only way my plan is going to work without causing further conflicts.

*He is still out for the count, like a baby. Priceless,* I think to myself as I walk into his office. I'm surprised no one has realized his current state.

I stop at the window, preparing to jump, but I hesitate. There is no way I can just walk out of the front door. The fall from this window to the floor looks longer than I expected. I know I am an ass-kicking half leech, but heights are never my thing.

F*ck, it's clear I didn't think this whole thing through. Like seriously, I don't do heights. I have only jumped out of a window once in my entire life, and that was when I was chasing after

Nicklaus. Oh well, no, twice. I almost forgot about the time that Mecca jumped out of a freaking skyscraper. She thought she was saving me.

I sigh in frustration. I really, really want to go talk to Mecca, but this is f*cking ridiculous. First things first, I don't know where I am going. Secondly, I don't know how to get there. Plus, I hate heights!

Nicklaus groans softly from the other side of the room.

F*ck, my time is almost up. Gosh, this is so f*cking annoying.

I start to think about how I am being ridiculous. I'm a half vamp for crying out loud, not to mention a soon-to-be queen. I literally just bought millions to their knees, and here I am really sitting here, scared to jump out of the window? What a f*cking irony!

Not thinking further, I grow a pair of balls and finally jump.

*     *     *

NICKLAUS

I wake up in my office in a daze and with a sharp pain in my neck, back, and head. If I didn't know any better, I would have thought someone snapped my neck. My father used to do it to me when I was younger, which was over 300 years ago. I hated it when he did that sh*t. He was always a dick.

I groan as I pull myself up off the floor.

*What the f*ck happened?*

Memories of the previous night come flooding back vividly in great detail, all the way up until . . .

*Claire! She . . . Oh f*ck, she snapped my neck! Of course, she did. I should have known that feisty beloved of mine would have her sweet revenge.*

My eyes travel from my unzipped jeans to my penis soaked in her scent. She didn't even allow me to finish soiling her with my seed. F*cking embarrassing! She is probably in our chambers laughing her ass off. How foolish could I be? The worst part is I'm still rock-hard, and I desperately need to be relieved. F*ck, f*ck, f*ck blue balls. How cruel can she be? Seriously, who snaps their beloved's neck right during sex?

*The human who spits in the vampire's face kicks him in his balls and tries to bite his dick off for attacking her,* my subconscious says, as I zip up my jeans. Yep, I should have expected that. In all honesty, I'm surprised Claire didn't murder me in my sleep.

I look at the clock, groaning.

*Great, we still have two hours before our departure.*

A tingling sensation, followed by a throbbing pain, rushes into my dick. There is no way I'm getting on that plane without release. I'm going to shove my entire dick into her wet and tight walls.

I smirk as I think about the first time she saw it. The lust she felt was automatic, not to mention her naughty little thoughts. She compared my dick with a horse's. All I could think about at that time was allowing her to ride me like a rodeo.

*F*ck, I miss hearing her thoughts. I'm going to f*ck the sh*t out of her.*

With that thought, I place my hands over my crotch and get out of my office, hoping and praying I don't run into one of the guys on my way to our chamber. If they see me like this, I'll be their entertainment for at least a century.

I almost make it to my wing undetected—seconds away actually—when out of nowhere, Marcellus walks down the long hallway.

F*ck my fate! Hopefully, he will just nod and let me be. Of course, he doesn't.

"My king," he calls, approaching me with a smirk.

490

I keep walking but acknowledge him with a nod. My dick is killing me.

"Where is that hot-ass queen of ours?"

My footsteps are muffled by the deeply layered royal-blue and gold carpet that leads to my wing. Marcellus places his hands on my shoulder. I groan and pinch the bridge of my nose—f*ck, f*ck, f*ck me. I'm sure the discomfort on my face is evident.

Marcellus squeezes my shoulder playfully. "Hey, man, you okay? You don't look too good."

"Yeah, I'm cool."

He removes his hand with a smirk. "Yeah, I can see that." He turns around, and for the first time in centuries, he surprises me.

Marcellus walks down the hall. And just when I think I've spared myself, he opens his big mouth. "You know I've dealt with a lot of witches," he says from the other end of the wall. "Do you want to know one thing they all have in common?"

"No," I respond, opening the door.

"Come on, Nicklaus, just guess."

I ignore the bastard. I don't have time for his games.

"Welp, I'll tell you anyway." He is now beside me.

F*ck, I've almost made my escape. It's almost impossible to use my speed in my current state.

"Bye, Marcellus."

He's mad. This fool somehow always pops up at the wrong time.

"Okay, okay," he says, acting like he is going to turn around.

But I know better. The moment I am about to close the door to the wing, he opens it and follows me in.

"Look, man, I have the perfect remedy for your problem," he offers, tailing me.

"What problem?"

"I tried to tell you, man." He smacks my back with the smirk of a devil. "I've dealt with a lot of witches, and all of them are good at . . . you know."

"I know what?"

"That thing . . ."

"What thing?"

F*ck he is starting to annoy me more than usual.

*No. You're annoyed because your dick is throbbing,* my subconscious states.

"Shut up!" I say out loud to Marcellus and to myself.

His smirk deepens. "Alright then," he says, finally taking his leave.

I sigh in relief and make my way down the other end of the hall, seconds away from my room.

"So I guess I'll tell everyone else how to deal with blue balls," Marcellus whispers—but loud enough for me to hear—as he reaches the west-wing door.

My monster growls and chases after him.

I've been chasing Marcellus for five minutes. He is truly a pain in my ass. He runs down the hallway and laughs like the idiot he is. Just wait until I catch him. If he were someone else, I would let him be. My dick is throbbing too damn hard to be chasing after anyone but Claire's tight pussy.

The servants seem petrified when they run into me, my men looking amused. Most of my security detail is used to us behaving in this manner when we are all together. The servants, on the other hand, believe that even when we are playing, a murder is likely to happen.

I have to catch Marcellus before he decides to stop running on this wing. The moment we get off this floor, the others will have known about what's happening to me. Who am I kidding? Knowing Marcellus, he must have mind-linked with them already. The entire household will be told about my misfortune by noon, so that's the push I need.

*     *     *

CLAIRE

My feet barely hit the ice-cold snow as I make my way through the forest. My inner monster has been in control of my body since the very moment I jumped out of the window, weirdly enough.

Right now, I'm lost in my own mind, enjoying the ride. My monster seems to know where she is going. Every once in a while she stops to take a deep sniff of the air, following the faint scent of damp earth through the forest and further away from the mountains. She doesn't seem worried about anyone following us, and I can feel more than tell she doesn't give a rat's ass if Nicklaus wakes up and figures out we have left.

It may sound strange to refer to her as her own person, but she is. I feel like I'm watching another entity control my body, which doesn't feel that odd to me. In fact, it's really amazing. I have this weird connection with her, as if I'm a part of her, and yet we are not the same person. We just share the same body. One will call us polar opposites, but we are connected in so many ways. Our souls are one, blending together in harmony. I'm sure it sounds crazy as f*ck. It's one of those things you have to experience firsthand to be able to fully grasp it.

The damp earth scent becomes stronger, mixing and mingling with many other aromas—mostly smells of things that remind me of nature. My sensitive ears pick up on the sound of low-level wolves starting their daily tasks. My monster drops to her knees and focuses her attention on the pack house through the gap of the trees. It is still about one hundred yards away, so I'm not worried about anyone sensing us at the moment.

Werewolves can sense vampires if they are in their true form but cannot pinpoint exactly where we are. At this moment, I

493

don't want them to be able to detect my presence. I'm relieved to see that no one has shifted because if they did, that would surely make the task at hand more difficult, not that my monster cares. She will gladly demonstrate her dominance, although I would prefer this not to get bloody. I am here to lead by example.

My monster's eyes travel up and down the massive pack house, searching for an entrance. I have to find a way to get in quietly.

After ten minutes or so, my monster allows me to take full control. Someone's frustrated, obviously, but I get it. This place is like a fortress. I really didn't think this through. F*ck! I want to mentally slap myself, and I'm sure my inner demon feels the same way. The house seems to be bigger than I can remember, with many windows and balconies closed. What remains open is one balcony, and of course it has to be the highest one.

*Nope, I'll pass. No need to deal with any more heights today.*

I stare at the balcony one more time, and f*ck my luck when I zoom in on the carved statue of Mecca. Nine times out of ten, that's the balcony that leads to the wing dedicated to her. No other place in that massive pack house has a statue of the lost Luna. If I remember correctly, not too many wolves are allowed in that section, so that's exactly what I'm searching for.

*An easy access with little attention*, I think and softly groan to myself. *Nope, I'll find another way. But . . . there is no other way.*

I start to pace back and forth, suddenly feeling defeated. Then my emotion takes a swift turn, and a roaring, fire-spitting rage burns through my chest and floods my veins. That can only mean one thing—correction, that means two things—Nicklaus is awake, and he is pissed with a capital *P*. F*ck, f*ck, f*ck. My time is up. Just my mother freaking luck!

My eyes scan the area one more time, then I take off.

\*      \*      \*

Yup, the f*cking bastard did exactly what I'd expected; he mind-linked with the others to tell them about my misfortune, so before I head back to my wing, let me finish beating the crap out of him. We are now on the lower level of the house. I caught up with his ass the moment my dick returned to its glory. Xander, Cloven, Vlad and most of the people in the household are present, rolling over, pointing, and dying in laughter as they watch me kick Marcellus's ass. The bastard even has the audacity to laugh as well. Thankfully, Claire hasn't decided to leave our wing to further add to my embarrassment. Not all odds are against me at the moment I guess.

I kick Marcellus in his left leg.

He falls down to the floor dramatically, covering his crotch. "Hey, hey, hey! Watch my balls," he laughs. "I don't want to end up like you," he jokes, making our friends and my backstabbing brother laugh louder.

Marcellus loves to put on a show—dickhead.

I continue to beat his ass, and everyone keeps on laughing for a little while longer.

Luckily for him, Xander decides to step in. "I think he had enough," he says, pulling me back.

I doubt that.

"Plus, we have to get ready for our departure."

Yeah, he's right about that. I punch Marcellus in the gut one last time before walking away.

"I'm surprised the queen didn't come down with the commotion and all," Cloven says, helping Marcellus picks his face up off the floor.

"I'm not," Vlad adds. "I ordered one of the servants to give her some pancakes."

"Your Highness," calls out a human.

495

I growl in response, my eyes in her direction. No human addresses me without permission. The servant girl rushes down the stairs. With one glance, it's obvious she is scared out of her mind, sweat dripping down her beady little nose. Her bright-blue eyes are wide with fear. Her tiny frame is shaking, not to mention her pounding heart. It's beating so goddamn loudly that my ears start to ring.

She jumps when the others turn to face her direction, but her eyes remain on us, on Vlad. This piques my interest. Usually when a human is in our presence, they refuse to look us in the eye. Claire was probably the first human in history that showed me different until now. I've been in this servant girl's presence more than once, and she tends to be extremely shy and well-mannered, so the disrespect catches me off guard. I don't like to be caught off guard.

I release another warning growl, and she realizes her mistake at once. She drops down to her knees and bow.

What the hell has gotten into this girl?

"Timid but sexy little thing," Marcellus speaks, too low for her human ears to hear. "She's probably a freak in the sheets."

"Shut up, Marcellus," Vlad snaps, surprising the f*ck out of me.

I turn to him, and I think he surprises himself based on the look that settles on his face.

The timid human's heart pounds louder, regaining my attention.

"Why are you in my presence?" I ask, sounding bored, I'm sure.

"My apologies, Your Highness, I didn't mean to intrude, but the queen . . ."

"What about the queen?"

She doesn't respond, not out loud at least.

*How am I supposed to tell him I can't find the queen? He will kill me. She didn't eat. Freak, why me? Why the hell did he assign me to that goddamn wing? My life is over. Oh Lord,* she mentally tells herself.

"What about the queen, girl?" I ask impatiently.

Her heart drops. "I can't find her," she whispers.

*I'm dead. F\*ck, I think I might piss myself,* she says inside her head.

I have to hold in my laughter. "You're dismissed," I tell her, without sparing the nerve-wracking human another glance.

*Good riddance! I'm saved by the bell. Now be a good girl and leave. He dismissed you. There's no need to tell him you can't find her anywhere. Nope, that's the opposite of being a good girl, and if he finds out I knew, he would most certainly kill me. I can see him now commanding, "Off with her head!"* she says to herself.

My God, this human overthinks everything.

"There's more," she says unexpectedly, further irking my nerves.

I don't feel like hearing her personal monologue out loud.

"Speak freely," Xander encourages. He must have been listening in.

"I can't seem to find her anywhere. I've asked around. Other servants haven't seen her either, and her food is cold."

"I'll go find her," Xander offers. "She is probably wandering around."

I nod in agreement, just because I have no worries. Claire cannot go too far. Now that we are one, I'll always be able to find her, always. She's trapped.

As if on cue, Raphael (my agent) asks for permission to mind-link. This is getting more annoying. They know than to bother me after a battle. Plus, my dick is starting to tingle again.

*"What?"* I snap inside my mind.

*"I'm sorry, Your Highness. We are running border patrol, and I think we just picked up on something strange—"*

*"Like what?"* I cut him off, making my way upstairs.

497

The others are no longer standing there. They most likely have gone to prepare for our departure.

*"The queen's scent is strong on the left side of the forest,"* he responds, stopping me in my tracks. *"And it just becomes stronger as we get farther away from the estate, but it smells different."*

Quicker than a human can blink, I'm out of the estate and head toward that end of the forest. A human servant unable to find Claire is one thing, but a well-trained vampire picking up on her scent where it shouldn't be is a whole another ball game. One may even say that's one hell of a coincidence.

My vision tints red the moment I enter the forest, my body burning. I am extremely pissed. Instantly, I smell my beloved's scent. It wouldn't be alarming—since all of us were out here last night—if it weren't for the fact that her milk-and-honey aroma is tainted, claimed. That only means Claire has been out here after we made love.

*"Sire, would you like us to follow the trail?"* Raphael's voice reappears.

*"Yes,"* my monster growls. *"I'm right behind you."*

# CHAPTER SIXTY-FOUR
## Friend or Foe

CLAIRE

My monster is on edge the moment I step foot in the pack house. My nerves are shot, and it's strange. I remember the last time I was here. I felt like this place was a highly desirable home—Utopia, or like heaven that's shielding and protecting us all from the hell of a world outside these walls. Now, it's different. It's as though I'm walking straight into a lion's den. My monster feels like I'm offering myself up to spend eternity in a dystopian state. She's acting paranoid, constantly making her presence known just in case she needs to save us both. In an attempt to calm her, I decide to walk in the opposite direction instead of taking the route Beta Rendell showed me. Hopefully, I can find a quicker exit.

The deeper I walk through the hall, the louder the pounding of my heart becomes. I immediately realize that coming this way is a huge mistake. I know the entire wing is dedicated to Mecca, but this area is more detailed and more private, I suppose. Her pictures cover every inch of the walls. In some photos, she is with Alpha Maddox, but in most of them, she is alone. She looks carefree and full of life, nothing like the wild and crazy ole Mecca that I've grown used to. She is so much more.

From day one, I had always felt like she was one of the most-beautiful women I'd ever seen. But I was wrong. The version of Mecca—the one in the photos—is much more beautiful, prepossessing in every pose. There are no cosmetics for beauty like happiness, and that's the energy she gives off in those pictures; it's her beauty. Now I truly understand why Alpha Maddox did not try to find a second-chance mate. With these photos alone, anyone can tell Mecca is everything to him. Every item reminds me of her. Even the walls are painted the color she told me was her favorite— midnight blue—and the roses in the vases are exactly what she smells like.

In between some of the pictures are oak-brown wooden shelves with words carved into them in a language I'm unable to understand or process. They are also filled with many different small knickknacks. My eyes scan each item, and an oak-brown figurine particularly grabs my attention. It's a wolf howling at a bright yellow moon reminiscent of Mecca's eyes when her wolf is present. It also resembles Mecca's real wolf. Right beside it is a brown wooden maple leaf, of which natural and refreshing look reminds me of Mecca's flawless milk-chocolate skin tone.

I walk further down the hallway, my monster becoming more agitated. To her, Mecca is not our friend, and this pains me. I just don't know how to feel about that. I understand why my monster feels the way she does. Mecca did try to kill me after I'd saved her life multiple times. She went a little overboard, but it would be one-sided if I refused to admit she had the right to. I understand the reasons behind her behavior. She had a happy life with the man whose love for her is as big as the sky, and this hallway is proof of that. However, vampires took everything from her. Nicklaus took what she had and ruined her. She also risked her happiness to come to my rescue, only to find that I have become one of the leeches, or like Nicklaus.

My inner battle goes on and on. My eyes settle on a photo, and it stops me in my tracks, washing my thoughts away. In the picture is Mecca, sitting in the passenger seat of a beat-up red car.

The vehicle is oddly old, but there is some weird sex appeal about it. Seriously, the car is hot.

In the driver's seat is another woman. She has chestnut-brown hair, coffee-colored eyes, and slightly tan skin. I realize the car is not the hot one but the woman behind the wheel. She looks soft and extremely delicate, yet there's something untamed and wild hidden in the depths of her eyes. She is just breathtakingly beautiful.

*Bella.*

Behind her is a man with his arms draped around the driver's seat, holding Bella. He is wearing sunglasses. A hood is pulled over his head—which to me is strange since the picture was taken on a warm sunny day—hiding most of his face. His smile is as bright as day. I'll definitely notice that smile anywhere. It's beautiful, wicked, and somehow gentle.

*Xander!*

My heart stops, then it starts thumping, and I suddenly feel light-headed. Xander told me they were all friends, but this picture paints differently. They're like family.

The smell of damp earth and roses unexpectedly overloads my senses, alerting me to a new presence. I turn around and Mecca's amber eyes meet mine. She seems surprised upon seeing me, but she doesn't say anything. All I can hear is the sound of my heart now beating softly. Neither of us utters a word. We just stand there, locked in place and looking at each other. Deadly silence is in the air. The moment is anything but sober. Mecca hasn't attacked me yet, so that's still a good sign.

No longer able to take the silent chills, I break the ice. "Hey," I begin.

"How did you get in here?" she asks, skipping formalities.

*Geez, what a grouch.*

"I broke in, silly," I tease her.

She just stares at me like I've lost my mind. Maybe I have.

501

*This is awkward. Shall I leave or try a different approach? Hmm,*
*I'll go with the latter.*

"You smell like a wet dog," I tell her, hoping she doesn't take it to heart.

She releases a growl and clenches her fists, and my hope is stomped on at once.

*Oops. Good job! Idiot Claire,* I mentally chastise myself.

"You think because you're a leech queen, you can just appear in my home and offend me?" she snarls, struggling to keep her control.

*Offend? Are you f*cking serious?*

She never took offense at my jokes before. There were never any filters in our communication.

"I wasn't trying to offend you. Why would I do that? I came all this way to check on you. It was a joke, you know." I take a step forward. "We always joke around."

Mecca knocks her head back like a madwoman, and laughter explodes out of her lungs. Usually, I would find this gesture entertaining, considering the fact that she is my creepy ole Mecca, but the blatant disrespect is clear.

"Get the f*ck out of my home now, leech queen!" she sneers.

My monster slowly creeps up on me, her lingering presence clutching at my mind like a disease. She doesn't like her tone. Through our eyes, Mecca is beneath her.

"Are you deaf, Queen of All Leeches?" Mecca mocks. "I said get the f*ck out of my home!"

My vision tints red while her eyes are now bright golden. I need to go now before my monster takes full control. I should have known nothing will ever be the same. Some things are the way they are for a reason. Predominantly, they are, when Mecca and I are involved. Her hatred runs too deep. We no longer share that type of connection.

Without fear, I stare into her eyes even though the pain of our ruined and lost friendship is breaking me down on the inside. Tears threaten to escape from my eyes, adding fuel to my inner fire. *Why did I come here? This is a mistake.*

"You know what? Screw this. Forget that I even came here," I say, walking away.

*If I don't leave now, things will surely get bloody.*

"Why did you come here, leech?"

By itself, my body snaps back in her direction. My monster or I don't like her throwing me the insult I use on the vampires.

*You are them,* says my subconscious. I tell myself to shut the f*ck up.

"Do not f*cking call me a leech, you dog!" I warn. This time I don't give a flying f*ck if she takes offense or not.

Mecca tilts her head to the side, sniffing the air. Her facial expression switches from hate to disgust. "My apologies, soon-to-be leech queen!"

The sarcasm in her voice starts to annoy me. I don't like it; my monster doesn't like it. "I told you not to call me that again."

"What are you going to do, cry?" she mocks.

"F*ck you!" I snap back, finally ready to give her a piece of my mind.

She knocks her head back, giving a sudden bellow of laughter. Creepy ole Mecca is starting to become a bitter, crazy b*tch in my book. I am trying to make this world a better place, so I'm not going to stoop to her level.

On that note, I take my leave, telling myself over and over that she is not worth it.

"You are already freshly f*cked," she spits.

I ignore her and continue to make my way out of the hall.

*How the f*ck does she even know that by the way? You know what? It doesn't matter.*

For once my monster and I are on the same page. We are unbothered, unfazed. We have no worries. My sensitive ears pick up on the other wolves coming our way. They know I'm here. At this point, I don't even care if this situation turns bloody. I dare any one of them to attempt to put their hands on me, and they will die. My sentimental human side has been altered at this moment. I'm officially bipolar, not to mention Nicklaus's anger is starting to consume my own. He already knows I am here, and he's on his way. One thing is for for sure, he is beyond pissed.

"That's right! Go back to your leech king!" shouts Mecca.

*Don't worry, I'm going, darling.* I want to shout back but nope. I raise my chin, straighten my shoulders, and keep it moving. There's no point arguing with the senseless.

"You're a fool! He is using you!"

Her words stop me right in my tracks.

*Using me?*

I turn back around. "What? You're crazier than I thought!" I holler.

She'd better tread lightly. Mecca has made it extremely clear we are no longer friends, and my monster doesn't like her speaking ill of Nicklaus.

"You have been warned. Now, get the f*ck out," she says.

"Make me," I challenge her, raising my eyebrow and reawakening her wolf. My monster's wicked presence becomes stronger, and this feeling of darkness taking over my light is starting to become my best comfort. I stare directly into Mecca's golden eyes, ready for her to pounce. My monster's dark presence is currently tainting my body, mind, and soul.

Amusement flashes in Mecca's eyes. "He is going to break you, just like how his brother broke her. They don't care about you. They only care about the power that you can wield." Her yellow eyes falter and then fade away, then they are back to their original amber shade as they focus on the pendant hanging from my neck. "And I'm the one who so foolishly gave it to you," she spits through clenched teeth.

504

"Is this what this is about?" I take a hold of the gift. "You were willing to kill me after everything I did for you." Now, I'm the one laughing. "You've got to be kidding me. All of this is because inside your sick and twisted mind, you really believe that Nicklaus turned me to possess this power."

Mecca doesn't respond, pissing me off further. She studies her gift for a while, then finally turns her back to me.

That does it.

"Answer me!" I snap, roughly grabbing her shoulder.

She snatches my arm. "You want answers, leech queen?" she taunts. "I'll give you answers. No, this isn't about the power you can wield. I didn't even know you could do it." Her voice turns dark—very dark—and cold as her eyes smoulder with hatred. "But I did know who you were to him. I knew you were his f*cking beloved the very moment you opened your mouth. Your defiance said it all."

We are now standing face-to-face, and the room seems to spin with every word she utters.

"If you were any other human, you would have been dead. He would have killed you, so it didn't take long for me to put two and two together. I planned to kill you the moment I was free." She tilts her head to the side, looking directly into my eyes and once again challenging me. "But then a better thought came to mind," she reveals. "Your leech and his brother had taken everything away from me, so it was only right to return the favor, starting by taking you."

The moment the words leave her mouth, my hands are around her neck within a second. The picture frames smash down onto the floor as I slam her body into the wall. My enhanced senses pick up on her mate and some other wolves rushing down the hall. How perfect! They'll get here just in time to watch the show I dare them to intervene. They shall die. She used me. She tried to take that happiness Nicklaus found by using me? How dare she use me?

505

She acted like my friend, but in reality she's been my foe. People pretend so well.

My monster wants blood. She wants revenge, and is it selfish that I slightly agree with my monster even after knowing how much Nicklaus truly stole from Mecca? Is it selfish to say I'm still hurt by her actions? Is it selfish that I want to kill her?

Every sane thought of mine is slipping away. The dark and menacing presence within me desperately wants to break free. A pitch of rage is threatening to taint my inner light.

Mecca continues to silently stare. She doesn't struggle. She doesn't fight back. Her glowing golden eyes just watch me, assessing me. Her mate and the other wolves are now behind me. I can feel their fear and sense their dilemma as I continue to battle with myself while looking into the eyes of the monster I once believed was my friend. My inner darkness wants to end her, which would be so easy. I can even destroy this entire pack by just uttering a single word. I can use the gift she gave me against her, ending her and everything she truly loves, but I won't because that would make me become like her.

Swallowing down my pride and holding back my tears, I throw Mecca into her mate, and they stumble into the wall. I make my way out of her wing, going slowly down the flights of stairs. Everyone in the entire house is out of their rooms, silently watching me. They are all forcefully bowing as I walk through the house full of wolves. Some humans are present as well, and none of them looks me in the eye—predictable enough. I'm a leech to them now, and humans don't look leeches in the eye.

How they feel about me is obvious. All of them fear me and hate me. I'm the leech queen that made their kind submit. That must be what they are all saying about me. I'm certain they've completely overlooked the fact that I made vampires submit as well, but it really doesn't matter. It's just hard to believe these are the same people who were praising me not even a week ago. It's funny how quickly they change. One day they tell you that you are their heroine, then the next they act like you're an evil villain.

I want to yell at them all and say, "Sure, I'll take that! Continue to paint me out to be the bad guy." But I can't. I stare straight ahead as though they were invisible, refusing to show them any sign of weakness. Beta Rendell is standing directly in front of the door as I make it down the last flight of stairs. He looks worried, but I know it's not genuine. He is just worried about the treaty.

"Your Highness." He bows when I reach him. Unlike the bowing of others, his doesn't look forced.

I ignore him and open the door. I can feel my beloved's presence becoming stronger. The energy and power of his monster radiate off him, beaming in the direction of this house.

"Claire"—Beta Rendell grabs my hand right before I step out of the door—"do you still think everything will work?"

My neck snaps in his direction. "I meant what I said in the meeting, Beta. If your pack decides to alter, be wise," I tell him, as I finally make it out of the front door.

# CHAPTER SIXTY-FIVE
## An Angry King

NICKLAUS

Xander mind-linked with me as soon as I realized Claire had taken off. The monster within me sensed my aggravation. I told Xander to head to the airport while I retrieve Claire. He wasn't happy about it. Actually, nobody was, but they agreed to go ahead without us. We couldn't afford to waste another moment.

Claire had to run off to chase after a pack of mutts. It wasn't a surprise when my men alerted me that her scent ended there. I know Claire has a soft spot for those mutts. I wasn't even taken aback when they told me she entered the pack house alone. My beloved doesn't fear anyone. What is surprising is the fact that she would leave me for this group of pathetic mutts she can't seem to shake. This is the second time she has done this sh*t, and it's unacceptable. I'm beyond the point of livid. The monster within me is ticking like a bomb, seconds away from exploding.

Claire willingly wandered into the territory of our enemies, and that thought alone cuts me deeper than I care to admit or show. The power she has over me is nerve-wracking and sickening. It's only been two hours or so since she snapped my neck, but it feels like I've been centuries away from her. I can't believe she did it to me and put herself in danger. I had done the same to her, but it was to make sure she was safe. There's a difference, and she needs to understand that her actions have necessary consequences. She is behaving like a disobedient child, not like a queen of an entire species. Why the f*ck would she go into their territory without protection?

My men have been watching the mutts's home from afar. They were ordered never to intervene unless they sense that Claire is in danger. So far, they haven't picked up on any activity.

My grip on the steering wheel tightens as I get closer to the Northern Pack's territory.

*"Sire, the queen has left the house,"* Raphael informs me through our mind link. *"What are your orders?"*

*"You can retreat. I'm arriving now."*

*"There is one more thing,"* he states.

Before I have the chance to tell him I didn't ask for further details, he quickly says, *"She is crying."*

That makes me want to laugh out loud. I shut him out after that.

Claire should be crying. She left me to go to the f*cking dogs. What the f*ck did she think would happen? That they would welcome her back with open arms? Foolish! She is half-vampire. We are their mortal enemies.

It's just been hours since she declared her loyalty to the vampires and to me, and she already broke my neck to go running to the f*cking vet house!

The nearer I am to the pack house, the more my body aches for her soul. My inner demon is reaching—calling to her.

As I drive down the filthy dirt path, I see her standing there with a fake smile plastered on her face. I almost lose it. After whatever the f*ck they did to her, she is still protecting them. She is so proud. She wouldn't even cry to me, her beloved. That is something I'm not going to go for. She is my queen, and I will end this entire world, if it means bringing her happiness. Still, she needs to learn I am also her king.

509

*    *    *

CLAIRE

My monster has retreated to the back of my mind, leaving me with my own thoughts. Mecca's hatred-filled eyes, the forced bows of the other werewolves, and the fearful faces of humans flicker in and out of my head as I stand in front of the pack house. I need some time alone, and thankfully, no one is outside at the moment.

My eyes start to water, and before I know it, moisture travels down the side of my cheeks. I can't get their faces out of my head, the way they looked down on me as if I'm the traitor or the one who did them wrong when it was Mecca who betrayed me despite after everything I have done for her and still trying to do for them. How could they? How could they look at me like I'm the enemy? I'm fighting for peace. Does that mean nothing to them?

The betrayal and judgment are way too deep, but Mecca's hateful words bleed me dry.

My heart skips a beat when a black *SUV* with dark-tinted windows pulls down the dirt path that leads to the pack house. I quickly turn away and wipe my tears with the sleeve of my shirt. I straighten up my posture and hold my head high.

Nicklaus will never agree to the treaty if he finds out what Mecca did or said to me. I can't and won't allow that, so I force myself to smile as though nothing happened. I am leaving a lion's den behind me only to patiently wait for another lion to approach me.

The scent of burning cedarwood and expensive cologne blows in the wind, wrapping around me like a cocoon as the window from the driver's side slides down. Nicklaus's bright red eyes lock on mine. The anger in them is so intense while the rest of his face remains emotionless. His silence sends chills down my spine, making the hair on the back of my neck raise. His impassive

510

expression is scaring me sh*tless. I can feel his dark, raw, and intense power clenching at the surface, waiting to be released.

I open my mouth to say something but then close it when his chin jolts with aggression.

"Get in," he demands. His stern tone leaves no room for argument or disobedience.

My fake smile drops, and my heart pounds hard, doing somersaults inside my chest.

I am about to say something again, but he holds his hands up, silencing me before I have a chance to speak.

"Don't make me get out of this car. Get in now!"

I want to move, but I can't. My feet are glued. The power booming around him is too much to take.

He tilts his head to the side, stalking me—his prey—like the predator he is, and I want to tremble under the eye of this wrathful king.

Once the car door flies open, a bolt of invisible lightning seems to strike within me. I am surprised he doesn't yank off the hinges of the car door. I'm sure he would have if the car had hinges. Does it have hinges? I have no idea.

He wastes no time and walks over to me with the grace of a predator. I have to fight the urge to flinch. The intense and raw power surrounding him is unbearable. For the first time in history, Nicklaus frightens me. Barely controlled hostile rage rolls off him in intense heat waves. His fists are clenched, and his beautiful midnight-black hair is pushed back but blows freely in the wind, making him look much wilder.

"Why the f*ck are you still standing right here?" he shouts, daring me to defy him. "I said get in!"

The ground seems to shake with his words. I get inside the car. I'm brave but I'm not stupid. Right now is not the time to disobey this vengeful king. Right now is not the time to go back and forth. Besides, my brain is a muffled mess at this point. I don't have the energy.

His eyes travel to the forest and then right back to me before he enters the car. Doom soars through me the moment he gets inside. His hands grip the steering wheel, and he speeds away from the pack house. I stare out of the window, silently watching the beautiful scenery go by. I sigh and hold back my tears. I'm going to miss it here. I'm going to miss her.

"Tell me, Claire," he spits out my name like acid boiling on the tip of his tongue. "Did you find what you were looking for?"

He is so dramatic.

"What is your problem?"

"You!" he yells, stepping on the gas pedal. "You're my f*cking problem. Your reckless and impulsive behavior can destroy the f*cking world."

Now, that's even more dramatic and extremely hypocritical, when you consider the fact that he was the one who destroyed the world in the first place. His reckless and impulsive behavior destroyed millions.

Instead of putting him in his place, I choose to ignore him.

"You need to behave like a queen. Your loyalty lies with me. You belong to me."

Eventually, he starts to argue with himself. I'm not entertaining his f*ckery. He wants me to act like a queen, then I'll show him queen. I'm ignoring this f*cking peasant.

My stare shifts to a glare as I continue to look out of the window. I move around on the cream leather seat until I find a comfortable position. Once satisfied, I place my elbow on the window and continue to tune him out.

"Did you hear anything I said?"

*Nope. I'm on my best queen behavior.*

"Claire?" His voice raises. "Claire!"

*"Did you hear that?"* I ask my inner monster.

*"Nope, I don't think so."*

She has checked out as well.

"Damn it, Claire!" Nicklaus slams on the brakes, and the car stops with a squeal. His threatening gaze is on me. He glares at me for a long while, but I continue to ignore him. He decides to place his foot back on the brake pedal seconds after and speeds off like a maniac.

Someone certainly has a serious case of road rage. I want to tell him so badly to slow down, but I choose to keep my mouth shut—it's called silent treatment. This time neither of us speaks.

\*　　\*　　\*

We arrive at the airport in less than thirty-five minutes. It should have been hours, but Nicklaus was speeding through their secret tunnels like a bat out of hell. The tension still hasn't melted away.

The airport is much smaller and a lot more private than the one back in the city. Nicklaus drives straight onto a tarmac where a big plane, along with three other luxurious-looking black *SUV*s, is waiting—the lives of these vampire kings!

Some of Nicklaus's men open the door for us the moment he stops the car. The others exit as well. Relief floods their faces and then comes anger, intense anger. They all look equally pissed—welp, most of them—whereas Marcellus seems to be wickedly delightful.

"Finally," Marcellus acknowledges Nicklaus. "What took you so long? Did you catch fleas or ticks?"

His comment irks me to no end.

Nicklaus ignores him and starts to give instructions to his men, disappearing behind the other end of the plane. I don't know what he's doing. The plane is too big.

"You're becoming reckless, brave one," Xander scolds me.

*And you're becoming a backstabbing traitor . . . who snaps necks.* I want to shout back, but I don't feel like speaking or even making eye contact.

Xander breathes a deep sigh. "You're so stubborn." He smirks, then he vanishes on the other end of the plane as well.

Vlad stands in front of me, as if shielding me from an invisible threat. He's not speaking either. I guess he's back to being Mr. Meany again. In all honesty, he seems lost in thought.

I don't see the red-eyed vampire. What's his name again? Oh yeah, Count Cloven. That's his name. He must have stayed behind.

Marcellus steps in front of Vlad. "My queen, we were worried sick. How was your trip to the vet? They didn't bite, now did they?"

"Could you please cut the dog jokes?" I snap. "They're annoying."

"Oh, is that so?" He raises his eyebrows.

I notice for the first time the ring on his eyebrow. It is kind of cool. Why didn't I see it before?

"Coming from the girl that has a century's worth of vampire jokes. Vlad told me about his unpleasant first encounter with you. I think you're just mad that you finally met your match."

"Is that so?" I turn to face Vlad.

He shrugs—what is his problem? He tells me he will be back shortly, then goes in the same direction where the others went.

A charming smile spreads over Marcellus's face.

He can't be serious. He is the devil's child. He's not fooling me with that smile.

"The king of games is no match for me." I flash him an innocent smile of my own.

"Of course not! I wouldn't dare challenge a professional ball kicker," Marcellus quips.

Nicklaus growls from the other end of the plane.

*Oh, so he's listening.*

Marcellus seems to be immune to Nicklaus's barbaric behavior; so am I. Okay, I'm starting to like him. If he keeps ruffling Nicklaus's feathers, we might just get along perfectly.

The captain and co-pilot came out to greet us. I thought they were going to be rude—with me being half-human and all— but they are actually pretty decent leeches. I wonder if they can sense I'm half-vampire.

"Do they know about me?" I whisper into Marcellus's ear.

He gives me a strange look. "No, half-breed queen," he whispers back, looking over his shoulder to confirm that no one is listening in on our conversation. "They would be dead if they did," he adds.

Normally, my stomach would have flipped, and I would have added Marcellus to my jeepers-creepers list. I might not be normal anymore because I don't feel a thing—not a single ounce of disgust for his bold statement.

Amusement swims in his clover eyes. "It's ironic, right?" His lips curl up into a knowing smirk.

"What's ironic?" My eyes move to the side of the plane, looking for Nicklaus, then back to Marcellus.

"That you didn't feel any remorse about me confessing that they would be dead if they knew about you."

I open my mouth to respond but close it quickly. I don't know what to say.

"Cat has your tongue?" Marcellus runs his hands through his icky dark hair. "Wow, that's a first," he teases.

"Actually, this is the second time today," I admit awkwardly.

What is it about these vampire kings? First, Xander and I formed a brother-and-sister bond, now Marcellus and I are chatting casually like we are good friends. After one genuine conversation with them, it seems like I can talk to them about anything. It's so weird.

"There is nothing wrong with change," he says, bringing me back to the current conversation. "A part of your human side died when the vampirism spread through your system. That's all. Your soul is just a little tainted," he bluntly states like it's normal.

The strange part is that it actually seems normal. I am tainted. Heck, I might need to add my name on my jeepers-creeper list.

"Nicklaus is upset that you snapped his neck," Marcellus slowly starts the conversation back up. "It's a pride thing."

We begin our short walk to the plane.

Is this what all of this is about? I don't get it. Nicklaus had snapped my neck, so I snapped his. What a big f*cking deal! For someone who has lived so long, he is sure behaving like a child. He's like hundreds and hundreds of years old for f*ck's sake!

The other men come around right before we head up the long ramp. Nicklaus's security detail all appear to be in a sour mood whereas Marcellus and I are wearing a sluggish grin. This seems to piss off Nicklaus even more. A rough storm is brewing up in his cerulean eyes. His angry but extremely handsome face is priceless, and I fight the urge to laugh.

I start to really, really, really like Marcellus. He's so fun unlike Nicklaus, who's a grouch. Well right now, he's an angry old man who happens to be a king. No! I'll take that back. Nicklaus is an ill-tempered old man who happens to be a hot king. He's smoking hot. I'll take my grouch of an old man over a fun buddy any day. I wouldn't admit that to him of course. Jealousy suits him.

Marcellus puts his hands on my back and ushers me up the plane. Welp, he tries to.

"Get your f*cking hands off her!" growls Nicklaus, snatching Marcellus hands off my back.

He moves so fast. We were a couple of feet away from each other moments ago.

His eyes are glowing, his body shaking. He needs some anger management courses. It's not that serious as I'm still turned on by his actions, but again, I will never admit it.

Marcellus doesn't respond. He raises his hands up in the air and flashes that charming smile of his. Passive-aggressive behavior at its finest, if you ask me. I'm starting to believe he has a death wish. For his sake, I hope Nicklaus doesn't grant it.

Nicklaus storms past him, gently pulling me by the arm and ushering me up the plane himself. I can feel his wrath within me. Meanwhile, Marcellus is acting jolly and carefree. He's going to die. I can literally see Nicklaus throwing him off the plane. I'm vividly visualizing the scene play out in my head.

Nicklaus guides me to the back of the plane. He opens a door, and stuffs me in a private room. "Don't move," he tells me, as he motions me to the bed.

I shoot him an angry glare. I don't care what he says to me, but I'm not speaking.

"If you need something, call me." He turns around to go back out of the door. "Oh, and stop acting like a child. It doesn't suit you," he adds, then leaves.

*Jealousy doesn't suit you!* I want to scream at the top of my lungs.

*Yes, it does,* my subconscious says to me.

*Arghhh, shut up!*

My own mind is a traitorous slut.

Instead of going after him to tell him off, kick his balls, and snap his neck, I decide to study my surroundings instead.

*This room is similar to the bedroom on the other plane I flew in. Correction, we flew in,* I think to myself, throwing my head back on the bed. *This reminds me of our first kiss—the feel of his savory tongue licking my bottom lip. Oh, my gracious.*

The plane takes off, and my ears start to pop. I stare out of the window, looking at the clouds. I continue to daydream about our first kiss.

Jeepers creepers! I'm whipped.

# CHAPTER SIXTY-SIX
## A Drunk Mind Speaks a Sober Tongue

NICKLAUS

I stand outside the door to listen to the rhythm of Claire's gentle heartbeats. She doesn't have to speak for me to be able to determine what she is currently feeling. Her heart rate gives her away every time, but I hate that she blocked me from feeling her emotions. She's so goddamn stubborn.

Her heart rate increases for a few seconds before it returns back to a steady rhythm.

*What is she thinking about? I wish I could still get inside that pretty little head of hers. I miss her thoughts. She's so entertaining. I wish she would speak to me, yell, shout, or scream. I'll take that. Her silence is killing me. I want to hear her velvety tone and fluent idiomatic expressions. Sarcasm just drips off her honey-laced tongue.*

Shortly after we take off, I make my way to the other side of the plane where a bar— equipped with a bartender—is situated. The men have been patiently waiting. I need a drink. Something strong, bitter, and full of toxins will be perfect. It is going to be a long flight, and we have many anticipated fights ahead of us. Alcohol is heavily required, so Jack Daniel's shall be my best friend. I'm sure the guys have already started their personal session.

As expected they are already sitting on the bar stools, entertaining one another. Xander and Marcellus have their drinks in their hands while bickering back and forth. Vlad is sitting a couple of stools down, lost in thought and downing poison. What the hell has gotten into him? I know he's not the friendly type, but he damn sure isn't a loner either.

I take a seat right beside him. Without being told, the bartender places a glass of Jack Daniel's on the rocks in front of me. She flashes me a flirty smile and attempts to start a casual conversation, but it only results in a big epic fail.

Rebecca the Train is a lower-level vampire slut. She gives blow jobs, makes good drinks, and loves to please me any way she can. She takes orders from me and only me. I allow the men to sow their royal oats if they want to in many of our trips.

*I forgot to fire her. If Claire finds out, she will be pretty goddamn pissed. Maybe I should kill this slut to avoid future conflict. Nope.*

Now that I think about it, that would make things a lot worse. Claire would feel sorry for her. She can't help it. My queen is the epitome of merciful. I, on the other hand, am not. That can be a great balance for our union, I suppose.

*But I'd rather get rid of this slut altogether.*

Knocking my drink back, I turn to face Vlad. He looks troubled, like a sorrowful man lost in the glass of hard liquor. He seems oblivious to me sitting beside him and watching him, which is so unlike him. Vlad is in charge of my security detail because of many things. One of the best qualities he possesses is his attention to details. Usually, he has a third eye but not right now.

"Hey, you alright?" I ask, taking another sip of the f*cking sting.

F*ck, that tastes great. It's nice to know that Rebecca is good for something other than an easy f*ck.

Vlad looks up from his glass of escape and sighs. "Yeah, I am, Your Highness."

"You can skip the formalities, Vlad." I take another sip. "You have earned your place at the table to be called brother." I put my free hand on his shoulder.

He looks taken aback. I can't blame him. Only a select few—mostly the other kings—are aware of this side of me. Vlad's loyalty and devotion to my queen and me are unquestionable.

"Yeah," Marcellus adds with a slur. "He got his ass kicked by Claire. He rightfully deserves to be a part of this brotherhood. Personally, I believe he deserves a medal or something special."

"Shut up, Marcellus," we all say in unison.

He's so f*cking annoying. The fool has the audacity to laugh. We all have our focus on the joker in the room. This man is a f*cking clown. He's still one of my best friends and the most-loyal man I could ever have. He's a headache, but he's a loyal joker to the very end. Loyalty means everything to me, that's why I'm so f*cked up with Claire. Her loyalty must belong to me regardless of my flaws and faults or the fake bonds they formed with her.

Now, don't get me wrong. I know Claire has a heart of gold, and her overall goal is peace. I get that, but Rome wasn't built in a day. Trust me, that adage is true. I saw the empire rise and crumble before my very eyes.

Marcellus is still hysterically laughing. His eyes are filled with happy tears. He's an idiot. F*ck, he is annoying. He's like the annoying little brother I never had.

I raise the glass over my head to propose a toast. "To brotherhood," I speak.

"To brotherhood," they all repeat.

We knock it back, and the toxin runs deep. Xander and Marcellus go back to whatever the hell they are discussing while Rebecca slides me another drink.

"Can I ask you a personal question?" Vlad queries with caution and skepticism.

He doesn't open up much. I have known him for centuries. I am his king, and he is my soldier. That's it, so the hesitation is expected.

"Go for it." I study his worried expression.

"Yeah, go for it," Marcellus chimes in.

521

"Shut the hell up!" snaps Vlad.

Marcellus just laughs in response.

Yup, Vlad is officially one of us.

He shifts his focus to Rebecca and then back to me. He doesn't want her to hear whatever he is about to say. It must be about Claire.

I nod in understanding. "Rebecca, how about you go show my brothers a good time," I instruct.

As soon as the words leave my mouth, she perks up. Her nipples visually get hard through her clothing that barely covers her body. "As you wish, Your Highness," she responds with that god-awful, flirtatious smile.

F*ck, I want to kill her.

Xander and Marcellus exchange looks as Rebecca stands in front of them and takes off her clothes, then she unzips their pants. Xander glares at me. He has never liked to ride Rebecca the Train. She throws it. He catches it and rejects it. That's just the way Xander is. He may snap her neck if she misbehaves in front of Claire. Correction, he *will* snap her neck tonight if she misbehaves in front of Claire.

"Take them elsewhere to relax," I lazily order.

Again, she follows my command, and Marcellus hops like a bunny. That fool is always down for Rebecca the Train.

Xander is still glaring.

*"It's for Vlad,"* I communicate with him inside my head.

*"I'm not touching that slut,"* he responds. *"I'd rather not touch someone I can potentially kill."*

That's what I thought. I know him so well. Good! He can take the worry off my hands.

Xander puts his glass down and rises from his seat. "Have fun. I'm going to check on the brave one." He disappears without another word.

Rebecca takes Marcellus by the hand, and they follow suit.

*Why did I ever touch that girl?*

522

My mind goes completely blank, and not one logical explanation comes to mind.

"What was that about?" Vlad asks.

I almost laugh at the evident disgust plastered on his face. I pick up my glass and take another sip of my drink. "Would you care to find out?"

"F*ck no." He studies the drink in his hand before finishing it altogether. "What made you accept Claire, Nicklaus? I mean before she was one of us, how did you deal with the fact that your beloved was a human?"

Out of all questions, I don't expect this one.

"Well, I didn't, at least not at first." I finish my drink and slam the glass down onto the bar. "Our bond was forged whether I wanted it or not. She was destined to be my queen, and there was nothing I could have done about it. Fate always wins."

Vlad stands up and slides over the bar. "How so?" He pops open a bottle of Johnny Walker and then chugs it down. He's a troubled man drowning his sorrows. Once he finishes downing the whiskey, he moves along to a bottle of Jägermeister, leaving Scotland and walking straight into Germany. Yeah, he's going through something. His lips host a ghost of a smile as he removes the now-empty bottle.

I stare into my empty glass. "Welp, Claire has that sort of effect on people," I confess, with the ghost of a smile of my own.

Claire has affected our entire world in the best way. She truly has no idea what type of power she holds, the type of power she holds on me alone. The world will truly crumble underneath the loss of her soft touch.

"Yeah, she does," he absentmindedly responds. "Claire plays a huge part in my inner battle."

His words rub me the wrong way. My monster is now present—that quick. "Vlad, you are my brother, and you have—"

"No." He picks up another bottle of Johnny Walker. "I love Claire as a friend, you know?"

"No, I don't." I shrug. "But I do understand."

My monster disappears, going back into the dark shadows of my mind. Yup, I've got a problem. One may even go as far as saying I am a little paranoid about losing her to another man, but Claire is just a great catch. Who wouldn't want her? Every one who has met her seems to fall at her feet.

Vlad chuckles softly. "You got it bad, man."

I'm not really surprised at his observation about my jealousy problem concerning Claire. He's right, I got it bad.

"You play another part in my inner battle," he admits, and this piques my interest.

"How so?" I find myself as the one asking him now.

He laughs into the bottle of Stolichnaya. Now he's embracing his Russian roots. "I found my beloved," he slurs, unexpectedly nearly losing his footing, although he was the one who said I got it bad.

We all do. We get blissfully f*cked the moment we find our beloveds.

Instead of questioning who or where she is, I decide to allow the drunken man to speak his sober heart.

"Her name is Abigail. She is sweet and shy, and she is a human." He pauses, visualizing his beloved in his mind, I'm sure. He takes another swig of his drink. "How can I keep her out of our world? I can't bring her into this. I'm not good for her, and she is no good for me. Our people will never accept her. She's too kindhearted to have to deal with me."

The more he speaks, the more I realize I was once like him.

"You have no choice," I tell him the honest truth.

He has that look in his eyes, the same one Cyrus and I had. How did I miss it?

"When I first met Claire, the pull I felt for her was automatic. I tried to stay away from her but still kept her close. She made me feel human emotions and has tamed my monster since

524

day one. I was also worried about her safety and how our people would react if I decided to claim a human to be my queen."

"You are our king, Nicklaus," he reminds me. "Your family name holds weight. You have people that will die for you. I've got no—"

"You have me. I told you, you are my brother. I will protect you and your beloved. No harm will come to her."

Vlad starts laughing like a madman, catching me off guard. Does he think I am a joke?

"I don't need anyone's protection, and nor do I want it." He grips the top of the bottle tightly while swallowing down its contents. Once he finishes, he tells me, "I would die for her. I would destroy our entire empire for her. I'm not worried about harm coming toward her, physically at least, but I'm worried about mental damage. Her soul is too pure."

"You're trying to protect her soul?"

He runs his hands through his hair. "I'm no good for her."

"She is good for you."

"No, she's not," he responds, slightly raising his voice. "Abigail is everything I'm not. She's far better than I deserve."

I sigh. "You're making the situation more problematic than it has to be," I point out. "Turn her, Vlad. Complete the bond. Don't fight fate. Trust me on this one."

"Her fate will be fatal alongside me. I must stay away from her at all cost."

Some things are unavoidable. Vlad will learn it by himself. Abigail already implanted her hooks in his soul. She is a goner, and so is he.

"Good luck."

I wish him the best—he's going to need it. The raw fire and undeniable passion in his eyes tell it all. He cannot live without her.

"Thanks." He finishes drowning his troubles. "I'm going to get some rest," he speaks after a while.

*     *     *

Claire is sound asleep when I return to our cabin. Xander's scent still hangs slightly in the air. He must have stayed here until she fell asleep.

I turn to place my undivided attention on my sleeping beauty, and once again, I find myself struck by her. She is inherently flawless in every aspect, luring my monster in. There's a blinding light inside her that demands obedience. No one can deny it. Claire is perfect. How the hell did I get so lucky?

I quickly take off my slacks and unbutton my shirt, then I anxiously slide behind her and place my arms around her tiny frame. I've been in desperate need to touch her. The size of the bed forces our bodies to mold as one. Claire rolls over to her side, unintentionally poking her little ass out. She's wearing nothing but my T-shirt and some red lace panties. Her swollen nipples poke out through my shirt, and my dick instantly hardens. F*ck!

I start to become more and more excited just staring at her, enjoying this extremely comfortable position and the amazing view of my seductress of a beloved. Out of nowhere, she scouts her round and full ass right onto my manhood.

Oh f*ck, my dick goes stone-hard! I bring my hands underneath the shirt and rub soft circles all over her smooth skin. She shivers in response, and her heart starts beating frantically. I might come on myself just from touching her. Without warning, she turns over and slings her leg over me, locking me in between her heat. My dick is growing harder by the second, and I know she feels the pressure.

I try to calm myself down and focus on anything but the sweet-tasting heat that lies between her legs—her kitty. I believe that's what she once called it. I concentrate more on her long, full eyelashes that are fanning her angelic face. She's mesmerizing. How the hell can I possibly find a distraction when I'm lying beside her?

526

Her plump pink lips are puckered as she slightly snores. I want to devour them with my own. They taste just as good as they look—sweet and satisfying.

After a while of staring at her like the creep I am, I come to the conclusion that there are no other distractions. She is the biggest distraction of all time. There's something foreign and intriguing about her features. Her soul calls to me, whether it wants to or not, like the beautiful melody of a siren singing and calling as it swims around freely in the sea. She's that extraordinary.

I settle my head on her chest, still telling myself over and over how lucky I am. I just want to listen to the rhythm of her heartbeats.

She squeezes her legs tighter around my frame.

Blood God! This woman would be the death of me—a death I'd willingly meet head-on. I had waited lifetimes to find her, and now that I have her, I will never let her go.

I continue to enjoy the warmth of her skin and the melody of her beating heart. She belongs to me for the rest of eternity. She's perfect. Again, how did I get so lucky?

*       *       *

I wake up feeling like the man of the year—this bliss, peace, and harmony. Claire is still asleep, snuggling closer beside me. I know we are fairly near to landing. I can sense my power surging through me. We, kings, are stronger in our kingdom and a force to be reckoned with in our own realms. Claire should experience this exact feeling the moment she awakes. Now that we are bonded, my power is hers as well.

I can feel the power in the emerald strengthening, getting ready for a fight. Claire and I don't share a one-sided bond, so this power is also mine. And Claire is strong. She doesn't truly understand what she possesses. To be quite candid, neither did I. At this exact moment I can feel her dominance rushing through my veins. Everything that was a blur—that I was blinded with—is now crystal clear. The queen has finally arrived. Claire was born to rule. She was made for this. She was made to stand by my side. The surging power which she carries within speaks for itself. Claire hosts it. She is the one; she has always been the one.

My people, this world that I have been born into, and the other kings are truly not ready for her. They aren't ready for us. It's really f*cking ironic. Since day one, I'd feared what my people and my parents would do to her if they found out who and what she is to me. Right now, however, I want to laugh at my own stupidity. My fear was a f*cking joke. Claire is the one they should fear. They should fear our union.

Even with that being said, the threats we are surely going to face are unsettling and weighing heavily on my mind, on our minds. I can feel the unease running through my connection with the other men. I sit on the edge of the bed for a while, really not wanting to leave her alone for a single second. I want to wake her. I want her beside me every moment of the day, every second before the hour. I need her. She is so goddamn intoxicating.

I take her hand and plant a gentle kiss on the back of her soft skin before finally heading out to get ready.

*     *     *

Once freshened up, I make my way to the other side of the plane where the others are most likely waiting. The moment I arrive, they are in the little lounge area. Rebecca the Train is nowhere to be seen, thank Blood God. The last thing we want is for Claire to burn the plane down right upon landing. That would be quite the entrance, and just thinking about it makes me chuckle to myself.

"She's still out," Marcellus begins like he knows what I'm thinking.

Everyone is sitting around as if the world were on their shoulders, but Marcellus tries to change the mood. "Man, let me tell you about the ride of my life."

"There is no point," Xander refuses. "We know all about the bumpy train ride from that wh*re. She certainly doesn't miss any stops," he says, as I take a seat.

I roll my eyes. It's too bad I can't erase my own memory. If I could, Rebecca the Train would have been long forgotten.

Desperate to avoid any further conversation about her, I get straight to the point. "Have any of the other kings contacted any one of you?" I ask.

"Their commanders contacted me," Vlad answers, "and they are all here."

"All of them?" Marcellus queries. He's asking about Cyrus without actually asking.

"All of them," Vlad confirms.

I understand Marcellus's doubts. Cyrus has every right to hate me. I would have killed his beloved with no remorse, and I still will if Claire's life is threatened.

Vlad closes his eyes. He is most likely communicating with the rest of our security detail.

"Don't forget to instruct someone to have pancakes ready before we land," I tell him, knowing he is still listening in on us. "I want to make sure Claire is fed before we enter the palace."

"You"—Marcellus points to me—"your royal f*cking ass is whipped."

"Officially," Xander adds with a low chuckle.

So now I'm the bid.

I'm about to remind them that Claire would beat the crap out of them when Vlad's eyes pop open.

"We may have a problem," he speaks, gaining everyone's attention. "Your sister is also here."

529

# CHAPTER SIXTY-SEVEN
## Cyprus Island Palace

CLAIRE

As soon as I open my eyes, the world seems different—well, I seem different. I'm perfectly aware I have changed and still changing. My senses are more heightened, and my sense quality is threefold better than before I fell asleep. An unsettling emotion booms through my core. Something is wrong, but for some reason, I don't feel afraid. In all honesty, I feel like I'm ready to take on the world. Whoever is dumb enough to come my way shall die.

My monster is no longer a different person. Someway, we became one overnight. Our minds are in sync as though we have an unspoken agreement, at least right now. Something has changed although I can't quite place my finger on it, not that I want to. The world around me looks different, and I love it. I've never felt so powerful and content in my life. All my worries from yesterday were left in yesterday. They are long gone. Today is a new day.

This taste of power coursing through my entire body is addictive. Even the one inside the emerald is going haywire. The electric currents flow within me, blending as one in perfect harmony. I can also feel a much darker and more primal power gushing through my veins, tainted with a hint of light. I welcome all this intoxicating power with open arms. This wicked, dark, and extremely delightful power is clenching on my soul. That bond I have with Nicklaus has been amplified. The need for him is at an all-time high. It's a craving I know I can't survive without.

Nicklaus's brothers are now my brothers, Vlad and Marcellus included. I can feel the loyalty, protection, and love they have for me as it runs deep inside my core. I can also feel their fear and unsettling nerves of the unknown. The dreadful feeling of what's to come is hanging heavily over their heads. All of them are worried about how the kings and other vampires would feel about me. I honestly don't care. I mean, I want to be accepted and connected to them all because Nicklaus's people are now my people. His friends and loved ones are now my friends and loved ones too. I don't really want to fight them. However, if it comes down to a threat against the ones who are loyal to me and the ones who aren't, help me God, we shall win.

Getting out of bed also feels foreign. My feet are quicker and abnormally stronger—trained to go. Somehow my appearance is much more delicate and softer than usual. I take a look in the mirror that hangs above the bed, and I almost don't recognize myself. Since day one of being a part of Nicklaus's world, I've felt prettier than usual. I know that my vampire genes have enhanced my beauty in ways that no one could understand but myself. The little insecurities I once had when I was still a human have been vanquished and are replaced with a different type of self-confidence. There is this inner knowing that I am far more beautiful than I have ever given myself credit for, and I can see that as I stare at my reflection in the mirror. My golden hair is longer, more golden, and is completely full—luscious even. My skin is blemish-free, and I'm glowing. *Flawless* would be an understatement.

The emerald glows all of a sudden, and my eyes flash electric green along with it.

OMG! Now, that's bewitching. Wait . . . bewitching? See what I mean? Even my vocabulary isn't my own.

I heave a sigh. My eyes travel to the window. The plane is preparing for landing. We are getting closer and closer to Nicklaus's kingdom. I just know. His home is calling my name, calling out to my soul. Just through the window, I can tell his kingdom experiences a lot of balmy days. The sun is shining brightly, and the morning sky is clear. The clouds, pure white and fluffy, seem thicker from right here. I stand beside the tiny window, observing the land beneath me. I can feel Nicklaus. He is on his way to me.

"How are you feeling?" he asks, opening the door. As soon as he steps into the room, it seems to melt in his presence.

"Content in my own skin," I quickly say, my eyes drenching him in.

Nicklaus is dressed to impress without dressing up all. He is wearing a crisp white T-shirt and dark denim designer jeans that do little to hide his well-toned legs. His shirt clings to his body like a second skin, clearly doing little work in concealing his nice, firm, cut-and-ripped ten-pack abs. Like I said, this man is dressed to impress unintentionally. It's not his fault. He is basically screaming he is all muscles, and I'm drooling. Freak, I can't help it.

"Claire," he calls, with a knowing smirk.

My face is on fire, and the blaze is soon followed by an ice blizzard. Oh God, I was just openly gawking at him, and of course, Nicklaus soaked up every second of my momentary weakness.

His smirk deepens. I want to kiss him to smack it off his tasty lips. Oh gosh! Damn him.

"You like what you see?" He gives me a flashback of the first time we met. He knew then that I really liked what I saw, just as I very much like what I am looking at right now.

"Of course not," I lie, the same as the first time.

"Liar," he calls me out, unlike the first time.

F*ck, he's a little cocky bastard. He knows his worth.

"How are you feeling?" I change the subject even though I already know the answer.

*Just look at him!*

532

"Content in my own element," he coolly answers.

*Yeah, I bet. You smug, handsome, cocky, arrogant vampire, I bet you are content in your own element. Geez, if I were you, I would be content too.*

Nicklaus flashes a charming smile as if he could hear my thoughts. I am so grateful those days are over.

"It's nice to hear you speak again. I missed your voice."

Out of all the things he could say.

I release a peal of bubbly laughter, a genuine one. "Really? You missed my voice?"

"Yes, your sweet and honey-laced voice," he whispers, pulling me into the warmth of his God-blessed body.

Secretly, I miss hearing his voice too, but I won't dare tell him that. It shall be my little secret. I've already boosted his ego enough during the last five seconds.

We stand for a while, locked in each other's embrace. His words about his being content in his element really register inside my head.

"Are you anxious to return home?" I rest my head on his chest.

*Gosh, he is so blessed.*

The amazing smell of burnt cedarwood and expensive cologne invades my senses. The heavenly feeling I get from this man still seems to amaze me.

"Yes, I am anxious to return to *our* home," he corrects me.

I smile at that, but what he doesn't know is that in his arms is where my true home is.

\*     \*     \*

We get off the plane to the summery weather of his kingdom—*our* kingdom. The familiar but foreign smell of salty water hangs in the air. The sun is blazing bright and strong while the breezy wind blows freely through my hair. The atmosphere is amazing, certainly a breath of fresh air. The walk through the airport is somewhat different than my first experience at airports altogether. For starters, the men in black, whom I have grown so accustomed to, are all around us. There are also vampire workers, just like at the last airport. However, the security seems a bit tighter than usual. Nicklaus's men have always been stone-cold, tight-faced, expressionless, and ready for business, but right now they seem to be more alert. It's as if they're searching for any sign of danger.

Nicklaus told me that the entire airport has been shut down until further notice, so besides a few selected workers, our little entourage is the only group of guests here.

The vampire workers remind me of the last ones I came in contact with. Just like the last bunch, they are doing whatever it takes to please the kings, but they don't seem to be stunned or amazed by Xander, Marcellus, or Nicklaus, unlike the ones I remember from North America. No, not at all. They are stunned and amazed by me. Yes, I can feel their eyes on me. Whenever they think I'm not looking, they watch and wonder who the hell I am to them—or should I say, they watch and wonder who the hell I am to Nicklaus?

Oh yes. Nicklaus has no problem demonstrating his affection in public. He has been holding my hand the entire way through the airport. He kisses my forehead and pulls me into the security of his manly body whenever he gets the chance. Like right now, he's rubbing soft, reassuring circles on my palm while we are waiting for a vampire attendant to haul some of the luggage I didn't realize we have. The poor attendant bows every time he completes a task, which has been about twenty times in the last five minutes. But who's counting?

Xander is standing on our left side, seeming bored; Marcellus on our right, looking extremely happy. He winks at every vampire attendant, and they all look willing enough to drop their drawers.

Vlad has disappeared. He has been meaner, ruder, and more on guard than usual. He is also burying himself in work, putting his best foot forward to make sure I'm overly protected. That is typical of him, but still something is different. What am I missing?

Nicklaus is in front of me. He presses gentle kisses on my forehead every so often. I love it when he does that. It makes me feel warm and safe. Well, they all make me feel really secure.

We are finally about to depart.

"Who is she?" whispers one of the vampire attendants standing close to the Airport Departures door.

Thanks to my newly enhanced vampire senses, I can clearly hear, see, and even smell everything going on around me. The vampire woman is a short brunette with sparkling blue eyes. Just like every vampire woman I have come across, she is beautiful. The other female vampire she is talking to is looking at me, without really looking at me. She is also a short brunette, her eyes a deep-brown shade.

"I don't know," she whispers back, "but she must not be a lady from one of the respected families." She boldly stares me up and down. "She must be the king's new mistress. Lady Gwen will have a fit if she knows our king is having an affair. It's not right."

Instantly, the color drains from my face. How quickly could I forget about the beach-blond, curvy, light blue-eyed leech b*tch that shoved her tongue down Nicklaus's throat?—down *my* throat, because any part of his body belongs to me. He belongs to me, not to her.

Proving me right, his deep voice seductively whispers, "Firecracker."

It sends a fit of electric chills to spark fire deep in my core. His smooth, soft, and wet lips gently touch the left side of my neck and immediately devour every inch of my skin hungrily, bringing forth the scent of my arousal.

"Yours," he proclaims for all to hear.

"Mine!"

Out of the corner of my eye, I see the two vampire leeches with their mouths agape, eyes wide.

"I'm down for a ménage à trois," Marcellus says to them, walking away. He is halfway out of the door when he pauses and then turns around. "Oh yeah, I always have spots open for mistresses inside my kingdom. Let me know, ladies. Let me know."

For the first time in history, no one tells him to shut up.

I flash the gossiping leeches the sweetest, innocent smile I could muster as Nicklaus and I, holding hand in hand, walk out of the airport. I see Vlad standing beside one of the many sleek and overly spacious black limousines that are already waiting outside.

"See you soon, brave one." Xander pulls me into his warm embrace.

He came to see me before I fell asleep last night. I didn't speak to him at first, being the stubborn person that I am, but no one can stay mad at Xander for too long. It's Xander. He gets on my everlasting nerve, and I still owe him a black eye for snapping my neck. Besides that, we are cool. I guess that's just the type of relationship brothers and sisters have.

"Aren't you going to meet us at the palace?" I ask him, as Nicklaus opens up the car door for me to get in.

They share a look I cannot decipher at the moment, but it doesn't go unnoticed.

Apparently, Marcellus, Xander, and Vlad are assigned to one limo. Nicklaus and I are riding in our own car, which doesn't make any sense. We are all going to the same place, so why not ride together? And why are they all acting like we are walking on eggshells?

"You're damn right, we are," Marcellus answers for Xander. "We just have to run some errands before the feast."

Oh right, the Feast of the Brothers. Maybe that's it.

"But if you insist, I'll be more than happy to ride with you alone," Marcellus adds.

536

Nicklaus growls threateningly.

*He is always growling like a dog. Some vampire king he is.*

I laugh to myself. Once again, I'm glad he can no longer hear my thoughts.

"Yeah, Claire, I think that might be a good idea," Marcellus continues with his mordant sense of humor. "We can do a lot of things together."

Nicklaus growls louder.

"Alone," Marcellus teases even more. "Just you, me, and my di—"

In the blink of an eye, Nicklaus's hands go around Marcellus's neck, cutting off his air supply. Nicklaus is giving him exactly what he asked for.

It's a major turn-on for me.

\*     \*     \*

We have been inside this ridiculously large vehicle for around an hour, silently watching the magical island of Cyprus pass by our window. Every once in a while, Nicklaus would order the driver to stop so he could show me an important landmark. We stopped by a place where a statue carved for him stands, which was a disappointment as it didn't capture his barbaric, boyish nature. It did not give justice to his handsomeness. I think we made it out in front of the statue long enough for the life-size sculptured version of him to learn how to really demonstrate his cocky-ass smirk. Then, we visited a private beach, where I truly enjoyed the feel of the sand underneath my toes, the actual smell of a hypnotic body of water up close, and the direct exposure to the blazing sun. The beach was soothing to me.

I had no idea what Nicklaus was feeling as he had shut off his emotions, but he seemed to have been lost in thought the entire time. Then I realized that our sightseeing was nothing but him stalling. I tried over and over to get inside the sweet, deranged head of his, but he continuously refused to let me in.

He provided me access to his emotions a second ago. Finally, we are officially on our way to his home, I mean our home. Tiny butterflies suddenly appear in my stomach, and it tingles with the excitement. Nicklaus places me on his lap and gives me soft kisses. I know he can feel that excitement traveling through my veins like I can feel the unease running through his. His emotions are nerve-wracking and filled with unspoken possibilities.

"My ass-kissing king," I say, planting a kiss on his neck.

His highly addictive scent covers me like a warm wool blanket. He smells so good.

"Yes, firecracker." He runs his gentle fingers through my hair.

"I love you," we both say in unison, and my heart swells.

The first time I went to his home I was asleep. When we left for North America, I was also asleep. So as we quickly approach his majestic abode, I try to stay wide awake and alert.

\*       \*       \*

I drench in *our* home. It feels like it's my very first time here. Cyprus Palace is eternally fit for the king of all vampire kings. I put that on my own scout's honor. The first word that comes to my mind is *astonishing* in every way; the second, *magnificent*; the third, *extraordinary*. My heart rate increases by a thousand pounds a second, just with the first glance. His mighty palace sits perfectly on top of the highest cliff, surrounded by the bright, vivid, aquamarine, sapphire, and deep-blue ocean. The ombre body of water is just the beginning of this impressive landscape.

We drive past a host of valleys filled with more exotic flowers I can count and cross over a massive stone bridge that finally leads us to the heavily guarded golden front gate. The stone-structured building is far from complex. It looks enchanting but

538

ancient—surely surviving centuries's worth of solid blazing sun and tropical storms of fresh rain. I'm truly impressed. Its top seems to reach the sky, seemingly inches away from the warming sun. The gigantic columns supporting and surrounding the arched roof entrance have intricately and beautifully carved capitals. Directly in front of the magical building is a massive golden fountain.

My heart starts to hammer in my chest when the men in black open the limousine door. Its beating only gets louder when Nicklaus holds out his hand to help me out of the car.

This is it. I've left his palace as his chosen, and now I am returning to *our* palace as his queen.

# CHAPTER SIXTY-EIGHT
## Say Thank You, Princess B*tch

The men in black open the door for us, and my heart sinks. The very moment we step inside the palace, Nicklaus's mood shifts drastically. Throughout the day he has already been on edge and on high alert, but around me he still showed his boyish nature, teasing tactics, and sinfully delighted spirit. Right now, his heavily guarded demeanor and blank stare don't make me feel at ease. If anything, it makes this experience extremely nerve-wracking.

As if he can read my mind, Nicklaus slips his hand into my own and then squeezes mine reassuringly. That one gesture instantly calms my nerves—actions speak louder than words.

The palace is quite busy, humming with all sorts of activities. Human slaves and vampire workers are everywhere, preparing for the arrival of other kings. Just like back at the airport, I can feel them all looking at me, without really looking at me. The difference is they know exactly who I am, except that they wouldn't dare to gossip about it, at least not right now. They will wait until we are not in hearing range so they can begin the talk of the century, I'm sure.

We walk through the massive palace, heading in the direction of Nicklaus's chambers. Everything looks the same—if not, better—and exactly how I remember it. The portraits of every single vampire king, with others or alone, still hang on the red-painted walls. The first time I walked through these hallways, I remember thinking to myself that all the vampire kings looked like family in the pictures. Now I know without a doubt they are certainly family, bonded without question. Hopefully, Nicklaus's claiming me as his beloved will not threaten their brotherhood.

The huge gold lights with rows and rows of diamonds (I now know for sure are called chandeliers) are hanging and dazzling bright above our heads. With every step we take, they seem to sparkle brighter.

The first time I walked through this grand place, I compared it to a picture out of a fairy-tale story. I remember feeling like this was all a dream. But as we walk past the several kitchens, three libraries, two pools, and numerous other rooms I'm still unable to identify, I realize this isn't an imaginary place from a magical story. No, this isn't a fairy-tale story at all. This is his home, our home.

I know I keep saying that, but it's true. Although, Nicklaus and my story will most likely be compared to a nightmare instead of a fairy tale, a beautifully grand nightmare I would never want to awaken from. I feel like that girl who lost her glass slipper.

What's her name again? Cinderella, I think.

We both share the same story except that my prince is a king. He would most likely slaughter the entire kingdom to find me instead of having a young maiden try on the shoe. Yes, he is that crazy, and yes, that's one reason why I love him. There's just something about his sinful nature that sparks a fire within my soul.

Nicklaus turns my hand, making it face upward. He entwines his fingers with mine as we get closer to the massive gold door that leads into his bed chambers. We are approached by a formal, stately-looking vampire in an expensive black suit. I don't remember seeing him before. He has fair-blond hair, similar to Vlad's, slicked back and brushed down to a T. His natural crimson eyes remind me of Count Cloven's. He has a blank expression.

"Welcome home, Your Majesty," he greets with a bow.

541

"Grand Harold," Nicklaus acknowledges him, as Grand Harold opens the door.

The strange familiarity that comes with stepping inside Nicklaus's chambers washes over me.

*This feels like home.*

"I haven't properly introduced you to my beloved," Nicklaus adds, as we step inside. "Grand Harold, this is my beloved, Claire. Claire, this is my royal butler, Grand Harold."

Grand Harold gracefully bows. If he is surprised by Nicklaus's introduction, his expression gives away nothing. "Your Majesty, Princess Daniela requests an audience with you at once. Duke Aldon is also present," he informs.

Nicklaus doesn't seem surprised or fazed on the outside, but what's on the inside says it all. I can feel the mixing pot of negative emotions stirring within my very own soul from him. Here comes the nerve-wrenching feeling again.

"We shall be in shortly," Nicklaus says, then he curtly dismisses Grand Harold with a single hand motion.

"Who is Princess Daniela?" I ask him, the moment Grand Harold steps out of the room.

He doesn't answer right away, allowing the monster within me to creep up on my surface. In a fatal attempt to settle her, I walk over toward the balcony. I missed the view. The way the sun blazes brightly over the many enchanting ombre shades of the deep-blue sea is mind-blowing.

I peek over my shoulder to get a glimpse of my beloved. He has a strange facial expression, and he seems to be lost in thought. This has happened a lot today, as if the weight of the world were on his shoulder. I don't like that. I don't want to be his burden. I wonder if Princess Daniela is one of the ladies from the respected vampire houses I read about. Hopefully, she is not one of his past suitors. I'm not in the mood to deal with seeing or hearing about any more of his past flings.

I mean, I trust him. Nicklaus belongs to me in every way. If he wanted one of those perfectly groomed leech wh*res, he would have taken them as his queen a long time ago, I'm sure. I'm not blind. I see how every woman in every species drools over him, including the werewolves, even if they never admit it. Nicklaus is just the type of man that can bring a woman to their knees, literally, with one commandment.

My monster gets more and more pissed just thinking about it. I don't want anyone else to claim him.

*Since when did I become so possessive?* I mentally ask myself. *I'll kill her.*

*Don't go there, Claire,* says my subconcious.

It's too late. My vision is already turning red. Oh how quickly one's mood can flip.

"Who the f*ck is this so called princess?" I ask him again. This time my voice is not my own.

"You're jealous," he taunts from behind me.

"Don't taunt me."

"I would never," he taunts again. "I'll only tell you about this beast of a princess if you admit that you're jealous."

He called her a beast. That's a good thing and enough to calm the monster within me. But he wants me to openly admit that I'm jealous, and that's one thing I refuse to do. My pride won't allow it.

"Come on, Claire. I know you are jealous. I can feel it."

Mother of f*ckship! He's got me there. I forget our link of emotions is open at this moment.

His bad mood shifts to a new one: amusement. He is f*cking amused at my jealousy. Oh great! Now, I really feel some type of way.

Out of nowhere, his strong arms wrap around my waist, once again instantly calming me down. His lips are dangerously close to my left ear, making me shiver in response. His touch seems to be the solution to any inner challenge I face.

After a minute of silence and warmth from his gentle touch, he speaks, "Daniela is my sister."

His sister . . . Jeepers creepers! I was just jealous of his sister. F*cking embarrassing.

"Sister? I didn't know you had a sister." I try to redeem myself.

Nicklaus's arms tighten around my waist. The mixing pots of negative emotions return, boiling with a vengeance. Something inside me is telling me there is a reason I never heard of his sister.

*       *       *

Stunningly brilliant gray eyes assess me from head to toe the very moment I step inside the room. Waist-length royal-purple hair, styled in a flawless elegant braid, flatters those long lashes and high cheekbones. Silver piercings are placed upon her perfectly plump lips, and I can't help but admire them. She is beyond beautiful. How in Nicklaus's right mind did he call her a beast? She is more like the beauty who captures the heart of a beast if anything. Princess Daniela is stunning, and I'm starting to believe the Vlad family's true curse is being dangerously beautiful with a bad attitude.

I received a better welcome from the vampire with scarlet-red eyes—Duke Aldon, who I assume is her beloved when I met him a few seconds ago. He is a tall man and is undoubtedly handsome. With his radiant smile and engaging personality, he is also such a charmer. It's strange to see him paired with such a b*tch. I mean I don't really know much about Princess Daniela, but first impressions are everything, right? She's acting like a b*tch. Who said physical appearance is everything? I guess Duke Aldon would disagree with that statement because the look of admiration that flickers inside his vivid crimson eyes tells it all—he loves her.

Marcellus and Xander just joined us seconds ago. They walked in just in time for the staring battle. Right now, Duke Aldon is looking dreamily at Princess Daniela while the princess is staring coldly at me. I'm staring blankly at her whereas Nicklaus is glaring at Princess Daniela, and so is Xander. Marcellus is just smirking. He is not participating, but he is damn sure getting a kick out of this silent battle of power.

My gut is telling me this is only the beginning. Obviously, Princess Daniela doesn't approve of our union and clearly no one gives a rat's ass. If she thinks burning me with her stare or pointing the tip of her delicate chin is enough to make me run away, she is wrong. Sister or not, I fear nobody.

With a smug grin plastered on my face, I continue to stare blankly into her eyes, refusing to be the one to break eye contact. The energy in the room is draining. I know Princess Daniela is trying to place her dominance over me. Nicklaus warned me about that, but she will not succeed in putting an ounce of fear in my heart.

I remember Nicklaus telling me, "My sister is the epitome of arrogance. She will try everything in her power to belittle and provoke you." Unfortunately for her, it's not working. I don't understand why supernatural women in power feel like they can scare me into submission—first, the lycan princess; then, the lycan queen; now, his sister.

I mentally shake my head. I will not bend, break, or bow to anyone.

Nicklaus places his hand on top of mine and then gives my cheek a soft peck. Princess Daniela raises her eyebrow, silently voicing her displeasure. Again, I don't give a rat's ass. I softly peck Nicklaus on his right cheek, just to ruffle her feathers more. This battle of dominance isn't my first one, and I'm sure it will not be my last.

I feel like we are going to be staring in silence for hours. I can't even enjoy the rich and fine decor that surrounds me. The tension inside this room is running so high that even the servants seem to want to run away from it. Like right now, the poor servant

545

girl's hands are trembling as she places down the first course. I want to assure her everything is okay and thank her for serving this delicious-smelling meal, but my proud and defiant monster within refuses to avert our eyes from our beloved's sister. She still has our undivided attention. Apparently, the princess has other plans. She flashes me an innocent smile—reminding me of a she-devil version of her brother's devilish smirk—then, she dives right into the fine meal prepared by the best chefs the world has to offer (I'm sure) without sparing me another glance.

Her blatant disrespect doesn't go unnoticed. Xander releases a small growl in response. Marcellus's jaw drops; he is so silly. Even Duke Aldon seems surprised by her actions. He gives her a look of disapproval, his already-pale skin now appearing transparent.

Everyone knows the king is the first one to eat. Nicklaus's face is anything but transparent. In fact, I'm almost certain it is many shades of red, like the devil ready to claim Princess Daniela's soul. She went too far.

The power radiating from my beloved is unbearable. If it weren't for his soft and gentle strokes on my hand, I would have fainted already. True to her last name, Princess Daniela doesn't look fazed and unbothered. There is no doubt she is a member of the Vlad family. Just like Nicklaus, she fears nothing. Just like him, she sure knows how to get under someone's skin. Just like him, she is an arrogant, prideful, and extremely conceited vampire. I must admit she has balls. And just like him, she would get kicked in the balls.

Nicklaus's hands clench into tight fists underneath the table. I know he is fighting with every fiber in his body to tame his monster. I can feel the demon clenching in my very soul. He wants blood. He wants her blood so bad I can taste it.

Before he acts on his truest natural desire, I decide to intervene by simply cutting the piece of steak on his plate, stabbing it with a fork. I place the meat directly in front of his mouth to show submission. The princess has scarred his pride, and I am the one to bandage his wound. I won't allow him to feed into her f*ckery. I once read that the biggest battles are won by doing absolutely nothing. Always feeding into one's ignorance makes you just as ignorant. Princess Daniela is beneath us. Whether she likes it or not, that's just the way the wind blows. She can play pretend all she likes, but every one in this room knows it.

The tension in Nicklaus's face dissolves as he takes a bite of his food. Out of the corner of my eye, I catch a glimpse of the reactions of others. Xander is smirking, and Marcellus has a mischievous grin on his face. Duke Aldon seems even strangely proud, as though a new line of respect has just been formed. Princess Daniela's lips thin, her eyes blazing bright red. She knows the point I have made: I just saved her life.

Say thank you, b*tch.

The rest of the lunch went well. The men already started engaging in pointless conversations a while back. The princess has not tried anything else so far, and she hasn't spared me another glance either. I wonder if she has given up with the big-bad-wolf act. It was so pointless.

Finally, Nicklaus has finished his meal. The others have to wait until we finish eating. They can't leave the table unless we dismiss them, so I'm grateful he is done. I feel so tired already, and I know that the Feast of the Brothers will be much worse. At least the princess has kept her mouth shut throughout the entire lunch. The others will show more than passive-aggressive behavior. I'm beat tired. Rest is much needed at this point.

Nicklaus rises from his seat and holds his hand out for me to join. Before I can take it, his sister decides to pull another stunt. She stands up. This time the room trembles with Nicklaus's growl.

"I already pardoned your foolish behavior once," he hisses. "Don't forget you are in my kingdom and are obliged to behave. Most importantly, don't forget your f*cking place."

547

"That's funny coming from you, Klaus," she spits through clenched teeth, "especially since you so foolishly declare a slave as our *supposed* queen."

"Enough, Daniela!" Nicklaus snaps, appearing in front of her.

They start to argue in a language I will never be able to understand. It sounds foreign and ancient yet so beautiful, and I'm sort of intrigued.

With every passing second, my monster claws harder to break free. She understands the dialogue word by word, and she doesn't like the tone of our beloved's sister. I try my best to keep her in check, but my head is already pounding and my skin starts to spark with the scene that is now playing in slow motion before me.

My eyes travel to Xander, and he stares directly into them while shaking his head from left to right as if he telling me, "No, don't do it." Then, they shift to Marcellus, who is also watching me with his head moving up and down as if saying, "Yes, do it, Claire. Get her." Next, my neck snaps in Duke Aldon's direction. The man seems oblivious to the power brewing within me. Finally, my eyes shift from my beloved and then to his pain-in-the-ass sister. They both are yelling at each other with blazing red eyes. The more I watch them, the more electricity sparks fire within my soul. I so desperately want to release the beast and snap Princess Daniela's fragile neck with my bare hands. It would be easy.

Nicklaus is losing control. I can see him ripping out her spine and draining every ounce of her royal blood. The luxury of the kill will be his wine within seconds if she doesn't tread carefully.

It amazes me how no one chooses to intervene. They, including Xander, are all watching with blank stares. And just when I decide to give in to my monster's craving, Xander once again looks at me. He wants this to stop, and he is depending on me. That's when I realize that all the men are waiting for my next move, like in a game of chess. This moment is a test of my true character. Should I put out the flame or add fuel to the already-blazing fire?

My monster chooses the latter, but that tad bit of humanity that keeps a glimpse of light within me refuses to cave in. Family is family no matter what, and that includes this selfish stuck-up b*tch.

"Say it one more time!" Nicklaus roars in English. His body is trembling, his eyes burning black coal. His left hand is tightly gripping the side of the table—I'm surprised it hasn't crumbled.

"You heard what I said. Should I address the peasant in a language she will understand?"

Princess Daniela's blazing red eyes move in my direction. "Not one respected vampire, servant, or even betrayer of the crown will accept you as our queen," she states.

"Then, every respected vampire, servant, and betrayer of the crown shall die," I declare, finally standing up.

Within a second, I'm in front of them both.

"Come, my love," I tell Nicklaus, as I rest my hand on his shoulder.

His body heat cools down by a long shot underneath my touch, and his stormy eyes blaze into my soul. Whatever she said has pushed him way over his limits.

"She is not worth it." I take his hand and lead him out of the room.

He follows my lead without hesitation.

Make no mistake. One more wrong move from Princess Daniela, and her life shall end.

For the second time within an hour, I've saved her life. Say thank you, Princess B*tch.

# CHAPTER SIXTY-NINE
## You Are the One

As we make our way out of the room, I can feel his anger rushing through my veins. Emotions boiling like hot lava swirl inside me. His power lingers in the air like a thick cloud of smoke; it's nearly impossible to breathe. I'm surprised I haven't choked.

*If Nicklaus had gotten his way, the princess would have been vanquished into a pile of ashes.*

With that in mind, I cling to his arms for her dear life. Princess B*tch really does owe me one.

The moment we're out in the hallway, I smash my body straight into Nicklaus's. Finally, I feel like I can breathe again. "Be calm, my ass-kissing king," I whisper softly in his ear before pulling his beautiful face to rest over my heart.

The intense rage causes a fever to form inside us, spreading quickly like wildfire, and the only way to turn down the heat is by allowing it to run its course. I know exactly what he needs, and it's me. I wrap my arms tightly around him, securing my position. Nicklaus's nostril flare widely as he takes in my scent. I cup his face with my hands, and he shivers. I run my fingers down the side of his neck, giving him time to enjoy the electric current that sparks out of my skin into his. Nicklaus growls softly when I release his face, only to run my hands through his velvety hair. Once again, my touch makes him shiver.

The sounds in the thriving palace seem to deaden, then silence soon envelops us. Nothing can be heard except the soft beating of my heart and our short, deep breaths. Quite a few servants, slaves, and men in black are walking around us, but none of them dares to stop or stare. They continue with their daily tasks as if we were invisible. There is no doubt in my mind that the little moment I and Nicklaus are sharing will be the new gossip in the slave quarters later on. But at this moment, it does not matter. Keeping him calm is my number one priority.

I continue to hold him close to my heart. I know its soft beating is his favorite sound. His distinctive cedarwood and expensive cologne aroma wash all over me. Out of concern for his pain-in-the-ass sister, I refuse to let him go. I still can't believe her. Actually, I'll take that back. I can believe her. She is her mother's daughter. Some genetic traits are inevitable. His sister is the demon child, birthed by the devil herself. How unfortunate!

*Well, let me not be a hypocrite because neither Nicklaus nor Xander is any saint. In fact, they might be the devil split in half.*

I quickly shake that thought out of my head. Right now isn't the time to be cracking jokes even if it's a truthful one.

After a short period of time of breathing in each other's scent, Nicklaus pulls away and brings his inhumanly beautiful face directly in front of my own. I almost whine from the loss of his skin contact. At this rate, I don't believe any amount of time touching him will ever be enough, not even an eternity of doing it will be long enough in my book. I'm utterly infatuated with him.

Nicklaus catches me off guard when he places a gentle kiss on the center of my forehead with his feather-like lips. "Thank you," he whispers huskily, his chiseled chin on top of my head.

"There is no need to thank me, my love." I slightly pull away and stare into his soul-snatching, piercing, chilling silver-cerulean eyes. I swear I can float adrift inside them. They are so beautiful. He's so beautiful.

"There is so much I should thank you for, Claire. You saved—"

I softly kiss his plump lips, cutting him off. "If anything, I have saved her."

"I'm not talking about Daniela, firecracker. I know you can kick my sister's ass."

"You're damn right, I can," I declare, "and yours too."

"Keep telling yourself that, Queen Claire."

"I shall," I respond. "Claire's Ass-kissing King Nicklaus." I just have to add it. My lips form into a silly grin as I try my best to replicate his sweet but sadistic smirk. "Don't forget I used to be a slave to you, leeches. I know how to deal with you all. And let me just say that the royal ones are by far the worst. They are a real pain in the neck."

A hearty chuckle escapes his lips. I love him. Only my ass-kissing king will catch on to my not-so-obvious leech jokes. "Oh yeah," he agrees, pulling me back into the warmth of his rock-hard chest.

Ouch! What the hell do they feed these vampire kings? Like seriously, his chest is made of steel. I know the answer to that question. Their favorite fruit is blood orange.

It's corny, I know.

"That's rich coming from the girl who can blend in with two species," he horribly jokes.

"Oh, that's funny, coming from the foolish king of all vampire kings, who is really a royal silly sucker."

His chest vibrates with his laughter. "Okay, you half-damned soul," he teases. "Or should I say, you ghost, in a half?" he mocks me.

I laugh at it. Gosh, I can't believe I said that when he first told me I was no longer human, or only half-human. This is the side of him that never ceases to amaze me. The powerful centuries-old king of all vampire kings—who sometimes behaves like an immature teenage human boy—has tainted and claimed my soul.

"On a serious note, Claire, I had waited lifetimes to find you. You are the beat to my still heart. Your existence is the sole reason for my existence," Nicklaus says, placing his lips softly onto my own. You saved me just by taking your first breath of air, and I'm forever grateful," he continues, then crashes his lips down onto mine.

The minty taste of his tongue invades my senses hard and strong. My pulse immediately quickens. I'm weak. The shower of his love pounds rapidly in my heart. The chemical reaction of our kiss is explosive, and I'm lost inside his element, blowing up like dynamite the very moment his lips touch mine.

He deepens the kiss, making it ten times harder for me to breathe. Our lips merging together as one is too much to take in. This extremely mind-blowing and intoxicating moment brings forth a mixture of many different things. The planets seem to align around me, the sun burns brightly above me, the moon glows within me, and the stars shine through me. Like a kaleidoscope of colors, so many beautiful emotions just rush through me.

Nicklaus said his sole reason for existence is me. In my eyes, he is my sole reason of existence. We were made for each other. This is our destiny.

He breaks the kiss and pulls away from me, giving our bodies some time to come back to reality. All I can think about is, How I did get so lucky? Thoughts of our unexpected bond run a marathon inside my head. Our love and bond came out of nowhere, formed so fast. He saved me in more ways than he could ever imagine. Before him, death was my way out, my way of gaining peace from this hell of a world. Now, Nicklaus is my only peace, and in his arms is my escape from reality. He is the only reason I breathe. My life would be pointless without him. He's my sanctuary.

How on earth did I ever get so lucky to be paired with him? Just thinking about the intoxicating connection we formed out of nowhere makes my eyes water.

Nicklaus must sense the sea of emotions suddenly pouring out of my soul as he pulls me back in and lifts my chin with the tip of his finger, then he asks, "What's going on in that beautiful twisted head of yours?"

*You.* I swallow down the truth.

"Nothing," I say, holding back my tears.

His eyes scan down and rest on my chest. "You know, even with that powerful emerald of yours, your heartbeat gives away when you're lying."

I sigh. "I know, but you can no longer read my thoughts," I tease. "And I'll never tell."

"Of course you won't, you little devil."

"I'm not a devil." I poke him in the chest.

Nicklaus flashes that beautiful sick, sadistic smile that I love so much. "No, you're not, firecracker. You're an angel, baby. I'm a devil. Together, we are a sinful angelic blend."

"We're twisted."

"I know." He winks.

Again, this is the side of him that never ceases to amaze me. I can stand here, acting like a child. I could tease and tell bad jokes to the end of time, as long as I do it with him.

I place my head back onto his chest, resting it there for a while longer as I enjoy his scent.

\*       \*       \*

Nicklaus walked me back to his chambers a while ago. I mean *our* chambers—a girl could never get used to that. He said he had some important tasks to complete before dinner. He made me promise not to wander off alone and ask the guards for anything I might need. He had his most-trusted men in black stationed at the red door that leads to our wing. Apparently, Commander Vlad is occupied, which typically won't be a bad thing. He is Mr. Meany after all. Well, he is not that bad even if he isn't the best company.

But without him, I have nothing to do. Who else am I supposed to bother? I can try my hand with the other guards. They don't seem so different from Vlad. Just like him, they are stoic robots who barely blink. Okay, Vlad does blink and is only stoical when he wants to be.

Wait a minute, I'm giving Mr. Meany a compliment? Boredom must really have struck because it damn sure has shocked the f*ck out of me.

Nicklaus promised to be back in time to escort me to dinner. Hopefully, he can return sooner. It has been over an hour since he left, and I can't relax. All I can think about is him. How bored I am without him! Gosh, I'm turning into one of those clingy leeches that act like they can't eat, sleep, or piss without their beloved. Oh my God, it's annoying. This craving for him is sweetly sickening. Maybe a little detox from his highly addictive presence is what I need. A little time alone never hurts anybody.

*Ding-dong, Claire. Yes, it can, because you're clearly hurting without him.*

My monster's presence is deadly silent without our beloved around. She might as well be announced dead. It's pathetic—I know—but that's just how it is. We are lost without him.

I pace back and forth in front of the balcony, practically sulking like a baby because I miss him. I have to try to focus on anything that would occupy my mind long enough to stop thinking about him. I stop pacing to admire the view. I really did miss island scenery. The sun is setting. The beautiful, burning amber star is hovering close over the sea. As the day turns into night, the usual ombre body of water resembles one shade—cerulean. It's absolutely breathtaking. It reminds me of Nicklaus's extraordinarily vivid eyes.

"Oh geez! Get a grip, Claire!" I scold myself out loud. I am beyond pathetic. I start pacing back and forth again. And let's not forget my nonstop sulking.

The sound of someone knocking on the door stops me in my tracks. My nostrils flare as I take in a unique delicate floral scent. It is water-fresh, clean, luxurious, and slightly powdery but not too sweet. It's just perfect.

"Who is it?" I call out from behind the door.

I know it's not one of the men in black because I wouldn't have missed that scent—they damn sure don't smell good. Plus, the guards won't allow just anybody to pass through. They wouldn't want to anger Nicklaus, but now for sure he would lose his sh*t.

They don't respond, increasing my curiosity. I strain my ears to hear any sound from the other side of the door. Whoever it is has a heartbeat, indicating that it is a human. However, no human I've encountered so far has smelled this good.

"If you don't tell me who you are, I will not grant you access."

Still they remain silent—what the hell! I know they are still there because their heart pounding like an alarm is giving them away. They're either excited or scared, but most likely scared out of their mind. That would explain their silence. There's no telling what rumors are floating around the palace about me.

I am about to open the door when the soft voice on the other side stops me.

"Claire, it's Jadis! Open the door. I was trying to surprise you."

My heart drops.

If it were a few days ago, I would have opened the door, jumped for joy, and pulled her into the tightest hug I could manage, smothering her. Now, I'm not so sure.

She knocks again.

"Go away!" I tell her.

I don't feel like dealing with this right now. What if she reacts the way Mecca did? What if she no longer wants to be friends with me?

"What? Are you crazy? If your cute ass doesn't open the door in five seconds, my cute ass is going to fly through it."

F*ck, I know she is good at it. This girl went from pet to chosen. She can do anything if she puts her mind to it, not to mention her being a maniac.

My heart starts to beat faster. I don't want to hurt her because of my cowardice. Before all of this, I never was the type to care about what people thought of me. It's not like I was the popular girl in school, but I never had friends then, so I guess that changes things. We all have our own insecurities, mostly formed from our past, some from the present. That's part of being human. After all, I'm still half-human.

With that in mind, I take a deep breath and open the door. Jadis rushes in and throws her arms around me, slightly cutting off my air supply.

"OMG, Claire! I missed you so goddamn much, gorgeous," she squeals, nearly tackling me down. "OMG! OMG! OMG! I missed you so much. Look at you," she says, pulling away from me. Her soft brown eyes are now filled with tears. "I missed you so, so much. I have loads to empty onto your back, my sweetest darling best friend. Speaking of which, why the hell did you tell me to go away?" She raises a curious brow, her hands on her hips.

I take a moment to look at her. She is wearing a sheer, floral-printed maxi dress that hugs her tiny frame like a sleeve. The dress is daring and demanding yet somehow still extremely elegant. It screams highly-favored chosen. Jadis looks beyond beautiful. She is flawless, as always.

"Uh. Hello, gorgeous. I'm talking to you!"

"Uh!"

Oh right. I have to explain why the hell I did not let her in at first, but I'm surprised she doesn't sense anything different about me. The other humans act like they did.

I take a much-needed breath. Okay, here goes nothing. "Uh, I thought . . . I thought . . ."

"Since when the hell does a cat hold Claire's tongue?" she teases, dropping her arms down to her sides. "You've gotta be kidding me! This is unbelievable! Ever since I got here, all the humans have been speaking about how you had become a legend overnight in the northern kingdom, and here you are, acting shy? The world knows you are far from that."

*Legend?*

"What do you mean by 'legend'?" I ask her. Now I'm confused.

Jadis rolls her eyes, then makes her way over toward the balcony. "Oh please. Now, you're being modest," she says. "The golden boy made it his point to tell the entire slave quarter about you saving King Cyrus's slave, not to mention Victoria, who told everyone that the two of you are now BFF."

*Victoria . . . golden boy . . . Wait! Is she referring to Alec? I forgot about him. How the hell did he get here?*

"Oh yeah," Jadis continues. "Then, there's the fact that the entire world is speaking about the golden-haired human that has stolen the heart of the king of all vampires kings."

I'm stunned. This is not what I expected at all.

"So, my dear friend," Jadis says, turning back around to face me with the biggest smile plastered on her angelic face, "are you going to explain to me what the hell is going on? All the humans are buzzing about you being the chosen one, and I'm here to tell you, baby, you are most certainly the one."

"I'm trying to figure out the same thing," I confess, making my way over to Nicklaus's oversized bed—*our* oversized bed.

Jadis sits down right beside me. Leave it to her to not have an ounce of fear of sitting down on Nicklaus's bed. She is just like Mecca, crazy as ever. Well, she is a maniac. The difference between her and Mecca is that there isn't any hatred in her pretty brown eyes as she stares at me just like she has stared at me since day one. The only thing I can identify is kindness and curiosity. She hasn't changed one bit, and I'm beyond grateful.

Unexpectedly, I throw my arms around her. "I missed you so much. You have no idea what I've been through."

"Hopefully a whole lot of f*cking." She giggles into the side of my neck.

Oh, she hasn't changed at all. She is still the crazy vampire-boy maniac that I met.

"I missed you so much," I tell her again.

"I missed you too, doll face," she responds, tightening our hug.

We stay like that for a while before Jadis decides to pull away.

"Now spill!" she says.

# CHAPTER SEVENTY
## I'll Never Kiss and Tell

For hours now, Jadis and I have been in my bedchambers, talking about everything. I mean *everything*. I started from the very beginning—my very first encounter with Nicklaus and all the other vampire kings at the auction. I explained how I saved Jasmine's life and then I went into great detail about how Xander is nowhere near the cold-hearted king he is rumored to be. I told her how he'd showed me he'd had my best interest in heart since day one, even when I was too stubborn to admit it.

Speaking about Xander's undying loyalty, devotion, and unconditional love brought tears to my eyes several times. I've never truly realized how much he had done for me until I said it out loud. He is truly the most-kindhearted person I've ever met.

After I spilled tears of joy, I cried my heart out over Mecca, and Jadis has been extremely interested in knowing more about my unexpected friendship of doom with the long-lost northern Luna. I shared our tragic tale from the very beginning, during the day when Nicklaus killed the slave girl in his sick and twisted way to save me and then I met the most beautiful wolf I'd encountered.

I told Jadis how Mecca bragged to the other northern wolves about me saving her, then I confessed that Mecca didn't truly understand that she was the one who actually saved me. I told her the stories Mecca had shared with me, which had given me hope to gain true freedom—the real type of freedom I could experience without my life being stripped away from this hellhole of a world.

I confessed that not only had Mecca told me stories about the world before the Awakening, but she had also gifted me with the opportunity to see the real world outside of chains and bondage. I explained my point of view about werewolves overall and described how beautifully insane they truly are. I stressed that they are so much more than the savage beasts. I explained their extraordinary culture, beliefs, and values to the best of my ability. Then my tears flowed freely again as I talked about my very first bonfire. I showed Jadis the beautiful pendant holding the fascinating emerald that is full of power I'm somehow able to wield. She stared at it in pure fascination, her eyes tearful and wide. She understood my pain.

After crying together, we started talking about our encounters with supernatural beings. I told her about Vlad, and when I talked about Marcellus, she laughed her ass off the entire time. Can you blame her? Who wouldn't? Just hearing the things that can come out of the man's mouth will make someone piss themselves.

Then I went into telling her about the influential wolf family—the Wildes. Jadis already heard about them, which wasn't a surprise, since they are royalty in the world of the wolves. However, she was shocked to learn about the ruthless king's beloved being an extremely beautiful, shy, and unique she-wolf by the name of Embry Wilde.

When I described the Alpha and the Beta from the Northern Pack, Jadis uttered, "F*cking delicious." She is so crazy about boys.

Her face quickly shifted from lust to disgust as I told her about the lycan king, queen, and princess. That was when I learned that there's a member of the lycan family I had the pleasure of not meeting. (Thank God.) His name is Prince Ethel. He is rumored to be the Almighty—and way past the point of arrogant—Prince.

Hmmm . . . sounds familiar. You know they say, "The apple sure doesn't fall far from the tree." Anyway, Prince Ethel and the legendary lycan beta named Rollin have recently traveled to King Cornelius's kingdom. Jadis doesn't like Prince Ethel. The Beta is pretty decent for her, and that he possesses the most-unusual shade of amethyst eyes she has ever seen. But other than that, she doesn't know much about him. He doesn't mingle much with others.

The prince is obnoxious and arrogant. Jadis made it her point to emphasize that he loves attention. He makes sure everyone in the room knows exactly who he is. He seems f*cking overrated, if you ask me. Jadis has a bad feeling about him, but she can't place her finger on it. King Cornelius has kept her far away from the prince during her stay.

Oh yes! I almost forgot King Cornelius and Jadis have shared plenty of steamy nights. Okay, let me just say they have shared every single night together since she arrived in his kingdom. Jadis is head over heels in love with the dominant, sadistic king. He still hasn't acknowledged her as his beloved, but she believes with all her heart that he has.

I've bitten my tongue on multiple occasions during our tell-it-all moment. I don't like King Cornelius. Let's be very clear with that. However, it isn't my place to meddle with their affairs even though I really, really want to. Jadis is a big girl, and she can handle it herself.

She is still talking about the soon-to-be love of her life at this very moment, while I am stuffing my mouth with buttermilk pancakes that have just been delivered—thanks to my beloved, for certain. He also made sure that the men in black had bought us a cute little dining glass table.

Thoughtful, right? I know.

King Cornelius ordered a servant to serve Jadis a huge plate of berries and some other fruits and vegetables and two humongous pots full of coffee. Apparently, Jadis can't live without

562

coffee. It is a must-have for her, just like pancakes are a must-have for me. It's just a staple of our lifestyles.

"Claire, are you listening?" Jadis asks me again, as I stuff a pancake into my mouth.

I try my hardest to keep my opinion to myself. I have a bad habit of doing that when Jadis is concerned. Plus, I feel the need to keep her out of harm's way. And my monster agrees with me. No one would get to hurt Jadis and get away with it.

"Of course," I lie, swallowing down the fluffy heaviness of pancake. Damn, that's good!

"You're a horrible liar." She places her mug down onto the table.

How does everyone seem to know when I am lying? I can't be that bad of a liar, right?

"I have told you my honest opinion about every single part of your journey. Is it really hard for you to do the same thing?" she questions me.

F*ck! Now, I feel bad. Jadis does have a point, though.

I drop my fork and look directly into her big brown eyes. "I think you deserve better Jadis," I confess. "You are truly beautiful inside and out. After everything you've been through, all I can think about is how you deserve nothing but happiness. You are kind, smart, and one of the best, if not the best person I've known." I pause, waiting for a reaction.

She doesn't seem to have taken offense at my words.

"King Cornelius—"

"Makes me happy, Claire," she interrupts me, standing up.

You can see the sun setting from the balcony behind her. The stunning view enhances her already-undeniable beauty. Now that I'm looking at her with my enhanced sight, it makes me realize that she is far more beautiful than I have thought. In fact, she is seriously, inhumanly beautiful. King Cornelius would be stuck on stupid if he ever hurt her. She truly is a rare jewel.

"He makes me happier than you could ever imagine. I know it seems strange from your perspective since King Nicklaus has openly declared you as his beloved, but you have to understand that all vampires don't have that luxury."

"What do you mean?" I ask, out of plain confusion.

I would get it if Cornelius was a typical vampire, but he is far from that. In fact, he is a royal and a direct descendant of a wealthy vampire house. Surely, he could claim whoever the hell he wants to claim as his beloved.

"From my understanding, King Nicklaus is a direct descendant of the Vlad family. From what Cornelius shared with me, Nicklaus's family is the real deal. Everyone respects them and is scared sh*tless of them. They have ruled over vampires long before the Awakening."

"He told you that?"

I can't believe King Cornelius would actually share their history with her.

"Yup." Jadis nods and smiles deviously. "We shared a lot of things with each other, on his bed, on the floor, in the shower, in the pool, in the balcony, on the roof—"

"Okay, okay, okay! I get it!"

No wonder she consumes so much coffee. She and King Cornelius obviously have been f*cking like bunnies. I'm surprised she isn't expecting, which wouldn't be out of place, considering what she has been doing and the environment she is in. No wonder he is the king of the Kingdom of Breeders. Good God!

"Jadis, you are kinky," I tell her how it is.

"Only for the dominant, sadistic king." She bites down onto one of her fingers with no shame. "I'll submit any day and any position he wants me to."

My mouth drops open.

*A submissive little son of a gun! Maybe, they are meant for each other.*

"Enough about me." Jadis takes her seat. "Tell me about how good King Nicklaus is in bed."

*Wait, what? She didn't just ask me that.*

My face is on fire. I didn't expect that one.

"He must be good. I heard all the kings are great in bed, but Nicklaus is rumored to be an incubus when compared to the other kings," she goes on.

Now my face is officially flaming, burned to a crisp. My monster, on the other hand, is annoyed. I can imagine her making a face inside my head. If it were anyone else, she would have snapped their neck. But it's Jadis.

"I'm not discussing that," I tell her, because I'm not.

At this point, I feel like I can tell Jadis anything, but when it comes to Nicklaus, I must draw the line. Something is off-limits; Nicklaus is off-limits. The private moments I spend with him are special, treasured, and dear to my heart. I'll guard them with my life. No one needs to learn about how skillful he is with his silky tongue or how inhumanly big his manhood is. That horse dick belongs to me, and I'm the only cowgirl that should know how riding his rodeo feels like.

"Such matter is off-limits, Jadis!"

"Oh"—she grins—"so you have engaged in such pleasures?"

"What? I have no idea what you're talking about."

"Bullsh*t," she calls me out. "You can see it up in your grill. Plus, you're the worst liar in this entire universe."

I really must be a bad liar.

"Your face screamed he has been f*cking the sh*t out of you," she says. "Not to mention your racing heart."

"How do you know my heart is racing?" I ask her, changing the subject.

She starts laughing. "Don't you dare try to change the subject."

Goddamn, she is good!

565

"It doesn't take a rocket scientist or supernatural creatures to see how fast your heart is hammering inside your chest." Jadis laughs harder. She has placed her hand over my chest before I even realize it. "See?" she teases, as my heart is pounding profusely. "Cross your heart and hope to die. Swear to God you wouldn't lie!"

*No, she did not . . .*

"You didn't just use the 'solemnly swear' on me," I say.

It has been so long since I heard that as a kid. When we were children, we used to solemnly swear inside those dreadful institutes we were placed in. Before the vampires got their hooks into us, we humans were pretty close—believe it or not—but that changed over the years. From what I know, all human children around the world use the "solemnly swear," just like we chant "Your fight is over" when one of our own is killed. It's been the way for as long as I can remember. Humans may have been placed in chains, but we do have a little culture. If only we can stick together, then our race—the human race—may be able to break the chains. I keep forgetting I'm no longer just human, but I will always be loyal to my race. Vampire queen and all, I will never forget where I came from.

*Things need to change for humans. I need to change things for them, for us.*

That reminds me that I still haven't told Jadis I'm no longer just human.

"Earth to Claire." Jadis waves her hands in front of my face. "It's that good, huh?"

"Huh? I'm lost. What are you talking about?"

"You know very well what I'm talking about." She hops off the bed, only to jump up and down like the little sex bunny that she is. "Damn! King Nicklaus must really be a demon."

*He's a demon.*

"You blanked out, just thinking about the things he has done to you." She sighs dreamily.

"I don't kiss and tell."

"So you have kissed?" She wiggles her eyebrows.

Oh gosh, who would have thought that Jadis is such a pervert?

"With tongue or without?"

*With!*

I refuse to say that out loud. Memories of our first kiss surface in my mind, making me redder than a dog in heat.

*Really, Claire, a dog in heat? Jadis is most certainly rubbing off on me.*

"Fine! Be that way." Jadis pouts her lips and crosses her arms, behaving like a five-year-old child—this is ridiculous. She pulls another cup of coffee. "If you don't tell, I won't tell," she speaks again.

"You already told me everything," I point out, holding in my laughter.

"No, I haven't. Trust me when I say there is much more where that came from."Jadis giggles inside her mug.

"I'm sure, buttercup."

There is no doubt in my mind about that.

"You damn Skippy, cherry pop!" she says to me.

The great irony of the pet name she gives me is too much to take, so I lean over and laugh my ass off. Jadis is such a joy. She has one of those personalities that just draws you in. Her soul is on fire. And when you consider all she has overcome, she is truly extraordinary. I admire everything about her. She is a special girl.

We sit in silence for a while, soaking up each other's company.

*It's getting late. We should be preparing ourselves for tonight's festivities.*

I shake my thoughts away before they run too deep. Right now, I just want to lavish myself with peace. This moment with Jadis was needed. No, it was mandatory, especially when the reality of what's to come starts to sink in. That reminds me.

"There is something I need to tell you," I begin.

567

Jadis perks up and her lips curve into a legendary, devious smile. Her mind is so dirty.

"No, it's nothing like that," I quickly tell her, before she starts asking questions about the many positions we have tried. "It's serious."

Jadis's promiscuous demeanor dissolves the very moment the word "serious" comes out of my mouth. She places her mug down and then gives me her undivided attention. My heart rate starts to pick up as I brace myself. I don't want to lose her like I lost Mecca. I don't want to see sunset inside her big brown eyes as I tell my truth.

"I'm all ears, cherry pop," she says, adding a soft smile that makes me form a tiny smile of my own.

I glance in the direction of the balcony, debating with myself whether I should really tell her—well, she will find it out one way or another, so I might as well tell her now. I take a deep breath, getting myself ready for the worst. "I am no longer human," I get out.

"What do you mean?"

Out of the corner of my eye, I can see her lean her head over to one side, watching me curiously.

"I am a vampire, well half-vampire." I turn to face her. "Vampires call my kind dhampirs. It means that I am half-human and half-vampire. Apparently, my kind is rare."

Jadis jumps to her feet, and my heart stops. "No f*cking way," she squeaks. "That's not fair. You get the king of all vampire kings, which makes you the queen of the entire world, then you become a cool kick-ass half vampire who can somehow wield power from a mysterious emerald? What the hell! I'm certainly Jell-O!"

Jell-O? She can't be serious. But her adorable pout says it all. Without, thinking I make my way over to her in vampire speed and give her the biggest hug I can muster.

"OMG, you're a freaking vampire, in real life! Oh f*ck, this is some cool sh*t!" Jadis throws her arms right around me.

"I love you, buttercup."

"Of course you do, cherry pop," she says, slightly pulling away. "Who wouldn't?"

She is right about that.

One thing is for certain and two things are for sure: Jadis makes it impossible for anyone not to love her. Earlier today, I was worried about King Cornelius hurting her. Now, I'm kind of concerned about him because Jadis is certainly a heartbreaker. Losing her friendship or love would certainly break anyone.

$$* \quad * \quad *$$

The last two hours have been hectic, most certainly fast and furious. Jadis has been running around like a chicken with her head cut off. She is taking full charge of getting me ready. The time is near. The sun has set, bringing forth the darkness of the night. I feel more powerful than I ever could imagine. I am officially a being of the night. My monster, which typically lingers and clings to me, is up front and center. She is here with me, and we are one once again.

Shortly after I confessed to Jadis I am no longer human, Grand Harold delivered two dresses and two pairs of heels, not that we needed them. I still have millions of dresses in my closet, with tags still on them, and more-than-enough shoes for me to walk in for the rest of eternity. Jadis and I are of the same size. We would be A-okay.

I still haven't seen the dress for me, so shower, hair, and makeup first—Jadis's orders.

"Come on, Claire. It's time," she tells me for the thousandth time, while I have been in the bathroom, procrastinating.

"Coming," I answer from behind the bathroom door, for the thousandth time as well.

"Get your cute ass out her now!"

I can tell she has become impatient. My sensitive ears can pick up on the tapping of her expensive heels. I groan and open the door. As expected, she is already standing in the middle of the room, tapping her left foot. Her one hand is on her hip, and the other hand is holding a hanger with a dress that's still covered.

Jadis's attire for the night is in plain view, flawlessly put on her to-die-for frame. She's stunning, and nothing or no one will ever be able to take that away from her. The dress is made for her. It's a sheer floor-length A-line gown embroidered with 3D crimson flowers. It fits her body like a glove and shows every inch of her delicate skin. But one great detail that brings the dress to life is the real rose petals that cover her kitty and nipples. Her shoulder-length chestnut hair is curled to perfection. Her face is beat for the gods. She is the true definition of exquisiteness.

"Oh darling." She flashes a dazzling smile. "If you think I look good, just wait until I place my magical hands on you," she squeaks as she unzips the dress.

My heart flutters and skips, then explodes.

*OMG! Queen me! Crown me. This is so unreal.*

# CHAPTER SEVENTY-ONE
## Then and Now

"Oh my God!"

My soft heart rate skyrockets, triplefold. The dress is a dress, the most-enchanting piece of fabric. Maybe that's not a big deal, knowing my upbringing and all. However, to say that it is the most-beautiful piece of clothing I've ever seen is an understatement. The seamstress has outdone herself, and that's for sure. Nicklaus has outdone himself.

It is a strapless, mermaid-style, floor-length tulle gown embroidered with crystals and pure gold, sewn to perfection and meant to draw attention from every angle. It is daring and inviting, just what the vampires like. It most certainly fits for a queen. Mind-blowing and magnificent, this dress was made for royalty for sure. Through the delicate but extremely elegant fabric, my skin shall surely glow and show—another big must-have for the vampire community.

The gown feels like liquid gold as it is touches my skin, melting my body in a united front and syncing onto my frame in perfect harmony. I'm grateful. No. That would be another understatement. I am beyond blessed. I feel like this dress was made for me, or more like made for me to stand alongside him. How did I get so lucky?

As usual, Jadis's magical hands begin their work, styling my hair in a very elegant deep wave updo before she paints a masterpiece on my face. She does it wonderfully that it makes me feel more beautiful than usual. She really does have a gift. She's perfected the craft of making others look dangerously desirable.

As I study myself in the mirror, I feel irresistible, like I can make anyone do whatever I want once their eyes are on me. The intense amount of raw power flowing through my veins would be a weird addition to the look, but only one word can describe my feeling: invincible.

"Thank you again, Jadis. You really outdid yourself."

"Nonsense, cherry pop," she replies, finishing up some last-minute touches on my hair.

"Ouch," I groan.

There are more-than-enough bobby pins to poke my brains out.

"Beauty is pain, Claire." Jadis pulls away from me and assesses me from head to toe.

"Yeah. A pain in the ass," I complain, taking in my appearance one last time.

*Wow! Jadis truly has outdone herself. Breathtakingly beautiful. The pain is worth it.*

I'll never admit that, not that I have to. The mischievous smile tugging on Jadis's lips tells it all. She already knows. She must be finally satisfied with her masterpiece because she makes her way over to the table to take a huge gulp of her coffee.

I study myself for a while longer. I'm not conceited or something. I'm just really impressed.

"I really didn't add anything but some liner, a red lipstick, and blush," Jadis suddenly says.

My face is flawless, even more flawless than a vampire face should be. My green eyes appear brilliant, and my red lips are plumper. My lashes are fuller, thicker, and longer. Those key points scream mascara, foundation, and concealer. I don't know much about makeup, but I do know those.

I turn to give her a wary look.

"Seriously, Claire," she continues, "I really didn't add that much." She places her mug down. (This girl seriously loves coffee.) "In all honesty, your makeup is extremely subtle. You don't even need it."

My ears pick up on the slow and steady beating of her heart. I don't know if she is lying or not.

"Your skin glistens naturally, and your features are to die for, literally," Jadis expresses. "It's really extraordinary if you ask me. You have always been beautiful, but now no one can compare to you. It's like you became a goddess during your trip."

*Nope! The only godly-looking individual would be Nicklaus. Now, that man!*

"I'm so jealous. Lady Gwen doesn't even hold a candle to your beauty, and Ive always felt like she resembled a baby doll."

*So have I, the baby doll that I would like to break.*

I decide to keep that comment to myself.

When I was in North America, I didn't even think about that leech b*tch. Now, her name keeps randomly coming up. Where the hell is she anyway? I'm sure the gossip about Nicklaus and his chosen has reached her ears by now. One can only hope she hides in a shell for the rest of eternity. If she knew what was good for her health, she would.

I turn to take a look at my drop-dead gorgeous best friend. "I'm the one who should be jealous of you, Jadis. My vampire traits may enhance my beauty, but you are human and are timeless to me."

"Yup, cherry pop." She takes another look at herself in the mirror. "We are some hot b*tches, and we're both totally getting laid tonight."

We burst out laughing.

Oh Jadis, my Jadis!

I can smell Vlad before the sound of his knuckles knocking on the door hits my sensitive ears.

573

"Your Highness, King Nicklaus and King Xander ordered me to escort you down to the dining hall," he says from the other side of the door.

*Since when did he become so formal?*

"He just called you, Your f*cking Highness," squeals Jadis. "It's about to go down."

She has no idea how true her statement is.

\*       \*       \*

"Chin up, brave one." Xander lifts my chin up with his finger, making sure my eyes meet his.

Xander had been waiting at the bottom of the grand staircase. When we arrived, he directed Vlad to escort Jadis to the dining hall. Chosens are required to be present before their king. I, on the other hand, will walk alongside my king, my beloved. Oh God, I don't believe I will ever get used to calling him *my* anything. But that's what he is—all mine.

Xander is preparing me to make my entrance. At this point, I just want to get it over with.

During our walk down to the dining hall, I almost lost it. My heart started pounding. Thankfully, he came to my rescue, like the knight in shining armor that he is. He's currently giving me a little pep talk.

"Who would have thought that a human girl who was so horrible in school would be eventually crowned as the queen of all kings?" he states, a charming smile playing across his lips. The pride shining in his icy silver eyes is hard to ignore.

"You have managed to defeat the odds many times, brave one. You have survived rape and mental and physical torture. You have survived constant bullying from your peers and constant harassment from my species. So many have tried to break you and bring you down." His eyes start to water, and so do mine. "So many

574

have tried to extinguish the fire that burns brightly inside you. So many have tried to put out your light—"

"Unfortunately for us, there's a blinding light inside you. No one can deny you."

I shiver as the words are whispered in my ear. I turn to face my breathtaking beloved. He is wearing a black tuxedo, and a waistcoat and bow tie encrusted with pure gold. It's almost identical to my gown. His hair, dark as the night sky, is slicked back, highlighting his soul-snatching silver-cerulean eyes. He looks phenomenal.

Everything and everyone around us fade away. I think Xander said something about giving us a moment alone, but I'm not that sure because all I can see, smell, think, and hear revolve around Nicklaus. My breath gets caught inside my throat, shutting down my ability to speak or breathe. This can't be real. The sight of him takes my breath away, and I'm literally fighting for air.

"You like what you see, firecracker?" he teases, winking.

Oh the torture. I'm having a panic (of the sight) attack, and he wants to taunt me about it? It's just like the first time he met me. He cannot be serious.

Nicklaus takes his place beside me before taking my hand. He knows exactly what to do. Now I feel like I can breathe again. His scent seeps through my pores, only to settle inside my heart. I suddenly feel all warm and cozy inside. I love his smell.

"You're an asswipe," I remark.

He chuckles and then brings my hand close to his lips, only to drop a soft and gentle kiss. "No, my love. I will kiss your ass, but I won't wipe it."

"Shut up!" I say, and I can't help but blush.

He continues smiling from ear to ear. "Don't' worry, firecracker. The sight of you makes my still heart skip a beat every single time I look at you."

Yeah, I bet. I know the feeling.

575

"Before we go in, I want to educate you about some of the kings."

I nod. I'm grateful. If there's anyone who can help me get through this, it will be him.

He starts telling me all I need to know about each and every vampire king.

* * *

Are you ready now, firecracker?" he asks, as we approach the door.

I nod. "As ready as it gets."

Nicklaus eyes me up and down, amusement evident on his handsome face. "Good! They damn sure aren't ready for you," he says.

The men in black open the doors, and my mind flashes back to my very first feast the moment we step into the dining hall. Just like before, there are servants everywhere, running around like chickens with their heads cut off. The room is somehow different even though the decor, dining room setup, and the expected guests are present.

When we dined with Princess B*tch earlier today, rows of crystal chandeliers sparked this dark room to life. Now, the many ivory candles placed all around the room are the only source of light, just like the very first feast. Once again, the dancing flames from the candles bounce onto the squeaky clean, sparkling marble floor. Xander is already present. He is standing by the table, smirking and appearing to be oddly proud. All of the chosens are already in positions, bowing in the name of obedience, elegance, and grace.

My eyes quickly scan the girls. First, they land on Jadis. She looks like a goddess, but I already know that. Next, they land on Victoria, who was once my enemy, but she is now sort of a friend. She is still extremely beautiful. She is wearing a sleeveless crimson

576

silk gown with deep plunging neck and back and has a high side split. It hugs her body and shows off her fair skin, just as vampires like it. She looks stunning, which is really nothing new. She always has been.

Finally, my eyes land on the one and only Jasmine. My monster is already clawing inside me, ready to sink our fangs into her delicate, flawless skin. She looks like the devil's wife with her sheer—barely there—painted-on like liquid, strapless, mermaid-style gown. It kind of resembles what Jadis is wearing. The only difference is that Jasmine's kitty and nipples are on full display—f*cking wh*re—but I must admit the girl has perfected the art of seduction. She's bewitching. Every single one of the chosens is ravishing, as expected.

The other kings have not shown up yet. They are expected to make their presence known after Nicklaus's arrival. Leave it for Xander to be the one to defy the rules.

Nicklaus and I walk over to the table in the center, holding hand in hand. The skin-to-skin contact sparks electric currents to flow between us. I can't get enough of this feeling; it's so welcoming.

As we draw closer to the table, Nicklaus turns to face me. "I love you, firecracker," he declares.

Butterflies swarm in my stomach as his soul-snatching eyes bore into my soul. He means every word. There is no denying that. God, how did I get so lucky?

"I love you too, my ass-kissing king," I tell him, my sensitive ears picking up on Jadis's fatal attempt of a sneaky laughter.

*Oh freak. Now I'm going to have to explain to her why I call him my ass-kissing king. She is too nosy.*

Nicklaus chuckles, as if he knows what I'm thinking.

Suddenly, many different scents hit me hard and strong that it's nearly impossible for me to distinguish one from another.

There are too many scents mingling, and they all are extremely pleasant. As a matter of fact, they smell delicious.

At first, I was under the impression that the servants were about to walk into the room with a million and one trays of mouthwatering desserts, until the door actually opens. King Cyrus is the first to present himself. He looks amazing with his new haircut and his naturally flawless and fair skin. His handsome face looks the same, and as usual, no emotion can be detected in it. His golden eyes are set on one and one only—me. And guess what? I blankly stare right back at him. The ruthless king should know by now he doesn't intimidate me, and no one can.

A ghostly hint of a smile tugs on his lips as he saunters into the room. The scent of wildflowers and damp earth hangs onto him like a second skin, blending in perfect harmony with his own natural mulberry spice aroma.

Embry immediately comes to mind. A part of me feels bad about what happened between us. The other part of me—the more monstrous part of me—still feels some type of way about her attempting to take my beloved's life. I don't know if I want to apologize to her or murder her. Nicklaus is also conflicted. I can feel his emotions running through my veins. He loves Cyrus, but at the same time, his monster is wary of him now. He explained to me that Cyrus is a member of the House of Ettore. That pacific wealthy house is known to always side with the House of Vlad, always. Nicklaus doesn't know what to expect or where they stand, and that troubles him. It troubles me too.

I rub the back of his hand with my fingertips, attempting to calm his nerves. Hopefully, the two of them can just let bygones be bygones. They have been friends for a very long time.

Next to enter is King Luscious, the barbaric and reckless king. Nicklaus told me he may be the hardest to persuade to stand by our side due to his upbringing. Apparently, his parents, who were very respected and treasured vampires from the Wealthy House of Akeldama, were murdered by a group of hunters.

Nicklaus said that hunters are humans with enhanced speed, strength, and more brainpower. They were created to protect the human race from the supernatural world. To be more exact, they were created to protect humans from vampires. Nicklaus seems to hate them more than he hates werewolves. He made them sound like some human superheroes who know how to kick some leeches's asses when he described them. I can't wait to meet one.

Anyway, King Luscious despises hunters, and every race related to them. Trueborn hunters, hunters, humans, and dhampirs are not his thing, so he will probably hate me. He is groomed from head to toe. He is wearing a black tuxedo and a black waistcoat. His sun-kissed skin appears too smooth to touch, and his dark features are trimmed, cleaned, and tamed. The thought of him being a wimp appears inside my head once again, just like the very first time I saw him. All I can say now is that looks can certainly be deceiving.

Nicklaus made it his point to stress the fact that King Luscious isn't to be underestimated. He is exactly what I thought him to be during my first feast—dangerous and very lethal. The closer he gets, the more I am able to identify that he smells like rosewood. His eyes are still locked on me. Unfortunately for him, he receives the same treatment as the king before him. Proud and defiant, I stare right into the milk-chocolate eyes of the savage vampire king. Despise me if he must, but he will respect me.

King Marcellus is the next one to saunter through the doors, smelling fresh like clean linen. He looks calm, cool, and collected—which kind of catches me off guard because I've grown so used to his turned-all-the-way-up and nonchalant behavior. It's sort of disappointing. He is the type of man that should never guard or shield who he truly is. Today, I learned that he is a descendant of the Wealthy House of Throne, who are known for their mischievous behavior.

Sounds familiar, right? It would be an honor to meet more members, I'm sure.

Nicklaus told me that Marcellus has always been Marcellus. He speaks out of turn. He says stupid sh*t and ruffles the feathers of other kings, purposely.

Just like the kings before him, Marcellus's eyes are fixed on mine. Unlike them, I can see love, respect, and devotion flicker in and out of his vivid green eyes, along with a shimmer of good ole malice. You've just gotta love it.

King Seneca is the fourth king to present himself. He looks cold, threatening, and mildly curious all at the same time. His aroma is clean and fresh, like Marcellus's, but earthy and spicy like King Luscious's. Overall, his scent reminds me of a rainy day in the forest. He seems bored, and he doesn't spare me a single glance unlike the ones before him.

Smart man!

Nicklaus also warned me about King Seneca's history. The members of the Wealthy House of Athan are cold and cunning. Before the Awakening, they lived among humans, learning our strengths and weaknesses. They played a major part in the downfall of human species. King Seneca is a violent and quick-witted man, both in theory and in practice. He is deadly and dangerous.

"Be mindful, as he likes to f*ck with people's heads," Nicklaus warned me before we walked into the dining hall.

If I learned one thing from Xander, it's how to play a good game of chess. I am a worthy opponent. I have no worries. Challenge accepted.

King Rufus comes in with a human on a leash he is dragging behind him. The sight of him turns my stomach. Memories of our first encounter burst inside my mind. I remember the poor, helpless human girl he killed, all because she had tripped over her own two feet. I remember the pain I felt when I dropped to my knees and recited the oath. I remember how none of them gave a single f*ck about him taking a human's life for such an illogical reason.

580

As my mind replays the events again and again, my dark and powerful presence becomes more alert within me. I don't like this king at all. Everything about him irks me to the very end—from his golden hair that goes so well with his tan skin to his handsome, boyish face that stirs venomous rage within me. Even his masculine cypress aroma makes me feel sick to my stomach, no matter how good it actually smells.

My eyes lock on King Rufus's predatory golden eyes. He is just as disgusted by me as I am disgusted by him. Good! The feeling is mutual. The short-tempered, ill-mannered king flashes his fangs at me, and I almost lose it. Nicklaus gently pulls me into him before I can actually act on it.

"Calm down, firecracker," he whispers in my ear, soothing me. "I already reminded you it will be bad business if the House of Baldassare started an uprising."

Who gives a f*ck? I surely don't care.

"Allow me to deal with him," he carries on. "All you have to do tonight is stand here and look pretty."

Yeah right! I roll my eyes at him, but I don't respond. In all honesty, he calmed me down the very moment he pulled me into the security of his body.

"Good, girl," he whispers.

Before I could tell Nicklaus to f*ck off, a soft, unique, floral aroma tainted with the distinctive scent of sandalwood grabs my attention. King Cornelius walks in like the man of the hour, smelling frighteningly similar to Jadis, which doesn't make sense at all. Yes, I'm aware he has been doing the nasty stuff with her, but their scents have never tainted until now. I'm confused.

All of a sudden, Nicklaus pulls out the chair for me to sit on. Then, he follows my lead. "You may come, slaves," he directs the chosens after the other vampire kings follow suit.

They move in unison, like a choir singing together in harmony.

"Now that we're all are seated," he announces, "we can feast and discuss the matter at hand."

"Cut the crap, Nicklaus! How about you enlighten us with why the hell you declared a chosen wh*re to be our queen?"

# CHAPTER SEVENTY-TWO
## Royal Traditions

My neck snaps in Cyrus's direction. Crimson-red blood immediately drips in my vision, and my chest blazes with scorching-hot rage.

"Mind your tongue, Cyrus!" Nicklaus growls.

The love and devotion in his features are long gone and are now replaced with passionate fury. I can feel his body go stiff beside me. His soft and delicate fingers, which were just entwining with my own, are now sharp claws digging deeper and deeper into my skin. Even with that, I refuse to let him go. My hand moves up his skin and grips his wrist.

"What?" Cyrus asks sarcastically, his red eyes fixed on me.

All I'm doing is voicing the concerns of the people. Cyrus can't be serious right now. Out of all the barbaric creatures in this room, he's the one I least expected to challenge Nicklaus, to challenge us.

The other vampire kings watch the scene with emotionless expressions.

"You and I both know this has nothing to do with how anyone feels, but you," says Nicklaus, my grip on his wrist slipping by the second. "Don't turn our petty dispute into a personal vendetta because it shall not end well for you," he warns.

Cyrus stands up. "I'll take my chances." (He is playing with fire.) "You're bringing filth to our throne, and you expect me to bite my tongue?" He stares Nicklaus directly in the eye.

"Cyrus."

My beloved's voice is low, but somehow, it still shakes the room. Nicklaus is losing control, and so am I. Fury crashes through my entire body like a tidal wave. The dark, menacing presence breaks free and floods my entire system. Without warning, pitch-black rage taints my inner light. My monster is in attendance—ready to pounce—and a storm of apprehended murder is brewing above our heads.

With each passing second, the room becomes deadlier and more silent. The air is filled with cruel and wicked anticipation. Cyrus's action is a wreck, a recipe of impending death. My beloved is shaking violently, so close to snapping. His rage is burning brighter than the desert sun. The darkness inside his soul invades my own that is darker than a fossil fuel of midnight coal.

Centuries's worth of memories with Cyrus consumes Nicklaus's brain. He is fighting his demon, attempting to spare the life of the king he considers a brother.

"Cyrus," I call, using a tone of reason out of respect for Nicklaus.

"You have no right to speak to me, slave," he mocks, sealing the deal.

With a chilling roar, Nicklaus releases the beast and moves in a blur. It is so quick that I don't even feel his wrist slip from my grasp. The scorching-hot heat burns brighter with the movement of his feet. Cyrus pounces in the air, meeting Nicklaus head-on. His fangs descend, and his talons swing as they swiftly go for blood. Nicklaus manages to avoid his attack, and with no hesitation, delivers a blow of his own. Deadly and lethal, they are both out for blood.

The chosens in the room scatter like ants while servants and slaves run for cover. No one wants to be in the middle of two vampires literally going at each other's neck. All watch them except King Rufus, who is staring at me with an annoying smirk on his handsome, devilish face. He is waiting for my reaction to this bloody battle that is currently making the chandeliers above our heads shake violently.

Ignoring his dire need for attention, my monster and I sit back and watch our beloved put the other monster in his place. We feel no fear. Our beloved can handle this on his own. Even if Cyrus somehow defeats the odds and gets the better of Nicklaus, he will still lose his life before my beloved loses his—that's for sure.

Cyrus's mulberry-scented blood fills the air as Nicklaus continues to rain deadly blows on him. Both are so quick, and I'm positive the humans in the room are unable to tell who is hitting who, but I can. Nicklaus isn't showing an ounce of mercy.

Is it wrong that I'm getting a kick of out this? Is it a mistake if I see no fault in Nicklaus's actions? Honestly, I don't give a sh*t. Screw whoever is against us!

Two strong hands rest on my shoulders, and the familiar, comforting touch consumes me. "Only you can stop this, brave one," Xander whispers in my ear.

Now, why would I do that?

Wordlessly, I look at him like he is crazy.

"I know he doesn't deserve your pity or protection!" My mate's vicious growls cover Xander's insane plea.

"Trust me when I say you don't want him to follow through with this," Xander coaxes.

Ignoring him, I continue to watch Nicklaus's monster show his dominance. The way he cleverly manages to invade any attack from his opponent obviously tells he is a beautiful but deadly creature. The way he brings forth the scent of spiced mulberry blood with a calculating, cruel smile on his face as a river of blood drips off his fangs is enchanting. I'm drawn to his wicked, wild, and wondrous monster that craves for blood like an addict.

"Claire!" yells Xander, gaining King Seneca's attention.

Except Marcellus, no other vampire king in this room has the slightest clue as to how powerful I really am. I know King Seneca is curious to learn why the hell Xander is begging me—out of all people—to save the ruthless king. He is a smart man. With one word, I know I can stop this and him, but one question remains: why the hell would I do that?

Play with fire and you get burned. Step out of line, and you'll be crushed. Go against my beloved, and you must be dealt with accordingly. Defy him if you must, but you shall die.

In the next moment, King Cyrus fights back with all his might. His and Nicklaus's ferocious monsters clash. They have been fighting for over ten minutes, but the battle has truly just begun. Nicklaus's monster starts to demonstrate his true nature. He moves with the same grace of a predator, which is something I have grown used to. His monster takes over completely, proving that he is a true force to be reckoned with. This is when I realize that he has been toying with Cyrus from the very beginning, and he still is.

"Please put an end to this," Xander pleads again.

"Now why would I do that?" I hiss, briefly looking into his blazing red eyes.

Can someone please tell me why?

"Yeah, why would she do that?" Marcellus mocks in a low voice, but no sound is low enough for my sensitive ears.

I don't have to spare him a glance to know that he is grinning like a Cheshire cat. He gets me; I don't want to save the ruthless king. I am in a dark place, and it goes blacker than black the moment Cyrus's talons unexpectedly sink into Nicklaus's chest, giving off a new scent to fill the air. The sweet and intoxicating scent of burning cedarwood and fresh berries with a hint of cinnamon, now mixed with the smell of blood, invades my nostrils. Quickly, I jump out of my seat with a roar, ready to lunge. I officially gain everyone's attention inside this room.

"What is she?" a voice says.

"Claire, my friend, is a f*cking queen. You motherf*ckers have no idea who you're dealing with," brags someone.

It might be Marcellus. I don't know, and I don't care. Right now I want blood.

"Claire!" Xander attempts to restrain me.

My skin starts to tingle while my slow heart rate increases rapidly. My neck itches intensely, further provoking my monster. She loves the raw and intense power flowing within me.

"Claire, believe me when I say, you don't want to do this," persuades Xander, holding me by the waist.

Yes, I do! He must be insane.

The power burns brighter as I'm trying my best to break free from his grip. Xander is stronger than he looks. I don't want to hurt him, but I will.

"This will only result in more bloodshed. You're better than us," he reasons with me.

A similar conversation we once had flashes inside my mind. "You are our savior," he once said.

Is this what he meant? Did Xander know right then I was Nicklaus's beloved? Of course, he did! That would explain everything.

I twitch my head back, focusing once again on the two barbaric kings delivering a series of deadly blows. My patience is wearing thin. At this point, it's hard to see who is winning.

"Get your hands off me, now!" I warn Xander. My voice is not my own, nor are my thoughts. My mind, body, and soul are clouded with a great deal of malice. Instinctively, I know it's more of Nicklaus's desire to kill than my own. Regardless, that doesn't make much difference since we are still one.

The fight is getting out of control in front of my soulless eyes. Cyrus's back is turned to me, presenting his body like a gift, and I have dibs on it.

"Claire!" yells Xander. "Please calm down."

587

In response, I release a menacing growl. My power continues to surge as the fight goes on. I draw it forth, ready to release my hell on Earth.

Then, Xander's next words register in my head: "Give Cyrus and Nicklaus the same respect we showed." What he said hits home, catching me by surprise. I manage to regain control within a second. His words mentally sting, forcing my monster to retreat. I take a moment to recollect my thoughts. It feels like it has been hours, but I know it's only been a second. Xander's truthful words ring over and over inside my head.

"I will not intervene in any way," I state calmly, turning to face him.

Disappointment sinks into his features, but he lets me go nonetheless. He knows I am woman enough to keep my word. "Don't forget who you are," he whispers, once again stinging me with his sharp tongue.

I nod in agreement and refocus on my battling beloved.

If Nicklaus was distracted by my little outburst, no one would know.

The fight continues, and crimson blood now stains the marble floor that was once squeaky clean. Roars and vicious growls ring loudly through the air as both Nicklaus and Cyrus move in a frenzy of bad blood. The contents in my stomach flip-flop, drop, and spin. I hate standing back and watching, especially after Cyrus has managed to draw blood.

Xander was right. I would have been crushed if Nicklaus had taken Mecca's life. Just thinking about that tragic ending brings me great distress. Despite my personal feeling toward Cyrus in this moment, I know very well that Nicklaus loves him dearly.

Out of the corner of my eye, I see all the vampire kings, besides Marcellus, once again watch me with great interest. It's strange that they seem more focused on trying to figure me out than care about their brothers attempting to take each other's life. It makes me wonder whether they really give a flying f*ck about either of them—or, are they just used to this type of brutality against one another?

Even Marcellus has no shame as he watches the show on the edge of his seat. The smug bastard lives for bloody glory. Let's face it, neither of the kings disappoints, with their sharp claws digging and making deep wounds where blood gushes.

The two monsters have been trying to kill each other for like hours now; then Cyrus slows down out of nowhere, becoming sloppier. Before my very eyes, I see the ruthless king's surge of power coming to an end when in a blur of lethal movement, Nicklaus buries his claws deep into his neck. My beloved lifts him off the floor with one hand. He growls triumphantly and plunges his sharp fangs into his best friend's neck before his bare hands rip into his chest. Chills from the thrill of his close kill flows through our bond like a ripple effect of a tidal wave. Victory belongs to him, and he revels in it, until a whirlwind of sadness nearly knocks me off my feet.

"Nicklaus, enough!" Xander speaks. "This is not our way."

Nicklaus looks at him, and a deep growl rumbles through his chest. He now has everyone's undivided attention. If the other vampire kings in this room disagree with his action, they don't show it. Still emotionless, they watch the scene unfold while sitting in audible silence.

My heart skips a beat when Nicklaus stares at me, his eyes blazing with fire. He doesn't want to do this, but he will for me. Reality comes crashing down, and my monster retreats to the back of my mind—as if nonexistent. I stand in silence as I look at him. The battle is coming to an end. I can see that he is a little bloody but in a way better condition than Cyrus, who could lose his life in a matter of seconds. Pain surges inside me. I realize that I can't let that happen. Xander is right; I must stop this.

Nicklaus breaks eye contact, and I know he is going for the kill.

"Nicklaus, please stop," I plead, barely hearing my own voice.

The other kings's eyes flicker from me to him. Nicklaus freezes once again, making eye contact. His eyes are asking me the obvious question.

With a deep reluctant sigh, I speak, "Cyrus is your family, our family. No matter what we go through, family is family."

Unexpectedly, King Rufus stands up and walks toward me, dragging his pet human on a leash. His body tenses. I can all but feel Xander crouch down protectively behind me.

Nicklaus tosses Cyrus's body to the side as if he were nothing, his eyes assessing his new enemy. "Rufus," he simply calls, but the tone of his voice is a warning. He is still struggling with his monster.

I don't think I have it in me to save another king if one attacks. In other words, I will not save King Rufus if he decides to target me. I don't like him at all, not even a bit. However, there is no need to go in with guns blazing for now.

I hold up one hand, hoping that my gesture will keep Nicklaus at bay. I can handle myself. All the vampire kings need to learn that I am also a force to be reckoned with. If Nicklaus continues to fight my battles, I will never gain respect for myself. I am the destined queen. No one, even Nicklaus, has to fight my battles. That's neither here nor there.

King Rufus doesn't give a sh*t about what's going on around us. He continues to make his way to me. His golden eyes are fixed on mine, his lips forming into a sickening smile.

With an innocent smile plastered on my face, I watch the fool walk straight into a death trap—me. When his hands reach his pocket, my monster reappears. He waits patiently. The raw intense power pumps through my veins. I'm ready. King Rufus is now inches away from me, hesitating for a second—as he should—then out of nowhere, he bows his head and kneels on his right knee.

What the hell is he doing?

"I pledge my loyalty to King Nicklaus and Queen Claire, the queen of all vampire kings," he declares, shocking the f*ck out of me.

# CHAPTER SEVENTY-THREE
## Pledge of Allegiance

NICKLAUS

My monster gets ready for another battle when Rufus makes his way over to Claire. I toss Cyrus's body to the side like a rag doll, focusing my attention on the possible new threat. "Rufus!" I warn, struggling to keep my monster at bay.

Screw that! There is no need. No one can be trusted, if you ask me. At this point, anyone can lose their life no matter what extent of pain it will bring me. Although I understand why Cyrus pushed my buttons, his actions cut me deep. For this reason, I brace myself to go to war with another man I once consider my brother.

Xander remains crouched in a threatening stance behind Claire. Marcellus's face is still emotionless. He is careful enough not to give away his loyalty to Claire as I instructed. However, his eyes tell another story. They flash a thrill of anticipation.

Claire holds up her hand, stopping me in my tracks. I know she feels my pain, which was why she prevented me from taking Cyrus's life in the first place. When Cyrus and I fought, I was able to observe everything. I never allowed my monster to take full control. There was really no need. Claire was the one to demonstrate true strength. Cyrus disrespected her, and disrespect is one thing vampires can't stomach, half-vampire or not. It roars through our toxic vampiric veins.

Claire herself used to purposely provoke my kind because of her idiotic death wish. Our monsters aren't strong enough to fight our demonic impulses, but Claire managed to defeat the odds by showing true strength once again. When she had every right to demand to have Cyrus's head on a platter, she requested mercy. That is the epitome of inner strength. Now look at her as she stands proudly with her chin pointed in the air and head held high. Her shoulders are straight as King Rufus approaches her. Claire's character draws people in. It makes them want to follow her lead. In a room full of predators, she somehow remains fearless and poised. She is a quintessential, courageous, confident woman— distinguished, dignified, and daring.

Slaves, chosens, servants, and vampires alike watch the scene in complete silence. I'm certain that even they can all agree. Maybe that's why Rufus is making his way to her. I can sense that his monster is not present. Could it be that he has decided to pledge his allegiance to both of us? Could it be that he is able to see what I can see?

Of course, it is. Once he bows his head and is in the process of kneeling on his right knee, my suspicions are confirmed. Claire stopping me from taking Cyrus's life is proof to him that she not only respects the bond of the kings, but she also cares about the well-being of our people, because one dead king can lead to the destruction of the entire vampire monarchy. Even a blind man can see that she is beautiful. And when Xander pleaded, she ignored him, which means that she can also be vicious.

Rufus's current action adds up when I think about everything Claire did throughout the fight.

"I pledge my loyalty to King Nicklaus and Queen Claire, the queen of all vampire kings," he declares.

Not even the proudest vampire, who has been bewitched and smitten by his beloved could understand how proud I am of my most-powerful and prized possession. I'm amazed. She has earned the short-tempered king's loyalty. Her astonishing regal bearing captivates me. I am blessed and certainly favored to be paired with a woman like her. This girl, who was once human and wasn't raised for royalty, continues to demonstrate how fit she is for it. This woman was born to rule. How could I ever doubt her? Since day one, she has demonstrated distinctive traits of a true queen.

I sit back and watch Claire as she continues to analyze the short-tempered king, then her smoky green eyes search for me. I burn her with my stare, tucking and hiding away all my emotions. This one is up to her. I will not direct her to accept his loyalty, nor will I hold anything against her if she declines it. She needs to make her own decision. She is my queen after all. She has to learn how to carry the crown and think for herself. Besides, I refuse to force a bond.

Once Claire realizes that the decision is in her hands, she shifts her gaze back onto the kneeling king and studies him for a long-drawn-out moment. I know how she feels about him. Will her personal opinion sway her away from him? I can't help but wonder what's going on in that pretty little head of hers. I miss reading her thoughts. Her stories were entertaining as hell. Thanks to her pendant, I no longer have the luxury of exploring her beautiful mind, unless she wants me to. Not only that, she has also learned how to conceal and when to reveal her emotions—another reason why I'm crazy about her. Her growth is impressive. She's got beauty and brains. How the f*ck did I get so lucky?

Without instructions, Claire places her hand on King Rufus's left shoulder, then she lifts his chin with her finger and stares him directly in the eye. "I accept your loyalty, King Rufus," she states, once again making my still heart skip a beat.

Xander's body instantly relaxes, and the thick tension inside the room dissolves.

Seneca follows suit, making his way to Claire to pledge his loyalty to his new queen.

I shared a little information about the kings to my beloved before this bloody dinner began. I wanted to make sure she was aware of whom and what she was dealing with, but I intentionally left important details out—for instance, I didn't tell her that Rufus and Seneca are cousins. I knew very well that if Rufus showed loyalty, Seneca would do the same, or vice versa. They are closer than they appear to be, and only the inner circle knows that.

I purposely left out that Rufus was enslaved by humans many centuries ago, and that's why Seneca willingly lived amongst humans to learn about their strengths and weaknesses for the vampires to be victorious during the Awakening. He played a part in enslaving a race to avenge his cousin. I'm not saying that makes it right, but it is what it is. We vampires are monsters, and the world knows that. We don't hide our true nature; we never did. "Don't judge a book by its cover," as they say. Nothing in our world is what it appears to be, and Claire will learn that fairly soon. Five out of eight kings have accepted her. We are now one step closer toward becoming unstoppable. And the council is not ready.

Seneca stops directly in front of Claire. He bows his head low and then kneels on his right knee. "I pledge my loyalty to King Nicklaus and Queen Claire, the queen of all vampire kings," he states.

A tiny peaceful smile tugs on Claire's lips. Her smoky green eyes are filled with warmth as she accepts his loyalty with no hesitation. I'm very well aware that she is curious about this legendary king. Seneca is known for his quick wit and violent nature, which can be very useful for Claire if something ever happens to me. She can learn a lot from him, if I must admit. That's doesn't necessarily mean that I will. I don't want her to feel like she needs anybody but me.

Cornelius stands up. His eyes briefly flicker in his chosen's direction before he confidently walks toward Claire.

Cocky little b*tch.

When Seneca rises to his feet, Cornelius lowers his head and kneels down as well. Claire's heart starts to beat wildly, her eyes briefly scanning the room for her friend. Cornelius's chosen winks at my beloved, almost causing her to laugh. I don't even want to know what that is about. That human is strange.

"I pledge my loyalty to King Nicklaus and Queen Claire, the queen of all vampire kings," Cornelius speaks, then turns to face me and winks.

I ignore the smug bastard, my eyes focusing on my friend King Luscious. His hatred for Claire's ancestry runs extremely deep, so I truly understand the dilemma evident in his deep brown eyes. Overall, he is a good man. Some old wounds are just too deep to heal.

"We shall see," he states harshly more to me than to Claire, breaking eye contact.

"That was quick."

I hear Marcellus say underneath his breath before he directs the slaves to come out of hiding and serve dinner.

Cyrus groans beside me, regaining my attention.

"Take him to the medical wing," I order some random servant, "and clean up this mess." I point to another slave. "There are still important matters to discuss. Everyone, please take your seat.

\*       \*       \*

CLAIRE

The energy in the room is charged with electricity as Nicklaus instructs everyone to take a seat, using that damn silky tone that makes my heart skip a beat. Tonight is a night to remember, for sure. I can't believe three vampire kings have pledged their loyalty to me, and it feels like a dream. Never in a

596

million years did I expect anything like this to happen to me. I'm absolutely stunned, surely in a trance, until Nicklaus makes his way to the center of the table—exactly where he belongs—and holds out his hand for me to take.

"My queen," he states, pride and love in his voice.

"My king," I walk toward him and stand by his side. It's as if this is where I always belong—paired with him.

We take our seats in unison.

"Now that we've solved that issue, let's focus on the problem we have to tackle," Nicklaus begins. His eyes roam over each and every king's face.

Sounds familiar?

"You all are already aware that Claire is my beloved. You all are aware that the council has summoned us and her," he continues.

Now, this is new. I didn't know the council summoned them or me. Why the hell did they summon me, and why the hell hasn't he mentioned this to me? Questions after questions start to pop up, but I know now is not the time or place to receive answers. He still has to give me answers by the end of the night. Trust and believe me when I say that he will.

"Does anyone have any questions?" Nicklaus asks them all rather harshly.

He should have said, "Speak now or forever hold your peace."

"The hunters in my kingdom whisper about the devil king's human beloved who has a soft spot for dogs, our natural enemies. Now why should I follow you?" King Luscious says.

He is the first to respond, just like he did during my very first feast. I'm starting to feel like I traveled to a past memory in a parallel universe, and once again, I recognize something dangerous and lethal lingering in his eyes while he directs his question to me.

I stare him directly in the eye, not even bothering to silently plead with Nicklaus to provide me with the right thing to say. I know King Luscious is testing me. "You are entitled to do as you please, King Luscious," I answer him curtly. "I will not beg, persuade, or demand anyone to follow me, and I damn sure will not explain my action to anyone; nor will I address any rumors."

He smirks.

Every soul currently sitting at the table seems to have some type of victory smile on their face, except Jasmine. She is a jealous woman, always and forever.

"Any more questions?" my beloved asks once more.

This time, no one seems to have anything to say, or so I thought.

"Why would the council summon Claire?" King Rufus queries.

It's strange hearing him casually utter my name with his foreign and unusual accent.

"That is one reason why I requested a feast," Nicklaus responds. "At first, I only assumed my father was aware of my bond with Claire. I didn't want any one of you to be caught off guard," he sarcastically explains. "After meeting with my lovely sister this past noon, I'm sure that my father is certainly aware now. I just can't figure out his end game."

"I tell you what, the council surely doesn't have a slightest clue. If they did, there would have been an uprising everywhere by now," King Cornelius states.

Xander sighs. "I also share your thoughts," he openly admits. "If the news had been disclosed to the public, there would have been hell out there by now. And at least one vampire would have attempted assassination."

*Hell out there? Um . . . News flash! Hell was already unleashed on Earth a long time ago, buddy, starting with the Awakening.*

Nicklaus stares at me with amusement, as if he knows what I'm thinking. "As what I observed at the airport, many people believe Claire is nothing but a mistress. They didn't recognize her to be my golden-haired chosen."

598

*Golden-haired chosen? Where did that come from?*

"The commoners believed she was another vampire lady. At this time, I don't see her as a threat since no one knows what or who she truly is," Nicklaus explains.

"Tell me, Nicklaus," King Luscious says, "what she exactly is."

My head snaps in his direction. He is referring to me as if I did not exist in the room, and my monster takes instant offense.

Nicklaus places his hand on my lap. He too has peeped what I just have. I can feel his monster on the horizon as well.

Swallowing my pride, I run my fingers along his hand. "We wouldn't want another episode to happen, now would we?

"To begin with, Claire isn't an it! She is your queen," hisses Nicklaus. His mood shifts quicker than one can flip a light switch.

"My apologies, Brother," Luscious speaks (bullsh*t).

I roll my eyes. He can shove that apology up his ass. He can't fool me.

I look at him, and of course, he smirks. He knows I know he is full of sh*t.

"I only asked because of safety concerns. Don't you fear for your queen's safety?"

See? I didn't miss his empathy for their queen. He is trying.

"Do you not fear for yourself?" I respond to his question myself.

King Luscious releases a chilling laugh. The tension inside the room returns. "You have balls. I'll never take that away from you, half breed."

Oh, so he does know what I am. Interesting.

"I hate to be the one to disappoint you, my dear, but your sharp tongue and vampirism aren't enough to make me or any other vampires to bend our knees, bow before you, or follow you blindly."

"Welp, she has certainly earned loyalty from just about everyone else," Marcellus says, coming to my defense.

"Yeah. Speak for yourself," King Rufus adds.

King Seneca doesn't respond. Instead, he rises from his seat and simply bows in my direction before he takes his seat once again. Xander is oddly quiet, but his blazing red eyes speak for himself. And for the second time tonight, Nicklaus's body tenses up beside me. He is offended, yet I might as well be a blind woman when it comes to King Luscious's pointless insults.

"Oh really?" I raise an eyebrow. "Interesting." With that being said, I stand up.

King Luscious stares at me boldly as I make my way toward him. With a smirk on my face, I embrace the feeling of tingling chills as they travel all over my skin. When my soft heartbeat starts to increase in speed, I ravish in pure delight and welcome the itching sensation buzzing throughout my neck.

# CHAPTER SEVENTY-FOUR
## The Storm

The raw and intense power within me continues to hum with every step I take. King Luscious watches me closely as though I were his prey. The crazy part of it all is that he is my prey. I'm the more dominant species, and he said I have balls. No! He is the one who has balls, which I'd be more than happy to rip out of their socket.

His smirk deepens, getting on my nerves more, if that's even possible. What is it with these kings always trying to get under my skin?

I can feel his monster brewing within him—good, because so is mine—then one strong hand gently grips my forearm, bringing blistering fire to my skin.

*"Claire,"* Nicklaus's silky voice enters my mind, as he holds me back.

How does he move so fast?

*"Don't feed into his game,"* he says in my mind.

*"What game? This is not a game. The power rippling through me is not a game. I am not to be played with."*

*"No, you're not, firecracker. You are a queen. You don't have to fight with any of those men. Leave the violence up to me."*

Look, who's talking?

*"I am not that type of queen, just like you're not that type of king. Allow me to deal with this on my own."*

601

*"I'll never allow you to deal with anything on your own, never!"*

*"You will with this one!"* I snatch my arm away from him and close my mind off completely.

He grinds his teeth. He doesn't stop me, but he does follow behind me angrily. I know he wants to protect me, but I can protect myself. None of them can put fear in my heart. I'm not the type of girl they can restrain, shove, or smack around without expecting to be smacked the hell back. I've never been that person and never will be. If King Luscious is surprised about Nicklaus standing down, he doesn't show it. He just continues to silently watch me—with a smirk—as I approach him. I'm starting to really hate that smirk, and I want to knock it off his face.

See? Nicklaus is right about one thing: King Luscious is certainly playing a dangerous game. This king thinks I'm weak. He believes I'm sort of a damsel in distress, not worthy enough to be called queen. This creep has no idea who he is dealing with. It's actually quite funny, if you think about it.

I can feel Nicklaus's soul-snatching eyes bore holes into my back. Well, everyone's eyes in the room seem to spit laser orbs through me—the way they are all watching me, as if anticipating what's to come.

"Now what did you say?" I ask King Luscious when I get to him.

"You heard what I said, half breed!" he snarls.

Nicklaus growls and the table shakes.

Luscious ignores him. "I will not bend the knee, bow before you, or follow you blindly."

"You don't have to, but you must learn to respect me."

"Respect is earned, not given, child," he hisses back with blood-colored eyes. "And you haven't earned sh*t."

My vision tints red. The dark presence inside me doesn't like his tone or choice of words one bit.

"Mind your tongue!" screams my beloved. He pulls me away and shoves me behind him.

My vision is still red, bright red, as I try my best to keep my composure. I place my attention onto the thick dark clouds outside the window. A storm is surely on the horizon.

"You don't frighten me, Brother!" he yells back, taking a step closer. "You know better than anybody that I say how I feel. I didn't say anything wrong. I spoke the truth. I will not just give away my loyalty without proper cause."

Lightning strikes. One might think that the emotions inside this room cause the sudden storm.

"You will do what I say," growls Nicklaus. "I am your king."

My chest starts to burn. I'm feeling not only my rage but also Nicklaus's fury that is now burning brighter than the morning star.

Lightning strikes again. The rain is coming.

"You are my king, and I will follow you to war. I will slaughter millions, if that's what it takes for you to keep your crown. I will do anything. In fact, I've done everything for you, but I refuse to follow your half-human beloved!" Luscious shouts back, staring me directly in the eye. His stone-cold gaze is filled with nothing but hatred.

My monster's presence appears, and I push her away. She wants to take him on, but I'm trying my best not to give in to my heart's true desires.

"Get the f*ck over yourself!" Marcellus pipes up, thunder now roaring. "No one gives a f*ck about how you feel!"

"Shut the f*ck up, Marcellus!" King Luscious snaps his neck in Marcellus direction.

"Or what?" Marcellus taunts.

All three of them are behaving like f*cking children. This dinner has gone from "war of the fangs" to "war of insults." My head is spiraling out of control. The first drop of rain drips into my eardrum as they continue to bicker back and forth in some foreign language I can't possibly understand, increasing my inner battle. My head is spinning, my heart rate increasing by the second.

"The last time I checked we were at the Feast of Brothers, and I have the right to speak freely."

King Luscious's voice draws me back in. My jaw clenches tighter with every word that comes out of his mouth. I'm trying.

"You don't have the right to question your king," Seneca states.

The chain tightens around my neck as the raw power inside its pendant alerts me of its presence. I'm still trying, really trying, to keep everything within me at bay.

Lightning strikes again. King Luscious's eyes lock on Nicklaus's as he speaks, "Is it wrong to second-guess your choice of queen when she is half-human and half-b*tch?"

Booming thunder roars louder, and lightning strikes increase the tension in the room. Without warning, Nicklaus slams his body into the wall, quicker than one can blink.

My breathing stops for a moment.

"I will not allow anyone to disrespect my beloved," Nicklaus spits in King Luscious's face, his entire body shaking uncontrollably. Scorching-hot fury blazing within him—within us—is shown in his eyes.

I feel every part of his intense emotions. I can barely breathe. The storm is officially here. This is exactly what he wants. He is playing King Luscious's game. He is losing control and acting as if I couldn't save or defend myself. This has to come to an end.

With every second, more heat blazes within me, and the sound of thunderous pounding along with flashing lightning strikes around me. Xander looks at me intensely, seeming to be waiting for something.

Xander and his games!

My head is spinning. I'm tired of having to prove myself over and over again. I'm exhausted. My heart rate increases slightly—not a lot but enough. The pendant squeezes tighter around my neck, almost completely cutting off my air supply.

"What's wrong, Nicklaus?" taunts King Luscious. "Can your queen not speak for herself? Is she really that weak?"

My vision turns red, and my monster comes out of hiding again. Between Nicklaus's rage and my monster's hunger, the power ripples within me, and I feel like I'm about to explode.

Nicklaus growls as he slams his fist directly into King Luscious's jaw, knocking him to the floor and instantly filling the air with rosewood-scented blood.

Luscious is back to his feet in no time and wipes his mouth. He smirks. "That's what I thought," he spits through clenched teeth.

I can feel his anger growing by the second as well. His monster is present—lethal and dangerous, as Nicklaus told me.

I pull in a sharp breath. There's way too much going on around me.

"Rip his bloody head off!" Marcellus growls, standing up.

The servants, slaves, and chosens become uneasy again. I can smell Jadis's fear, pushing my monster further. She shouldn't fear anything.

Thunder rolls.

"Shut up, Marcellus!"

"F*ck up!" Marcellus hisses back.

Luscious ignores him, addressing Nicklaus instead. "You want me to follow a b*tch that cannot protect herself?" He knocks his head back with laughter. "Who would have thought the king of all vampire kings would be paired with a weak queen?"

That's it! I'm done with this. Like Nicklaus, I lose all control. My skin starts to tingle, my heart pounding louder than a beating drum. The itching sensation zaps like lightning, bringing me back to life.

"Enough!" I scream. I allow all my sinfully sweet energy to break free. "Follow my every command until I tell you all otherwise."

A bright emerald-green light flashes, and an unknown force freezes everything around me. And when I say *everything*, I mean everything. Even the pouring rain that can be seen through the window completely stops.

I narrow my eyes at Nicklaus and Luscious, who are both frozen in place—stuck at a standstill. Their eyes are what only seem to move, ablaze with bright-red fury, as they stare at each other.

I tear my blazing-hot gaze away from them and briefly study the faces of everyone else. Xander is sitting in the chair, frozen. He has a smirk plastered on his face, his eyes beaming with unhidden excitement. I kind of feel like he is secretly giving me a high five mentally. Victoria, who is standing behind him, is scared out of her mind. I swear if she could move, she would be a shaking bag of bones. King Cornelius is seated on Xander's right side, his face expressionless. Jadis is on his lap, clinging to him like he is her life support—I make a face at that. Surprisingly, King Rufus is not paying the scene any attention. He just stares at me wide-eyed.

Ha! I bet he is thankful for choosing the right side.

King Seneca doesn't seem that surprised at all. His head is tilted to one side. He is assessing me as expected. I can tell he is trying to understand how I pulled off what I pulled off.

Marcellus, who is supposed to be sitting on his left side, is out of his seat, frozen with the face of a devil. His usually vivid green eyes are now an unusual shade of scarlet. He is pissed, not at me of course, but at the situation overall. I can't blame him.

"Pay close attention!" I order, the voice not my own.

All heads snap in my direction in unison. This is actually kind of fun; welp, excluding the humans who are forced to also follow my commands. Let's fix that, shall we?

"All the humans in this room, except Jadis and the chosens, please take your leave."

All of them leave the room, practically running out of the door.

"Jadis, you are free from my command," I whisper, trying not to scare her with my monster's voice.

Her body relaxes instantly.

I turn to face her, and she surprisingly doesn't look frightened at all. "Would you like to stay, or do you want to go?" I quietly ask her, ignoring the impatient vibes that the vampire kings are dishing out.

And trust me, they are all very impatient. I can feel Nicklaus trying to break free from my control; all of them are. They don't like this one bit.

"I'm fine," Jadis says with a smile.

She really is not scared. I thought she would be, but now that I think about it, Jadis is insane. Of course she doesn't fear me. She doesn't have all her marbles.

The vampire kings's annoyance increases by the second, and I can't hold back my smirk.

Good. This is exactly what they get. The looks on their faces are priceless. I'm sure if I were in my right state of mind, I would hurl myself at them and burst out in laughter. Unfortunately for them, I'm not.

"Now that I've got everyone's undivided attention," I state out loud, my eyes traveling over each and every one of their faces, "and I have proven to all of you that I'm more than capable of defending myself." I turn to King Luscious. "I'm asking you all nicely if we can please continue the feast without any further bullsh*t." I walk to the center of the room, and their eyes follow behind my steps like lost dogs. "We're going to play a game of Simon Says," I joke, just for the heck of it.

Oh man, this power is remarkable.

"Claire Says," Jadis corrects me.

Funny. I'm starting to believe Jadis is meant to be my other half. She is always on point.

I twitch my head to the side and study the kings one by one. "Yes, Jadis, you are right. A game of Claire Says. Now, nod if you promise to get along with your brothers," I tell them, as if they were my sons.

All seven heads move up and down.

"Good." I squeal, may be a little happy. "Now, Claire says nod again if you promise to respect one another."

All seven heads move up and down.

"Perfect."

This is fun, really fun.

I turn to face King Luscious. "Now, Claire says, nod if you understand that I am the chosen one."

All seven heads move up and down.

"Claire says, nod if you understand that I am the only one."

All seven heads move up and down.

"Perfect! Now, Claire says, nod if you understand that I am your true queen."

Each king nods their head one by one, including King Luscious.

Checkmate! I won. Six out of all seven kings, and plus Nicklaus, have bowed down before me. With that being said, I think my work is done.

"You are all free from my command."

The power within me roars to life, lighting up the room with an emerald-green glow. It's beautiful, and we all stare in awe at it.

Nicklaus is in front of me within a second, his soul-snatching eyes meet mine. "Meeting is adjourned," he declares. "We have a problem," he whispers in my ear.

*"We need to get this resolved,"* I say to him inside his head.

He places his entire body closer to mine. I can feel his horse of a dick poking through the confinements of his pants. "Oh, we have bigger challenges in hand," he tells me. He picks me up off the floor and rush out of the room, carrying me.

# CHAPTER SEVENTY-FIVE
## The Pleasure-filled, Passionate Night

The moment he steps inside the room, his tongue hits the back of my throat—straight like that! He kisses me without permission, not that he needs it, and takes my breath away without warning. I'm caught off guard to be honest, suddenly stuck in haze and lost in a blue dream of his love. The way his silky, savory tongue sends heat to the center of my core and hungrily swirls with my own, sucking, nibbling, and greedily tasting my mouth is bliss. I love how it devours me whole and how his sweet, minty taste is currently making my taste buds explode. I love his teasing, when he slightly pulls apart, only to roughly suck and then gently peck my lips with his extremely soft ones that feel really smooth against mine. I'm a goner. I'm in the zone. I'm hypnotized. I am in another universe where only he and I exist. I am his and I belong to him. He belongs to me.

Oh my! The eruption of pleasure from our tongues moving in sync alone makes me want to cum. I am so wet, hot, and ready. I want him with every fiber in my body. I need him. I'm cold. This is a never-ending battle of love. I'm starving and craving to feel his horse dick plunge in and out of me. He will have all of me. I'll give him all.

I place my hand on his head, pulling him closer and deepening our kiss. I need more. Nicklaus doesn't disappoint. He allows me to swallow his tongue. I moan from his taste, enough to make any woman's panties drench. I'm soaked.

By the time he pulls away, I'm breathless. For the second time tonight, I've found myself gasping for air because of him.

Nicklaus throws me onto the bed and watches me, his eyes fixed in my figure. He enjoys my struggle while I feel naked underneath his steady stare. This man basks in the glory of leaving me breathless.

"You wanted all eyes on you, did you not?" he asks, his voice deeper and huskier than usual.

I'm stuck. How is that even possible?

I stare at him blankly. For some strange reason, I can't find my voice.

His lips curve in their legendary, beautiful, sadistic smirk.

I love it. No. I hate it. Uuuhhhh . . . My brain is discombobulated. I can't function. Something is missing. I'm a loose screw right now.

He leans his head over to the side. "Cat got your tongue," he teases.

*No! But you do.*

I gulp. His steady stare shifts into a full-blown evaluation. Those soul-snatching eyes drench me in from head to toe. The way his mesmerizing cerulean orbs linger on my most-feminine parts would make one think I'm naked.

A minute or a second goes by. I'm not really sure. I still can't seem to think or find my words. I'm flustered and can barely breathe. This is what this king does to me. I can feel his lust for me flowing through his sturdy and cut-by-a-god frame. All I can think about is his magical hands, exploring every inch of me. In my mind, he is touching me, without him actually touching me. I shiver from the anticipation. My chest moves up and down as I continue catching my breath.

"We're going to play Simon Says," he quips.

I swallow the lump in my throat.

*Oh boy! What have I done?*

"Or should I say Nicklaus Commands?"

I'm still speechless. Out of nowhere, my vocal cords are paralyzed.

"Since my firecracker of a queen is lost for words, how about we utilize head motions?" he teases. He places his hand on top of his crotch and grabs his dick.

*Oh mother of f\*cking horses, please save me,* I mentally pray.

"No one can save you, Claire." He starts removing his tux.

*F\*ck. F\*ck. F\*ck. F\*ck my life.*

"I'm very much want to f\*ck your life away," he says.

I still can't speak, but his words make my soft heart skip a beat.

*How the hell did our roles get reversed? He's a god of a man, and the size of his penis can really be compared to a horse's—half-god, half-horse!*

"I told you once before, little firecracker, that I'm far from a god."

*He's right. He is the devil.*

"And that makes you the devil's wife. Besides, I believe God is a woman, a strong, desirable, pleasure-filled, and highly favored woman like yourself," Nicklaus continues, still drenching me in.

Meanwhile, I'm over here still struggling for air. If I weren't trying to catch my breath, I'd roll my eyes at him. How can he leave me this speechless?

*"Stay out of my head,"* I mentally state.

Our kiss really does things to me. I think I'm having a panic attack.

"Now why would I do that, my love, when exploring your mind is so much fun?" The devil beloved of mine has the nerve to wink. "Let's get back to the game, shall we?" he proudly says.

*I'm royally screwed.*

"You have no idea how well this royal is about to screw you. Nod if you want to be devoured, my love," he directs, as he removes his waistcoat.

What a waste of coat! He looks much better without it.

"I said nod, Claire, not drool."

My mouth falls slightly, but my head moves up and down.

Since when have I become so submissive?

"Good job!" Nicklaus says, "Nod if you want me to plunge this horse dick so deep in your walls that it shall invade your guts." He removes his bow tie and subdued shirt.

*Oh mother of leeches!*

My eyes flicker up and down, taking in his glorious chest— when I say "glorious," I mean G-L-O-R-I-O-U-S—then my head goes up and down of its own accord.

Why I'm enjoying this so much? I'm super soaked.

He smirks. "Good job, baby." He jumps on the bed and pulls me into him.

He is still half-naked. I am fully dressed, yet my body quickly melts in his touch. The once enchantment of a gown that felt like liquid gold clinging to my skin now feels like acid. I want to rid of it and be free. I want to be naked with him.

I moan when Nicklaus's magical hands cup my face.

"Your ass-kissing king says, nod if you want me to suck and lick your honey-sweetened kitty."

My juices flow instantly. Helpless, I surrender. I need him now.

Nicklaus's nostrils flare widely as he takes a deep sniff of air. "I can smell your arousal, firecracker."

I purr, my kitty throbbing. I can't take it anymore. "Please, f*ck me," I beg. Screw the meaning behind "Patience is a virtue." I've got other valuable qualities.

Wasting no time, he discards his pants and strips me down. First, he rips my gown and then reaches back and unclamps my black lace bra. He then brings his lips and trails kisses all the way down to my black lace panties. Once there, he frees my kitty with his teeth and stares at my pink folds with hooded eyes. I can feel his savory tongue flicking before he actually flicks onto my clit.

*Not right now. I want the dick.*

Reading my mind, Nicklaus makes his way back up to me. He grips his dick and places it directly over my belly-button. His rock-hard, long, and thick penis pokes my stomach as he snatches off his boxers. He climbs on top of me, and my body screams. My craving for him is obvious.

His mouth clashes with my own, and once again, he devours me whole. I moan inside his mouth and squirm underneath him. My dying need of him hurts so badly, like a knife being shoved inside my core. I'm physically hurting all over, because he is not inside me. I need his dick, like I need air to breathe.

He breaks our kiss, only to press sweet kisses all over my bare skin. Every peck is sparks flying all over me. It's magnetic. And when he removes his lips from my skin, it feels like he is pulling my soul away with them.

I arch my back. *"Please, enter me,"* I silently plead.

"Behave, firecracker." His minty breath fans my skin.

"I don't want to behave," I moan. "F*ck me now."

"My pleasure."

Talk about pleasure. He fills me with all of his cock, and my eyes roll back. My nails dig deep into his skin as he plunges his horse dick deep into my core. He hammers in and out of my tight folds, making me drip.

"F*ck, Claire, you're f*cking soaking," he whispers, then he grips a chunk of my hair and goes deeper. He feels so f*cking damn good as he slams hard and fast—rough, just how I want it. His dominance in the bedroom is undeniable. "Mine," he declares, slamming harder.

Suddenly, he is out of me. He flips me over and demands my ass in the air. My heart is beating so fast that I'm afraid it might fall out of my chest and land onto the bed. Without warning, he shoves every inch of him inside me, then yanks my hair back and thrusts.

I scream so loud. Surely, all the windows burst.

"Scream for me, Claire," he roars.

I can feel his dick twitch and flip inside me. My submission is turning him on. He is teaching me my place by burying his dick deep inside my core and touching my guts as promised. I meet him halfway, throwing it back and making my ass jiggle. He smacks it, and my tits swing freely, bouncing around like two bunnies.

*Oh my God.*

"Not God, baby!" he yells over my screams. "I told you I'm the devil, and you're captured, an angel captured by the devil himself."

"Yes, capture me," I moan.

The tip of his dick is the first part of his manhood that catches my climax, followed by the remainder of my sweet juices soaking his entire horse. Nicklaus's soft and firm hands cup my tits as he pounds harder. Each stroke feels like a match, sparking fire inside me. He is burning me alive, and I am exploding.

I arch higher, bringing the feeling of him inside me to a new height. I don't want to come down. He holds my waist and then digs his nails into my flesh, and I scream louder.

"Nicklaus," I then moan. "I'm coming."

My vision turns red, matching my beloved's now crimson orbs. Our monsters are ready to take control, and we give them exactly what they want.

My nails turn to talons as I wrap my legs around him and flip him over. Now, I'm on top, bouncing up and down. I grind and prepare his dick like a rodeo rider. His monster growls and covers my nipple with his mouth. He sucks slowly, flicking his tongue over my nipple, and gently grazes on my bare skin with his sharp fangs. The slight sting buzzes and blazes to life inside me. Amplifying my need for speed, I drive faster. My hands roam freely, exploring

614

every inch of his manly chest. He pulls his body up, aiding his dick to go further. It feels so good. He feels so good.

All of a sudden, my breath gets caught inside my chest. A tingling sensation spreads throughout my body, making my toes curl. I start to feel numb as an unknown force takes over. "Oh, Nicklaus!" I scream.

"That's it, baby," he utters. "I found your G-spot. Oh f*ck, Claire. Stay right there."

His husky voice makes the feeling inside me go haywire. I don't know what a G-spot is, but this and the position of his dick make me drive harder. I don't want this feeling to ever go away. I'll ride him for the rest of eternity whatever it takes.

My mind, body, and soul are now in a utopian state. I'm almost there, screaming so loud that I'm sure the entire house can hear me. If I were still human, I'd be a sweaty mess—the way I'm working out on his body. Nicklaus buries his face in the crook of my neck, and I go crazy as he inhales my scent. The feel of him breathing down my skin is too much to take.

"Open your mind to me," his monster demands, as he puts his hand over my head.

I obey, and nothing in life has ever seemed so clear. Nicklaus's memories rush inside my mind, sending tidal waves to crash deep into my heated core—I'm flushed. I can see and feel every one of his emotions he holds for me. I'm experiencing every ounce of his love as it flows within my blood and soils into my tainted soul. The pleasure is too much to bear. His desire for me runs so deep, anchoring my soul and tying our spirits together. Everything my heart has once known is represented—the pleasure, the passion, the desire. I now know everything that my soul has always remembered.

His words from his memory float inside my head. *"I love her full, luscious lashes that highlight her smoky green eyes. I'm in love with how peaceful she looks when she is asleep. Just watching her sleep makes me feel at peace. I'm in love with her. I'm infatuated with this human girl,"* he once thought.

My tears flow freely as the sensation continues to increase. His memories of me dance gracefully in my mind's eye. I see everything he erased. He has confirmed on numerous occasions that I am his beloved. He shows me his talents and shares his family history. Since day one, he has always loved me. I have been his forever from first glance.

The built-up sensation is now glowing dim like an ember as my tears continue to stream down my face. The world spins around me. The tingling inside me comes crashing down, taking my breath away. I knock my head back with a moan. My body instantly goes numb, and I fall onto the bed with heavy eyes. I'm done.

Nicklaus pulls me close, and I have never felt this safe and warm.

\*     \*     \*

I wake up in my beloved's arms. The sun is shining high in the sky, beaming a bright light through the balcony. I squint my eyes and turn to face him. He is still asleep. He looks peaceful and stress-free. I can smell the scent of expensive cologne, burning cedarwood, and milk and honey. The evidence of our sex lingers in the air.

"You're awake," Nicklaus suddenly says, pulling me closer to him. "Why are you watching me sleep?"

"For the same reasons you had when you watched me sleep," I tell him, as memories of last night resurface.

"Fair point." He trails his finger down my bare skin.

I take a deep breath. I smell like him, and it really is the best kind of smell. I lay my head on his chest, using his body as my personal pillow. "We need to get ready for today," I state. "We need to finish discussing our plans with the others and our upcoming meeting with the council. Speaking of the council, why didn't you tell me they summoned me?"

"Because no one cares about the old leeches summoning anyone," he answers, lying through his sparkly white teeth.

I laugh anyway. I never thought he would ever use the word *leeches*.

"I'm rubbing off on you." I laugh into his chest.

"You can rub all over me, firecracker, whenever and wherever you want."

"Pervert!"

"Sure I am the pervert who wants to rock your world again." He brings his penis close to my kitty.

Ignoring my craving for him, I continue, "Business comes before pleasure, Nicklaus. And you're not off the hook. Why didn't you tell me about the summons?"

"You are my business, and pleasure. You come before all."

He makes my cheeks blaze with natural heat. Leave it to him to stop important matters, only to handle his personal desire. Leave it to him to place pleasure before business. He is supposed to be putting plans in motion and lay down the law, not moving his body against my own and positioning his pipe. He is an absolute ruler, unchecked and unrestrained. He's a tyrant and barbaric ruler who does what he wants when he wants it. He is the type of man who takes what he wants when he wants to take it. Right now, he wants all of me, and I shall give it to him again. What the king desires, the king gets.

Nicklaus knows exactly what he wants, and that one fact alone is turning me on. Some women would most likely respect a man that handles business and places their livelihood before quality time, but I am not that woman. I prefer a man that craves me more than anything else and whose priorities are set on me. I know it sounds selfish, but you can't blame me. I've been nothing but selfless ever since I could remember. When you have spent half of your life pleasing others and putting their needs above your own, it's astonishing to see someone else give you the same treatment in return. It's fulfilling to be craved and wanted so badly by a king, especially the king of the ones I was raised to please, and that he would stop an important task just for you. It's an honor.

He can order a city to remain silent and listen to my moans—he is that powerful—and they will follow. They will stand quiet and watch if he orders them to.

Am I crazy for also feeling turned on by that scenario? If I am, oh well, with that that being said, I give in. I climb on top and once again give him my all.

# CHAPTER SEVENTY-SIX
## The Highly Favored

We spent most of the day in bed, just he and I, and I'm still in cloud nine because of it. Our bedchamber is our heavenly sanctuary. It is still filled with our twisted and blended passionate lovers's scent of cedarwood and honey. I couldn't get enough of Nicklaus. When he showered, I showered right beside him—naked. When I became hungry, he fed me himself, then I fed him. Well, I served him the water like jewel in between my legs.

My face catches on fire every time I think about Nicklaus telling me that my kitty is his favorite dish. I miss him. He left a few minutes ago. I, on the other hand, am still trying to get myself together. It was hard getting ready with my beloved constantly touching me. Every time I found something to wear, he would distract me by bringing his body close to mine, kissing my lips, and nibbling on my ear. He's so touchy. If he'd had it his way, we would still be exploring the depths of each other's body. As tempting as it sounded, I reminded him that our royal obligations should come first.

Tonight is the night before we take our departure for Nicklaus's homeland Sighişoara, Romania, and I couldn't be more excited.

During our time in bed, Nicklaus and I took a stroll down memory lane. He completely opened his mind up to me, filling my head with six hundred and nineteen years of memories—too many to be revealed in a day. I saw more than enough to last me a lifetime. I enjoyed learning his history. I can't believe he is that old. It's like I'm dating a walking corpse.

Haha. I still crack myself up.

Nicklaus's mind holds centuries's worth of time stamps. It was an amazing experience. It was as if I stepped into a time machine while lying in bed with him with his hand over my head. He has seen so much in his life. He has encountered many legendary figures in history—kings, queens, knights, revolutionists, scientists, musicians, artists, great poets and explorers; you name it. He has helped build empires and also watched them fall. He has spent many days painting alongside a man seeking perfection, watching him create the Mona Lisa smile. He has befriended many men, sailors included. In fact, one of his most-pleasant memories was when he and an old friend spent a beautiful summer afternoon at a place named Radio City Music Hall. They partied hard. They danced for hours with many beautiful women—most certainly intoxicated with alcohol. Hours later, Nicklaus found himself in a crowd, watching his friend share an iconic kiss that was once said brought a world war to end. Overall, his life has been fascinating—a beautiful creation indeed—and it amazes me.

I was deeply interested in learning about all his phenomenal encounters. Out of the characters in the stories his memory painted a vivid picture of, one piqued my interest the most. Her name was Queen Elizabeth. She was lavishly dressed and had a pale face and flame-red hair. She was beautiful and absolutely a darling. Based on what I witnessed through his memories, she was also a strong ruler. Apparently, she was once considered a legend in the human world, especially in Marcellus's kingdom of Europe. Nicklaus believes that I and the queen would have hit it off. He deeply respected her even though she was a human, and I admit I felt a little jealous when I saw how he used to look at her. He admired the so-called virgin queen.

620

Every time I asked him if she was really a virgin, which I did several times, his eyes would sparkle with amusement. He said, "Maybe you should question Marcellus about his golden days during the Golden Age." Whatever the hell that's supposed to mean.

Nicklaus also showed me how the human world was like before the Awakening. Humans used to roam the world freely, without restrictions or chains, but still followed the laws of the land. From what I saw, it was a whole nother world, like a parallel universe, and everything was so different.

Nicklaus claimed that the human world before the Awakening was not all it's cracked up to be. Humans were free on paper, but the laws of the land also held them in chains. He stated the only difference between now and then is that human world leaders, governments, and political figures were the masters back then. Vampires lived in the shadows and were too afraid to make their existence known for the most part. If they weren't a member of one of the wealthy houses, they would have to depend on humans for protection, shelter, and even food. Humans were in constant war with other species, and even with their own species.

Nicklaus has seen enough bloodshed. He has been through so much and has done so much. He has fought alongside humans, just for the fun of it, and has killed millions of people just because he wanted to. He is a monster, and there is no denying that. However, that doesn't change how I feel about him or who he is to me. I knew who he was before I officially met him. If that makes me the devil's wife, so be it.

I also am who I am. I cannot allow my species to continue to live in chains while I live freely. I will never forget where I came from. I didn't discuss this with Nicklaus. I decided it's best to bring up the circumstances of my race after the meeting with the council. Besides, I know there are a lot of trials and tribulations I will have to face when it's time to go down that path. I must be ready if I'm going to bring forth New World Order. And trust me when I say that I am. That should start with getting educated on both of my species's true histories. Only then can I decide how to make the future better than the past and present.

That's exactly what I'm about to do. I'll be in the library while Nicklaus attends to some important matters. In our conversation today, he stressed that without true knowledge of the past, there is no future. That's one of the reasons those dreadful vampire academies are ordered not to teach students about the history of humans—another thing that needs to change, but change is coming.

My beloved also gave me a rundown on his family tree. To sum it all up, his mother hates Xander, for he is a constant reminder of her past as human. Can you believe the Queen of Damned was once a human wh*re? I couldn't, but that's neither here nor there. Their sister is favored by his legendary father because she is ruthless, cunning, and conniving. Nicklaus doesn't trust her at all.

Talk about family drama.

Nicklaus shared with me the true reason why their family's name holds weight in the vampire world. Vampires believe that the House of Vlad are descendants of the Vampire God.

I remember reading the book *Curse of the Vlads* and thought it was just about a superstitious bullcrap. Boy, I was wrong. It's more of a spiritual belief. The Vampire God's name is Vlad. Some vampires worship him by the name of Dracula. Vampires think that going to war without the House of Vlad's blessing or against the House of Vlad is an offense to their God, who is thought to be Nicklaus's great-grandfather. Nicklaus is not only the king of all vampire kings in their eyes but is also possibly the great-grandson of the Vampire God. His family is considered blessed and highly-favored in the world of vampires. It's crazy, right?

After going into the closet for like the thousandth time today to change, I grab the first piece of clothing I see. Every item is fit for royalty, so what I get really doesn't matter, just like this one dress I've absentmindedly grabbed—a royal-blue taffeta dress that crashes down to the floor. I style my golden hair in a fancy updo and put some makeup on my face, all the while recalling Jadis's instructions every step of the way. Once done, I admire myself in the mirror. Jadis has taught me well. If the world were how it used to be, she would have surely done well for herself as a stylist. She has an impeccable style, and she damn sure knows how to pass on her knowledge. I've got to hand it to her. She would have made a killing.

I quickly leave, anxious to make it to my destination. As expected, Mr. Meany is standing by the door when I exit our chambers. Lately, he has been meaner and more distant, very distant, than usual. I wonder what's going on with him.

"Long time no see," I greet him, as we make our way out of the private wing and down the enormous hallway. "Where have you been lately?" I ask him without looking in his direction.

"You just saw me yesterday, Your Highness."

"Claire!" I correct him and continue to walk.

"Oh yes, Claire!" he says, a little bit too overenthusiastically for my liking. "Anywho, I thought you would like to know that the entire castle is buzzing about your little 'Claire Says' game last night."

My lips form into a half-smitten smirk. *I bet they are,* I think.

"Among other things . . ." he trails off.

I stop right in my tracks and turn to face him. "Other things? Other things like what?" I slightly raise an eyebrow.

Commander Vlad's face remains expressionless as usual. His cool, icy blue eyes tell it all—he is amused. "Oh nothing, really. Just something about 'Nicklaus says scream at the top of your lungs and burst every window out in the castle' game."

My jaw drops to the floor.

As we continue to make our way through, Commander Vlad's hearty laugh still bounces off the walls.

"Finally!" shouts Jadis. She jumps off one of the many maroon velvet couches as I walk into the library. She almost trips over her court-train bright-red gown while making her way to me.

Victoria is also present. She looks lovely as ever with her knee-length emerald-green satin dress. She stands up when she notices me and then slightly bows.

I have one word for it: awkward.

Her fiery-red hair is tamed and curled to perfection. The life of a chosen, I tell you.

Commander Vlad slips into the library after me and disappears, most likely scouting out the area.

We are in one of the libraries in the east wing of the palace. It is one of the places open to guests. Commander Vlad insisted that I utilize the private libraries, and I repeatedly told him no just to irk him.

Payback's a b*tch.

"What took you so long?" Jadis starts to drill me. "We have been waiting for you in this dreadfully boring room for over twenty minutes."

I take a moment to view my surroundings. Nothing about this place is dreadful or boring. The library is actually quite the opposite. Smooth, solid, and light hardwood spreads through the massive room. Rows and rows of maroon-colored bookcases matching the many maroon velvet couches in the sitting area are filled with century's worth of oakwood bookshelves. They stand tall and proud, almost reaching the glass ceiling. Thick-framed golden portraits of the royal family hang in their glory all around the oak-brown walls. In the center is a maroon ladder-like staircase which leads to each and every section of the deep oakwood bookshelves. The interior design is to die for. Everything coordinates in every way, but each item in this room has its own beauty.

"Earth to Claire," Jadis calls out to me, crossing her arms across her chest in the process.

"How did you know I was coming?" I walk toward the couch where Victoria is standing close. I can hear her heartbeat picking up. She is still bowing, looking like she is about to piss herself. I'll repeat, *awkward*. I'm trying my hardest not to laugh, and so is Jadis.

"You don't have to bow to me," I tell Vctoria as I take a seat.

"You're not the only one around here with powers," responds Jadis, plopping down beside me.

I raise my eyebrow while staring in her big brown eyes. "And what type of power do you have?"

"Power of persuasion, cherry pop," she brags, turning to face Victoria. "Victoria, can you please stop acting so weird?" she says to her, and I couldn't be happier.

"My apologies, Your Majesty."

"Claire," I correct her. "Victoria, please take a seat and relax. I'm not going to bite you. I'm only half-leech."

"Yeah," Jadis adds. "Claire is still the same person, just a little more badass than before, but she is the same ole Claire, who now just happens to be a fan of a game called Nicklaus Says."

My eyes bulge, heart skips a beat, and face drops. She just said that, didn't she?

Before I can respond, Mr. Meany reappears and nods, indicating that this room is safe for me. "I'll be right outside if you need me," he tells me, then he makes his way to the door.

"What about me, Mr. Hot Stuff?" Jadis asks with a giggle.

Victoria and I laugh along with her. This girl sure knows how to lighten the mood.

"I need you. I need some Mr. Hunky in my life. Come to mama," she quips.

Commander Vlad rolls his eyes before he walks out, closing the door behind him.

Jadis is the first to stop laughing. "So out of all the fantastic rooms you have access to, why in leech's earth did you choose to spend the day in here?" she questions me.

"I want to learn more about our history." I stand up and walk toward one of the many bookshelves.

"History," she repeats the last word.

Even though my back is to her, I can tell she is making a funny face behind me.

"Yes *our* history." I begin my search. My fingers absently scan the back of the cool-textured and ancient-looking books as I stroll through the Historical Nonfiction section of the library. My lips form into a slight smile as I rememner Nicklaus's words. "Without true knowledge of the past, there is no future," I recite his words verbatim.

"How boring!" huffs Jadis. She dramatically throws herself down on the sofa.

"I think it sounds fun," Victoria pipes up.

Surprised, both Jadis and I turn to look in her direction.

"What?" She throws her arms up in the air. "I love to read, not to mention it would be pretty cool to learn about who and where we came from. Just think about it. This is a once-in-a-lifetime opportunity. How many humans can you name know our true history?"

"Yeah, how many, Jadis?" I chime in.

"Welp, one plus one shall equal two." Jadis stands up. (She just can't sit still.) "You guys have fun with that. I'm going to go bribe one of the guards to let me get a peek of that sexy new prisoner."

"What prisoner?" I ask.

Jadis and her boy-crazed mind.

"Some human from King Cyrus's land," she responds way too quickly. "He is super hot and his eyes . . . they are like smoky green smoke bombs. Victoria, you know him, right? What's his name again?"

626

"Smoky green eyes?" I ask them both.

Victoria's heart skips a beat.

Jadis's big brown eyes widen as she continues, "He is absolutely perfect . . . bulky, muscular frame, smokin'! Golden sun-kissed hair, smokin'! A bit bloody and bruised from what I hear, but still smokin' . . ." she rambles on.

Hmmm. It's interesting, very interesting.

Victoria's face is transparently pale, and her palms are extremely sweaty, increasing my suspicions. She has some explaining to do.

I shift my focus back to Jadis. "I thought you were destined for bigger things."

"I am." She flashes a brilliant smile. "But sometimes girls just want to have fun."

Classic. If the circumstances were different, I'd be rolling.

"Hmmm. Yeah. How about you do that? You do have the power of persuasion."

Jadis is already heading out of the room before I can even turn back to look at her.

"You bet, I do," she says, getting out of the door to harass Commander Vlad before she leaves, I'm sure.

"So . . ." I look at Victoria, studying her for a while once Jadis's scent becomes less potent.

She moves around and starts to fiddle with the hem of her dress. Her heart rate increases by a long shot. The sweet scent of her fear awakens a very dangerous part of me.

Ignoring my new sudden thirst, I decide to concentrate on anything but her. "Why does it sound like Jadis is describing Alec?" I get straight to the point.

"Because . . . she is referring to . . . Alec," she hesitantly answers, her head held down.

"How long has he been here? How long has he been in their custody?"

She remains silent. I walk toward the window, and she follows behind me. The sun has completely disappeared, bringing forth the young night. We shall be departing sooner than later. Watching from right here, I can see the roaring waves disappearing into the steady, sliding sand. What a breathtaking view!

"And why hasn't this been brought to my attention before?" I ask.

She gulps from behind me.

"I asked you a question," I remind her after a couple of seconds, raising my voice slightly.

She flinches and takes a step back, on the verge of breaking down in tears. "Because you weren't supposed to know. The king ordered everyone not to say anything to you, or else—"

"Which king?" My monster is on the horizon. I know the answer, but I need her to confirm it. I need her to say it out loud.

Victoria's heart beats louder and louder by the second.

"I asked you which king!" I am seconds away from ripping her head off her neck, figuratively speaking of course.

"King Nicklaus," she gets out, her voice no more than a whisper.

Of course, he did.

"Claire, you don't understand. The king is still the king. I have to follow orders. We all do. It's different for you."

"That may be true, but you were never content with being a slave. You did what you had to do to survive," I say her words to her. "A night of new beginnings, right?" I remind her. I take a deep breath, looking out of the window. "You're dismissed."

I don't feel like talking to her anymore. I'm disappointed with her.

I can hear her high heels clicking. Her heart rate is skyrocketing. She really is scared out of her mind.

"And Victoria," I call out to her as my sensitive ears pick up on her hand touching the door knob, "this discussion stays inside this room. No one should know that I am aware of Alec's condition, not even your chosen king."

"You have my word, Your Majesty."

I stand in front of the window, watching the crashing waves for a while longer.

*Nicklaus, Nicklaus, Nicklaus . . . what am I going to do with you?*

# CHAPTER SEVENTY-SEVEN
## The Chosen One

I pace around in the library, pondering over the information Victoria has revealed to me. A bright firepit of rage courses through my veins.

How could he? No. That would be a dumb question. The real question should be, Why would he? No. That would be another dumb question. I know why Nicklaus did what he did. I know firsthand what he is capable of. Placing Alec in the dungeons because of a little crush is just ridiculous. He has gone overboard.

*No. Killing him would be a little overboard,* my subconscious speaks up.

*Shut up!* I mentally tell myself.

Alec means nothing to me. Well, I don't have any feelings for him, but I do care for him. I don't know why I feel connected to him. The point is that Nicklaus knows it, and that's exactly why the boy is chained in the first place.

*New flash! They are all in chains,* my subconscious speaks again.

*Arghhh. Shut up,* I snap at myself.

I'm going f*cking crazy. My monster doesn't agree with my anger. She thinks it's a waste of time. I'm sure she does because she is a leech. The human side of me is really bothered about this whole ordeal. Nicklaus shouldn't have thrown someone in the dungeon because he felt like it. No one should. Every human or vampire must be granted with some type of chance to explain themselves. This is exactly what I meant. I can't allow my species to continue living in chains while I live freely. I guess Nicklaus and I shall have this conversation sooner than later. I do need to learn more about both my species first to be able to tidy up the mess my beloved created.

My eyes scan the massive rows of books in the Historical Nonfiction section once again but shoot to the door when I hear the sound of it being opened.

"Your Highness, what's wrong?" Commander Vlad comes in. "I can feel your frustration through our bond."

"Claire!" I snap.

How many times do I have to remind him to call me Claire?

"And what did you just say to me?" I lean my head over and turn my entire body in his direction. "What do you mean you can feel my emotions through our bond?"

Commander Vlad closes the door behind him. "The moment you accepted my loyalty, I became a part of you. Any vampires you accept shall be bonded to you. Normally, it takes a while before the bond is sealed, but things are always different when you are concerned," he explains.

"I don't get it. A sealed bond gives any and every one front-row seats to my emotions?"

"Precisely. Well, something of the sort. We can feel what you feel when you want us to feel it. We can communicate with you if you grant us access. Right now, you're like an open book."

My frustration increases.

*This is what I meant. I don't know much about what I am, where I came from, or whom I came from. How the hell am I supposed to lead two entire species when I'm completely blind?*

My head starts pounding as I think about it, then all of a sudden, the weight of the world is on my shoulders. Commander

Vlad is watching me with a strange expression. He is most likely trying to understand the sudden change of my mood.

Join the club! So am I. My emotions are all over the place.

Ignoring his concerned stare, I ask, "And how long have you been able to feel my emotions?"

"This is the first time I really feel them. King Nicklaus can feel them as well. He has been trying to speak with you, but you blocked him out."

*You're damn right. I did. He's lucky I haven't found his ass. I would have fried him to a crisp.*

"Where is he?" I turn to face the window. Right now, I wish I could go adrift, lost in the sea, stress- and worry-free.

"All the kings are running over the plan with the security detail. He shall be in shortly after."

"How much time do we still have before departure?"

"Maybe an hour or so. Is this what this is about? Are you nervous about the summons?"

I almost die from laughter.

*Sure, I am.*

My hand starts to fiddle with the pendant.

Commander Vlad's eyes are fixed on my hand movement. "Are you sure you're okay?" he asks cautiously.

I almost snap at him when the library door swings open, and the intoxicating scent of fresh, burning cedarwood and expensive cologne invades my lungs. I don't need to turn around to know who's coming in. Xander's and Nicklaus's scents are quite similar but oddly different. I'll be able to identify their distinctive scents even without my sense of smell, even in my sleep. I'm in love with their scent. It's my favorite.

"Brave one"—Xander enters the room—"your emotions are driving your foolish beloved crazy. What's going on?"

I don't really feel like being bothered, so I ignore him. Tears threatening to escape as I continue to watch the crashing waves. I can feel the heat blazing from Xander's and Vlad's burning stares. Refusing to allow anyone to see me cry, I hold my tears back and raise my head in Xander's direction. "I'm fine." I look at him without giving away my emotions.

"You're an awful liar," he calls me out, seeing right through me. "Leave us," he orders.

"Your Highness," says Commander Vlad, ignoring Xander's command, only to ask for my approval.

I nod, signaling that he can leave. He obeys with no complaints.

*Look at that! Commander Vlad's loyalty is with me after all.*

"You officially has his loyalty," Xander voices my thoughts out loud.

"Yeah." I slightly open the window. The sound, smell, and feel of the ocean and fresh wind float in the room.

We stand in silence for a while, listening to the wind. We take deep breaths and embrace the bright moon along with the twinkling stars and purplish and dark-bluish sky.

"Claire," Xander finally speaks, "there is no need for you to continue this charade of acting, as if nothing were wrong. I can feel your tornado of emotions spiraling out of control. What is going on in your pretty little head, brave one?"

*What isn't?*

I sigh, and Xander watches me intensely.

*I know he isn't going to drop it. I know him, just as well as he knows me. In fact, he is most likely the only vampire who truly understands me.*

With that in mind, I ask him, "How can the blind lead the blind?"

"Claire is speaking in riddles, out of all people. I wonder where you got that from."

I laugh slightly, and playfully shove his chest. "I learned from the very best leech the leeches have to offer."

"Damn right, you did." He smirks, beautifully.

Damn him and that beautiful smirk of his.

633

"No, seriously, brave one, could you elaborate? I don't understand the meaning behind your words." He sits down and pats the seat beside him, inviting me to sit as well.

I plop down beside him. "I don't know where I came from, just like most humans in this day and age. I don't know much about your people's history, our people's history rather. The only thing a blind leader can do is lead their followers astray. Things need to change, Xander. How can I convince two entire species to be receptive to change when I don't even understand how to adapt to the changes my body is going through?" I heave a deep sigh. "How can I expect other vampires to show some humanity when their king, himself, doesn't give a glimpse of this?"

"What do you mean?" he asks, confusion evident on his handsome face.

"It doesn't really matter, now does it. Once a monster, always a monster."

"I see," Xander responds sheepishly, then he stares into space.

We sit in silence, and my mind continues to wander. What's understood doesn't have to be explained. Xander knows I'm right.

I start to play with the cool emerald attached to the pendant. The jewel feels good against my skin. Its power is truly highly addictive. So far, I've been able to do whatever I want to do with it. I have made people follow my every command.

Out of nowhere, a thought suddenly appears: *I can force Nicklaus and others to coexist. That would be perfect. We can all live in harmony. I can force the much-needed change with one word.*

I wonder if that's the route I need to take. I think over the idea. Everything will be like it should be—equal and balanced. The only problem is that if I go down that route, I'll be no better than any of them. I would be forcing them against their will. To stop violence is one way—to use the power of the emerald so as to prevent bloodshed and to protect the ones I love— but using this for personal gain no matter how much good it would bring is a whole nother ball game. Things need to change, and they shall. It is inevitable. However, there is a way to go about things. Sometimes it's better not to fight fire with fire.

My mind continues to drift. I think about everything I have been through and every obstacle I have overcome.

Xander's cool hand being placed on my lap chases my thoughts away. "Do you remember what I told you that day I took you out of the dungeon?" he suddenly asks.

"Which part?"

"The part that applies to you in this very moment." He puts his hand over mine. "I admitted that your fearless nature awakened something inside me that had been long buried. I declared that you were my savior, our savior. And I meant every word. There's a reason why I'm called the cold-hearted king. In a day and without trying, you melted the frozen wall I had enclosed my heart with for centuries. You can achieve the impossible, Claire. Don't ever forget that."

I lower my head, allowing his words to sink in.

Xander gets up and makes his way toward the door. Before he exits, he turns. "Nicklaus selected you as his chosen because he was too afraid to accept you as his beloved. How quickly has that changed?" he asks, regaining my attention. "I once told you that the players are too focused on the king. They truly underestimate the power of the queen. How many people have underestimated you since that day? And how many times have you proven them wrong?"

"I disagree, but sometimes it's best to just agree to disagree," I recite the same exact words I said to him for what seems like so long ago.

He flashes a charming smile. "I agree with that, brave one, because I truly believe in you, even when you don't believe in yourself."

With those last words, he leaves me alone with my own thoughts. I stay back in the library and think about everything

Xander has said to me. His points are always valid, but they're still *his* points of view. I feel how I feel, and no one can change that.

It has been five minutes since he left, so I decide to get up and finally do what I came here to do: read about the histories of humans and vampires.

As I stroll down different sections of the library, the unfamiliar power of the emerald hums around my neck. My hands, seeming to have a mind of their own, grab many different books without me even paying attention to the titles. The power from the precious gemstone buzzes to life with each book selected, but it zaps when my hands touch the spine of one book that contains a one-word title in a language I don't understand.

"Electus," I say it out loud. I carry the book to a table at the end of the section, all the other books falling from my hand. With the first touch, its dark-brown cover sparks underneath my fingers.

The book looks ancient. It is thick and massive from the outside and appears worn from old age. However, everyone knows not to judge a book by its cover.

Excited to start, I absentmindedly flip open the crisp and freshly reserved first page that is white in color. "This book is dedicated to the Chosen One," I read the fancy cursive writing out loud.

As soon as the words fall from my lips, everything around me goes in slow motion. My neck itches, my heart starts thudding, and my skin begins to tingle. A bright emerald-green light flashes— the unfamiliar power awakens. The wind is knocked out of me as a thousand scenes and memories float in my head. The world shifts around me, then comes a soft, sweet voice from the other end of the table. "We meet at last, my sweet Claire, the Chosen One!"

# CHAPTER SEVENTY-EIGHT
## The Witch

I turn and see a drop-dead gorgeous, raven-haired woman with pink cheeks. Her radiant green eyes are reading me from head to toe like a book. Her face is enchanting, and she oozes confidence. She is sitting in a chair on the other end of the table.

"Who the hell are you, and where did you come from?" I jump out of my seat.

Her plump lips curl into a ridiculously beautiful smile. "That's neither here nor there, Electus," she responds, her voice sexy and powerful. She has a rich and thick accent. I never heard anything like it before, but strangely enough I know it's a Romanian accent.

*Who is this woman?*

"Who are you?"

*No, wait!*

"Where did you come from?"

*No, wait, what did she just call me?*

"What did you just call me? I ask question after question, batting them out of my scrambled thoughts.

"Electus," she quickly responds.

*Electus?*

"What the hell does that mean?"

"The chosen one."

*The chosen one? I don't get it. The chosen one . . .*

My eyes flicker to the book and then back to her. "Electus," I repeat. "The chosen one . . ." Within the next second, everything clicks. "The book!"

"Yes, my child. The book belongs to me, among other things," says the mysterious woman. She stands up and struts in my direction.

I prepare myself. I watch her every move, patiently awaiting her approach. Strangely, I don't feel threatened, but at the same time I instinctively know she is a major threat. She's dressed too impressively in a stunning sleeveless lace gown that shows off every inch of her tall frame and curvy figure. It has a split on the left side that trails up to her thigh, exposing her flawless skin and well-toned legs. Her waist-length jet-black hair is cascading down her back like a steady-flowing river.

The deep V-neck portion of the dress serves her breasts justice. They sit up high and perky, bouncing in unison as she struts. The way she walks would make people want to stop what they are doing just to look at her. The power this mysterious woman possesses is a force to be reckoned with—an elemental force, for sure. Her every step demands attention, obedience, and respect. Her potent essence is undeniable. She is a living example of how a strong and powerful woman is supposed to carry herself.

*My God! Nicklaus's belief about God being a woman seems pretty accurate in this moment.*

Her smile brightens, as if she knows what I am thinking. That's when I pick up on the familiar aura surrounding her. It's beaming a mile radius with each step she takes. As soon as I notice it, time seems to stop. I can no longer feel the night breeze from outside the window. I can no longer hear the sound of the waves breaking on the shore. She is still heading my way at the exact same pace. I search for my monster's presence. For some strange reason, I can't feel my predator's dark and tainted soul.

*What the f*ck!*

No one else to rely on, I grab the pendant. For the first time in history, I don't feel the buzzing electric energy that typically comes along with one touch. I focus, trying my hardest to draw forth the power I know I can wield, but to no avail. There is nothing—no tingling of the skin and pounding of the heart, and no ghost-like figure of unknown power looming around me.

Caught off guard, I immediately open my mind up to Nicklaus.

*"Nicklaus, something is wrong."*

He doesn't respond.

*"Nicklaus . . . Nicklaus."*

Three seconds later.

*"Nicklaus."*

Five seconds later.

*"Nicklaus."*

Still there is no answer. The woman is now less than three steps closer to me.

I completely break down the mental barrier that prevents anyone from entering my mind.

*"Vlad,"* I call out in my head, *"I need you now."* I wait for him to respond, but I'm met by silence.

"They can't hear you, Claire," the woman says to me, now standing right before me.

*What the f\*ck is going on?*

A tiny shiver runs down my spine. Even with that, I refuse to show a single ounce of fear or any sign of weakness. I size her up, staring her directly in the eye—shoulders straightened and head held high.

"How the hell do you know my name, and who the f\*ck are you?" I sneer.

Her cat-like eyes glow with excitement. They study every inch of my face, then roam down to my neckline before settling on the pendant. Then, they make their way back to my face again. She looks me in the eye. "Such a stunning and brave girl," she remarks. "Your ancestors would certainly be proud of you."

"My ancestors?"

"Yes," she answers quickly. "I am very familiar with your bloodline."

"I don't understand," I mutter.

Her head turns in the direction of the door. "Just in time," she says.

As if on cue, the door flies open. The fresh scent of burning cedarwood and expensive cologne wraps around me, then seconds later, I'm being shoved behind *his* back.

\*     \*     \*

NICKLAUS

It's only been thirty minutes or so since I left Claire alone in our chambers, but I can still taste her milk-and-honey essence on the tip of my tongue. I can still feel her juices dripping off the tip of my dick and the pain and pleasure of her monster digging those talons deep into my skin. I can still hear her honey-laced tone screaming my name for the world to hear. I miss her. If I had my way, we would be still be exploring the depths of each other's body. She reminded me that our royal duties should come first, and that's exactly what I'm doing now in my office—fulfilling some bullsh*t royal obligations.

First, I have to go over security measures just in case some idiot decides to attack my kingdom during my departure, which I doubt. No one has the balls. But like Xander says, "It's better to be safe than sorry." I also have to double-check security measures for our trip, just in case someone decides to attack us during our departure, which I triple doubt. No one is that stupid. And if someone actually does wish a cruel death, God bless their for-sure-dead and ripped-to-shreds soul.

I also need to review some documents—whoop-dee-f*cking-doo!—then meet with the other kings, which is the most-dreadful part of the night, if you ask me. Nonetheless, we must do what we have to do. I've got to oversee some last-minute preparations with all of them before we leave. I also need to discuss with them some things about the summons. I'm really f*cking annoyed about that. Well, I'm annoyed about all of my obligations at this point. All I want is to be around Claire.

Don't get me wrong. The well-being and safety of my subjects are a priority. They always have been, and that's a problem. I have lived centuries putting my species before my happiness, but Claire changes all of that. I'd rather live the rest of my existence with her in my arms. In fact, I'm actually considering to force her to be around me every second, minute, and hour of the day. I imagine her now sitting on my lap as I sit on my throne, listening to the problems of our people. I can see myself touching her hair and whispering in her ear that she is mine. The life I tell you.

However, Claire would never allow it. She is an ideal queen, a leader. She wants to be actively involved in the affairs of our land. I'm convinced that's the reason why she is destined to be my beloved. When I f*ck sh*t up, she finds a way to fix my faults. When I lose my temper, she remains cool. When I misjudge others, she reevaluates and resolves it. She is my balance. F*ck, I miss her.

*"Commander Vlad,"* I call out, having entered his mind.

*"Your Highness."*

*"Enough with the pleasantries. You are my brother. Where is the queen?"*

*"You sound like Claire. She hates me when I call her with her title."*

I laugh to myself.

*"We are in the east-wing library, and she is currently being interrogated by King Cornelius's chosen. If I must say, that's one strange human,"* Vlad says.

I chuckle. Yes, she is.

*"Claire refused to go to the private library, just to irk me,"* Vlad continues.

Sounds like Claire.

My lips curl into a soft smile. I picture my beautiful beloved making silly faces at Vlad and cracking leech jokes just to get under his skin. You've just got to love her.

*"Your Highness, I would like to speak to you about Abigail."*

*"Speak freely, and I order you to never call Claire or me with our titles in private again."* I sit down at my desk. I pick up a document and briefly scan it.

*"My apologies. It's an old habit,"* he explains.

I nod. I know what he means. I have had the same circle of friends for centuries. Vlad is one of the first and most likely the last addition.

*"I would like to be relieved from active duty and be assigned as part of King Cyrus's security detail."*

I place the useless document down and sit back. I knew this was coming the very moment he confided in me about Abigail. *"And how do you think the queen will take this information?"*

*"I don't know,"* he answers honestly.

*"She won't take it well. You are the only vampire other than me, Xander, and Marcellus that she actually trusts. After we handle the summons, they will return to their kingdom. She will—"*

*"With all due respect, Nicklaus, I'm not asking for your permission."*

I smirk.

*"I'm loyal to my queen and loyal to my king. I'd prefer to have both of your blessings. If not, then I will take my leave one way or another."*

There it goes.

I laugh to myself. *"As I stated before, Vlad, you are my brother. Skip the pleasantries, and go get your girl."*

*"Thank you, Brother."*

I can hear the relief in his voice.

*"I'll leave right away when we return from our trip,"* he says.

642

*"Agreed."* I briefly stare at the moon, figuring out its position in the sky. It's time. *"I have a meeting with all of the kings. I'll discuss your reassignment with King Cyrus at once."*

Mad or not, Cyrus will welcome Vlad to his army with open arms. Vlad is one of the only commanders who have lived to tell the tale of fighting lycans by himself. Cyrus needs him.

*"Thank you,"* he tells me again.

*"Don't thank me yet."* I laugh through our mind link. *"You have to break the news to Claire."*

He chuckles in response.

\*     \*     \*

I'm sitting in this god-awful and uncomfortable chair, rubbing my temple. My mind is racing. This meeting should have been a quick one, but we've been running over our plan with the lower-level security detail for more than an hour now. They are not to be trusted. My personal guards, which are an army alone, are the only ones who know everything. It's like in every kingdom, our lower-level security detail are our guinea pigs—better yet, the first to die. We use them as subjects in our experiments. Whenever we have an upcoming war, we break them down into tiny groups and provide each with different information, just in case we have a traitor among our ranks. This method has been very effective in sniffing them out. For example, a group of pussies is afraid to go up against the council. Xander thought it would be best to tell them and only them the truth about Claire, just to see how they would react. They were scared sh*tless. To them, going against the council is like going against the Blood God himself. They all fear my father.

Xander wanted to know how loyal this group of men would remain if a war between the kings and council actually began. At first, I thought it was a pretty good idea; now, not so much. In fact, it's a f*cking nightmare. They all will have to die before we take off, and that's less than an hour away.

"So I'm going to say this one more time"—Marcellus looks each assigned comrade in the eye—"the queen's safety is our number one priority. You shall all protect her with your lives against whomever."

"But it's the council, sire," says some foolish soldier.

Before I have a chance to snap the idiot's neck with one swift movement, Rufus beats me to it.

"I don't give a f*ck if it's the Vlad's man pope!" He throws the pussy's head onto the table. "No one touches the queen. Do I make myself clear?"

Fear is evident in their eyes.

Claire has been blocking me out for a while now. She's f*cking pissed, and I don't have the slightest clue why. I can feel her anger, frustration, and displeasure twisting like a tornado inside my brain. I can't get to her, and it's driving me crazy. This is exactly what I meant earlier. When it comes to Claire, I could care less about royal obligations. These are a bunch of bullsh*t.

*"What the hell is going on with Claire?"* I growl through our connection. *"I've been attempting to communicate with her. Tell her to unblock me now!"* I slam my fist onto the table.

All eyes inside the room dart to me. Xander stands and leaves, going to check on Claire for sure. What the hell would I do without him?

"What?" I snap at everyone. "Carry the f*ck on!"

Of course, everyone obeys.

About fifteen minutes later, Xander mind-links with me. *"She's fine,"* he confirms.

*"What's the matter with her?"*

He sighs. *"That's not my place to tell. All I can say is that you need to be careful with her."*

*Be careful with her? "What the f*ck is that supposed to mean?"* I snarl.

*"Exactly what it is, Nicklaus!"* he retorts. *"Don't underestimate the power she holds over you. I'm not just talking about the power of the*

*emerald. I'm talking about the power of the bond as well. Claire is still half-human. Remember that.*"

I am just about to tell him to mind his goddamn business when out of nowhere, a bright green light blinds me, and an unknown force sends me flying through the room. My ears start ringing, then a word is whispered in my ear: *"Somnum* (Sleep)."

Everything goes blank.

*   *   *

CLAIRE

*Xander!*

He moves faster than I have ever witnessed even with my enhanced senses. "I knew it was you!" he snaps. His voice is low and dangerous, threatening. "What are you doing here, Aurora?"

*Aurora? I heard that name before.*

The mysterious woman's radiant green eyes narrow in displeasure, not bothered showing how annoyed she is. "Waiting for you, cold-hearted king."

"What do you want from Claire?" Xander hisses. Right now, he is not the man I have grown used to but the monster that everyone talks about.

"Shut up!" she straight up tells him, and his mouth literally shuts. "Move out of my way."

The air cracks with electricity, and Xander's body goes flying across the room—literally flying—before it slams into the front door.

"Somnum," she orders.

Xander's eyes close instantly.

Without thinking, I charge into the woman's direction. I could give a rat's ass who or what she is. We all shall fight with or without my powers.

In the next instant, Aurora is in front of me—now, that's fast. I swing my leg out, attempting to kick her. She meets my assault with a backflip on the other end of the room. I charge again. And before I can carry out my next attack, she appears right beside me, catching me off guard.

*What the f\*ck? She was just right . . .*

She rests her hand on my shoulder, and electricity zaps within me. My heart starts pounding. Her touch makes my skin tingle—chilled tingles. A sudden itch rushes through my entire body. I gasp for air when the chain with the emerald pendant tightens around my neck.

"*Mitescere, Electus* (Calm down, Chosen One)," she says to me in a language I can now somehow understand. "I am not here to hurt you. I am here to help, guide, and warn you." Emerald-green light glows through her eyes and enters into my soul.

"The pendants belongs to you!" I gasp.

"No, my dear." She removes her hand from my shoulder. "The emerald belongs to you, to your bloodline. My magic is just the primary source."

# CHAPTER SEVENTY-NINE
## The Untold Story

"I don't understand."

"In time you shall." Aurora walks toward the table. "Now, sit. We've got so much to discuss in such little time."

My feet follow her command, and I grind my teeth in frustration.

*This brings back old memories, the bad memories of when Nicklaus used to compel my surface.*

"You don't like to be controlled." She reads my mind out loud, doing another thing I absolutely hate.

"I don't like you or any other person invading my privacy!" I sass her as I take a seat beside her. Once again, I've got no control over my own body.

She flashes a dazzling smile.

*Geez louise, she is so beautiful!*

"Thank you, Claire. However, if you don't like something, change it. If anyone has the power to defeat all odds, then it's you."

"What is that supposed to mean?"

"Exactly what it is. You have the power to defeat all odds."

*Uh-huh.* I stare at her blankly.

"Love is a force as powerful and as strange as the power of the emerald, my dear," she says, horribly attempting to elaborate.

I still don't get it. My head starts to spin. Ah yai yai! The riddles, the mind games, the impossible puzzles—all of these are draining my cat.

*She is just like Xander.*

"I'm nothing like the cold-hearted king," she tells me, obviously reading my mind again.

"No, you're not, because he understands how to honor one's wishes!"

"Oh really?" She raises her eyebrow and flashes another dazzling smile.

*She is so beautiful. What is she?*

Her smile brightens. Of course, she is reading my mind, but this time she decides not to speak on it—smart woman.

"Give me your hand, my dear," she directs, her cat-like eyes entering my soul.

This time, my hand doesn't follow her instruction. Now I've got complete control over my body.

True to my nature, I do what I do best: defy. "I'm not giving you sh*t until you wake Xander up. I don't trust you."

I do trust her. I don't know why, but I do. There's something safe about her presence and aura. It's actually calming, and I feel connected to this strange woman in every way.

She continues to stare into my eyes for a long while, the silence between us strangely comforting. I don't understand it at all, but I'm trying my hardest to figure it out, figure her out. But I can't, no matter how hard I try. My brain is fried.

*"Evigilare faciatis* (Awaken)," she finally speaks, waving her hand in Xander's direction.

Xander's eyes pop open. The room is now filled with the familiar, bright, electric emerald-green light.

"Aurora!" Xander exclaims.

His penetrating growls fill the air within a second. His eyes narrow, and his posture goes dangerously stiff. Before I know it, he's already standing right beside me. His eyes bleed fifty shades of red blood, fire, and ash. I've never seen him so mad.

"What the f*ck do you think you're doing? I swear on every child you have birthed, they shall meet their Maker by the night's end," he threatens.

"Don't bother making useless threats, cold-hearted king," she nonchalantly replies. She smiles sweetly, obviously unconcerned. "Now, Claire, we are running out of time. Please give me your hand."

"She's not giving you sh*t!" Xander damn near snatches me out of the seat and then slides his arms around me protectively.

Aurora's eyes glow electric green. "If you continue to prevent me from completing my task, you shall meet your Maker, for that I promise," she retorts, her voice deadly. Her body suddenly goes stiff, and her expression turns cold.

Talk about a mood shift.

"You had your chance to protect, love, and connect with her spirit, but you failed! I will not allow history to repeat itself for the thousandth time."

"What the f*ck are you talking about? I've protected and loved Claire since day one. She is my brother's beloved."

"I see." She looks him up and down. "If you had listened to my warning before, this moment in time would not be happening. If only you had found it in your frozen heart to love, protect, and connect with—"

"Don't you dare bring her into this!" Xander shouts. His anger floods the room like a tsunami, his rage pouring down.

"She has everything to do with this. Your decision has been affecting us all. Because of you, the war of the world is to come. Now, stand down before I end you."

"I don't fear you, cold-hearted b*tch!" he spits through clenched teeth.

"You don't have to fear me to die, " she responds. The hatred her eyes hold for him is undeniable.

"Try me b—"

"Enough!" I bark. They are confusing me to no end.

*What is it with these two fighting like children? I'm starting to learn that all of the supernatural species fight against one another like children. Who's really older, me or them? Goodness gracious!*

"You're older than them," Aurora states loud and clear.

"What?"

*She cannot be talking to me.*

"I am talking to you, and I'm answering your unspoken question," she says, once again giving me her undivided attention. "When your spirit is placed into the equation, you are older than most."

I'm f*cking lost, but at least I'm not the only one. Xander stares at Aurora like she has grown two heads.

"What do you mean by my spirit?"

"Your spirit mingles with many spirits, and that's why you were able to wield my power the very moment the pendant was placed upon your skin. The spirits within you remember the time they had lived long before you."

"What the f*ck are you talking about?" Xander asks.

She turns to face him. "You are in no position to ask me any questions!" she spits.

"My position is first in line when the challenge concerns Claire!" he spits back.

They bicker back and forth once again. I tune both of them out and rethink over Aurora's words.

*"Your spirit mingles with many spirits."* What does that mean? The Chosen One . . . how so? *"When your spirit is placed into the equation, you are older than most."*

Now, that sounds creepy. I don't understand any of it, but I now understand one thing—the power I can somehow wield is most certainly her power, which means she's the only one who can explain why I can wield it.

"Show me," I finally speak up, regaining their attention.

"Are you crazy?" scoffs Xander. His anger is now directed toward me. "You're not going anywhere near her."

"I had protected Claire long before you were born," she says, her thick Romanian accent stained with malice. "I'll never harm her. You have my word. This is my final warning, so stand down, Xander."

"Over my dead body! Your word is useless," he growls, adding fuel to her brewing flame.

"Stand down, Xander," I say, as I walk around him.

"Hell no!" Xander yanks my arm, preventing me from taking another step. This is the first time he's ever handled me with force.

I yank my body away from him. "I'm your queen, and I'm ordering you to stand down."

"You don't know her, Claire! She can't be trusted."

"You pledged allegiance to me, did you not?" I stare him directly in his eye. I can see his inner battle.

Xander is only trying to protect me. However, he knows that once I've made up my mind, nothing or no one can stop me.

"Never trust a witch," he says after a second passes, then he lets go.

Aurora watches our encounter in silence. Although her face doesn't show any emotion, something is hidden and buried within her sight—pride, if I'm not mistaken.

Finally, I make my way to her, and she patiently waits for me to take her hand.

"Open your mind," she instructs, the moment I reach her.

Instantly, I break down all my mental barriers, and follow her command. A thick cloud of emerald smoke enters into my mind, as the feeling of power within her touches my skin. It runs through my blood, then consumes my mind.

\*     \*     \*

*A long time ago in a place so far away, there was once a girl named Jazlyn. She was beautiful—heavenly divine. She had full, luscious long dark hair, electrifying green eyes, and thick, heavy lashes that fanned her angelic face.* She lived with her father, sister, and mother in the village spread out across a bright green valley with many huts settled upon a collection of steep hills. The climate there was moist and wet, thick enough to taste. The massive valley was full of dark green trees. A dark river poured through it, flowing all the way out to the blackest sea. The mountains surrounding the village were so high, fading into the thick, clear blue clouds and sun-kissed, moist sky.

Jazlyn wasn't like the other village girls. Although she was a little rebellious and extremely brave, she also had a heart of gold. She was the type of person who would defend the weak and befriend the sick. Her parents had to tell her to do the opposite of what they actually wanted done. She excelled in whatever she strived to achieve, which made her their favorite. She was their diamond in the rough.

*One day, the village children were playing a game of ostrakinda.* Jazlyn was the only child given the black stone, *indicating that she was the only child on team night.* The other children figured that the best way to beat her was by teaming up against her. *But Jazlyn was determined to win. She hid in the bushes at a hut on the far-east side of the village. At that hut lived a girl—a supernatural beauty with pink cheeks, raven hair, radiant green eyes, and enchanting face. Despite being beautiful, all the villagers stayed away from her. They believed she was cursed,* so *Jazlyn knew that all the children were not brave enough to search for her there.*

Two seconds after hiding, Jazlyn heard a high-pitched scream. She wasn't the type of person who would run away from trouble. No, she wasn't like that at all, so she ran directly toward where that scream came from. She entered the strange girl's hut, not fearing whatever lay ahead. During those days, it was unusual for a girl to live alone.

*Jazlyn found the girl lying unconscious on the floor, with a dagger plunged into her heart. She was minutes away from death.* Walking away would be against Jazlyn's nature, so without thinking, she rushed to the girl's side. She instantly knew what to do because her mother was a healer. However, the odds were stacked against her. If the girl was going to survive, she would have to move fast, and so she did.

*Jazlyn put a cloth around the wound to stop the bleeding, then she quickly searched the hut to locate herbs she could use to sterilize it. Once she found them, she had only a few minutes to boil some water, remove the dagger, and bandage the wound.*

*Somehow, someway, she defeated the odds! Once the girl was stable, Jazlyn carried her to their hut with all her strength. She begged her mother to nurse her back to good health, without her father's knowledge as he would never allow it.* Her mother was hesitant, but she couldn't just let the girl die. She agreed, only if Jazlyn promised to care for her when she could not.

For months, Jazlyn watched over the girl, fed her, bathed her, and shortly after befriended her. She learned that her name was Aurora. The strange girl had no idea who or where she came from. Jazlyn learned that she had nightmares of many faces she had never encountered, and odd things she could never explain always happened around her.

The girls became tighter than a bark on a tree. Many memories of the lives they once lived flashed in great speed. They did everything together and shared a sister-like bond. Both of them blossomed into phenomenal women.

# CHAPTER EIGHTY
## The Premonition

Jazlyn grew up to be an outspoken woman. She had a free spirit and was as stubborn as a mule, still refusing to follow rules. Other women envied her and men were head over heels in love with her. She was declared as the fairest in the village. Many men fought for her attention and affection, but she fell for only one. He was a tall, strong, and handsome man who was easy on the eyes and smooth with his words. He and Jazlyn spent many passionate nights together. She gave him her mind, body, and soul. He gave her his body, but he refused to give away his heart. He whispered sweet things in her ear, slid into her bed when the village was fast asleep, then returned to his wife's bed before sunrise.

Aurora, on the other hand, left the village as she reached maturity, in hopes of getting the answers of who she was and where she came from. During her journey, she discovered her heritage. She learned that she came from a family of powerful women—a coven, they call themselves—and that her nightmares were not nightmares at all. In fact, they were visions. She was gifted with the power of sight, amongst other things.

Many seasons had come and gone, and the girls continued to grow and venture out. One day after Aurora mastered her gift of clairvoyance, she had a vision of Jazlyn's destined tragic ending. Her good friend would be cursed by a gypsy, as a consequence of having an affair with the gypsy's husband.

Aurora rushed back to the village. She knew she couldn't intervene with fate—it always wins. She just hoped she would be able persuade Jazlyn to alter foreseen decisions. She would do everything in her power to convincer her. She would guide and save her.

Even before Aurora arrived, the gypsy was long gone. She was a coward. She knew she was no match for her. What Aurora didn't know was the gypsy had foreseen her intentions and had already carried out her plans. She had cursed Jazlyn and her offspring and their many generations to come.

"I missed you so much." Jazlyn embraced her dearest friend with open arms.

"I missed you more." Aurora returned the hug. "You have truly become the fairest of all."

Jazlyn giggled at her friend's response. "Come let's go for a swim for old time's sake."

The two girls reminisced about their childhood and told each other about everything going on in their lives. They also talked about their plans for the future. It didn't take them long to reveal their darkest secrets. Aurora confessed she was a witch, and Jazlyn admitted having a scandalous affair.

"I denied Alaric's request to become his doxy, Aurora," said Jazlyn. "But I must admit my heart bleeds for his touch."

"Don't be foolish, Jazlyn." Aurora desperately wanted to reveal to her friend her dire fate if she continued down that path. "The fairest maiden in the village shouldn't settle for the fishwife's husband, Jazlyn," Aurora calls her out. She flashes a smile, then jumps into the water.

Jazlyn didn't respond. Instead, she played with the pendant hanging from her neck while blankly staring into space. Her electric green eyes spoke a thousand unspoken words.

Aurora quickly swam back up to the top of the river. Her cat-like eyes settled on the pendant. "How did a farmer's daughter obtain such a treasure?" she asked.

"It's my family's most-prized possession, passed along to generations," she revealed.

"I see," Aurora replied, diving back in.

Aurora stayed in the village for many months and continued to try to convince Jazlyn to let Alaric go. She told her that no good would come from stealing another woman's husband. Jazlyn argued, using the excuse that his wife was already gone. And even though he already refused to marry her, Jazlyn didn't stop sleeping with him.

"You reap what you sow," Aurora warned. "There are consequences for every action."

Jazlyn didn't listen. Her fate was sealed. She indulged in her true heart's desire, no matter how many times she was warned. Aurora even utilized her power to sway both of them away, but it only further pushed them into each other's bed. So she decided to change her tactics and searched for the gypsy. She figured if she couldn't stop Jazlyn and Alaric, then she would just eliminate the threat. Unfortunately for her, she never found the gypsy, and never heard of or saw her again. She must have disappeared from the face of Earth. Jazlyn got pregnant shortly after.

One night, when the wind was blowing strong and the air was filled with a thick cloud of mist, Jazlyn entered Aurora's hut with a tear-stained face, as predicted. "I'm in need of your aid. I'm carrying his child," she confessed to Aurora, her heavenly divine face painted with pain. "Alaric refused to admit that he is the father of the child. He said that if a woman hopped in a married man's bed, she would hop in any other man's bed," she cried in between words. "I shall be shamed if I do not rid this, so please help me."

Aurora stared at her with sympathetic eyes. She knew this was coming. She came back to this village for this exact moment in history. She wanted to be there for the girl that had saved her life. Aurora didn't want to take this route, but Jazlyn left her with no other choice. She stood in front of her and placed a gentle but firm hand on her growing belly. This was what she had been trying to prevent. Aurora knew that using her power of death for personal gain would turn her into a dark witch. Her pure soul would be tainted for the rest of eternity, and there was no going back. Her coven would hunt her down and end her. That would be their only option, for she was too powerful.

Desperate to save her friend, Aurora decided to give up her life in exchange for Jazlyn's. She closed her eyes, calling forth the power within her to bring death. Time slowed down around them as a bright, electric, emerald-green light flashed through the hut, and an unknown force zapped through the air around them. Aurora saw a vision the moment her power touched the unborn child's soul. It was the premonition of imminent world disaster if the child was never going to be born. The child's daughter from generations to come would be the chosen one, and she had to be born, or else . . .

Instant tears brimmed in Aurora's eyes. "I cannot!" She gasped, removing her hand from her dear friend's belly. For the first time since learning how to use her gift, she was caught off guard.

Jazlyn's lips quivered. Fear was evident in her eyes. "You told me you have the power to bring death. My father would disown me. I will be banished. Please, my friend, I'm begging you."

Aurora hesitated for a second. She so desperately wanted to help Jazlyn. She would give her life in exchange for her friend's happiness—if only life had been that easy.

Finding the courage, Aurora told her friend what needed to be told. "I also possess the gift of clairvoyance. I have seen the future. Your offspring will be the cause of many wars and will spark the flame of a lifetime of fiery battles. But she is also going to be the light that will give back everything that darkness shall have stolen."

"What are you saying?" Jazlyn asked through tears.

"Your daughter's daughter down the line will be a free-spirited individual with a sharp tongue and shall host the power to break free from all chains. Your daughter's daughter will never bend or break for anyone."

Jazlyn cried hysterically. "Aurora, please."

"Generations on top of generations will pass, and one of your descendants shall be paired with a cold-hearted king. Her nature shall be anything but well-behaved and extremely untamed. Her aura will be wild and gentle. He will deny his heart's true desire and force her to accept a second-chance mate. That event alone will lead to tragedy—the Awakening. From that generation later, from your bloodline, the Chosen One shall come. She shall host all of your spirits. She will be the only female descendant of your bloodline to have golden hair."

*  *  *

## CLAIRE

A thick cloud of emerald-green smoke once again appears then disappears from my mind altogether. The feeling of Aurora's power leaves my skin, is dispensed from my blood, and relinquished from my mind. My skin tingles, my heart beats rapidly, and my neck suddenly itches. Xander is now standing beside me, a troublesome look plastered all over his handsome face. Aurora's inhumanly beautiful face comes back into view.

"Impossible!" I say to her, taking my hand away from her grasp.

*What she just showed me couldn't be true.*

"You know deep down inside what I showed you was the truth," she says, her stare as hard as stone. "Your mother once revealed herself to you."

I quickly think over her words. Automatically, my mind flashes back to the day when Xander and I were alone, the day when he told me his side of the story.

*    *    *

*"King Luke of the lycans was her second-chance mate."*

*His words literally knocked the wind out of my body. Abruptly, the pendant around my neck seemed to tighten, completely cutting off my air supply. My skin tingled, the hair on the back of my neck standing. Xander instantly placed a gentle but firm hand onto the pendant. It burned through his flesh like acid, but he refused to let go. For the first time, I felt another presence. The pendant hosted another extremely wild and powerful presence. I closed my eyes, only to be met with coffee-colored eyes that then disappeared so fast. She was gone. My eyes snapped open, and Xander came back into view, looking like he'd seen a ghost.*

*    *    *

My breath catches in my lungs, and the world around me starts to spin. All of a sudden, a million and one memories of many beautiful, wild, and courageous women dance gracefully across my memory.

*My ancestors's memories . . .*

"Claire," Xander calls, starting to panic. He pulls me into the security of his arms. "What have you done to her?" he shouts at Aurora as the world continues to spin.

The room shakes as the memories continue to come crashing down. One second they are so vivid and bright, then the next they start to gleam like an ember as a bright green light glows out of my skin. The familiar force rushes through me, shaking the entire room.

Aurora's soft voice rings through my ears. *"Electa causa* (You were chosen for a reason). *Mane vero apud te* (Stay true to yourself)."

My head pounds harder, her voice ringing louder.

*"Sunt venire* (They're coming). *Meminisse debes* (You should remember)."

Those are the last words I hear before I lose consciousness.

# CHAPTER EIGHTY-ONE
## The Timeline of Events

"Why the hell would you allow that b*tch anywhere near my beloved?"

I hear my beloved roar, sounding way past the point of livid. His scent lingers in the air like smoke. I'm lying on an extremely comfortable bed, my body tangled in fine silk sheets. They don't smell like him, so I know that I am not in our bed, yet it feels like home. I can hear the soft sound of crashing waves and can smell the scent of the sea—they make me feel at peace. We are still in our kingdom. I feel, hear, and smell everything around me, but my mind is halfway there, elsewhere.

"I swear on my life, blood, and soul that if she doesn't wake up, I'll end you, brother or not!"

All eight kings are present. I can feel their concern for me circling through our bond.

"Your beloved!" Xander hisses. "Your beloved!"

Somehow I know they are spitting venom into each other's face. Both of them need to calm down.

I'm unable to open my eyes, but I'm fine.

"Since day one, I've protected Claire, even when you did not claim her as your beloved because you were being such a pussy," Xander's voice booms, and I swear the bed shakes underneath me. "Claire is like a sister to me. I would give her all the air in my body just so she can continue to breathe. I'll give her my heart just so hers can beat louder. I will give her my life for her to live. I'd been there for Claire before your b*tch ass grew some balls and gained the courage to admit that you actually cared for her."

"Ouch, I know that hurts," Marcellus pipes up, not even trying to whisper.

Xander and Nicklaus growl at the same damn time.

God, I love Marcellus. He sure knows when to crack a joke.

"Mind your tongue!" my beloved spits, his monster taking control.

Even with my eyes glued shut, I know his are bloodshot red. I can't tell if he is speaking to Xander or Marcellus.

Out of nowhere, a sudden ache throbs viciously in my skull. Unable to stand the pain, my entire body trembles.

"What's happening to her?" one of the kings asks, sounding worried.

I can't identify the owner of the voice. I'm losing focus. My soft heartbeats feel gentler than usual, almost silent. My mind shifts from past to present. One minute, memories of a tragedy plague my brain, then the next, my panicking beloved's shouting of my name reels me back in.

Nicklaus scoops me into the safety of his arms, his electrifying touch sparking fire within me. He holds me close to his Greek sculpture of a chest. "Firecracker," he whispers in my ear.

I shiver. My head rolls back freely, and I feel his soft and pleasure-filled hands cup my face.

"Open your eyes for me," he says, his voice sounding distant.

I can hear the others barking orders and scattering around like ants around me. For the life of me, I can't open my eyes.

"Where the f*ck is the healer?" one of them yells.

"Her heart is slowing down," another speaks.

"Perhaps, she is in a dream state," someone suggests— maybe Marcellus? "That's got to be it. One of Aurora's daughters did it to me before. She was a clever and freaky little witch. She put me to sleep by casting a spell on me, quite often!"

That has to be Marcellus.

"Lay her down," says an unknown voice.

I can feel the vibrating sensation from Nicklaus's chest, indicating that he has growled. The wind rushes around me, making it harder for me to hear them. Then someone or something tugs at my body, pulling me away from him, and I whimper.

*"Nicklaus."*

I try to call him, but I can't. His presence seems to disappear, and I feel empty and cold. My mind begins to shift, and many memories start to flicker in and out. I'm drifting. A thick emerald smoke smothers and clouds my mind; I can't think. Once again the intense power sinks into my skin, runs through my blood, and consumes my mind whole. Jazlyn's and Aurora's beautiful faces come into view again.

"If so many bad things are coming from my sin, why are you refusing to help me?" Jazlyn asks her friend, rubbing her now swollen belly. She is sitting on a cot while watching her friend cleaning their home.

Aurora stops what she is doing and stares at her for a long while, the silence deafening. She walks over toward Jazlyn and places her hand over Jazlyn's belly. "The child is meant to be born. Many sins will eventually become the world's blessing. *Fato signatus est* (Fate has been sealed)."

Aurora has been teaching Jazlyn how to speak and understand her native tongue.

"My offspring's fate seems to be a curse. No child should have to pay the price because of their mother's sins. If I had your gifts, I would live forever to protect—"

"You aren't immortal, but I am. I promise to love, cherish, and protect each and every member of your bloodline for generations to come. Your bloodline shall wield my power)."

"I don't understand."

"Let me show you." Aurora places her free hand onto the pendant hanging from Jazlyn's neck. "The accouchement is set in stone. I've ensured that you will live forever without actually living forever. You will be around spiritually for many generations to come. Only your direct descendants can wield my power. The jewel I'm going to create shall be the host."

A bright, electric, emerald-green light glows out of Aurora's hand and into the pendant. The small jewel is replaced with a powerful stone, not just any stone. Jazlyn watches the scene with amazement with tear-filled eyes as Aurora creates an emerald! It is a pear-shaped emerald surrounded by pave-set diamonds.

"Thank you," she says.

"You don't ever have to thank me." Aurora cups her friend's beautiful face. "Have you decided on a name?" she suddenly asks.

"Morgan. It is my tribute to you."

Morgan was the name of Aurora's mother. Jazlyn never met her, but Aurora's coven spoke highly of the legendary witch named Morgan.

"I love you, Jazlyn," Aurora says, tears streaming down her face.

They share a feverish kiss only lovers would share.

Memories of their final days together flick in great speed.

Aurora cares for Jazlyn during her entire pregnancy. She watches her once-friend turned lover grow sick. For months, she feeds her when she is too weak, bathes her like Jazlyn once did for her, and uses her savory tongue to put Jazlyn to sleep every single night.

"She's coming!" Jazlyn screams. She is curled over with pain, breathing fast and hard. Her baby is arriving sooner than expected. Jazlyn is nothing but belly and a bag of bones. The hut shakes from her thunderous screams.

"You can do this," encourages Aurora while wringing out the warm rag. She rushes toward Jazlyn and places it over her head.

She helps her get comfortable on the cot. "All you have to do is push. I'll do the rest."

"I can't do this," Jazlyn responds through her fatal attempt to breathe. "I'm not strong enough," she huffs through her pained cries.

"You are the strongest woman I know. Now, push," Aurora coaxes, as Jazlyn screams louder.

"Something's wrong," she sobs after pushing for what seems like hours, blood flowing like a river down her legs. "I can't feel her."

"Push!" Aurora stucks her hand in between Jazlyn's legs. "I can feel the head. She's almost here."

Jazlyn continues to push with all her might. Her blood stains the sheets. It drips down onto the floor and splashes all over the walls. Shortly after, the cries of a newborn fills their hut.

"She's beautiful," Aurora whispers, tears rolling down her cheeks. "Morgan is beautiful."

Jazlyn's chest moves up and down as she gasps for air. "Thank you for everything," she says, amidst her struggle to breathe.

Aurora quickly wraps Morgan up and places the newborn in her mother's arm

Jazlyn takes in her daughter for the very first time. "Take care of her," she mutters. "Take care of them all," are her final words.

The day Aurora helped deliver the beautiful baby girl Morgan is the same day she buries her longtime friend—her sister, her heart, her lover, her paramour, her everything.

She raises the girl as her own and protects her, but fate strikes once again as Morgan grows into a woman. Just like her mother, Morgan makes unwise decisions despite Aurora's warnings. And just like her mother, she pays for it with her life. The day Morgan's daughter takes her first breath is the same day Morgan has her last, and the cycle continues for centuries. Each and every one of them shares a similar, cruel fate.

Aurora honors Jazlyn's last words. She has protected them, guided them, and loved them unconditionally. One in particular gives her the most trouble. She is a girl with chestnut-brown hair and coffee-colored eyes. Her beauty is timeless.

"If you continue to play with fire, you shall be burned," Aurora tells the girl. "Don't allow heartbreak or a change in your plans change your ultimate goal."

"What goal? Gosh, it's just a date. You should be telling me that I'm young and need to explore my options and not settle for scum, like a normal mother would."

"You're not normal, and I'm not a normal mother, Isabella,"Aurora speaks the truth. "Your decisions affect us all. I hate to admit it, but you are destined to be with Xander."

"Xander"—she snorted—"wants nothing to do with me. Luke is my second-chance mate. Fate brought us together. I'm his destiny, and we're destined—"

"Destined for doom," Aurora cuts in.

"F*ck off!" Bella hisses. It is too hard for her to accept the truth.

"Mind your tongue!" Aurora raises her voice.

"Worry about your own goddamn daughters, Aurora!"

"You are my daughter."

"No, I'm not!" she snaps. "My mother is dead, and her soul is trapped inside this emerald"—she holds up the pendant—"right along with all the souls of my other ancestors, thanks to you!" She walks out of the house and slams the door behind her. *"Sigillum* (Seal)," she commands.

That light from the gemstone flashes through the midnight sky, and an unknown force seals the door shut. Bella knows Aurora can easily break the spell. It is her magic after all, but she also knows her words hurt Aurora badly. She hates hurting her, but she can't help it. Hurting people can't help; it can only hurt people.

Bella is no longer the pure little girl who lived her life to the fullest. She is tainted, dark, and hurt.

Bella rushes toward her best friend's beat-up red car, the wind blowing her hair. The rare gem hanging from her neck glistens underneath the moonlight with every step she takes.

"Hurry your cute ass up before your mother casts a spell of death on me!" a girl with milk-chocolate skin and long jet-black hair yells out of the window on the driver's side.

"Shut up, Mecca!" responds Bella, as she gets into the car. "Now, hurry up before she comes. Luke keeps texting me."

"Are you sure you want to go through with this?" Mecca asks, skeptically. "I mean, I get it that Xander f*cked up big time, but Luke is no better. He has already chosen another and calls her queen. He didn't even wait for his mate. Plus, he's a lycan."

Bella glares at her best friend. "You know like I know that most lycans aren't lucky enough to meet their 'destined.' He can't spend centuries waiting for something that may have never come. His people needs a queen."

"So you're going to spend the rest of your life playing mistress of your second-chance mate? How is that fair to you?"

"Of course not! He promised to denounce their mating."

"Bella, get out of the car now!" Aurora interrupts them, appearing out of thin air. Her eyes lock on Mecca's. "I told you to stay the hell away from her, mutt," she says spitefully.

Mecca's eyes flash bright yellow, but she bites her tongue. She knows better than to argue with a witch, especially Aurora.

"You're acting like the wicked witch of the west!" Bella yells out from the window.

The wind zaps with unseen electricity, becoming more charged. Aurora's cat-like eyes glow like a night light as she lifts up her hands. The engine of the car roars to life, without Mecca starting it up. It begins shaking, then a thick cloud of emerald smoke rises from under the hood and floats in the air.

"You haven't seen wicked!" Aurora spits, as a circle of dark-green fire burns brightly around the vehicle.

*"Exstingue* (Extinguish)!" Bella hisses, and the fire immediately disappears. "What is your problem?" she yells. She opens the car door and makes her way toward Aurora. "You're treating me like a prisoner. I'm no longer a child, so let me live!"

"You're making childish decisions, Isabella. How many times do I have to tell you that you're blessed and cursed with two paths? Each one will end differently, and you're choosing the wrong one."

"They are my paths to take, are they not?" Bella challenges, the fire in her eyes burning brighter than the sun. "Allow me to live. You have better things to do than worry about my future, like worrying about your own blood that you abandoned. Your daughters need their mother, and here you are playing mommy to someone else's child! And you wonder why they hate you?" she mocks.

Bella's words surely cut too deep. She has gone overboard. Aurora's eyes spark with electric current, the ground underneath them shaking from her rage. But Bella holds her head high, her posture straight. She continues to stare Aurora directly in the eye. She is a defiant little thing. She fears nothing or no one, even the most-powerful witch. She holds her ground, and that is the day her fate is officially sealed.

Aurora keeps on reminding Bella, just like she did for her ancestors. However, unlike them, Aurora pushes her away. History once again repeats itself, but this time the outcome would be fatal for the entire world. Everything is about to change, drastically.

\*   \*   \*

NICKLAUS

"She is fine," the healer confirms for the thousandth time, while I listen to the soft beating of Claire's heart for the nth time.

"King Marcellus was correct. The witch has put a spell on her, which is why she can't wake up, but she should awaken shortly."

I have been sitting beside my beloved for several hours, going through hell. She has been in constant pain, shaking, whimpering, and hyperventilating every couple of hours. Her suffering tortures me.

"How could a sleeping spell have this sort of effect on her body?" I ask the healer, holding Claire's hand.

My monster had long retreated to the back of my mind. He knows that Claire needs us to stay level-headed to help her get through this. Whenever her body undergoes an episode, my touch seems to be the only thing that can calm her—like the antidote to a disease. I am her remedy.

"I'm not sure, my king," the healer responds. "But I am a hundred percent positive that she is experiencing a sleeping spell. From what I was told, she has suffered far worse."

My sensitive ears pick up on some commotion outside the wing.

Hours ago, I kicked everyone out and blocked them from communicating with me. Their worry for Claire didn't do anything but make my monster increasingly on edge. It's hard for me to control my monster in this moment. He has almost murdered the entire palace many times throughout the last several hours. Being alone with Claire seems to be the only thing that keeps him at bay right now.

Plus, the other kings and I argued nonstop about the summons. I told them to go ahead without me. Considering my title, I don't have to answer the goddamn summons, but they do. Of course, they refused to leave while their queen is not in good health. Every single one of them disobeyed my orders, including Cyrus, which kind of caught me off guard. We even had a heart-to-heart talk, and he said he was upset about what happened to Embry. He felt betrayed, and he wanted me to feel what he felt. I told him how childish and foolish he was. However, in the end, I admitted that I understood him.

"We have a problem!" Vlad shouts, interrupting my train of thought as he barges into the room.

Claire's body jumps in her unconscious state as my neck snaps in his direction—that quick. My vision shifts to a bright and vivid shade of red. He has a death wish.

"My apologies." His words come out in a hurry. "I wouldn't have bothered you if it wasn't important. You need to see this."

"I thought I made myself very clear that no one should bother me!" my monster snaps, nothing personal. I have no patience for anyone in this moment, and they all know it. All I care about right now is Claire. All I can think about right now is Claire. Claire! Claire! Claire! I feel uneasy because of her condition. No one is safe around me in this moment, and they know this. I might as well be deemed as a madman.

"The palace will soon be under attack, and many prisoners have somehow escaped from the dungeon. I can't seem to reach some of my men outside the palace gates. I think it's safe to say we have been invaded."

The very idea is laughable. In fact, that's exactly what I do: laugh. I laugh so goddamn hard. I've never laughed like this in my entire centuries of existence. He can't be serious.

"Nicklaus—" Vlad attempts to continue.

Xander storms into the room. "Your traitorous b*tch of a sister has freed dangerous prisoners, killed some of our best men, and is now on her way back here with an army, the council, and most importantly your father," he speaks bitterly.

# CHAPTER EIGHTY-TWO
## The Position of the Moon

CLAIRE

I'm lost in my own mind, stuck in a dream, as I watch the life Bella once lived. My mother was extremely beautiful and courageous. She wasn't the type of girl to take sh*t from anybody, but she was also the girl that would give a stranger the shirt off her back. There was truly something wild and gentle about her soul. She was a sweetheart and a badass—all in one. Everyone loved her. The supernatural community seemed to be drawn to her. Vampires, werewolves, lycans, and even hunters were very fond of her.

My mother was amazing, and I am honored to call myself her daughter. Watching her journey has been a phenomenal experience. However, there are some moments of her life that I wish I could fast-forward, like right now. My stomach turns as I'm forced to watch her make love to the lycan king, Luke. Watching the woman I now know to be my mother as she makes love to a man who made it his business to hit on me is disturbing as hell. Even as disgusting as that sound, I somehow know that I have to. I must pay attention to every single detail no matter how gruesome it may be. Aurora brings me here for a reason.

I watch Xander suffer when my mom makes love to Luke. He is a broken man. Witnessing his humanity slip away in front of my very eyes breaks my heart, and it is bleeding for him. However, there is a lesson in every experience.

I never really understood how Xander earned the title the Cold-Hearted King. It never added up to me until now. My mother moving on and bonding with another makes Xander become uncharitable and detached. His soul is slipping away, but my mother's and her second-chance mate's souls are thriving. Having to admit that the lycan king is good for her pains me. He is the healer of her broken heart, and they are content, but just for a while. I guess there's truth in the saying "Nothing lasts forever."

Eventually, Luke places his people before his destined heart. He never denounces his mating with the lycan queen. He stays with her, using the excuse that he fathered children with her. As predicted, my mother becomes his mistres and plays that role for years, telling herself that she can't find it in her heart to reject him.

But that all changes the day she walks in on Luke and his wife making love. With her heart broken yet again, my mother decides to travel the world. She leaves the supernatural world and everyone she ever loves along with it behind her. I must say I don't agree with her cutting all ties with Mecca or Aurora even though I understand why she is doing it—she wants a fresh start, and she finds it. During her travels, she meets a human named Alec and falls for him. He has golden-blond hair and soul-snatching, unique green eyes. He is extremely handsome. She isn't his beloved or destined. He isn't her soul mate or second-chance mate for that matter, but he is hers. She finds love and is finally happy living her life with the man of her dreams in a city called City of Love. That is the happiest time of her life.

"I love you, Alec," she says to him, after they've shared another passionate, steamy night.

"*Je t'aime davantage,* Isabella (I love you more, Isabella)," he responds, with his thick French accent.

672

She blushes. I can tell she loves it when he speaks to her in his native tongue. They stay in bed, tangled in each other's embrace and enjoying the sweet silence of their peace.

"How do you feel about children?" Alec suddenly asks, taking the air out of her lungs.

Having a child is out of the question for Bella, obviously. She is very aware of our family's curse. She doesn't want to bring a child into the world, only to leave them motherless.

My mom's face pales. "I don't want children." She jumps out of the bed.

"Why not, *mon amour* (my love)?" He follows behind her and manages to grab her waist before she has time to exit the room. "Just imagine our daughter, chasing after her brother in our apartment. She shall be the spitting image of you, and our son shall be the spitting image of me. His name will be Alec, and her name will be Claire. They will be perfect," he says dreamily.

"There is no point of speaking of children that will never exist." Bella pulls away. "I don't want kids."

"Okay, okay, mademoiselle," he teases, holding his hands up high in the air. "For now, no more talk about children. Now get your hot ass back into our bed." He bites down onto his lip, and she blushes again.

I guess it's safe to say that my mom was a sucker for him biting down on his lip. She would never admit that, I'm sure.

"Why Claire?" she asks him out of nowhere, piquing my interest. *Yeah, why Claire?*

"I mean, I understand why you would want to name your firstborn
son after you, but why Claire?"

Alec flashes a heartrending smile. "It's my mother's name. She died while giving birth to me."

My mother's heart skips a beat. "We have found something else in common, my love." She slides back into bed with him, and they spend the rest of the night making love.

I place my hands over my eyes. I'm tired of watching her make love. Thankfully, it works, and a new memory surfaces.

My mother is walking toward a shop displaying a green circle logo with a woman in the center of it. (I believe it reads, *Starbucks*.) Unintentionally, she bumps into a man.

My heart stops when I realize it's Xander. I can all but see the world shift around the both of them.

My mother's heart misses a beat. All it takes is one look into Xander's icy silver eyes to spark a million flares inside her soul. Just one word from his heart-shaped lips sends wildfire to spread through the center of her core. Just one touch from him shaking her hand sends an inferno of fire to spread up her legs. It happens so fast. Her self-control literally alters, and all the feelings Xander thought he had long buried for my mom seem to suddenly reappear. He is giving her the look—the same look that Nicklaus gives me. He is still in love with her. This is the day he agrees to claim her, and she agrees to accept immortality willingly. Their destiny awaits them.

For two entire months, they are so happy, and it brings tears to my eyes. Then time comes for my mother to be gifted with immortality. On that day, the pendant around her neck brings forth a vision. (I watch attentively.) It reveals her giving birth to a golden-haired girl and boy with electric green eyes.

*Twins! OMG, I'm a twin! What the actual f*ck? I have a brother? Where the hell is he?*

I know she really is my mother. I can feel it. But so many things still don't add up, like the fact that she had lived over a hundred years before I came into existence. A million and one questions roam in my head.

*Hold up, is Xander my father? No, that can't be. That would mean that Nicklaus is my uncle, right?*

My face turns pale, and the sudden urge to puke kicks in.

*I need answers, now!*

So I pull myself together and continue to watch.

674

My mother touches her belly, and mixed emotions—love, devotion, confusion, fear—can be seen and felt. Fear flickers in her eyes. She has the same question, Who is the father, Xander or Alec? Granting she has made love to Xander for many nights, but the babies in the vision are the spitting image of her human lover, Alec.

*I am the spitting image of Alec.*

Not having an idea who fathers her twins, my mother suddenly has a mini panic attack. She decides to flee. The day she leaves is the exact day her second-chance mate leads an attack, slaughtering millions of vampires. It is a nightmare. Nicklaus is also there, and he almost gets murdered.

My blood starts to boil. My vision shifts red.

*"Focus,"* a voice commands in my ear.

I jump and turn around, only to find no one. I shake my head and do what I am ordered to do—I focus.

After the bloodshed, it is too hard to believe that the attack is a coincidence. If Xander was cold-hearted before, now he is frozen. He swears on his life he would have his vengeance.

*We all know how that part of the story ends.*

Memories continue to flicker.

"Aurora, I need your help," my mother says, holding her now round belly as she steps into her childhood home she hadn't visited in years.

Aurora stares at her with the same sympathetic eyes she had when she looked at my great-great-great-grandmother. She knew my mother was coming, and for that I'm certain.

"You know very well I can't rid your baby," Aurora responds.

"I'm not asking you to. I know my family history. I've accepted and understand the path I've chosen and I'm more than happy to give my life in exchange for theirs."

"Theirs? What do you mean?"

My mother's coffee-colored eyes start to water. "I am pregnant with twins, a girl and a b—"

675

"Impossible!" Aurora places her hand on my mom's growing belly, and electric currents of energy instantly shoot from my mother's belly into her hand. "Impossible!" she exclaims again.

"My children will have a different shade of golden hair and electric green eyes," my mother speaks, as tears continue to spill from her eyes.

"The Chosen One." Aurora quickly embraces her.

"Yes, my daughter shall be the Chosen One. Her name shall be Claire and her brother's name shall be Alec, the names their father would have wanted."

"Would have? Where is the father the offsprings, my dear?"

"He's dead. Xander killed him."

My heart drops.

$$*\qquad*\qquad*$$

NICKLAUS

"Who did she free?" I ask Derek, one of the station guards, as we make our way through the dungeon.

Marcellus, Cyrus, and Cornelius are following close behind us. We are all in our fighting attire. Rufus and Seneca are currently preparing our soldiers for the battle. Luscious and a private team are currently setting up ground defenses and are scouting the palace grounds while Xander is making last-minute preparations. Vlad is in my wing, protecting Claire, who is still in a dream-like state. I refused to leave her unguarded. Vlad is the only other person apart from Xander that I trust with her life. He has proven himself.

"All the captured lycans, a dozen of vampires who are against your rules, and one human boy," he reports.

"Human boy . . ." I stop in my tracks.

*Why the hell would my sister waste her time freeing a human?*

"Why the hell would Daniela free a human?" Cornelius voices my curiosity out loud. "Which human?"

"The human that was brought in from King Cyrus's kingdom," Derek answers quickly.

"Claire's human friend?" questions Marcellus.

*What the f\*ck does she want from him?*

I turn to face Cyrus.

"I'm already on it," he says, making his way toward the exit of the dungeon—to reach out to his lieutenant, I'm sure.

We need to figure out who the slave boy really is. From the looks of things, he sounds like a spy.

*I'm going to kill him!*

"Where's the report of every prisoner they freed?" I ask, as we start to walk back.

"It is right here, Your Majesty," another guard acknowledges, handing over the document.

I briefly scan through the list of prisoners who have escaped. "They're right," I speak to Marcellus and Cornelius, "that b\*tch has freed all the lycans, those pathetic humans, and most of the vampires who are against my rule." I hand over the document to Cornelius.

"Since when has Master Azazel been against your rule?" Cornelius asks as he scans the document.

"When I yanked off his dick," I respond nonchalantly. "Today is the day that I kill him too. That pathetic, waste-of-a-life raped Claire."

The dungeon is filled with Cornelius's and Marcellus's growls. Today is certainly the day Master Azazel shall meet his end.

"I am going to kill him," Marcellus spits through clenched teeth.

"No! His life is mine to take," I declare, as we walk up one of the many flights of stairs.

"What I can't seem to understand is why the f*ck the council would go to war over a f*cking summons?" Cornelius's monster hisses.

Luscious enters my mind. *"They are drawing closer,"* he warns and then disappears.

Instantly, everything around me turns red—my monster has made her presence known. "This isn't about a goddamn summons," I state the obvious. "This is about Claire."

Both their monsters release a war-ready growl.

"They're almost here!" my monster snarls, as we exit the dungeon.

*   *   *

CLAIRE

My emotions are all over the place as I watch the memories of my mother's final days unfold.

*My birthday shall be her last day.*

Aurora cares for her during her entire pregnancy, just like she did for all of my ancestors. And like the others before her, my mother eventually becomes very ill.

"I need a favor," she says to Aurora.

"Anything, my love." She helps her out of the bed.

My mother is nothing but skin, bones, and belly—just like the rest of them once were. "I want you to give the pendant to Mecca," she states, as soon as she is comfortable.

"Absolutely not!"

"Aurora, please. The war between the lycans, wolves, and vampires has been vicious. If anything happens to her because of my beloved, I would never forgive myself. Please—"

"The pendant will not protect her. The emerald belongs to your bloodline and your bloodline only. She will never be able to wield its power."

"She doesn't have to. She just needs to wear it. You know like I know just wearing it would be enough to scare any supernatural beings off."

"I said no, and that's final!" Aurora walks toward the window, her aggravation evident.

"If anyone could understand how it feels like to be unable to protect someone you care about dearly, it's you," my mother mutters. The fire in her eyes could burn down the room.

"I said no, Isabella. We witches do not get involved in other supernatural affairs, and you know that."

"Fine! I'll do it myself." She tries to get out of bed, but she collapses the very moment her two feet hit the floor.

Within a second, Aurora is by her side. "Isabella," she says, scooping her into her arms. There is so much pain in those glowing cat-like eyes as she picks her up off the floor, careful enough not to hurt her.

My mother releases a soft groan

Once again, tears roll down my face as I'm forced to watch her suffer.

Aurora's eyes are already a watery mess. "I'll give the pendant to her," she promises, as she places my mother back down onto the bed. Then, she suddenly freezes, her eyes glowing like a night light. "The year 2041 will be a dangerous year for the she-wolf. The life she currently lives will be snatched away," Aurora speaks again, putting her hand down on the emerald. "Your daughter shall be the one to free her."

"And how do you know this?" my mother asks with a hushed voice.

Aurora lies on the bed beside her, then she starts stroking her hair gently. "Because it's a part of her destiny," she replies in a soothing voice. "She will break many chains."

\*     \*     \*

679

The palace is in complete chaos. Servants and slaves are running around everywhere to seek sanctuary. The guards and soldiers are rushing to their assigned positions, preparing themselves. Marcellus, Cornelius, and I are heading toward the front entrance of the palace. Our security detail is walking on our outside perimeter. The other kings are already outside of the palace gates, patiently waiting. Everyone is bracing themselves for what's to come. The smell of promised death and fear fills the air. The sound of humans panicking and vampires praying rings in my sensitive ears. The scene before me bleeds crimson red as my monster paces around inside me. We are ready for this.

"Cornelius," says a voice over all the chaos. "Cornelius," it calls out again.

Cornelius tenses up. He stops, and we all stop. "I told you to stay in my chambers," his monster hisses, turning around to face the source of the voice.

It is his chosen, Jadis, Claire's friend. She is running in our direction. The red-haired human girl is hot on her heels. Both their hearts are booming, sounding like war drums.

"Don't go," Jadis pleads.

If my monster wasn't on the verge of surfacing, I would roll my eyes. How cliche?

"We don't have time for this!" I snarl. "Take the both of them to my chambers," I order one of my men.

I'm actually glad that they appear. Claire would have my head cut off if anything happened to any one of them, especially Jadis.

Cornelius releases a warning growl. "Don't touch her!" he threatens, intervening before any of my men has a chance to move. His monster is also on edge.

680

This time I do roll my eyes. I know he has feelings for this human, but this is absolutely ridiculous. "Cornelius, we don't have time for this," I remind him warningly.

"Give me a second," he requests.

My monster's patience is running thin, but out of respect for Cornelius, I keep him at bay and nod. The very moment Cornelius is in front of the human girl, he wastes no time smashing his lips down onto hers. Everyone watches the scene in pure shock but me. I know who she is to him. His monster is currently craving her touch. She is his peace. Trust me when I say I know that feeling.

Cornelius breaks the kiss, and she whimpers. "You will be safe with them. I'll be back to you soon, little bird," he coos. He catches the single tear trailing down her face with his thumb.

"Then, I'll be waiting," she responds, pulling herself together.

Before we leave, Jadis drops down to one knee. She kisses Cornelius's left hand and then his right. "I wish you good fortune," she says. "I wish you all good fortune."

Then the war bell rings.

\*      \*      \*

CLAIRE

The night sky is pitch black, with a hint of dark-purple hue. The stars shine bright like diamonds, and the soothing shiny rays of the full pink moon radiate intense power. I can feel the magic in the air. It is the night, when my mother draws her last breath, and I draw my first—my birthday.

My heart beats a million times per second as I watch the scene before me with wide eyes. My mother is hunched over in a clearing, her body drenched in sweat. The powerful presence of the moon can be felt as it beams radiant light onto her skin, making it shimmer and glisten. Her hair is a wild, wet mess. She is wearing a simple ivory silk slip dress with a wide neckline. She has never been lovelier in her natural state. Her whole life has led up to this moment. This is her legacy. I am her legacy.

She is in the center of many equally lovely women, witches from Aurora's coven, who each has their own powerful presence. They form a circle around my mother, their legs crossed and elbows placed down onto their knees.

"No, it's too soon!" my mother screams, her breathing shallow and rapid. "It's too soon for them to come out."

"The position of the moon is set, my love. It is time." Aurora looks at each and every witch's face. "No matter what happens, continue to chant," she demands.

Suddenly, fluids rush down my mother's legs, followed by a waterfall of blood.

"They are coming," announces Aurora. "It has begun."

The other witches stare into the night sky and chant, *"In nomine electi unus* (In the name of the Chosen One).*"

"It's too soon," my mother hisses through clenched teeth. She is in a supine position. Her hips and knees are flexed and thighs are apart, and a witch with rich dark-brown hair, perfect brows, glowing skin, and different eye color is holding her hand.

"Don't be afraid," Aurora coaxes, using her hands to spread open my mother's legs.

The chanting becomes louder. "In nomine electi unus."

"I feel no fear," my mother says through her fatal attempt to breathe. "I'm strong enough," she screams as a soft whimper escapes her.

The unknown woman places a cloth in her mouth and instructs her to bite down on it. "It's strong enough," she reassures her.

Aurora nods. She puts her hand inside my mother's jewel, and she screams in response. "Stay calm, my child. The moon shall guide us all. Repeat after me," she commands. "In nomine electi unus."

"In nomine electi unus," my mother shouts through clenched teeth. "In nomine electi unus."

Gallons of blood gushes out as Aurora turns her hand. My mother's body starts to shake.

I panic.

# CHAPTER EIGHTY-THREE
## The Warning

Magic sparks life in the air, and the chanting becomes louder.

"In nomine electi unus. In nomine electi unus. In nomine electi . . ."

"Keep pushing! You can do this," the witch holding her hands encourages her over the chants.

My mother screams and chants louder, "In nomine electi unus."

"The baby's head isn't showing yet," Aurora speaks. "I can't detect any heartbeats. Push, Bella."

Another witch with fire-colored hair breaks through the circle. "You must push, Bella. You must push."

The chanting grows louder and louder. "In nomine electi unus."

"I can't. I caaan't!" my mother screams again, the ground shaking with her roars. Crimson cascades down her legs, leaving a puddle of blood spreading across the forest floor. "Something's wrong! I can't feel them."

"Continue to repeat after me, Bella. In nomine electi unus. Push." Aurora stucks her hand further in between my mother's legs.

The witch holding my mother's hands further encourages, "Push, Bella, push."

The witches around keep chanting louder and louder and louder. My mother pushes harder, harder, and harder. Her blood stains the grass, drips onto the ground, and splashes all over Aurora's arms. Still, every one of them continues to chant, "In nomine electi unus. In nomine electi unus . . ."

"The moon is in position!" a witch shouts, as she leans her head back to stare at the night sky. "She has granted us access. Now is the time."

"Aurora, you must get them out," another witch shouts.

My mother's breathing becomes more shallow, void of life. She is losing way too much blood, her heart slowing down and the fire in her eyes burning out.

"Stay with me, Bella," Aurora begs.

"She's dying," screams one of them. "The babies must draw their first breath before she takes her last, or we will all lose them."

"Alizon," Aurora yells out, "you must take over."

A witch with striking blond hair and ocean-colored eyes appears out of thin air.

"Mother," yells the witch holding my mother's hands. Her eyes glow pure white as she speaks, "Death is knocking at her door. We have less than five minutes."

My heart flip-flops inside my chest. I knew this was coming. I know I never met her, but that doesn't make this any easier to watch. She is still my mother.

In a hurry, Aurora strips off all her clothing and throws herself on top of my mother's barely conscious body. "Place them into me," she demands.

"Mother, we can't."

"Now!" she says, as the chanting continues. "They must live. The Chosen One must live."

"A witch's pregnancy can last for over a hundred years!" shouts Alizon. "Are you certain you want to go through with this?"

"Get on with it," Aurora orders, her radiant eyes glowing a fascinating shade of neon green.

"Mother, I beg you to reconsider," states the witch with rich dark-brown hair.

A bright, electric emerald-green light suddenly strikes throughout the night sky.

"Now, Evanora!" Aurora screams over the other witches's chants.

My mother starts to hyperventilate underneath Aurora's body. Foam drenches the side of her mouth, and blood drips into her ears and onto the grass.

"Nooo!" I scream out loud and fall to my knees.

The witch, who I now know to be Evanora, turns (in my direction). "Electus," she whispers, and I freeze. "The Chosen One's soul is present," she announces, her different-colored eyes glowing pure white. "This is the way." She stands up and places a hand on Aurora's back, firmly pressing it down while my mother's body continues to shake.

Tears keep rolling down my cheeks. I close my eyes and bury my face into my hands. It feels like my soul is being snatched out of my body, literally ripped. I understand that I never met my mother, and I never will, but to see the woman who gave her life, for me to live, is torturing my soul.

"In nomine electi unus," the witches chant continuously.
"In nomine
electi unus. In nomine electi . . ."

"*Tua vita mea est* (Your life is mine)," declares Evanora, as the other witches around her keep on chanting.

The words suddenly ring a bell. The wind starts to whoosh around me and a bright, electric emerald-green light beams from the full pink moon down into my skin. I feel the raw power within me, the magic forcefully being knocked into me. My skin tingles, my heart beats fast, and my neck suddenly itches as the emerald radiates bright green light into the center of the field.

Aurora takes one deep breath as my mother blows out her last. Her swollen belly becomes Aurora's to carry.

The energy around me shifts. Time slows down around us all.

My mother's eyes lock on my own. "Break the curse. I love you," she says to me before she is officially gone.

The memory and everyone inside it disappears.

*     *     *

NICKLAUS

The other kings are already waiting in the clearing outside the gates of the palace. They are all masked, emotionless. Xander has ensured that tents are placed on this end of the battlefield. They are set up a couple of feet away from the palace. Our best men shall be stationed here. This is the last line of defense, just in case we lose, and Vlad needs time to make his great escape with Claire. Our men have been instructed to alert him if they see any sign of threats.

The sky is pitch black. The moon—the only source of light— is shining brightly. The sand is blowing around us due to the strong wind. The waves are roaring, crashing down and singing their own war song. The war bells continue to ring, alerting the kingdom that danger is coming. The chaos around me seems to have no end. My sensitive ears pick up on the sound of the other army marching. They are only seconds away.

We all enter the war tent prepared for planning, even though the time to discuss tactics has been used up.

"What are we up against, Luscious?" I get straight to the point.

He throws a map down onto the table in the center of the room, and we gather around it. "They have split into four groups," he begins. "This group is the group of lycans." He points at a red circle he made on the map. "They will come in from the west, the Beta is leading them.

"This," he says, pointing at another red circle, "is your sister's personal guard. She is also commanding the group of vampires Princess Daniela freed, the ones who are against your rule. They are attempting to sneak up behind us and come in from the south."

"So this must be my father's personal guard and the council's army?" I point at the circle in the middle. "They are the ones marching down on us in this moment, am I correct?"

He nods. "The lycan prince is marching along with them."

"So, who's leading the fourth group?" Xander speaks, his eyes searching the entire map.

Luscious's body goes visibly stiff. I can see hesitation swimming around in his eyes.

"Who is it?" I ask.

"It's your—"

"Mother," a familiar voice says from behind us all.

We all turn around, only to find Lady Gwen, Master Azazel, and no one other than my mother.

\*     \*     \*

CLAIRE

I'm still here now, standing in the middle of the clearing. After the last memory has disappeared, no other memory surfaces. I'm numb. I'm in shock. I still can't believe that my mother saw me, let alone spoke to me. Her last words couldn't have been for me.

"It's impossible."

"Nothing is impossible, Claire," a voice suddenly says.

I turn around and come face-to-face with Aurora, the drop-dead gorgeous, pink-cheeked, raven-haired witch with radiant green eyes and enchanting face—the witch who has done so much for my family. She stares at me with sympathetic eyes, the same way she did at all of my ancestors before me.

Without thinking, I throw myself into her warms, and she welcomes me. She gently strokes my hair, being the anchor of my comfort just like she had been to so many other women who shared the blood that flows through me. I can't stop my tears from falling. This is what I need right now.

"Why did you bring me here just to watch her die?" I ask with a broken voice. "I don't understand the point."

She slightly pulls away from me and lifts my chin with a single finger. "You needed to know where you came from so you can know where you're going, my dear. You needed to see that you came from a line of powerful women. You needed to understand that you are truly the blessing that came from generations of the cursed."

"I still don't understand," I admit, tears now flowing like a river down my cheeks.

Aurora's posture straightens as she lets go of my chin. Her eyes scan me up and down before they settle onto my stomach for a brief second, then they make their way back up to my face. "Come, my child," she instructs, walking off without another word.

My feet seem to be glued in place. The way she just analyzed me was kind of unsettling.

"Come," she calls out, now standing on the other side of the clearing. "They are coming."

"Who's coming?" I suddenly able to move my feet again.

She ignores me and continues to walk into the forest around the clearing, her memories dancing along with the shadows of the trees as I catch up with her. "You were created with a human that came from many cursed women who held no fear. You were blessed by a coven of the world's most-dangerous witches. You were carried and birthed by the world's most-powerful witch to ever exist. You were chosen, Claire."

"But, why me?"

She flashes that inhumanly beautiful smile of hers. "I already told you, dear. You're the Chosen One."

"But what does that mean, Aurora?" I ask, not bothering to hide my frustration. After everything that I've seen and learned, I still feel blinder than a bat—not to mention that she has been talking in riddles.

*Chosen on this and chosen on that. Can someone please cut me some slack?*

"The energy to heal the world can be obtained through love," she explains without really explaining anything at all. "As I told you before, love is a force as powerful and as strange as the power of the emerald."

"I still—"

"Once your blood mother passed away, I carried the two of you in my very own womb."

The memory of the time she is talking about plays before our eyes.

"I carried you and your twin brother from the year of 2040 and birthed you in the year of 2163."

"Impossible!" I gasp.

"I told you that nothing is impossible, Claire. A witch's pregnancy isn't like a human's. Our pregnancy can last over a century if need be."

I remember one of the witches saying that to Aurora on the day when my mother died.

"Did my brother survive?" I finally ask the question I had been holding back. I was too afraid to learn the truth. I don't think I really want to know. Even if he did make it, there's no telling if he is still alive. We entered the world way after the Awakening. As we all know, these are dangerous times for humans, especially males.

"Yes." The memory of the time when my mother was pregnant with us continues to flicker. "I believe you have already met him," she says, stopping me in my tracks.

I lean my head over to one side. "Met . . . ?"

690

"His name is Alec," she answers my obvious question. "He was assigned to King Cyrus's kingdom when it was time for him to be auctioned off."

*Wait, what? Alec? She couldn't be speaking about who I'm thinking about, could she?*

My mind goes back to the time when I first met Alec, the slave boy. He looked smoking hot—perhaps in his mid-twenties, but he might be younger. He had a face of a god. His golden-blond hair was somewhat similar to my golden shade, just a few shades darker. However, that was not what gained my attention. No, not at all. His eyes resembling my own did, making me halt right in my tracks. It felt like staring at the male version of myself in the mirror. His unique green shades shocked my soul.

"No, impossible!" I blurt out, holding back my sudden urge to puke.

"I told you child, nothing is impossible. Don't worry about the physical attraction you felt toward him. It's the bond. Just look at it as your soul recognizing your other half."

OMG! I think I'm about to faint.

Suddenly Aurora freezes, her eyes glowing like a night light. I know that look. She is having another vision.

*Oh no! No, not right now.*

I touch her shoulder in attempt to snap her out of it. "Aurora, what were you saying about my brother?" I shake her.

"He is in danger!" she says out loud. "They all are in danger! It has begun."

\*     \*     \*

NICKLAUS

The other vampire kings crouch down, ready to attack. Lady Gwen and Master Azazel follow their lead. My mother,

691

Xander, and I remain cool. My mother is wearing a crown—a crown that belongs to the future queen.

She and her f*ckery.

"Why are you here? How did you make it past our defenses without being detected?" I question her, mind-linking with my guards at the same time. If they slipped through, anyone can.

"I'd lived in this palace way before you were born, Nicklaus, and so had your father. Take heed to that." She walks all the way into the tent and takes a seat like she owns the place.

My mother has no fear. She believes I would never harm her because she is my mother. I hate to be the bearer of bad news, but she is now my enemy. And you know they say that once you cross that line, you need to stay there.

"It's nice to see you too, honey dumpling," says Lady Gwen, flashing that god-awful plastic smile. She looks as lovely as ever, her platinum waves hanging freely down her back. She has her all-silver armor on, her cloak and lips complementing each other— they are the shade of crimson-red blood.

I give it to the woman. She is beautiful, but she might as well be a ghost. I ignore the b*tch, my eyes on Master Azazel instead. I lean my head over to one side, assessing the dickless brute. He shall finally meet his Maker today. Out of the corner of my eye, I notice Marcellus, Cornelius, and Xander staring at him. Yup, Master Azazel is as good as dead.

"Nicklaus," calls my mother, regaining my attention.

"Yes, Mother Dearest."

The disgust in my voice doesn't go unnoticed. She smirks and then focuses her attention on the other vampire kings. She looks them up and down, challenging them all before placing her attention back on me.

"Leave us," she orders, finishing her horrible attempt of intimidation.

As expected, no one moves.

"Who the f*ck do you think you are?" I spit through clenched teeth.

"I am your mother," she spits back. "That's the only reason you're still alive. You should be thanking me," she says, as her eyes lock on Xander's. "The both of you should be thanking me."

The f*cking audacity of this woman!

"Thanking you for what?" Xander mocks. "The only thing you ever did was giving birth to us. Other than that, you should be considered dead."

Within a second, she is in front of him. "You were never supposed to exist. So yes, my boy, that's exactly what you should be thanking me for, you ungrateful piece of sh*t."

Xander's eyes flash bright red. "That's rich coming from a wh*re. Why are you here, Mother?" he taunts. "We all know that the war field is not the best place for you. You're so much safer in Apollyon's bed as you patiently wait to slop his dick down."

She raises her hand. "How dare you, you weak piece of sh—"

I'm in front of them both in a flash before my mother's hand collides with Xander's face. "Enough!" I snap.

This sh*t is pointless. Who the f*ck has a family feud before war?

"Leave us," I order everyone.

*"She's trying to distract us,"* I tell Xander in our mind link.

His eyes spit fire, and his chest heaves up and down. My mother on the other end is smiling from ear to ear. She just loves getting under his skin.

*"Brother, get ready. They will be attacking at any moment,"* I continue to speak inside his head.

Without another word, Xander and the other kings disappear.

"What do you want, Mother?" I spit the moment they leave the room.

Master Azazel and Lady Gwen are still present, obviously too afraid to move. They should be.

"I came to warn you, Nicklaus."

Haha. She can't be serious.

"What a fine time to warn somebody." I walk to the table, taking a swig of whiskey—f*ck, it's good!

"Nicklaus, I'm serious. You still have time to put an end to this foolishness. The council doesn't want this, your sister doesn't want this, and your father doesn't want this," she coaxes.

"Right," I sarcastically state, "yet all of them are currently marching down, not only an army but also my father's personal guard. You fools also teamed up with the lycans, just to take me down. From the looks of things, Mother Dearest, all of you certainly want to die," I hiss, my blood boiling.

"There will be no bloodshed, my sweet boy, not if you surrender and accept your father's proposal."

Yup, it's official. My mother is f*cking deranged, I know.

Laughter explodes out of my chest. "I'll never surrender to anyone, Mother. You know that!"

"Please, honey dumpling."

The ghost decides to speak. Her voice has never been so f*cking annoying.

"Please, just hear us out," the ghost goes on.

"Did I grant you permission to speak?" I turn to face Lady Gwen. My voice is so cold that she shivers in response.

Master Azazel steps in front of her as if he could protect the wh*re. The fool can't even protect himself.

"How cute!" I smirk like a maniac. "How about the two of you go f*ck yourselves? Oh right, Azazel you can't—"

He growls and takes a step forward.

I burst out laughing. "You don't have the balls," I spit, "literally."

"Nicklaus," my mother calls, raising that annoying voice of hers, "you need to listen to me and listen to me clearly. You will stop this foolishness! You will surrender! You will give the lycan prince the mutt that Cyrus stole from him," she says. "You will denounce the fraudulent claim of that chosen wh*re being your queen," she lies. She turns to face Lady Gwen, taking the crown off her head in the process. "And you will claim this trueborn as your queen." She puts my beloved's future crown on Lady Gwen's head—the nerve of this woman.

My monster releases a loud roar. My chest burns into fury, and red hues dim my eyes. My monster has heard enough of this and is ready to go to war. He wants to end every last one of them right now.

I lower my eyes for a brief second.

"Calm down, honey dumpling. Your father's proposal is a good one. We shall rule together, and all shall be forgiven."

"Is that right?" my monster questions, drawing the plastic b*tch in just so I can snatch my beloved's crown off her head.

The dummy actually draws closer while nodding in approval. She even has the nerve to wrap her arms around me, and the urge to rip them out of their sockets courses through my veins. My eyes remain fixed on the crown—Claire's crown.

"Gwen," my mother warns.

The fool doesn't listen. She continues, "So what do you say, honey dumpling? You know like I know that I'm more than capable of making you happy. I am meant for you, not her." She smiles coyly. The jealousy she holds for my beloved is buried deep in her skin. "The chosen wh*re shall be publicly executed, of course. That's nonnegotiable," she says.

That does it. Without warning, my hand slams through her chest, pushing past her rib cage, then I grab her unbeaten heart.

"Gwen!" my mother calls out, a little too late.

Lady Gwen's eyes are wide with fear. Within a second, they are void of life as I pull her heart out of her chest and secure my beloved's crown of course before throwing her lifeless body onto the ground—f*ck, that feels good!

My monster is pleased. "F*ck your proposal!" he spits, and the tent explodes.

# CHAPTER EIGHTY-FOUR
## The Queen Has Awakened

CLAIRE

"Who's in danger?" I ask Aurora.

"Your destiny awaits you," is her response. "It has begun."

*Destiny? I'm so sick of the words "destiny" and "chosen."*

"What the hell are you talking about?" My patience with her, this bullsh*t witch business, and chosen-one f*ckery is wearing thin. "Nothing you say makes a lick of sense. You swear I'm the chosen this and chosen that, yet you still refuse to tell me what the f*ck it even means. You know what? Screw this." I've had it with this bullsh*t! I walk off in the opposite direction even though I don't have the slightest clue of how I'm supposed to get out of this f*cking dream-state—a creepy witch's spell.

"The war of all of the species is coming," she says from behind me, and my feet suddenly stop working. "Your union with the vampire king is far from being welcomed. Many shall fight against it. Many will die to protect it and because of it."

I am about to tell her to go f*ck herself, but she continues, "That's why you are the Chosen One. You're the light who will give back everything the darkness has taken away. You will give back everything your beloved has stolen."

"I still don't get it."

"In due time you shall," she answers proudly. Once again, her eyes scan me up and down, then they settle on my stomach for a brief second before they make their way back up to my face. "You are brave enough to explore the darkness." She walks over to me. "You hold the infinity power of light."

"But I—"

"Always remember that love is a force as powerful and as strange as the power of the emerald, my child," she says, before I have a chance to question her further. Her eyes flicker to the pendant hanging from my neck, then her delicate hands touch the emerald—I swear I can feel the intense, raw power traveling from her very soul and directly into the pendant. She suddenly pulls me into her arms and gives me a big loving squeeze, just like a mother would. "Your first challenge is to show them what happens when they challenge the reign of the true queen. The gypsy is praying for your speedy recovery. It's time to go," she says, sounding amused.

"What gypsy?"

She flashes that beautiful smile of hers. "Remember all that you were told, my dear, and everything that you have learned before this. Everything that you have experienced in life is for a reason, especially your encounters with the vampire kings."

Before I can respond, time slows down around us and gravity shifts. My skin instantly tingles, my heart starts to pound rapidly, and my neck suddenly itches.

"Make me proud," she says.

A bright, electric emerald green light blinds me, and an unknown force knocks me down to the ground

\*       \*       \*

NICKLAUS

"Get the f*ck up, now!"

Xander's yells overpower the ringing sound in my ears. My head is pounding viciously, and the smell of fire, blood, and death smothers my senses. I must've blacked out from the force of the blast. I remember Xander yanking me out of the tent just in time, giving me his hand to take, and pulling me up to my feet.

*How long have I been out?* I ask myself, the ringing in my ears still hasn't stopped. *Claire's crown is nowhere to be found. F\*ck, I must have lost it in the blast.*

I take a look at my surroundings. Piles of lifeless bodies are all around us. The other kings are currently engaged in a full-fledged battle. The war has officially begun. The song of clashing swords and cries of death blow in the wind. My personal guards are all around me. For a while, the ringing inside my ears is all I can focus on until Xander yells, "The palace has been invaded!"

*Claire . . .*

I break off in the direction of the palace gates. I should have known better. My father has never been the type to play fair. All our preparations are for nothing. I won't be surprised if he is hiding in my home, watching everything that transpires from the shadows the entire time. He could give a f\*ck about honor and attack a man head up. He's the type of man that hits you from the back, slithering like the snake that he is, and I know this. If anything happens to Claire because of my stupidity, I'll never forgive myself.

I open up our bond to check on my beloved, but I feel nothing at all. I swear my unbeaten heart suddenly skips thousands of beats per second. I could only pray that she's still safe in my wing, lost in a dream.

*"Vlad,"* I reach out.

There is no response.

*"Vlad, get Claire out there right f\*cking now!"* I roar through our connection but still no response.

My monster instantly increases our speed despite my condition. I can hear Xander following close behind me and the

699

other kings taking lives all around me. I'm literally seconds away from the gates when something suddenly slams into me and knocks me down to the ground.

"Not so fast, Big Brother," my sister hisses as she lunges on top of me.

Another bomb goes off.

*     *     *

CLAIRE

My eyes pop open. Loud roars and the sound of crashing waves and pure chaos ring loudly in my ears.

*What the hell is going on here?*

The stench of fire, blood, and death floats around me. Nicklaus isn't with me, but I can feel he is near. I pull my body up and quickly scan my surroundings. Jadis and Victoria are present, holding each other in a chair on the other side of the room. They seem to be praying, their hearts pounding in alarm.

"What the hell is going on?" I ask, my voice sounding hoarse.

Jadis's neck snaps in my direction. Her big brown eyes widen in surprise. "It worked!" she says. She jumps out of her seat and rushes over to the bed.

That's when I notice her mascara sliding and smudging underneath her beautiful big eyes. She looks like a train wreck. Her dress is all wrinkled, and her chestnut hair is a mess. The sound of bombs, people dying, and gunshots enter my sensitive ears. I can feel my monster inside me coming back to life, slowly but surely awakening. Before Jadis can reach me, I'm up and out of the bed.

"What the f*ck is going on?" I ask her, as I look out of the window.

There are bodies everywhere, the sand painted with blood. The waves seem to be singing their own war song, crashing down in perfect harmony with the war bells as the smell of fear floats freely in the air.

*Where the hell is Nicklaus?*

I open up our bond to check on those who are loyal to me. All I can feel is scorching hot wrath throughout our connection. That's it; that's all.

"We are under attack, cherry pop," Jadis states the obvious. "There are guards outside our door. The king ordered that we stay in this room. I was just praying for your speedy recovery while Victoria was praying that you would wake up so we could all make a sweet escape, if need be. Our prayers have been answered."

*"The gypsy is praying for your speedy recovery."* Aurora's words ring loud and clear.

My head snaps in Jadis's direction.

*No, she couldn't be talking about Jadis. That's impossible!*

*"Nothing is impossible, Claire."* Aurora's words enter my mind again.

I stare at my friend in a new light. Now that I'm paying attention, she does look different. I mean she looks like she's been through hell, but underneath the surface I can see so much more. There's an aura of vibrant colors surrounding her outwardly contagious soul.

"Jadis," I begin. I hear sudden commotion from the other side of the door, so I step outside of the closet, and Jadis foolishly follows behind me.

"Get behind me now!" my monster barks at the both of them, and they follow her command with no argument.

Seconds later, hinges fly off the door.

*     *     *

NICKLAUS

I roll over just in time to prevent Daniela's sharp claws from sinking into my skin, and the bomb from blowing my head off. I'm back to my feet within a second, and she attacks again without warning. She reaches out to claw me, but I sidestep her and swiftly smack her hand away.

"Come on, Daniela," I taunt. "I taught you better than that, Little Sister."

"Today's the day the student becomes the teacher, Big Brother," she taunts back. Before she lunges again, her sharp and long claws dig deep into my skin. It draws blood, but the pain doesn't faze me.

Another bomb goes off. I do a backflip in the air, kicking her square in the stomach in the process with little force. It sends her flying before she falls flat on her ass. In a flash, I'm in front of my sweet little sister, ready to teach her a lesson. She swooshes out her right leg and manages to knock me down to the ground, then she is back to her feet and goes for the kill. She throws her fist into my chest, but it is another epic fail. Once again, I roll over, and my head knocks back with laughter. Before she can blink, I jump off the ground, sidestep her, and grab a big chunk of her hair—all in one process. I yank her by the hair, swinging her body into mine and dragging her little ass.

"Who's teaching who?" I ask, placing my lips dangerously close to her ear. "You're a good fighter, Daniela, but you're no match for me."

"Is that right?" She kicks her leg back and rams me square in my dick.

"F*ck," I hiss. I let her go as I fall down to my knees.

"Classic," she brags. She flashes a cocky smile, then charges in my direction again.

\*　　　\*　　　\*

CLAIRE

702

Hinges fly off the door, and splinters of wood splatter everywhere. My monster is fully present. She is crouching down in a defensive stance Nicklaus once showed me, ready for whomever. My crimson eyes lock on Commander Vlad, who is all bruised and bloody. He is holding his arm over his stomach.

"We must go at once," he hisses. He grabs my left arm with his free hand and drags me out of the room.

Death is all I can see. Bodies of the guards who were left to protect us are scattered all around. This is war. The screams of the innocent from the other side of the palace fill my ears, and a thick cloud of black smoke enters my lungs. Jadis and Victoria break into a fit of coughs from behind me.

"The council is here. I must get you to safety. Take them to safety," I order Commander Vlad, shying away from his embrace.

"No, I cannot leave you unprotected. The council is—"

"No match for me!" I snatch the *M1 Garand* from one of our dead men's hands.

"Your Highness, please. My duty is to protect you."

"Your duty is to follow my command," I remind him, turning to face Jadis and Victoria, who both currently look like they want to sh\*t on themselves. "I need you to locate the human named Alec. Victoria and Jadis know exactly who he is."

"The king's sister has him," he tells me quickly, earning a growl from my monster.

Vlad watches me curiously as I continue, "Take as many humans and servants as you can to safety. Don't engage with the enemies unless it's absolutely needed."

Vlad grinds his teeth, but he doesn't dare to disobey me.

"Here, buttercup." I hand Jadis a gun and then turn to Victoria to give her the other one. "If anything happens to Vlad and you find yourself alone, use this."

Just thinking about something happening to Vlad sets my monster off. She doesn't like it one bit, and neither of us likes the thought of these girls being left alone.

"It will not kill a vampire, but it shall slow one of us down," Vlad continues for me.

I know he can feel my uneasiness through our connection.

"I don't know how to use it," Victoria whispers in a shaky voice.

"Just pull the trigger and let it loose," I instruct, showing her how to cock the gun back. "The bullets are laced with pure, undiluted silver. This can paralyze a vampire and cause crippling pain," I state, earning a skeptical look from the both of them.

Vlad remains expressionless, but the pride blooming through our connections speaks a million of emotions.

"Thank you, cherry pop." Jadis pulls me into a tight hug.

Victoria joins in, hanging onto me for dear life.

"I wish you good fortunes," adds Jadis. She pulls away and kisses my hands.

I smile slightly.

*Jadis and her blessings remind me . . .*

The potent smell of burning cedarwood suddenly invades my nostrils, causing my entire body to shift. At first whiff, I thought it was Xander's or Nicklaus's. However, the flowery fragrance that mingles with it tells me otherwise. The new smell doesn't belong to either Xander or Nicklaus no matter how similar their scents are.

I can see tension roll through Commander Vlad's features. He smells it as well, and by the look of things, he knows exactly to whom it belongs.

"Go now," I order them.

Vlad's disapproval soars through our bond, but a command is a command. "As you wish, Your Majesty," he spits through clenched teeth, then he begins to usher the girls in the opposite direction.

"Oh, and Vlad," I call out, the newcomers a couple of minutes away, "take care of them and yourself."

He bows. "As you wish, Your Highness." His hesitation to leave me behind is evident.

"Now, go." I turn my back to all of them and face the direction of our enemies, who are now less than a minute away.

"Claire!" Vlad shouts, to my surprise. He barely calls me by my name. "It has been my honor to serve you, and as long as I've got breath in my body, I will always serve you."

"Take care, Mr. Meany."

He flashes a million-dollar smile. "Kill them all, Your Highness."

Within a flash, they are all gone. I brace myself, patiently awaiting the intruders who dare to declare war inside my home. Seconds later, a party of ten unknown vampires, Nicklaus's b*tch of a mother, and a vampire with a creepy smile, soaked-in-blood blond hair, and a pair of bright green eyes come into view. Master Azazel, the sick and sadistic piece of sh*t, is standing in front of them all.

*　　*　　*

NICKLAUS

Xander catches Daniela in midair—by the neck—then slams her body onto the ground with a loud thud. "Go to Claire," his monster roars, eyes on me. "I'll handle your light work." The cold gleam in his eyes tells me that in this moment he is not my brother; he is none other than the cold-hearted king.

*"Leave her alive,"* I request inside his head.

*"That isn't your decision to make, Little Brother."* He lunges in Daniela's direction and snaps her neck with little effort, then he sinks his fangs into our dearest sister's skin.

Daniela screams while attempting to break free from Xander's hold as he continues to down the contents of her blood. Unable to watch my sister's fate, I take off into the direction of the palace gates. From afar, I can see Cyrus freeze at the door. That's the exact moment I feel them—the council. The raw, authentic power that forms in their presence is hard to miss. The fighting around us all ceases to exist.

*"Go to Claire,"* I tell Cyrus in our mind link. *"If they are here, this is where I need to be."*

*"Your place is to stand beside our queen. She needs—"*

*"The threat against her life has been eliminated. Go to her now! We will handle them."*

He nods, then disappears into the castle.

Finally, I turn. Orpheus is the first one I come to face. He is already covered in blood. He is watching the scene before our eyes with malevolent anticipation, his soulless marigold eyes fixed on mine. He flashes a small smile, and I return it with a cocky smirk of my own. Council Member Astron's electric-blue eyes are also on me as he licks the blood of her enemies off her hands. Her platinum hair and ruby lips are also drenched in crimson, her features void of emotions. She has no fear or care for this matter at all. She is here for one thing and one thing only—to feed.

Draven, one of the most-powerful among them, remains blood-free. He is not known to take pleasures in the thrill of the kill. He doesn't indulge in such activities, but believe me when I say that it is a good thing as he is extremely deadly. Just like the others, his face is void of emotion, and cruel anticipation can be seen inside his pale-blue eyes. His attention is placed on Apollyon, my father—the most-powerful of them all. He is standing alone in the center of the field, proud and tall. Behind him stand the Lycan Prince Ethel, the Lycan Beta Rollin, Lord Athan—Lady Gwen's father—and Duke Aldon, the traitorous ass.

I search through my bond with Claire one last time, and now I feel her. My beloved's monster is wide awake, and the power within her touches each and every soul of our inner circle. We can all feel her. The queen has awakened, and more importantly, is out of harm's way. The other kings, painted with the blood of our

706

enemies, growl in approval. They are circling around me while being surrounded by my guards, who are using their own bodies as our shield. Xander makes his way into the circle, dragging Daniela by the hair.

All the council members's eyes snap in the direction of the palace, indicating that they can also feel her power. My father's lips curve into a smirk as his eyes start to roam over each and every vampire king for a long-drawn-out moment. Once done, they land on Xander, then on his precious and barely breathing daughter before they finally fall on me.

Daniela releases a soft whimper. Surprisingly enough, my father remains unbothered. The fact that he looks so relaxed, as if he already won the battle, disturbs me. He must have something up his sleeve.

My father is stronger, faster, and holds more power than me, but he knows I'm not the one to be underestimated. Something's off. He appears so calm, way too calm. And I will not lie, that makes me nervous. However, no one should ever know that. If there is something my father and I have in common, it is the fact that we both hate losing. So no matter what he has in store for me, I'll fight till death for my win. There will be no draw or surrendering. Today is the day that one of us shall die.

"Kill them all."

His voice is carried in the wind, and they start to charge.

I rush in an inhuman speed to the front line. "For the queen!" my monster roars, sparking electricity into the night sky.

"For the queen!" my men shout from behind me, as they run toward our enemies.

\*       \*       \*

CLAIRE

"Look what we found," states Azazel, sounding extremely proud of himself. His electric green eyes spark with excitement, and his disgusting smile deepens. He has no idea what he has just gotten himself into.

"Hello," I respond sweetly, flashing the most-innocent smile I can muster. He shall die first.

I see Nicklaus's mother; she is wearing a crown—my crown I suppose. "What took you so long, my mother-in-law?" I ask, choosing my words carefully just to get underneath her ancient skin.

She spits on the marble floor. "You aren't and will never be my daughter, slave!"

"That may be true." I take my first step toward her. "However, I am your queen, and you will bow down before me one way or another."

She releases a monstrous growl. "Kill her now!" she orders.

All her minions charge in my direction except the one I want the most, but that's fine. I guess we shall save the most-desirable kill for last.

My monster instantly takes full control, and I welcome the bright, vivid, and intense shade of crimson as it stains my vision. The familiar power of the emerald presents itself and comes into my awareness. My monster and the magic are once again in perfect accord. For the first time, I don't fear the raw, intense power; nor do I try to fight the darkness tainting my soul. Instead, I welcome the feeling with open arms. I await the thrill that shall come from my enemy's sweet and delicious blood as it soaks onto my tongue.

I sit back and watch my monster play as she takes them all head-on, moving with no fear. None of them can touch us. Within a second, she lands on her first victim in inhuman speed and plunges our sharp talons into a soldier's neck, ripping his head out of it. The metallic, salty smell of his blood fills the air.

*One down, nine to go.*

On instinct, our fangs sink into our next victim. His blood tastes sweeter than sweet. His screams and pointless pleas for mercy add fuel to our burning fire. And before a second ends, he is already dead.

*Two down and eight to go.*

One of the soldiers manages to strike. He digs his claws deep into our skin, drawing blood. This angers my monster, so I give her the urge to end their lives quicker. She grabs him and dangles his body high in the air. Another one leaps, but she catches him as well and then she buries our fangs into his flesh. However, we don't get to enjoy the thrill of the kill—nope—so in a blur, she yanks the other soldier's heart out of his chest. So far, my monster has killed three, leaving seven more lives to claim.

*Four down, six to go.*

I continue to count as I watch the scene in the back of our head, completely amazed. My monster moves like a blood-thirsty angel, eager to shed blood. The world seems to shake with her roar while she brings our body to slide through the hallway with our claws blazing, slicing two more soldiers's legs and bringing them down to their knees. Seconds later, she is back on our feet and twists both of their heads in an awkward angle until the sound of necks being snapped rings in our ears; then I see heads flying in the air and bounce off the walls, their bodies hitting the ground with a loud thud.

*Five down.*

*Six down.*

*Seven down.*

I shout inside our head as my monster slings a soldier into our body, tugging him into a hug. She swiftly bites deep down into his skin and devours him whole in less than a second. She throws the lifeless body to the side and wipes off the corner of our mouth.

*Eight down.*

The last two minions stand stuck in place, their heads moving back and forth—from us, then to each other.

709

"End her now!" Nicklaus's mother pointlessly shouts.

"End me now," my monster mocks. She is having way too much fun.

One of the vampires looks at her and then at his fellow comrade. "Run for your life!" he orders, and they break off into a full sprint in opposite directions.

*Uh-uh. Not so fast.*

I turn to face them while calling forth the power of the emerald. Instantly, time stands still. My skin starts to tingle, my heart pounds rapidly, and my neck itches.

*"Tua vita mea est* (Your life is mine)," I recite the words I remember from the dream.

That familiar light flashes, and the unknown force knocks the two minions down to the ground.

*Priceless. Both of their lives belong to us. Too bad, too sad, they are dead.*

My enhanced senses pick up on a new scent of wildflowers and damp earth blending in perfect harmony with the mulberry spice aroma, in the same exact moment a certain set of words floats inside my head: "Rule number one, never take your eyes off your enemy." As if on cue, I turn back around just in time to catch the sick and sadistic sh*t who raped me. Of course, the coward tries to attack me from behind.

# CHAPTER EIGHTY-FIVE
## Bow down, B*tches

Master Azazel's body is now resting in my hands, literally.

"Well done, Your Highness," says Cyrus, finally making his presence known. He creeps up and snatches Lady Akasha by the neck. He holds her in place, forcing her to watch the grand finale. "This belongs to our queen," he says, taking my crown off her head.

"Cyrus, let me go at once. Apollyon will have your head for this. He will have both of your heads, starting with the chosen wh*re," she spits another round of pointless threat.

Choosing to ignore her, I stare directly into Master Azazel's eyes—his soul is mine to take. I tilt my head over to one side, and I swear I can hear his frozen heart skipping a million and one beats. "I can hear your heartbeat, you know," I recite the words he once said to me.

He struggles to break free, and I laugh in his face.

*My, my my! Look how quickly the tables have turned.*

"You know the best part about humans coming out of those facilities?" I ask him the same question he once asked me.

His mouth is moving, but he doesn't speak, and he doesn't blink. He barely breathes, and he does piss himself.

Nicklaus's mother is having a fit, attempting to break free from Cyrus's arms.

"I wonder how he can pee with no dick." Cyrus laughs so hard.

My neck snaps in his direction, and he laughs harder.

"Nicklaus rid him of his manhood as a consequence of his sick desire," Cyrus states.

*I love my king.*

"Did it hurt, Azazel the Dickless?" I quip.

He doesn't respond.

"Answer me," I bark, just like he once did to me.

"Please, please, show mercy."

*Oh, now he wants to beg. I remember when I once begged, but he shoved his dick into me instead.*

"Address me properly! What's my name?"

"Please, Your Majesty, show mercy."

"Nothing can do, you weak sick and sadistic piece of sh*t!" I say in my own voice, pushing my monster to the back of my mind—this kill belongs to me. "Now, let's have a little fun, shall we? I remember when you picked me up by the back of my neck and abruptly dunked my head into a tub full of water. Do you remember that?" The power from the emerald sparks within my very soul.

Azazel shakes his head.

"Awe, but I do. *Aqua* (Water)," I hiss, then a bucket of water appears out of thin air. I pull Azazel by the hair. "Gasp for air, just like I once did." I plunge his head into the bucket of water. *"Spiritus tuus ad me pertinet* (Your breath belongs to me)."

Instantly, Azazel the Dickless struggles to breathe as I hold his head underwater. I remember how my eyes started to sting and how I desperately kicked my feet out behind me, trying to fight the unexpected attack, before my body eventually went limp just like his body now. He pulled me back up by the hair, so I return the favor. I gasped for air right after, just like he is doing in this exact moment. He plunged my head back into the water, and once again I return the favor, doing the same to him. I remember how my head

712

hit the bottom of the tub and my vision blurred. That was the moment the clear water turned bright red, just like now.

"Bleed for me)," I hiss.

His blood floats on the top of the bucket, and it overflows. Red-colored water spills all over the already-bloody floor. Azazel the Dickless is drowning. Can you believe that? A vampire is drowning—haha. Meanwhile, Cyrus and Nicklaus's mother watch the scene in utter shock.

"This was the moment I thought that my wish was finally coming true," I roar. I'm no longer a blood-thirsty angel but an avenging one, seeking vengeance that shall be granted by his blood.

"And then you lifted me up for air once again," I whisper, continuing my game of tit for tat.

He is gasping for air and a bloody mess—it's such a beautiful sight.

"And you remember what you said to me next, Azazel the Dickless?"

His head rolls from one side to the other.

"Answer me!" my monster shouts. She's back.

He rolls his head again, refusing to look me in my eye.

"Oh no, you don't, slave. Death is too good for you," she reminds him.

"Claire, please." Azazel manages to speak.

"It's *Your Majesty* to you. Now, die slow."

Once again, time stands still, and my skin starts to tingle. "Tua vita mea est," I recite the exact words the witch said in my dream, my heart pounding and my neck itching.

"*Cinis cinerem, pulvis in pulverem* (Ashes to ashes, dust to dust)," I spit.

The sound of his scream fills the air, and another bright, electric emerald-green light pours into the hall. My inner fire turns his body into nothing but a pile of ashes, slowly burning him alive in my very hands. Soon enough, silence replaces his screams. I dust my hands off when it's all done, as if nothing ever happened. My beloved's b*tch of a mother is now all alone.

"What are you?" she asks, her eyes are now wide with fear.

"I am your queen, Mother Dearest," I mock, as Cyrus places my crown on top of my head.

I've officially instilled fear of death in my not-so-sweet mother-in-law's frozen heart. She starts to literally shake. In the back of my mind, I kind of feel bad. She is my beloved's mother after all. But my monster likes the b*tch being on the verge of bowing down and grovelling before me.

"Take me to my beloved at once," I order Cyrus, not sparing Lady Akasha a single glance, "and bring her with us."

He nods and forcefully shoves her ahead. We walk through the palace with no fear of our enemies making an appearance. I push my monster to the back of my mind as my eyes scan the massive pile of lifeless bodies we pass. Too many have lost their lives tonight, humans and vampires alike. My soft heart beats faintly inside my chest with every step I take. I don't recognize anyone I know, but the pain of lives lost still affects my human side nonetheless.

"This is a disaster," I mumble as we get closer to the other wing of the palace.

"These are the casualties of war," my beloved's mother corrects me.

Cyrus continues to shove her ahead.

"And this is only the beginning. No vampire of great status will ever accept you as our queen, no matter how powerful you may be!"

*Someone's brave again. Now that was fast.*

I turn around to face her. "Then every vampire of great status shall die," I hiss back, allowing my monster to briefly take control. I walk ahead of them, but I stop right in my tracks when I detect sudden movement. My human side plays at the back as my monster returns, front and center and on high alert. We utilize our advanced senses to determine if this newcomer is a friend or foe, and that's when I hear a random heartbeat from my left.

Hiding behind the grand piano is a human. Cyrus takes a step toward it, and I hold up my hand. From the sound of things, whoever he or she is, they are scared out of their mind. If Cyrus touches the human, it may cause them to have a heart attack.

"You can come out," I say. "I will not allow anyone to hurt you."

The human's heart skips a beat.

"I promise you will be safe. You have my word."

"Claire," the human calls out.

I instantly recognize his voice, and my mind drifts back to the conversation I had with Aurora.

*"Did my brother survive?"* I remember asking the question I had been holding back, too afraid to learn the truth.

*"Yes,"* she answered, and the memory of the time she was pregnant with us continued to flicker. *"I believe you have already met him,"* she said, stopping me in my tracks.

I leaned my head over to one side. *"Met . . . ?"*

*"His name is . . ."*

My mind comes back to reality. Now it's my heart's turn to skip a beat as I walk around the piano.

\*         \*         \*

NICKLAUS

So it begins. The war has officially started. Lifeless bodies are scattered all around. This time, there are no strategies; there is no need for command. My men and my father's men all see eye to eye in the moment. We all share one common goal: to eliminate each other.

I charge in my father's direction. Once he falls, they all shall fall.

The Lycan Prince Ethel roars and then comes at me head-on. "Find Embry!" he shouts to his beta while picking up speed.

*Why the f\*ck is he here, for Cyrus's beloved? You know what, that's irrelevant. He will die before he gets his hand on Claire or Embry.*

He breaks one of my men's neck and jumps in the air, shifting into his full-fledged lycan form—all in one process.

Xander and Marcellus appear by my side, coming for the one who dares to come for me. I swoop down to grab a pistol from one of my lifeless men. Seconds later, silver bullets fly in my father's direction. He moves his head from side to side, dodging a choir of bullets. With the eye of a predator, I memorize his movement, and I am quickly able to predict his next step.

He lunges at me, and I mimic his actions, letting loose in the process just in time to shoot him at the side of his head. The bullet only grazes his ear, but it does the trick. He's not down for good, but he is down for now. From my peripheral vision, I see Xander and Duke Aldon engaging in a deadly battle. I so desperately want to intervene—his death is personal—but my monster keeps his eye on the prize.

My father stands in the center, his face showing only a subtle hint of anger. His intense gaze settles on me. He raises a single finger, gesturing it back and forth. He is telling me to get closer, silently challenging me.

Ah yes, I sure will.

I continue to charge in his direction, increasing my speed. Sudden uncontrollable rage made of ashes and fire burns me alive on the inside, slowing me down. Instantly, I decipher that the intense power belongs to Claire, and that can only mean one thing—someone is attacking her; she's in danger. I shift courses and head for the palace, but all too soon I realize my mistake as I'm snatched by the neck from behind.

"The b*tch makes you weaker than weak," my father whispers in my ear before plunging his fangs into the side of my neck.

*     *     *

CLAIRE

His similar, unique green eyes stare straight into my own, never failing to shock my soul.

"Alec!" I immediately pull him into my arms.

He hesitates for a while but eventually returns the hug.

"Thank God you're okay."

He is a bloody mess, beaten from head to toe. But he is alive, and that is all that matters. My brother is alive.

I take a deep whiff of the scent. For the first time, I realize that he smells like honey and lemon, quite similar but also different from my own.

"Get away from her!" Cyrus spits, pulling Alec away while still holding onto Nicklaus's mother.

*What the hell is up with all of these possessive vampire kings?*

"What the hell, Cyrus? Explain yourself."

"He cannot be trusted. Princess Daniela freed many of our enemies before the attack started, and he was one of them."

*Why would she free him? He is a human.*

I step around Cyrus to demand further explanation when a unknown scent alerts my monster. Cyrus crouches down in a defensive stance and pushes me behind him. My beloved's b*tch of a mother takes advantage of the moment, trying to make her escape. Cyrus yanks my arm, allowing her to get away.

"What the f*ck are you doing? She will warn them of my gift."

"Then how about you go after her, half-breed queen," says an unknown voice from the other side of the room.

717

We turn and come in contact with a god of man who possesses the most-unusual shade of amethyst eyes. By his woodsy scent, I can tell he is not a vampire. His aura tells me he is too powerful to be a werewolf, which means he is a lycan. And if my memory serves me right, he is the personification of the lycan beta that Jadis once described.

"What the f*ck do you want, Rollin?"

Cyrus's words confirm my suspicions.

*So, Jadis was right. He is a wondrous sight after all.*

"Where is the Wilde she-wolf?" Rollin asks, catching me off guard.

*Embry . . . Why the hell is he looking for Embry?*

Cyrus growls, and the Beta braces himself for an attack.

*We don't have time for this.*

I step around Cyrus. "The Wilde she-wolf is under my protection," I state.

"My fight is not with you, half-breed queen," he hisses, his unusual shade of amethyst eyes flickering in my direction. "I'm only here to claim what rightfully belongs to my prince."

"She belongs to me," Cyrus speaks.

Beta Rollin ignores him and continues to stare in my direction. "Besides, you have bigger challenges at hand," he says.

"Claire." Cyrus drops down to his knees.

Before I can catch him, throbbing pain is forcefully and invisibly being plunged into my chest, then it hits me next: Nicklaus is hurt. Another jolt strikes like lightning within me and takes my soul out of my chest, officially bringing me down to my knees. And that's when I feel it—absolute emptiness. Our bond is snatched out of my chest.

"Nooo!" I scream. Darkness swallows me whole—my monster swallows me whole—and all I can see is red.

\*       \*       \*

## NICKLAUS

His bite is paralyzing, completely taking away my ability to move. If he releases his venom, I'm dead. I can't let that happen. I won't let that happen. Blood is pouring out from the side of my neck as my father greedily takes his fill of my life force, roaring from time to time.

F*ck no! I refuse to go down without a fight. I use my last bit of strength to knock my head back and hit him square in the face, ripping my flesh in the process. He stumbles back, which gives me the chance to break away. Fire consumes my entire body and burns brightly in the center of my chest. My monster completely takes over, my whole body now under his command. He wastes no time and goes for the kill, striking our sharp talons across my father's face. In defense, he leaps back, and we miss him by a second. Not pausing at all, he issues a series of deadly blows of his own, coming at me with all his might.

I duck and dodge a few of his ruthless assaults, only to be struck by the deadliest one of all. He kicks me in the rib cage, sending me flying back. With lightning speed, he jumps in the air and then grabs me by the neck. Finally, he uses his centuries's old worth of obtained strength to slam me down into the ground. He growls in victory as his sharp talons dig deep, extremely deep, into my open wound. The pain is blinding. My monster struggles to break free from him. The more I move, the deeper he digs, applying more pressure. Using all my strength, I swing my legs in the air and hook them around his neck, tightly squeezing them.

It is not one of my grandest ideas, especially with me getting injured, but f*ck it. I successfully pull myself up, thanks to the strength of my quads. However, I instantly realize I have made another my mistake. My eyes lock on my father's crimson orbs, and the all-too-familiar feeling of him using his higher power to compel me and restrict my movement consumes me. That's when he slams me once again onto the floor—the power does its job. Pain flushes through my entire nervous system, making me feel like I'm moments away from death. Thankfully, my mind has long been immune to this. I can still think and comprehend, but that's about it.

"Your heart bleeds for the wh*re, does it not?" he says, once again lifting me up off the ground.

All I can do is glare at my dick of a father. F*ck I hate him.

"Do you know the best thing about becoming bonded, my son? Through the bond, they can feel all your pain, even when they are human," he tells me, as if I didn't know that yet. "You see, it would be extremely fun to make you kill your beloved wh*re, but then you will be broken and useless to my rule. As my heir, I can't have that, but I can deal with ridding you of your humanity."

*What the f*ck does he mean?*

My sudden thought is cut short the moment his hand collides with my chest. I let out a loud growl of anguish. He smirks while crushing my heart with his bare hands.

"That's right, son. She shall feel your pain. She'll think you're dead, and the b*tch will come running to your rescue," he reveals his master plan.

It makes realize how I foolishly played right into his hands. That's when I see her. For all to hear, she roars. She declares war. Her monster is blinded by rage. Her eyes spit fire; her stare spits ice. She has never looked this dangerous as she stares into the sky. My sensitive ears pick up on her faint chanting, in Latin I believe, or maybe I've just lost way too much blood.

"Bow down, b*tches," she commands, the voice not her own.

A bright, electric emerald-green light flashes in the sky, and an unknown force sends a tidal wave to boom throughout the battlefield. Every single soul but one—my father—drops like flies around her.

My father raises me high in the air. "Checkmate," he says. "Good job, son. You have a little witch on your hand. Now, the real fun shall begin." He forces me to stare directly into his hypnotizing red orbs. "Play dead," he commands, compelling me to obey.

I hit the floor, and it all goes blank.

*     *     *

CLAIRE

My chest is on fire, and there is so much pain. Claire is long gone. All my monster seeks is vengeance. I walk out of the palace gates, passing each and every one of our men and my enemies without sparing them a single glance. I see the other kings, and I can feel their pain through our bond. They are fighting for vengeance. They are fighting to destroy and kill all. They are fighting for revenge against the army of our enemies with every ounce of their strength. Death trails behind them.

*My kings . . .*

I don't have time to view who they're fighting with in the moment, and I really don't care. My mind is set on one thing and one thing only: death to all. They all shall pay. I raise my head and call forth the power of the moon, which I know to be the primary power source of the emerald.

"*Omnia reddent. Omnia reddent. Omnia reddent.* (All shall pay. All shall pay. All shall pay.)"

The chant rolls freely off my tongue. The fight starts to go in slow motion all around me.

"Bow down, b*tches," I order, the voice not my own.

The emerald-green light flashes in the midnight sky, and I push the force within me to bring my enemies down to their knees. All but one bow before me. My eyes lock on the sore thumb out of the bunch. I instantly recognize who he is. Their resemblance is haunting—angular features, thick lashes, heart-shaped lips, and extremely handsome face. Apollyon is certainly Nicklaus's father,

721

not to mention those silver-cerulean eyes that pierce straight into my soul. Directly beside him lies the body of my beloved, and suddenly my heart drops.

*My king, my heart and soul . . . He's gone.*

In the very next moment, the dark and menacing presence has broken all chains. It floods my mind, body, and soul, and it's welcomed. Pitch-black rage taints my inner light—game over. I charge through the sea of bent bodies with a loud roar, and he meets my attack with a charge of his own. We clash. Instinctively, my leg kicks out and collides with his rock-hard chest, but he doesn't fold, move, or flinch.

"Try harder, chosen wh*re!" he spits.

With a rush of the wind, I strike again, using all my force. He delivers deadly defense attacks, and my anger grows. With quickness, I swing my sharp talons out and manage to strike the armor across his chest. He stumbles back, and this officially pisses him off.

Here is my chance to end this once and for all. I utilize the strength of my monster. I jump in the air, kick, and swing my left leg out. Somehow, he intercepts my foot in midair and slings me across the battlefield. Unfortunately for me, my head lands on something sharp. With my blurry vision, I see Nicklaus's father charging toward me. His eyes are all red now, and dark-blue veins run all around his extremely pale skin. Through my dizzy state, I struggle to get up. He immediately leaps and lands on top of me. He viciously sinks his fangs into the side of my neck, and I release an ear-piercing scream. He growls. His bite becomes sharper as he takes my life essence with every sip. I can feel my power slipping, and everyone around me becomes free from my control.

He has won. I've lost; we've lost. I struggle to break free from his grasp as he bites down harder. I can feel the other kings attempting to get to me, but they are not strong enough. My body is going limp, and my life suddenly flashes before my eyes. Everything spools out of my mind—all the abuse I've gone through, the bullying, the sexual assaults; everything, I mean everything. All my pain was for nothing. My mother's sacrifice was for nothing. I've failed her.

I'll miss them all, starting with Xander, who believed in me when no one else did. "The players are too focused on the king. They truly underestimate the power of the queen," he once said. I will miss his encouraging words.

I'll miss Jadis, the most-bomb friend that anyone would be extremely lucky to have. "You reminded me that our lives are worth fighting for. You reminded me that dying is better than living in chains," she once said. Hopefully, she finds a way to break them.

I'll miss Mecca, the bravest she-wolf one will ever meet. "I once told you that there was something about you. For the life of me, I couldn't place my finger on it," she once said to me. She never did get to tell me what she meant, and now she never will.

I'll miss Mr. Meany, Cyrus, Marcellus's epic ass, and even Victoria—the red-headed slut.

Most importantly, I'll miss Nicklaus, my ass-kissing king. I'll give anything to see his face for one last time. I'll give anything to feel the phenomenal feeling that spreads through my body with just one touch from him. But I cannot. I'm dead. Aurora was wrong. I am not the Chosen One.

Finally giving up, my eyes close. Nicklaus's father is seconds away from taking away my last ounce of blood. I can feel him. One-half of my soul is being ripped, the other half being sewn. I'm about to give up. I've lost.

That's exactly how I feel until a hot-and-cold gentle touch brushes my soul. I feel my life source, my beloved. Nicklaus is alive. I can feel his soul calling out to me.

*"Fight firecracker."* His words suddenly appear inside me head. *"Fight for our love."*

Something inside me clicks. My skin starts to tingle, and instincts take over. I find the strength to push Appolyon off me. I jump to my feet and slam my hand straight into his chest—that's right. His life is now in my hands. I squeeze his barely existing heart with all my might while staring straight into his now bright crimson eyes.

*Should he die or live?*

"Die." I can hear Marcellus's voice.

"Live." I can hear Xander's voice.

"You choose." I can hear Nicklaus's voice.

At least, I think I can.

What's a girl should do?

I close my eyes, thinking over my decision. Out of nowhere, Aurora's inhumanly beautiful face appears inside my head.

*"Your first challenge is to show them what happens when they challenge the reign of the true queen."*

That's it! A decision has been made. My heart starts to hammer in my chest, and my neck suddenly itches.

*"Et arcum,* b*tch (Bow down, b*tch)," I hiss. That bright, emerald-green light flashes out of my entire body and enters into his soul.

Finally, he bows before me. Checkmate! I've won. What's done is done.

*       *       *

NICKLAUS

*Two weeks later*

The battle was won, but the war has just officially begun. My father and the rest of the council members have been detained, but my not-so-sweet baby sister and b*tch of a mother somehow managed to escape, taking the traitorous b*tch Duke Aldon with them. That's just the start of our problems.

My union with Claire seems to piss off the entire globe. The werewolves basically said, "F*ck the treaty." And it all started with the dog b*tch Mecca. We recently discovered that she had done a lot of eavesdropping during her time in the dungeon and used all the information she'd obtained to stir up trouble in South America. Apparently, the only way she was able to sway the werewolf community was by forming a new treaty with the hunters. Together they have freed more than a thousand of future slaves from the boarding schools in North America over the last two weeks. The b*tch's plan has made her a hero to humans, an asset to hunters, and a war goddess to the werewolves. She is now rumored to be the commander of the new werewolf army, and thanks to the lycan prince's infatuation for Cyrus's beloved, Embry. The lycans not only blessed the she-wolf's path of vengeance, but they also decided to join her on her path to destruction.

The she-wolf b*tch has officially become a royal pain in my ass. North America and South America are really spiraling out of control. To make matters worse, I learned all about this information only two nights ago. Luckily for Claire, my dog-loving beloved, she was the one to receive the news from Count Cloven, and instead of notifying me and the other kings right away, she burned the letter—in an attempt to keep this information from getting to us. She believed she would be able to get the situation under control in secret. She thought she could handle it in a peaceful way.

When I was first informed about it and confronted Claire, she rolled her eyes and stated, "The slaves aren't going to be slaves for much longer anyway, Nicklaus. Get over it."

Get over it? I swear I could have f*cked her to death, making her tight walls fold while she'd be screaming, "I apologize, Nicklaus! I'm sorry, my king."

She is so stubborn. She believes her pet Mecca would soon calm down and won't take it too far. "She is a good person, Nicklaus. She will eventually see reason," she told me. Oh boy, was she wrong? As a consequence of her actions, the werewolves were able to attack and raid Cyrus's estate. They killed any and every vampire on sight, including Cyrus's aunt. My best friend won't ever be able to bury her properly. Count Cloven informed us that the werewolves had ripped her to shreds. He made it back to us this morning, seconds away from death with a box stringed around his neck. Inside the box was the head of Cyrus's darling aunt, Lady Katherine, with a note attached that read, "Death to all leeches. And oh, f*ck your treaty gift."

It doesn't take a rocket scientist to learn who created the nickname for vampires. Thankfully, Cyrus doesn't blame my hard-headed beloved. He understands that she has a gentle heart. Even so, there is no excuse for the loss we suffered because of her lack of judgment. What's done is done, but we will not rest until we rid the world of their kind, with the exemption of Embry of course. Cyrus didn't even wait for my permission to once again declare war. Honestly, he didn't have to because at this point the declaration is set in stone.

Lady Katherine was not only his aunt but was also a second mother to all of us. She was a legend in the vampire community. Every single low and respected households loved her. The council members, including my father, respected her. Before he met my mother, Lady Katherine was his chosen queen many moons ago. She was the perfect candidate. To be quite frank, I think he should have picked her. A lot of things would have been different if he had. She was everything my mother is not, and I mean that in the most-humble way. I loved her. Claire would have loved her too. She will truly be missed.

This morning when we received the news, I was blinded by rage and completely lost my cool. I told Claire I made the wrong choice, and that she was a disgrace of a queen. That was just the start. I said a lot of things to break her heart, and I'm not proud of it. But again, what's done is done.

Claire really doesn't understand that her foolish attachment to the dog can be our downfall. The she-wolf b*tch is bitter as f*ck. She won't rest until she makes all of us vampire kings suffer and feel what we've made her feel—pain and loss—over the last century.

I made Claire pick a side, which is completely against her nature. However, in this moment we don't need a tender-hearted queen. We need a ruthless one who refuses to show mercy and won't stop until all our enemies are dead. Claire chose the latter. She chose me as she should.

Keeping the information from us has made her appear to be an accomplice to the she-wolf's crimes. If her betrayal is discovered, the vampire community will never accept her, nor will they continue to follow our rule. F*ck, they are already rebelling against us, which brings me to problem number two. Over the last couple of weeks, trouble has been brewing in the circling kingdoms. As a result to the council's arrest, the respected families have been stepping out of line. They demanded the release of the council members, most importantly my father.

No can do. My outright refusal led to another awakening. The slaves call it the New Awakening. Humans were massacred all around Europe, Africa, and Asia. Well, at least a few humans in Asia were able to survive. At this point, all humans there may officially be extinct. To add to the equation, my mother and sister were the number one instigators to that problem. They even started a campaign with the slogan "Death to the hybrid queen," resulting in problem number three. My mother and sister's campaign has caused multiple riots and numerous death threats against Claire, and many whisper about the rebellion that's surely on the horizon. It has been hell—a f*cking disaster!

The other kings and the queen are exhausted. I am exhausted. Claire and I are barely able to spend quality time together, not to mention our arguments today. Basically, the palace is full of tension, and let's not forget about the fact that Xander completely abandoned us. Yup, he took the f*ck off after learning that his late beloved was Claire's birth mother. I believe the pain of Claire being the daughter of Bella and her human lover was just too much for him to bear. Claire believed otherwise. She said she felt a change in Xander through their bond. She thinks he feels like he failed her when my father almost ended her life.

I can only hope she is right, and I am wrong because if I am right, there is a huge possibility that Xander has lost his humanity and returned to his old roots, once again claiming the title the Cold-Hearted King. And if that is the case, so help whatever soul that he crosses.

The other kings and I were shocked when Claire retold the story that had been presented to her during her dream-state. I mean she is special. I've known that since day one; we all have, but none of us expected she would be proclaimed the Chosen One. Whatever the f*ck that's supposed to mean.

Plus, Aurora was supposed to be her surrogate mother. I mean Aurora is Claire and her twin's surrogate mother. Who would have thought about that? I kind of felt bad that I almost killed her brother. Sike! I just told Claire I did and apologized just to make her happy. The truth is if I knew what I know now and was presented with the same situation, I would drain that human of every ounce of blood, just like I told him I would the very moment Claire left us alone. I also said to him to go with Cyrus when it was time to depart, or else . . . I don't trust him, and I want him to be as far away from Claire as possible, brother or not.

There is a reason why my sister freed him, and I will get to the bottom of it. As they say what's done in the dark will be brought to the light. Claire is the light, and I am the darkness that will bring her all the heads of our enemies lurking in the shadows. Mark my words! Whoever goes against me and the true queen shall die.

To end all this bullsh*t going on, Cyrus and Luscious returned to their kingdoms to wage war against the hunters and werewolves. Vlad tagged along, as expected. Claire's brother was forced to go, but she doesn't know that. Marcellus, Rufus, and Seneca also returned to their kingdoms to regain control, with orders to use force if need be. Xander is off the map while Cornelius and Claire's friend, Jadis, are still here for the time being, which has everything to do with Jadis of course. She refused to leave Claire, who needs her the most. I'm really starting to like this girl. I admit she has spunk.

This brings me to the final problem we must solve. Due to the urgent departure of the other kings, we were forced to postpone Claire's crowning ceremony. In other words, she is not the legal queen, on papers anyway. Yup. In the moment we are royally screwed. That's exactly why I am in my study, drowning my troubles. Thanks to my other close friend, gold ole Jack.

"Nicklaus, I need to talk to you," says Claire, as she barges into my study, officially putting an end to my train of thought.

"Of course, you do." I quickly spin my chair around and pretend to be looking out of the window. I can't look at her.

Claire is wearing a ruby-red silk slip dress that does little justice to hiding her goddess-given curves. The piece of clothing— its lack of material—was created to make my dick hard. Claire's face is fresh, with absolutely no makeup, just as I like it. Her hair is in its natural state, loose golden waves flowing all the way down to that firm ass of hers. She looks like magic.

*F\*ck, f\*ck, f\*ck, I am hard. Goddamn her.*

"Don't turn your back to me, you f\*cking fanger!" she insults, using that tone that makes my dick twitch.

*Fanger! What? Looks like someone came up with a new insult.*

"Fanger," I quote, turning around to face her, with my legendary smirk.

She growls at me. She hates how much she loves my smirk.

"Come on, Claire, you can do better than that."

"Would it be better if I called you a blood-sucking lee—"

"You'd better not state those words out of your mouth ever again!" I raise my voice, hopping out of my chair quicker than one could blink.

"My apologies," she responds, sounding guilty.

She should be.

"I was just coming in to say that I . . . that I . . ." her voice trails off, starting to crack, "that I . . ." She tries to continue as her eyes become watery.

"Shhhhh." I stand in front her and catch a single tear with my finger before it has the time to fall down her beautiful face. Immediately, I take her into my arms. My unbeaten heart breaks. I don't like seeing her cry, or worse being the primary source of her tears. "Don't you dare say another word, firecracker."

She slightly pulls away. "No. You need to hear—"

I pull her back into my arms with a soft growl, completely cutting her off. "My word is final, Claire. I don't want to hear more. What's done is done, my love. It's time to move on."

"But you said—"

"Let it go."

"But I—"

"I said let it go, Claire. Yes, you made a wrong decision, but who am I to judge? I've also made many decisions that I am not proud of. I have caused so many deaths. I have left children fatherless, left children motherless, and murdered entire families. All of us vampire kings have done barbaric things. The vampire race in general has done terrible things.

"Losing Katherine was nowhere near the amount of bad karma we deserve," I confess, telling her the truth that I would never admit to anyone.

Claire is now back in my arms where she belongs, crying a river.

F*ck, I f*cked up!

"Firecracker," I say, pulling away and lifting her chin up with my finger, "stop what you're doing at once." I look at her, and I fall straight into those smoky forest-green eyes.

Claire is a perfectly cut diamond—beautiful, luminous, and strong. I am so blessed to have her.

She cups my face, and her silk-like touch feels otherworldly.

"You are an angel. No. Better yet, you are a goddess. Please forgive me for my sins."

"I thought I was the devil's wife, Nicklaus," she responds, reeling me in with her melodic voice, like a siren singing to sailors and forcing them to crash their ship.

I sink.

"You are, baby," I tease. "That you are."

She hooks her arms around my neck, making my monster purr from her golden touch. God of all blood, I swear on everything that I love, I'm way past the point of being in love with this girl.

"But you don't have faith in my rule," she states. Her mesmerizing smile turns upside down. "You don't believe I'm fit to rule," she repeats the exact words I said to her during our argument earlier today.

"I didn't mean any of those things, Claire. I am an idiot, absolutely the biggest dickhead on this entire planet. I don't deserve you. Claire, you are courageous, beautiful, kindhearted, headstrong, and brave. I am a coward, cold-hearted, somewhat tractable, and not so brave."

"Oh, and you're a monster," she adds, with a soft smile.

There it goes. Her happiness means ten times more than my pride.

"You're right, firecracker. I am very much so a monster. I am a tyrant in my own right. You see, the world knows me as the most-barbaric of all the vampire kings. Unfortunately for you, that funny word called fate decide to say, 'F*ck you,' and chose you to be my beloved, the Chosen One and the true queen."

"How unfortunate?" she teases.

"Yes, how unfortunate," I say.

She crashes her lips into mine, making me lose focus and taking my breath away. F*ck, fate is so good, so good! How the hell did I get this lucky? The taste of milk and honey washes all over my tongue—so sweet, so thick, and so refreshing. Again, I find myself lost. Our kiss is long and desperate—exactly what we need.

I pull away, slightly on desperate need of air. My penis is as hard as a rock. If I hadn't stopped, I would have taken her right here hard and fast, which wouldn't be a problem if she wasn't still a little banged up. She whines, like she always does, totally oblivious to the effect she has on me or my body.

"Our children shall be the unfortunate ones," I joke, earning a growl from her.

"Don't you dare say such a thing," she scolds me, looking absolutely adorable. "Our children will be surrounded by love. They will be kind, well-mannered, and brave. They won't take sh*t from anybody, that's for sure. We shall be the best parents we can be, that is when I find a way to break this stupid ass curse."

"You will make a good mother," I tell her God's honest truth, while making my way down to her tummy. "I, on the other hand, will need a lot of preparation for the task." I kiss her belly, only to come to a complete halt.

"Nicklaus?"

My heart falls out of my chest.

"Nicklaus?"

*No, I must be mistaken.*

"Nicklaus, what's wrong?"

*I'm dead literally; a stake has been plunged into my heart.*

"Nicklaus, you're freaking me out."

I lean a little closer, tightening my hold onto her belly in the process.

"Nicklaus, what the—"

"You're pregnant!"

In that exact moment I hear her soft heart skip a beat, and my child's heartbeat pick up. No. Our children's heartbeats pick up. Claire is pregnant with twins. She faints upon knowing it.

# BONUS CHAPTER ONE
## The Luna

MECCA

*Hudson, New York*

Goddess Luna has been very good to me. She has delivered me from evil, placed me in a position of greater power, and most importantly has guided me during my journey back home to once again stand alongside my mate. And I'm forever grateful. She has forced me to humble myself and taught me patience.

You see before the Awakening, I was stuck in my ways and bigheaded like many other wolves. I was as arrogant as a lycan and was physically, emotionally, and mentally weak like a human. If that wasn't enough, I was just as selfish as a hunter. Eventually, that all changed.

During my time of incarceration, I was knocked off my high horse. Every day, the leeches found new ways to break me. They starved me to death, refused to give me even a single drop of water. They beat me with silver whips on a daily basis. Once done, they would insert a needle into my skin that released different amounts of silver liquid inside my veins.

The worst part of it all was after the punishment, all I could do was think. It drove me crazy at first. I constantly thought about my mate, my pack, the life that I could only dream of living once again, and my revenge. This was my day-to-day life the entire time I was held captive. My wolf's nature was almost nonexistent, my human body was broken, and my mind was lost.

That was the weakest point of my life. I remember dropping down to my knees with a tear-stained face, begging Goddess Luna to release me from my pain. I remember questioning her plan and doubting her true power. Lucky for me, she was gracious enough to answer my questions. She came to me in a dream and whispered, "Pay attention." I didn't understand what she meant, but I chose to follow her command. I paid attention. I watched the hellfire inside the dungeon burn brighter. I watched the leeches claim the world as their playground and put many species—werewolves, hunters, lycans, humans, and even some gypsies—in chains. Witches were the only ones excluded, and that's only because no one messes with them. No one!

I watched their eagerness to form a new world order and dominate other species. I watched them treat others like scum and a pile of horse sh*t. I watched them make many, many enemies, so I decided to make my enemies my friends. Now, I have a number of friends. I formed alliances with different creatures from all walks of life, and one in particular was a highly respected hunter from South America named Forrest. We had served a life sentence together, and had had constant discussions about what we would do if we ever had a chance to get our revenge. One day, we talked about forming a treaty between werewolves and hunters. We made a promise that if either of us was able to escape, we would set plays in motion to achieve our ultimate goal.

Forrest actually managed to escape. Ironically enough, so did I shortly after. Our plan to form an alliance worked out better than we had anticipated. Together, we successfully freed many humans, raided the estate of the ruthless leech and killed his precious darling aunt—yeah, payback's a b*tch! The best part is that it's only the beginning. When it comes to the leech kings, I can only swear on the Goddess herself that it shall get worse, much worse. Luna's passing day is on the horizon. Before it comes, I promise my wolf that vengeance shall be ours.

Today is the day that Forrest's hunter group, all four werewolf packs of North America, and the lycans shall come together and discuss our plans to bring forth retribution on the leeches and devise a plan to end their world domination altogether. I'm now walking through the pack grounds, waiting for word of their arrival.

"Luna!" calls Rendell, walking up from behind me. "I mean Commander. I mean Luna."

"Luna is fine." I turn around to face him.

This has been happening to me all week. The wolves from my pack don't know the best way to address me.

"I may be a commander now, but I've always been your Luna."

Rendell offers a small smile.

"Now, what can I help you with?" I ask, as we continue to walk.

"Alpha Maddox wanted me to inform you that our guests have arrived."

"Great! And did all the expected to attend arrive?" I ask, as we walk toward a group of pups playing hide and hunt.

"Luna! Luna! Luna!" the pups shout as soon as they sense our approach, stopping our conversation.

This is another thing that's been happening all week. The pups cannot get enough of me, which sometimes makes it harder for me to step into my role as commander. We werewolves don't place our problems on our pups's backs, unlike leeches, who from day one fill the heads of their young with hatred. We are better than them. The were-people refuse to taint our young's innocence. We value their childhood and goodness. We allow our pups to be pups.

I lower my body and scoop all six of them into my arms, then I give them a big hug. Beta Rendell steps to the side with a wolfish grin, and patiently waits for me.

736

"Luna, I am going to grow up and be just like you," says Quebell, Omega Nicholson's daughter.

"I'm going to be better than you, Luna," her twin sister Bluebell says right after.

Beta Rendell chuckles. I give him one look, and his laughter disappears immediately. But the wolfish grin goes absolutely nowhere.

The redhead Bell twins of the Northern Pack are known to be two legendary identical little devils. They are beautiful, bubbly, and brave. However, they are also a tornado and hurricane all in one—double trouble!

"Is that right?" I ask Bluebell. I turn my head to face her and release the group.

The other pups all run off to continue their game of hide and hunt, but the Bell twins stay.

"Yup," Bluebell responds, popping her *p*. "My father said I should always strive for greatness. You are great, Luna, so I shall be greater. I will be greater than you," she declares without an ounce of doubt.

"Father also said that the only person you should try to be better than is the wolf you were yesterday, Blue," reminds Quebell. "You should compete with yourself only."

"No one asked you, Que!" Bluebell's eyes glow bright yellow. Her little wolf wants to come out to play.

"So what, Blue? I said what I said, and I mean what I say," Quebell states, starting to size her sister up.

You see what I mean? A tornado and a hurricane all in one, double trouble. When they come, you shall seek shelter.

"Hey, hey, hey! No wolf-poking," I scold the two little devils, pushing them apart. "I believe that we all can agree on your father being extremely disappointed if he was told that the two of you have gotten into another fight. Am I right?"

"Yes, Luna," they answer, bowing their heads in unison.

"I also believe we all can agree that your father would be extremely upset if he was told that the two of you were bothering your Luna instead of playing hide and hunt. Am I correct?"

"Yes, Luna," they answer in unison again.

"And I believe we all can agree that your father would be extremely wolf-ruffled if he was told that the two of you had once again managed to sneak into the kitchen and ate up all of the dessert again before dinner. Am I correct?"

"Yes, Luna."

"Wait!" Bluebell shouts out, lifting up her head. "We didn't sneak into the kitchen."

"Yeah." Quebell catches on last. "We have been out here playing all day. You can ask the other pups and the human kids that you brought back home with you."

"Yeah." Bluebell crosses her arms. "We have a witness."

Beta Rendell loses control and bursts out laughing, and I laugh along this time.

"Oh, is that right?"

"Yes, Luna. We swear on our tails," Quebell adds.

I lower myself to be at their eye level. "Well, I guess the two of you have an alibi then." I shrug. "That means mama wolf's sweet cherry pie is just sitting on the kitchen counter all by itself. A pup is going to sneak a piece sooner than later, and their parents's tails are going to go up.

"Awe, someone is going to get in trouble," they say.

"Yeah, they are!" I widen my eyes. "But it won't be you two because you have an alibi."

Their thunderstorm-like eyes meet and then come their cute little smirks. Without another word, the twins run off in the direction of the pack house.

*Two little devils!*

"They are going to do great things one day," Rendell acknowledges, watching them run off.

"Yeah, they are." I stand back up. "Destruct and destroy."

He laughs at that and then he gets straight back to business. "All who were expected to attend have arrived, including the strange group of hunter friends."

Now, it's my turn to laugh. The hunters are great soldiers, but their way of life is very strange.

"Even though they are strange," he continues, "I believe your idea to form an alliance with them was genius. You really do have a gift of making the right friends, Luna."

I nod, and we continue our walk through the pack grounds.

"Claire was also a great person. I hope she is okay," he suddenly says, riling up my wolf.

My eyes glow bright yellow. "I told you to never utter the name of the leech's lover ever again!" I spit, walking ahead of him.

"My apologies, Luna." He chases after me. "It's just . . . Claire is—"

"The leech queen!" I quickly turn back around to face him.

This is another thing that has been happening all week. Beta Rendell defends Claire every chance he gets, and it's really starting to tick me off. He knows what she has done to me.

"She made her choice, and she chose them," I remind him for what seems like the thousandth time. "She is young and naïve." My head falls back, laughter exploding from my chest. "How are you defending a person you don't even know?" I question him, my tongue laced with sarcasm.

"Claire may be young, but she is far from naive," he states.

Between me and Goddess Luna, that human may have more worldly knowledge and experience than some centuries-old werewolves I know. She has greater appreciation and understanding of things than any other human I've met in this century. That human has an old soul.

"She was brainwashed, like many other humans," is his next defense, and all I can do is laugh harder.

Oh boy! He really doesn't know Claire. One thing's for certain: Claire's mind or body will never be willing to break or bend for any soul on this earth, not even for her leech king.

Beta Rendell's frustration is evident. The wolf has got it bad for the brave little human.

"Does Farrah know about your little high school crush?" I tease, in between my laughter. "Your liking to the leech queen is obvious. Our Goddess has granted you a second-chance mate, yet your mind is thinking about someone else. How could you be so ungrateful?"

His eyes flash bright yellow—look at that. I hit a spot!

"How could you turn your back on the person who broke bread with you when no one else cared when you starved? How could you turn your back on someone who risked her life in an attempt to save yours? She freed you, Luna. If it hadn't been for her, you wouldn't be here; we wouldn't be here. She deserves our loyalty. She deserves you to be the friend she was to you," he speaks out of line, crossing all boundaries.

Without warning, my hand grabs his neck, and before he has time to react, I have slammed him straight into a tree. My wolf's claws dig deep into his skin. She doesn't like his tone or appreciate his choice of words, and neither does my human side. I am his superior. Beta Rendell seems to have forgotten his place.

"Do I need to remind you who the hell you are speaking to?" I and my wolf release a growl. I stare him directly in the eye, daring his wolf to challenge mine.

He immediately lowers his neck to show complete submission. "No, Luna. Please, forgive me."

"Good," I hiss through clenched teeth. I let him go and storm off. My wolf wants to rip off his head, so I need to get out of here fast.

"Luna, wait!" Rendell once again runs after me.

"What is it?" I snap.

This is another thing that has been happening all week. If a pack member calls my name, I have to answer them, mad or not.

"I apologize for offending you. It's just I can't help but feel like the leeches forced Claire to accept immortality," he carries on.

I give it to him! He is persistent—foolish but very persistent. Beta Rendell truly is a fool in love.

My head knocks back with laughter once again. "One cannot be forced to become a leech, Rendell. They have to accept it," I state, educating him. "Claire becoming a leech was by choice not by force, trust me."

He lowers his head in defeat.

"Now, if you don't have any more questions, I'll have to excuse myself and go prepare for the meeting."

This time Beta Rendell allows me to walk away in peace, or at least I thought so.

"We could just eliminate the leech kings, Luna. They are the real threats."

"Once again, you're wrong. With that attitude, we will lose the war. We can't place all of our focus on the kings," are my last words. I walk back to the pack house in a hurry, praying to my Goddess that I don't run into any more pack members. Being a Luna can be overwhelming at times, and right now I just need a few moments alone.

Once I walk through the house and come into contact with the familiar midnight-blue walls, my wolf purrs within me. Out of all the places in the entire mansion, my private wing is the only area where I can let my hair down. This is the only area in the house where I can have privacy and take a moment to worry about myself. I have my mate to thank for that.

My eyes travel over the wall filled with photos of my life before the Awakening, and I take a trip down memory lane.

*So much has changed; I've changed. Back then, I was a wolf more in tune with my human side. I even had human friends, and lived a reckless and carefree life. I was so naive.*

741

"What's troubling you, my goddess," my mate, Maddox, asks from behind me. He wraps his strong arms around my waist, his woodsy and pine scent covering me whole.

My wolf does somersaults inside my chest.

"Nothing much. I'm just pondering, papa wolf. There is nothing to worry about." I lean my head back and slide my hands down his pants.

Whenever we're alone, all we want to do is f*ck. The beasts within our bodies crave each other's touch. My pussy is always on fire around my mate, and his dick has no problem extinguishing the flame. F*ck, just thinking about it makes me wet.

Maddox's nostrils flare widely, and his magnificent eyes flash that fascinating shade of golden that I love so much.

*Thank Goddess for pairing me with a Wilde wolf. They are the hottest werewolf men that have ever existed—another reason I am forever grateful for.*

"Someone wants to get f*cked," Maddox huskily whispers.

"I always want to get f*cked," I howl.

"And I'm always wiggling to f*ck that sweet little pussy of yours into submission. But first, we must discuss what you were just thinking about, then I'll let the dog out."

My head falls back in laughter, my eyes filled with tears of joy. I turn around and wrap my arms around his neck.

*Thank you, thank you, thank you, Moon Goddess once again.*

"That is your decision to keep that 'Cane Corso' inside your pants, but I don't feel like talking about unimportant matters."

"Anything that flows through your beautifully deranged head is important, Mecca. I told you to never forget that."

"Hmmmm." I sigh, laying my head onto his chest.

"Hey, look at me," he demands, forcing me to actually look up at him.

My papa wolf doesn't like any wolf to disobey an order, including his mate. Maddox is prideful, dominant, and demanding.

He doesn't take disrespect lightly. This characteristic is exactly what turns me on.

"I was just thinking about the leech queen. Beta Rendell spoke on her behalf again, but this time he crossed boundaries."

My mate's eyes swirl ultraviolet radiation as his alpha aura comes forth. "Then he shall be dealt with," he growls, moving his body away.

"I already dealt with him." I grab his arm to prevent him from leaving. "He showed his submission."

"As he should. The little f*ck is lucky he is still alive after the sh*t he pulled off with my niece. My brother wolf still wants his blood. The only thing that is saving him is our friendship and our Goddess's pairing, although I still don't understand why she would pair the two as second-chance mates."

"It isn't your place to question our Goddess, papa wolf," I say, teaching him what I've been taught. "Everything happens for a reason, and Hunter needs to let it go. This is not the time to fall apart and beef with one another. This is the time that we wolves stay united."

He pulls me back into his arms and kisses my forehead. Once again, my wolf purrs. We love it when he does that.

"You're correct, my goddess. Now, can you finally tell me what Beta Rendell said that poked your wolf."

My mate is also the type of wolf that doesn't let sh*t go, so I might as well tell him.

"It wasn't what he said. It was how he said it," I confess. "My wolf was only upset because he questioned my heart. He threw everything that Claire has done for me at my face. Rendell doesn't understand that destroying her isn't something I want to do but have to."

"And why do you have to do that, my goddess?" he asks cautiously. "I know you feel betrayed. You have every right to, but we can bring them down and grant her mercy."

"A king is nothing without his queen. Without her, he will fall. Without him, they all shall fall, like I said. I have no choice but to end her. Trust me, Claire is the one to focus on. The reason why he stayed on top is because he had no weakness, but that all changed when he found her. Claire is his weakness. I just hate that she is his beloved," I explain, my tears suddenly starting to flow.

Maddox doesn't respond. He just holds me and allows me to have a moment of weakness, and we stand like this for a long while.

"I understand that you feel like you owe the leech queen," he finally speaks again, "but if we are going to declare war and then freeze up in battle, you have to get over her, my goddess. Your mind has to be clear."

"I know, I know." I wipe away my tears and turn my back to him, focusing back on the wall filled with photos. My eyes lock on the picture of the cold-hearted leech king, Bella, and me.

I remember that day as if it were yesterday. She was so upset that I wouldn't drive that beat-up red car. She cursed me out for hours, only to stop when the cold-hearted king placed his arms around her neck and said, "Smile." Only Goddess knows how much I miss her.

Then, my eyes travel to the picture of Claire and me, captured by one of the older she-wolves. It was the day of the bonfire. She looks beautiful and extremely happy. I remember her making silly faces at me whenever I made eye contact and how she would stare directly in the eye at any supernatural being that dared to display dominance over her. She showed no fear, and that was when she was my brave little human, and deep down inside she always will be. I will always love her even after I end her.

# BONUS CHAPTER TWO
## The Cold-Hearted King

XANDER

*Elephant Island, Antarctica*

I'm shattered, just like the old-fashioned glass of whiskey I've thrown at the thick brick wall of my palace. I'm hurt, constantly searching for ways to end this never-ending cycle of unbearable pain. I'm trying my hardest to fill the void I've been feeling for over a century. I'm broken—beyond damaged and officially marked as irreparable. I'm a lost cause, and no one can do anything to fix it.

I was under the impression that Claire could help me. In all honesty, I believed she somehow managed to fix the shattered pieces of me, and maybe in some ways she did. Her defiant and brave nature awakened a more genuine side of me that I had long buried. Her gentle touch brought my humanity back to life. Her clever and stubborn nature drove my monster crazy. She made me feel emotions again, for the first time in over a century; she flipped my humanity switch back on.

However, she fixed me only to break me, unintentionally of course. She will never deliberately hurt me. Claire can't control who her mother is. She can't control the fact that I was the idiot that allowed her mother's soft touch slip through my fingers. It was my fault. That's exactly why I'm sitting here in my frozen palace, drowning my sorrows and shattering the glass shortly after. Claire can't control that I'm a waste of life. She doesn't even have the slightest clue that I'm this weak, that I am a wreck. Just like her mother, she loves me for all my flaws—like mother, like daughter.

F*ck, I hate my life. I can feel myself sinking back into darkness, burying my true nature underground. My humanity is slowly but surely slipping away. I want to give in. I want to unleash further hell onto this wasteland of an earth. I want to burn down cities, take my fill of whoever and whatever blood, and make others feel the pain I feel. As fun as that may sound, I can't and will not allow that to happen.

See? That's my problem. I'm miserable, and we all know that misery loves company. My biggest issue is I refuse to make Claire my miserable companion because that is exactly what will happen if I allow my humanity to slip. She will be miserable, and that's out of the f*cking question. Losing my humanity won't do anyone any good, especially her. In fact, it may just make things ten times worse. The world is already in complete chaos. Hunters, werewolves, and lycans have all teamed up to come against us, kings.

On top of that, vampire kingdoms are spiraling out of control, starting with nonstop riots and the free-the-council bullsh*t campaigns—not to mention the fact that human death count is skyrocketing by the day, which I wouldn't give two sh*ts about if it weren't for Claire.

F*ck, I'm officially going crazy. All of it is too much. I'm battling with myself, with my inner demon. My people need me. Nicklaus and Claire need me. The other kings need me. Every-f*cking-body needs me, but who the f*ck can I run to in my time of need? Who the f*ck can I run to when I feel my control altering? Who can I run to when times get hard? You know who? No-f*cking-body, ever since Isabella—my love, my heart, my soul,

746

my reason for existence—disappeared from the face of this dreadful earth.

Ever since she was gone, I've been in pain and been dealing with venomous rage. She meant so much to me, but all we had is nothing but history and painful memories. I haven't been the same ever since. Well, at least I wasn't until Claire came into the picture. And she happens to be my beloved's daughter, fathered by another man. F*ck!

I throw another glass at the wall. It shatters, becoming nothing but a reflection of my soul.

I'm so f*cking sick of it all. Who would have ever thought that Bella is Claire's mother? Let's not also forget that Aurora, the witch b*tch, carried my beloved's offspring in her womb for over a century, only to drop her load off out of nowhere. Like seriously, what the actual f*ck! I feel like that b*tch did that to spite me. I hate her. She was always against my and Bella's union after I f*cked up. That b*tch acted as if a person doesn't make mistakes. She was another reason why my Bella ended up with children with another man. If it hadn't been for that goddamn cloaking spell she placed on Bella, I would have located her sooner, then none of this would have happened.

*Could you blame her?* my inner voice of reason states.

*Oh, shut the hell up!*

I feel like I have two different beings on my shoulder—a devil and an angel. Both of them are attempting to sway me into their direction. Yup, it's official, I'm going crazy.

*Who am I kidding? It's not her fault. It's still my fault,* I think to myself, smashing yet another glass.

This is how I'm dealing with the pain. My head is spinning. I am going numb. How could I ever be so stupid? All I had to do was accept her. F*ck, I miss her. I'll always miss her.

\*      \*      \*

"Brave one," I called out to my beautiful beloved as I walked into our chambers.

The sight of Isabella always took my breath away, and that day was no different. She forever had that effect on me. I remember the first time I laid eyes on her. I was walking through the human-infested streets of New York City so I could take a ferry to New Jersey. At the time, my brother was staying in one of his many estates there, and I missed him gravely. It would have been much easier for me to travel through the forests, but then I would have risked running into one of the many werewolf packs of America. I didn't really have the patience or time to deal with those dogs, so I had no choice but to blend in with human society.

I walked into Starbucks—one of their many coffee shops of humans—to buy a cup of their overly priced coffee. I had to stand in their ridiculously long-ass line, and to say I was annoyed would be an understatement; I was pissed.

By the time I reached the register, I pulled my sunglasses down to avoid humans from seeing my bloodshot-red eyes. That was the moment when the most-intoxicating scent of spicy cinnamon invaded my senses with no warning, forcing me to silently search the entire surroundings. I took a deep whiff of the scent that was driving my inner monster crazy, only to come face-to-face with a woman. She was curvy in all the right places and had chestnut-brown hair and coffee-colored eyes. The sight of the human operating a cash register took my breath away, literally. I was stunned.

At first, she seemed surprised that all of the other humans just randomly decided to leave, but she looked relieved, until she saw me. "Why the hell are you wearing sunglasses in the middle of December?" the human girl asked. "Never mind. That's none of my business. What can I get for you?"

I couldn't respond. I was in shock.

"Hello, buddy, are you deaf?" She waved her hand in front of me like I was a statue. "I asked you a question."

748

"And I chose not to answer," I told her, when I finally managed to find my voice.

"Well, in case you are pretending to be blind as well," she responded with a smirk, "I have . . . you know . . . You are at my register, and it is my job to take your order."

"I don't want you to take my order," I shot back, and really I meant that. I'd prefer to be taken into the bathroom and be allowed to sink my fangs into her delicate flesh.

The human girl started tapping her foot. She had zero to no patience and a low tolerance for bullsh*t. But for some strange reason, that only seemed to turn me on.

"Look here, buddy, I don't have time for your games. You can order now like a normal person, or get the hell out of my line!"

"Isabella!" warned a short, fat, and bald human beside her.

"Aww, shut the hell up," she snapped at him. She obviously hated her job.

I couldn't help but smile. She sure did have a little temper, a mean and feisty little thing.

"You know what, John, I've had it with this sh*t. I quit!" she yelled, then threw her apron at his face. "I'd rather live with my nuisance of a mother for the rest of my life than deal with this sh*t."

Yup, she was most certainly feisty. Now, typically I would be disgusted with a woman behaving in such a manner, but Isabella's behavior made me feel quite the opposite. She drew me in.

"Oh and you, thank you for being such a dick," she mocked, taking her frustration out on me again. "You have really done me a huge favor," she said, horribly attempting to show gratitude. "In fact, I owe you a free drink."

Now that caught me off guard. I was the customer who pissed her off so bad that she quit, and what did she do?

"Really?" I remember saying.

"Bella," the human man warned her once again.

"I sure do," she sassed him, then completely ignored him. She flashed a wicked smile that made her coffee-colored eyes glint. "Take this," she hissed and threw a cup of lukewarm coffee directly at my face.

What the f*ck just happened? I couldn't believe it. No human ever had the balls to do anything to me. In fact, they were typically too afraid to get close to any vampires. It was like they had a sixth sense telling them to stay far away from us. But not her. She had no fear. She was certainly the bravest human I'd ever encountered, and I was undeniably infatuated with her—even if she was the most-impatient, ill-mannered, or irrational person I'd ever met in my centuries of existence. Little did I know that the brave little human's throwing a drink in my face was only the beginning.

"I hate it when you call me that," Bella complained, turning around to face me and bringing me back to the present. Her eyes flicker with annoyance. "I so much prefer something like heroic hero, captain courageous, or brave bell."

"Brave bell," I teased. I wrapped my arms around her tiny but curvy frame and then pull her into my arms.

She wrapped her arms around my neck.

"It actually has a nice ring to it."

"Yeah, it does," Bella teased, rolling her eyes and making funny faces.

*I thank the Blood God for bringing this woman back into my life. I have been lost without her. I have been foolish.*

"I was a fool for not claiming you right away," I confessed my deepest regret while staring directly into my beloved's beautiful and bold eyes.

"Yeah, you were," she teased again, her mouth curving into a coy smile.

Even a deaf man could hear how serious she sounded.

"Yeah, I was." I lowered my head down and placed my lips closer to her plump and delicious ones.

750

"And now you have to spend centuries's worth of time chasing after me." Her coy smile deepened.

"Now that I can, brave bell, I'll follow you to the ends of the world."

"Really?"

I could see the wicked glint in her irises. She was up to something. She was always up to something.

"Let's test that theory, shall we?" challenged Bella.

This woman loved to challenge me. She was so goddamn infuriating, always had been and always would be. I'd never met a creature so hell-bent on driving me into the brink of insanity until Bella walked into my life. Well, I walked into her life, but that would defeat the purpose. I was just so lucky.

I captured her soft lips with my own, officially turning the tables around and taking her breath away—it worked like a charm every time. She allowed me to have my way with her for just a second, following my lead. It did not last long, for Bella loved taking control. This was how it started. I kissed her and then she took over. It didn't bother me, though. In fact, I loved it. I loved everything about this infuriating girl.

Bella's cinnamon spice scent sank into my senses, and my inner monster went crazy. Her smell was like my favorite drug. She was intoxicating. I wanted to hold my breath and imprint her aroma inside my nose forever. I wanted to hold her and never let her go. As expected, she deepened our kiss and took full control. She sucked and nibbled gently on my bottom lip, only to turn around to seal the deal with a single slick across my top lip with the tip of her savory tongue. I loved it when she did that sh*t. Shivers ran through my entire body, taking me to my happy place. This woman did sweet things to me. I was so in love.

"I love you, babe," she whispered huskily.

I'd used to hate pet names until she had one for me.

"I love you more, brave bell."

"Impossible," she said, pecking my lips gently one last time.

"Nothing is impossible."

"Don't say that," she stopped me, scrunching up her little nose. "You sound like my mom."

I rolled my eyes at that. Bella had a bad habit of comparing me to her witch b*tch of a mom. "And you're acting like my mother."

Her eyes grew wide. "I hate to break it to you, babe, but your mother is the devil's wife. No one is that evil," she commented.

Laughter exploded from my lungs.

"Not even Daniela and the world knows that she is one wicked b*tch," she added.

"Hey, hey, hey! She is still my mother," I said in between my fit of laughter.

"How unfortunate you are!" she quipped.

Both of us knew damn well that she was speaking nothing but the truth. My family was f*cked up.

"Did you mean it when you said you would chase me to the ends of the earth?" Bella asked. The wicked glint in her eyes returned.

I lowered my head to kiss her soft and gentle lips once again. "Of course, I did, brave bell."

"Good! Then, I guess you'd better start." She turned around.

The next thing I knew, Bella was already breaking out of the room. I watched my beloved with a smile on my face.

God, I love that woman.

*　　　*　　　*

"Look at yourself. You're a wreck! Get the hell up," says the last person I've expected to hear in my godforsaken kingdom, smacking me back to reality.

I open my eyes only to see the one and only Aurora. She is standing directly in front of me with her hands placed on both sides.

"How the hell did you get inside my palace?" I ask her with a slur.

"Did you really believe your weak-ass witch protection wards are strong enough to keep me out?" She rolls her eyes. "Get yourself together now. Claire needs you."

I struggle to pull myself up off the ground—when and how did I get this drunk? F*ck, my head hurts.

"You smell like a bucket of whiskey," she scolds me, like she gives a f*ck. "You're a f*cking idiot. Bella would be so disappointed."

"Don't you dare!" I snap, finally managing to stand to my feet. "Don't you dare speak her name in my presence!"

Who the hell does she think she is?

She smirks. "Oh please, you're a pathetic excuse for a king," she says, trying to provoke me, as she always does. She just loves to piss me off. "Don't sit here and pretend like you weren't just dreaming about my child. Don't sit here and pretend like you're not a drunken fool because of the self-pity you feel, all because you were too coward to claim her," she continues, calling me out. "Don't sit here and pretend like you didn't leave Claire in her time of need because the pain of her being the daughter of Bella and her human lover is too much for you to bear."

"Shut up!" I snarl, my eyes blazing. "Shut the f*ck up!"

"Why? Because I speak the truth? If you can't handle the truth, that's your problem," she hisses through clenched teeth.

F*ck, I hate this woman.

"Get the hell out of my kingdom before I end you!"

She bursts out laughing. "You know, like I know, that you are no match for me, cold-hearted king."

"Get out!" my monster growls, seconds away from losing it.

Aurora looks my monster dead in the eye. "I warned you once, and I'll warn you again. Don't fight fate. Your destiny is to stand beside the Chosen One. Your destiny is to protect her from the monster you created."

"The monster I created? I haven't done anything but protect Claire. I had nothing to do with her becoming a dhampir, and just because she is one, that doesn't mean she is a monster!" I snap. "Claire is the purest soul I've ever encountered, dhampir or not."

"I'm not talking about Claire, you fool," she mocks, raising her voice. "I'm talking about the mutt you imprisoned. She is coming after Claire with everything she has, and she won't stop until Claire's head is on a spike."

I burst out laughing like a madman. "That dog is no match for Claire. To be quite frank, Claire would make the entire pack rip their own hearts out and hand them to her, if she wanted to."

"You, out of all people, should know not to underestimate the influence of pain, cold-hearted king," she scolds me yet again. "That wolf's heart has already been ripped out of her chest over and over again, thanks to you and your barbaric companions. Plus, she is smarter than you think. She knows Claire's weakness is her gentle heart."

"The mutt won't lay a finger on her!" my monster roars. "If you care so much about Claire, why don't you put the dog down yourself, since you feel like she is such a threat?"

"You know very well I cannot intervene with fate. And even if I could, I wouldn't kill the mutt. She was a good friend to Claire's mother. She is only acting up because of the bullsh*t you forced her to endure. Plus, you need to stop running away from your problems and right your wrongs."

754

"I did right my wrongs! I made sure Claire and Nicklaus accepted each other. I protected Claire and will continue to protect her."

"As if those were enough. You really are pathetic. You didn't even apologize to Claire for hurting her mother or killing her father," she further provokes.

I turn my back to her and stare out of my window. I don't have the energy to go back and forth with Aurora, and in all honesty, she is right. I owe Claire a lifetime of apologies. I owe her a lifetime of me righting my wrongs. I know this.

"Why don't you just tell Mecca who Claire's mother is?" I silently ask.

"Why don't you?" she silently asks me back. "She is with a child, you know," she adds, regaining my attention.

I turn back around. "Who's with a child?"

Suddenly, a bright green light blinds me, and an unknown force sends me flying throughout the room. Instantly, my ears start ringing, then I hear Aurora's final words before she disappears: "By the way, your second-chance mate won't wait around forever. Claim her before they find her. Don't make the same mistake twice."

My blood turns to ice, and I swear my frozen heart skips several beats.

*How the hell did she know about her? Better yet, what did she mean by . . . ?*

I scramble to my feet and run through my palace. I have to get to Isis now. I know Aurora better than anyone. "Claim her before they find her" was a warning. Someone else knows about Isis, and they are searching for her. I can't allow anyone to find her.

Within a second, I'm in front of the cozy little cottage on the far end of Elephant Island I built for Isis before she even had a chance to take her first breath of air. She has lived here with her sister since the day she was born. I wanted to make sure that no one would know she existed, and I have been doing a damn good

755

job of hiding it for nearly eighteen years. F*ck, I'd even hidden it from Nicklaus. He just found out about her a couple of months ago, but he still doesn't know the full truth about her.

I take a look at the home I had built for Isis. It could need some work. It's winter here in Antarctica. The weather is harsher than usual this time of year, and by the look of things, it has been an extremely harsh winter for the two of them. It's time to move them from here.

"Why are you here?" asks Alice, as she closes the cottage door behind her.

She is Isis's older half sister. I lied to Nicklaus and the others when I told them she was a human. She is actually a witch.

"It's time for you two to move. It's not safe here, and this place is falling apart," I reason with her. "I built another cabin in Alexander Island. I'll send my lieutenant to escort the both of you there at once."

"Isis can't travel with this weather," she hisses through clenched teeth, "let alone travel with one of your people. The fact that the old lady keeps coming around is already bad enough. Whenever she leaves, I have to erase that part in Isis's memory, and even that is becoming a hassle. She becomes more and more powerful each day."

"Wait, what old lady?" I ask.

"Nannie."

*What the hell is Nannie doing here?*

"Your kin, that old woman, is so goddamn stubborn. She refuses to stop coming around no matter how many times I threaten to cast a spell on her ass."

"I had no clue she was visiting," I admit. F*ck, I don't even know how she gets here.

"A part of our deal was that you would stay away," she reminds me, switching the subject.

"I don't need a reminder," I hiss. "Since you feel the need to remind me of my end of the bargain, how about I remind you that you were supposed to keep the witches from finding out about her?"

Alice's stormy eyes catch on fire. "And I have," she responds, slightly raising her voice. "I have killed many of my own kind to keep Isis safe."

"So how did the most-powerful one of you all find out about her?" I query, slightly raising my voice right back at her.

"Aurora doesn't know sh*t. You have my word."

"Your word is bullsh*t! Why the hell do you think I'm here? Now, where is she?" My patience is running thin. I need to see her. I need to make sure she is okay.

I push Alice to the side and barge right through the front door. She follows right behind me with an angry stride of her own. I know she is pissed. She knows like I know that this is a bad idea, but I could give a f*ck about how she feels. I have to see Isis. The aroma of juicy peaches, dew-covered leaves, and a hint of vanilla makes my monster purr loudly within me. She smells better than I remember. I freeze the moment I lay eyes on her. Isis is lying across the couch, sleeping peacefully. I stand stuck in place, admiring the beautiful woman she has grown to be.

I haven't physically laid eyes on her since the day she was born, and now that I have, I realize how bad of an idea this actually is. Her plump lips part slightly as she releases gentle snores. Her long and wavy fiery hair hangs freely. Her full and long lashes gently fan her flawless face, preventing me from viewing her icy eyes she inherited from her mother's side of legendary family. How I so desperately wish she would open them!

"You need to go now," Alice whispers from behind me. "Go, before she awakes. You don't want her learning the fact she is mated to a monster."

I turn to face her, seconds away from giving the witch a piece of my mind. That's when the most-beautiful sound reaches my sensitive ears.

"Alice," Isis calls out from behind me.

"Start packing," I hiss inside her sister's ear.

I'm gone within a second, leaving Alice and my sleeping beauty behind. I can't allow her to see me. At least right now I can't. There is just too much going on. It's not safe for her. But I will certainly take Aurora's advice this time around. I am coming back for my second-chance mate. I am coming back to claim my second-chance beloved.

# EXCLUSIVE BONUS CHAPTER
## We're Coming: Part I

CLAIRE

*A week after the announced pregnancy*

"Stop moving, or I'll pluck your eyeballs out," growls Jadis.

She seems highly devoted to completing the task of making sure my eyebrows look perfect. However, she's attempting to achieve the impossible. My eyebrows are currently in beast mode, just like every other area on my body where hair sprouts: my legs, which need a good waxing; my armpits, where the hair keeps growing like little golden brussels sprouts no matter how many times I shave them; and let's not forget my chest. I know that sounds gross, but it is what it is. My chest has gone from beauty to beast within a week. My kitty, most certainly, also needs yet another good shaving. It reminds me of Mecca. I remember teasing her about her hairy crotch.

You see how karma works? Welp, I do. Who knew that pregnancy could make someone so goddamn hairy?

Jadis and Victoria are in my private dressing chambers to prepare me for a date I was not supposed to know about, but of course Jadis opened her big ole mouth. That girl can't keep a secret. Apparently, Nicklaus plans to take me out tonight to help me with clearing my mind. He's worried about me, and for the first time ever, I understand his side of things.

I'm woman enough to admit that I've been a complete "flip-flop." One minute I'm crying, and the next minute I'm smiling. One minute I'm worried, and the next minute I'm worry-free. You'll never really know which Claire you're going to get. My emotions have been at an all-time peak. One may even say I've been extremely discombobulated; and haven't had a chance to relax, which is completely unacceptable according to Nicklaus—that one being, my beloved. According to him that's not good, so as a result he tried to forbid me from tagging along to North America—key word: tried. But I'm going, whether he likes it or not. There is no way I'm allowing him to go without me. He will do more bad than good. So, yes we're going back to North America and guess what? All the kings's horses and men are expected to hit up North America again.

Haha. Now that's a good one. We and the other kings are expected to make our way to Cyrus's kingdom. We're supposed to be leaving tomorrow. Nicklaus is really eager to get to Cyrus, who has officially lost his marbles. Yup, Cyrus has officially declared war. He's been slaughtering the werewolves left to right, night and day, attacking each and every werewolf pack without mercy. The Kingdom of North America is literally a battlefield, and the mysterious hunters have also joined in the war, working alongside the werewolves. So, King Luscious of South America has made his way up to North America to wreak even more destruction. It's been a mess, a complete mess.

Nicklaus claims he is going to defuse the situation and end it once and for all. He thinks I'm stupid, but I know very well he wants to go just to join in the action. He is going to destroy what Embry and I have planned. I won't allow it, pregnant or not. I will not stand for the bullsh*t any longer. I'm going to North America for one reason and one reason only—end this petty ass dispute.

760

Nicklaus has no idea that Embry sent me a letter. She is planning something really big, and she needs my help to pull it off. If we have it our way, the packs of North America will change forever, and the vampire kings will have no choice but get in line with the New World Order. We are going to put every last one of them in their place, and I can't wait. I guess it's safe to say that sh*t is about to go down, and if that won't take the cake . . . this will!

It's also time for the annual blood gathering. It is one vampire tradition that my crazy ass beloved is set on having. I don't know why, but he is, even though the entire world has been in complete chaos.

The blood gathering is a masquerade ball, where all the important vampire houses discuss the well-being of their futures. Considering all the riots and free-the-council campaigns that have been going on, I can bet my bottom dollar that sh*t is about to hit the fan, that's why my beloved is acting so paranoid. He wants to make sure I'm safe, but he does not really need to worry. I'm safe. The real question is, Are they safe from me?

"You can't harm her. She's carrying our babies," Victoria scold Jadis, reeling me back into their conversation.

I shift my eyes in her direction. She's holding up another one of my dresses against her body as she stares at her reflection in the mirror. She is supposed to be picking out my dress, not trying them on, but it's Victoria we are talking about. She's the queen of raiding my closet. Nicklaus had to order two items of everything I love the most, just in case it magically disappears in my closet and goes into hers.

"No, you can't harm me." I stick my tongue out at Jadis.

Thanks to her handy-dandy tweezers, her hands sting like a b*tch, so I push them away from my eyebrows.

"Babies on board, remember?" I continue, as I head over toward the other side of the room. I need to get as far away as possible from Jadis and her deadly tools.

"What do our babies have to do with my plucking your eyeballs out?" Jadis shouts, leaning her head back to look up at the ceiling. "You don't have to see to deliver them. Blind breeders pop out babies all the time. Our little prince and princess will be just fine."

"And what makes you think they are a girl and boy?" questions Victoria, picking up another one of my dresses.

Actually, it's my favorite dress, so I need to watch out for that one.

"Yeah, what makes you think they are a girl and a boy?" I take a seat in the fluffy stool in front of the vanity set.

Hopefully, they're both girls. I don't want another man in my life. All the kings are already a handful, especially the one that calls me his firecracker. There is no need to add something to that equation.

"Just call it a hunch. We will have a boy and a girl," predicts Jadis. "How perfect!"

Wait a minute, we? Why do they keep saying *our* babies? They are *my* babies, not theirs. I'm not sharing them with anyone. I don't even want to share them with Nicklaus, so I'm damn sure I'm not sharing the twins with the two of them.

When Nicklaus told me I was pregnant, it scared me sh*tless. Literally, I fainted. Who could blame me? I'm only eighteen, and becoming a teen mom was never in my agenda. Welp, becoming a mother was never the plan because all I ever wanted was to be the Queen of Death. That was my dream. Yup, it sure was to be shipped off right into the motherland of the bleeders.

I never thought in my wildest dreams that I would be expecting, as Jadis likes to say; or better yet, I never thought that instead of a bleeder, I would become a breeder to the king of all vampire kings, the father of my kids by the way. Here I am living in this reality. I am months away from having babies, only for them to be possibly snatched right out of my arms and be handed to Jadis and Victoria.

Uh-uh, I don't think so. They will have to kill me first.

*That's not funny,* snaps my subconscious.

It's really not, considering my current situation. Seriously, I really wasn't expecting life to throw this type of wicked curve ball in my direction. I, Claire, is having twins! Do you know how that feels like to be suddenly announced pregnant at the drop of two heartbeats? It's scary as hell, not to mention the fact that just a couple of weeks ago I also found out that I'm a direct descendant of a line of beautiful, cursed women who died during every childbirth. That's just outrageously a pitty. It's downright crazy if you really think about it.

I used to pray every day and night for my eighteenth birthday just so I could wake up and die. I still pray every day and night that I find a way to break this godforsaken curse so I can live to see my children grow up.

Do you see how life works? I do, and it sucks, big time. I'd never truly understood the true meaning of "Be careful what you wish for" until I became the one regretting my wish. I should be thankful I've got two friends who will willingly play mother hens to my chicks. I know they will love my babies without them actually coming from their kitties.

"Do you guys really mean it?" I suddenly yelp, jumping out of my seat. I just need their reassurance.

Bipolar, I know. But it's alright because I already confessed that I've been a complete flip-flop. It's okay. I can blame it on my pregnancy mood swings. At this moment, I'm panicking.

"Did we mean what, Claire?" asks Victoria, looking rather puzzled. She is most likely caught off guard by my sudden outburst.

Jadis drops her flat iron and stares at me long and hard. She is wearing one of those "let me make sure my bestie isn't going crazy" type of face.

"Did you mean that my babies are *our* babies?" I clarify, feeling stupid for saying that out loud.

"Um, Claire"—Jadis walks over toward me—"are you feeling sick, honey?" she asks, sounding like a breeder. She looks extremely focused as she pats my forehead with the back of her hand, as if she could read my temperature with it.

"No, I'm not sick." I smack her hand away from my face and stomp my feet like a child.

Come on, man, I'm trying to have a serious moment here.

"Good." Jadis sighs and goes back to whatever she was doing. "Because Nicklaus will have my head if you mysteriously fall sick before your date," she mumbles underneath her breath. "I thought morning sickness only occurs during the daytime. I need to do more research."

"If you're not sick," says Victoria, as she hangs another one of my dresses up close to her frame, "why asked such a silly question? We already called dibs on the twins."

"Yeah, Claire, don't be stingy. There are two of them, and that's more than enough to share," adds Jadis. "I can take morning shift while Victoria can take the night, and you can have the afternoon. See how that works?" she says to herself. "Unless you and Nicklaus just carry them away. Wait a minute!" she exclaims, her big brown eyes growing wide. "Please, tell me you're not going all cheetah mother on us, are you? I mean, it's okay to be a mama bear. They are just a tad bit overprotective, but don't go cheetah. There is no need to raise the twins in isolation. It's okay to share them."

What is she talking about? I don't even know what that means.

"No, Jadis, that's not what I want to do," I respond, my voice now breaking. "I want you both to be there for them. I want you both to promise me you two will take care of the twins when I—"

"Don't you dare say it!" Victoria is the one to catch on. She drops the dress, quickly runs over, and smashes my face into her chest. "Don't you dare complete that sentence. Don't you dare."

764

She slightly pulls me in and plants a soft kiss on my forehead. "We will all be here to take care of the twins, all of us." She pulls me close to her heart.

I rest my head on her chest and release my tears. I just can't.

"Awe, Claiiire," says Jadis, sighing heavily. She runs over to join in our hug. She hooks her tiny arms around Victoria and my frame and then tightly pulls the both of us in. "Don't cry, cherry pop. It will be alright."

We stand in place, simultaneously embracing one another for what seems like forever. I don't mind, though. I need it. I need my girls.

It seems like I've always needed a group hug these days.

"Victoria is right, Claire. We will all be here to care for the super duper cute prince and princess of ours. I promise." Jadis breaks the group hug.

"How can you promise that, Jadis? After everything I shared with the two of you, you can't possibly believe that."

She knows that she can't. They both know I'm doomed. I told them about my curse. They are probably only saying that to make me feel better. They are my friends, so they feel obligated to do so.

"I can, and I do," responds Jadis with a shrug.

"No, you can't," I argue.

"Yes, I can," she argues back.

"No, you can't."

"Yes, I can!" she snaps back, and that's . . . that voice tone.

I sigh in defeat. Jadis is the queen of believing in the impossible.

"You're right," I admit. "I must have faith, for their sake."

Jadis flashes me a dazzling smile—she is so f*cking pretty. "I know I am." She starts searching for another one of her deadly beauty tools, I'm sure. "Oh, and you should have faith. I'll make sure of it if it's the last thing I do. We will get through this together.

We will find a way, because we are the chosen wh*res, and the chosen wh*res are the most-powerful creatures that walk the vampire-soaked-in-blood earth."

"Yes, we are the chosen wh*res," Victoria shouts excitedly, making her way back toward my dresses.

I can't help but burst out laughing.

"Wait a minute, chosen wh*re, why do we have to be chosen wh*res? I'm sick of the stereotypes," sulks Victoria. "I'm already a red-headed slut just because I'm a redhead, and I don't like that name."

"No. You are a red-headed slut because you are a redhead that happens to be a slut," corrects Jadis, making me laugh harder. "Don't blame that on stereotypes, baby."

"And you're a snob," Victoria insults Jadis right back. "A snobby, control freak, nerdy brunette snob,"

"How dare you!" Jadis fakes insult, placing her hand over her heart, just to add a dramatic effect. "How dare you call me a freak without adding that I'm a freak in the sheets? Now that's just insulting," says Jadis with a wink, officially making me almost die from laughter.

They are f*cking crazy.

"What's so funny, Claire the Bear?" Victoria asks. "You dumb blond," she horribly insults.

I'm just about to tell her she needs to come up with some better snapbacks when suddenly an unexpected gust of wind blows the fresh scent of expensive cologne, burning cedarwood, and a hint of cypress aroma into the room, stopping my laughter at once. I turn my head immediately in the direction of the balcony door. I know that smell. I'll be able to identify that in my sleep. Actually, I'll be able to identify that scent even if I didn't have a sense of smell. It is that familiar; he is that familiar to me.

"Claire," calls Victoria as her heart rate increases in speed. "You know I was just kidding, right?"

"Shhh," I hush Victoria, making her jump.

Little sucker!

"What is it, Claire?" Jadis looks out of the balcony. "Do I need to get the gun?"

"No, Jadis, you don't. Everything is alright," I tell her, holding back my laughter.

Ever since the battle, Jadis has become the little rebel, ready to take on the world. My little gypsy has a dark side.

My sensitive ears pick up on a chuckle—his chuckle—from the other side of the balcony door.

"Can you girls give me a moment alone, so I can—"

"Absolutely not," Jadis cuts in, both her hands on her hips. "I'm not leaving you alone, Claire, ever! You need me, so you're stuck with me. You're stuck with us. Plus, you have to get ready for your date."

"Speak for yourself, crazy lady," Victoria says. "I'll go. In fact, I'm going to go get the pregnant lady something to eat. You want pancakes? Of course, you do," acknowledges Victoria, damn near running out of my room.

"She is such a pussy," Jadis taunts. "Now come on, we have a date to get you ready for."

As if on cue, a unique soft floral aroma mixed with the distinctive scent of sandalwood floats underneath the door. I'm saved by the bell. It's time for Jadis and Cornelius's daily quickie, and there is no way in hell she's turning that down. It does not matter what time it is or how much I need her, when Cornelius is ready to put on his daily horse-dick show, Jadis is quick to ride till she can't no more.

In a flash, I'm in front of the door and open it. "Take your beloved," I instruct.

"Oh, I plan to." Cornelius walks right in my room and scoops Jadis up right into his arms. "I plan to take her outside, in the garden, directly underneath the moon."

"Daddy, I told you I can't have our start-of-the-night quickie." Jadis pouts. "Our king has given me a very important task to complete."

"And I told you I don't give a f*ck about that." He throws her on his shoulder. "I'm about to tap that ass, baby girl," he teases. "Plus, Claire has a visitor," he reminds me, as he takes my crazy best friend to her dick appointment.

I shake my head and make my way to the balcony door. My soft heartbeat picks up slightly. I haven't seen him ever since he found out about my mom. I miss him. I miss . . .

"Xander!" I gasp, as I walk out onto the balcony. I waste no time and crashes my body into his.

# EXCLUSIVE BONUS CHAPTER
## We're Coming: Part II

Xander embraces me without any hesitation. "Brave one," he says, holding onto my tiny frame as if I could disappear.

I'm not complaining because I'm holding onto him tightly as well, as if he was going to disappear. I missed him so, so much. I was worried that his humanity switch was flipped. Nicklaus explained to me that when a vampire switches off their humanity, that means they are cutting off their ability to feel. He said vampires can become emotionless creatures, which didn't really make much sense to me because in my eyes most vampires are already are. But according to Nicklaus, I've got no idea how emotionless a vampire can become. He made it his point to educate me about it.

He also told me that whenever a vampire has completely shut down their humanity, they become carefree and remorseless about their actions and impervious to guilt and conscience, turning them into merciless, calculating killers. He said that Xander is the king of turning off his emotions. That's how he acquired the title the Cold-Hearted King. If he has flipped the switch, Nicklaus would forbid me to see him until he comes back to his senses. "Xander is dangerous and deadly when he becomes like that, Claire," Nicklaus told me. "You have to stay away from him by any means necessary."

Blah, blah, blah.

Xander will never hurt me, humanity on or off. I don't care what anyone has to say or think, but he is a good man. He's my brother, and I will never stay away from him. Nicklaus acts like Xander doesn't need anybody. We all need somebody. Everyone goes through a rough patch, Almighty Vampires included.

I begged Nicklaus to go find Xander. I argued that we needed our brother, and that he needed us, but Nicklaus downright refused. He responded, "I have way too much stress on my shoulders right now. There is no way I'm going to go hunt down a king, brother or not. Xander will come around when he is ready. He always finds his way back home, trust me." Nicklaus then gave a goddamn devilish smirk.

Urg, I could have strangled him. I still hate that smirk—uh, that sexy and sadistic smirk. I couldn't believe him, and I couldn't believe he would leave me all alone to deal with Xander. Oh, that reminds me.

Suddenly, I ram my knee straight into Xander's manhood.

"Ouch." He groans like a little b*tch, dropping to his knees and cupping his "ding-a-ling." "F*ck, Claire, that hurts," he cries.

"Serves you right." I cross my arms over my chest like a spoiled brat or more like an insubordinate child. "That's how I felt when you left me. How could you do that to me?" I ask, slightly raising my voice—yeah, I'm pissed off right now. "You left me all because of who my mom is, like I could control that?" I tell him, my voice now breaking.

And here come the tears. I swear these mood swings of mine are going to drive me to the brink of insanity.

"I was worried sick. I thought you were never coming back, and that you flipped the switch or whatever the hell . . ." I trail off, holding back my tears. I try not to say how I really feel out loud, but I am who I am, and there is no way that I will ever bite my tongue. "You hate me now, don't you?" I cover my face with my hands. (He hates me. I know he does.) "You hate me because I'm the daughter of one of my mother's other lovers."

"Claire," calls Xander. Within a rush of wind, his arms are wrapped back around me. "Look at me," he demands.

I can't. I want to, but I can't.

"Look at me." He lifts my face with a single finger and gives me no choice.

I look at him for a long-drawn-out moment, tears streaming down my face. Gosh, I'm so goddamn emotional now.

"I could never hate you," he whispers, staring directly into my eyes. "You are the purest soul I've ever known. You are brave and beautiful. If there is anything I hate about myself, it is that I did so much wrong to you before I even met you. I killed your father and hurt your mother. I . . . I just . . . I just . . . didn't want to face you. I'm sorry," he gets out. "You have every right to hate me, not the other way around. I was a coward."

"Yeah, you are," I state between my hiccups. "You are a big ole coward."

"A huge one," he adds.

"An enormous one."

"Gigantic one," he says back.

I can't help but smile. "I can never hate you. I love you, Xander."

He stares at me long and hard with his glassy, icy eyes. He studies every inch of my face, and we stand like this for what seems like forever.

"I love you more, brave one," he finally speaks.

"That's impossible." I once again smash my face into his rock-hard chest.

Xander and I are not blood-related, but he will forever and always be dear to my heart. He's my first real friend and protector. He is my everything, and I'll always love him.

"Your mother would be so proud of you," he whispers in my ear, making my softly beating heart skip a beat.

I could only hope so.

771

"So," comes an amused voice suddenly from behind us, "this is who you ditch me for, the king's brother? How kinky!"

Xander and I turn to face the one and only Jadis. She is smiling from ear to ear, her head popping out of the balcony door.

"Actually, you ditched me," I respond. I guess her dick appointment is over.

"You know, you can tell me if you're sleeping with both of them. I won't judge. It will be our dirty little secret. I'll be your diary. Jadis a.k.a Claire's Vampire Diary," she so boldly states.

I choke on my own spit. This girl.

"Hello, Jadis," greets Xander, flashing her a gorgeous grin.

Jadis returns his grin with a dazzling smile, then she walks onto the balcony and grabs my arm. "She's late! She's late for a very important date. No time to say hello. Good bye," she says to Xander.

And within the next second, I'm being dragged back into the room by my very determined best friend. I hear Xander's laughter from the balcony all the way into the bathroom.

"Now, you're going to sit down and let me work my magic, otherwise . . ." she states, practically throwing me into the bathtub.

"Hey, be careful. Baby on board," I remind her.

"Baby on board?" repeats Xander with a shocked voice.

"Babies!" yells Jadis, overly excited.

The next thing I hear is a loud thump. Jeepers creepers!

"I think he has fainted," whispers my best friend.

"Serves him right," I whisper right back. "That's what he gets for leaving me."

"True."

Jadis and I burst into a fit of giggles.

\*     \*     \*

I stand in front of the mirror, frozen in place. Jadis has damn sure outdone herself. Her hands always create magic, and I don't think I could get used to seeing myself looking like this.

"Beautiful," Jadis comments, buckling up my left heel. "You look beautiful, darling. Nicklaus is going to eat you all up, literally."

I blush. Oh Jadis and her sadistic tongue.

"I wonder if it's possible to get pregnant while you're already pregnant, because, baby, he most certainly shall shoot his seed all the way up your fallopian tubes tonight."

"Cut it out, Jadis," I scold her, blushing harder.

"What? You know I'm right. You're sexy, and you know it."

I don't respond. She does have a good point, thanks to her applying a bright ruby-red lipstick on my plump lips and bringing out the color of my eyes with the dark and daring smoky eye-shadow look. It really makes my unique green eyes appear much, much brighter; they actually pop.

She has also tamed my golden waves, straightening them right out and then sleeking it down into a ponytail. The dress of my choice—a sexy sequin maxi dress—has a huge plunging *V*-neckline, so my pendant falls in the middle of my chest while the emerald glows brightly, sitting pretty. Both sides of the dress are cut out, and so is the waist. It reveals a lot of my skin, not to mention the high, double front slits that show off my freshly shaved legs. Victoria does know how to pick out a dress. Seriously, that girl is also good.

*I'm sexy, and I know it.*

"Come on, Queen Conceited," Jadis speaks, checking me out.

"Thank you, Jadis. You really are the best."

She is indeed good at what she does.

773

"Ah duh. I'm the best goddamn makeup artist slash adviser there is to have," she self-proclaims. "Now, hurry your cute ass up. Grand Harold is about to knock on the door for you."

As if on cue, Grand Harold's scent hits my nose, and we hear a knock on the door. I look at myself in the mirror one last time and then head out of the door, finally making my way to the one and only Nicklaus, my ass-kissing king.

*    *    *

NICKLAUS

The past couple of weeks has been very theatrical. Cyrus and Luscious have been on a warpath of vengeance and destruction in North America, mercilessly killing anyone that gets in their way. They've been slaughtering werewolves and hunters left and right. My brothers have once again proven why these dogs shouldn't f*ck with us vampire kings, especially the ruthless and barbaric ones. I can't wait to join in the fun. I'm ready to go.

Hiding my plan from Claire to go destroy those dogs has been a complete nightmare and a little overwhelming. I'm ready to get this sh*t over with. I've got to before she miraculously finds a way to stop me. Claire is so clever and goddamn stubborn. She has been snooping around my office every chance she gets, attempting to decipher my next move. If she were anyone else, she would probably be dead, but she is my beloved. I know her loyalty is with me, although I also know she is searching for a way to end this without bloodshed.

However, there is no other way. Things are about to get a little bloody, and that's exactly how I want it. Those dogs need to learn their place. They need to know that declaring war on any king I consider my brother is a suicide mission. I am also aware that my sweet little beloved has been writing to Embry in secret. They use code words so as not to get caught. And I must admit they are smart, maybe a little too smart for their own good. They are planning something. Cyrus knows it, and I know it, but we don't really care. Neither of them will partake in the final battle or will even be in that continent when it's time for everything to go down, so they can have their little secret letters. It's all for nothing.

Claire shall only be in North America for a couple of days, for appearance's sake of course, then off to another continent she goes. There is no way I'm allowing my pregnant beloved to be in danger. She's f*cking crazy—downright insane—for believing that I will eventually give in. I've been working on a master plan to make sure we can get her out of the continent before she can utilize her powers to stop us. Now, that's the hard part. We all know she would kick our asses, so I have to come up with a way to completely blindside her and Seneca, the smart-ass who proposed that we host a grand extravaganza, so we're going to have a ball—our annual blood gathering to be exact.

My beloved believes that I actually give a f*ck about following traditions. She thinks I truly value playing dress-up and discussing politics with those totally useless, disloyal, privileged pricks. What she does not know is it's all a distraction to get her to safety. She's going to be pissed, but I can take her being pissed as long as she's safe. I just hope I don't end up with blue balls for an entire century because of it.

The commotion outside my study doors knocks away my train of thought, then comes a very familiar scent. Ah, Xander is back. And by the sound of things, he knows that Claire is pregnant. Now, here comes the bullsh*t.

"Why the f*ck didn't you tell me that Claire is pregnant?" Xander shouts, storming through my door, followed by two royal guards who look like they want to piss themselves.

I was very clear that no one should disturb me, unless it was my firecracker, whom I intentionally made sure was occupied. There is no way she's getting away from Cornelius's spunky little beloved when it's time to play dress-up.

I pinch the bridge of my nose and then dismiss my two guards with a wave of my hand. "It's nice to see you too, Brother," I mock, rising to my feet to grab a drink. I'm going to need it. Xander is pissed, and I'm already agitated. I don't have time for this sh*t, nor do I have the patience. But Claire would be super duper pissed if I attacked Xander on his first day home, so I must remain calm, or at least try to be calm.

*Keep calm,* I mentally say to myself. *Keep calm.*

"Nicklaus, this is not a joke!" he snaps, now pacing back and forth in front of the window.

I roll my eyes. *No sh*t, Sherlock, it's not a joke.*

"She's Bella's daughter!" he roars. "Do you have any idea what that means? She's cursed. Why the f*ck are you sitting here planning a war, sending out party invitations and all this bullsh*t when her life is in danger?" he goes on. "Claire's safety is our number one priority. F*ck everything else!"

I raise an eyebrow and stare at my brother without uttering a single word. I do not appreciate him indicating that Claire's safety, or better yet health, is not my first priority. If anyone knows how important Claire is to me, it's Xander. His little rant is insulting.

*Keep calm, Nicklaus. Keep motherf*cking calm.*

"Nicklaus," Xander almost shouts, "are you listening to what I'm saying?"

"Of course, I am. Sh*t, Sherlock," I say, knocking my drink back. F*ck, that's good.

"Sh*t, Sherlock?" Xander raises his eyebrow. He makes his way over to make a drink himself. "Claire is rubbing off on you."

I smile at that. Yeah, she is. I've never felt this young or carefree in my entire existence. Claire brings this calm, cool, and collected demeanor out of me. She has changed me for the better. The world should be more grateful to her.

"So, I take it that you already have a plan?" he asks. "I mean you have to, with your being all calm and sh*t." He takes a seat on the leather sectional behind the bar. "Care to explain?"

I sit right beside him. I feel a rippling wave of excitement flow through our bond as I tell my brother my master plan.

*     *     *

"I'm going to be an uncle!" exclaims Xander as we make our way down the grand staircase.

It is like a thousandth time he has said that after I told him everything. And this is the first time in centuries he has actually been impressed with me. He agreed that my plan was a masterpiece all the way around the border. He then teased me about how badly Claire would kick my ass after I get her out of dodge, because we both know she is going to flip.

As for my twins and Claire's curse, that's also been taken care of, thanks to Cornelius. The moment we get the girls into his kingdom, he will personally hunt down every gypsy to locate the bloodline of the gypsy b*tch. I will rid her from this world and that stupid ass curse once and for all. I can't wait to kill that bitter f*cking hag. Like seriously, who would curse someone's entire generation as getting back because she couldn't keep another woman out of her husband's bed? "Yeah, she f*cked your husband! Get over it, stupid gypsy b*tch." That's exactly what I'm going to say. F*cking cunt!

We have more than enough time, thanks to Claire being a dhampir. Her human side will drag the length of her pregnancy out—giving her months into her due date—unlike vampires who give birth in a matter of weeks. But her vampire side will heal any damage her pregnancy will cause her body. I know most people would be worried because she's cursed, but Claire isn't a weak and fragile human girl. My beloved is the strongest woman I've known. And if there's anyone capable of defeating this curse, then it's her. It's Claire that we're talking about. We shall get through this. Trust me.

"Wow! An uncle," my brother says again as we finally reach the bottom of the staircase.

"Yeah," I acknowledge. "I'm also going to be a father."

I'm having children with the most-selfless and powerful woman who has ever walked this godforsaken planet. How the f*ck did I get so lucky?

Not even a second elapses, and the sweet, potent, and intoxicating milk-and-honey scent invades my nostrils. It causes my still heart to somehow skip a beat, as always. My entire body begins to hum with highly anticipated pleasure. Every time I see Claire, it always feels like seeing her for the first time. I still get the same feelings. I'm still head over heels in love with this phenomenal woman.

I look up and there she is. My baby looks smoking hot with all her curves on full display. The dress she's wearing complements her at every angle. Her silky, soft golden waves have been straightened out—tamed—to perfection. Her new hairstyle provides me with full access to her stunning features and highlights her smoky green eyes, if that's even possible, which have always been and always will be stunningly brilliant. I hope our children inherit her eyes. In fact, I hope that our children look exactly like her.

To this day, I'm still infatuated with this woman. You can even say I'm obsessed. And guess what? I really am. I'm so blessed and honored to be the man matched with her. She is everything to me. Our children are everything to me. I swear she still really doesn't have any idea how much control she has over me, how much control all three of them have over me.

"You look breathtaking, firecracker." I take her hand into mine and plant a single kiss on it.

She blushes. "You don't look too bad yourself," she lies. She knows damn well I look good.

"Are you kidding me? He looks f*cking smoking hot," Jadis calls her out. "He's such a stud," she comments, earning a growl from her very pissed-off beloved, who has appeared out of nowhere from behind her.

"Oh, cut it out, Cornelius," says my beloved's very spunky best friend.

My brother picks her tiny frame up off the floor and throws her over his shoulder before smacking her ass.

"Bad girls must be punished."

I hear him say as he disappears, carrying Jadis with him.

I'm surprised she has not gotten pregnant yet. I swear they f*ck damn nearly every second of the day.

I place my attention back to my own sex goddess.

" Are you ready to go?" she asks me, smiling from ear to ear.

"As long as you are coming, I'm ready. I'll always be ready," I tell her the truth, earning a small chuckle from my brother.

"I never thought that I'll live to see the day," he speaks.

"See the day for what?" I place my hand on the door knob to escort Claire out.

"To see the day when you become—"

"Whipped," an unexpected and very annoying voice pipes up in the exact moment the front door flies open.

"Marcellus!" my beloved shouts overexcitedly, as she jumps into the fool's arms.

Her actions earn a growl from me.

F*ck, I should have known his ass would pop up here instead of taking it straight to North America like he was told to.

"Claire," he says back, wrapping his arms around her waist—my beloved's waist!

"Get you're f*cking arms off her before I remove them out of their sockets!" I spit through clenched teeth.

"You see what I mean?" he whispers inside my beloved's ear right before he lets her go. "He's *whipped,* butter cream whipped," he adds.

I growl at him.

779

All of a sudden, I'm no longer too excited about our upcoming trip to North America, especially if I have to spend a long and dreadful plane ride with this fool. I forget how f*cking annoying this clown could be. But that wouldn't change anything because tomorrow is the day that I'm reuniting with all my brothers. Those dogs have no idea what's heading their way. We're coming.

"Come on, my ass-kissing king," Claire teases, as she struts toward the car.

Damn, she looks good. I'm still in the middle of the doorway, staring at her like a lovesick puppy. She's so beautiful.

Marcellus bursts out laughing. "Aww, man, you really are whipped," the fool teases yet again, now standing right beside me.

"Shut up, Marcellus!" I snap, following my beloved.

"Whiiipped," he teases more, and I flip him off.

But he is right.

Do you like vampire stories?
Here are samples of other stories
you might enjoy!

GEORGIA ALEXIOU

THE *Lovely* BITE

# CHAPTER 1

I sit on the roof, watching the sun rise over the horizon. The coffee steam blowing away with the wind, just like my thoughts. It's another relaxing morning as usual. I always admire the sun rising, beginning everybody's day. It's a signal to begin our lives, give us a brand-new chance, a new change.

A change in something good.

"Adeline, hurry up! I'm going to be late!" Mom shouts through the open window of my bedroom, breaking my thoughts. Every morning, I usually go on the roof to watch the sunrise. Not in the winter, though. Two years ago, I slipped and fell on to the ground, tearing a muscle in my shoulder which required surgery.

Mom sticks her head out of my window and hands me my backpack. She knows the deal. I get up, balancing on the slanted bottom while trading my mug of coffee for my backpack.

I put the straps over my shoulders, walking to the edge of the roof and crouching down. Mom tells me to be careful while I wrap my legs around the rope that Dad made so I can slide down.

I grab on, clenching on to the rope and sliding down till I reach the ground. The spring weather gives my bare legs a chill while I walk to the car. It is always breezy in the morning which is something to get a grip from my sleepiness.

Mom comes out from the front door, then Dad locks it. They kiss each other goodbye before parting ways. Dad goes to his car while Mom and I go in hers. He leaves the driveway before we do, turning the other way where school is.

"Do you have any exams today?" Mom asks while I'm staring down at the screen of my cell phone. I'm on Instagram, staring at the picture of my ex-boyfriend and his new girlfriend. I frown at the caption he wrote.

*"Missing my baby a little extra today."*

"Is that John?" I flinch at Mom's words. She tries to peek at my screen while driving at the same time. "His girlfriend is cute."

"Wow, thanks Mom. I like your comments once, even if he was *my* boyfriend," I scoff, switch the screen off, and place it on my lap. There's a bit of grief that pits in my stomach when she said that. I don't get emotionally hurt often, since I usually tend to avoid it however, this heartbreak *did* hurt.

"But it's not like you two hate each other now." She is right. John moved away in the middle of fall and I knew a long-distance relationship wasn't going to work. He didn't seem that upset when we broke up, but I guess now he seems to be happy with his new girlfriend.

I sigh, slipping my phone in my bag when I realize that we are in the school's parking lot. Seeing a load of students jump out of the buses and rush in through the school's doors makes my stomach drop. Today is the last semester after our one week of spring break.

"I'll get over it."

"You seem like you already have," Mom says, stopping in front of the curb. I gaze at the school before I bring my attention back to her.

"It still bothers me." I step out of the car and grab my backpack.

Before I could shut the door, Mom calls out, "Listen, Adeline. Love takes time, you will find that boy . . . *soon.*"

"I'm not in a rush either. I'm seventeen," I inform her and she shrugs at my comment.

"I met your father when I was still a freshman in college." Her eyes glow with smothering love, probably from thinking about my dad. She isn't wrong though. The connection they both have is unbelievable. I've never met a pair of parents with an undying love so strong that it's still going at the age of forty. Sometimes I cringe from all the snuggling and loving they do around the house in my presence, but in the end, they laugh when I make a gagging noise or tell them to make room for Jesus.

"Yeah, when there was no social media and only love letters." She chuckles at my comment and I can't help but grin. "Bye Mom."

"Oh wait, honey!" Once my back is towards her, I stop again to face her. I hear the final bell ring for first period from the welcoming doors.

"There might be something wrong in the school's system about you. It was supposed to be taken care of before the break ended, but there was a little hiccup along the way."

I nod to her in a weird way, trying to understand what she means. She looks at me with a stern face, her eyebrows furrowing. "Adeline?"

"Yeah, Mom, sure. I have to go." I shut the door and walk into the school where I'm greeted by loud students and chattering teachers.

\*       \*       \*

My first four classes went by strangely. My teachers would look at me, back to their computer, then back to me. I found it unusual in this situation, especially when it's quiet and everybody seated in class is staring at me.

My math teacher pushed his glasses up to the bridge of his nose and goes *"umph"* without giving an explanation. Whispers go across the class between people and I would narrow my eyes at them.

Before fifth period started, Rebecca, my close friend meets me at my locker while we walk to lunch together. We both stop at the table we usually sit at and I drop my bag on the floor. A group of our friends meet us, and we all sit together before I let out a deep breath to catch Rebecca's attention.

"You look flustered."

"I am," I start, pulling out snacks from my bag. "Teachers are acting very strange around me, and I don't know why."

"Did you fail an exam?" I shoot my eyes up to her and frown. Her sharp eyes are staring back at me and her lips are curled in a serious way.

"What?"

"Rebecca, I'm being serious. My mom also said something to me earlier in the morning that didn't make sense."

She realizes that I am actually stressed, and cautiously sits down across from me. She brings her hand to mine that's resting on the table.

"Hey, I'm sure it's nothing and that everything is okay."

I look around my surroundings, where some are paying attention towards me while others are talking like I don't exist.

"You're right. I probably am just overthinking things," I admit before peeling the plastic wrapping of my granola bar in half. "Just distract me," I willingly say because before I brought this up, Rebecca seemed pretty eager to tell me something. It takes a moment or two for her to eventually kill the dark mood and lighten it up.

"So, Jordan told me that he wants to hit you up at the party tomorrow," she whispers to me and from afar I can see Jordan looking our way. We suddenly make eye contact and he winks at me with a smirk.

I turn my gaze back at Rebecca, taking a bite into the bar.

"Tell him I'm not interested." I chew on the granola, making her jaw drop.

"Are you really denying Jordan?"

Let me tell you something. Jordan is the biggest flirt in my school who can grab any female's attention. Who else can say no to a jock and a smart academic man?

No one . . . but me.

"Come on, you need to jump around now since you and John are done. I don't like this moody Adeline," she teases with pouty lips.

John and I were a young couple, dated for two years. I guess because he was my first love, it's hard to forget.

"Is it that bad if I say no?" I snap in defense, eventually swallowing the remains in my mouth.

"You are out of your mind," she spits out while shaking her head like a lunatic. I run my hands through my hair, ignoring the knots, and stare back into her brown eyes.

"Well sorry that I don't get down with every guy in our grade like you," I say sarcastically but meaning it at the same time. Rebecca widens her eyes, throwing a goldfish at me.

"You b*tch." She laughs and I purse my lips into a fine line.

"The truth hurts right?"

"Well, at least I'm living. Expanding my sex life with males and females." Rebecca came out as a bisexual a year ago during pride month. Since she has no preference, she just explores both genders.

Personally, I feel like there should be no reason to have sex with every guy at every party. In my school, it's not a "who got an A on their test," but a "who can have the most sex in one week" type of thing. It's sickening, actually.

"Whatever, I'll wait when it's time for the next boy I'm going to date," I reply with passion in my voice while Rebecca shrugs back.

"Whatever you say Adeline. It would give you at least five points to get with Jordan. You aren't begging at his feet; he's crying at yours."

"Okay but I don't even find him attractive," I start to argue because this conversation is actually getting on my nerves.

"I know, I know, I'm just saying." Her voice is laced with a b*tchy tone and it's irritating my skin like fire.

*Does anybody else have that best friend that can still annoy you? Yes? No? Only me?*

I roll my eyes, getting up and grabbing my backpack. I leave Rebecca, who ended up initiating conversation with our other friends at the lunch table and I throw the rest of my food in the nearest garbage bin.

*Can this day get any worse?* I think to myself while leaving the cafeteria. I love Rebecca to death, but she has no right to tell me who I should be intimate with.

*I'm right, right?*

I go into the bathroom to fix my hair. As I'm washing my hands, I look at myself in the mirror. I stare into my bright faded green eyes, yawning at the thought of sleeping. I didn't drink enough coffee. I dry my hands and the bell suddenly rings, signaling to the students to get to their next class.

I crash into the crowded hallway and go to my US Government course. I make it into class a little late due to being on the other side of the building.

Everyone is seated and when I walk in, some students are staring. The class goes silent and my teacher, Ms. Haverly glances at my entrance with a surprise look on her face.

I ball my hands into fists when I see everybody's stupid look on their faces. It's been irking me all day for no reason.

"Oh Adeline, you're still here?" I pause, standing in the middle of the classroom while the air between us lace in silence.

"What do you mean?" I ask her and she starts typing on the keyboard of her computer.

"I don't know, I thought you switched classes." She brings her lips down into a curious pout and raises an eyebrow, looking confused herself.

I furrow my eyebrows, walking closer to her desk.

"Why would I switch classes? It's the fourth quarter. There's no reason for me to change my class."

"I know, that's why but I also thought you took the initiative and moved."

"How so?" I'm taken aback from her words, my voice raising in a tone of anger and fear.

"You aren't on my roster anymore." I stand next to her while she turns her computer screen to me. The attendance for this class is up on the tab and her mouse points at where my name is usually at.

Well . . . now it's not there.

If you enjoyed this sample, look for
**The Lovely Bite**
on Amazon.

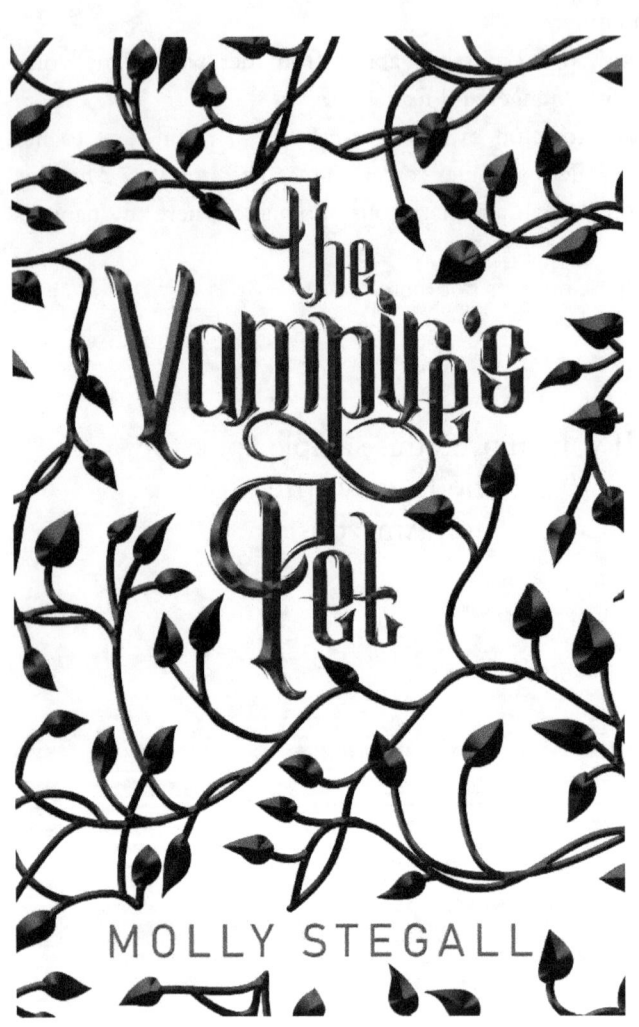

# The Vampire's Pet

MOLLY STEGALL

# CHAPTER I

The bell that hung above the door of the pet shop rang as it opened, shaking back and forth before finally settling. A tall man wearing a suit entered. His nose scrunched up as the unpleasant smell of the shop entered his nose.

The shopkeeper lifted his head from his paperwork, as he lowered the pen to the desk and turned to look at who had entered. His mouth stretched into a thin smile as his fingers ran through his thinning brown hair.

"Ah, Lord Henry. What a pleasant surprise," he said in a formal, rehearsed voice. The shopkeeper went over to shake the man's hand. A few of the pets rolled their eyes in disgust.

The vampires who started the uprising long ago were the respected lords of today. They took millions of dollars and enslaved billions of humans in the process.

"I'm looking for a new pet," Henry said as he looked around the room, not particularly paying attention to what the shopkeeper was saying. Dim lights caused the hue of the room to be an ugly, disgusting, faded yellow, and unfortunately, the lack of windows allowed the color to remain. In the middle, where the vampires would walk, was a concrete walkway, while the floor of the cages was dirt. The pets knew better than to throw filth on the concrete.

Many eyes peered through the cage bars, staring at Henry. Some averted their eyes quickly; others stared right at him, almost challenging him.

"Of course. Do you want a boy or a girl?" the shopkeeper asked as he started to walk.

"Girl," Henry said as he scanned a few cages. One had a girl sitting against the wall, staring in the opposite direction. Another had a girl that was drawing in the dirt, trying to pass the time.

The cages were so small that a child's head would barely touch the top of it. Each had three cement brick walls and a metal bar door.

"Do you have anything in mind?" the shopkeeper asked as he continued walking, not bothering to look into the cages.

"No," Henry said as he looked into a few more. The pets varied in ages: some were as young as six, others were as old as fifty. Each age had its own advantages and disadvantages in terms of housekeeping or being a blood pet. Henry stopped suddenly as something caught his eye. "What about this one?" he asked as he peered through the bars.

The shopkeeper stopped and knew which human was in there. "Oh, her name is Rose," he said in disgust.

"Rose," Henry said to himself, almost in a whisper. He stared at the back of the sleeping girl on the dirty floor. Her body was slowly falling and rising with each breath. She was curled up in a small ball as if it would protect her. Her shirt, though big, showed off her ribs as it pressed against her.

"If you wish my lord, I could wake her," the shopkeeper said as he peered into the cage.

"Yes, please," Henry said as he moved to the left a little, giving the shopkeeper more room. Despite the movement, his eyes never left the sleeping girl.

"As you wish," the shopkeeper said as he laid his hands on a chain that was connected to the door and attached to the metal collar around Rose's neck. The chain was there to remind the pets that they were nothing but pets.

The shopkeeper yanked on the chain, harder than needed. Rose was dragged across the dirt floor, waking her with a jolt of fear and pain. She rolled on her side, coughing and gasping for air as her hands tried to relieve the tension the collar was creating. Her rasping, strained breaths echoed throughout the air before it turned to whimpers.

"This," the shopkeeper pulled the chain again, this time even harder, "is Rose." Before Rose could stop or try to lessen the impact, her body collided with the solid metal, earning another pain-filled whimper. A cloud of dirt rose around her before it settled on her skin and clothes. The shopkeeper moved to the side so Henry could get a better look. The former started to kick some of the dirt that had come onto the concrete back into her cage.

Rose looked down to avoid eye contact with him, but Henry put his finger under her chin and tilted her head up. Her bottom lip began to quiver as he touched her. His hand, however, didn't strike her or harshly grab her, rather it gently touched her skin. Strands of her matted brown hair fell in front of her green eyes. Though they seemed to be the only light-colored eyes in the pet shop, they looked broken, in pain and completely devoid of any life that should have been gifted to her. Her clothes were ripped, old, and covered in dirt, and the stench emanating off of them told Henry that this was the only pair of clothes that she had. His nose twitched again at the funk. Slowly, her dull green eyes raised to meet his red ones.

Henry's dark brown hair was neatly styled on top of his head, with the sides cut shorter. Like every other vampire, his eyes were red, but a different kind of red. They weren't a dark, violent maroon color like her old master's, but a soft, kind red that she had never seen before on a vampire. His eyes were the only ones that seemed to sparkle in the dull light. The black suit he was wearing seemed to comfortably hug his figure, unlike Rose's tattered loose clothes.

"There are bruises on her. What from?" Henry asked as he tilted her head to the side. His eyes scanned over her arms and neck. A variety of blues and purples rested on top of her once tan skin.

"Those are from her old master," the shopkeeper said with a hint of satisfaction in his voice that was only noticeable to himself and Rose.

"You mean she was owned before?" Henry asked as he raised an eyebrow, glancing back at the shopkeeper.

"Yes sir. She actually got back about two weeks ago," the shopkeeper said, dropping the hint of satisfaction, scared that Henry could sense it.

"Why?" Henry asked as he turned his head back to Rose. She had dropped her head downwards, avoiding eye contact again.

"Her master didn't say. He just didn't want her anymore," the shopkeeper said, using his professional voice again.

"How old is she?" Henry asked. The pet shop lighting and dirt, not to mention the bruises she had on her, made Rose's age hard to determine.

"Nineteen," the shopkeeper responded.

Henry's eyebrows rose. "Has she been drunk from yet?" His eyes looked at her neck, trying to find any bite marks.

"No sir," he said, still a little surprised that she hadn't been drunk, especially with her blood type.

"What's her blood type?" Henry asked. Not that he cared. It was just the questions everyone asked. It almost came like second nature.

"AB negative," Henry's eyebrows rose again. AB negative blood was a very rare blood type.

Henry sat there for a few seconds, thinking as he stared at Rose. Rose stared at the ground, her bottom lip started to quiver again, but she didn't dare move. *Please don't pick me. I can't handle another master. Please don't pick me,* Rose pleaded to herself as tears formed in the corners of her eyes.

"Does she have any family?" Henry asked.

"No sir," the shopkeeper replied, his lips forming a straight line.

"I think I'll take her," Henry said as he stood up and fixed his suit and tie.

"Are you sure? She is very shy."

"Yes, I am sure," Henry said in an irritated tone. He firmly stared at the shopkeeper, almost daring him to question him again.

The shopkeeper swallowed. "Okay," he said as he opened the squeaking rusty door of the cage. He unchained Rose and attached a leash to her collar, which he always kept with him.

Rose got out of her cage and stood up too fast. Blackness clouded her vision, and her legs began to give out, nearly sending her stumbling into Henry.

The shopkeeper yanked her towards him before she hit Henry. "Behave," he said through gritted teeth. He pushed her away from him, earning a whimper. "Will you please follow me, sir," the shopkeeper said as he started to walk towards the back room with Rose behind him and Henry at her side.

As they were walking, a torturous scream echoed behind them. They all turned around. Henry's and the shopkeeper's faces showed no emotion as the scene unfolded. A girl was being dragged by a fairly big man across the floor by her hair. Her hands were wrapped around the man's arm, using all her strength to release the pressure.

"I'm sorry, I'm sorry. I didn't mean it!" she begged as she struggled. The man had no trouble dragging her across the smooth concrete.

"You need to learn not to talk back!" the man yelled as he harshly stomped his foot down on the girl's stomach. She started to gasp for air as every ounce of fight left her body. He took the opportunity to drag her with more ease into a room that was strictly used for disciplining pets. A lock sounded after he shut the door. The blood-curdling screams echoed again from within the room.

Henry's and the shopkeeper's face remained the same.

Rose's eyes were tightly shut, and her face was contorted in pain as if she were experiencing what the girl was going through. Her skin somehow became paler, and her breath began to grow heavier.

"Can we please continue," Henry said in an annoyed voice, making it more of a command than a question.

The shopkeeper snapped away from Rose and warmly smiled. He turned around and tugged the leash on Rose's collar. She was too caught up thinking about the disciplining room to notice that he had begun to walk. He pulled harder and she stumbled after him.

They entered the back room. "Would you like any other accessories?" The shopkeeper motioned his hands at a wall that had leashes, collars, muzzles, and nicknacks.

Henry put his finger under her chin, tilting her head up. "These won't be necessary, correct?" She quickly shook her head. He nodded and went to the wall, picking out a blue-colored collar and leash. "Just these," Henry said as he handed them to the shopkeeper.

"Okay. I will need you to sign these papers, and I'll exchange the collars and leashes," the shopkeeper said while Henry nodded. Henry walked to a table to sign the papers as the shopkeeper made his way to Rose.

He unlocked the collar to reveal raw, tender skin on her neck. The cold air bit and nipped at her skin, but she knew better than to move.

"I don't want to see you back here. I don't need something as pathetic as you taking up some space," he whispered into her ear as he fastened the collar as tight as it could go before clipping it on the leash. "Here you are, my lord." Henry signed the last paper before he took the leash. The shopkeeper slid the price to the lord, who merely glanced at it before pulling out the necessary payment.

While humans were considered next to worthless animals, they were not cheap.

"Thank you," Henry said as he nodded a little. He grabbed the leash and started to walk out of the building with Rose behind him.

Rose drudgingly walked behind her new master, knowing that she was going to have to start a new life.

If you enjoyed this sample, look for
**The Vampire's Pet**
on Amazon.

# ACKNOWLEDGEMENTS

Thank you ancestral spirits for guiding me back to my roots. I write to escape; I escape when I write. Once again, I want to thank you for guiding me to stepping into my full potential.

Dear Cody, Cyon, Dalila, Riley, Chase, and Rio—this is for you. I would like each one of you to vividly see that dreams do come true. All of you motivated me to go above and beyond. You are my greatest gifts, my air, my breath, and my lungs. This story is proof that anything is possible.

To the love of my life, Russell Williams, thank you for believing in me as well. You are my diary. Without you, I won't have been able to stay sane enough to write this series, let alone complete it. May you sleep in peace.

To the women that raised me, Demeque Johnson and Hallums Benson, I would also like to say thank you for being in my life. Both of you have taught me everything I know. Without you, I will be nowhere.

And to my family, this is only the beginning. We made it. Who would have ever thought that Sondreen would create so much Black Girl Magic.

# ABOUT THE AUTHOR

Sondreen J. has won over millions of hearts from her strong-willed characters and thrilling unpredictable stories. She's known to first draw her readings in with the skills of her pen and then capture their hearts with her never-ending mysterious wonders of her mind. She knows how to create a connection, a true connection between her readers and her characters and has been commended on numerous occasions for mastering the skill of having the ability to not only inspire her readers, but also captivate their minds. Her strong-willed background allows her to create power within her characters in a way that's both thought to be motivating and astonishing.

www.ingramcontent.com/pod-product-compliance
Lightning Source LLC
Chambersburg PA
CBHW050116030726
47505CB00007B/1899